THE FIREBRAND

MARION ZIMMER BRADLEY

A ROC BOOK

ROC
Published by New American Library, a division of
Penguin Group (USA) Inc., 375 Hudson Street,
New York, New York 10014, USA
Penguin Group (Canada), 90 Eglinton Avenue East, Suite 700, Toronto,
Ontario M4P 2Y3, Canada (a division of Pearson Penguin Canada Inc.)
Penguin Books Ltd., 80 Strand, London WC2R 0RL, England
Penguin Ireland, 25 St. Stephen's Green, Dublin 2,
Ireland (a division of Penguin Books Ltd.)
Penguin Group (Australia), 250 Camberwell Road, Camberwell, Victoria 3124,
Australia (a division of Pearson Australia Group Pty. Ltd.)
Penguin Books India Pvt. Ltd., 11 Community Centre, Panchsheel Park,
New Delhi - 110 017, India
Penguin Group (NZ), 67 Apollo Drive, Rosedale, North Shore 0632,
New Zealand (a division of Pearson New Zealand Ltd.)
Penguin Books (South Africa (Pty.) Ltd., 24 Sturdee Avenue,
Rosebank, Johannesburg 2196, South Africa

Penguin Books Ltd., Registered Offices:
80 Strand, London WC2R 0RL, England

Published by Roc, an imprint of New American Library, a division of Penguin Group (USA) Inc.
This is an authorized reprint of a hardcover edition published by Simon & Schuster, Inc. For infor-
mation address Simon & Schuster, Inc., 1230 Avenue of the Americas, New York, New York 10020.

First Roc Printing, May 2003
15 14 13 12 11

ROC REGISTERED TRADEMARK—MARCA REGISTRADA

Roc Trade Paperback ISBN: 978-0-451-45924-4

The Library of Congress has catalogued the hardcover edition of this title as follows:

Bradley, Marion Zimmer.
    The firebrand.
    1. Cassandra (Greek mythology)—Fiction. 2. Trojan War—Fiction. I. Title.
    PS3552.R228F5 1987 813'.54 87-17283

Printed in the United States of America

PUBLISHER'S NOTE
This is a work of fiction. Names, characters, places, and incidents either are the products of the
author's imagination or are used fictitiously, and any resemblance to actual persons, living or dead,
business establishments, events, or locales is entirely coincidental.
    The publisher does not have any control over and does not assume any responsibility for author
or third-party Web sites or their content.

FOR MARY RENAULT

"Oh Troy Town! Tall Troy's on fire!"

—ROSSETTI

"Before the birth of Paris, Hecuba, Queen of Troy, dreamed that she had given birth to a firebrand who would burn down the walls of Troy."

PROLOGUE

ALL DAY the rain had been coming down; now heavy, now tapering off to showers, but never entirely stopping. The women carried their spinning indoors to the hearth, and the children huddled under the overhanging roofs of the courtyard, venturing out for a few minutes between showers to splash through the brick-lined puddles and track the mud inside to the hearthside. By evening, the oldest of the women by the hearth thought she might go mad with the shrieking and splashing, the charging of the little armies, the bashing of wooden swords on wooden shields, the splintering sounds and quarreling over the broken toys, the shifting of loyalties from leader to leader, the yells of the "killed" and "wounded" when they were put out of the game.

Too much rain was still coming down the chimney for proper cooking at the hearth; as the winter day darkened, fires were lighted in braziers. As the baking meat and bread began to smell good, one after another the children came and hunched down like hungry puppies, sniffing loudly and still quarreling in undertones. Shortly before dinner, a guest arrived at the door: a minstrel, a wanderer whose lyre strapped to his shoulder guaranteed him welcome and lodging everywhere. When he had been given food and a bath and dry clothing, the minstrel came and seated himself in the place accorded the most welcome guests, close to the fire. He began to tune his instrument, leaning his ear close to the tortoise-shell pegs and testing the sound with his finger. Then, without asking leave—even in these days a bard did as he chose—he strummed a single loud chord and declaimed:

> I will sing of battles and of the great men who fought them;
> Of the men who lingered ten years before the giant-builded
>   walls of Troy;
> And of the Gods who pulled down those walls at last, of
>   Apollo Sun Lord and Poseidon the mighty Earth Shaker.
> I will sing the tale of the anger of powerful Akhilles,
> Born of a Goddess, so mighty no weapon could slay him;
> Even the story of his overweening pride, and that battle
> Where he and great Hector fought for three days on the plains
>   before high-walled Troy;
> Of proud Hector and gallant Akhilles, of Kentaurs and Ama-
>   zons, Gods and heroes,
> Odysseus and Aeneas, all those who fought and were slain on
>   the plains before Troy—

"No!" the old woman exclaimed sharply, letting her spindle drop and springing up. "I won't have it! I'll not hear that nonsense sung in my hall!"

The minstrel let his hand fall on the strings with a jangling dissonance; his look was one of dismay and surprise, but his tone was polite.

"My lady?"

"I tell you I won't have those stupid lies sung here at my hearth!" she said vehemently.

The children made disappointed sounds; she gestured them imperiously to silence. "Minstrel, you are welcome to your meal and to a seat by my fire; but I won't have you filling the children's ears with that lying nonsense. It wasn't like that at all."

"Indeed?" the harper inquired, still politely. "How do you know this, madam? I sing the tale as I learned it from my master, as it is sung everywhere from Crete to Colchis—"

"It may be sung that way, from here to the very end of the world," the old woman said, "but it didn't happen that way at all."

"How do you know that?" asked the minstrel.

"Because I was there, and I saw it all," replied the old woman.

The children murmured and cried out.

"You never told us that, Grandmother. Did you know Akhilles, and Hector, and Priam, and all the heroes?"

"Heroes!" she said scornfully. "Yes, I knew them; Hector was my brother."

The minstrel bent forward and looked sharply at her.

"Now I know you," he said at last.

She nodded and bent her white head forward.

"Then perhaps, Lady, *you* should tell the story; I who serve the God of Truth would not sing lies for all men to hear."

The old woman was silent for a long time. At last she said, "No; I cannot live it all again." The children whined with disappointment. "Have you no other tale to sing?"

"Many," said the harper, "but I wish not to tell a story you mock as a lie. Will you not tell the truth, that I may sing it elsewhere?"

She shook her head firmly.

"The truth is not so good a story."

"Can you not at least tell me where my story goes astray, that I may amend it?"

She sighed. "There was a time when I would have tried," she said, "but no man wishes to believe the truth. For your story speaks of heroes and Kings, not Queens; and of Gods, not Goddesses."

"Not so," said the harper, "for much of the story speaks of the beautiful Helen, who was stolen away by Paris; and of Leda, the mother of Helen and her sister Klytemnestra, who was seduced by great Zeus, who took the form of her husband the King—"

"I knew you could not understand," the old woman said, "for, to begin, at first in this land there were no Kings, but only Queens, the daughters of the Goddesses, and they took consorts where they would. And then the worshipers of the Sky Gods, the horse-folk, the users of iron, came down into our country; and when the Queens took them as consorts, they called themselves Kings and demanded the right to rule. And so the Gods and the Goddesses were in strife; and a time came when they brought their quarrels to Troy—" Abruptly she broke off.

"Enough," she said. "The world has changed; already I can tell you think me an old woman whose wits wander. This has been my destiny always: to speak truth and never to be believed. So it has been, so it will ever be. Sing what you will; but mock not my own truth on my own hearth. There are tales enough. Tell us about Medea, Lady of Colchis, and the golden fleece which Jason stole from her shrine—if he did. I dare say there is some other truth to that tale too, but I neither know it, nor care what the truth may be; I have not set foot in Colchis for many long years." She picked up her spindle and quietly began to spin.

The harper bowed his head.

"Be it so, Lady Kassandra," he said. "We all thought you dead in Troy, or in Mykenae soon after."

"Then that should prove to you that at least in some particulars the tale speaks not the truth," she said, but in an undertone.

Still my fate: always to speak the truth, and only to be thought mad. Even now, the Sun Lord has not forgiven me. . . .

Apollo's Call

1

AT THIS TIME of year, the light lingered late; but the last glow of sunset had faded now in the west, and mist had begun to drift in from the sea.

Leda, Lady of Sparta, rose from her bed, where her consort, Tyndareus, lingered still. As usual after their coupling, he had fallen into a heavy sleep; he did not notice when she left the bed and, throwing a light garment about her shoulders, went out into the courtyard of the women's quarters.

Women's quarters, the Queen thought angrily, *when it is my own castle; one would think that I, not he, was the interloper here; that he, not I, held land-right in Sparta. Earth Mother knows not so much as his name.*

She had been willing enough when he came and sought her hand, even though he was one of the invaders from the north, worshiper of thunder and oak and of the Sky Gods, a coarse, hairy man who bore the hated black iron on spear and armor. And yet now his kind were everywhere, and they demanded marriage by their new laws, as if their Gods had flung down from Her celestial throne the Goddess who owned land and harvest and people. The woman wedded by one of these bearers of iron was expected to join in the worship of their Gods and to give her body only to that man.

One day, Leda thought, the Goddess would punish these men for keeping women from paying due homage to the forces of Life. These men said the Goddesses were subservient to the Gods; which seemed to Leda a horrible blasphemy and a mad reversal of the natural order of things. Men had no divine power; they neither bred nor bore; yet somehow they felt they had some natural right in the fruit of their women's bodies, as if coupling with a woman gave them some power of ownership, as if children did not naturally belong to the woman whose body had sheltered and nourished them.

Yet Tyndareus was her husband and she loved him; and because she loved him she was even willing to indulge his madness and jealousy, and risk angering Earth Mother by lying only with him.

And yet she wished that she could make him understand that it was wrong for her to be shut up in the women's quarters —that as a priestess she must be out and around the fields to be sure that the Goddess was given Her due of service; that she owed the gift of fertility to all men, not to her consort alone; that the Goddess could not restrict Her gifts to any one man, even if he called himself a King.

A distant muttering of thunder reverberated from far below, as if it had risen from the sea, or as if the Great Serpent who now and again caused the earth to shake might be stirring in Her depths.

A riffle of wind stirred the light garment about Leda's shoulders, and her hair flew wildly like a solitary bird in flight. Faint lightning suddenly flared all the courtyard alight, and silhouetted against the squared light of the doorframe she saw her husband coming in search of her. Leda shrank inwardly; would he berate her for leaving the women's quarters, even at this hour of the night?

But he did not speak; he only moved toward her, and something in his step, the deliberate way he moved, told the woman that despite the well-known form and the features now clearly visible in the moonlight, this was not her husband. How this could be she did not know, but around his shoulders a flicker of errant lightning seemed to play, and as he walked his foot struck the flagstones with the faintest sound of faraway thunder. He seemed to have grown taller, his head thrown back against the levin-light which crackled in his hair. Leda knew, with a shudder that bristled down the small hairs on her body, that one of the stranger Gods was now abroad within the semblance of her husband, riding him as he would mount and ride one of his own horses. The lightning-flare told her it was Olympian Zeus, controller of thunders, Lord of Lightning.

This was nothing new to her; she knew the feel of the Goddess filling and overflowing her body when she blessed the harvests or when she lay in the fields drawing down the Divine power of growth to the grain. She remembered how she seemed to stand aside from her familiar self, and it was the Goddess who moved through the rites, dominating everyone else with the power within Her.

Tyndareus, she knew, must now be watching from within, as Zeus, the master of his body, moved toward his wife. She knew, because Tyndareus had once told her, that of all his Gods it was for the Thunder Lord that he felt most devotion.

She shrank away; perhaps He would not notice her and she could remain unseen until the God departed from her husband. The head that now was the God's head moved, that flicker of lightning following the loose flying movement of his hair. She knew He had seen her; but it was not Tyndareus' voice that spoke, but a voice deeper, softer, a profound bass rumble filled with the distant thunders.

"Leda," said Zeus Thunderer, "come here to me."

He put out His hand to take hers, and obediently, mastering the sudden inner dread—if this God bore the lightnings, would His touch strike her with the thunder-stroke?—she laid her hand in His. His flesh felt cold, and her hand shivered a little at the touch. Looking up at Him, she perceived on His face the shadow of a smile wholly unlike Tyndareus' stern and unbending look, as if the God were laughing—no, not at her, but with her. He drew her in under His arm, casting the edge of His mantle over her, so that she could feel His body's warmth. He did not speak again, but drew her along inside the room she had quitted only a few moments ago.

Then He pulled her close to Him, inside the mantle, so that she could feel His manhood rising against her body.

Do the laws against lying with any other man ban a God in my husband's very shape and form? she wondered wildly. Somewhere inside, the real Tyndareus must be looking out at her:

jealously, or pleased that his woman found favor with his God? She had no way to know; from the strength with which He held her she knew it would be impossible to protest.

At first she had felt His alien flesh as chill; now it seemed pleasantly warm, as if fevered.

He lifted her and laid her down; a single swift touch and somehow she was already open, throbbing and eager. Then He was over and within her, and the lightning played around His form and face, its echo deep in the pounding rhythms of His touch. For a moment it seemed that this was not a man, that in fact it was nothing human at all, but that she was alone on a great windswept height, encircled by beating wings, or a great lapping ring of fire, or as if some beast swept round her and ravished her with confusion and ecstasy—beating wings, thunder, as a hot and demanding mouth took possession of hers.

Then suddenly it was over, as if it had been a very long time ago, a fading memory or a dream, and she was lying alone on the bed, feeling very small, chilled and abandoned and alone as the God towered over her—it seemed, to the sky. He bent and kissed her with great tenderness. She closed her eyes, and when she woke, Tyndareus was fast asleep at her side and she was not sure she had ever left her bed. It was Tyndareus; when she put out her hand to be sure, his flesh was warm—or cool—and there was not the faintest crackle of lightning in the hair that lay on the pillow beside her.

Had she only dreamed it, then? As the thought crossed her mind, she heard from far outside the house the ripple of thunder; wherever He had gone, the God had not wholly left her. And now she knew that however long she might live with Tyndareus as his wife, she would never again look on her husband's face without searching in it for some sign of the God Who had visited her in his form.

2

HECUBA THE QUEEN never went outside the walls of Troy without looking back in great pride at this fortress of a city, rising up, terrace upon terrace, above the fertile plain of the green-flowing Scamander, beyond which lay the sea. She always marveled at the work of the Gods that had given her the rulership over Troy. Herself, the Queen; and Priam as her husband, warrior and consort.

She was the mother of Prince Hector, his heir. One day her sons and daughters would inherit this city and the land beyond, as far as the eye could see.

Even if the child whom she was soon to bear should be a daughter, Priam would have no cause to complain of her. Hector was now seven, old enough to learn arms-play. His first suit of armor had already been ordered from the smith who served the royal household. Their daughter Polyxena was four years old, and would someday be pretty, with long reddish hair like Hecuba's own; one day she would be as valuable as any son, for a daughter could be married to one of Priam's rival kings and cement a firm alliance. A king's household should be rich with sons and daughters. The palace women had borne him many sons and a few daughters. But Hecuba, as his Queen, was in charge of the royal nursery, and it was her duty—no, her privilege—to say how every one of the King's children should be brought up, whether born to her or to any other woman.

Queen Hecuba was a handsome woman, tall and broad-shouldered, her auburn hair drawn back smoothly from her brow and dressed in long curls at her neckline. She walked like the Goddess Hera, carrying her child (low and near to birth) proudly before her. She wore the low-cut bodice and tiered skirt, with a pattern of brilliant stripes, that was the common dress of the noblewomen of Troy. A gold collar, as wide as the palm of her hand, gleamed about her throat.

As she walked through a quiet street near the marketplace, a woman of the people, short and dark and coarsely dressed in earth-colored linen, darted out to touch her belly, murmuring, as if startled at her own temerity, "A blessing, O Queen!"

"It is not I," Hecuba responded, "but the Goddess who blesses you." As she held out her hands, she felt above her the shadow of the Goddess, like a tingling in the crown of her head; and she could see in the woman's face the never-failing reflection of awe and wonder at the sudden change.

"May you bear many sons and daughters for our city. I pray you bless me also, Daughter," Hecuba said seriously.

The woman looked up at the Queen—or did she see only the Goddess?—and murmured, "Lady, may the fame of the prince you bear outshine even the fame of Prince Hector."

"So be it," murmured the Queen, and wondered why she felt a small premonitory shiver, as if the blessing had somehow been transmuted, between the woman's lips and her ears, into a curse.

It must have been visible on her face, too, she thought, for her waiting-woman stepped close and said in her ear, "Lady, you are pale; is it the beginning of labor?"

Such was the Queen's confusion that for a moment she actually wondered if the strange sweating chill that seized her was actually the first touch of the birth process. Or was it only the result of that brief overshadowing by the Goddess? She did not remember anything like this with Hector's birth, but she had been a young girl then, hardly aware of the process taking place within her. "I know not," she said. "It is possible."

"Then you must return to the palace and the King must be told," said the woman. Hecuba hesitated. She had no wish to return inside the walls, but if she was truly in labor, it was her duty—not only to the child, and to her husband, but to the King and to all the people of Troy—to safeguard the prince or princess she bore.

"Very well, we shall return to the palace," she said, and turned about in the street. One of the things that troubled her when she walked in the city was that a crowd of women and children always followed her asking for blessings. Since she had become visibly pregnant they begged for the blessing of fertility, as if she could, like the Goddess, bestow the gift of childbearing.

With her woman, she walked beneath the twin lionesses guarding the gates of Priam's palace, and across the huge court-yard behind them where his soldiers gathered for arms-drill. A sentry at the gate raised his spear in salute.

Hecuba watched the soldiers, paired in teams and fighting with blunted weapons. She knew as much about weapons as any of them, for she had been born and raised on the plains, daughter of a nomad tribe whose women rode horseback, and trained like the men of the cities with sword and spear. Her hand itched for a sword, but it was not the custom in Troy, and while at first Priam had allowed her to handle weapons and practice with his soldiers, when she became pregnant with Hector he had forbidden it. In vain she told him that the women of her tribe rode horseback and worked with weapons until a few days before they were delivered of their children; he would not listen to her.

The royal midwives told her that if she so much as touched edged weapons, it would injure her child and perhaps the men who owned the weapons. A woman's touch, they said, especially the touch of a woman in her condition, would make the weapon useless in battle. This sounded to Hecuba like the most solemn foolishness, as if men feared the notion that a woman could be strong enough to protect herself.

"But you have no need to protect yourself, my dearest love," Priam had said. "What sort of man would I be if I could not protect my wife and child?" That had ended the matter, and from that day to this, Hecuba had never so much as touched the hilt of a weapon. Imagining the weight of a sword in her hand now, she grimaced, knowing that she was weak from women's indoor work and soft from lack of training. Priam was not so bad as the Argive kings who kept their women confined inside their houses, but he did not really like it when she went very far outside the palace. He had grown up with women who stayed indoors at all times, and one of his most critical descriptions of a woman was "sunburnt from gadding about."

The Queen went through the small door into the cool shadows of the palace and along the marble-floored halls, hearing in the silence the small sound of her skirts trailing against the floor and her waiting-woman's soft footfalls behind her.

In her sunlit rooms, with all the curtains flung open as she preferred to keep them, her women were sunning and airing linens, and as she came through the doors they paused to greet her. The waiting-woman announced, "The Queen is in labor; send for the royal midwife."

"No, wait." Hecuba's soft but definite voice cut through the cries of excitement. "There is no such hurry; it is by no means certain. I felt strange and had no way of knowing what ailed me; but it is by no means sure it is *that*."

"Still, Lady, if you are not sure, you should let her come to you," the woman persuaded, and the Queen at last agreed. Certainly there was no need for haste; if she was in labor there would soon be no doubt about it; but if she was not it would do no harm to speak with the woman. The strange sensation had passed off as if it had never been, nor did it return.

The sun declined, and Hecuba spent the day helping her women fold and put away the sun-bleached linens. At sundown Priam sent word that he would spend the evening with his men; she should sup with her women and go to bed without waiting for him.

Five years ago, she thought, this would have dismayed her; she would not have been able to go to sleep unless she was encircled in his strong and loving arms. Now, especially this late in pregnancy, she was pleased at the thought of having her bed to herself. Even when it crossed her mind that he might be sharing the bed of one of the other women of the court, perhaps one of the mothers of the other royal children, it did not trouble her; she knew a king must have many sons and her own son Hector was firm in his father's favor.

She would not go into labor this night at least; so she called her women to let them put her to bed with the expected ceremony. For some reason the last image in her mind before she slept was the woman who had asked her for a blessing that day in the street.

SHORTLY BEFORE midnight, the watchman outside the Queen's apartments, drowsing on duty, was awakened by a frightful shriek of despair and dread which seemed to ring throughout the entire palace. Galvanized to full awareness, the watchman stepped inside the rooms, yelling until one of the Queen's women appeared.

"What's happened? Is the Queen in labor? Is the house afire?" he demanded.

"An evil omen," the woman cried, "the most evil of dreams —" and then the Queen herself appeared in the doorway.

"Fire!" she cried out, and the watchman looked in dismay at the usually dignified figure of the Queen, her long reddish hair unbound and falling disheveled to her waist, her tunic unfastened at the shoulder and ungirt so that she was half naked above the waist. He had never noticed before that the Queen was a beautiful woman.

"Lady, what can I do for you?" he asked. "Where is the fire?"

Then he saw an astonishing thing; between one breath and the next, the Queen altered, one moment a distraught stranger, and the next, the regal lady he knew. Her voice was shaking with fear, even though she managed to say quietly, "It must have been a dream. A dream of fire, no more."

"Tell us, Lady," her waiting-woman urged, moving close to the Queen, her eyes alert and wary as she motioned to the watchman. "Go, you should not be here."

"It is my duty to be sure that all is well with the King's women," he said firmly, his eyes fixed on the Queen's newly calm face.

"Let him be; he is doing no more than his duty," Hecuba told the woman, though her voice was still shaking. "I assure you, watchman, it was no more than an evil dream; I had the women search all the rooms. There is no fire."

"We must send to the Temple for a priestess," urged a woman at Hecuba's side. "We must know what peril is betokened by such an evil dream!"

A firm step sounded and the door was thrust open; the King of Troy stood in the doorway, a tall strong man in his thirties, firmly muscled and broad-shouldered even without his armor, with dark curling hair and a neatly trimmed curly dark beard, demanding to know, in the name of all the Gods and Goddesses, what was all this commotion in his house.

"My lord—" the servants backed away as Priam strode through the door.

"Is all well with you, my lady?" he asked, and Hecuba lowered her eyes.

"My lord husband, I regret this disturbance. I had a dream of great evil."

Priam waved at the women. "Go and be certain that all is well in the rooms of the royal children," he commanded, and the women scurried away. Priam was a kindly man, but it was not well to cross him on the relatively rare occasions when he was out of temper. "And you," he said to the watchman, "you heard the Queen; go at once to the Temple of the Great Mother: tell them that the Queen has had a dream of evil omen and is in need of a priestess who can interpret it to her. At once!"

The watchman hurried down the stairs and Hecuba held out her hand to her husband.

"It was truly no more than a dream, then?" he asked.

"No more than a dream," she said, but even the memory of it still made her shiver.

"Tell me, love," he said, and led her back to her bed, sitting beside her and leaning forward to clasp her fingers—hardly smaller than his own—between his callused palms.

"I feel such a fool for disturbing everyone with a nightmare," she said.

"No, you were perfectly right," he said. "Who knows? The dream may have been sent by some God who is your enemy—or mine. Or by a friendly God, as a warning of disaster. Tell me, my love."

"I dreamed—I dreamed—" Hecuba swallowed hard, trying to dispel the choking sensation of dread. "I dreamed the child had been born, a son, and as I lay watching them swaddle him, suddenly some God was in the room—"

"What God?" Priam interrupted sharply. "In what form?"

"How should I know?" Hecuba asked reasonably. "I know little of the Olympians. But I am sure I have not offended any of them nor done them any dishonor."

"Tell me of his form and appearance," Priam insisted.

"He was a youth and beardless; no more than six or seven years older than our Hector," Hecuba said.

"Then it must have been Hermes, the Messenger of the Gods," Priam said.

Hecuba cried out, "But why should a God of the Argives come to me?"

Priam said, "The ways of the Gods are not for us to question. How can I tell? Go on."

Hecuba spoke, her voice still uncertain. "Hermes, then, or whichever God it may have been, leaned over the cradle, and picked up the baby—" Hecuba was white, and beads of sweat stood on her brow, but she tried hard to steady her voice "—it wasn't a baby but—a child—a naked child, burning—I mean it was all afire and burning like a torch. And as he moved, fire came and invaded the castle, burning everywhere and striking the town . . ." She broke down and sobbed. "Oh, what can it mean?"

"Only the Gods know that for certain," Priam said, and held her hand firmly in his.

Hecuba faltered, "In my dream the baby ran before the God . . . a newborn child, running all afire through the palace, and after him, as he passed, all the rooms took fire. Then he ran down through the city—I stood on the balcony overlooking the town, and fire sprang up behind him as he ran, still flaming, so that Troy was burning, all on fire, from the high citadel to the shore, and even the sea was all afire before his steps . . ."

"In the name of Poseidon," Priam murmured under his breath, "what an evil omen . . . for Troy and for all of us!"

He sat silent, stroking her hand, until a slight sound outside the room announced the arrival of the priestess.

She stepped inside the room and said in a calm, cheerful voice: "Peace to all in this House; Rejoice, O Lord and Lady of Troy. My name is Sarmato. I bring you the blessings of the Holy Mother. What service may I do the Queen?" She was a tall, sturdily built woman, probably still of childbearing age, though her dark hair was already showing streaks of gray. She said to

Hecuba, smiling, "I see that the Great Goddess has already blessed you, Queen. Are you ill or in labor?"

"Neither," said Hecuba. "Did they not tell you, priestess? Some God sent me an evil dream."

"Tell me," said Sarmato, "and fear not. The Gods mean us well, of that I am certain. So speak and be not afraid."

Hecuba recounted her dream again, beginning to feel, as she told it, now she was fully awake, that it was not so much horrible as absurd. Nevertheless, she shivered with the terror she had felt in the dream.

The priestess listened with a slight frown gathering between her brows. When Hecuba had finished, she said, "You are sure there was nothing more?"

"Nothing that I can remember, my lady."

The priestess frowned, and from a pouch tied at her waist she drew out a small handful of pebbles; she knelt on the floor and cast them like knucklebones, studying and muttering over their arrangement, casting them again and yet a third time, finally gathering them up and returning them to the pouch.

Then she raised her eyes to Hecuba.

"Thus speaks the Messenger of the Gods of Olympos to you. You bear a son under an evil fate, who will destroy the city of Troy."

Hecuba caught her breath in consternation, but felt her husband's fingers clasping hers, strong and warm and reassuring.

"Can anything be done to avert this fate?" Priam asked.

The priestess shrugged. "In seeking to avert fate, men often bring it closer. The Gods have sent you a warning, but they have not chosen to tell you of what you must do to avert this doom. It might be safest to do nothing."

Priam frowned and said, "Then the child must be exposed at birth," and Hecuba cried out in horror.

"No! No! It was but a dream, a dream . . ."

"A warning from Hermes," said Priam severely. "Expose the boy as soon as he is born; hear me!" He added, in the inflexible formula which gave the words the force of laws carved into stone: "I have spoken; let it be done!"

Hecuba crumpled weeping on her pillows, and Priam said tenderly, "I would not for all Troy have given you this grief, my dearest, but the Gods cannot be mocked."

"Gods!" Hecuba cried, frantic. "What kind of God is it that sends deceitful nightmares to destroy an innocent little child, a newborn babe in the cradle? Among my people," she added resentfully, "a child is its mother's, and no one but she who carried it for most of a year and brought it to birth can say its fate; if she refuses to suckle it and bring it up, that is her own choice. What right has a *man* over children?" She did not say *a mere man*, but her tone of voice made it obvious.

"The right of a *father*," Priam said sternly. "I am master of this house, and as I have spoken, so shall it be done—hear me, woman!"

"Don't say *woman* to me in that tone of voice," cried Hecuba. "I am a free citizen and a Queen and not one of your slaves or concubines!" Yet for all that, she knew that Priam would have his way; when she had chosen to marry a man from those who dwelt in cities and assumed rights over their women, she knew she had consented to this. Priam arose from her side and gave the priestess a piece of gold; she bowed and departed.

Three days later, Hecuba went into labor and gave birth to twins: first a son, then a daughter, as like as one rosebud to another on the same branch. They were both healthy and well formed, and cried lustily, although they were so tiny that the boy's head fitted into Hecuba's palm, and the girl was smaller still.

"Look at him, my lord," she said fiercely to Priam when he came. "He is no bigger than a kitten! And you fear *this* was sent by some God to bring disaster on our city?"

"There is something in what you say," admitted Priam. "Royal blood is, after all, royal blood, and sacred; he is the son of a King of Troy . . ." He considered for a moment. "No doubt it would be enough to have him fostered far away from the city; I have an old and trusted servant, a shepherd on the slopes of Mount Ida, and he will bring up the child. Will that content you, my wife?"

Hecuba knew that the alternative was to have the child

exposed on a mountain, and he was so small and frail that he would die quickly. "Let it be so, then, in the name of the Goddess," she said with resignation, and handed the boy to Priam, who held the child awkwardly, as one unused to handling babies.

He looked into the child's eyes and said, "Greetings, little son." Hecuba sighed with relief; after having formally acknowledged a child, a father could not have it killed, or expose it to die.

Hector and Polyxena had been allowed to come and speak with their mother. Hector said now, "Will you give my brother a royal name, Father?"

Priam scowled, thinking it over. Then he said, "Alexandros. Let the girl be called Alexandra, then."

He went away, taking Hector with him, and Hecuba lay with the dark-haired baby girl in the curve of her arm, thinking that she could comfort herself with the knowledge that her son lived, even if she could not rear him herself, while she had her daughter to keep. *Alexandra,* she thought. *I will call her Kassandra.*

The princess had remained in the room with the women and now edged close to Hecuba's side. Hecuba asked, "Do you like your little sister, my darling?"

"No; she is red and ugly, and not even as pretty as my doll," said Polyxena.

"All babies are like that when they are born," said Hecuba. "You were just as red and ugly; soon she will be just as pretty as you are."

The child scowled. "Why do you want another daughter, Mother, when you have me?"

"Because, darling, if one daughter is a good thing, with two daughters one is twice blessed."

"But Father did not think that two sons were better than one son," Polyxena argued, and Hecuba recalled the prophecy spoken by the woman in the street. Among her own tribe, twins were thought to be, in themselves, an evil omen, and were invariably put to death. If she had remained with them, she would have had to see both infants sacrificed.

Hecuba still felt a residue of superstitious fear; what could have gone amiss to send her two children at one birth, like an animal littering? That was what the women of her tribe believed must be done; yet she had been told that the true reason for the sacrifice of twins was only that it was all but impossible for a woman to suckle two children in a single season. Her twins at least had not been sacrificed to the poverty of the tribe. There were plenty of wet-nurses in Troy; she could have kept them both. Yet Priam had decreed otherwise. She had lost one child —but, by the blessing of the Goddess, only one, not both.

One of her women murmured, almost out of hearing, "Priam is mad! To send away a son and rear a daughter?"

Among my people, Hecuba remembered, *a daughter is valued no less than a son; if this little one had been born in my tribe, I could rear her to be a warrior woman! But if she had been born to my tribe, she would not have lived. Here she will be valued only for the bride-price she will bring when she is married, as I was, to some King.*

But what would become of her son? Would he live in obscurity as a shepherd all his life? It was better than death, perhaps, and the God who had sent the dream and was therefore responsible for his fate might yet protect him.

3

LIGHT GLEAMED in eye-hurting flashes from the sea and the white stone. Kassandra narrowed her eyes against the light and tugged softly at Hecuba's sleeve.

"Why do we go to the Temple today, Mother?" she asked.

Secretly she did not care. It was a rare adventure for her to be allowed outside the women's quarters and rarer yet to go outside the palace altogether. Whatever their destination, the excursion was welcome.

Hecuba said softly, "We go to pray that the child I am to bear this winter will be a son."

"Why, Mother? You have a son already. I should think you would rather have another daughter; you only have two of us girls. I would rather have another sister."

"I am sure you would," said the Queen, smiling, "but your father wants another son. Men always want sons so they can grow up to fight in their armies and defend the city."

"Is there a war?"

"No, not now; but there are always wars when a city is as rich as Troy."

"But if I had another sister she might be a warrior woman, as you were when you were a girl, and learn to use weapons and defend the city as well as any son." Then she paused to consider. "I do not think Polyxena could be a soldier; she is too soft and timid. But I would like to be a warrior woman. Like you."

"I am sure you would, Kassandra; but it is not the custom for women of Troy."

"Why not?"

"What do you mean, why not? Customs *are*. There is no reason for them."

Kassandra gave her mother a skeptical look, but she had already learned not to question that tone in her mother's voice. She thought secretly that her mother was the most queenly and beautiful woman in the world, tall and strong-looking, in her low-cut bodice and flounced skirt, but she no longer quite believed her all-knowing like the Goddess. In the six years of her life, she had heard something similar nearly every day and believed it less with every year; but when Hecuba spoke like that, Kassandra knew she would get no further explanation.

"Tell me about when you were a warrior, Mother."

"I am of the nomad tribe, the riding women," Hecuba began. She was almost always willing to talk about her early life —more so, Kassandra thought, since this latest pregnancy. "Our fathers and brothers are also of the horse-folk, and they are very brave."

"Are they warriors?"

"No, child; among the horse-tribes, the women are the warriors. The men are healers and magicians, and they know all kinds of wisdom and about the lore of trees and herbs."

"When I am older can I go to live with them?"

"The Kentaurs? Of course not; women cannot be fostered in a man's tribe."

"No; I mean with your tribe, the riding women."

"I do not think your father would like that," said Hecuba, thinking that this small, solemn daughter might well have grown to be a leader among her own nomad people, "but perhaps someday it can be arranged. Among my tribe a father has authority only over his sons, and it is the mother who decrees the destiny of a daughter. You would have to learn to ride and to use weapons."

She took up the small, soft hand in hers, thinking that it was hardly the hand of a warrior woman.

"Which Temple is that—up there?" Kassandra asked, pointing upward to the highest of the terraces above them, indicating a building that gleamed brilliantly white in the sun. From where they stood, Kassandra, leaning on the wall that guarded the winding stairway upward, could look down and see the roofs of the palace and the small figures of the women laying out washing to dry, small trees in tubs, the bright colors of their clothing and the mats where they lay to rest in the sun; and far below that, the city walls looking out over the plain.

"It is the Temple of Pallas Athene, the greatest of the Goddesses of your father's people."

"Is She the same as the Great Goddess, the one you call Earth Mother?"

"All the Goddesses are one, as all the Gods are one; but they show themselves with different faces to mankind, in different cities and at different times. Here in Troy, Pallas Athene is the Goddess as Maiden, because in Her temple under the care of Her maidens is guarded the holiest object within our city. It is called the Palladium." Hecuba paused, but Kassandra, sensing a story, was mouse-silent, and Hecuba went on in a reminiscent tone.

"They say that when the Goddess Athene was young she had a mortal playmate, the Libyan maiden Pallas, and when

Pallas died Athene mourned her so greatly that she added her name to her own and was thereafter known as Pallas Athene; She fashioned an image of Her friend and set it up in the Temple of Zeus on Olympos. At that time, Erechtheus, who was King in Crete—your father's forefather before his people came to this part of the world—had a great herd of a thousand beautiful cattle, and Boreas, the son of the North Wind, loved them, and visited them as a great white bull; and these sacred cattle became the bull-Gods of Crete."

"I did not know that the Kings of Crete were our forefathers," Kassandra said.

"There are many things you do not know," Hecuba said in reproof, and Kassandra held her breath—would her mother be too cross to finish the story? But Hecuba's frown was fleeting, and she went on.

"Ilos, the son of Erechtheus, came to these shores and entered the sacred Games here. He was the victor in the games, and as his prize he won fifty youths and fifty maidens. And rather than making them his slaves, he said, 'I will free them, and with them I will found a city.' And so he set forth in a ship at the will of the Gods—and he sacrificed to the North Wind to send him to the right place for his city, which he meant to call Ilion; which is another name for the city of Troy."

"And did the North Wind blow him *here?*" Kassandra asked.

"No; he was blown from his course at sea by a whirlwind, and when he came to rest near the mouth of our holy Scamander, the Gods sent one of these cows, a beautiful heifer, a daughter of the North Wind, and a voice came to Ilos, crying out, 'Follow the cow! Follow the cow! Where the cow lies down, there establish your city!' And they say that the cow wandered to the bend of the river Scamander and there she lay down; and there Ilos built the city of Troy. And one night he awoke hearing another voice from Heaven, saying, 'Preserve the image I give you; for while Pallas dwells within your city, your city shall never fall.' And he woke and beheld the image of Pallas, with a distaff in one hand and a spear in the other, like Athene's self. So when the city was built, he built this Temple first, on the high place, far up here, and he dedicated it to Athene—She was quite a new face of the Goddess, then, one of the great Olympians, worshiped even by those who honor the Sky Gods and the Thunderer—he made Her the patron of the city. And She brought to us the arts of weaving and the gifts of the vine and the olive, wine and oil."

"But we are not going to Her Temple today, Mother?"

"No, my love; though the Maiden Goddess is also patron of childbirth and I should sacrifice also to her. Today we seek the Sun Lord Apollo. He is the Lord of the Oracles as well; he slew the great Python, the Goddess of the Underworld, and became Lord of the Underworld as well."

"Tell me, if the Python was a Goddess, how could she be slain?"

"Oh, I suppose it is because the Sun Lord is stronger than any Goddess," her mother said, as they began to climb the hill at the center of the city. The steps were steep, and Kassandra's legs felt tired as she struggled up them. Once she looked back; they were so high, so near the God's house, that she could see over the wall of the city to the great rivers where they flowed across the plain and came together in a great flood of silver toward the sea.

Then for a moment it seemed to her that the surface of the sea was shadowed and that she saw ships blurring the brightness of the waves. She wiped her eyes and said, "Are those my father's ships?"

Hecuba looked back and asked, "What ships? I see no ships. Are you playing some game with me?"

"No; I really see them. Look there, one has a gray sail. . . . No, it was the sun in my eyes; I cannot see them now." Her eyes ached, and the ships were gone—or had they ever been more than the glare on the water?

It seemed to her that the air was so clear, filled with little sparkles like a thin veil, that at any moment it might tear or slip aside, revealing a glimpse into another world beyond this one. She could not remember ever seeing anything like this before. She felt, without knowing how, that the ships she had seen were there in that other world. Perhaps they were something she was going to see someday. She was young enough not to think this in any way strange. Her mother had moved on ahead, and for some reason it seemed to Kassandra that it would disturb the Queen if she spoke again about the ships she had seen and could not see now. She hurried after her mother, her legs aching as she strained up the steps.

The Temple of Apollo Helios the Sun Lord stood more than halfway to the summit of the hill upon which was built the great city of Troy. It was overlooked only by the great height of the Temple of Maiden Athene far above; but it was itself the most beautiful of the Temples of the city. It was built of shining white marble, with tall columns at either side, on a foundation of stonework set up—so Kassandra had been told more than once—by Titans before even the oldest men in the city were born. The light was so fierce that Kassandra shaded her eyes with her hands. Well, if this was the very home of the Sun God, what would be its nature if not strong and perpetual light?

In the outer court, where merchants were selling all manner of things—animals for sacrifice, small clay statues of the God, various foods and drinks—her mother bought her a slice of sweet melon. It slid deliciously down her throat, dry from the long and dusty climb. The area under the portico of the next court was cool and shadowy; there a number of priests and functionaries recognized the Queen and beckoned her forward.

"Welcome, Lady," said one of them, "and the little princess too. Would you like to sit here and rest for a moment until the priestess can speak with you?"

The Queen and the princess were shown to a marble bench in the shade. Kassandra sat quietly beside her mother for a moment, glad to be out of the heat; she finished her melon and wiped her hands on her underskirt, then looked about for a place to put the rind; it did not seem quite right to throw it on the floor under the eyes of the priests and priestesses. She slid down from the bench and discovered a basket where there was a quantity of fruit rinds and peelings, and put her rind inside it with the others.

Then she walked around the room slowly, wondering what she would see, and how different the house of a God would be from the house of a King. This, of course, was only His reception room, where people waited for audience; there was a room like this in the palace where petitioners came to wait when they wanted to ask a favor of the King or bring him a present. She wondered if He had a bedroom or where He slept or bathed. And Kassandra peered through into the main room which, she thought, must be the God's audience chamber.

He was there. The colors in which He was painted were so lifelike that Kassandra was not really aware for a moment that what she was seeing was a statue. It seemed reasonable that a God should be a little larger than life, rigidly upright, smiling a distant but welcoming smile. Kassandra stole into the room, to the very foot of the God, and for a moment she thought she had actually heard Him speak; then she knew it was only a voice in her mind.

"Kassandra," He said, and it seemed perfectly natural that a God should know her name without being told, *"will you be My priestess?"*

She whispered, neither knowing nor caring if she spoke aloud, "Do you want me, Lord Apollo?"

"Yes; it is I who called you here," he said. The voice was great and golden, just what she imagined that a God's voice would be; and she had been told that the Sun Lord was also the God of music and song.

"But I am only a little girl, not yet old enough to leave my father's house," she whispered.

"Still, I bid you remember, when that day comes, that you are Mine," said the voice, and for a moment the motes of golden dust in the slanting sunshine became all one great ray of light through which it seemed that the God reached down to her and touched her with a burning touch . . . and then the brightness was gone and she could see that it was only a statue, chill and unmoving and not at all like the Apollo who had spoken to her. The priestess had come to lead her mother forward to the statue, but Kassandra tugged at her mother's hand.

"It's all right," she whispered insistently. "The God told me He would give you what you asked for."

She had no idea when she had heard this; she simply *knew* that her mother's child was a boy, and if she knew when she had not known before, then it must have been the God who told her, and so, though she had not heard the God's voice, she knew that what she said was true.

Hecuba looked down at her skeptically, let her hand go and went into the inner room with the priestess. Kassandra went to look around the room.

Beside the altar was a small reed basket, and inside, as Kassandra peeped in, a suggestion of movement. At first she thought it was kittens, and wondered why, for cats were not sacrificed to the Gods. Looking more closely, she noted that there were two small coiled snakes in the basket. Serpents, she knew, belonged to Apollo of the Underworld. Without stopping to think, she reached out and grasped them in either hand, bringing them toward her face. They felt soft and warm and dry, faintly scaly beneath her fingers, and she could not resist kissing them. She felt strangely elated and just faintly sick, her small body trembling all over.

She never knew how long she crouched there, holding the serpents, nor could she have said what they told her; she only knew that she was listening attentively to them all that time.

Then she heard her mother's voice in a cry of dread and reproof. She looked up, smiling.

"It's all right," she said, looking past her mother to the troubled face of the priestess behind Hecuba. "The God told me I might."

"Put them down, quickly," said the priestess. "You are not used to handling them; they might very well have bitten you."

Kassandra gave each of the serpents a final caress and laid it gently back in the reed basket. It seemed to her that they were reluctant to leave her, and she bent close and promised them she would come again and play with them.

"You wretched, disobedient girl!" Hecuba cried as she rose, grabbing her by the arm and pinching her hard, and Kassandra drew away, troubled; she could not remember that her mother had ever been angry with her before this, and she could not imagine why she should make a fuss about something like this.

"Don't you know that snakes are poisonous and dangerous?"

"But they belong to the God," Kassandra argued. "He would not let them bite me."

"You were very lucky," said the priestess gravely.

"*You* handle them, and you are not afraid," Kassandra said.

"But I am a priestess and I have been taught to handle them."

"Apollo said I was to be His priestess, and He told me I might touch them," she argued, and the priestess looked down at her with a frown.

"Is this true, child?"

"Of course it is not true," Hecuba said sharply. "She is making up a tale! She is always imagining things."

This was so unfair and unjustified that Kassandra began to cry. Her mother grabbed her firmly by the arm and pulled her outside, pushing her ahead and down the steep steps so roughly that she stumbled and almost fell. The day seemed to have lost all its golden brilliance. The God was gone; she could no longer feel His presence, and she could have cried for that even more than for the bruising grip of her mother on her upper arm.

"Why would you say such a thing?" Hecuba scolded again. "Are you such a baby that I cannot leave you alone for twenty minutes without your getting into mischief? Playing with the Temple serpents—don't you know how badly they could have hurt you?"

"But the God said He would not let them hurt me," Kassandra declared stubbornly, and her mother pinched her again, leaving a bruise on her arm.

"You must not say such a thing!"

"But it is true," the girl insisted.

"Nonsense; if you ever say such a thing again," said her mother crossly, "I shall beat you." Kassandra was silent. What had happened had happened; she had no wish to be beaten, but she knew the truth and could not deny it. Why couldn't her mother trust her? She always told the truth.

She could not bear it, that her mother and the priestess should think she was lying, and as she went quietly, no longer protesting, down the long steps, her hand tucked tightly in the larger hand of the Queen, she clung to the face of Apollo, His gentle voice in her mind. Without her even being aware of it, something very deep within her was already waiting for the sound.

4

AT THE NEXT full moon, Hecuba was delivered of a son, who was to be her last child. They named him Troilus. Kassandra, standing by her mother's bed in the birth chamber, looking on the face of her small brother, was not surprised. But when she reminded her mother that she had known since the day of her visit to the Temple that the child would be a son, Hecuba sounded displeased.

"Why, so you did," she said angrily, "but do you really think a God spoke to you? You are only trying to make yourself important," she scolded, "and I will not listen to it. You are not so little as that. That is a babyish thing to do."

But that, Kassandra thought angrily, was the important thing: she had *known*; the God had spoken to her. Did He speak to babies, then? And why should it make her mother angry? She knew the Goddess spoke to her mother; she had seen the Lady descend on Hecuba when she invoked Her at harvest time and in blessing.

"Listen, Kassandra," said the Queen seriously, "the greatest crime is to speak anything but the truth about a God. Apollo is Lord of the Truth; if you speak His name falsely, He will punish you, and His anger is terrible."

"But I am telling the truth; the God *did* speak to me," Kassandra said earnestly, and her mother sighed in despair, for this was not an unknown thing either.

"Well, I suppose you must be left to Him, then. But I warn you, don't speak of this to anyone else."

Now that there was another prince in the palace, another son of Priam by his Queen, there was rejoicing through the city.

Kassandra was left very much to herself, and she wondered why a prince should be so much more important than a princess. It was no use asking her mother why this should be so. She might have asked her older sister, but Polyxena seemed to care for nothing except gossip with the waiting-women about pretty clothes and jewelry and marriages. This seemed dull to Kassandra, but they assured her than when she was older she would be more interested in the important things of a woman's life. She wondered why these should be so important. She was willing enough to look at pretty clothes and jewelry, but had no desire to wear them herself; she would as soon see them on Polyxena or her mother. Her mother's waiting-women thought her as strange as she thought them. Once she had stubbornly refused to enter a room, crying out, "The ceiling will fall!" Three days later, there was a small earthquake and it did fall.

AS TIME PASSED and season followed season, Troilus began first to toddle and then to walk and talk; sooner than Kassandra thought possible, he was almost as tall as she was herself. Meanwhile, Polyxena grew taller than Hecuba and was initiated into the women's Mysteries.

Kassandra longed fiercely for the time when she too would be recognized as a woman, though she could not see that it made Polyxena any wiser. When she had been initiated into the Mysteries, would the God speak again to her? All these years she had never again heard His voice; perhaps her mother was right and she had only imagined it. She longed to hear that voice again, if only to reassure herself it had been real. Yet her longing was tempered with reluctance; to be a woman, it seemed, was to change so irrevocably as to lose all that made her herself. Polyxena was now tied to the life of the women's quarters, and seemed quite content to be so; she no longer even seemed to resent the loss of her freedom, and would no longer conspire with Kassandra to run away down into the city.

Soon enough, Troilus was old enough to be sent to the men's quarters to sleep, and she herself was twelve years old. That year she grew taller, and from certain changes in her body she knew that soon she too would be counted among the women of the palace and no longer allowed to run about where she chose.

Obediently, Kassandra allowed her mother's old nurse to teach her to spin and weave. With the help of Hesione, her father's unmarried sister, she let herself be coaxed into spinning the thread and weaving a robe for her clay doll, which she still cherished. She hated the drudgery, which made her fingers ache, but she was proud of her work when it was done.

She now occupied a room in the women's quarters with Polyxena, who was sixteen and old enough to be married, and Hesione, a lively young woman in her twenties, with Priam's curling dark hair and brilliant green eyes. Under the seemingly senseless rules of conduct set forth by her mother and Hesione, Kassandra was to stay indoors and ignore all the interesting things that might be happening in the palace or the city. But there were days when she managed to evade the vigilance of the women, when she would run off alone to one of her secret places.

One morning she slipped out of the palace and took the route through the streets that led upward to Apollo's Temple.

She had no desire to climb to the Temple itself, no sense that the God had summoned her. She told herself that when that day came, she would know. As she climbed, halfway up she turned to look down into the harbor, and saw the ships. They were just as she had seen them the day the God spoke to her; but now she knew that they were ships from the South, from the island kingdoms of the Akhaians and of Crete. They had come to trade with the Hyperborean countries, and Kassandra thought, with an excitement that was almost physical, that they would reach the country of the North Wind, from whose breath were born the great Bull-Gods of Crete. She wished she might sail north with the ships; but she could never go. Women were never allowed to sail on any of the great trading ships, which, as they sailed up through the straits, must pay tribute to King Priam and to Troy. And as she stared at the ships, a shudder, unlike any physical sensation she had known before, ran through her body. . . .

She was lying in a corner on a ship, lifting up and down to the motion of the waves; nauseated, sick, exhausted and terrified, bruised and sore; yet when she looked up at the sky above the great sun-shimmering sail, the sky was blue and gleaming with Apollo's sun. A man's face looked down at her with a fierce, hateful, triumphant smile. In one moment of terror, it was printed forever on her mind. Kassandra had never in her life known real fear or real shame, only momentary embarrassment at a mild reproof from her mother or father; now she knew the ultimate of both. With one part of her mind she knew she had never seen this man, yet knew that never in her life would she forget his face, with its great hook of a nose like the beak of some rapacious bird of prey, the eyes gleaming like a hawk's, the cruel fierce smile and the harsh jutting chin; a black-bearded countenance which filled her with dread and terror.

In a moment between a breath and a breath, it was gone, and she was standing on the steps, the ships distant in the harbor below her. Yet a moment ago, she *knew*, she had been lying in one of those ships, a captive—the hard deck under her body, the salt wind over her, the flapping sound of the sail and the creaking of the wooden boards of the ship. She felt again the terror and the curious exhilaration which she could not understand.

She had at the moment no way of knowing what had happened to her, or why. She turned around and looked upward to where the Temple of Pallas Athene rose white and high above the harbor, and prayed to the Maiden Goddess that what she had seen and felt was no more than some kind of waking nightmare. Or would it truly happen one day . . . that she would be that bruised captive in the ship, prey of that fierce hawk-faced man? He did not resemble any Trojan she had ever seen. . . .

Deliberately putting away the frozen horror of her—nightmare? vision?—Kassandra turned away and looked inland, to where the great height rose of the holy Mount Ida. Somewhere on the slopes of that mountain . . . no, she had dreamed it, had never set foot on the slopes of Ida. High above were the never-melting snows, and below, the green pasturelands where, she had been told, her father's many flocks and herds grazed in the care of shepherds. She rubbed her hands fretfully over her eyes. *If she could only see what lay there beyond her sight . . .*

Not even years later, when all things which had to do with

prophecy and the Sight were second nature to her, was Kassandra ever sure whence came the sudden knowledge of what she must do next. She never claimed or thought she had heard the voice of the God; *that* she would have known and recognized at once. It was simply *there*, a part of her being. She turned round and ran quickly back to the palace. Passing through a street she knew, she glanced almost wistfully at the fountain; no, the water was not still enough for that.

In the outer court, she spied one of her mother's women, and hid behind a statue, fearing that the woman might have been sent to search for her. There was always a fuss now whenever she went outside the women's quarters.

Such folly! Staying inside did not help Hesione, she thought, and did not know what she meant by it. Thinking of Hesione filled her with a sudden dread, and she did not know why, but it occurred to her that she should warn her. *Warn her? Of what? Why? No, it would be no use. What must come will come.* Something within her made her wish to run to Hesione (or to her mother, or to Polyxena, or to her nurse, anyone who could ease this nameless terror which made her knees tremble and her stomach wobble). But whatever her own mission might be, it was more urgent to her than any fancied or foreseen dangers to anyone else. She was still crouched, hiding, behind the pillar; but the woman was out of sight. *I was afraid that she would see me.*

Afraid? No! I have not known the meaning of the word! After the terror of that vision in the harbor, Kassandra knew that nothing less would ever make her feel fear. Still she did not wish to be seen with this compulsion upon her; someone might stop her from doing what *must* be done. She hurried to the women's quarters and found a clay bowl which she filled with water drawn fresh from the cistern, and knelt before it.

Staring into the water, at first she saw only her own face looking back, as from a mirror. Then as the shadows shifted on the surface of the water, she knew it was a boy's face she looked on, very like her own: the same heavy straight dark hair, the same deep-set eyes, shadowed beneath long heavy lashes. He looked beyond her, staring at something she could not see. . . .

Troubled with care for the sheep, each one's name known, each footstep placed with such care; the inner knowledge of where they were and what must be done for each of them, as if directed by some secret wisdom. Kassandra found herself wishing passionately that she could be trusted with work as responsible and meaningful as this. For some time she knelt by the basin, wondering why she had been brought to see him and what it could possibly mean. She was not aware that she was cramped and cold, nor that her knees ached from her unmoving posture; she watched with him, sharing his annoyance when one of the animals stumbled, sharing his pleasure at the sunlight, her mind just touching and skimming over the occasional fears—of wolves, or larger and more dangerous beasts . . . she *was* the strange boy whose face was her own reflection. Lost in this passionate identification, she was roused by a sudden outcry.

"Hai! Help, ho, fire, murder, rape! Help!" For a moment she thought it was he who had cried out; but no, it was somehow a *different* kind of sound, heard with her physical ears; it jarred her out of her trance.

Another vision, but this one with neither pain nor fear. Do they come from a God? She returned with a painful jolt to awareness of where she was: in the courtyard of the women's quarters.

And she suddenly smelled smoke, and the bowl into which she still stared clouded, tilted sidewise, and the water ran out across the floor. The visionary stillness went with it, and Kassandra found that she could move.

Strange footsteps clattered on the floor; she heard her mother scream, and ran into the corridor. It was empty, except for the shrieking of women. Then she saw two men in armor, with great high-crested helmets. They were tall, taller than her father or the half-grown Hector; great hairy, savage-looking men, both of them with fair hair hanging below their helmets; one of them bore over his shoulder a screaming woman. In shock and horror, Kassandra recognized the woman: her aunt Hesione.

Kassandra had no idea what was happening or why; she was still halfway within the apartness of her vision. The soldiers ran right past her, brushing so close to her and so swiftly that one all but knocked her off her feet. She started to run after them, with some vague notion that she might somehow help Hesione; but they were already gone, rushing down the palace steps; as if her inner sight followed, she saw Hesione borne, still screaming, down the stairs and through the city. The people melted away before the intruders. It was as if the men's gaze had the quality of the Gorgon's head, to turn people to stone—not only must they avoid looking on the Akhaians, but they must not even be looked upon by them.

There was a dreadful screaming from the lower city, and it seemed that all the women in the palace like a chorus had taken up the shrieks.

The screaming went on for some time, then died away into a grief-stricken wailing. Kassandra went in search of her mother —suddenly frightened and guilty for not thinking sooner that Hecuba too might have been taken. In the distance she could faintly hear sounds of clashing warfare; she could hear the war-cries of her father's men, who were fighting the intruders on their way back to the ships. Somehow Kassandra was aware that their fighting was in vain.

Is what I saw, what I felt, that which will happen to Hesione? That terrible hawk-faced man—will he take her for his captive? Did I see—and worse, did I feel—what will happen to her?

She did not know whether to hope that she herself need not suffer it, or to be ashamed that she wished it instead upon her beloved young aunt.

She came into her mother's room, where Hecuba sat white as death, holding little Troilus on her lap.

"There you are, naughty girl," said one of the nurses. "We were afraid that the Akhaian raiders had gotten you too."

Kassandra ran to her mother and fell to her knees at her side. "I saw them take Aunt Hesione," she whispered. "What will happen to her?"

"They will take her back to their country and hold her there until your father pays ransom for her," Hecuba said, wiping away her tears.

There was the loud step at the door that Kassandra always

associated with her father, and Priam came into the chamber, girt for battle but with some of his armor's straps half-fastened as if he had armed himself too quickly.

Hecuba raised her eyes and saw behind Priam the armed figure of Hector, a slender warrior of nineteen.

"Is it well with you and the children, my love?" asked the King. "Today your eldest son fought by my side as a true warrior."

"And Hesione?" Hecuba asked.

"Gone. There were too many for us and they had gotten to the ships before we could reach her," Priam said. "You know perfectly well that they care nothing for the woman; it is only that she is my sister and so they think they can demand concessions and freedom from harbor tolls—that is all." He set his spear aside with an expression of disgust.

Hecuba called Hector to her, fussing over him till he moved away and said irritably, "Have done, Mother—I am not a little one still holding your skirts!"

"Shall I send for wine, my lord?" Hecuba asked, putting down the child and rising dutifully, but Priam shook his head.

"Don't trouble yourself," he said, "I would not have disturbed you, but I thought you would like to know that your son came honorably and unwounded from his first battle."

He went out of the room, and Hecuba said between her teeth, "Battle indeed! He cannot wait to get to his newest woman, that is all, and she will give him unmixed wine and he will be ill! And as for Hesione—much he cares for *her*! As long as they do not disturb his precious shipping, the Akhaians could have us all and welcome!"

Kassandra knew better than to ask anything further of her mother at that moment; but that night when they gathered in the great dining hall of the palace (for Priam still kept to the old custom in which men and women dined all together, instead of the new fashion whereby women took their meals separately in the women's quarters—"so that the women need not appear before strange men," as the Akhaian slaves put it), she waited until Priam was in a good humor, sharing his finest wine with her mother and beckoning to Polyxena, whom he always petted, to come and sit beside him. Then Kassandra stole forward, and Priam indulgently motioned to her.

"What do you want, Bright Eyes?"

"Only to ask a question, Father, about something I saw today."

"If it is about Aunt Hesione—" he began.

"No, sir; but do you think the Akhaians will ask ransom for her?"

"Probably not," said Priam. "Probably one of them will marry her and try to claim rights in Troy because of it."

"How dreadful for her!" Kassandra whispered.

"Not so bad, after all; she will have a good husband among the Akhaians, and it will perhaps for *this* year stave off war about trading rights," Priam said. "In the old days, many marriages were made like that."

"How horrible!" Polyxena said timidly. "I would not want to go so far from home to marry. And I would rather have a proper wedding, not be carried off like that!"

"Well, I am sure we can arrange that sooner or later," said Priam indulgently. "There is your mother's kinsman young Akhilles—he shows signs, they say, of being a mighty warrior. . . ."

Hecuba shook her head. She said, "Akhilles has been promised to his cousin Deidameia, daughter of Lykomedes; and I would as soon my daughter never came into that kindred."

"All the same, if he is to win fame and glory . . . I have heard that the boy is already a great hunter of lions and boars," countered Priam. "I would gladly have him for a son-in-law." He sighed. "Well, there is time enough later to think of husbands and weddings for the girls. What did you see today, little Kassandra, that you wanted to ask me?"

Even as the words crossed her lips, Kassandra felt she should perhaps keep silent; that what she had seen in the scrying-bowl should not be spoken; but her confusion and her hunger for knowledge were so great she could not stop herself. The words rushed out: "Father, tell me, who is the boy I saw today with a face so exactly like my own?"

Priam glared at her so that she quivered with terror. He

stared over her head at Hecuba and said in a terrible voice, "Where have you been taking her?"

Hecuba looked blankly at Priam and said, "I have taken her nowhere. I do not have the faintest idea what she is talking about."

"Come here, Kassandra," said Priam, frowning ominously and pushing Polyxena away from his knee. "Tell me more about this; where did you see the boy? Was he in the city?"

"No, Father, I have only seen him in the scrying-bowl. He watches the sheep on Mount Ida, and he looks exactly like me."

She was frightened at the abrupt change in her father's face. He roared, "And what were you doing with a scrying-bowl, you little wretch?"

He turned on Hecuba with a gesture of rage, and for a moment, Kassandra thought he would strike the Queen.

"You, Lady, this is your doing—I leave the rearing of the girls to you, and here is one of my daughters meddling with scrying and sorceries, oracles and the like—"

"But who *is* he?" Kassandra demanded. Her need for an answer was greater than her fear. "And why does he look so much like me?"

In return, her father roared wordlessly, and struck her across the face with such force that she lost her balance and skidded down the steps near his throne, falling and striking her head.

Her mother shouted with indignation, hurrying to raise her. "What have you done to my daughter, you great brute?"

Priam glared at his wife and rose angrily to his feet. He raised his hand to strike her, and Kassandra cried out through her sobs, "No! Don't hit Mother; she didn't do anything!" At the edge of her vision she saw Polyxena looking at them wide-eyed but too frightened to speak, and thought with more contempt than anger, *She would stand by and let the King beat our mother?* She cried out, "It was not Mother's fault, she did not even know! It was the God who said I might—He said when I was grown up I was to be His priestess, and it was He who showed me how to use the scrying-bowl—"

"Be silent!" Priam commanded, and glared over her head at Hecuba. She could not imagine why he was so angry.

"I'll have no sorceries in my palace, Lady—do you hear me?" Priam said. "Send her to be fostered before she spreads this nonsense to the other girls, the proper maidenly ones . . ." He looked around, and his frown softened as his eyes rested on the simpering Polyxena. Then he glared at Kassandra again where she still crouched, holding her bleeding head. Now she knew there was *really* some secret about the boy whose face she had seen.

He would not talk about Hesione. *He does not care. It is enough for him that she will be married to one of those invaders who carried her off.* The thought, coupled with the fear and the shame of the vision—if that was what it had been—made her feel a sudden dread. *Father will not tell me. Well, then, I shall ask the Lord Apollo.*

He knows even more than Father. And He told me I was to be His own; if it were I and not Hesione, He would not have let me be carried away by that man. It is enough for Father that she will be married; if that man carried me off, would he let me go to a marriage like that? Her vision of the man with the eagle face was never to leave her. But to block it out, she closed her eyes and tried to summon up again the golden voice of the Sun Lord, saying, *You are Mine.*

5

KASSANDRA'S BRUISES were still yellow and green, the moon faded to a narrow morning crescent. She stood beside her mother, who was laying a few of her tunics in a leather bag, with her new sandals and a warm winter cloak.

"But it is not winter yet," she protested.

"It is colder on the plains," Hecuba told her. "Believe me, you will need it for riding, my love."

Kassandra leaned against her mother and said, almost in tears, "I don't want to go away from you."

"And I will miss you, too, but I think you will be happy," Hecuba said. "I wish I were going with you."

"Then why don't you come, Mother?"

"Your father needs me."

"No, he doesn't," Kassandra protested. "He has his other women; he could manage without you."

"I am sure he would," Hecuba said, grimacing a little. "But I do not want to leave him to them; they are not as careful of his health and his honor as I am. Also, there is your baby brother, and he needs me."

This made no sense to Kassandra; Troilus had been sent to the men's quarters at the New Year. But if her mother did not wish to go, there was nothing she could say. Kassandra hoped she would never have children, if having them meant never doing what you wished.

Hecuba raised her head, hearing sounds down in the courtyard. "I think they are coming," she said, and took Kassandra's hand in hers. Together they hurried down the long flight of stairs.

Many of the housefolk were gathered, staring at the women who had ridden their horses, white and bay and black, right into the court. Their leader, a tall woman with a dark, freckled face, vaulted down from the back of her horse and ran to catch Hecuba in her arms.

"Sister! What joy to see you," she cried. Hecuba held her, and Kassandra marveled to see her staid mother laughing and crying at once. After a moment the tall stranger let her go and said, "You have grown fat and soft with indoor living; and your skin is so white and pale, you might be a ghost!"

"Is that so bad?" Hecuba asked.

The woman scowled at her and asked, "And these are your daughters? Are they house-mice too?"

"That you will have to decide for yourself," Hecuba said, beckoning the girls forward. "This is Polyxena. She is already sixteen."

"She looks too frail for an outdoor life such as ours, Hecuba. I think perhaps you have kept her indoors too long; but we will do what we can with her, and return her to you healthy and strong."

Polyxena shrank away behind her mother, and the tall Amazon laughed.

"No?"

"No; you are to have the little one, Kassandra," said Hecuba.

"The little one? How old is she?"

"Twelve years," Hecuba answered. "Kassandra, child, come and greet your kinswoman Penthesilea, the chief of our tribe."

Kassandra looked attentively at the older woman. She was taller by several finger-breadths than Hecuba, who was herself tall for a woman. She wore a pointed leather cap, under which Kassandra could see tucked-up coils of faded ginger-colored hair, and a short tight tunic; her legs were long and lean in leather breeches which came below the knee. Her face was thin and lined, her complexion not only burnt dark by the sun, but spotted with thousands of brown freckles. She looked, Kassandra thought, more like a warrior than a woman; but her face was enough like Hecuba's own that Kassandra had no doubt that this was her kinswoman. She smiled at Kassandra good-naturedly.

"Do you think you will like to come with us, then? You are not frightened? I think your sister is afraid of our horses," she added.

"Polyxena is afraid of everything," Kassandra said. "She wants to be what my father calls a proper good girl."

"And you don't?"

"Not if it means staying in the house all the time," said Kassandra, and saw Penthesilea smile. "What is your horse's name? Will he bite?"

"*She* is called Racer, and she has never bitten me yet," said Penthesilea. "You may make friends with her if you are able."

Kassandra went boldly forward and held out her hand as she had been taught to do with a strange dog so that it could smell her scent. The horse butted its great head down and snorted, and Kassandra stroked the silky nose and looked into the great loving eyes. She felt, returning that wide-eyed gaze, that she had already found a friend among these strangers.

Penthesilea said, "Well, are you ready to come with us, then?"

"Oh, *yes!*" Kassandra breathed fervently. Penthesilea's thin stern face looked friendlier when she smiled.

"Do you think you can learn to ride?"

Friendly or not, the horse looked *very* large, and very high off the ground; but Kassandra said valiantly, "If you could learn and my mother could learn, I suppose there is no reason I cannot."

"Won't you come up to the women's quarters and share some refreshment before you must go?" asked Hecuba.

"Why, yes, if you will have someone look after our horses," Penthesilea said. Hecuba summoned one of the servants and gave orders to take Penthesilea's horse and those of her two companions to the stables. The two women with her, dressed as she was dressed, the Amazon leader introduced as Charis and Melissa. Charis was thin and pale, almost as freckled as the Queen, but her hair was the color of brass; Melissa had brown curly hair and was plump and pink-cheeked. They were, Kassandra decided, fifteen or sixteen. She wondered if they were Penthesilea's daughters but was too shy to ask.

Climbing to the women's quarters, Kassandra wondered why she had never noticed before how dark it was inside. Hecuba had called the waiting-women to bring wine and sweets, and while the guests nibbled at them, Penthesilea called Kassandra to her and said, "If you are to ride with us, you must be properly dressed, my dear. We brought a pair of breeches for you. Charis will help you to put them on. And you should have a warm cloak for riding; when the sun is down it grows cold quickly."

"Mother made me a warm cloak," Kassandra said, and went with Charis into her room to fetch the bag of her possessions. The leather breeches were a little big for her—Kassandra wondered who had worn them before this, for they were shiny in the seat with hard wear. But they were astonishingly comfortable once she had grown used to their stiffness against her legs. She thought that now she could run like the wind without tripping over her skirts. She was threading the leather belt through the loops when she heard her father's step and his boisterous voice.

"Well, kinswoman, have you come to lead my armies to Mykenae to recover Hesione? And such splendid horses—I saw them in the stable. Like the immortal horses of Poseidon's own herd! Where did you find them?"

"We traded for them with Idomeneus, the King of Crete," said Penthesilea. "We had not heard about Hesione; what happened?"

"Agamemnon's men from Mykenae, or so we thought," Priam said. "Akhaians anyhow, raiders. Rumor says Agamemnon is a vicious and cruel King. Even his own men love him not; but they fear him."

"He is a powerful fighter," said Penthesilea. "I hope to meet him one day in battle. If you yourself will not lead your armies to Mykenae to recover Hesione, wait only until I summon my women. You will have to give us ships, but I could have Hesione back to you by the next new moon."

"If it were feasible to go against the Akhaians now, I would need no woman to lead my army," Priam said, scowling. "I would rather wait and see what demands he makes of me."

"And what of Hesione, in Agamemnon's hands?" asked Penthesilea. "Are you going to abandon her? You know what will happen to her among the Akhaians!"

"One way or another, I would have had to find her a husband," said Priam. "This at least saves me a dowry, since if it is Agamemnon who has taken her, he cannot have the insolence to ask a dowry for a prize of war."

Penthesilea scowled, and Kassandra too was shocked: Priam was rich; why should he begrudge a dowry?

"Priam, Agamemnon already has a wife," said Penthesilea: "Klytemnestra, the daughter of Leda and her King, Tyndareus. She bore Agamemnon a daughter who must be seven or eight years old by now. I cannot believe they are so short of women in Akhaia that they must resort to stealing them . . . nor that Agamemnon is so much in need of a concubine that he would carry one off when he could have any chief 's daughter within his kingdom."

"So he married the daughter of Leda?" Priam frowned for a moment and said, "Is that the one who was, they said, so beautiful that Aphrodite would be jealous, and her father had to choose among almost forty suitors for her?"

"No," said Penthesilea. "They were twins, which is always ill fortune. One was Klytemnestra; the other daughter, Helen, was the beauty. Agamemnon managed to inveigle Leda and Tyndareus—God knows how he managed it—into marrying Helen off to his brother, Menelaus, while he married Klytemnestra."

"I don't envy Menelaus," said Priam. "A man is cursed who has a beautiful wife." He smiled absently at Hecuba. "Thank all the Gods you never brought me that kind of trouble, my dear. Nor are your daughters dangerously beautiful."

Hecuba looked at her husband coldly. Penthesilea said, "That could be a matter of opinion. But from what I know of Agamemnon, unless rumor lies, he is thinking less of woman's beauty than of power; through Leda's daughters he thinks to claim all Mykenae, and Sparta too, and call himself King. And then, I suppose, he will seek to gain more power to the north—and make you look to your own city here in Troy."

"I think they are trying to force me to deal with them," Priam said, "to recognize them as Kings—which I will do when Kerberos opens his doors and lets the dead out of Hades' realm."

"I doubt they will seek gold," said Penthesilea. "There is gold enough in Mykenae—though rumor has it that Agamemnon is a greedy man. If I should make a guess, it would be that what Agamemnon will demand is that you give him trading rights through the strait yonder"—she pointed to the sea—"without the toll you charge."

"Never," said Priam. "A God brought my people here to the banks of the Scamander; and whoever wishes to pass beyond to the country of the North Wind must render tribute to the Gods of Troy." He stared crossly at Penthesilea and demanded, "What is it to you? What has a woman to do with the government of countries and the payment of tribute?"

"I too dwell within the lands where the Akhaian raiders dare to come," said the Amazon Queen. "And if they should steal one of my women, I would make them pay for it, not in gold or dowries alone, but in blood. And since you could not stop them from carrying off your own sister, I repeat: my warriors are at your service if you wish to lead them against those pirates."

Priam laughed, but bared his teeth as he did so, and Kassandra knew that he was furious, though he would not say so to Penthesilea. "On the day when I call upon women, kin or no, for the defense of the city, Troy will be in evil straits, Kinswoman; may that day be far away indeed." He turned round and saw Kassandra in her leather breeches and heavy cloak coming into the room. "Well, what's this, Daughter? Showing your legs like a boy? Have you resolved to become an Amazon, Bright Eyes?"

He sounded surprisingly good-natured; but Hecuba said quickly, "You bade me send her to be fostered away from the city, Husband, and I thought my sister's tribe as good as any."

"I have found you to be the best of wives, no matter where you came from, and I have no doubt your sister will do well enough by her," said Priam, and bent down to Kassandra. She flinched, half expecting another blow; but he only kissed her gently on the forehead.

"Be a good girl, and forget not that you are a princess of Troy."

Hecuba took Kassandra in her arms and hugged her hard.

"I shall miss you, Daughter; be a good girl and come back to me safely, my darling."

Kassandra clung to her mother, Hecuba's former harshness forgotten, aware only that she was going away among strangers. Then Hecuba released her. She said, "I have my own weapons for you, Daughter," and brought out a leaf-shaped sword in a green scabbard, and a short metal-tipped spear. They were almost too heavy to lift, but struggling with all her strength and pride, Kassandra managed to fasten their belts about her waist.

"They were mine when I rode with the Amazons," said Hecuba. "Carry them in strength and honor, my daughter."

Kassandra blinked away the tears that were forming in her eyes. Priam was frowning, but Kassandra was accustomed to her father's disapproval. She defiantly took the hand Penthesilea held out to her. Her mother's sister could not be too unlike her mother, after all.

When the Amazons reclaimed their horses in the lower courtyard, Kassandra was disappointed to be lifted to Racer's back behind Penthesilea. "I thought I was to ride a horse by myself," she said, her lip quivering.

"You will when you learn, my child, but we have no time to teach you at this minute. We want to be far from this city by nightfall; it does not please us to sleep within walls, and we do not want to camp in the lands ruled by men."

That made sense to Kassandra; her arms gripped hard around the woman's narrow waist, and they were off.

For the first few minutes it took all her strength and attention to hold on, rocked up and down by the bumpy gait of the horse on the stones. Then she began to get the feel of letting her body sway and adjust itself to the motion, and began to look around and see the city from her new perspective. She had time for one brief look backward at the temple atop the heights of the city; then they were outside the walls and descending toward the green waters of the Scamander.

"How will we get across the river, Lady?" she asked, leaning her head forward, close to Penthesilea's ear. "Can the horses swim?"

The woman turned her head slightly. "To be sure they can; but they will not need to swim today; there is a ford an hour's journey upriver." She touched her heels lightly to the horse's sides, and the animal began to run so swiftly that Kassandra had to hold on with all her strength. The other women were racing alongside, and Kassandra felt a kind of elation through her whole body. Behind Penthesilea she was a little sheltered from the wind, but her long hair blew about so wildly that for a moment she wondered how she would ever manage to comb and tidy it again. It didn't matter; in the excitement of the ride she forgot it at once.

They had ridden for some time when Penthesilea pulled her horse to a stop and whistled, a shrill cry of some strange bird.

From a little thicket up ahead, three horses, ridden by Amazon women, emerged.

"Greetings," one of the newcomers called. "I see you are come safe from Priam's house; you were so long gone, we were beginning to wonder! How is it with our sister?"

"Well, but she grows fat and old and worn with childbearing in the King's house," said Penthesilea.

"Is this our fosterling—Hecuba's daughter?" asked one of the newcomers.

"It is," said Penthesilea, turning her head toward Kassandra. "And if she is truly her mother's daughter, she will be more than welcome among us."

Kassandra smiled shyly at the newcomers, one of whom held out her arms and leaned over to embrace her.

"I was your mother's closest friend when we were girls," she said.

They rode on, toward the gleam of the river Scamander. Dusk was falling as they drew their horses up at the ford; in the last glow of sunlight Kassandra could see the rapid flicker of the sun on the shallow ripples, the sharp stones in the streambed where the river ran fast and shallow. She gasped as the horse stepped over the steep edge down into the water, and was again admonished to hold on tight. "If you fall off, it will be hard to get you again before you are bashed about."

Having no desire whatever to fall on those sharp rocks, Kassandra held on very tightly, and soon the horse was scrambling up at the far edge. They galloped during the few minutes of light remaining; then they pulled to a stop, gathered their horses in a circle and dismounted.

Kassandra watched with fascination as without discussion one of the women built a fire, and another, from her saddlebags, pulled a tent and began unfolding it and setting it up. Soon dried meat was bubbling in a caldron and smelled very savory.

She was so stiff that when she tried to come forward to the fire, she tottered like an old woman. Charis began to laugh, but Penthesilea scowled at her.

"Don't mock the child; she hasn't whimpered, and it was a long ride for one unused to horseback. You were no better when you came to us. Give her something to eat."

Charis dipped up a cup of stew and handed it to Kassandra in a wooden bowl.

"Thank you," she said, dipping the horn spoon they handed her into the mixture. "May I have a piece of bread, please?"

"We have none," Penthesilea said. "We grow no crops, living as we do with our tents and herds." One of the women poured something white and foaming into her cup; Kassandra tasted it.

"It is mare's milk," said the woman who had introduced herself as Elaria, Hecuba's friend. Kassandra drank curiously, not sure that she liked either the taste or the idea; but the other women drank it, so she supposed it would not do her any harm.

Elaria chuckled, watching the cautious look of suppressed disgust on Kassandra's face. She said, "Drink it and you will grow as strong and free as our mares, and your mane as silky." She stroked Kassandra's long dark hair. "You are to be my foster-daughter as long as you dwell with us. In our village you will live in my tent: I have two daughters who will befriend you."

Kassandra looked a little wistfully at Penthesilea; but she supposed that if the woman was a Queen she would be too busy to care for a little girl, even her sister's daughter. And Elaria looked kind and friendly.

When the meal was finished, the women gathered around the campfire. Penthesilea appointed two of them to stand watch.

Kassandra whispered, "Why do we post sentries? There is no war, is there?"

"Not as they would use the word in Troy," Elaria whispered back. "But we are still in the lands ruled by men; and women are always at war in such lands. Many—most men would treat us as lawful prizes, and our horses too."

One of the women had started a song; the others joined in. Kassandra listened, not knowing the tune or the dialect, but after a time she was humming along on the choruses. She felt tired and lay back to rest, looking up at the great white stars far above; and the next thing she knew she was being carried through the dark. She woke up, startled. "Where am I?"

"You fell asleep at the campfire; I am taking you to my tent to sleep," said Elaria's voice softly, and Kassandra settled down and slept again, waking only when there was daylight in the tent. Someone had taken off her leather breeches, and her legs were chafed and sore. As she woke, Elaria came in. She smoothed some salve on the sore places and gave Kassandra a pair of linen drawers to wear under the leather, which helped a great deal. Then she took a comb carved of bone and began combing out the tangles in Kassandra's long, silky hair; then she braided it tightly and gathered it up under a pointed leather cap like those all the women wore. Kassandra's eyes watered as the comb jerked out the knots, but she did not cry, and Elaria patted her head approvingly.

"Today you will ride behind me," Elaria said, "and perhaps today we will reach our own grazing grounds, and we can find a mare for you and begin to teach you to ride. A day will come, and not too far from now, when you will be able to spend all day in the saddle without weariness."

Breakfast was a chunk of leathery dried meat, gnawed upon as she clung to the saddle behind Elaria. As they rode, the character of the land changed gradually from the fertile green of the riverbed to a barren windswept plain rising higher and higher from the low-lying fields. At the edge of the plain were round bald hills, brown all over, with great rocks jutting from their slopes, and beyond them sheer-rising cliffs. On the side of one of the hills she could see flecks moving, larger than sheep. Elaria turned and pointed.

"There our horse-herds graze," she said. "By nightfall we will be at home in our own country."

Penthesilea was riding beside them. Very softly, she said, "They are not our herds. Look there, and see the Kentaurs, riding among them."

Now Kassandra could see more clearly; she made out the hairy bodies and bearded heads of men, rising among the herds. Like all city children, Kassandra had been reared on stories of the Kentaurs—wild, lawless creatures with the heads and upper bodies of men and the lower bodies of horses. Now she could see the origin of the old stories. They were small men, and browned from their outdoor life; the long, unkempt hair down their backs gave the very impression of a horse's mane, and their brown bodies blended into the horses' bodies, their bowed legs curled up around the horses' necks: upper body of man, lower body of horse. Like many little girls, Kassandra had been told that they stole women from cities and villages, and had been admonished by her nurse, "If you are not a good girl, the Kentaurs will carry you off."

She murmured, frightened, "Will they hurt us, Aunt?"

"No, no, of course not; my son lives among them," Penthesilea said. "And if it is Cheiron's tribe, they are our friends and allies."

"I thought that the Amazon tribes had only women," Kassandra said, surprised. "You have a son, Aunt?"

"Yes, but he lives with his father; all our sons do," Penthesilea said. "Why, silly girl, do you still believe the Kentaur tribes are monsters? Look, they are only men; riders like ourselves."

Nevertheless, as the riders came closer, Kassandra shrank away; the men were all but naked, and looked wild and uncivilized indeed; she shrank behind Elaria on her horse where they would not see her.

"Greetings, Lady of the Horse-women," called out the foremost rider. "How fared you in Priam's city?"

"Well enough; as you see, we are back safe and well," Penthesilea called. "How is it with your men?"

"We found a bee tree this morning and have taken a barrel of honey," the man said, leaning close and embracing Penthesilea from horseback. "You shall have a share, if you will."

She pulled away from him and said, "The cost of your honey is always too high; what do you want from us this time?"

He straightened and rode alongside her, smiling in a good-natured way. "You can do me a service," he said, "if you will. One of my men became besotted with a village girl a few moons ago, and carried her away without troubling to ask her father for her. But she's no good for anything but his bed. Can't even milk a mare or make cheese, and weeps and wails all the time; now he's sick to death of the blubbering bitch, and—"

"Don't ask me to take her off your hands," Penthesilea interrupted. "She'd be no good in our tents either."

"What I want," the man said, "is that you take her back to her father," and Penthesilea snorted.

"And let us be the ones to face her tribesmen's wrath and swords? Not likely!"

"Trouble is, the wench is pregnant," said the Kentaur. "Can't you take her till the babe's born? Seems like she might be happier among women."

"If she'll come with us, with no trouble," said Penthesilea, "we'll keep her till the child's born, and if it's a daughter, keep them both. If it's a son, do you want him?"

"To be sure," said the man, "and as for the woman, once the child's born you can keep her or send her back to her village or, for all I care, drown her."

"I am simply too good-hearted," Penthesilea said. "Why should I get you out of trouble you made for yourselves?"

"For a half barrel of honey?"

"For a half barrel of honey," said Elaria, "I'll look after the girl myself, and deliver her child *and* get her back to her village."

"We'll all share it," Penthesilea said, "but next time one of your men seeks congress with a woman, send him to our tents and no doubt one of us will satisfy him, with no such complications. Every time one of your men goes after a girl out of season and goes into the villages, all the tribes get the backlash; more tales about how lawless we all are, men and women alike."

"Don't scold me, Lady," the man said, hiding his face briefly with his hands. "None of us is more than human. And who is that, hiding there behind your companion?" He looked around Elaria, and winked at Kassandra; he looked so droll, with his hairy face screwed up behind his matted hair, that she burst out laughing. "Have you stolen a child from Priam's city?"

"Not so," Penthesilea said. "It is my sister's daughter, who is to dwell with us for a few seasons."

"A pretty little thing," said the Kentaur. "Soon all my young men will be fighting over her."

Kassandra blushed and hid behind Elaria again. In Priam's palace, even her mother freely admitted that Polyxena was "the pretty one," while Kassandra was "the clever one." Kassandra had told herself that she did not care; still, it was pleasing to think someone found *her* pretty. "Well," Penthesilea said, "let us see this honey, and the woman you want us to take off your hands."

"Will you feast with us? We are roasting a kid for the evening meal," the Kentaur said, and Penthesilea glanced at her women.

"We had hoped to sleep this night in our own tents," she protested, "but the kid smells savory and well roasted; it would be a shame not to take our share." And Elaria added, "Why not rest here for an hour or two? If we do not get home tonight, tomorrow is another day."

Penthesilea shrugged. "My women have answered for me; we will accept your hospitality with pleasure—or perhaps just with greed."

The Kentaur beckoned and rode toward the central campfire, and Penthesilea motioned to her women to follow. A young woman knelt before the fire, turning the spit where a kid was roasting. The fat dripping on the fire smelled wonderful, and the crisped skin sizzled. The women slid from their horses, and after a time the men followed.

Penthesilea went at once to the woman turning the spit. Kassandra noticed with horror that both her ankles had been pierced and that her feet were hobbled together by a rope passed through the wounds, so that she could not take large strides. The Amazon Queen looked down at her, not unkindly, and asked, "You are the captive?"

"I am; they stole me from my father's house last summer."

"Do you want to return?"

"He swore when he pierced my feet that he would love me and care for me forever; will he cast me off now? Would my father have me back in his house crippled and my belly swelling with a Kentaur's child?"

"He tells me you are not happy here," Penthesilea said. "If you wish to come with us, you may dwell in our village until your child is born, and then return to your father's house or wherever you wish to go."

The woman's face twisted with weeping. "Like this?" she said, gesturing toward her mutilated ankles.

Penthesilea turned to the Kentaur leader and said, "I would have taken her willingly, had she been unharmed. But we cannot return her like this to her father's village. Wasn't it enough for your young man to carry her away and take her virginity?"

The Kentaur spread his hands helplessly. "He swore he wanted her forever, to keep and cherish, and feared only that she might manage ever to escape him."

"You should know, after all these years, how long that kind of love endures," chided the Amazon Queen. "It seldom outlasts the taking of the maidenhead. An eternal love sometimes lasts as long as half a year, but never survives pregnancy. Now what can we do with her? You know as well as I, she cannot be returned to her father's village this way. This time you have gotten yourself into something from which we cannot extricate you."

"At this point my man would pay to be rid of her," the Kentaur said.

"So he must. What will he give, then, to be rid of her?"

"A good mare in foal as indemnity to her father, or for a dowry if she wishes to marry."

"Perhaps for that we can manage to be rid of her when she can walk again," Penthesilea said, "but I promise you, this is the last time we solve your love troubles. Keep your men away from the village women and perhaps you will not bring us all into disrepute like this. And it had better be a good mare or it will not be worth the trouble."

She sniffed appreciatively. "But it would be a pity for the kid to burn or roast too done while I scold you. Let's have a slice of it, shall we?"

One of the Kentaurs took a big knife and began to slice chunks of meat and crisp skin off the kid. The women gathered and sat on the grass while the food was handed round, with wine from leathern jacks, and chunks of honeycomb. Kassandra ate hungrily; she was tired of riding, and willing to recline on the grass as she ate, and drank the wine. After a time she felt dizzy and lay back, closing her eyes drowsily. At home she was allowed to drink only well-watered wine, and now she felt a little sick. Nevertheless, it seemed that no meal eaten within walls had ever tasted so good to her.

One of the young men who had ridden next to the Kentaur leader came to refill the cup in her hand. Kassandra shook her head. "No more, I thank you."

"The God of Wine will be cross with you if you deny His gifts," said the boy. "Drink, Bright Eyes."

That was what her father called her in his rare affable moods. She sipped a few more swallows, then shook her head. "Already I am too dizzy to sit my horse!"

"Then rest," the boy said, and pulled her back to lie against his shoulder, his arms around her.

Penthesilea's eyes rested on them and she said sharply to the boy, "Let her be, she is not for you. She is the daughter of Priam and a princess of Troy."

The Kentaur chief laughed and said, "He is not so far beneath her, my lady; he is the son of a King."

"I know your royal fosterlings," said Penthesilea. "I recall too well when Theseus took our Queen Antiope from us, to live within walls, and die there. All the same, this maiden is in my care, and anyone who touches her must first deal with me."

The boy laughed and let Kassandra go. "Perhaps when you are grown up, Bright Eyes, your father may think better of me than our kinswoman does; her tribe does not like men, nor marriage."

"Neither do I," said Kassandra, pulling away from him.

"Well, perhaps when you are older you will change your mind," the boy said. He leaned forward and kissed her on the lips. Kassandra pulled away and wiped her mouth vigorously, as the Kentaurs laughed. Kassandra saw the crippled village woman watching her, frowning.

The Amazon Queen called her women to their horses, helping one of them load the promised honey on her mare's back. Then she cut the rope binding the crippled woman's ankles, and helped her to the back of a horse, speaking to her gently. The woman was not crying now; she went willingly with them. The Kentaur embraced Penthesilea as she mounted her horse.

"Cannot we persuade you to spend the night in our tents?"

"Another time perhaps," Penthesilea promised, and heartily returned his embrace. "For now, farewell."

Kassandra was confused; were these men and boys the terrible Kentaurs of the legends? They seemed friendly enough. But she wondered just what their relations were with the Amazons. They did not treat the women the way her father's soldiers spoke with the women of the household. The handsome boy who had kissed her came and looked up, smiling, at her.

"Perhaps I shall see you at the roundup?" he said. Kassandra looked away, blushing; she did not know what to say to him. He was the first boy except her own brothers she had spoken to.

Penthesilea motioned the women to follow her, and Kassandra saw that they were riding inland, and that the slopes of Mount Ida towered over them. She thought of the vision she had had of the boy with her face herding sheep on the slopes.

He may herd sheep, but I am to learn to ride, she thought, and, still dizzied with the unaccustomed wine, she leaned forward, balancing herself against Elaria, and fell asleep, rocked by the horse's swaying gait.

6

THE WORLD was bigger than she had ever thought; though they rode from first daylight till it was too dark to see, it seemed to Kassandra that they were simply crawling over the plains. The hills of Troy could still be seen behind them, no farther away than before; in the clear air it sometimes seemed she could reach out and touch the shining summit of the city.

Within a very few weeks it seemed to Kassandra that her life had always been lived with the horsewomen of the tribe. From day's beginning to day's end she did not set her feet to the ground, but even before breaking her fast was already in the saddle of the chestnut mare they had allotted to her use, whom she called Southwind. With the other girls her age she stood watch against invaders, and at night kept the horses together, watching the stars.

She loved Elaria, who cared for her as she did her own daughters, girls of eleven and seventeen; Penthesilea she worshiped, although the Amazon Queen rarely spoke to her except for a daily inquiry as to her health and welfare. She grew strong, bronzed and healthy. In the endless burning sun on the plains she saw the face of Apollo Sun Lord, and it seemed to her that she lived her life under His eyes.

She had lived with the horsewomen for more than a moon when one day as the tribe dismounted, in view of the now distant Mount Ida, for their frugal noon meal of hunks of strong mare's-milk cheese, she found herself telling Penthesilea all about the curious vision.

"His face was as like to mine as is mine to my own face reflected in the water," she said, "yet when I spoke of him, my father knocked me down; and he was angry with my mother too."

Penthesilea paused for a long time before answering, and Kassandra wondered if the silence of her parents was to be repeated. Then the woman said slowly, "I can well see that your mother, and especially your father, would not wish to speak of this; but I see no reason you should not be told what half of Troy knows. He is your twin brother, Kassandra. When you were born, the Earth Mother, who is also Serpent Mother, sent my sister Hecuba an evil omen: twins. You should both have been killed," she said harshly. When Kassandra shrank away, her lips trembling, she reached out and stroked the girl's hair. "I am glad you were not," she said. "No doubt some God has laid His hand on you.

"Your father felt, perhaps, that he could escape his fate by exposing the child; but as a worshiper of the Father-principle—which is, in truth, a worship of male power and ability to father sons—he dared not wholly renounce a son, and the child was fostered somewhere far from the palace. Your father did not wish to know anything of him because of the evil omen of his birth; so he was angry when you spoke of him."

Kassandra felt tremendous relief. It seemed to her that all her life she had walked alone when there should have been another at her side, very like her but somehow different.

"And it is not wicked to wish to see him in the scrying-bowl?"

"You do not need the scrying-bowl," Penthesilea said. "If the Goddess has given you Sight, you need only look within your heart and you will find him there. I am not surprised you are so blessed; your mother had it as a girl and lost it when she married a city-dwelling man."

"I believed that the —Sight—was the gift of the Sun Lord," Kassandra said. "It first came to me within His Temple."

"Perhaps," said Penthesilea. "But remember, child: before ever Apollo Sun Lord came to rule these lands, our Horse Mother—the Great Mare, the Earth Mother from whom we all are born—she was here."

She turned and laid her two hands reverently on the dark earth, and Kassandra imitated the gesture, only half understanding. It seemed that she could feel a dark strength moving upward from the earth and flowing through her; it was the same kind of blissful strength she had felt when she held Apollo's serpents in her two hands. She wondered if she were being disloyal to the God who had called her.

"They told me in the Temple that Apollo Sun Lord had slain the Python, the great Goddess of the Underworld. Is this the Serpent Mother of whom you speak?"

"She who is the Great Goddess cannot be slain, for She is immortal; She may choose to withdraw Herself for a time, but She is and will remain forever," said the Amazon Queen, and Kassandra, feeling the strength of the earth beneath her hands, took this in as absolute truth.

"Is the Serpent Mother, then, the mother of the Sun Lord?" she asked.

Penthesilea, drawing a breath of reverence, said, "She is mother to Gods and men alike, mother of all things; so Apollo is Her child too, even as are you and I."

Then . . . if Apollo Sun Lord sought to slay Her, then was He seeking to kill His mother? Kassandra's breath caught with the wickedness of the thought. But could a God do wickedness? And if a certain deed was wicked for men, was it wicked also for a God? If a Goddess was immortal, how then could She be slain at all? These things were mysteries, and she set her whole being into fierce resolve that one day she would understand them. Apollo Sun Lord had called her; He had given her His serpents; one day He would lead her to knowledge of the Serpent Mother's mysteries as well.

The women finished their noon meal and stretched out to rest on the green turf. Kassandra was not sleepy; she had not been accustomed to sleep this way at midday. She watched the clouds drifting across the sky and looked up to the slopes of Mount Ida rising high above the plain.

Her twin brother. It made Kassandra angry to think that everyone knew this when she, whom it concerned most closely, had been kept in ignorance.

She tried to remember deliberately and consciously the state she had been in when she had first seen her brother in the waters of the scrying-bowl. She knelt motionless on the grass, staring upward at the sky, her mind blank, searching for the face she had seen but once, and then only in a vision. For a moment her questing thoughts settled on her own face, seen reflected as if in water, and the golden shimmer which she still called, in her mind, the face and breath of Apollo Sun Lord.

Then the features shifted and the face was a boy's, her own and yet somehow subtly *not* her own, filled with a mischief wholly alien to her, and she knew she had found her brother. She wondered what he was called, and if he could see her.

From somewhere in the mysterious linkage between them, the answer came: he could if he wished; but he had no reason to seek her, and no particular interest. *Why not?* Kassandra wondered, not yet knowing that she had stumbled on the major flaw in her twin's character: a total lack of interest in anything that did not relate to himself or contribute in some way to his own comfort and satisfaction.

For an instant, this puzzled her enough that she lost the fragment of vision; then she collected herself to call it back. Her senses were filled with the intoxicating scent of thyme from the slopes of the mountain, where the bright light and heat of the Sun Lord's presence gathered together the fragrant oils of the herb and concentrated their scent in the air. Looking out of the boy's eyes, she saw the crude brush in his hand as he combed the sleek sides of a great bull, smoothing the gleaming white hair of the flanks into patterns like waves. The beast was larger than he was himself; like Kassandra, he was slight and lightly made, wiry rather than muscular. His arms were sun-burnt brown as any shepherd's, his fingers callused and hard with endless hard work. She stood there with him, her arm moving like his, making patterns on the bull's sides, and when the hair was suitably smooth and wavy, she put aside the brush. With another brush she dipped into a pot of paint that stood at his side, laying the coat of smooth gilt paint across the horns. The bull's great dark eyes met her own with love and trust and a touch of puzzlement, so that the beast shifted its weight res-tively. Kassandra wondered if somehow the animal's instincts knew what her brother did not: that it was not only his master who stood before him.

The combing and gilding finished, Paris (she did not ask herself how she now knew his name, but she knew it like her own) tied a garland of green leaves and ribbons around the animal's broad neck, and stood back to survey his handiwork with pride. The bull was indeed beautiful, the finest that she had ever seen. She shared his thoughts, that he could honestly regard this fine animal, on whose looks and condition he had spared no effort in all the past year, as the finest bull in the fair. He tied a rope carefully around the animal's neck and gathered up a staff and a leather pouch in which there were a hunk of bread, a few strips of dried meat and a handful of ripe olives. Having tied the pouch at his waist he bent to slip his feet into sandals. He gave the great bedizened bull a gentle smack with the staff on its flank, and set off down the slopes of Mount Ida.

Kassandra found herself, to her own surprise, back in her own body, kneeling on the plain, among the sleeping Amazons. The sun had begun to decline a little from its zenith, and she knew the tribe would soon wake and be ready to ride.

She had heard that in the islands of the sea kingdoms far to the south, the bull was held sacred. She had seen in the Tem-ples little statues of sacred bulls, and someone had told her the story of Queen Pasiphae of Crete, of whom Zeus had become enamored. He had come to her as a great white bull and they said that she had subsequently given birth to a monster with a bull's head and the body of a man. He was called the Minotaur, and he had terrorized all the sea Kings until he was slain by the hero Theseus.

When Kassandra was a little girl, she had believed the story; now she wondered what truth, if any, lay behind it. Having learned the reality behind the legend of the Kentaurs, she believed there must be some such truth, however obscure, within all such stories.

There were deformed men who were bestial in both looks and manner; she wondered if the Minotaur had been such a man, with the mark of his father's animal disguise in body or mind.

She was eager to see what had become of Paris, and of his beautiful white bull. Young women, particularly from the royal house, were never allowed to attend the cattle fairs, held all over the countryside, but she had heard of them and was intensely curious.

But the women were stirring, and in a few minutes the movements about her, and their voices, dispelled the quietness she needed to remain in the state where she could follow him. She sprang up, with only a little regret, and ran to catch her mare.

Once or twice in the next day or two she caught a glimpse of her brother, driving the garlanded bull; fording a river (where he spoiled his sandals) and falling in with other travelers driving cattle bedecked like his own; none of the animals was quite so fine or so handsome.

The moon grew round, lighting the whole sky from sunset to sunrise. During the day the sun blinded, the white dust glittered. Drowsing on horseback while the mares moved steadily, grazing in their close-kept ring, Kassandra watched the dry dust devils lifting up and swirling across the grass before they blew away. She thought of the restless God Hermes, lord of the winds and of deception and artifice.

Daydreaming, she saw one of the little whirlwinds shiver and tremble and draw itself upright into the form of a man; and so she followed the shifting restless wind westward across the plains to the very foot of Mount Ida. In the blinding sunlight, a beam of gold shifted and altered in the glow and became a man's form; but taller and brighter than any man, with the face of Apollo Sun Lord; and before the two Gods walked a bull.

Kassandra had heard the story of the bulls of Apollo—great shining cattle, more beautiful than any earthly beast; and surely this was one of them; broad-backed, with shining horns needing no gilt or ribbons to make them gleam with light. One of the oldest ballads sung by the minstrels of her father's court had to do with how the infant Hermes had stolen Apollo's sacred herd, and then turned away Apollo's anger by fashioning for Him a lyre from the shell of a tortoise. Now the brightness of the sacred bull's eyes and the bright luster of its coat dimmed the memory of the bull Paris had decorated with so much toil. It was not fair; how could any mortal bull venture to be judged alongside the divine cattle of a God?

She leaned forward, her eyes closed; she had learned to sleep on horseback, yielding her body bonelessly to the animal's movement. Now she drowsed, her mind ranging out in search of her brother. Perhaps it was the sight of Apollo's bull that drew her to the animal Paris led to the fair.

Kassandra looked out from her brother's eyes on the great body of assembled beasts and ran in his mind over their faults and virtues. This cow had flanks too narrow; that one, an ugly mottled pattern of brown and pink on its udder; this bull had horns twisted askew and not fit for guarding its herd; that one, a hump above its neck. Near or far, Paris thought with pride, there was none to match the bull from his own herd, which he had garlanded with such pride and brought here; he could declare the honors of the day to his foster-father's own bull. This was the second year he had been chosen to judge the cattle, and he was proud of his skill and proud of the confidence his neighbors and fellow herdsmen felt in him.

He moved among the cattle, motioning gently to bring one forward so he could see it better, or to take an animal not seriously being considered out of his range of vision.

He had chosen the finest heifer and calf, and then, to mur-

murs of acclaim, the finest cow; it was a splendid cow indeed, its hide pale white with patches of gray so subtle that it was all but blue; its eyes were mild and motherly, its udder smooth and uniformly pink as a maiden's breasts. Its horns were small and wide-spread, and its breath fragrant with the thyme-scented grass.

Now it was time to judge the bulls. Paris moved with satisfaction toward his foster-father's own Snowy, the beast he had tended and decorated with such care. In a whole day of judging cattle he knew that he had honestly seen no beast to match it, and he felt justified in awarding the prize to his foster-father's animal. He had actually opened his mouth to speak when he saw the two strangers and their bull.

As soon as the younger one—Paris supposed he was the younger—began to talk, Paris knew somehow that he was in the presence of the more-than-mortal. It was his first such encounter, but the blaze of the man's eyes from under his hat, and something about the voice, as if it came from very far away and yet very close, told him this was no ordinary man. As for Kassandra, she would have recognized anywhere the unearthly shimmer around the golden curls of her God; and perhaps without Paris' knowing it consciously, something crept through to him from the mind of his unknown sister.

He said aloud, "Strangers, bring the bull closer so I may see him. I have never seen such a fine animal." But perhaps the bull had some fault not apparent, Paris thought, walking around it from all sides. No, the legs were like pillars of marble; even the tail moved with an air of nobility. The horns were smooth and broad, the eye fierce yet gentle; the animal even suffered, with a look of boredom, Paris to open its mouth gently and look at the perfect teeth.

What right has a God to bring his perfect cattle to be judged among mortal men? Paris wondered. Well, it was Fate, and it would be arrogant to set himself against Fate.

He beckoned again to the man who held the rope around the bull's neck, and said with a regretful glance at Snowy, "I am sorry to say it, but never in all my life have I seen a bull so fine. Strangers, the prize is yours."

The glowing smile of the Immortal blurred into the sun; and as Kassandra woke, she heard a voice—no more than an echo in her mind: *This man is an honest judge; perhaps he is the one to settle the challenge of Eris.* And then she was alone in her saddle and Paris was gone, this time beyond any recall at her command. She did not see him again for a long time.

7

NO SOONER had they reached the country of the Amazons than the weather changed. One day, there was blinding sun from early morning to sunset; overnight, it seemed, there was day-long rain combined with damp, dripping nights. Being on horseback was no longer a pleasure, but toil and exhaustion; to Kassandra every day was a constant battle against cold and damp.

The Amazons kept up the fires in their sheltered camps; many lived in caves, others in heavy-walled leather tents set up in thick-leaved groves. Small children and pregnant women stayed inside all day, huddling close to the smoking fires.

There were times when the warmth tempted her, but among the tribe, girls Kassandra's age counted themselves among the warriors, so she covered herself with a heavy robe of thick oil-surfaced wool, and endured the dampness as best she could.

As the rainy season dragged by she grew taller, and one day when she dismounted for a rare hot meal in the camp around the fire she realized that her body was rounding, small breasts sprouting under the rough loose garments.

From time to time as they rode, there slipped into her mind visions of the boy with her face. He was taller now; the woven tunic he wore barely covered his thighs, and she shivered in sympathy when he tried to cover himself with his too-short cloak. Surrounded by his flock, he lay on the slopes of the mountain, and once she saw him at a festival, one of a group of boys garlanded and moving in a dance. Another time she sat within him before a blazing fire as he was given a new warm cloak and his long hair was cut for the altar of the Sun Lord. Was he too under Apollo's protection?

Once in spring, silent in a cluster of other boys, he watched a group of little girls—though most of them were as tall as or taller than he—wrapped in bearskins, dancing a ritual dance to the Maiden.

Now she seldom even thought about indoor life except for a vague constant nag of memory of a time when she was confined to the palace and never allowed outside. Curious sensations attacked her body; the roughly woven wool of her tunic rubbed her nipples raw and she begged from one of the other women an undergarment of soft cotton cloth. It helped, but not enough; her breasts were sore most of the time.

The days shortened, and a pale winter moon stood in the sky. The herds circled aimlessly, searching for food. Later the mares' milk failed, and the hungry beasts moved restlessly from exhausted pasture to exhausted pasture.

The loss of the mares' milk, the Amazons' staple food, meant there was even less to eat; what there was was saved by custom for the pregnant women and the youngest children. Day after day, Kassandra knew little but sharp hunger; she kept her small allotment of food to eat before she slept, so that she would not wake dreaming of the ovens in Priam's castle and the rich warm smell of baking bread. In the pastures, as she watched over the horses, she searched endlessly for dried-out fruits or stringy berries clinging to dead vines; like all the other girls, she ate anything she could find, accepting that about half of the food so found would make her sick.

"We cannot stay here," the women said. "What is the Queen waiting for?"

"Some word from the Goddess," said the others, and the older women of the tribe went to Penthesilea, demanding that they move on to the winter pastures.

"Yes," said the Queen, "we should have gone a moon ago; but there is war in the countryside. If we move the tribe with all our children and old women, we shall be captured and enslaved. Do you want that?"

"No, no," the women protested. "Under your will we will live free, and if we must we will die free."

Nevertheless, Penthesilea promised that when the moon was full again she would seek counsel of the Goddess, to know Her will.

Seeing her own face once in the water after a hard rain, Kassandra hardly recognized herself; she had grown tall and lean, face and hands burnt brown by the unremitting sun, her features sharp and more like a woman's than a girl's—or perhaps like a young boy's . . . There were freckles on her face too, and she wondered if her family would know her if she should appear unannounced before them, or whether they would ask "Who is this woman from the wild tribes? Away with her." Or would they, perhaps, mistake her for her exiled twin?

Despite the hardship, she had no wish to return to Troy; she missed her mother sometimes, but not the life in the walled city.

One night at sunset, the young girls, returning to the camp for dry clothing and a share-out of such food as could be found —usually astringent boiled roots, or some hard wild beans— were told not to take the horses out again, but to remain and gather with the other women. All fires in the camp but one had been extinguished, and it was dark and cold.

There was not so much as a mouthful of food to be shared out, and Elaria told her fosterling that the Queen had declared that all must fast before the Goddess was petitioned.

"That's nothing new," Kassandra said. "I should think we had done enough fasting in this last month to satisfy any Goddess. What more can She ask of us?"

"Hush," said Elaria. "She has never yet failed to care for us. We are all still alive; there have been many years when there was raiding, and many outlaws in the countryside, when we did not leave our pastures till half our young children were dead. This year the Goddess has not taken so much as a babe at the breast, nor a single foal."

"So much the better for Her," Kassandra said. "I cannot

imagine what use dead tribeswomen would be to the Goddess, unless She wishes us to serve Her in the Afterworld."

Aching with hunger, Kassandra got out of her damp riding leathers and slipped into a dry robe of coarsely woven wool. She tugged a wooden comb through her hair and braided it, coiling it low on her neck. In her exhausted and semistarved state, the very feel of dry clothing and the heat of the fire was sensuous pleasure; she stood for some time simply feeling the warmth soak into her body, until one of the other women shoved her aside. In the close air of the tent, the smoke was gradually filling the entire space, and she coughed and choked until she felt that she would vomit, if her stomach had not been so empty.

Behind her in the tent, she felt the pressure of other bodies, the silent rustle of women and girls and children: all the women of the tribe seemed to be gathered in the dark behind her. They squatted around the fire, and from somewhere came the soft thump of hands on taut skins stretched across a hoop, the chattering of gourds with dry seeds, shaken and rattling like the dry leaves, like the rain pattering on the tents. The fire smoked with little light, so that Kassandra could feel only the faint streams of discouraged heat.

Out of the dark silence next to the fire, three of the oldest women in the tribe rose up and cast the contents of a small basket on the fire. The dried leaves blazed up, then smoldered, flinging out thick white clouds of aromatic smoke. It filled the tent with its curious, dry, sweetish perfume, and as she breathed it in, Kassandra felt her head swimming, and strange colors moved before her eyes, so that she no longer felt the dull pain of her hunger.

Penthesilea said from the darkness, "My sisters, I know your hunger; do I not share it? Anyone who is unwilling to remain with us, I freely give you leave to go to the men's villages, where they will share their food if you lie with them. But do not bring daughters so born back to our tribe, but leave them to be slaves, as you have shown yourselves to be. If there are any who wish to leave now, let them do so, for you are not fit to stay while we petition our Maiden Huntress, who cherishes freedom for women."

Silence; within the smoke-filled tent no woman stirred.

"Then, sisters, in our need let us summon Her who cares for us."

Again silence, except for the fingertip drumming. Then out of the silence came a long eerie howl.

"Oww—ooooo-ooooo-ooooow!"

For a moment Kassandra thought it was some animal lurking outside the tent. Then she saw the open mouths, the strained-back heads of the women. The howl came again, and again; the faces of the women no longer looked quite human. The howling screams went on, rising and falling as the women swayed and yelled, and were joined by a sharp short "Yip-yip-yip-yip-yip . . . yip-yip-yip," until the noise filled the tent; it beat and battered at her consciousness, and she could only harden herself to remain apart from it. She had seen her mother overshadowed by the Goddess, but never in the midst of mad commotion like this.

At that moment, for the first time in many moons, Hecuba's face was suddenly before Kassandra's eyes and it seemed she could hear Hecuba's gentle voice:

It is not the custom . . .

Why not?

There is no reason for customs. They are, no more . . .

She had not believed it then and she did not believe it now. There must be a reason why this weird howling should be thought a suitable way to summon the Maiden Huntress. *Are we to become as the wild beasts She is hunting?*

Penthesilea rose, stretching out her hands to the women; between one breath and the next, Kassandra saw the Queen's face blur, and the brightness of the Goddess shone through the very skin, the voice altered beyond recognition. She cried out, "Not to the south, where the men's tribes wander! Ride to the east, past the two rivers; there remain until the spring's stars fall!"

Then she crumpled forward; two women of the tribe's elders caught her and supported her in a fit of coughing so violent that it ended in weak retching. When she raised herself, her face was her own again.

She asked in a hoarse whisper, "Did she answer us?"

A dozen voices repeated the words she had spoken while she was overshadowed:

"Not to the south, where the men's tribes wander! Ride to the east, past the two rivers; there remain until the spring's stars fall!"

"Then we ride at dawn, sisters," Penthesilea said, her voice still weak. "There is no time to lose. I know of no rivers to the east, but if we turn our backs on Father Scamander and follow the east wind, we will surely come to them."

"What meant the Goddess when She spoke of 'until the spring's stars fall'?" asked one of the women.

Penthesilea shrugged her narrow shoulders. "I do not know, sisters; the Goddess spoke but did not explain Her words. If we follow Her will, She will make it known to us."

Four of the women brought in baskets filled with coiled roots and passed around leathern bottles of wine. Penthesilea said, "Let us feast in Her name, sisters, and ride at dawn filled with Her bounty."

Kassandra realized how long food must have been hoarded for this midwinter feast. She tore into the tasteless boiled roots like the starving animal she felt herself to be, and drank her share of the wine.

When the baskets were empty and the last drop had been squeezed from the wineskins, the tribe's few possessions were gathered: the tents taken down and bundled together; a few bronze cooking kettles, a store of cloaks worn by former leaders. Kassandra was still seeing the Goddess' face through and over Penthesilea's own, and hearing the curious alteration in her kinswoman's voice. Kassandra wondered if one day the Goddess would speak through her own voice and spirit.

The tribe of women drew their horses into a line of march: Penthesilea and her warriors at the head; the elderly or pregnant women and the smallest girls at the very center, surrounded by the strongest young women.

Kassandra had a spear and knew how to use it, so she took a place among the young warriors. Penthesilea saw her and frowned, but she said nothing; Kassandra took her silence as leave to stay where she was. She didn't know whether she hoped for her first battle or whether she was inwardly praying that the journey would be completely uneventful. Dawn was breaking as Penthesilea called out the signal to ride; a single star still hung in the dark sky. Kassandra shivered in the wool robe she had worn at the ceremony. She hoped there would be no rain this night; she had left her riding leathers in the tent, and they had been packed somewhere among the leather bags and baskets.

Her closest companion, a girl of fourteen or so whom her mother called "Star," riding next to her, made no secret that she was hoping for a fight.

"One year when I was small there was a war against one of the Kentaur tribes—not Cheiron's band, they're our friends, but one of the tribes from inland. They came down on us just as we left our old camp and tried to steal away the strongest of our stallions," Star told her. "I could hardly see them; I was still riding with my mother. But I heard the men screaming as Penthesilea rode them down."

"Did we win?"

"Of course we won; if we hadn't, they'd have taken us to their encampment and broken our legs so we couldn't run away," Star said, and Kassandra remembered the crippled woman in the men's camp. "But we made peace with them, and we lent them the stallion for a year to improve their herds. And we agreed to visit their village that year instead of Cheiron's; Penthesilea said we have become too closely akin to his people by now and should skip a few years because it is not wise to lie with our own brothers and fathers for too many generations. She says when we do, the babies are weak and sometimes they die."

Kassandra did not understand, and said so. Star laughed and said, "They wouldn't let you go anyhow; before you go to the men's villages, you must be a woman, not a little girl."

"I am a woman," Kassandra said. "I have been old enough for bearing for ten moons now."

"Still, you must be a tried warrior; I have been grown now for a year and more, and I am not yet allowed to go to the men's villages. But I'm not in a hurry; after all, I might be pregnant for nine moons and bear only a useless male, who must be given to his father's tribe," said Star.

"Go to the men's villages? What for?" Kassandra asked, and Star told her.

"I think you must be making it up," Kassandra said. "My mother and father would never do anything like that." She could understand a mare and a stallion; but the thought of her royal parents engaging in such maneuvers seemed disgusting. Yet she remembered, unwillingly, that whenever her father summoned one of the many palace women into his sleeping quarters, sooner or later (more often sooner than later) there would be a new baby in the palace, and if it was a son, Priam would visit the palace goldsmith, and there would be handsome gifts, rings and chains and gold cups, for the newly favored woman and for her child.

So perhaps this thing Star was telling her was true after all, strange though it seemed. She had seen children born, but her mother had told her it was not worthy of a princess to listen to the tattle of the palace women; now she remembered certain gross jests she had not understood at the time and felt her cheeks burning. Her mother had told her that babies were sent into the wombs of women by Earth Mother, and she had wondered sometimes why the Goddess did not send her one, because she dearly loved babies.

"That's why the city-dwellers keep their women locked up in special women's quarters," Star said. "They say that city women are so lecherous that they cannot be trusted alone."

"They're not," said Kassandra, not sure why she was so angry.

"They are too! Or why would their men have to keep them locked up inside walls? Our women aren't like that," Star said, "but city women are like goats—they will fornicate with any man they see!" With an ill-natured smile at Kassandra, she said, "You are from a city, aren't you? Weren't *you* locked up to keep you away from men?"

Kassandra's knees tightened on her horse; she lunged forward and flung herself on Star, howling in rage. Star clawed at her, and Kassandra jerked Star's roughly braided hair, trying to

drag the girl from her horse. Their mounts neighed and snick-
ered as they fought, slapping and clawing and yelling; Kassandra
felt the girl's elbow connect with her nose and blood begin to
drip as her nails raked into Star's cheek.

Then Penthesilea and Elaria were both there, laughing as
they nudged their horses between the girls. Penthesilea dragged
Kassandra from her saddle and held her under her arms while
she flailed angrily.

"For shame, Kassandra! If we fight like this among ourselves, how can we hope to have peace with other tribes? Is it so
you treat your sisters? What are you fighting about?"

Kassandra hung her head and would not answer. Star was
still grinning that disgusting grin.

"I said to her that city women are kept locked up because
they fornicate like goats," Star jeered, "and if it were not true,
would she have bothered to fight me about it?"

Kassandra said angrily, "My mother is not like that! Tell her
to take it back!"

Penthesilea leaned close to her and said in her ear, "Will
your mother be different for her saying it, true or lie?"

"No, of course not. But if she says it—"

"If she says it, you fear that someone will hear it and believe
it?" Penthesilea asked, raising a delicate eyebrow. "Why give her
that much power over you, Kassandra?"

Kassandra hung her head and did not answer, and Penthesilea, scowling, cast her eyes on Star.

"Is this how you treat a kinswoman and guest of the tribe,
little sister?"

She leaned from her horse and touched her finger to Star's
scratched and bleeding cheek. "I will not punish you, for you
are already punished; she defended herself well. Next time,
show more courtesy to a guest of our tribe. The goodwill of
Priam's wife is valuable to us." She turned her back on Star and
leaned toward Kassandra, still holding her tight against her
breast. Kassandra could feel the laughter in her voice. "Are you
old enough to ride alone without getting into trouble, or must I
carry you before me like a baby?"

"I can ride alone," Kassandra said sulkily, though she was
grateful to Penthesilea for defending her.

"Then I shall set you on your horse again," said the Amazon Queen, and gratefully Kassandra felt Southwind's broad back beneath her. Star caught her eye and wriggled her nose at Kassandra, and she knew they were friends again. Penthesilea rode to the head of the line of march and called out, and they rode.

A chilly drizzling rain was falling, and gradually soaked through everything. Kassandra drew her striped wool robe up over her head, but her hair was still wet and clinging. They rode all day and pressed on into the night. Kassandra wondered when they would reach the new pastures. She had no idea where they were going, but rode in the damp darkness, following the tail of the horse ahead of her.

She rode in a dark dream, and felt curious sensations attacking her body which she could not identify. Then the flow of a fire appeared before her eyes, and she knew she was not seeing it with her own eyes at all. Somewhere Paris sat before this fire, and across the fire he was looking at a slender young woman with long fair hair loosely tied at her neck. She wore the long, loose tucked-up gown of the mainland women, and Kassandra sensed the way in which Paris could not take his eyes from her, the sharp hunger in his body which confused her enough that she took her eyes from the fire, and then she was riding again, feeling the dampness of her cloak dripping cold water down her neck. Her body was still alive with the tug of what she knew, without understanding, to be desire. It was the first time she had been so wholly aware of her own body . . . yet it was not her own. The memory of the girl's great eyes, the tender curve of her cheek, the swell of her young breasts where the robe stood away from her body, the way in which these memories aroused totally physical sensations, troubled her; in a flash she began to associate them with the troubling things Star had been saying, and she was filled with dismay and something she was still too innocent to identify as shame.

Toward morning the rain stopped and the dark ragged clouds blew away; the moon came out, and Kassandra could see that they were passing through a narrow gorge of rock, high up; she looked down on broad plains below, covered with small twisted trees and orderly plowed fields enclosed by stone walls.

They moved slowly down the steep slope, and gradually the leading horses slowed and stopped. The tents were unpacked, and the fire pot, wrapped in a damp cloth, was set in a central place. Already the first rays of a red sun were coming up across the gorge they had crossed in the night. They sent the young girls to look for dry wood. There was little to be found after days of soaking rain, but under the thick twisted olive trees Kassandra found a few dry chips where the rain had not penetrated, and she ran back with them to the fire.

The sun came up as they sat there, in a flood of red which told of more rain to come, so they sat there enjoying the damp heat and drying their hair and robes. Then the older women started to supervise the setting up of the tent and took a woman about to give birth inside; the warriors told the young girls to set the herds to grazing, and Kassandra went with them.

She was very tired and her eyes burned, but she was not sleepy; a part of her mind was back in the tent where the women clustered, encouraging the laboring woman, and a part of her was still far away, sharing with Paris. She knew he was on the hillside with his flocks, and that his thoughts remained with the girl whose memory obsessed him. She knew the girl's name, Oenone, the sweet mortal sound of it, and knew hauntingly how Paris clung to the memory that wiped out all awareness of what should have been uppermost in his thoughts, his duty to his flock. And even before Paris sensed it himself, she heard—or felt, or smelled—the presence of the girl stealing toward him through the groves of trees on the mountainside.

The bitter scent of juniper was all around them. Kassandra hardly knew which of them, Paris or the girl, first saw the other, or who moved first to run and crush the other into eager arms. The touch of hungry kisses almost jolted her back into her own body and her own place, but she was ready for it now, and clung to her awareness of *his* emotions and sensations. The next thing she knew, Oenone was sprawled on the soft grass, while Paris knelt above her, pulling at her garments.

Suddenly aware that this was not a moment to be shared even with a twin sister, she pulled back and away and was astride her own horse with drops of a rain shower on her face. She longed for the sunshine of her own country, Apollo's own sunshine, and for the first time since she had ridden away with the Amazons wondered when she would return.

She felt sick; her eyes burned, and a queasiness attacked her. The memory of what she had shared answered some of the many questions in her mind, but she was not sure whether it was her brother with whom she had shared this curious experience, or the girl Oenone, whether she was lover or beloved.

She was not certain now that she was within her own body, or whether she was still lying in the soft grass on Mount Ida with her brother and the girl, their bodies still locked in the afterglow of desire. Her mind would not stay within the confines of her body, but spread far beyond her, so that a part of her was here in the circle of horses and young women, and a part of her extended downward into the birthing tent, where the woman knelt in a ring of women watching her, crying out instructions and encouragement. The rending pains seemed to be attacking her own inexperienced body. She was racked by confusion, felt the blood leaving her cheeks, heard her own breath rasp in her throat.

She turned wildly around; she pulled so hard on the reins that her mare almost stumbled, and dug her heels into the horse's flank, fleeing across the plain, as if by fierce physical effort she could bring all her consciousness back into her own body. Penthesilea saw her riding away from the camp and quickly jumped to the back of her own horse, and raced after her.

Kassandra, stretched out along the mare's back desperately trying to shut out everything outside herself, sensed the pursuit and dug her heels harder. Nevertheless, Penthesilea's horse was longer-legged, and she was by far the better rider; gradually the gap between the two riders narrowed and the Amazon drew abreast of the girl, seeing with dismay Kassandra's flushed face and terrified eyes.

She held out her arms and scooped Kassandra from the back of her mare, holding her limp on the saddle before her.

She could feel the girl's forehead fire-hot as if with fever. Almost delirious now, Kassandra struggled against her, and the older woman held her tight in her strong arms.

"Hush! Hush! What ails you, Bright Eyes? Why, your fore-

head feels as if you were sun-stricken, yet it is not a hot day!"
Her voice was kindly, yet Kassandra felt that the older woman
was mocking her, and struggled frantically to be free.

"Nothing is wrong—I did not mean to—"

"No, all is well, child. No one will hurt you; no one is angry
with you," Penthesilea said as she held her, soothing her. After
a moment Kassandra abandoned her struggles and went limp in
her kinswoman's arms.

"Tell me about it."

Kassandra blurted out, "I was—with him. My brother. And
a girl. And I couldn't shut it out, anything, anywhere in the
camp . . ."

"Goddess be merciful," Penthesilea whispered. At Kassandra's age she too had borne the gift (or curse) of the wide-open
seeing. Sharing experiences for which the mind or body was
unprepared could indeed touch upon inner madness, and there
was not always a safe return. Kassandra was lying in her arms
only half conscious, and her kinswoman was not sure what to
do for her.

First she must get her back to the camp; so far from the
other women, or the horses, there were likely to be strange
lawless men in these wilds, and in Kassandra's present state,
such an encounter might drive her sheer over the edge of sanity.
She turned about, holding the reins of Kassandra's mare so it
would follow her. She cradled the girl against her breast, and
when they were within the circle of the camp, lifted her down
and carried her inside the tent, where the new mother was resting beside her sleeping infant. Penthesilea laid Kassandra down
on a blanket and sat beside her, her firm hand on her niece's
brow, covering her eyes, willing her to shut out all the intrusions
into her mind.

Kassandra's sobbing subsided and she slowly grew calm,
turning her face into Penthesilea's hand like a baby, curled up
against her.

After a long time, the Amazon Queen asked, "Are you better now?"

"Yes, but—will it come again?"

"Probably. It is a gift of the Goddess, and you must learn to live with it. There is little I can do to help you, child. Perhaps Serpent Mother has called you to speak for the Gods; there are priestesses and seeresses among us. Perhaps when it is time for you to go underground and face Her . . . ."

"I do not understand," Kassandra said. Then she remembered when Apollo had spoken to her and asked that she be His priestess. She told Penthesilea of this, and the older Amazon looked relieved.

"Is it so? I know nothing of your Sun Lord; it seems to me strange that a woman should seek a God rather than the Earth Mother or our Serpent Mother. It is She who dwells underground and rules over all the realms of women—the darkness of birth and death. Perhaps She too has called you and you have not heard Her voice. I have heard that sometimes it is so with the priestesses born: that if they do not hear Her call, she will set Her hand on them through the darkness of evil dreams, so that they may learn how to listen to Her voice."

Kassandra was not certain; she knew little of Penthesilea's Serpent Mother, yet she remembered the beautiful serpents in Apollo's house and how she had longed to caress them. Perhaps this Serpent Mother had called her too, not only the bright and beloved Sun Lord.

She had hoped that her kinswoman, who knew so much about the Goddess, would tell her what she must do to be rid of this unwanted Sight. Now she began to realize that she must herself control it, must find a way within herself to shut the floodgates before the visions overwhelmed her.

"I will try," she said. "Are there any who know about these things?"

"Perhaps among the servants of the Gods. You are a princess of two royal houses: ours of the Amazons', and your father's; I know nothing of those Gods, but a time must come when as one of us, you must go underground to meet the Serpent Mother, and since already She has called you, it should be sooner rather than later. Perhaps at the next moon; I shall speak to the elders and see what they say of you."

Perhaps, Kassandra said to herself, *this is why the God called me to be His servant.* Yet she had herself opened these doors; she should not complain that she had been given the gift which she had asked.

DAY AFTER day the tribe rode, into the fierce winds and the raw icy rain. The weather grew colder and colder, and at night the women wrapped themselves in all their woolen garments and blankets. Kassandra curled up next to her horse, sheltering in the warmth of the big sleek body. Eventually the skies grew clear and brilliant and the rain stopped. Still to the east the tribe traveled; when the women asked their leaders when they would rest and find pasture for their horses, Penthesilea only sighed: "We must first pass two rivers, as the Goddess has decreed."

The moon had waxed and waned again when they sighted the first human beings they had seen on this journey: a small band of men dressed in skins to which hair clung, so that the women guessed that the art of tanning skins was still unknown to them.

There are pastures here, Kassandra thought; *this might be the place to rest our herds and remain. But not with these men . . .*

The men stared open-mouthed and loutish at the women, and Penthesilea drew up her horse beside them.

"Who owns these flocks and herds?" she asked, pointing to the sheep and goats grazing on the bright green vegetation.

"We do. What kind of goats be ye riding?" asked one of the men. "Never did we see goats so big and healthy."

Penthesilea started to say that they were not goats but horses; then decided that in their ignorance there might be some advantage for the tribe. "They are the goats of Poseidon, God of the Sea," she told him, and he asked only, "What be the sea?"

"Water from here to the horizon," she said, and he gasped, "Oh, my! Never do we see water but what's in some muddy hole that dries in the summer! No wonder they look rich and fat!" Then he smiled craftily and asked in his rude dialect if the ladies would care to pasture their herds beside his own.

"Perhaps for a night or two," said Penthesilea.

"Where be yer menfolks?" he asked.

"We have none; we are free of all men," said the Amazon, "but we will accept the hospitality of your pasture for this night, since we have been riding for a long time. Our animals are weary and will welcome a little of your good grass."

"They are welcome to it," replied one of the men, who seemed a little cleaner than the rest, and his garment a little more whole.

As they were dismounting, Penthesilea whispered to Kassandra that they must be wary, and not sleep, but watch their horses even through the night. "For I do not trust these men, not even a little," she whispered. "I think, as soon as we are sleeping, or they think we are sleeping, they will try to steal our horses, and perhaps attack us."

The men tried to edge their way into the circle of women and to steal furtive touches, and Kassandra thought if they had been city women, inexperienced in guile, they would not have realized what the men were doing. She rose with the other young girls to begin spreading out their blankets. She slipped hobbles over her horse's feet, so that it could not go far away in the night, loosened her leather belt and lay down in her blanket, between Elaria and Star.

"I wonder how far we will ride," Star murmured, hugging her blanket around her thin shoulders against the dampness. "If we do not soon find food, the children will begin to die."

"It is not as bad as that," Elaria remonstrated. "We have not even begun to bleed the horses. We can live on their blood for at least a month before they begin to weaken. Once when there was a bad year we lived on the mares' blood for two months. My first daughter died, and we were all so near starving that when we went to the men's village, none of us became pregnant for almost half a year."

"I am hungry enough that I would drink mares' blood—or anything else," Star grumbled, but Elaria said, "That cannot be until Penthesilea gives orders; and she knows what she is doing."

"I am not so sure," Star muttered. "Letting us sleep here among all these men—"

"No," said Elaria, "she bade us *not* sleep."

Slowly the moon rose above the trees, climbing higher and

higher. Then across her lowered eyelids Kassandra saw dark forms stealing through the clearing.

She was waiting for Penthesilea's signal when suddenly the stars above were blotted out by a dark shadow and the weight of a man's body was suddenly across hers; hands were tearing away her breeches, fumbling at her breast. She had her hand on her bronze dagger; she struggled to free herself, but was pinned down flat. She kicked, and bit at the hand that covered her mouth; her attacker yelped—like the dog he was, she thought fiercely—and she thrust up hard with the hilt of the dagger, striking his mouth; he yelped again and Kassandra felt a spray of blood and curses from his broken lips. Then she got the dagger right way round and struck; he yelled and fell across her, just as Penthesilea shouted and all over the grove women sprang to their feet. Someone thrust a torch into the dying coals and the firelight flared up, reflecting light on bronze daggers naked in the men's hands.

"Such is your hospitality to guests?"

"I have taken care of one of them, Aunt!" Kassandra cried out. She scrambled free, pushing the groaning man off her body. Penthesilea strode toward her and looked down.

"Finish him," she said. "Don't leave him to die slowly in pain."

But I don't want to kill him, Kassandra thought; *he can.t hurt me now, and he didn't do me any real harm.* All the same, she knew the law of the Amazons: death for any man who attempted to rape an Amazon; and she could not violate that law. Under the cold eyes of Penthesilea, Kassandra bent reluctantly over the wounded man and drew her dagger hard across his throat. He gurgled and died.

Kassandra, feeling sick, straightened and felt Penthesilea's hand hard on her shoulder. "Good work. Now you are truly one of our warriors," she murmured, and strode forward into the torchlight toward the assembled men.

"The Gods have decreed that the guest is sacred," Penthesilea chided. "Yet one of your men would have ravished one of my unwilling maidens. What excuse can you give for that breach of hospitality?"

"But who ever heard of women to be riding alone this way?" the leader argued. "The Gods protect only women who are decent wives, and you're not; you don't belong to anyone."

"What God told you that?" Penthesilea inquired.

"We don't need a God to tell us what just stands to reason. And since you had no husbands, we decided we'd take ye in and give ye what ye needed most, men to look after ye."

"That is not what we need nor what we seek," the Amazon declared, and gestured to the women surrounding the men with their weapons.

"Take them!"

Kassandra found herself rushing forward with the rest, her dagger raised. The man she rushed against made no particular effort to defend himself; she pushed him down and knelt over him with her knife at his throat.

"Don't kill us!" the leader of the men cried out. "We won't hurt you!"

"*Now* you won't," Penthesilea said fiercely, "but when we were sleeping and you thought us helpless, you would have killed or raped us!"

Penthesilea held the edge of her dagger at his throat, and he cringed. "Will you swear by your own Gods never again to molest any women of our tribes—or any other—if we let you live?"

"No, we won't," said the leader. "The Gods sent you to us, and we took you, and I think we did what was right."

Penthesilea shrugged and cut his throat. The other men screamed that they would swear, and Penthesilea motioned to the women to let them go. One by one, they knelt and swore as required.

"But I do not trust even their oath," said Penthesilea, "once they are out of sight of our weapons." She gave orders for their possessions to be gathered together and for the horses to be saddled, so that they could ride at dawn.

After her sleepless night, Kassandra's eyes burned and her head ached; it seemed that she could still feel the man's gross hands on her. When she wished to move she could not; her body was rigid, locked; she heard someone calling her name but the sound was very far away.

Penthesilea came to her, and the touch of her hand brought Kassandra back to herself.

"Can you ride?" she asked.

Wordlessly, Kassandra nodded, and she pulled herself up into the saddle. Her foster-mother came and embraced her, saying "You did well; now you have killed a man, you are a warrior, fit to fight for us. You are a child no more." Penthesilea called out the signal to ride, and Kassandra, shivering, urged her horse into motion. She wrapped her blanket over her shoulders.

Ugh, she thought, *it smells of death.*

They rode, chill rain in their faces; she envied the women who were carrying covered clay pots of hot coals. Eastward, and farther eastward, they rode, the wind chilling and growing colder. After a long time the sky lightened to a pale gray, but there was no true daybreak. All around her Kassandra heard the women grumbling, and she ached with hunger and cold.

Penthesilea at last called for a halt, and the women began setting up their tents for the first time in many days. Kassandra clung to her horse, needing the heat of the animal's body; the aching cold seemed to seep into every muscle and bone of her body. After a time there were fires burning at the center of the encampment, and she went like the others and crouched close to the tongues of warmth.

Penthesilea gestured near where they had been riding, and the women saw, with astonishment, green fields of half-ripened grain. Kassandra could hardly believe her eyes: grain at this season?

"It is winter wheat," Penthesilea said. "These people plant their grain before the first snow falls, and it lies through the winter under the snow, and ripens before the barley harvest. For this cold climate, they have two grains, and it is the rye I seek."

The Amazon Queen beckoned to her kinswoman, and Kassandra came to her side.

"What land have we come to, Aunt?" she asked.

"This is the country of the Thracians," Penthesilea told her; "and northward"—she gestured—"lies the ancient city of Colchis."

Kassandra remembered one of her mother's stories. "Where Jason found the golden fleece, by the aid of the witch Medea?"

"The same. But there is little gold there, these days, though there is much witchcraft."

"Are there people living hereabout?" asked Kassandra. It seemed impossible that anyone would choose to live in this desolate place.

"Fields of wheat and rye do not plant themselves," Penthesilea reproved her. "Where there is grain, there is always someone, man or woman, to plant it. And here there are people, and also"—she pointed—"horses."

Far away on the horizon, hardly visible, Kassandra made out small moving flecks which seemed no larger than sheep; but from the way they moved, she could see they were horses. As they surged nearer, Kassandra made out that they were very different from the horses that she and the other Amazons rode; small and dun-colored, with heavyset bodies and thick shaggy hair almost like fur.

"The wild horses of the North; they have never been ridden or tamed," Penthesilea said. "No God has touched them to mark them for mankind or women. If they belong to any God or Goddess, they are the property of the Huntress Artemis."

As if moved by one spirit, the whole herd wheeled and dashed away, the lead mare pausing with its head up to stare, nostrils dilated and eyes shining, at the women.

"They smell our stallion," said Penthesilea. "He must be watched; if he scents a herd of mares, he might well try to add them to our own, and these horses are no use to us. We could not feed them, and there would not be enough pasture."

"What are we doing here?" Kassandra asked.

"The Goddess is wise," her kinswoman replied. "Here in the country of the Thracians, we can trade for iron and replenish our weapons. There will be grain for sale in the city of Colchis, if not nearer; and we have items for trade: leatherwork

—saddles and bridles, and more. We will go this afternoon to the village and see if we can buy food."

Kassandra looked at the gray sky and wondered how anyone could tell whether it was morning or afternoon. She supposed that Penthesilea had some way of knowing.

Later that day, Penthesilea summoned Kassandra and one of the other young maidens, Evandre, and they rode toward the village which lay at the center of the grainfields. As the women entered the village—only a few small, round stone houses, and a central building open to the sky where women were working at the shaping of pots—the inhabitants came out to see them.

Many of the women were carrying spindles with wool or goat's hair wrapped around them. They wore long, loose skirts of woven goat's hair dyed green or blue; their hair was dark and ragged. Some had children in their arms, or clinging to their skirts.

Kassandra saw, with a little thrill of horror, that many of the children were curiously deformed. One little girl had a raw-looking cleft through her lip, running up through her face till her nostril looked like an open sore; another had but a thumb and one deformed finger on her tiny hand, which looked like a claw. She had never seen living children like this; in Troy, a child born deformed was immediately exposed on the slopes of Mount Ida for wolves or other wild beasts to destroy. Women and children hung back without speaking, but looking curiously at the Amazons and their horses.

"Where are you going?"

"Northward at the will of our Goddess, and at the moment, to Colchis," said Penthesilea. "We would like to trade here for grain."

"What have you to trade?"

"Leather goods," said Penthesilea, and the women shook their heads.

"We make our own leather from the hides of our horses and goats," said a woman who appeared to be a leader among them. "But sell us a dozen of your little girls and we will give you all the grain you can carry."

Penthesilea's face turned pale with anger.

"No woman of our tribe is ever sold into slavery."

"We do not want them for slaves," said the woman. "We will adopt them as our daughters. A sickness has raged here, and too many women have died in childbirth, while others cannot bear healthy babies; so you can see, women are very precious to us."

Penthesilea was paler than ever. She said softly to Evandre, "Pass the word back that no woman is to dismount from her horse for an instant in this village; not for any purpose, no matter what the need. We will ride on."

"What is the matter, Aunt?" Kassandra asked.

"We must touch none of their grain," Penthesilea said, and then, to the woman: "I am sorry for your sickness; but we can do nothing to help you. Nevertheless, if you would be free of it, cut down your standing grain and burn it; do not even let it lie to fertilize the fields. Get yourselves fresh seed corn from somewhere south of here. Examine the seeds carefully for any trace of blight; it is this which has poisoned the wombs of your women."

As they rode away from the village, Penthesilea, riding through the rye fields, bent down and plucked a few of the green stalks. She held them up, pointing to the place where the seeds would be forming.

"Look," she said, indicating the purplish threadlike fibers at the tips of the stalks as she held them toward Kassandra. "Smell it; as a priestess you must be able to recognize this whenever you encounter it. Do not taste it, whatever you do, nor eat of it even if you are starving."

Kassandra sniffed, and experienced a curious moldy, slimy, almost fishy smell.

"This rye will poison any who eat fresh grain, or even the bread which could be baked from it; and the worst form of poisoning is that it kills the children in the womb and can destroy a woman's fertility for years. That village may already be doomed. It is a pity; their women seem handsome and industrious, and their spinning and weaving work is notable. Also, they make fine pots and cups."

"Will they all die, Aunt?"

"Probably: many of them will eat the poisoned grain and not die of it, but no more healthy children will be born in that village, and by the time they are desperate enough to enforce, perhaps, a year's famine on their people, it may be too late."

"And the Gods permit this?" Kassandra asked. "What Goddess is angry enough to blight the grain in the village?"

"I do not know; perhaps it is not the doing of any Goddess at all," said her kinswoman. "I only know that it comes, year after year, especially when there has been too much rain."

It had never occurred to Kassandra to doubt that the grain of the fields was watched over and made to grow through the direct agency of Earth Mother; this was a frightening heresy, and she put it out of her mind as quickly as possible. She was aware again of hunger—she had been without substantial food for so long that she had almost ceased to be aware of it for days at a time.

As they rode, they began to see small animals darting into and out of burrows in the ground. A young girl quickly strung her bow and loosed a hunting arrow, shaped of fire-hardened wood instead of metal, and the animal it struck fell over and lay kicking. The archer leaped off her pony and clubbed it over the head. A flight of other arrows followed the first, but only one or two found their mark. At the thought of hare roasted on the spit, Kassandra's mouth watered.

Penthesilea drew the riders to a halt with a gesture.

"We will camp here, and I promise you, we will not ride on until we are all fed somehow," she said. "You warriors, take your bows and hunt; as for the rest of you, set up the targets and practice with your arrows. We have neglected practicing our hunting and fighting skills in these days while we ride. Too many of those arrows went far from the targets. In my mother's day, that many arrows would have brought down enough hares to feed us all."

She added, "I know how hungry you all are—I am no more fond of fasting than any of you, and it has been as long for me as for any of you since I have eaten a good meal. Yet I beg you, my sisters, if you have found—or stolen—any grain or anything made of it, or any food at all in that village, let me see it before you eat of it. Their grain is cursed, and those who eat of bread made from it may miscarry, or your child may be born with one eye or only one finger."

One woman defiantly pulled out a hard and somewhat moldy loaf from beneath her tunic. She said, "I will give this to some woman past childbearing age who can eat of it safely. I did not steal it," she added; "I bartered an old buckle for it."

One of the oldest women in the tribe said, "I will take it in exchange for my share of the hare I brought down with my arrow; it has been too long since I tasted bread, and I will certainly never bear any more children to be damaged by it."

The sight of the bread made Kassandra so hungry that she felt she would rather risk miscarriage or damage to a child she might bear someday far in the future; but she would not disobey her kinswoman. Other Amazons brought forth items of food they had bartered for—or stolen—in the village, almost all of which Penthesilea confiscated and threw into the fire.

Kassandra went to shoot at targets while the seasoned warriors rode away to seek game and the old women spread out across the flat countryside to seek food of any sort. It was too far into the winter for berries or fruit, but there might be roots or some edible fungus somewhere.

The short winter day was darkening into twilight when the hunters returned, and soon the cut-up hares were seething in a caldron with flat wild beans and some roots; chunks hacked from a larger beast—it had been skinned, but Kassandra suspected it was one of the rough-furred wild horses, and was hungry enough not to care—were roasting over a great fire. For that night at least they would have their fill, and Penthesilea had promised there would be plenty of food in Colchis.

8

"THERE IT LIES," Penthesilea said, and pointed. "The city of Colchis."

Accustomed to the fortified cyclopean walls of Troy, rising

high above the rivers of the fertile plain, Kassandra was not at first sight impressed by the walls of sun-hardened baked brick, dull in the hazy sunlight. This city, she thought, would be vulnerable to attack from anywhere. In her year with the Amazons, she had learned something—not formally, but from the other Amazons' tales of sieges and war—of military strategy.

"It is like the cities of Egypt and the Hittites," said Penthesilea. "They do not build impressive fortifications; they do not need them. Inside their iron gates you will see their Temples and the statues of their Gods. These are greater than the Temples and statues of Troy as the walls of Troy are greater than the walls of Colchis. The story goes that this city was founded by the ancient ship-people of the far South; but they are unlike any people here, as you will see when we enter the city. They are strange; they have many curious customs and ways." She laughed. "But then, that is what they would say of us, I suppose."

Of all this, Kassandra had heard only *iron gates*. She had seen little of the metal; once her father had shown her a ring of black metal which he told her was iron.

"It is too costly, and too hard to work, for weapons," he said to her. "Someday when people know more about the art of forging it, iron may be of use for plowing; it is much harder than bronze." Now Kassandra, remembering, thought that a city and a people who knew enough of iron to forge it into gates must indeed be wise.

"Is it because the gates are of iron that the city has not been taken?" she asked.

Penthesilea looked at her and said in some surprise, "I do not know. They are a fierce people, but they are seldom involved in war. I suppose it is because they are so far from the major trade areas. All the same, people will come from the ends of the world for iron."

"Will we enter the city, or camp outside the walls?"

"We will sleep this night in the city; their Queen is all but one of us," Penthesilea said. "She is the daughter of my mother's sister."

So, thought Kassandra, *she is my mother's kinswoman too, and mine.*

"And the King?"

"There is no King," Penthesilea said. "Imandra rules here, and she has not chosen yet to take a consort."

Behind the city, rust-red cliffs rose, dwarfing the gates. The path leading to the city was paved with gigantic blocks of stone, and the houses, with stone steps and arches, were constructed of wood and lath and brightly plastered and painted. The city streets were not paved, but muddy and trampled, and strange beasts of burden, horned and shaggy, moved between the houses, laden with huge baskets and jars. Their owners whacked them aside as the Amazons, drawn up in almost military formation, rode through the streets. Kassandra, conscious of all the eyes on her, braced her spear against the weariness of riding, and sat erect, trying to look like a warrior.

The city was very different from Troy. Women went everywhere freely in the streets, carrying jars and baskets on their heads. The women's garments were long, thick and cumbersome, but for all their clumsy skirts and their eye paint, the women looked strong and competent. She also saw a forge where a woman, dark-faced and soot-stained, with a warrior's thick muscles, was working. Bared to the waist to tolerate the fierce heat, she hammered on a sword. A young woman, not much more than a girl, worked the bellows. Kassandra had, in her months with the Amazons, seen women doing many strange things, but this was the strangest of all.

The sentries on the walls were women too and might well have been members of the Amazon company, for they were armed and wore breastplates of bronze, and carried long spears. As the Amazons rode through the streets, the sentries set up a long, whooping battle cry; and before long half a dozen of them, with their spears laid at rest in token of peace, appeared in the streets before them. Their leader rode forward and embraced Penthesilea from the saddle.

"We greet you rejoicing, Penthesilea, Queen of Mares," she said. "The Lady of Colchis sends you greeting and welcomes your return to us. She bids your women make camp in the field within the Southern Wall, and invites you to be her guest in the palace with a friend, or two if you wish."

The Amazon Queen called back the news the sentry had brought.

"And more," the woman of Colchis said: "the Queen sends your women two sheep as a gift, and a basket of bread baked this day in the royal ovens; let your women feast here while you join her at the palace." The Amazons sent up a great cheer at the thought of all this long-untasted food.

Penthesilea saw her women encamped in the field, their tents raised and the sheep slaughtered. Kassandra, standing by as a good rump portion was burnt for the Huntress, noted that the sheep were quite ordinary-looking, like the sheep of Troy. Penthesilea, watching her, said, "What is it? Were you expecting to see the sheep of Colchis with golden fleeces? They do not grow that way; not even the herds of Apollo Sun Lord are born so. But the Colchians lay their fleeces in the stream to catch the gold that still washes down the rivers; and though there is less gold than, perhaps, in Jason's day, still before you depart from Colchis you shall see these fleeces of gold. Now let us dress to dine at a Queen's table."

The Amazon Queen went into her own tent, took off her riding clothes and put on her finest skirt and boots of white doeskin, with a tunic leaving one breast bare as the custom was here. Told to dress in her best, Kassandra put on her Trojan dress—it was too short for her now, and came only halfway down her calves—and her sandals.

Penthesilea had taken a stub of kohl from her pack and was smudging her eyes; she turned and said, "Is this the only dress you have, child?"

"I'm afraid so."

"That will never do," said Penthesilea. "You have grown more than I thought." She dug into her own saddlebag and pulled out a worn dress dyed pale saffron. "This will be too big for you, but do the best you can."

Kassandra dragged the dress over her head and fastened it with her old bronze pins. She felt so awkward and encumbered by the skirts about her knees that it was hard to remember that once she had worn this kind of garment every day.

Together they walked up through the paved streets of Colchis. It was so long since Kassandra had been inside city walls, she felt that she was gaping at the tall houses like a barbarian.

The palace was built somewhat like the palace of Troy, of the local gray marble. It stood on the high place at the center of the city, and not even a Temple stood above it; Kassandra, raised in the custom in her land that the dwellings of men might not rise so high as the Temples of the Gods, was a little shocked.

As they stood on the palace steps, they could look out over the sea. *Just as it is in Troy*, thought Kassandra; only this sea was not the intense blue she remembered from her home, but dark gray and oily. Men were peacefully loading and unloading the ships lying at anchor in the harbor; they were not pirates or raiders, but merchants. This many ships near Troy would be a sign of disaster or war.

Yet she could see them lying off Troy, ships so many that the blue of the sea was darkened. . . .

With an effort she brought herself back to the present. There was no danger here . . .

Penthesilea touched her arm. "What is it? What did you see?"

"Ships," Kassandra murmured. "Ships—threatening Troy . . ."

"No doubt, if Priam goes on as he has begun," her kinswoman said drily. "Your father has attempted to grasp power he is not strong enough to hold, and one day that power will be tested. But for now we must not keep Queen Imandra waiting for us."

Kassandra had never thought to question her father's policies; yet she could see that what Penthesilea said was true. Priam exacted tribute from all ships that went through the straits into this sea; thus far, the Akhaians had paid it because it was less trouble than mustering a navy to challenge it. She looked at the iron gates and realized that they meant a whole new way of life, sooner or later.

She told herself she was unrealistic; her father was strong, with many warriors and many allies; he could hold Troy forever. *Perhaps one day Troy too will have iron gates, like this city of Colchis.* As they passed through the wide corridors, women guards in bronze breastplates and leather helmets inlaid with metal raised their fists in token of salute. Now they came into a high-ceilinged room with a skylight inlaid with translucent green stone, and at the center a high marble seat where a woman was sitting.

She looked like a warrior herself, with a beaten silver breastplate, but under it she was clad in a fine robe of brocade from the Far South, and a light chemise of Egyptian gauze, the kind that was known as "woven air." On her face she wore a false beard, gilded and tied like a ceremonial wig: token, Kassandra felt, that she ruled not as a woman but as King of the city. Around her hips was a belt inlaid with green stones, and a fine sword hung from the belt. She wore leather boots embroidered and dyed, which came up to her calves. Just below her breastplate, about her waist, was a curious belt which seemed to rise and fall with her breathing; as they came nearer, Kassandra realized that it was a living snake.

As they approached, the Queen rose and said, "I greet you rejoicing, Cousin. Have your warriors been properly welcomed and feasted? Is there anything more I can do to make you welcome, Penthesilea, Queen of horsewomen?"

Penthesilea smiled and said, "Indeed we have been welcomed, Lady; now tell me what you want of us. For I have known you since we were girls, and I know well that when not only I, but all my warriors are made welcome and feasted, it is not just for courtesy's sake. Kinship alone would require that I put myself and my women at your service, Imandra; ask freely what you desire of us."

"How well you read me, Penthesilea; indeed I have need of friendly warriors," Imandra said in her husky and pleasing voice, "but first let us share our dinner. Tell me, Cousin, who is the maiden? She is a little too young to be either of your daughters."

"She is the daughter of our kinswoman Hecuba of Troy."

"Oh?" Imandra's delicately painted eyebrows went up in an elegant arch.

She beckoned to a waiting-woman and snapped her fingers lightly; this was the signal for a number of slaves bearing jeweled dishes covered with an assortment of food to come forward:

roast meat and fowl in various delicious sauces, fruits in honey, sweets so richly spiced that Kassandra could not even guess what they were made of.

She had been hungry so long that all this food made her feel slightly sick; she ate sparingly of the roast fowl and some hard cakes of bread, then at the Queen's urging tasted a rich sweetmeat spiced with cinnamon. She noted that Penthesilea too ate little, and when the trays had been carried away and rose water poured over their hands, the Queen of Colchis said, "Cousin, I thought Hecuba had long forgotten her days as a warrior. Yet her daughter rides with you? Well, I have no quarrel with Priam of Troy. She is welcome. Is it she who is to marry Akhilles?"

"No, that I had not heard," said Penthesilea. "I think Priam will find, when he tries to find a husband for this one, that the Gods have claimed her for their own."

"Perhaps one of her sisters, then," said Imandra indifferently. "If we have need of a King in Colchis, perhaps I will marry my own daughter to one of Priam's sons; I have one of an age to be married. Tell me, Priam's daughter, is your oldest brother yet pledged in marriage?"

Kassandra said shyly, "Not that I have heard, Lady, but my father does not confide his plans to me. He may well have made some such arrangement many years ago that I have not heard about."

"Honestly spoken," said Imandra. "When you return to Troy, my envoys shall go with you, offering my Andromache for your father's son; if not the eldest, then another—he has fifty, I believe, and several are the sons of your royal mother, are they not?"

"I do not believe there are as many as fifty," said Kassandra, "but there are many."

"Be it so, then," said Imandra, and as she stretched out her hand to Kassandra, the serpent coiled about her waist began to stir; it crawled up onto her arm, and as Kassandra put out her own hand, the creature thrust out its nose, and its coils followed; it began to wind itself around Kassandra's wrist like a slender bracelet.

"She likes you," Imandra said. "Have you been taught to handle snakes?"

Kassandra said, remembering the serpents in the Temple of Apollo Sun Lord, "They are not strange to me."

"Take care; if she should bite you it would make you very ill," said Imandra. Kassandra felt no fear, but a sense of elation as the snake crawled along her arm, the soft dry sliding of the scales distinctly pleasurable to her flesh.

"And now to a serious matter," said Imandra. "Penthesilea, did you see the ships in the harbor?"

"Who could help seeing? They are many."

"They are laden with tin and iron from the North, from the country of the Hyperboreans," she said, "and naturally, it is coveted by my fellow Kings. Since I do not, they say, sell them sufficient tin for their bronze—they say I fear the weapons they will make, whereas the truth is I have little enough for myself, and they have nothing I crave—they have taken to attacking my caravans of tin and carrying it off without payment. In this city, there are too few trained warriors. What payment will you ask, to bring your warriors to guard my shipments of metal?"

Penthesilea raised her eyebrows. "It would be simpler—and cheaper, I suspect—to sell them what they want."

"And let them arm themselves against me? Better that my smiths make weapons and let them pay with gold for such weapons as they want. I send some tin and lead and also iron south to the Hittite Kings—those who are left of them. Those caravans too are robbed. There is gold in it for you, then, and for your women if they crave it."

"I can guard your caravans," said Penthesilea, "but the price will not be small. My women have traveled here under an omen and are not eager for war; all we want is to return to our own pastures in the spring."

Kassandra lost track of the conversation; she was absorbed in the snake that was coiling around her arm, gliding into the front of her dress, curling up warm between her breasts. She looked aside to one of the slave women juggling three gold-colored balls, and wondered how the girl managed it. When she returned to paying attention to what was happening, Penthesilea and Imandra were embracing, and Imandra said, "I shall await your warriors the day after tomorrow; by that time the caravans will be loaded and the ships sailing away again to the secret mines in the northern countries. My guards will escort you back to the field where your women are encamped; the Goddess give you a good night; and you too, little kinswoman." Then she held out her hand. "My snake has abandoned me. Bid her return to me, Kassandra."

With a certain reluctance, Kassandra reached into the bosom of her dress and scooped out the snake, which draped itself loosely over her hand, twining around her wrist. She loosened it awkwardly with her other hand.

"You must come back and play with her again; usually if I ask someone to hold her for me, she is likely to bite," said Imandra. "But she has taken to you as if you were a priestess. Will you come?"

"I would find it a pleasure," Kassandra murmured, as Imandra scooped the snake from her wrist; it crawled swiftly up her arm and slithered down into the Queen's dress.

"Then I shall welcome you another day, daughter of Hecuba. Farewell."

As they returned, with the women guards walking two paces behind them, Kassandra thought they were more like prisoners being escorted than honored guests being protected. Nevertheless, as they walked through the busy streets, she heard scufflings in alleys and once a muffled scream, and felt that here in this strange city it might not, after all, be entirely safe for women who were not a part of Colchis.

9

TEN DAYS later, Penthesilea rode out of Colchis with a picked group of Amazon warriors, Kassandra among them. They would accompany the caravans of tin, unloaded from the har-

bor ships, on their way southward to the faraway country of the
Hittite Kings.

Secretly Kassandra was remembering the words spoken in
prophecy: "There remain till the spring stars fall!" Was her kinswoman, then, defying the command of the Goddess? But it was
not her place to ask questions. Across her shoulder she carried
the Scythian bow, formed of a double span of horn, strung with
the braided hair of her horse's tail. At her side was the short
metal-tipped javelin of an Amazon warrior. Riding next to Star,
she remembered that her friend had already fought in a battle.

Yet it seemed so peaceful this morning, the bright clear air
adazzle with pale sunlight, a few clouds flying overhead. Their
horses' hooves made a muffled sound on the road beneath, a
counterpoint to the heavy rumble of the carts, each drawn by
two teams of mules, piled high with the wrapped bundles and
crude ingots of the dull/shiny metal and covered with black
cloth as heavy as a ship's sail.

The night before, she had stood, with the other warriors,
guarding the loading of the wagons; remembering the dense
blackness of the ingots of iron, the dullness of the lumps of tin,
she wondered why this ugly stuff should be so valuable. Surely
there was enough metal in the depths of the earth that all men
could have a share; why should men—and women—fight wars
over the stuff? If there was not enough for those who wished
for it, certainly it would be easy enough to bring more from
the mines. Yet it seemed that Queen Imandra took pride in the
fact that there was not enough for everyone who wanted a
share.

That day was uneventful; the Amazons rode along in single
file over the great plain, slowed to the pace of the trundling
wagons. Kassandra rode beside one of the blacksmith-women of
Colchis, talking with her about her curious trade; she discovered
to her surprise that the woman was married and had three
grown sons.

"And never a daughter I could train to my trade!"

Kassandra asked, "Why can you not teach your sons your
trade of a smith?"

The small muscular woman frowned at her.

"I thought you women of the Amazon tribes would understand," she said. "You do not even rear your own men-children, knowing how useless they are. Look, girl: metal is ripped from the womb of the Earth Mother; what would be Her wrath should any man dare to touch or mold Her bounty? It is a woman's task to shape it into earthly form for men to use. No man may follow the smith's trade, or the Earth Mother will not forgive his meddling."

If the Goddess does not wish this woman to teach her sons her craft, Kassandra thought, *why did She give the woman no daughters?* But she was learning not to speak every thought that crossed her mind. She murmured, "Perhaps you will yet have a daughter," but the blacksmith grumbled, "What? Risk bearing again when I have lived almost forty winters?" and Kassandra made no answer. Instead she pulled her horse ahead to ride beside Star. The older girl was cleaning dirt from under her fingernails with a little chipped-bone knife.

"Do you really think we shall have to fight?"

"Does it matter what I think? The Lady thinks so, and she knows more about it than I do."

Rebuffed again, Kassandra withdrew into her own thoughts. It was cold and windy; she drew her heavy mantle about her shoulders and thought about fighting. Since she had lived among the Amazons, she had been set every day to practice shooting with the bow, and had some skill with the javelin and even with the sword. Her eldest brother, Hector, had been in training as a warrior since he was old enough to grasp a sword in his hand; his first set of armor had been made for him when he was seven years old. Her mother too had been a warrior maiden, yet in Troy it had never occurred to anyone that Kassandra or her sister, Polyxena, should learn anything of weapons or of war. And although like all Priam's children she had been weaned on tales of heroes and glory, there were times when it seemed to her that war was an ugly thing and that she was better out of it. But if war was too evil a thing for women, why, then, should it be good for men? And if it was a fine and honorable thing for men, why should it be wrong for women to share the honor and the glory?

The only answer she could summon to her perplexity was Hecuba's comment *It is not the custom.*

But why? she had asked, and her mother's only answer had been *Customs have no reason; they simply are.*

She believed it no more now than she had believed it then.

Withdrawing into herself, she found herself seeking inward, for her twin brother. Troy, and the sunny slopes of Mount Ida, seemed very far away. She thought of the day when he had pursued, and caught, the girl Oenone, and the curious passionate sensations their coupling had roused within her. She wondered where he was now and what he was doing.

But except for a brief and neutral glimpse at the sheep and goats grazing on the slopes of Mount Ida, there was nothing to see. Usually, she thought, it is men who travel and women who remain at home; here I am far afield, and it is my brother who remains on the slopes of the sacred mountain. Well, why should it not be so once in the world?

Perhaps she would be the hero, then, rather than Hector or Paris?

But nothing happened; the carts trundled along slowly and the Amazons rode behind them.

When the early winter sunset stretched the shadows to ragged wavering forms, and the Amazons gathered their horses in a tight circle surrounding the wagons, to camp, Penthesilea voiced what had been in all their minds.

"Perhaps, with the caravan so guarded, they will not attack at all; perhaps we shall simply waste a weary long journey."

"Wouldn't that be the best thing that could happen? For them never to attack at all, and the caravan to reach the end of its journey in peace?" one of the women asked. "Then it would be settled without war . . . ?"

"Not settled at all; we would know they were still lurking, and the moment the guard was withdrawn they would swoop down again; we could waste all the winter here," another said. "I want to see these pirates disposed of once and for all."

"Imandra wants the lesson taught that the caravans from Colchis are not to be attacked," said one of the women fiercely. "And that lesson will be a good thing."

They cooked a stew of dried meat over the fires and slept in a ring around the wagons; many of the women, Kassandra noted, invited the men from the wagons into their blankets. She felt lonely but it never occurred to her to do the same. Little by little she heard the camp fall silent, until there was no sound except the eternal wind of the plains; and everyone slept.

It seemed that the same day was repeated over and over again; they crawled like an inchworm wriggling across a leaf, keeping pace with the heavy wagons, and at the end of that time Kassandra, looking back over the vast plain, thought they seemed no more than a single good day's ride on a good fast horse from the iron-gated city of Colchis and its harbor of ships.

She had lost count of the tediously limping days that brought no greater adventure than a bundle falling from a wagon, and the whole line of wagons coming to a halt while it was gathered up and laboriously hoisted back up again.

On the eleventh or twelfth day—she had lost count, since there was nothing by which to mark the time—she was watching one of the tied bundles inching its way slowly backward under the tarpaulin that covered the load. She knew she should ride forward and notify the caravan master, or at least the wagon driver, so that it could be lashed tighter, but when it fell, at least it would be a break in the monotony. She counted the paces before it would become unbalanced and tumble off.

"War," she grumbled to Star. "This is hardly an adventure, guarding the caravans; will we travel all the long way to the country of the Hittites? And will it be any more interesting than this?"

"Who knows?" Star shrugged. "I feel we have been cheated —we were promised battle and good pay. And so far there has been nothing but this dreary riding." She twitched her shoulders.

"At least the country of the Hittites will be something to see. I have heard that it never rains there; all their houses are made of mud bricks, so that if there *was* ever a good rain, houses and Temples and palaces and everything would wash away and their whole Empire would fall. But here, there is so little to think about that I am half tempted to invite that handsome horse-keeper into my bed."

"You would not!"

"No? Why not? What have I to lose? Except that it is forbidden to a warrior," said Star, "and if I had a child, I should spend my next four years suckling the brat, and washing swaddling clothes, instead of fighting and earning my place as a warrior."

Kassandra was a little shocked; Star spoke so lightly of such things.

"Haven't you seen him looking at me?" Star insisted. "He is handsome, and his shoulders are very strong. Or are you going to be one of those maidens who are vowed to remain chaste as the Maiden Huntress?"

Kassandra had not thought seriously about it. She had assumed that for years at least she would remain with the Amazon warriors who took chastity as a matter of course.

"But all your life, Kassandra? To live alone? It must be well enough for a Goddess who can have any man she will," said Star, "but even the Maiden, it is said, looks down from Heaven now and again and chooses a handsome youth to share her bed."

"I do not believe that," said Kassandra. "I think men like to tell those tales because they do not like to think any woman can resist them; they do not want to think that even a Goddess could choose to remain chaste."

"Well, I think they are right," said Star. "To lie with a man is what every woman desires—only among us, we are not bound to remain with any man and keep his house and wait on his wishes; but without men we would have no children, either. I am eager to choose my first; and for all your talk I am sure you are no different from any of us."

Kassandra remembered the coarse shepherd who would have violated her, and felt sick. At least here among the Amazons, no one would insist that she give herself to any man unless she chose; and she could not imagine why any woman would choose such a thing.

"It's different for you, Kassandra," Star said. "You are a princess of Troy, and your father will arrange a marriage with any man you wish; a King or a prince or a hero. There is nothing like that in my future."

"But if you want a man," Kassandra asked, "why are you riding with the Amazons?"

"I was given no choice," Star replied. "I am not an Amazon because I wished for it, but because my mother, and her mother before her, chose that way of life."

Kassandra said, "I can imagine no better life than this."

"Then you are short on imagination," Star said, "for almost any other life I can imagine would be better than this; I would rather be a warrior than a village woman with her legs broken, but I would rather live in a city such as Colchis and choose a husband for myself than be a warrior."

It did not sound like the kind of life Kassandra would wish for, and she could not think of anything else to say. She returned to watching the heavy wagon's bundles as they shifted, and she was half asleep in her saddle when a loud yell startled her and the wagon driver fell over headlong to the trail, an arrow through his throat.

Penthesilea shouted to her women, and Kassandra slung her strung bow swiftly to her breast, nocked an arrow and let fly at the nearest of the ragged men who were suddenly swarming on the plain, as if they had sprung like dragon's teeth from the sand. The arrow flew straight to its target; the man who had sprung up beside the driver fell off screaming, and at the same moment the heavy bundle clanged to the rocky path, crushing one of the attackers who was trying to pull himself up on the wagon. Man and metal rolled together down the slope, and one of the warriors leaped from her horse and ran toward him, thrusting quickly with her javelin.

One of the running men grabbed at Kassandra's saddle straps and hauled at her leg; she kicked, but he grabbed her off, and she struggled to get her knife free.

She thrust upward and he fell across her, blood streaming from his mouth; another thrust, with the javelin this time, and he fell lifeless across her body. She struggled to get herself free of his weight. Then there was a javelin aimed at her throat; she thrust upward with her knife to knock it aside and felt a tearing pain in her cheek.

A man's hand was gripping her elbow; she knocked the elbow into his mouth and felt blood and a tooth sprayed into her face. Over her shoulder she could see many men hauling at the bundles of metal, flinging them down into the roadway; she could hear Star screaming somewhere and the sound of arrows singing in flight. All around her was the high shrilling of the Amazon battle cry. Kassandra thrust her javelin and the man attacking her fell dead; she jerked the weapon free and found it covered with blood and entrails. Hastily unslinging her bow again, she began shooting at the invaders, but as every arrow flew she was afraid it would hit one of her companions.

Then it was all over; Penthesilea ran toward the wagon, beckoning her women to rally close. Kassandra hurried to catch her horse, which, to her amazement, had come through the thick of the flying arrows untouched. The driver of the wagon was dead, lying back along the roadway. Star lay half crushed under her fallen horse; the beast had been slain by half a dozen of the strangers' arrows. Shocked, Kassandra ran to try to heave the horse from her friend's body. Star lay still, her tunic torn, the back of her head smashed into a reddish mess, her eyes staring straight ahead.

She wanted a battle, Kassandra thought. *Well, she had one.* She bent over her friend and gently closed her eyes. Not till then did she realize how badly she herself was wounded; her cheek torn open, blood dripping from the flap of skin and flesh.

Penthesilea came to her and bent over Star's body.

"She was young to die," said the Amazon Queen gently. "But she fought bravely."

That was not, Kassandra thought, much good to Star now. The Amazon Queen looked her straight in the face and said, "But you too are wounded, child. Here, let me tend your wound."

Kassandra said dully, "It is nothing; it doesn't hurt."

"It will," said her kinswoman, and took her to one of the wagons, where Elaria washed the torn cheek with wine, and then dressed it with sweet oil.

"Now you are truly a warrior," said Elaria, and Kassandra remembered having been told that on the night when she had killed the man who tried to ravish her. But she supposed that a real battle made her more truly a fighting woman. She bore the wound proudly, the mark of her first battle.

Penthesilea, her face smeared with blood, bent close to

examine the cleansed wound and frowned. "Bind it carefully, Elaria, or there will be a dreadful scar—and that we must not have."

"What does it matter?" Kassandra asked wearily. "Most Amazon warriors have scars." Penthesilea herself was dripping blood from an open slash on her chin. Kassandra touched her cheek with careful fingers. "When it is healed it will hardly show. Why make a fuss about it?"

"You appear to be forgetting, Kassandra, that you are not an Amazon."

"My mother herself was once a warrior," Kassandra protested. "She will understand an honorable scar of battle."

"She is a warrior no longer," Penthesilea said grimly. "She chose a long time ago what she would be; that she would live with your father, keep his house, bear his children. So if your father is angry—and angry, believe me, he will be if we send you back to him with your beauty marred—your mother will be greatly distressed, and her goodwill is very valuable to us. You will go back to Troy when we head south in the spring."

"No!" Kassandra protested. "Only now am I beginning to be of some use to the tribe instead of a burden. Why should I go back to being a house-mouse"—she pronounced the words disdainfully—"just when I have shown myself fit to become a warrior?"

"Think, Kassandra, and you will know why you must go," Penthesilea replied. "You are becoming a warrior; which would be well and good were you to spend the rest of your life with us. I would welcome you among our tribe, a true warrior and a daughter to me as long as I live. But this cannot be; soon or late, you must return to your life in Troy—and since it must be so, then for your own sake it had best be soon. You are old enough now to be married; indeed, your father may already have chosen a husband for you. I would not send you back so changed that you would be miserable all your life if you must spend it within city walls." Kassandra knew this was true, but it seemed to her that she was being punished for becoming one of them.

"Don't look so downcast, Bright Eyes; I am not sending you away tomorrow," her kinswoman said, and drew the girl to her breast, stroking her hair. "You will remain with us at least for another moon, perhaps two, and return with us to Colchis. Nor have I forgotten the promise I made you. The Goddess has called you to Her service, has set Her hand upon you as priestess born; we could not claim you as warrior in any case. Before you depart from among us, we shall see you presented to Her."

Kassandra still felt that she had been cheated; she had worked so long and bravely to be accepted as an Amazon warrior, and it was that very hard work and bravery in battle which had lost her the coveted goal.

The scene of the battle was being cleared; the bodies of the Amazons—besides Star, two other women had been slain by arrows and one crushed beneath a fallen horse—were being dragged away to be burnt. Penthesilea pushed Kassandra gently down when she would have risen.

"Rest; you are wounded."

"Rest? What are the other warriors doing, wounded or not? May I not bear the part of a warrior at least while I still remain among you?"

Penthesilea sighed. "As you will, then. It is your right to see those you have slain sent to the Lord of the Underworld." With tenderness she touched the girl's wounded cheek.

Goddess, Mother of Mares, Lady who shapes our Fates, she thought, *why did You not send this one, the true daughter of my heart, to my womb, rather than to my sister, who had chosen to give her to a man's dominion? She will know no happiness there, and I see only darkness lying before her; darkness, and the shadow of another's fate.*

Her heart yearned for Kassandra as never for her own daughters; yet she realized that Hecuba's daughter must bear her own destiny, which she could not abate, and that the Dark Goddess had set her hand on the girl.

No woman can escape her Fate, she thought, *and it is ill done to seek to deprive Earth Mother of Her appointed sacrifice. Yet for love of her, I would send her to serve Earth Mother below, rather than sentence her to serve the Dark One here in mortal lands.*

10

KASSANDRA SAW her companions consigned to the flames without any visible display of emotion; when they made camp that night, at their insistence she spread her blankets between those of Penthesilea and Elaria.

It did filter through her mind that without consulting her, a decision had been made. Now that the worst of the danger was over, they seemed suddenly to have remembered that she was *a princess of Troy*, and she was now to be carefully protected. But she was no more and no less a princess than she had been two or three days ago.

She missed Star, though they had not, she supposed, really been friends. Yet there was a subdued horror in Kassandra at the thought that every night on this journey she had spread out her blankets on the trail close beside this girl whose body now lay burned to ashes after having been smashed into ruin and pierced with arrows.

A little less luck, an opponent a little more skilled and the javelin that had torn her cheek would have gone through her throat; it would have been her body burned tonight on that pyre. She felt vaguely guilty, and was too new to the warrior's world to know that every one of the women lying around her felt exactly the same way: guilty and troubled that it was she who was alive and her friend who had died.

Penthesilea had spoken of the Goddess' laying Her hand upon her, as if this were a fact like any other, and Kassandra found herself wondering if she had been spared because the Goddess had some use for her.

Her torn cheek itched with maddening ferocity, and when she raised her hand to try to ease it by scratching or rubbing, a sharp pain kept her from touching it. She shifted the cloak she had wadded under her head and tried to find a comfortable position to sleep. Which Goddess had laid a hand on her? Penthesilea had told her once, casually, that all the Goddesses were the same, although each village and tribe had its own name for

Her. There were many: the Moon Lady, whose tides and daily shifting rhythms laid Her compulsion on every female animal; the Mother of Mares, whom Penthesilea invoked; the Maiden Huntress, whose protection was on every maiden and everyone who shot with the bow, guardian of warriors; the Dark Mother of the under-earth, Snake Mother of the Underworld . . . but She, Kassandra thought in confusion as her thoughts began to blur into sleep, had been slain by Apollo's arrows. . . .

As often before sleep, she reached out in her mind for the familiar touch of her twin's thoughts. There was the riffle of a wind from home, and the thyme-scented air of Mount Ida drifted through her senses; the darkness of the shepherd's hut she had never, in her own body, entered was around her; she wondered what he would have thought of the battle. Or would this have seemed commonplace to him? No; for now she, a woman, had more experience of battle than he had. Shadowed darkly at her side she could see—or sense—a sleeping form she identified as the woman Oenone who had for so long been the center of her—of *his* fantasies. She had become accustomed in the last months to this curious division of herself and her twin, till she was no longer sure which sensations and emotions were hers and which Paris'. Was she asleep and dreaming? Was he?

The moonlight illuminated the softly shining form of a woman standing in the shadowed doorway of the shepherd's hut, and she knew she looked on the form of the Lady; a Queen, regal and shining; now the shining one shifted, and the light streamed from the silver bow, with arrows of moonlight filling the little room.

The moonlight seemed to pierce through her body—or his —running through the veins, weaving around her like a net, drawing her toward the figure in the doorway. It seemed to her that she stood, facing the Lady, and a voice spoke from behind her left shoulder . . .

"Paris, thou hast shown thyself a fair and honest judge." Kassandra saw again for an instant the bull Paris had awarded the prize at the fair. "Judge thou therefore among the Goddesses, which is the fairest."

"Truly"—she felt Paris' reply come as if from her own mouth—"the Lady is most fair in all her guises. . . ."

Boyish laughter echoed at her shoulder. "And canst thou worship Her with perfect equality in all the Goddesses, without preferring one above another? Even the Sky Father shies from such a difficult balance as that!" Something smooth and cool and very heavy was put into Paris' hands, and golden light shone up upon his face. "Take thou this apple, and offer it to the Most Fair Goddess."

The figure in the door shifted slightly; the full moon crowned it with a shining halo, and its robes shone like polished marble. Sky Father's Queen stood there, Hera, stately and majestic, rooted in earth but reigning over it. "Serve me, Paris, and you will be great. You shall rule over all the known countries, and the wealth of the world shall be yours."

Kassandra felt Paris bow his head. "Truly you are fair, Lady, Most Powerful Queen." But the apple still lay heavy in his hand.

She looked up cautiously, fearing the Lady's wrath, but now the moon seemed to shine through a golden haze, glinting from the helmet and shield the Lady bore. The golden light radiated from Her as well, and even the owl on Her right shoulder shone with reflected glory.

"You will have much wisdom, Paris," Athene said. "Already you know that you cannot rule the world unless you first rule yourself. I shall give you knowledge of self, and build upon it all other knowledge. You will have wisdom to live well, and achieve victory in all battles."

"I thank you, Lady, but I am a shepherd, not a warrior. And there is no war here; who would dare to challenge the rule of King Priam?"

Kassandra thought she saw a look of scorn on the Lady's face, but then She moved, coming close enough so that Kassandra felt she could reach out and touch Her. Her shield and helmet had disappeared, as had Her pale draperies, and light radiated from Her perfect body. Paris brought up his hands, still clasping the apple, to shield his eyes. "Bright Lady," he murmured.

"There are other battles a shepherd can easily win—and what victory can there be without love and a lady to share it? Thou art fair, Paris, and most pleasing to all the senses." Her breath brushed against his cheek and he felt dizzy, as if the entire mountain were spinning around him. The air around him was warm; he shone brilliantly, bathed in the Lady's golden glow. Her voice continued, soft and seductive, pulling him toward Her. "Thou art a man any woman would be proud to marry—even such a woman as Helen of Sparta, the most beautiful woman in the world."

"Surely no mortal woman could compare with You, Lady." Paris looked into Aphrodite's eyes, and Kassandra had the curious impression that she and he were drowning together, washed away in the tide of light that shone from the eyes of the Queen of Love.

"But Helen is not entirely mortal; she is a daughter of Zeus, and her mother was fair enough to tempt Him. She is almost as beautiful as I am, and she holds Sparta as well. All men desire her; all the Kings among the Argives sued for her hand. She chose Menelaus, but I assure you that one look at you would make her forget that choosing. For you are beautiful, and beauty draws all to itself."

Kassandra thought of Oenone, lying entranced at Paris' side; *What does he want of a beautiful woman? He has one already*—but Paris appeared unaware of her presence. The apple seemed feather-light in his hand as he handed it to the Goddess Aphrodite, and the golden glow brightened as if it would consume him. . . .

The sunlight was shining in her eyes through the tent flap that Elaria had just opened. "How are you feeling this morning, Bright Eyes?"

Kassandra stretched warily, slitting her eyes against the light—only sunlight, after all, not the brilliant arrowed moonlight of the Goddess. Had it been a vision, or only a dream; and had it been her dream, or her brother's? Three Goddesses—but not one of them had been the Maiden Huntress. Why not?

Perhaps Paris has no interest in maidens, she thought flippantly. But neither had there been any sign of Earth Mother—

or was Earth Mother the same as Hera? No, for Earth Mother is Goddess by Her own right, not wife even to a God, and those Goddesses were all defined as wife or daughter to Sky Father. Are those, then, the same as the Goddesses of Troy?

No, they could not be; why would a Goddess agree to be judged by any man—or even by any God?

None of these Goddesses is the Goddess as I know Her—the Maiden, Earth Mother, Serpent Mother—nor even Penthesilea's Mother of Mares. Perhaps in a land where the Sky Gods rule, can only those Goddesses be seen who are perceived as servants to the God? This left her more confused than ever.

It cannot have been my dream, for if I had dreamed of Goddesses I would have dreamed of those Goddesses I worship and honor. I have heard of these Goddesses; Mother told me of Athene with Her gifts of olive and grape; but they are not mine, nor of the Amazons.

"KASSANDRA? Are you still sleeping?" asked Elaria. "We are to return to Colchis, and Penthesilea has been asking for you."

"I am coming," said Kassandra, pulling on her breeches. As she moved, the tension of the dream—or vision—seemed to slip away, so that in her mind was only the curious memory of the alien Goddesses.

The vision is my brother's, not mine.

"Say to my kinswoman that I am coming," Kassandra said. "Let me but brush my hair."

"Let me help you," Elaria said, and knelt beside her. "Does your head hurt? The bandage has come away from your face: Ah, good—there is no sign of a scar; it is healing cleanly. The Goddess has been kind to you."

To herself Kassandra wondered, *Which Goddess?* but she did not speak the question aloud. In a few minutes she was in the saddle, and as they turned toward Colchis for the long ride, Kassandra saw before her in the brilliant sunlight the faces and forms of all the world's Goddesses. *But what did these Goddesses of the Akhaians want with my brother, or with me? Or with Troy?*

11

RIDING AT their own pace and no longer held to the slow lum-
bering of the clumsy tin-bearing wagons, Penthesilea, Kassandra and the others who were returning to Colchis left the
caravan to make its way to the faraway country of the Hittites.
Kassandra's face ached, and the jolting of her horse made it
worse. She wondered what fortune the rest of the warriors
would have on their journey and almost wished she could ride
with them to that unknown land, even if only to join them in
battle or death. But, she thought, I should not complain; I have
already traveled farther from my home than any other woman
of Troy has ever traveled, farther than any of my brothers, or
even Priam himself.

Penthesilea seemed unconcerned about attack as they retraced their way toward the city; perhaps the Amazons were not
worth attacking without the metal they guarded. And who, Kassandra wondered, would guard the next caravan, with so many
of the Amazons gone to guard this one? But she knew it was not
her affair.

Now that she thought about it, she was eager to see more
of the city of Colchis; Penthesilea's oracle had commanded her
to remain for some time. All she had to look forward to after
this was a return to Troy. Now she understood what her kinswoman meant in saying that she should return before she was
completely unfit for the ordinary life of a woman of Troy. But,
thought Kassandra, it is already too late for that.

*I shall go mad, prisoned inside house walls for the rest of my
life.*

And then she remembered her vision of the Goddesses and
of her brother. With this gift, she would always have a way of
going outside her immediate surroundings, and thus she was
more fortunate than many other women.

But was it any kind of substitute for actual change? Or
merely a mockery, that her mind should escape the prisoning
walls when her body could not?

She felt she would like to talk about this at length with her mother, who had lived both lives and might understand. But would her mother be willing to talk about it freely, having made her own irrevocable choice? What had her mother gained for all she had given up? Would she still make the same choice?

Yet Kassandra knew she would never really have that opportunity. To Hecuba it was important that she be seen as powerful, and to this end she would never admit to Kassandra—or to anyone else—that she might have made a choice that was less than perfect.

Who else was there to talk to? Was there anyone to whom she could confide her confusion and distress? She could think of no one. It was unlikely that Penthesilea would be ready for such a discussion; Kassandra was sure her kinswoman loved her, but that she regarded Kassandra as a child, not an equal with whom she would talk freely.

Even though they were traveling at the best speed of their horses, the ride to Colchis seemed all but endless. Even though at the end of the first day they came within sight of the high walls of the iron-gated city, there was still a long way to go: days in the saddle from first light, broken at noon for the usual cheese or curds. At least it was better than the hunger in the southern pastures. It was sunset of the third or fourth day when at last the tired riders passed beneath the great gates and towers. They set up a cheer in which Kassandra joined, but opening her mouth to cheer made the bandaged cut on her face ache. It was growing cold, and rain was threatening.

Within the shadow of the walls, a messenger from the palace came and spoke to Penthesilea, after which she beckoned to Kassandra.

"You and I are bidden to the palace, Kassandra; the rest of you, join the others in the camp."

Kassandra wondered what the Queen wanted of them. They trotted slowly through the cobbled streets, gave up their horses at the palace gates and were conducted by Queen Imandra's women into the royal presence.

She was waiting for them in the same room where she had greeted them before. A young girl with coils of dark curls arranged low on her neck sprawled beside her on a rug.

"You have done well," Imandra said, beckoning them forward; seizing Penthesilea's hand, she slid onto it a bracelet of carved golden leaves, set with bits of green stone. Kassandra had never seen anything so beautiful.

"I will not keep you long," said the Queen. "You will be wanting a bath and dinner, after your long journey. Still, I wanted to speak with you for a little."

"It is our pleasure, Kinswoman," Penthesilea said.

"Andromache," said Queen Imandra, turning to the girl on the rug beside her, "this is your cousin Kassandra, daughter of Hecuba of Troy. She is the sister of Hector, your promised husband."

The dark-haired girl sat up, flinging her long curls to one side. "You are Hector's sister?" she inquired eagerly. "Tell me about him. What is he like?"

"He is a bully," Kassandra said forthrightly. "You must be very firm with him or he will treat you like a rug and walk all over you, and you will be no more than a timid little thing perpetually yessing him, as my mother does my father."

"But that is suitable for a husband and wife," said Andromache. "How would you have a man behave?"

"It's useless to talk to her, Kassandra," said Queen Imandra. "She should have been born to one of your city-dwelling women. I had intended her for a warrior, as you can tell from the name I gave her."

"It's useless to say that to Kassandra," said Penthesilea; "she speaks no language but her own."

"It's horrible," Andromache said. "My name means 'Who fights like a man'—and who would want to?"

"I would," said Penthesilea, "and I do."

"I don't want to be rude to you, Kinswoman," said Andromache, "but I don't like fighting at all. My mother can't forgive me that I was not born to be a warrior like her, to bring her all kinds of honor at arms."

"The wretched girl," Imandra said, "will have nothing to do with weapons. She is lazy and childish; she wants only to stay indoors and wear pretty clothes. And already her mind is full of men. When I was her age I hardly knew there were men in the world except for my arms-master, and I only wanted him to be proud of me. I made the mistake of letting her be brought up by women, indoors; I should have turned her over to you, Penthesilea, as soon as she could sit a horse. What sort of Queen is this for Colchis? Good for nothing except to marry—and what good is that?"

"Oh, Mother!" said Andromache, crossly. "You must accept that I am not like you. To hear you talk, one would think that there was nothing to life except war and weapons and the ruling of your city, and beyond that, trade and ships beyond the borders of your world."

Imandra smiled and said, "I have found nothing better. Have you?"

"And what of love?" asked Andromache. "I have heard women talk—real women, not women who are pretending to be warriors—"

Imandra stopped her short by leaning over and slapping her face.

"How dare you say 'pretending' to be warriors? I am a warrior, and no less a woman for that!"

Andromache's smile was wicked, even though she put her hand to her reddening cheek.

"Men say that women who take up weapons are pretending to be warriors only because they are unable to spin and weave and make tapestries and bear children—"

"I did not find you under an olive tree," interrupted Imandra.

"And where is my father to say so?" asked the girl impudently.

Imandra smiled. "What does our guest say? Kassandra, you have lived both ways . . ."

"By the girdle of the Maiden," Kassandra said, "I would rather be a warrior than a wife."

"That seems to me folly," said Andromache, "for it has not brought happiness to my mother."

"Yet I would not change with any woman, wedded or unwedded, on the shores of the sea," said Imandra; "and I do not know what you mean by happiness. Who has put these sentimental notions into your head?"

Penthesilea, speaking for the first time, said, "Let her alone, Imandra; since you have decided she is to be married, it is just as well she should be contented in that state. A girl that age does not know what she wants, nor why; that is so among our girls as well as yours."

Kassandra looked down at the soft-skinned, rosy-cheeked young girl at her side. "I think you are quite perfect as you are; I find it hard to imagine you otherwise."

Andromache lifted her hand toward Kassandra's bandaged cheek. "What have you done to yourself, Cousin?"

"Nothing worth mentioning," Kassandra said. "No more than a scratch." And indeed before Andromache's soft eyes she felt it truly nothing, a trivial incident she should be ashamed to mention.

Imandra leaned forward, and as she did so, Kassandra saw the small squarish head sliding out of her bodice. She put out her hand. "May I?" she asked, pleading, and the snake glided forward to slide around her wrist. Imandra guided the snake into Kassandra's hand.

"Will she speak to you?"

Andromache looked on with a frown. "Ugh! How can you touch those things? I have such a horror of them."

Kassandra brought the snake caressingly to her cheek. "But that is foolish," she said. "She will not bite me, and if she did, it would do me very little harm."

"It has nothing to do with fear of being bitten," Andromache said. "It is not right, not *normal* to be unafraid of snakes. Even a monkey that has been kept in a cage all its life, and never seen a living snake, will cry and shiver if you so much as throw a piece of rope into the cage, thinking it is a snake. And I think men too are intended by nature to be afraid of snakes."

"Well, perhaps, then, I am not normal," Kassandra snapped. She bent her head close to the snake, crooning to it.

Imandra said gently, "It is not for everyone, Kassandra. Only for such as you, who are born with the link to the Gods."

"I do not understand this," Kassandra said, feeling sullen and inclined to contradict everything that was said to her. Petting the snake, she said, "I dreamed the other night—or perhaps it was a vision of some sort—of the Goddesses. But the Serpent Mother was not one of them."

"You dreamed? Tell me about it," said Imandra, but Kassandra hesitated. Partly she felt that to tell her dream might dilute the magic; it had been sent to her as a sacred secret and was not intended for anyone else. She cast a pleading look at Penthesilea, for she did not want, either, to offend the Queen who had been so good to them.

"I advise you to tell her, Kassandra," said the Amazon Queen. "She is herself a priestess of Earth Mother, and perhaps she can tell you what this means to your destiny."

Thus encouraged, Kassandra began, detailing every moment of her vision, ending with her confusion that neither the Maiden, nor Earth Mother, nor Serpent Mother had appeared among the Goddesses. Imandra listened intently, even when Kassandra, momentarily overcome by the memory, let her voice sink to a whisper.

When she finished, Imandra asked quietly, "Was this your first encounter with any of the Immortals?"

"No, Lady; I have seen the Mother Goddess of Troy speak through my mother's mouth, though I must have been very small indeed at the time. And once"—she swallowed, lowered her head and tried to steady her voice, knowing that if she did not she would break into wild weeping without knowing why— "once . . . in His own Temple . . . Apollo Sun Lord spoke clearly to me."

She felt Imandra's gentle fingers rest on her hair.

"It is as I thought when first I spoke with you; you have been called as a priestess. Do you know what that means?"

Kassandra shook her head and tried to guess.

"That I must live in the Temple and care for the oracles and the rites?"

"No, it is not as simple as that, child," Imandra told her. "It means that from this very day you must stand between men and Immortals, to explain the ways of the one to the other. . . . It is not a life I would choose for my own daughter."

"But why have I been chosen?"

"Only Those who called you know the answer to that, little one," Imandra said, and her voice was very gentle. "On some of us They lay Their hand in a way we cannot mistake. They do not explain Their ways to us. But if we try to escape Their will They have ways of forcing us to Their service, forget it not. . . . No one seeks to be chosen; it is the Gods who choose us, not we who seek to give our service to Them."

Yet, thought Kassandra, *I think I would have sought this service. At least I do not come to it unwilling.* The snake seemed to have fallen asleep in a heavy puddle on her arm; Imandra leaned forward and scooped it up still sleeping, letting it slide as if melting down the front of her dress.

"When next the moon shines full, you shall seek Her," she said. And Kassandra felt an omen in the way she spoke.

12

"I KNOW so little of being a priestess," Kassandra said. "What must I do?"

"If the Goddess has called you, She will make it clear to you," said Penthesilea, "and if She has not, it does not matter what you do or do not do; it will be all the same."

She patted Kassandra on the head and said, "You must get yourself a snake, and a pot to keep it in."

"I would rather keep it inside my dress, as the Queen does."

"That is all very well," said Penthesilea, "but any animal must have a place that is all its own, as a refuge."

Kassandra could very well understand that. And so she went to the market with her kinswoman, seeking a pot for her snake; tomorrow, she told herself, she would go into the countryside, seeking a snake for herself. It did not seem suitable to buy one at the market for money, though she supposed she could speak with the people who raised snakes for the Temple.

Perhaps Imandra could be persuaded to tell her what she should know.

She searched among the pot-sellers in the marketplace, and finally found a vessel tinted blue-green and decorated with sea creatures; on one side stood a priestess offering a serpent to some unfamiliar Goddess. It seemed to Kassandra that this was the perfect pot in which to keep her snake, and she at once bought it with the money that Penthesilea had given her. There were many pots decorated exactly like it, and she wondered if they were all put to the same use.

That evening as the sun set, she stood with Andromache on the palace roof, looking down into the darkness of the town as one by one, lights were kindled in the city below.

"You cannot go before the Goddess in leather Amazon breeches," said Andromache. "I will lend you a robe."

Kassandra frowned. "Is the Goddess a fool? I am what I am; do you think I can deceive Her by changing my garment?"

"You are right, of course," Andromache said soothingly, "it cannot matter to the Goddess. But other worshipers might see and be scandalized, not understanding."

"That is another matter," Kassandra agreed, "and I understand what you mean; I will wear a robe if you are kind enough to lend me one."

"Certainly, my sister," said Andromache, then hesitated, saying almost defensively, "You will be my sister if I marry your brother, and when I come to Troy I will have a friend in your strange city."

"Of course." Kassandra slipped her arm around the younger girl, and they stood close in the darkness. "But Troy is no stranger than *your* city."

"Stranger to me, though," said the young girl. "I am accustomed to a city where a Queen rules. Truly, does your mother Hecuba not rule the city?"

Kassandra giggled a little at the thought of Hecuba ruling over her stern father.

"No, she does not. And your mother—has she no husband?"

"What should she do with a husband? Two or three times

since my father died, she has taken a consort for a season and sent him away when she was tired of him. That is what is right for a Queen to do if she has desire for a man—at least in our city."

"And yet you are willing to marry my brother and be subject to him as our women are subject to their men?"

"I think I shall enjoy it," Andromache said with a giggle,. and then cried out, "Oh, look!"

Across the sky a line of brilliant light slashed and was gone.

Another followed it swiftly, and another, so brightly that for a moment it seemed that the earth itself reeled as the sky displaced itself. Star after star seemed to lose its moorings and fall, as the two girls watched. Kassandra murmured, " '. . . . there remain until the spring's stars fall.' "

In the darkness a shadow separated, became two, and Queen Imandra and Penthesilea appeared on the roof.

"Ah, I thought perhaps you were here, girls. It is as She told us," said Penthesilea, looking up at the shimmering heavens, as star after star appeared to detach itself from the sky and shimmer downward; "a shower of falling stars."

"But how can the stars fall? Will they all fall out of the sky?" Andromache asked. "And what will happen when they are all gone?"

Penthesilea chuckled and said, "Never fear, child. I have seen the star-showers every year for many years; there are always plenty left in the sky."

"Besides," Imandra added, "I cannot see how it would affect us here on earth if they all fell—except that I should be sorry not to have their light."

"Once," said Penthesilea, "when I was a very young woman, I was with my mother and her tribe—we were riding on the plains far to the north of here, among the iron mountains —and a star fell close to us, with a great crackling and sizzling noise and light. We searched all the night, in the smell of the burnt air, and at last we found a great black stone, still glowing red; that is why many believe that the stars are molten fire which cools to rock. My mother left me this sword, which I saw forged of the sky-metal."

"Sky-iron is better than iron ripped from the earth," confirmed Imandra, "perhaps because it is not under the curse of the Mother—it has not been torn from the earth, but is a gift of the Gods."

"I wish I could find a fallen star," murmured Andromache; "they are so beautiful."

She was still encircled in Kassandra's arm, and her tone was so wistful that Kassandra murmured, "I wish I could find one and give it to you as a gift worthy of you, little sister."

Penthesilea said, "So we are free to return to our own plains and pastures; we do not yet know why the Goddess sent us here."

"Whatever the reason," said Imandra, "it was my good fortune; perhaps the Goddess knew I had need of you here. When you go southward, you shall ride with my gifts. And if some of your women choose to remain and instruct the women of my guards, they shall be well paid." She looked upward, where the stars were still tumbling and dancing across the sky, and murmured, "Perhaps the Goddess has sent this as an omen for your journey before Her, Kassandra. There was no such omen for me when I sought Her far country to offer my service," she added, almost enviously.

"Where must I go?" asked Kassandra. "And must I journey alone?"

Imandra touched her hand gently in the dark. She said, "The journey is of the spirit, Kinswoman; you need not travel a single step. And although you will have many companions, every candidate journeys alone, as the soul is always alone before the Gods."

Kassandra's eyes were dazzled by the falling stars, and in the curious mood of the night it seemed that Imandra's words had some profound meaning stronger than the words themselves implied.

"Tell me more about the metal from the sky," said Andromache. "Should we not search for it, since it is falling all around us? Then we would not need to mine it, nor send for it on the ships from the northern lands."

Imandra said, "My court astrologers foretold this star-shower, and they will be watching from a field outside the city, with swift horses, so if a star should fall nearby, they will go out and search for it. It would be impious to let a gift of the Gods go thus unclaimed or to let it fall into the hands of others who would not treat it with due reverence."

It seemed to Kassandra that hundreds of stars had fallen; but looking into the dark light-sprinkled heavens overhead, she saw quite as many as ever. Perhaps, she thought, new stars grow when these fall. The spectacle was beginning to seem quite ordinary, and she turned her eyes from the sky, sighing.

"You should go to bed," Penthesilea said, "for tomorrow you will be taken with the others who are to seek the Goddess in Her country. And eat well before you sleep, for tomorrow you will be required to fast the day through."

"She will sleep in my room this night," Andromache said, "because I have promised to lend her a robe for tomorrow, Mother."

"That was a kindly thought for your kinswoman," Imandra said. "Get you to bed, then, girls, and do not lie awake long talking and giggling together."

"I promise," Andromache said, and drew Kassandra to the dark staircase leading down into the palace. She took Kassandra to her own rooms, where she called one of her serving-women to bathe them both and bring bread and fruit and wine. When they had bathed and eaten, Andromache leaned on the window-sill.

"Look, Cousin, the stars are still falling."

"No doubt they will do so all the night," Kassandra said. "Unless one falls through the window into our chamber, I cannot see that it makes any difference to us."

"I suppose not," said Andromache. "If one should fall here, Kassandra, you may have it for a sword like Penthesilea's; I have no desire for weapons."

"I suppose I have no need for them either, since it seems I am not to be a warrior, but a priestess," said Kassandra, sighing.

"Would you rather be a warrior for all your life, Kassandra?"

But Kassandra set her teeth and said, "I do not think it ever matters what I would rather; my destiny has been set, and no one can fight Fate, no matter what weapons she may bear."

When both girls lay side by side in Andromache's bed, and even the intermittent light of the falling stars had dimmed toward morning, Kassandra sensed through her fitful sleep that someone stood in the door; she half roused to murmur a question, but she was still held in sleep and knew she made no sound. Drowsily she knew that it was Penthesilea who stole quietly into the room to stand looking down at them in the moonlight for a long time, and then reached down to touch her hair for an instant as if in blessing. Then, although Kassandra did not see her leave the room, she was gone and there was only moonlight there.

13

THE DAWN was just paling in the sky when a woman entered the room, unannounced, and flung open the draperies. Andromache buried her head under the blankets against the light, but Kassandra sat up in bed and looked at her. She was a woman of Colchis, dark and sturdily built, with the self-confident bearing of one of Penthesilea's warrior women; she wore a long robe of bleached linen, pure white and unadorned. About her wrist coiled a small green serpent, and Kassandra knew she was a priestess.

"Who are you?" Kassandra asked.

"My name is Evadne, and I am a priestess sent to prepare you," she said. "Is it you or your companion who is to face the Goddess this day? Or, perhaps, both of you?"

Andromache uncovered one eye and said, "I was initiated last year; it is my cousin only." She shut her eyes and seemed to sleep again. Evadne gave Kassandra a droll smile, then became very serious again.

"Tell me," she said, "all women owe service to the Immortals, and all men too; do you mean that you will do Them service when They ask it of you or that you will devote your life to serving Them?"

"I am willing to devote my life to that service," Kassandra said, "but I do not know what it is that They ask of me."

Evadne handed her the robe Andromache had laid over a bench. "Let us go into the outer room so we will not disturb the princess," she said. When they were in the outer chamber she said, "Now tell me, why do you wish to become a priestess?"

Kassandra then told the story again of what had happened to her in the Sun Lord's House, for the first time speaking without an instant of hesitation; this woman knew the Immortals, and if anyone alive could understand, she would be the one. Evadne listened without comment, smiling slightly at the end.

"The Sun Lord is a jealous master," she said at last, "and it comes to me that He has called you. All the same, the Mother owns every woman, and I cannot deny you the right to face Her."

Kassandra said, "My mother told me that Serpent Mother and the Sun Lord are ancient enemies. Tell me, Lady"—the term of respect came naturally to her lips—"she said that Apollo Sun Lord fought Serpent Mother and that He slew Her; is this true? Am I disloyal to the Sun Lord if I serve the Mother, then?"

"She who is the Mother of All was never born; and so She can never be slain," Evadne said, making a reverent gesture. "As for the Sun Lord, the Immortals understand one another, and They do not see these things the way we might. Earth Mother, so they say, first had Her shrine where Apollo built His Oracle; and they say that while the shrine was abuilding, a great serpent or dragon came out of the very navel of the earth, and the Sun Lord—or perhaps His priest, it makes no difference— slew the beast with His arrows. And so, I think, some ignorant folk put it about that He had had a quarrel with Serpent Mother; but the Sun Lord, like all other created beings, is Her child."

"Then, although it is the Sun Lord who has called me, I may answer the call of the Mother?"

"All created beings owe service to Her," said the priestess, repeating her reverent gesture, "and more than that I may not say to the uninitiated. Now, I think, you should wash and make yourself ready to join the others who will make this journey with you. Later, if you wish, I can tell you some tales of the Goddess as She is worshiped here."

Kassandra hastened to obey, neatly arranging the gown she had so quickly thrown on. Andromache's robe was too long for her, and hung loose about her ankles; she tucked it up through her girdle so that she could walk easily. Then she combed her dark hair and left it unbound, as she had been told was seemly for virgins in this city, though it was troublesome to feel it hanging loose and blowing in the wind instead of being neatly braided.

She could hear, outside in the street, the sounds of the festival; women were coming out of the houses and were running about carrying green branches and bunches of flowers. Evadne came and led her into the throne room, where a number of girls about her own age were gathered; the throne was empty today, covered with a cloth of woven gold, on which coiled Imandra's great snake.

"Look," whispered one of the girls. "They say the Queen is also a priestess who can transform herself into a snake."

"What nonsense," Kassandra said. "The Queen is elsewhere and has left her serpent on the throne as a symbol of her power."

Penthesilea was among the women waiting. Kassandra stole to her kinswoman's side, and the Amazon Queen took her hand and held it tight; although Kassandra was not exactly frightened, she was glad of the reassurance of the touch. Imandra was there among them too, but at first Kassandra had not recognized her, for the Queen wore the ordinary dress of a priestess. This seemed reasonable to Kassandra—it was also the custom in Troy that the Queen should be the mortal representative of the Great Goddess.

She was surprised not to find Andromache also among them; if her cousin had been initiated last year, why did she not join the other priestesses? Still, it seemed Andromache was not particularly involved in religion; was this, she wondered, another reason Imandra hesitated to have her daughter succeed her as Queen? She had not known this was how Imandra felt till now; but she was growing accustomed to knowing or hearing the unspoken and seeing the invisible.

Imandra gestured the chattering girls to silence; the women who were already initiated priestesses gathered around her. Kassandra realized that she was the eldest of the candidates remaining; probably it was the custom in this city to initiate women somewhat younger. She wondered whether all these girls were to dedicate their lives to the Goddess, or only to "offer service when it was asked of them," which was the alternative Evadne had suggested. Either way, this was a preliminary initiation and taken for granted, it seemed, as a first step to service to the Immortals.

The older women gathered the uninitiated girls into a circle in their midst, with Imandra at their center. Behind them Kassandra heard from somewhere the beating of a drum, a soft, incessant sound like a heartbeat.

"At this time of the year," Imandra intoned, "we celebrate the return of Earth's Daughter from the underground where She has been imprisoned during the chill of the winter season. We see Her coming as the green of spring spreads over the barren lands, clothing the meadows and woods with the brightness of leaves and flowers."

Silence, except for the unending thrumming of the drums beaten by the women behind them.

"Here we sit in darkness, awaiting the return of Light; here we shall descend, each of us, to seek Earth's Daughter, into the realms of darkness. Each of us shall be purified and learn the ways of Truth."

The story went on in a monotone, telling the tale of Earth's Daughter, and how She had been lured into the underground realms, and how the serpents had comforted Her and sworn that no one of them would ever harm Her. Kassandra had heard only scraps of the story before this, because it either was not known to the uninitiated, or was not considered suitable hearing for outsiders. She listened intently, fascinated, her head aching with the sound of the drums that went on and on, never ceasing, behind the voices.

It began to seem that she was caught in a dream that went on and on for many days, knowing she was awake, but never fully conscious. Some time later she became aware, without the slightest idea how or where it had happened, that they were no longer in the throne room, but in a great dark cave, with water trickling from damp walls that rose far overhead into great echoing spaces which made the voices ring hollow and drowned even the sound of the drums.

Somewhere there was a reed flute whispering thin music and calling to her in a voice she almost knew. Then she felt— for it was too dim for her to see anything—a flat pottery bowl with raised design being passed from hand to hand, each girl in turn raising the bowl to her lips, drinking and passing it on. She could never remember afterward what they had said when she was bidden to drink. She thought, till she touched her lips to the brew, that it was wine.

She tasted a curious slimy bitterness which made her think of the smell of the blighted rye Penthesilea had bidden her remember; as she drank she thought her stomach would rebel, but with a fierce effort she controlled the queasiness and brought her attention back to the drums. The story had ended; for the life of her she could not remember how it had ended, or what had been the fate of Earth's Daughter.

After a time her disorientation became so great that it seemed she was no longer within the circle of women in the cave; she had no idea where she was, but she did not wonder about it. It did cross her mind that perhaps the brew had been some kind of drug, but she did not wonder about that either. She touched the chilly damp ground and was surprised that it felt like ordinary paving stone; had she moved at all? Strange colors crawled before her eyes, and it seemed for a moment that she was walking through a great dark tunnel.

Share with Earth's Daughter the descent into darkness, a voice guided her from afar; whether a real voice or not she never knew. *One by one you must leave behind all the things of this world which are dear to you, for now you have no part in them.*

She discovered that she was wearing her weapons; she would willingly have taken an oath that she had left them behind this morning. Through the sound of the drums the guiding voice came again:

This is the first of the gates of the Underworld; here you must give up that which binds you to Earth and the realms of Light.

Kassandra fumbled with the unfamiliar girdle of the robe she was wearing and unfastened the jeweled belt which held her sword and spear. She remembered Hecuba admonishing her to wear them always with honor; but that had been very far away and had nothing to do with this dark chamber. Had Penthesilea too come to this dark doorway and yielded up her weapons? She heard the sword and spear slide to the floor and strike there with a metallic sound within the noise of the drums.

Why did her hands move so slowly—or had she moved them at all? Was it all an illusion of the drums, or was she still crouched motionless in the dark circle, even while she strode boldly down the dark tunnel, clad in Andromache's long ungirt robe, which somehow did not trip her up at all.

Somewhere there was an eye of fire. Flames below her? Or was she looking into the slitted eye of the serpent?

It surveyed her unblinking, and a voice demanded:

This is the second Gate of the Underworld, where you must give up your fears or whatever holds you back from traveling this realm as one of those whose feet know and tread the Path in My very footprints.

The serpent's eye was close now; it moved, caressing her, and in a flicker of memory—centuries ago, in another life perhaps?—she remembered how she had caressed the serpents in the Sun Lord's House, and embraced them without fear. It was as if she embraced them again, and the eye came closer and closer; the world narrowed further till there was nothing in the dark with her except the serpent's embrace. Pain stabbed through her until she was certain she was dying, and she sank into death almost with relief.

But she was not dead; she was still moving through the fiery darkness alone; but there was a voice heard through the thrumming of the drums which went on until her whole head was ringing with it.

Now you are in My kingdom, and this is the third and final Gate of the Underworld. Here there is nothing left to you but your life. Will you lay that down as well to serve Me?

Kassandra thought madly, *I can't imagine what good my life would be to Her, but I've come so far, I won't turn back now.* She thought that she spoke aloud, but a part of her mind insisted that she made no sound, that speech was an illusion, like everything else which had happened to her on this journey—if it was indeed a journey and not a curious dream.

I will not turn back now, even if it means my life. I have given all else; take this as well, Dark Lady.

She hung senseless in the darkness, shot through with fire, surrounded by the rushing sound of wings.

Goddess, if I am to die for You, at least let me once behold Your face!

There was a little lightening of the darkness; before her eyes she saw a swirling paleness, from which gradually emerged a pair of dark eyes, a pallid face. She had seen the face before, reflected in a stream . . . it was her own. A voice very close to her whispered through the drumming and the whining flutes:

Do you not yet know that you are I, and I am you?

Then the rushing wings took her, blotting out everything. Wings and dark hurricane winds, thrusting her upward, upward toward the light, protesting, *But there is so much more to know . . .*

The winds were ripping her asunder; a lightning-flash revealed cruel eyes and beaks, rending, tearing—it was as if something alien flowed through her, filling her up like deep dark water, crowding out all thought and awareness. She looked down from a great height on someone who was and at the same time was not herself, and knew she looked on the face of the Goddess. Then her tenuous hold on consciousness surrendered, and still protesting, she fell into an endless silent chasm of blinding light.

SOMEONE WAS gently touching her face.

"Open your eyes, my child."

Kassandra felt sick and weak, but she opened her eyes to

silence and cool damp air. She was back in the cavern . . . had she ever left it? Her head was pillowed in Penthesilea's lap; the older woman's face was blurred with such a halo of light that Kassandra shielded her eyes with her hands and blurted out, "But you—*you* are the Goddess . . ." then fell silent in awe before her kinswoman. Her eyes hurt, and she closed them.

"Of course," the older woman whispered; "and so are you, my child. Never forget that."

"But what happened? Where am I? I was—"

Penthesilea quickly covered Kassandra's lips with a warning hand.

"Hush; it is forbidden to speak of the Mystery," she said. "But you have come far indeed; most candidates go no further than the First Gate. Come," Penthesilea murmured. "Come."

Kassandra rose, stumbling, and her kinswoman steadied her.

The drums were silent; only the fire and a thin wailing. Now she could see the flute player, a thin woman hunched behind the fire. Her eyes were vacant, and she swayed faintly as if in ecstasy; but the fire and the flute at least had been real. In a circle around them, about half the maidens still lay entranced, each watched over by one of the older priestesses. There were vacant spaces in the circle. Penthesilea urged her to make her way carefully, touching no one, toward the entrance of the cavern. Outside, it was raining, but from the dim twilight she could tell that the day was almost over. The drops of rain felt icy and clean on her face. She felt sick and fiercely thirsty; she tried to catch rain in her hands and sip the drops, but Penthesilea led her through a door she vaguely remembered seeing, and then she was in Imandra's lamp-lit throne room, where the magical journey had begun. She still walked carefully, as if she were a fragile jar filled to the brim with alien wine which would spill if she made a careless movement. Queen Imandra came from somewhere and embraced her, clasping her tightly in her arms.

"Welcome back, little sister, from the realms where the Dark One walked with you. Your journey was long, but I rejoice for your safe return," said the Queen. "Now you are one with all of us who belong to Her."

Penthesilea said, "She passed all three Gates."

"I know," Imandra answered. "But this initiation was long delayed. She is priestess born, and it is late for her."

She stood back and took Kassandra by the shoulders as her mother might have done. "You look pale, child; how are you feeling?"

"Please," said Kassandra, "I am so thirsty." But when Penthesilea would have poured her some wine, the smell sickened her, and she asked for water instead. It was clear and cold and relieved her thirst, but like everything she would eat or drink for many days, it had a pervasive slimy-fishy taste.

Imandra said, "Be sure to notice what you dream this night; it will be a special message from Earth's Daughter." Then she asked Penthesilea, "You will be returning south soon, now you have Her word?"

"As soon as Kassandra is able to ride, and Andromache prepared to return with her to Troy," answered the Amazon Queen.

"Be it so," Imandra said. "I have readied Andromache's dower, and many to travel with her. And for our young kinswoman, the priestess, I have a gift."

The gift was a serpent; a small green one very like Imandra's own, but no longer than her forearm and about as thick as her thumb. Kassandra thanked her, tongue-tied.

Imandra said softly, "A suitable gift from priestess to priestess, child. She is hatched from an egg of one of my own serpents; and besides, what else should I do with her? Give her to Andromache, who would flee from her? I think she will be happy to travel south with you in that beautiful pot, and to serve with you at the shrine in Troy."

That night Kassandra lay long awake, troubled at the thought of what she might dream; but when she fell asleep she saw only the rain-washed slopes of Mount Ida, and the three strange Goddesses; and it seemed that They struggled with one another not for Paris' favor, but for hers, and for Troy.

14

THEY SET FORTH in carts as clumsy and slow as the tin-bearing wagons had been, laden with Andromache's bride-gifts and dowry and with gifts from the Queen to her Trojan kindred from the treasures of Colchis: weapons of iron and bronze, bolts of cloth, pottery and gold and silver and even jewels.

Kassandra was unable to imagine why Queen Imandra was so eager to have her daughter allied with Troy, and even less able to imagine why Andromache was willing—no, eager—to comply. But if she must return to Troy, she was glad to have with her something of the wide world she had discovered here.

Also, she had come to love Andromache; and if she must part from Penthesilea and the women of the tribe, at least she would have with her one true friend and kinswoman in Troy.

The journey seemed endless, the wagons crawling day by day at a snail's gait across the wide plains, moon after moon fading and filling as they seemed no nearer to the distant mountains. Kassandra longed to mount and ride swiftly at the side of the Amazon guards, leaving the wagons to follow as best they could; but Andromache could not, or would not, ride, and fretted at being alone in the wagons. She wanted Kassandra's company; so reluctantly, Kassandra accepted the confinement and rode with her, playing endless games of Hound and Jackal on a carved onyx board, listening to her kinswoman's simple-minded chatter about clothing and jewelry and hair ornaments and what she would do when she was married—a subject which Andromache found endlessly fascinating (she had even resolved on names for the first three or four of her children), till Kassandra thought she would go mad.

On her outward journey (it seemed to her that she had been immensely younger then), Kassandra had never realized the enormous distances they had covered; only when summer arrived again and they were just beginning to see the distant hills behind Troy was she fully aware of how long this journey had been. In Troy, Colchis was popularly regarded as being halfway around the world. Now she was old enough to take account of the many months of travel; and of course with the wagons, they were traveling more slowly than the riding bands. She was in no hurry to see the end of the journey, knowing that her arrival in Troy would close the walls of the women's quarters around her again, but she wondered how things fared in the city, and one night while Andromache slept, she reached out in her mind to see, if not Troy, at least the mind of the twin brother whom she had not visited for so long. And after a time pictures began to form in her mind, at first small and faraway, gradually enlarging and becoming all of her awareness. . . .

FAR TO the south on the slopes of Mount Ida, where the dark-haired youth called Paris followed his foster-father's bulls and cattle, on a day in late autumn, a group of well-dressed young men appeared on the mountainside, and Paris, alert to any dangers to the herd he guarded, approached them with caution.

"Greeting, strangers; who are you, and how may I serve you?"

"We are the sons and the servants of King Priam of Troy," replied one of them, "and we have come for a bull; the finest of the herd, for it is a sacrifice for the Funeral Games of one of Priam's sons. Show us your finest."

Paris was somewhat troubled at their arrogant manner; nevertheless, his foster-father, Agelaus, had taught him that the wishes of the King were law, and he did not wish to be thought lacking in courtesy.

"My father is Priam's servant," he said, "and all that we have is at his disposal. He is from home this day; if it will please you to await his return, he can show you what we have. If you will rest in my house out of the heat of the noonday sun, my wife will bring you wine, or cool buttermilk; or if you prefer, mead from the honey of our own bees. When he returns, he will show you the herds and you may take what you will."

"I thank you; a drink of mead will be welcome," replied one of the newcomers from the city, and as Paris led the way to the little house where he lived with Oenone, he heard another one whisper, "A handsome fellow; and I had not thought to find such manners so far from the city."

As Oenone, bright and pretty in her working-day tunic,

with her hair tied up under the cloth she wore mornings for sweeping the house, fetched mead in wooden cups, he heard the other muttering, "And if nymphs as lovely as this are in abundance on the mountainsides, why should any man stay within city walls?"

Oenone looked sidewise at Paris, as if wondering who these men were and what they wanted; but he knew little more than she, though he had no desire to say so in their hearing. "These men have business with my father, my dear," he said. "Agelaus will return before the noon hour, and then they can settle it with him, whatever it may be." If they had wanted goats or even sheep, he would have felt qualified to deal with them himself, even if they were specially wanted for sacrifice; but the cattle were his father's special pride and joy. So he sipped at the mead Oenone had poured and waited, finally asking, "Are you all King Priam's sons?"

"We are," replied the elder of them. "I am Hector, Priam's eldest son by his Queen, Hecuba; and this is my half-brother Deiphobos."

Hector was unusually tall, almost a head taller than Paris himself, who was not a small man. He had the broad shoulders of a natural wrestler, and his face was strong-featured and handsome, with brown eyes set wide apart over high cheekbones and a stubborn mouth and chin. He bore at his waist an iron sword which Paris at once coveted, although until recently he had thought there could be no finer weapon than the bronze dagger Agelaus had given him as a special gift when he had gone out into a late-winter snowstorm and brought back a dozen weakling lambs who all would otherwise have perished.

"Tell me about these Funeral Games," he said at last. He noticed the way Hector was looking at Oenone and did not like it. But he also noticed that Oenone was taking no notice whatever of the stranger. *She is mine*, he thought; *she is a good woman and modest, not one to go about staring at strange men.*

"They are held every year," Hector said, "and they are like any other games at festivals. You look strong and athletic; have you never competed in such games? I am sure you could carry off many prizes."

"You mistake me," Paris said. "I am not a nobleman like yourselves, with leisure for sport; I am a humble shepherd and your father's servant. Games and the like are not for me."

"Modestly spoken," said Hector. "But the Games are open to any man not born a slave; you would be welcome."

Paris thought about it. "You spoke of prizes . . ."

"The major prize is a bronze tripod and caldron," Hector said. "Sometimes my father gives a sword for special valor."

"I would like that prize for my mother," said Paris. "Perhaps if my father gives me leave I will go."

"You are a grown man; you must be fifteen or more," said Hector, "quite old enough to come and go without permission."

And as Paris heard the words, he thought it must be so indeed; but he had never gone anywhere without Agelaus' leave and had never thought he would. He noticed that Hector was staring at him fixedly, and raised questioning eyebrows.

Hector coughed nervously. "I am wondering where I have seen you before," he said. "Your eyes—they seem to remind me of someone I know well, but I cannot remember where."

"I go sometimes to the marketplace on errands for my father or my mother," Paris said, but Hector shook his head. To Paris it seemed that a curious shadow hung over him; he felt an instinctive dislike for this large young man. Yet Hector had been in no way offensive, but had treated him with perfect courtesy, so he did not understand it.

He rose restlessly and went to the door of the house, peering out. After a moment he said, "My foster-father has come home," and after a few moments Agelaus, a small, slight man who still moved quickly despite his age, came into the room.

"Prince Hector," he said, bowing, "I am honored; how is it with my lord your father?"

Hector explained their errand, and Agelaus said, "It's my boy can help you with that, my prince; see, he knows the cattle better than I do, does all the cattle-judging at fairs and such. Paris, take the gentlemen out into the cattle-field and show them the best that we have."

Paris chose the finest bull of the herd, and Hector came and looked into the beast's face.

"I am a warrior and I know little of cattle," he said. "Why choose this bull?"

Paris pointed out the width of the bull's shoulders, the breadth of its flank. "And his coat is smooth without scars or imperfections; fit for a God," he said, and inwardly thought: *He is too good for sacrifice; he should be saved for breeding. Any old bull will do to strike off his head and bleed on an altar.*

And this arrogant prince comes and waves his hand and takes the best of the cattle my father and I have labored long and hard to raise. But he is right: all the cattle belong to Priam, and we are his servants.

"You know more than I of these matters," Hector repeated. "So I accept your word that this bull is the fittest for sacrifice to the Thunder Lord; now I must have a virgin heifer for the Lady, His consort."

Instantly Paris saw in his mind the fair and stately Goddess who had offered him wealth and power. He wondered if She bore him a grudge that he had not awarded Her the apple; perhaps if he chose for Her the finest creature in all the herd, She would forgive him.

"This heifer," he said, "is the finest of all; see her smooth brown coat, and her white face, and see how beautiful her eyes are; they seem almost human."

Hector patted the little animal's smooth shoulder and called for a tie rope.

"You don't need it, my prince," Paris said. "If you're taking the herd bull, she'll follow you like a puppy."

"So cows are not unlike women, then," Hector said with a crude laugh. "I thank you, and I wish you would reconsider coming to the Games. I am sure you would carry off most of the prizes; you look a natural athlete."

"It is kind of you to say so, my prince," Paris said, and watched Hector and his entourage as they descended the mountain toward the city.

Later that evening, when he went with his foster-father to fetch the goats for milking, he mentioned Hector's invitation. He was not at all prepared for the old man's response.

"No; I forbid it! Don't even think of it, my son; something terrible would be sure to happen!"

"But why, Father? The prince assured me that it did not matter that I was not nobly born; what harm could there be? And I would like to have the caldron and tripod for Mother, who has been so good to me and has no such things."

"Your mother don't want no caldrons; we want our good son safe here at home where nothing could happen to you."

"What could possibly happen to me, Father?"

"I am forbidden to tell you that," the old man said seriously. "Surely it should be enough for you that I forbid it; you have always been a good and obedient son to me before this."

"Father, I am no longer a child," Paris said. "Now when you forbid me something, I am old enough to know the reason."

Agelaus set his mouth sternly.

"I'll have no impudence and I don't have to give you no reasons; you'll do as I say."

Paris had always known that Agelaus was not his real father; since his dream of Goddesses, he had begun to suspect that his parentage was higher than he had ever dared to believe. Now he began to think that Agelaus' prohibition had something to do with this. But when he put the question, Agelaus looked more stubborn than ever.

"I can't tell you nothing at all about that," he said, and stamped off to milk the goats. Paris, following his example, said no more; but inside he was fuming.

Am I no more than a hired servant, to be bidden here or there? Even a hired servant is entitled to his holiday, and Father has never denied me leave before. I will go to the Games; my mother at least will forgive me if I bring her back a caldron and tripod. But if I carry off the prize and she does not want it, I will give it to Oenone.

He said nothing that night; but early the next morning, he put on his best holiday tunic (it was in fact coarse enough, though Oenone had woven it of their finest wool and dyed it with berry juice to a soft red color) and went to bid her farewell. She looked at him, her mouth contorted in distress.

"So you are going? In spite of your father's warning?"

"He has no right to forbid me," Paris replied defensively; "he is not even my father, so it is no impiety to disobey him."

"Still, he has been a good and kindly father to you," she

said, her lip quivering. "This is not well done, Paris. Why do you wish to go to their Games anyway? What is King Priam to you?"

"Because it is my destiny," he retorted hotly. "Because I no longer believe that it is the will of the Gods that I sit here all my days keeping goats on the mountainside. Come, girl, give me a kiss and wish me good fortune."

She stood on tiptoe and obediently kissed him, but she said, "I warn you, my love, there is no good fortune for you in this journey."

He scoffed, "Why, are you now going to speak as a prophetess? I have no love for such warnings."

"Still I must give it," Oenone said, and threw herself weeping into his arms.

"Paris, I beg you, for love of me, stay." She put her hand shyly over her swollen small belly and entreated timidly, "For *his* sake, if not for mine?"

"It is for his sake all the more that I must go and seek good fortune and fame," Paris said. "His father will be something more than Priam's herdsman."

"What is wrong with being the son of a herdsman?" Oenone asked. "I am proud to be a herdsman's wife."

Paris scowled at her and said, "Beloved, if you do not give me your blessing, I must go even without it; would you wish me ill?"

"Never, my love," she said seriously, "but I have the most terrible feeling that if you go you will never return to me."

"Now, that is the greatest folly I have ever heard," he said, and kissed her again. She clung to him still, so at last he gently disengaged her clinging hands and set off down the mountain; but he knew that she watched him till he was out of her sight.

KASSANDRA SLOWLY became aware again of where she was: in the darkness of the wagon, not the bright autumn sunlight of Mount Ida. And they were hardly into summer; they would reach Troy in the autumn, perhaps. At her side Andromache still slept quietly; cramped and cold, Kassandra crept into the blankets beside her, grateful for the warmth of her cousin's body.

He is in Troy. Perhaps he will be in Troy when I come there; I shall see him at last. The thought was almost too exciting to endure; Kassandra slept no more that night.

15

IT WAS ANDROMACHE rather than Kassandra who first saw the great high walls of Troy rising in the distance. She sounded overwhelmed as she said, "It really is bigger than Colchis."

"I told you so," Kassandra remarked.

"Yes, but I didn't believe you; I could not believe that any city could *really* be bigger than Colchis. What is the shining building high at the top of the city? Is that the palace?"

"No; it is the Temple of the Maiden; in Troy the highest places are reserved for the Immortals. And She is our patron Goddess who gave us the olive and the vine."

"King Priam cannot be a truly great King," Andromache said. "It is forbidden in Colchis for any house—even a Goddess' house—to be higher than the royal palace."

"And yet I know your mother is a pious woman who respects the Goddess," said Kassandra. She recalled that when she had first come to Colchis, it had seemed blasphemy to her to build a mortal's house so high. Her eyes sought out the Sun Lord's house with its golden roofs, rising a terrace above the palace; she pointed out the palace to Andromache.

"It is not built so high; but it is as fine a palace as any in Colchis," she told Andromache. Now that they were actually within sight of the city, Kassandra examined her own feelings warily, like biting on a sore tooth: she did not know how she felt about returning to Troy itself after her time of freedom. She realized that she was almost painfully eager to see her mother and her sister, Polyxena, and without trying, she felt her mind reach out for that insubstantial and confusing link with the twin brother who was at times even more real than her self.

I will not be caged again. Then she emended it a little: *I will never let them cage me again. No one can imprison me unless I am willing to be imprisoned.*

She looked round at her escort, half wishing she might return to the Amazon country with them. Penthesilea was not among them; she said that after their long absence she must remain to set the affairs of the tribe in order. Kassandra knew that if she had been dwelling among the Amazons now, she would be sent with the other women of childbearing age to the men's villages to bear a child for the tribe. She felt she would even be willing to observe that custom, if it was the price of remaining with Penthesilea's tribe; but that was not among the choices offered to her.

"But what is happening?" Andromache asked. "Is it a festival day?"

Processions were coming forth from the gates, long lines of men and women in holiday garments, animals garlanded with ribbons and flowers, whether for show or sacrifice she could not tell. Then she saw Hector and some of her other brothers wearing only the brief loincloth in which they competed on the field and knew it must be the Games. These were no business of women—though her mother had told her once that in ancient times women had competed in the footraces and in casting of spears and in archery too. Kassandra, who was a good shot, wished she were still small-breasted enough to pretend to be a boy, and shoot with the archers; but if she had ever been capable of such disguise, she was not now. Resignedly, she thought, *Well, one day my skill at weapons may still be of use to my city —in war, if not at Games*—and then saw, near the end of the procession, a chariot bearing the shrunken but still impressive figure of her father, Priam. She was about to throw herself headlong from the wagon and embrace him, but the sight of his gray hair shocked her; this old man was all but a stranger to her!

Behind him, riding in a smaller chariot, and wearing the insignia of the Goddess, Kassandra saw her mother; Hecuba seemed not to have changed by a single hair. Kassandra got down from the wagon and came forward, bending low before her father in token of respect, then hurrying to throw herself into her mother's arms.

"You are come at a good hour, my darling," Hecuba said. "But what a woman you have become! I would hardly have known this tall Amazon for my little daughter." She drew Kassandra up on the chariot beside her. "Who is your companion, my child?"

Kassandra looked at Andromache, who was still seated on the forward seat of the wagon. She looked very much alone, and out of place. This was not how she had intended to introduce her friend to Troy.

"She is Andromache, daughter of Imandra, Queen of Colchis," said Kassandra slowly. "Imandra, our kinswoman, sent her to be a wife to one of my brothers. She has a wagonload of treasure of Colchis for a dowry," she added, and as she spoke, her words seemed crude, to betoken a mere matter of purchase and queenly expediency, as if Imandra had sent her daughter as a bribe for Priam. Andromache deserved better than that.

"Now I see she has the look of Imandra," said Hecuba. "As for a marriage, that is for your father to say; but she is welcome here, marriage or no, as my kinswoman."

"Mother," said Kassandra seriously—after coming all this way Andromache should not be rejected—"she is the only child of the ruling Queen of Colchis; my father has sons and to spare, and if he cannot find one of my brothers to marry her for such an alliance, he is not as clever as he is reputed to be." She hurried to fetch Andromache, helping her down from the wagon and presenting her to Priam and Hecuba; Hecuba kissed her, and Andromache smiled and dimpled as she made a submissive bow to them. Priam patted her cheek and took her up on the stands beside him, calling her Daughter, which seemed a good start. He seated her between himself and Hecuba, while Kassandra wondered why Andromache was being so submissive. She asked, "Where is my sister, Polyxena?"

"She has stayed in the house like a proper modest girl," Hecuba reproved in a whisper. "Naturally she has no interest in seeing naked men competing at arms."

Well, Kassandra thought, *if I ever had any doubt, now I know I am home again. Am I to spend the rest of my life as a proper modest girl?* The thought depressed her.

Kassandra watched the opening contest, which was a foot-race, with tepid interest, trying to pick out those of Priam's sons whom she knew by sight. She recognized Hector at once, and Troilus, who must now, she thought, be at least ten years old. As they set off, Hector quickly took the lead, and he remained there throughout the first lap; then behind him a slighter, dark-haired youth began to gain. Almost easily, he overtook him and flashed past, touching the mark an instant before Hector's out-stretched hand.

"Bravely run!" shouted the other contestants, clustering around him.

"My dear," Priam said, leaning across Andromache to Hec-uba, "I do not know that young man, but if he can outrun Hector he is a worthy contestant. Find out who he is, will you?"

"Certainly," Hecuba said, and beckoned to a servant. "Go down and find out for the King who is the young man who won the footrace."

Kassandra shaded her eyes with her hand to look for the winner, but he had disappeared into the crowd. The contestants were now fitting strings to their bows. Kassandra, who had be-come an expert archer, watched with fascination, and suddenly, dazzled by the sun, felt confused: surely she was herself on the field, nocking an arrow into the bowstring—*My parents will be so angry* . . . Then, looking down at the strong bare arm so much more muscular than her own, she knew what had hap-pened: that her thoughts had again become entangled with those of her twin brother. Now she knew why the young winner of the footrace had seemed almost painfully familiar to her: this was her twin brother, Paris; and as she had foreseen, she was indeed present at his homecoming to Troy.

With that curious double sight, it seemed she was at once on the field and in her seat above it, looking up at Priam as if it were for the first time, seeing him at once as her father and as a strange, frightening old man with the unfamiliar majestic look of royalty. There were also old men whose names neither of them knew—Paris deduced, rightly, that these must be the Tro-jan King's advisers; a sweet-faced old woman he was sure was the Queen; a gaggle of young boys in expensive bright clothing, whom he assumed—correctly—to be Priam's younger sons, not old enough yet to take part in these contests, and some pretty girls who caught his eye mostly because they looked so different from Oenone. He wondered what they were doing here—perhaps the palace women were allowed to watch the Games. Well, he would give them something to watch. Now he was being beckoned forward to shoot at the mark.

Paris' first shot went wide because he was nervous, and his second flew far beyond the target. "Let the stranger shoot again," Hector said. "You are not accustomed to our targets; but if you can shoot so high and so far, surely you cannot be incapable of a proper shot." He pointed out the target and explained the rules.

Paris prepared to shoot again, thoroughly surprised at Hector's courtesy. He let fly his arrow, this time straight into the center of the target. The other archers shot one by one, but not even Hector could better his shot. Hector was not smiling now; he looked cross and sullen, and Kassandra knew he was regretting his impulsive generosity.

There were other contests, and Kassandra, pulling herself back into her own mind and body with a fierce effort, watched with interest and pleasure as her twin won them all. He threw Deiphobos almost effortlessly at wrestling, and when Deiphobos got up and rushed him, stretched him out insensible, not to rise till the Games were over. He cast the javelin farther even than Hector, listening to the shouts of "He is strong as Herakles" with ingenuous smiles of pleasure.

A servant came to the King and Queen with a message, and Kassandra heard her father repeat aloud, "He says that the young stranger is called Paris; he is the foster son of Agelaus the shepherd."

Hecuba turned white as bone. "I should have known; he has the look of you. But who could have believed it? It has been so long, so long . . ."

The contests now were ended, and Priam gestured for Paris, as the winner, to come forward. Then he rose.

"Agelaus," he called aloud, "you old rascal, where are you? You have brought back my son."

The old servant shuffled forward, looking pale and ill at ease. He bowed before the King and muttered, "I didn't tell him he could come today, Sire; he came without my leave, and I'd perfectly well understand if you were angry with me—with us both."

"No, indeed," Priam said graciously, and Kassandra saw her mother's knuckles unclench their painful grip over her heart. "He's a credit to you, and to me too. My own fault for listening to superstitious rubbish; I have only thanks for you, old friend." He took a gold ring from his own finger and put it on Agelaus' work-gnarled finger.

"You deserve more reward than this, my old friend, but this is all I have for you now. Before you return to your flocks I shall have a better gift for you."

Kassandra watched in astonishment as her father, who had slapped her to the ground even for inquiring of the existence of this brother, embraced Paris and awarded him all the prizes of the day. Hecuba was weeping and came forward to clasp her lost son.

"I never thought to see this day," she murmured. "I vow an unblemished heifer to the Goddess."

Hector frowned at the sight of his father bestowing lavish gifts on Paris: the promised tripod (which Paris said he wished to send to his foster-mother); a crimson cloak with embroidered bands, of the palace women's weaving; a fine helmet of worked bronze; an iron sword.

"And of course you will return to the palace and dine with your mother and me," he invited at last, smiling expansively. As Priam rose, gathering his cloak over his arm, one of the old men in the circle surrounding him came up and whispered urgently to him. Kassandra recognized the man as an old palace hanger-on, one of the priest-soothsayers in his circle.

Priam scowled and waved the man away.

"Don't talk to me of omens, old croaker! Superstitious rubbish; I should never have listened to them."

Kassandra could feel the shock—partly fear—that went through Paris at the words. Of course; he would know of the omens which had exiled him from the palace and his birthright —or was he only now learning of them?

Hector said into his father's ear—but clearly audible to Paris: "Father, if the Gods have decreed that he is a danger to Troy—"

Priam interrupted: "The Gods? No; a priestess, a reader of chicken guts and dreams; only a fool would have deprived himself of a fine son at such a one's blitherings. A King does not listen to the omens of a breeding woman, or her fancies. . . ."

Kassandra felt torn, half in sympathy for the twin whose fear and insecurity she could not but feel as if they were her own, half for her mother's dread. She wanted to step forward and draw her father's anger to herself; but before she could speak, Priam's eyes fell again on Andromache.

"And now I'll put right my old mistake and bring home my lost son. How say you, Hecuba: shall we marry the Colchian Queen's daughter to our wonderful new son?"

"You cannot do that, Father," said Hector, even as Kassandra felt Paris' eyes rest greedily on Andromache. "Paris has a wife already; I beheld her myself in the house of Agelaus."

"Is this true, my son?" Priam asked.

Paris looked sullen, but he understood the implied threat. He spoke politely: "It is true; my wife is a priestess to the River God Scamander."

"Then you must send for her, my son, and present her to your mother," Priam said, and turned to Hector. "And to you, Hector, my eldest son and heir, to you I give the hand of Queen Imandra's daughter; tonight we shall solemnize the marriage."

"Not so fast, not so fast," said Hecuba. "The child needs time to make her wedding clothes like any other girl; and the women of the palace must have time to prepare for this most important feast in a woman's life."

"Rubbish," said Priam. "As long as the bride is ready, and the dower arranged, any clothes can be worn for a wedding. Women are always worrying about such trivial things."

All this may be a foolish thing, Kassandra thought, *but it is crude of Priam to disregard it. What would the Queen of Colchis think to have her daughter's wedding tacked onto the end of the festival?*

She bent close to Andromache and whispered, "Don't let them hurry you this way. You are a princess of Colchis, not an old cloak to be given as an extra Games prize or a consolation for Hector because he did not win!"

Andromache smiled and whispered to Kassandra, "I think I'd like to have Hector before your father changes his mind again or decides he can use me as a prize for someone else." She looked up and murmured in a small and timid voice which Kassandra had never heard her use before, so false Kassandra did not see why Priam did not laugh at her, "My lord Priam . . . my husband's father . . . the Lady of Colchis, my mother the Queen, sent with me all kinds of clothing and linens; so if it pleases you, we can hold the wedding whenever you think proper."

Priam beamed and patted her shoulder.

"There's a fine girl," he said, and Andromache blushed and looked down shyly as Hector came and looked her over—Kassandra thought, just as he had looked over the virgin heifer Paris had chosen for the sacrifice.

"I shall be most content to take the daughter of Queen Imandra for wife."

THE LONG day was drawing to a close. Priam and Hecuba were helped into their chariots for the return to the palace. Kassandra found herself walking at Paris' side; she was deeply distressed because as yet he had not addressed a single word to her nor acknowledged in any way the bond between them which to her was so important. How could he ignore it?

She wondered if he too was under the special protection of the Sun Lord, that he could come and face the father who had intended to expose him at birth, and now acknowledged him and intended to restore him to his rightful place in the family.

Hector was walking close to Andromache; he turned and laid his hand on Kassandra's shoulder, then gave her a rough hug of welcome.

"Well, Sister Kassandra, how brown and sunburnt you are —though after all these years with the Amazons I should not be surprised. Why did you not gird on your bow and go into the field to shoot with the archers?"

"She could have done so, never doubt it," said Andromache, "and bettered your shot."

"No doubt," said Hector. "I was not at my best this day; and"—he coughed and lowered his voice, casting a quick look over his shoulder at Paris—"I would rather be beaten by a girl than by that upstart." He turned to Deiphobos, who was still holding his head as if it hurt him. "Tell me, Brother," he said, "what are we to do with this fellow? I cut my teeth on that old story about how Father exposed him because he was a threat to Troy. Am I to overlook it because Father saw fit to bribe me with a beautiful wife?"

Deiphobos said, "It seems Father is already besotted with him. He should take a lesson from King Pelias when he was confronted with his lost son Jason; I recall he sent Jason on a quest to the far ends of the world, to seek the Golden Fleece . . ."

"But there is no longer any gold in Colchis," said Andromache.

"Well, we must devise some way to rid ourselves of him," Hector said. "Perhaps we could persuade Father to send him to use some of that charm on Agamemnon and persuade him to return Hesione."

"A good thought, that," said Deiphobos. "And if that fails, we can send him—oh, to talk the sirens out of their sea-hoards, or to shoe the Kentaurs where they dwell—or to harness them to pull our chariots . . ."

"Or anything else that will take him away a thousand leagues from Troy," agreed Hector. "And this for Father's own benefit, if the Gods have decreed he is not a boon to Troy—"

"Nor, certainly, to us," said Deiphobos. But Kassandra had heard enough. She stepped out of the path and dropped back to walk at Paris' side.

"You," he said, looking at her rudely, "you—I thought you were a dream." And as their eyes met for the first time, she again felt the bond establish itself between them; was he too aware of how they were linked, within the soul?

"I thought you were a dream," he repeated, "or perhaps a nightmare."

The rudeness of his words was like a blow; she had hoped he would embrace her in welcome.

She said, "Brother, do you know they are plotting against

you? You have no welcome in Troy from our brothers." She reached for contact again, only to feel him draw back from her angrily.

He said, "I know that; do you think me a fool? After this, Sister, keep your thoughts to yourself—and stay out of mine!"

She recoiled with pain at the harshness of being shut out of his mind. Ever since she had known of his existence and the bond between them, she had fancied that when they met he would welcome her with joy and thereafter she would be special and even precious to him. Now, instead, he rebuffed her, thought of her as an intruder. Did he not even see that she was the one person here ready to welcome him with acceptance and love even greater than Priam's own?

She would not weep and beg him for his love.

"As you will," she snarled. "It was never my wish to be bound to you this way. Do you think, then, that perhaps our father would have exposed the wrong twin?" She flung herself away from him, hurrying down the path to rejoin Andromache, all the joy of her homecoming spoiled.

16

THROUGHOUT the evening, Kassandra thought that this was more of a celebration of Paris' welcome to the family than a wedding feast for Hector and Andromache, though once Priam had decided to solemnize the marriage he went to considerable trouble to leave nothing undone. He sent to the royal cellars for the best wine, and Hecuba went to the kitchens for delicacies to be added to the evening meal: fruits, honeycomb, all kinds of sweetmeats. Musicians, jugglers, dancers and acrobats were assembled for entertainment.

A priestess from the Temple of Pallas Athene was summoned to supervise the sacrifices which were such a necessary part of a royal wedding. Kassandra stayed close to Andromache, who, now that it was actually at hand, looked pale and frightened—or perhaps, Kassandra thought, with an irony which astonished her, this was Andromache's idea of how a properly modest woman should behave on the day of her wedding.

As they stood together in the courtyard, solemnly watching the sacrifices being gathered, Andromache leaned toward Kassandra and whispered, "I should think the Gods would have had enough sacrifices for one day. Do you suppose they ever get bored with watching people kill animals for them? A slaughterhouse wouldn't entertain *me*." Kassandra had to choke back a giggle which would have been scandalous; but it was true: there had already been many sacrifices at the Games. The couple stood side by side, hands clasped on the sacrificial knife, and Hector bent and whispered to Andromache. She shook her head, but he insisted, and it was her hand that drew the knife unhesitatingly across the throat of the white heifer. To Kassandra, who had eaten nothing since early morning, the smell of the roasting meat was like ambrosia.

After that it was only a few minutes till they went inside and Hecuba sent serving women to Andromache and Kassandra to dress them for the feast. They were in the room that Kassandra had shared with Polyxena when they were little children; but it was no longer a simple nursery. The walls had been painted in the Cretan fashion with murals of sea-creatures, strange curving squid and tentacled octopus entangled in coils of seaweed, and nereids and sirens. The tables were of carven wood, littered with cosmetics and scent bottles of blue glass blown into the shapes of fish and mermaids. There were curtains at the windows, Egyptian cotton, dyed green, through which the late sunlight entering the rooms came in as if through waves, giving a curious underwater light.

The wagonload of gifts from Colchis had been unloaded and carried into the palace, and Andromache rummaged in the boxloads for a suitable wedding gift for her new husband. The Queen sent up for Kassandra a fine gown of Egyptian gauze, and Andromache found among the chests from Colchis a gown of silk, full-skirted but so fine that the entire garment could be pulled through a ring, and dyed with the priceless crimson of Tyre.

The Queen also sent her own maids, who set out tubs of warmed water and bathed and perfumed both girls. They curled their hair with heated tongs, then sat them down and painted their faces with cosmetics. They put on red lip-salve that smelled of fresh apples and honey; then they applied kohl from Egypt to darken their brows and underline their eyes, and painted their eyelids with a blue paste that felt like powdered chalk but smelled of the finest olive oil. Andromache accepted all this attention as if she had been accustomed to it all her life, but Kassandra made nervous jokes as the women tended her.

"If I had horns, I am sure you would gild them," she said. "Am I a guest, or one of the sacrifices?"

"The Queen ordered it, Lady," said one of the waiting-women. Kassandra supposed that Hecuba had ordered all of this so that the Colchian princess might think Troy no less luxurious than her own faraway city.

The waiting-woman said, "She ordered that you should be no less fine than herself; and rightly so, for the old song says every lady is a Queen when she rides her bridal cart. And this is the way I have dressed the Lady Polyxena for every festival since she first was grown."

She frowned as she rubbed Kassandra's hands with scented oil that smelled of lilies and roses. "Your hands are callused, Lady Kassandra," she said reprovingly; "they will never be as soft as the princess' hands, which are like rose petals—as a lady's should be."

"I am sorry, there is nothing I can do about it," Kassandra said, twisting the maligned hands. It was at that moment that she first realized how much she would miss the outdoor life, as she already missed her horse. Penthesilea had given her a fine mare as a parting gift; but Kassandra's last act of the journey had been to send the horse back with the Amazon guard. She knew she would not be allowed to ride freely, and she did not want to see her noble companion penned up in the stables or, worse, given to one of her brothers to pull a chariot.

The sun was setting, and the waiting-women lighted

torches. Then they put a gold brooch on the shoulder of Kassandra's tunic, and laid a new cloak of striped wool over her shoulders. Andromache slid her feet into gilded sandals.

"And here is a pair for you, just like them," she said, bending to put them on Kassandra's feet.

"You will be as fine as the bride," said the attendant; but Kassandra felt that Andromache, with her shining dark curls, was more beautiful than any other woman in all of Troy.

The two girls hurried out to the stairs; but Kassandra could not run in the elaborate sandals, and they had to walk carefully step by step down the long flights of stairs.

The great feasting hall glowed with many torches and lamps. Priam was already seated on his high throne, and looked displeased because they were late. But when the herald called out, "The Lady Kassandra and Princess Andromache of Colchis," Priam stretched out his hand good-naturedly to the girls to approach him. He seated Andromache in the favored position beside him, sharing his own gold plate and goblet.

Hecuba signaled to Kassandra to sit beside her, and whispered, "Now you truly look a princess of Troy, not a wild tribeswoman, my darling. How pretty you are."

Kassandra thought she must look like a painted doll, like the little effigies that came from Egypt and were intended for the tombs of Queens and Kings. That was what Polyxena looked like; but if her mother was pleased, she would not protest.

When everyone was seated, Priam proposed the first toast, raising his cup.

"To my splendid new son Paris, and to the kindly fate which has restored him to me and his mother, a comfort in our old age."

"But Father," Hector protested in an undertone, "have you forgotten the prophecy at his birth, that he would bring down disaster on Troy? I was only a child, but I remember it well."

Priam looked displeased; Hecuba seemed about to cry. Paris looked unsurprised; Agelaus must have told him. But it was rude of Hector to mention it at a feast.

Hector was in his finest robes, an elaborate tunic with gold embroidery which Kassandra recognized as the work of the

Queen's own hands; Paris too had been given a fine robe and a new cloak like Kassandra's, and looked splendid. Priam surveyed them both with satisfaction as he said, "No, my son, I have not forgotten the omen which came not to me, but to my Queen. But the hand of the Gods has restored him to me, and no man can argue with Fate or the will of the Immortals."

"But are you certain," Hector persisted, "that it was the Gods, and not perhaps the work of some evil Fate bent on destroying our royal House?" Paris' dark face looked like a thundercloud, but Kassandra could not read her twin's thoughts now.

Priam said with a frown of warning which made Kassandra cringe, "Peace, my son! On this subject alone I will not hear you. I had rather see all Troy perish, if it came to that, than any harm come to my splendid newfound son."

Kassandra shuddered. Priam, who scorned prophecy, had just uttered one.

He smiled benevolently at Paris, who was seated at Hecuba's other side, his fingers tightly clasped in hers. Her face was wreathed in smiles, and Kassandra felt a stab of pain; the discovery of Paris meant that such further welcome as her mother might have given her was quite lost. She felt sad and heart-sore, but told herself that in any case Penthesilea had become her true mother; among the Amazons a daughter was useful and welcome, while here in Troy a daughter was always thought of only as not being a son.

Priam urged Andromache to drink every time the cup went round, forgetting that she was a young girl who would ordinarily not be allowed or encouraged to drink this way. Kassandra could see that already her friend was a little fuddled and tipsy. *Just as well, perhaps*, she thought, *for at the end of this feast she is to be sent quite unprepared to my brother Hector's bed. And he is quite drunk too.*

It suddenly occurred to her to be glad that Andromache was not marrying Paris as had been suggested; with the mind-link between them, she probably could not have avoided sharing in the consummation of the marriage. The thought made her hot and cold by turns; her sensitivities were burning. Where was

Oenone? Why had Paris not bidden her, as his wife, to the wedding?

Hector, perhaps because he was drunk, chose to pursue the subject. "Well, my father, you have chosen to honor our brother; will you not consider that he should be allowed to earn the honor you have bestowed upon him? I entreat you to send him at least on a quest to the Akhaians, so that if the evil prophecy still stands, it may be diverted to them."

"That's a good thought," murmured Priam, himself now the worse for a good deal of wine. "But you do not want to leave us already, do you, Paris?"

Paris murmured correctly that he was eternally at the disposal of his father and his King.

"He has charmed us all," replied Hector, not without malice. "So why not let him try this irresistible charm upon Agamemnon and persuade him to ransom the Lady Hesione?"

"Agamemnon," said Paris, looking up sharply. "Is he not the brother of that same Menelaus who married Helen of Sparta? And is he not himself married to the sister of the Spartan Queen?"

"It is so," Hector said. "When these Akhaians came from the North with their chariots and horses and their Thunder Gods, Leda, the Lady of Sparta, wedded one of these Kings, and it was rumored, when she bore him twin daughters, that one of them had been fathered by the Thunder Lord Himself.

"And Helen married Menelaus," Hector continued, "although it was said that she was fair as a Goddess, and could have married any King from Thessaly to Crete. There was, I heard, much dissension at Helen's wedding, so that it nearly resulted in a war then and there. You are not ill-looking, my Andromache," he said, coming close and looking attentively at her face, "but not so beautiful, I think, that I will need to keep you imprisoned lest all men envy me and covet you." He took her chin in his hands and looked down at her.

"My lord is gracious to his humble wife," said Andromache with a small grin which only Kassandra recognized as sarcasm.

Paris was watching Hector so closely that Kassandra could not but notice. What was he thinking? Could he be jealous of

Hector, who was neither as handsome nor as clever as he? With a beautiful wife like Oenone, he could hardly envy Hector Andromache just because she was a princess of Colchis. Or was he envious of Hector because Hector was the older, and his father's established favorite? Or was he angry because Hector had, after all, insulted him?

She sipped slowly at the wine in her cup, wondering how Andromache really felt about this marriage; she could not imagine her overjoyed at being married to the bullying Hector, but she supposed Andromache was not displeased at eventually being a Queen in Troy. Surreptitiously—her mother had always warned her that it was not proper to stare at men—she looked around the room, wondering if there was any man there she would willingly marry. Certainly none of her brothers, even supposing she were not their sister; Hector was rough and contentious; Deiphobos was shifty-eyed and a sneak; even Paris, handsome as he was, had already neglected Oenone. Troilus was only a child, but when he grew up he might be gentle and kindly enough. She remembered how even among the Amazons the girls had talked all the time about young men, and there too she had felt the weight of being *different* on her heart. Why was it she cared nothing for what was so important to them?

There must be something worthwhile in marriage, or why would all women be so eager for it? Then she remembered the words of Queen Imandra: that she was *priestess born*. At least this was a valid reason for her difference.

Kassandra's eyelids were drooping, and she blinked and sat up straight, wishing this were over; she had been awake and traveling before daylight, and it had been a long day.

Priam had called Paris to his side, and they were talking about ships, the route for sailing to the Akhaian islands and how best to approach Agamemnon's people. Andromache was half asleep. This was, thought Kassandra, the dullest feast she had ever known—though after all, she had not attended so many.

Finally Priam was proposing a toast to the wedded pair, and calling for torches to escort Hector and his bride to the bridal chamber.

First among the women, Hecuba led the procession with a

flaming torch in her hand. It flickered and flared brilliantly colored lights along the walls as the women, with Kassandra and Polyxena on either side of Andromache, escorted her up the stairs, followed by every woman in the palace, Priam's lesser wives and daughters, and all the servants down to the kitchen maids. The torches smoked and hurt Kassandra's eyes. It seemed to her that they were flaming high, that there was a dreadful fire beyond the walls, even within the bridal chamber; that they led Andromache forth to some dreadful fate . . .

Clasping her hands to her eyes as if to shut out the sight, she heard herself screaming, "No! No! The fire! Don't take her in there!"

"Be quiet!" Hecuba gripped her wrists till Kassandra writhed with the pain. "What is the matter with you? Are you mad?"

"Can't you hear the thunder?" Kassandra whispered. "No, no, there is only death and blood . . . fire in there, lightning, destruction—"

"Be still!" Hecuba commanded. "What an omen at a bride's bedding! How dare you make such a scene?"

"But can't they hear, can't they see . . ." Kassandra felt as if she brimmed with darkness and could see nothing but darkness shot through with fire. She pressed her hands against her eyes to shut it out. Was it no more than the smoking torches, distorting her sight?

"For shame!" Her mother was still scolding as she dragged her along. "I thought the princess of Colchis was your friend; would you spoil her bridal night with this fuss? You have always been jealous whenever anyone else is the center of attention; but I thought you had grown out of that . . ."

They led Andromache into the bridal chamber. It too had been painted with sea-creatures so realistic that they seemed to wriggle and swim on the walls. Hecuba had told her at supper that workmen from Crete had been in the palace for a year, redecorating the walls in the Cretan style, and that the carved furniture was tribute from the Queen of Knossos.

On the table beside the bed there was a little carved statue of Earth Mother, Her breasts bared over a tightly laced bodice, a flounced skirt, a serpent clasped in either hand. Andromache, as the women were stripping off her bridal finery and putting her into a shift of Egyptian gauze, whispered to Kassandra, "Look, it is Serpent Mother; She has been sent from my home to bless me this night . . ."

For a moment the dark flooding waters inside Kassandra again threatened to swell up and take over. She was drowning with fear; it was all she could do to keep from shrieking out the terror and apprehension that threatened to strangle her: *Fire, death, blood, doom for Troy . . . for all of us . . .*

Her mother's face, stern and angry, held her silent. She embraced Andromache with a numb dread, thrusting the beautiful little statue at her and murmuring, "May She bless you with fertility, then, Little Sister." Andromache seemed no more than a tall child in her shift, her hair brushed out of its elegant curls and streaming over her shoulders, her painted eyes enormous and dark with the kohl smudged around the lids. Kassandra, still submerged in the dark waters of her vision, felt ancient and withered among all these girls playing at weddings without the faintest idea what lay beyond.

Now they could hear the chanting of the men as they escorted Hector up the stairway to claim his bride. Andromache clung to her and whispered, "You are the only one who is not a stranger to me, Kassandra. I beg you, wish me happiness."

Kassandra's throat was so dry she could hardly speak.

If only it were as easy to bestow happiness as it is to wish it. She murmured through dry lips, "I do wish you happiness, Sister."

But there will be no happiness—only doom and the greatest grief in the world. . . .

She could almost hear the shrieks of anguish and mourning through the joyous singing of the marriage hymn, and as Hector, escorted by his friends, came into the room, the streaked red torchlight made their faces crimson with blood . . . or was it only the bones of their faces illuminated like skulls?

The priestess standing beside the bed gave them the marriage cup. Kassandra thought, *That should have been my task,* but her face was frozen in dread, and she knew she would never have had the heart to set it in her friend's hand.

"Don't look so woebegone, Little Sister," Hector said, touching her hair lightly. "It'll be your turn soon enough; at supper our father was talking of finding you a husband next. Did you know, the son of King Peleus, Akhilles, has made an offer for you? Father says there's a prophecy that he'll be the greatest hero of the ages. Maybe marriage to an Akhaian would settle these stupid wars—though I'd rather fight Akhilles and have the glory of it."

Kassandra gripped frantically at Hector's shoulders.

"Have a care what you pray for," she whispered, "for some God may grant it to you! Pray that you never meet with Akhilles in battle!"

He looked at her in distaste and firmly removed her hands from his shoulders.

"As a prophetess, you are a bird of ill omen, Sister, and I would rather not hear your croakings on my wedding night. Get you to your own bed, and leave us to ours."

She felt the dark waters drain away, leaving her hollow and empty and sick, without the slightest idea what she had been saying. She murmured, "Forgive me; I mean no harm. Surely you know I wish you nothing but good, you and our kinswoman from Colchis . . ."

Hector brushed her forehead with his lips.

"It has been a long day, and you have traveled far," he said. "And the Gods alone know what madness you have been taught in Colchis. It is no wonder you are all but raving with weariness. Good night, then, Little Sister, and—*this* for your omens!" He took the torch beside the bed and swiftly crushed out the flame. "May they all come to nothing, just like this!"

She turned away, unsteady, as the remaining women raised their voices in the last of the marriage songs. She knew she should join in, but felt that for her very life she could not utter a single note. On groping feet she blundered away from the bed and out of the marriage chamber, hurrying to her own room. She fell on her bed, not even bothering to take off her finery, or wipe the smeared cosmetics from her face. She fell into sleep as the dark waters surged over her again, drowning out the remaining echo of the joyous hymns.

17

FOR MANY DAYS now the harbor had rung with the sound of hammers and adzes as the ship grew in the cradle where the keel had been laid, and harpers had come almost every evening to the Great Hall to sing the lay of Jason and the building of the *Argo*.

For weeks provisions had been loaded for the voyage, while sailmakers stitched with their huge needles on the voluminous sail where it was laid out on the white sand of the beach; to dry or smoke barrels of meat, fires burned night and day in the courtyard; baskets of fruits were brought, and great jars of oil and wine, and always more and more weapons. It seemed to the women that for months now all the smiths in the kingdom had been hammering away at arrowheads of bronze, swords of bronze or iron, armor of all kinds.

Dozens of Priam's best warriors were going with Paris, not to make war but in case they encountered pirates in the crossing of the Aegean, whether the notorious plunderer Odysseus (who came sometimes to Priam's palace to sell his loot, or sometimes only to pay the toll Priam exacted of all ships northbound through the straits) or some other pirate. This expedition, laden with gifts for Agamemnon and the other Akhaian Kings, was not to be plundered; the mission, or at least so Priam said, was to negotiate an honorable ransom for the Lady Hesione.

Kassandra watched the ship growing under the builders' hands, and wished passionately that she were to sail in her with Paris and the others.

On two or three days while the warriors were training in the courtyard, she borrowed one of Paris' short tunics and, concealing herself under a helmet, practiced with them at sword and shield. Most people believed it was Paris fighting; since he seldom appeared on the practice field, she was not at once discovered. Even though she knew it was pretense, she enjoyed it immensely, and for a considerable time her long-limbed skill and muscular strength kept her identity unknown.

But one day a friend of Hector's matched her and knocked her down, and her short tunic flew up above her waist. Hector himself came and jerked the helmet from her head; then, angrily, wrested the sword out of her hand, turned it edgewise and beat her hard on the backside with it.

"Now get inside, Kassandra, and tend to your spinning and weaving," he snarled at her. "There is enough women's work for you to do; if I catch you masquerading out here again, I will beat you bloody with my own hands."

"Let her alone, you great bully," cried Andromache, who had been watching from the sidelines; she had been fitting a crimson cushion to Hector's chariot and tacking the last bits of gold thread on it. Hector turned on her angrily.

"Did you know she was here, Andromache?"

"What if I did?" demanded Andromache rebelliously. "My own mother, and yours too, fights like a warrior!"

"It's not suitable that my sister, or my wife, be out here before the eyes of soldiers," Hector said, scowling. "Get inside, and attend to your own work; and no more conniving with this wretched hoyden here!"

"I suppose you think you can beat me bloody too!" Andromache said pertly. "But you know what you shall have from me if you try!" Kassandra saw, in astonishment, the line of embarrassed crimson that crept upward in her brother's face.

Andromache's dark hair blew out around her face in the fresh wind; she was wearing a loose tunic almost the same color as her wedding gown, and looked very pretty. Hector said at last, so stiffly that Kassandra knew that he was stifling whatever he really wanted to say as not being suitable before an outsider, even a sister: "That's as it may be, Wife. Nevertheless, it is more seemly for you to go to the women's quarters and mind your loom; there is plenty of women's work to be done, and I would rather you do it than come out here learning Kassandra's ways. Still, if it makes you feel better, I shall not beat her this time. As for you, Kassandra, get inside and attend to your own affairs, or I shall tell Father, and perhaps he can put it in such a way that you will mind his words." She knew that the sulkiness on her face reached him, for he said, a little more kindly, "Come, Little

Sister, do you think I would be out here wearing myself into exhaustion with shield and spear if I could stay cool and comfortable inside the house? Battle may look good to you when it is only playing with spears and arrows with your friends and brothers, but look." He bared his arm, rolling up the woolen sleeve of his tunic past the bright embroidered edgework, and showed her a long red seam, still oozing at the center. "It still pains me when I move my arm; when there are real wounds to be given and received, war does not look so exciting!"

Kassandra looked at the wound marring her brother's smooth and muscular body, and felt a curious sickening tightness under her diaphragm; she flinched and remembered cutting the throat of the tribesman who would have raped her. She almost wanted to tell Hector about it—he was a warrior and would certainly understand. Then she looked into his eyes, and knew she would not; he would never, she thought, see beyond the fact that she was a girl.

"Be glad, Little Sister, that it was only I who saw you stripped like that," he said, not unkindly, "for if you were revealed as a woman on the battlefield . . . I have seen women warriors ravished and not one man protest. If a woman refuses such protection as is lawful for wives and sisters, there is no other protection for her." He pulled down his helmet and strode away, leaving the women staring after him, Kassandra angry and knowing she was supposed to be ashamed, Andromache suppressing giggles. After a moment, the giggles escaped.

"Oh, he was so angry! Kassandra, I would have been terrified if he had been that angry with *me*!" She drew her white shawl around her shoulders in the fresh wind. "Come, let's get out of the way. He's right, you know; if any other man had seen you"—she drew down her mouth into a grimace, and said with an exaggerated shudder, "something terrible would certainly have happened."

Seeing no alternative, Kassandra followed her, and Andromache linked her arm through her sister-in-law's.

Kassandra for the first time in days became aware of the prophetic darkness, filling her up inside.

While she had been on the field with a weapon, she had not

been conscious of the thing which had made her cry out on the night of the wedding. Now, through that dark water she saw Andromache, and all around her something else, overlaid with a cold and frightening fire of grief and terror, but enough joy before the sorrow that it made her lay her hand urgently on Andromache's arm and say softly, "You are with child?"

Andromache smiled; no, thought Kassandra, she glowed. "You think so? I was not sure yet; I thought perhaps I would ask the Queen how I could be sure. Your mother has been so kind to me, Kassandra; my own mother never understood or approved of me, because I was soft and a coward and I did not want to be a warrior; but Hecuba loves me, and I think she will be happy if it is so."

"I am sure of that, at least," Kassandra said, and then because she knew Andromache was about to ask "How do you know?" she fumbled for words she could use instead of trying to explain about the dark waters and the terrible crown of fire. "It seemed for a moment," she said, "that I could see you with Hector's son in your arms."

Andromache's smile was radiant; and Kassandra was relieved that for once she had given pleasure instead of fear with her unwanted gift.

In the days following, she did not again take up her weapons, but went out often, unrebuked, to see how the ship was progressing. It grew daily on the great cradle on the sand, and almost before Andromache's pregnancy was visible to unskilled eyes, it was ready for launching, and a white bull was sacrificed for the moment when it slid easily down the ramp toward the water.

At that moment Hector, standing between his wife and Kassandra, said, "You who prophesy unasked all the time, what do you see for this ship?"

Kassandra said in a low voice, "I see nothing. And perhaps that is the best omen of all." She could see the ship returning in a golden glow like the face of some God, and nothing more. "But I think it lucky that you are not sailing, Hector."

"So be it, then," said Hector. Paris came to bid them goodbye, clasping Hector's hand warmly and embracing Kassandra with a smile. He kissed his mother and leaped on board the ship, and his family stood together, watching it drift out of the harbor, the great sail bellying out with the wind. Paris stood at the steering oar at the back, straight and slender, his face alight with the westering sun. Kassandra shook off her mother's arm and walked away through the cheering crowd; she went straight to where a tall woman stood with her eyes fixed on the sail as it dwindled to the size of a toy.

"Oenone," she said, recognizing her from the moment when, with Paris, she had held the girl as if in her own arms, "what are you doing here? Why did you not come to bid him farewell with the rest of his kin?"

"I never knew when first I loved him that he was a prince," said the girl. Her voice was as lovely as she was, light and musical. "How could a common girl like me come up to the King and the Queen when they were saying goodbye to their son?"

Kassandra put her arm around Oenone and said gently, "You must come and stay at the palace. You are his wife and the mother of his child, so they will love you as they do Paris himself." *And if they do not*, she thought, *they can just behave as if they do, for the honor of the family. To think he went away without bidding her goodbye!*

Oenone's face was flooded with tears. She clutched Kassandra's arm. "They say you are a prophetess, that you can see the future," she said, weeping. "Tell me that he will come back! Tell me that he will come back to me!"

"Oh, he will come back," said Kassandra.

He will come back. But not to you.

She was confused at the depth of her own emotions. She said, "Let me speak to my mother about you," and went, with Andromache, to Hecuba. Andromache said in gentle reproach, "Oh, Kassandra, how can you? A peasant girl—to bring her to the palace?"

"She's not; she's as well born as either of us," Kassandra said. "You've only to look at her hands to see that. Her father is a priest of the River God Scamander."

She repeated this argument to Hecuba, whose first impulse had been to say, "Of course, if she is carrying Paris' child—and how can you be so sure of that, my dear?—we must see that she is well provided for and not in want. But to bring her to the palace?"

Nevertheless, when she met Oenone she was charmed at once by her beauty, and brought her to a suite of rooms high up in the palace, light and airy and looking out on the ocean. They were empty, and smelled of mice, but Hecuba said, "No one has used these rooms since Priam's mother lived here; we will have workmen in and have them redecorated for you, my dear, if you can manage with them this way for a night or two."

Oenone's eyes were large and almost disbelieving. "You are so good to me—they are much too fine for me—"

"Don't be foolish," Hecuba said brusquely. "For my son's wife—and soon his son—there's nothing too fine, believe me. We'll have workmen from Crete—there are workmen here painting frescoes in some houses in the city, and others painting vases and oil jars. I'll send a message to them tomorrow."

She was as good as her word, and within a day or two the Cretans came to plaster the rooms and paint festival scenes on the walls, great white bulls and the leaping bull-dancers of Crete, in realistic colors. Oenone was delighted with the pretty rooms, and pleased in a childlike way when Hecuba sent women to wait on her. "You must not overexert yourself, or my grandson may suffer," Hecuba said bluntly when Oenone tried inarticulately to thank her.

Andromache was kind to Oenone too, though in a careless way, and at first Kassandra spent a great deal of time with them, confused by her own feelings. Andromache now belonged to Hector, and Oenone to Paris; she had no close friends, and though every day or so Priam spoke of the necessity of finding her a husband, she was not sure that was what she wanted, or what she would say if he asked her—which he probably would not.

She did not understand why Oenone's presence should affect her this way; she supposed it was because she had shared Paris' emotions (but if Paris felt this way about Oenone, why had he been willing to leave her?) toward the girl when he made her his wife. She felt a great desire to caress the other woman, and comfort her, while at the same time she drew away from her, self-conscious even of the kind of careless embrace customary between girls.

Confused and frightened, she began to avoid Oenone, and this meant that she avoided Andromache too; for the two young wives now spent a good deal of time together, talking of their coming babes, and weaving baby clothes, a pastime that appealed to Kassandra not at all. Her sister Polyxena, never a friend, was not yet married, although Priam was haggling for the best possible alliance for her and she thought and spoke of little else.

Kassandra fancied that when Paris returned she might be less obsessed with Oenone; but she had no idea when that might be. Alone under the stars on the high roof of the palace, she sent out her thoughts seeking her twin, and achieved no more than fresh sea breezes and a blinding view of the deep darkness of the sea, so clear that she could see the pebbles on the sea bottom.

One day, choosing a time when Priam was in a good humor, she went to him and carefully emulating Polyxena's kittenish behavior, asked softly, "Please tell me, Father, how far is Paris going, and how long a journey is it till he will be back?"

Priam smiled indulgently, and said, "Look, my dear. Here we are on the shores of the straits. Ten days' sail this way, southward, and there is a cluster of islands ruled by the Akhaians. If he avoids shipwreck on reefs here"—he sketched a coastline—"he can sail southward to Crete, or northwesterly to the mainland of the Athenians and the Mykenaeans. If he has fair winds and no ship-breaking storms, he could return before the summer's end; but he will be trading and perhaps staying as a guest with one or more of the Akhaian Kings . . . as they call themselves. They are newcomers to this country; some of them have been there no more than their fathers' lifetimes. Their cities are new; ours is ancient. There was another Troy here, you know, Daughter, before my forefathers built our city."

"Really?" She made her voice soft and admiring like Polyxena's, and he smiled and told her of the ancient Cretan city that once had risen not more than a day's sail south along the coast. "In this city," he said, "were great storehouses of wine and oil, and they think this may have been why the city burned when great Poseidon Earth Shaker made the sea rise and the ground tremble. For a day and a night there was a great darkness over the whole world, as far south as Egypt; and the beautiful island Kallistos fell into the sea, drowning the Temple of Serpent Mother and leaving the Temples of Zeus the Thunderer and Apollo Sun Lord untouched. That is why there is now less worship, in the civilized lands, of Serpent Mother."

"But how do we know it is the Gods who have shaken the lands?" Kassandra asked. "Have They sent messengers to tell us so?"

"We do not know," Priam said, "but what else could it be? If it is not the Gods, there would be nothing but chaos. Poseidon is one of the greatest Gods here in Troy, and we petition Him to keep the earth solid beneath our feet."

"May He long do so," Kassandra murmured fervently, and since she saw that her father's attention had wandered to his wine cup, made a courteous request to go; her father nodded permission, and she went out into the courtyard, with much to think about. If indeed it had been the great earthquake (which she had heard about during her childhood—it had been several years before Priam's birth), then perhaps this was sufficient reason that the worship of Earth Mother had been discredited, except perhaps among the tribeswomen.

The courtyard was abustle; it was a brilliant day. Workmen were moving about. The people painting friezes high up in the rooms assigned to Oenone for Paris were grinding new pigments and mixing them with oil; tally-men were counting jars of wine brought in as tithes on one of the ships lying out in the harbor; some of the soldiers were practicing at arms. Far out beyond the city, Kassandra could see a cloud of dust which was probably Hector exercising the horses of his new chariot. She wandered among them like a ghost unseen; *it is as if I were a sorceress and had made myself invisible*, she thought, and wondered whether she could make herself so in truth, and whether it would make any difference if she did.

For no reason at all, her eyes fell idly on a young man who

was dutifully marking tallies with a notched stick and pressing wax on the sealing ropes of great jars, oil or wine—pressing the seal that indicated these had been taken for the King's household.

He seemed a bit restless under her scrutiny, turning his eyes away, and Kassandra, blushing—she had been taught it was unmaidenly to stare at young men—looked away. Then her eyes were drawn back. The young man seemed to glow. His eyes grew very strange, almost vacant; then they focused, and he drew upright. He seemed to grow taller, looming over her; yes, it was she, Kassandra, whom he fixed with his eyes, and in a flash she recognized what God possessed him, for she was looking again into the face of Apollo Sun Lord.

His voice reverberated as thunder, so that she wondered, with a scrap of wandering consciousness, how the other workers could go quietly on with their work.

Kassandra, daughter of Priam, have you forgotten Me?

She whispered under her breath, "Never, Lord."

Have you forgotten that I have set My hand upon you and called you for My own?

Again she whispered, "Never."

Your place is in My Temple; come, I bid you.

"I will come," she said, half aloud, gazing on the luminous form. Then the overseer strode through the yard, and the young man shimmered, wavered in the sun, which blurred Kassandra's eyes. . . .

The vision was gone, and for a moment Kassandra wondered if she had indeed been bidden to the Sun Lord's Temple. Should she fetch her cloak and her serpent, and climb up to the High Place of the Gods at once? She hesitated; if she had actually dreamed it and it had never happened, what would she say in the Temple to the priests and priestesses? Surely there were penalties for blasphemy of that kind. . . .

No. She was Priam's daughter, a princess of Troy, and she had been made a priestess of the Great Mother. She might be mistaken, but it was certainly no blasphemy, nor anything to be ignored. Silently she went into the palace, under her breath whispering, "If I have not been called, Sun Lord, send me a sign."

On the great stairway, she encountered Hecuba, dressed in a workaday smock, frown lines drawn between her brows making her look older.

"You are idle, Daughter," Hecuba rebuked her. "If you cannot find any way to keep yourself occupied, I myself will find you some task; henceforth you will not leave the women's quarters on any morning until your share of spinning and weaving is done. For shame, to leave your work to your sister. Was it only laziness you learned among the women of my tribe?"

"I am not idle!" Kassandra replied angrily. Was this the sign for which she had asked? "I have been sent for by the God, and I am required in His Temple."

Hecuba frowned at her, narrowing her eyes.

"Kassandra, the Gods choose Their priestesses from among simple folk; They do not call to a princess of Troy."

"Do you think me less worthy than another?" Kassandra flared out. "I have known since I was a child that Apollo Sun Lord wants me for His own, and now He has summoned me!"

"Oh, Kassandra," Hecuba sighed, "why do you talk such nonsense?" But Kassandra was no longer listening to her. She turned away and ran down the stairs and out through the great gates, hurrying up the hill toward Apollo's Temple.

18

KASSANDRA RAN up the steps of the street that traversed the city from lower to highest ground, hardly realizing that the women who dwelt in the crowded houses built along the steep street had all come out, in a flutter of brightly dyed dresses, to watch her precipitate flight. The pounding of her heart forced her to slow her steps to a walk, and then to a full stop.

She bent over, half sick. She had been rigidly schooled always to maintain her decorum before strangers; she pressed the loose sleeve of her dress over her lips, trying to control the nausea and sharp pain in her chest, and sought a step where she could sit and catch her breath. She did not want to appear on the doorstep of the God as a disheveled fugitive.

A kindly voice said "Princess . . . " and she looked up to see an aging woman bent over her, holding a clay cup in her hand. "You have climbed too far, and too swiftly, in this sun. May I offer you a drink of water? Or I can fetch you some cooled wine, if it would please you to step inside."

The thought of going into the cool shaded interior was tempting, but Kassandra was ashamed to show or admit weakness.

How can I be overcome by the sun? I am the beloved of Apollo Sun Lord . . . but she did not say this aloud, murmuring her thanks and setting the cup to her lips. The water tasted a little of clay and was not overcool, but it felt good to her parched lips and throat.

"Will you rest for a moment inside my house, Princess?"

"No, thank you." She kept her eyes averted. "I am quite well; I will sit here and rest for a moment." The light hurt her eyes; she shaded them with her hand, looking down at the clear dazzling reflection of the harbor. For a moment the sun blurred her sight; then she saw clearly, and all but cried out: the clear blue of the sea was dark with the sails of many ships.

So many! Where had they come from?

They were not her father's ships, and as she tried to focus on any one of them, she was suddenly no longer sure it was there. After a few moments of this, the harbor burned empty with dazzling blue sea, broken only by the shape of one old Cretan ship which had been unloading paints and lumber for the past three days.

It had been only a vision, then; a hallucination.

She wrenched her aching eyes from the illusory sea, slowly got to her feet and began to climb upward. She kept her eyes slitted narrowly against the sun, which glared like fire spreading down across the walls of Troy, and kept climbing, slowly, against a growing sense that to run away like this was folly, that one did not flee to a God like a strayed goat bolting from the flock. She should have come, oh, yes, but she should have come like a princess of Troy, suitably attended, and bearing the proper gifts for the House of the God.

Nevertheless, it would be wrong to turn back now. *Unless the deceitful vision of ships had been meant as a warning . . . ?* No; even so, she could not take back her commitment to the God.

She climbed on, approaching the Temple of the Sun Lord.

A flare of light, haloed by a flash of summer lightning, drew her eyes to the heights, where the Temple of Pallas Athene stood, and suddenly doubt assailed her. She had been made priestess of the Goddess, sent into the Underworld to seek Her, and had been accepted; was it not Earth Mother who had called her since her earliest childhood, and spoken to her with the voice of prophecy? Was she, then, abandoning her loyalty to the Divine Mother, Maiden and protectress of maidens, forsaking Her for the beautiful Sun Lord?

Sudden panic flooded her, so that for a moment she again thought she would vomit, and she swallowed spasmodically; her whole body was filled with a fear she could all but taste. She heard hard steps pursuing her, and for a moment the sky above her was dark, and one thought filled her mind to the brim, submerged in the dark waters: *I must reach the Temple of the Maiden; there alone will I be safe. . . . No man would dare lay hands on any whom She protects. . . .*

Kassandra blinked incredulously. There was no peril, no flame, no pursuer. The harbor gleamed empty and blue; the street around her contained only a few women, watching her climb sedately toward the great gates of the Sun Lord's Temple.

Is it the God who has sent madness on me? She paused to catch her breath and stepped over the threshold into the Temple of Apollo.

There was a sudden rush of wind, as if a giant hand pushed her across the threshold. Kassandra, patting her hair distractedly into place, looked about, almost disappointed that no one seemed to take notice. *What did I expect? That the God Himself would come out and make me welcome?*

An old woman in the ordinary dress of a priestess—a white tunic and a veil dyed with saffron to a sunny golden color—raised her head and looked at Kassandra, then stood up and came toward her. She said, "Welcome, daughter of Priam; have you come here for an oracle or an omen, or to offer sacrifice?"

"None of these things," Kassandra said, self-consciously, not knowing how to say what she had some to say. "I came—because the God has called me to come—to be His priestess . . ." And she broke off, feeling more than a little foolish.

But the older woman smiled in a kindly way and said, "Yes, of course; I remember that you came once to us when you were only a little girl, and seemed so much at home here, I thought perhaps one day the Sun Lord would call you. So now come inside, my dear, and tell me all about it. First, how old are you?" she asked. "You seem well grown to womanhood."

"My mother tells me that I shall be sixteen soon after Midsummer," Kassandra answered as they went inside. She remembered the waiting room where many years ago she had eaten a piece of sweet melon while her mother awaited the oracle, and found it hard to believe that it had changed so little in so many years. She wondered about the serpents she had seen and caressed at that time. They had been of a short-lived species; probably they were long dead. The thought saddened her.

The priestess gestured to her to sit.

"Tell me about yourself," she said. "Tell me all that makes you think you have been called to our Temple."

When Kassandra had finished, the priestess spoke again. "Well, Kassandra," she said, "if you wish to be one of us, you must live for a year here within the Temple, to learn to interpret the oracles and the omens and to speak for the God."

Kassandra said, feeling a surge of upswelling happiness, "I shall be happy to live in the house of the God."

"Then you must send one of the Temple servants to fetch your belongings: only a few changes of clothing and perhaps a warm cloak, for you must wear the common dress of a priestess; we are all as sisters here, and you may not wear jewels and ornaments while you dwell in the shrine."

"I do not care for jewels," Kassandra said, "and indeed, I have very few. But why is it not permitted?"

The old woman smiled. "It is a rule of the Temple," she said, "and I do not know why it is so. Perhaps it is because many of the folk who come here to consult us are poor, and if we were hung with jewels they might feel that we were enriching ourselves upon their offerings.

"My name," she said, "is Charis, which is one of the names of Earth Lady. I have dwelt in the house of the Sun Lord since I was nine winters old, and now I am seven-and-forty. We are long-lived here, unless we are chosen to bear a child to the God and it should chance that we die in childbirth; but that does not happen often, and many of our brothers and sisters are healer-priests. Have you your mother's or your father's leave to dwell in the house of the God?"

Kassandra said, "I think my mother will agree to it. As for my father, he has so many sons and daughters, I do not think he will know or care whether I am in the God's house or his. I have never been one of his favorites.

"But tell me," she asked the old priestess, "may I have my serpent to live with me in the Temple? She was a gift from Imandra, Queen and priestess of Colchis, and no one else in Troy loves her; I fear she will be neglected if I am not there to care for her."

"She will be welcome," Charis said. "You may have her brought here."

The old priestess now summoned a servant, and Kassandra instructed her as to which of her possessions she wanted fetched from the palace. "And go to my mother, Queen Hecuba," she said, "and tell her that I beg for her blessing."

The servant bowed and went away. "And now, if you wish," Charis said, "I will show you the chambers where the virgins of Apollo sleep."

So BEGAN the time that Kassandra remembered later as the happiest and most peaceful of her entire life. She learned to consult the oracles, to read the omens and to serve the shrine with the appointed offerings. She cared for the sacred serpents, and learned to interpret the meanings of their movements and behavior.

As she had foreseen, her mother made no difficulties; she sent by the servant the requested belongings, and a message: "Say to my daughter Kassandra that I bless her and approve what she has done; tell her I send her many kisses and embraces."

Very soon she found many friends at the shrine, and after

only a few months there were many clients and supplicants who came to deal with her and preferred that it be she who accepted their offerings and gave them advice. Once she asked an older priest: "I do not understand: why do they come to the God to ask these foolish questions for which they do not need a God's advice, but only the common wits they were born with?"

"Because so many of them are born fools or worse," said the old priest bluntly; "they think the Gods have nothing better to do than trouble Themselves with human affairs. Myself, I believe the Gods have enough concerns of Their own, in the land of the Immortals, not to worry Themselves very much with the business of ordinary men. Perhaps with the doings of Kings and the great ones; but"—and he lowered his eyes and spoke almost in a whisper—"I have seen little evidence even of that, daughter of Priam."

Kassandra was a little shocked by this blasphemy, but felt that if the priest had little faith in the God, it was more his loss than anyone else's. As for herself, while she dwelt in the shrine she had a great and often overpowering sense of the presence of her God, as in the moment when first He had called her.

This was not to say that her time in the Temple was entirely carefree. Some of the maidens in the shrine were openly jealous of her because she was a favorite with the older priests and priestesses, and spoke to her, or of her, with unkindness or spite; but she had never been popular with girls of her own age, not even with her sister and half-sisters, except among the Amazons, and had become resigned to that before she was out of childhood.

Mostly she felt she was surrounded with loving attention; what else could it be when she dwelt in the house of her God? There were many women in the shrine who spoke of the Sun Lord as other maidens spoke of a husband or lover; in fact, one of the common names for the priestesses was "brides of the God." One of the women, Phyllida, was regarded as having been the bride of the God in truth: she had borne a child who was accepted as a son of Apollo.

When Kassandra first heard this, she was annoyed and disgusted with what seemed obvious nonsense.

Is the girl simply a fool, deceived by some quite ordinary seducer? Or was she telling a tale to make up for some forbidden adventure of her own? Kassandra wondered, for the virgins of the God were forbidden to have anything to do with men; they were carefully watched and not allowed to receive visits or gifts or to meet with even their own brothers or fathers except in the presence of one of the governesses, who chaperoned and cared for the maidens of the Sun Lord. *If I wished to be the bride of any mortal man,* she thought, *my father would be all too happy to arrange a marriage for me.*

Sometimes Kassandra would half awaken at night, hearing the unmistakable voice of the God when He had called to her, a shining Immortal who was something more than mere man. More than once she dreamed that she lay fainting within the arms of her God, an ecstasy more than human sweeping through all her senses; from listening to the other girls talk (though out of shyness she took little part in this gossip), she learned that she was not the only girl favored with such dreams.

Once when one of the young maidens was telling her latest dream, filled with erotic detail which Kassandra thought only romantic imagining, she said: "If you dream so much of lying with a man, Esiria, why not send for your father and ask him to find you a husband? Otherwise, can you not find something else to occupy your thoughts and something more useful to talk about?"

"You are only jealous because He does not seek to lie with you even in a dream," Esiria retorted. "And if He did, would you then refuse Him?"

A curious chill went over Kassandra.

"If He should seek to lie with me," she declared, "I should try to be very certain that it was in truth the God, and not some lecherous man bent on deceiving a foolish and credulous woman, or romantic girl, who mistakes a mere lecher for a God's deputy. I know there are men in this Temple who would not be above taking advantage of a silly girl that way; or do you think priests are eunuchs because they have taken a vow of chastity?"

Esiria would say no more, and Kassandra held her peace;

but the next day when the women went to draw water at the well, she sought out Phyllida and asked to see her child. Like all mothers, the young woman (for she was not yet Kassandra's age) was eager to show her little boy.

He was pretty indeed, with big blue long-lashed eyes and a crop of golden curls which made it easy to believe that he was indeed a child of the Sun Lord. Kassandra admired and kissed him, then asked Phyllida in a sufficiently awed tone, "How did you know it was the God who had come to you?"

"At first I did not know," the girl said. "I thought it was a man in the mask of the God, and I opened my mouth to cry out for one of the governesses. But then—have you ever heard the voice of the God, daughter of Priam?"

Kassandra felt a catch in her throat, remembering that voice. She said, "I have heard . . ." and could not go on.

"Then, if it happens to you, you will know," said Phyllida abruptly, and said no more.

Kassandra looked again at the little boy and said, "He is beautiful; may I hold him for a moment?"

"Certainly." The child had fallen asleep, though his baby mouth, like a half-opened rose, still clung to his mother's nipple; Phyllida lifted him and put him into Kassandra's arms. He stirred and whimpered, but she jiggled him a little as she had seen his mother do and he was quiet. His weight, damp and soft in her arms, was unlike anything else she had ever felt; even among the Amazons she had never held quite so young a baby. She bent over close to him, touching the soft skin with her lips; it felt exactly like rose petals.

For a moment a vast content came over her; then it seemed as if a cloud covered the sun, and a cold wind blew over her, though she was still sitting in the warm bright court under a sun which almost burned her, so that she drew the end of her veil over the baby lest it damage his eyes or burn his skin. She recognized the darkness of vision and, motionless, awaited what she could not avoid.

Suffering and grief were the essence of it. Somehow she slid through time and knew that years had passed since this quiet moment; the child who lay against her breast was her own, the little head at her bosom was dark and curly, and even as that strange inward surge of happiness touched her it was clouded with despair, the memory of this very moment and an angry revulsion. The vision was so strong that for a moment she was paralyzed; then she knew again where she was. Once more she had managed to prevent the dark waters from drowning her.

She saw Phyllida's wide childish eyes regarding her in something like dread as she put the babe back into his mother's arms. Phyllida whispered, "You looked so faraway and strange, Kassandra. They say you can see into the future. What did you see for my child?" And as Kassandra was silent, she entreated, "You would not curse my baby?"

"No, no, of course not, little one," Kassandra said.

"Will you bless him, then, daughter of Priam?"

Kassandra wished to reassure her, and reached within herself for the distant touch of the Goddess, to draw upon that power for blessing. Instead, she heard herself say: "Alas, there is no blessing for any child of Troy born in this inauspicious year; but perhaps Apollo, his father, will bless him where I may not." She rose quickly and went away, leaving Phyllida staring after her in wordless dismay.

19

A FEW DAYS later, a messenger arrived with gifts for the Temple from King Priam's house and a message for Kassandra herself.

"Your father and mother have asked that you may make a visit to your home for the wedding of your half-sister Creusa."

"I shall have to ask leave," Kassandra told him, but permission was readily granted—perhaps too readily. Kassandra knew that it would not have been so swiftly given for any of the other young priestesses, and she really wished to be treated as one of them. But she could not fault the priests and priestesses that they did not wish to offend Troy's King. They only insisted that since she was not yet a full priestess but still in the probationary year, if she wished to spend the night in her father's house she be properly accompanied and chaperoned by a senior priestess.

The priestess who heard her request said, "It lies in your power to confer a favor, daughter of Priam: whom will you have to accompany you?"

Kassandra was not totally a stranger to this sort of courtly intrigue; whomever she chose, others might feel slighted. Making a choice no one could fault or envy, she chose the elderly Charis, who had first welcomed her to the house of the God.

Dressing herself in the most festive of the few simple dresses she had with her, and with the older woman at her side, she went quietly through the streets, attended only by one of the Temple slaves.

Charis, a lifelong dweller in the house of the Sun Lord, was nevertheless impressed as they approached the Great Citadel of Priam, and said little.

Kassandra was silent too, for she had looked down from the heights and seen again the dark ships in the harbor, not knowing whether they were really there or were yet to come.

As they entered the forecourt, Hecuba came to greet them. Kassandra bent to embrace her mother—Hecuba was a tall woman, but now Kassandra was taller still, and Hecuba lamented as she turned her face up to her tall daughter, "You cannot be still growing! Why, you are taller than most warriors, Kassandra! A man might not wish to have you near—"

"What does it matter, Mother? Since I am not to be married, but to dwell in the house of the God . . ."

"That I shall never accept," said Hecuba with spirit. "I want to see your children before I die."

But you never will, Kassandra suddenly knew. With the memory of holding Phyllida's child in her lap came the painful knowledge that before she could hold her grandchild—*the bitterness, the despair*—Hecuba's eyes would forever have closed on this world.

"Mother, let's not speak of that. If you want a wedding, you have Creusa now to marry off; and Polyxena's older than I am and still unwed. Find her a husband," she said, "and do not be concerned with me. Tell me now about Creusa's betrothed."

"She is to marry Aeneas, son of Anchises," Hecuba said—
"so handsome, they say he is truly a son of foam-born Aphrodite."

"She is a Goddess of whom I know nothing," Kassandra said, before she remembered the beautiful one in Paris' dream —the Goddess of Love and Beauty.

"If his father claims to be the lover of Aphrodite, I should think the Goddesses would be angry with him," said Kassandra. "I must see this marvel of a man."

"Well, Creusa is content with him, and so is your father," said Hecuba, "and in my youth I would have been more than happy with such a husband." She turned a little anxiously to Kassandra and said, "Please try not to prophesy doom at this wedding, dear; it upsets people so much."

Does she think I prophesy for the pleasure of doing it? Kassandra thought with a surge of anger. But her mother looked so troubled that her anger faded; she kissed her again and said, "I will certainly try not to see any disasters; if the Gods are kind, I may be able to foretell something better."

"Gods grant it," murmured Hecuba piously. "Well, come in, my dear; I have missed you very much."

After a moon spent in the house of the Sun Lord, everything in the palace seemed smaller and gaudy; yet dear and familiar. Andromache, dressed for the wedding in flame-dyed finery, ran out to greet Kassandra. Her pregnancy was very obvious now, and she waddled with the typical walk of a pregnant woman, tilting her body backward for balance. Kassandra, thinking of the lithe young girl in Imandra's house, felt saddened, but Andromache embraced her joyously.

"Oh, I am so glad to see you! I wish you would marry and come home so we could be together! Just think, in another moon I will have my son in my arms!"

"Where is Oenone? Should she not be among us? A pregnant woman is the luckiest of all guests at a wedding."

"She is not pregnant now," said Andromache. "Have you not heard? She bore Paris a son four days ago, and she is still in bed; she had a dreadful time, poor thing—your mother said she was so slender she should have known better than to have a child at all. But when I asked how she could have avoided it, she would not tell me—she said Hector would not like it. Oenone has called her son Corythus. . . . So if Creusa wants a pregnant woman at her wedding, she will have to make do with me."

"Creusa is fortunate to have you among her guests," Kassandra said.

Andromache smiled like a kitten lapping cream and said, "I hope she thinks so too."

"I should go and see Oenone," Kassandra said.

Andromache took Kassandra's hand and drew her along the stairs. "You had better not," she said; "she has been very strange lately. When I went to see her, she would not speak to me. She said I was her husband's enemy because Hector had sent him away."

They went into the upstairs suite where the women were dressing the bride. It was the beautiful room with the Cretan murals of bull-dancers, and Kassandra said, "But this is the room my mother had made ready for Oenone."

"She would not stay in it," Andromache said. "She said she did not want to lie here day after day looking out on the sea which had borne Paris away from her, so she insisted on moving into a room at the back of the palace where she can look upon Mount Ida, her home. But never mind that now; come and help dress the bride."

Far below they could hear the sounds of the men in the hall, drinking and toasting the wedding.

Creusa was being covered with an embroidered veil; she put it back for a moment and came forward to greet Andromache with a bow, then kissed Kassandra coolly and said "Welcome, Sister."

She was not Hecuba's daughter, but Priam's by the most important of his palace women. Strictly speaking, by court etiquette it was for Kassandra first to claim sisterhood; but she was not interested at the moment in preserving protocol. She warmly returned Creusa's embrace and said, "May Earth Mother and the Bright Ones bless you, Sister."

"Can you see good fortune for me, Kassandra—you who are a prophetess?"

"I will know that when I have seen your husband," said Kassandra elliptically.

"When you have seen him, I think you will envy me," Creusa said.

Kassandra smiled and said, "Indeed I hope so, Sister. Mother told me how handsome he is."

"And he is rich too, and a prince in his own country," said Creusa. "Surely no woman can be luckier than I."

"Do not say such things, lest the Immortals be jealous," reprimanded Charis. "Remember the fate of the woman who said her spinning was as fine as that of Pallas Athene, and Athene made her a spider, who should spin her webs forever to be torn down by housewives!"

"Come, come," said Andromache, who was the first of the bride-women. "Let us finish dressing her quickly, or the men will all be drunk before she comes. Kassandra, your fingers are nimblest; will you put the flowers in her hair?"

Kassandra quickly tied the blossoms into a wreath and fastened them into Creusa's bright curls.

"Now she is ready; let us lead her down."

Taking her by the hands, the women surrounded the bride and led her down the steep staircases of the palace, holding her carefully lest she stumble and begin her marriage with a false step—the worst of omens.

They lifted up their voices in the oldest of marriage hymns, the one to Earth Mother, and Kassandra felt surrounded with as much joy and gaiety as if it were her own wedding. *For once,* she thought, *I can be as carefree as any other young girl.* She was briefly aware that others did not observe themselves in this way; what was the difference? Bur for once she had an answer to that painful sense of difference. *I am a priestess and need not be like the others; if I can somehow manage to seem like the rest, it is enough.*

They were at the very threshold of the feasting hall when they heard a cry of surprise and welcome.

Priam called out, "Odysseus, you old cheat! Right enough, you know just when to come to sample our best wine for a wedding! Come in and have a drink, old comrade!"

Kassandra reached out and pulled Creusa back.

"Let our father welcome his guest first."

Creusa said sulkily, "I didn't want that old pirate at my wedding!"

Andromache whispered, "I have heard all my life of the stories he can tell; he has sailed farther than Jason and has many traveler's tales. He visited my mother in Colchis and brought her a mother-of-pearl comb that he said was given him by a mermaid."

"Perhaps he has brought you a wedding gift too, Creusa," Kassandra said. "In any case, even the Gods must show hospitality. Let us go in."

She sang the first line of the hymn to the Maiden, always sung at weddings, and the other girls joined in. Priam looked up and beckoned them forward. Kassandra saw a handsome young man, tall and slender, with curly light brown hair and with a scattering of dark freckles just gilding his face. She supposed, from the ornate crimson tunic he wore, that this was the bridegroom. Just approaching the high seat was a short, burly man of middle age with crisply curled hair and a red face, weatherbeaten and hook-nosed, with deep-set blue eyes that seemed to look out on immense distances. She supposed, even before she saw the recognition in Andromache's eyes, that this was the famous seafarer and pirate, her father's old friend Odysseus.

The seafarer turned and cried out, "What a bunch o' beauties, old friend. These cannot all be your daughters, Priam; or can they? I seem to remember you've somewhat more'n your share of womenfolk."

Priam summoned them to him with a wave of his hand.

Kassandra found herself enveloped in a great bear hug.

"Your second daughter, isn't it? Is this the bride? Well, why not, in the name of all the demons?" He smelled of salt air and faintly of wine. She could not be offended by the embrace; it was as kindly and enthusiastic as a gust of the sea wind. "You'd like one as beautiful as this, wouldn't you, Aeneas, my friend?"

Kassandra could see that Aeneas' eyes rested on her with appreciation, and that Creusa was almost crying.

She pulled back from Odysseus, gently, and said, "Don't,

sir. I am not for any man; I am a virgin of Apollo Sun Lord, and content to be so."

"Hellfire!" His swearing was enormous as everything else about him. "What a waste, Beautiful! I'd marry you myself, except I have a wife already back in Ithaca, and Hera, my protecting Goddess, is a Goddess of marital fidelity; I'll have trouble with Her if I go sniffing round other women. Not that I haven't had my share; but I couldn't marry anyone else—and besides, you want some beautiful young fellow, not an old walrus like me." She giggled; with his huge mustaches, he really did look like a walrus.

"And this is Hector's bride?" he said, turning to Andromache. "Hector, you won't mind if an old man kisses your wife, will you? Customary in my part of the world, you know." He took Andromache by the arms, patted her bulging belly. "Can't get close enough to you now for a real kiss, can I, girl? Well, some other time, maybe." He kissed her smackingly on the cheek.

"I brought some things in my pack—loot from a Cretan ship: bride-gifts for your daughter, Priam, and gifts for that fine grandson this pretty girl here's going to give you in a few days— no? And since this one won't marry, I'll give gifts to the Sun Lord's Temple for her."

"In Apollo's name I thank you, sir," said Kassandra courteously, but Odysseus pulled her down to sit at his side.

"Here, sit beside me, drink from my cup; you're the only unattached girl here, and such flirting as I can do before your father and mother will do you no harm, hey?"

"My sister Polyxena is not married," Kassandra said with a glimmer of mischief, and Odysseus said, laughing, "Won't be long, if I know your father, my girl; Polyxena's pretty enough, but just between you and me, I like a girl with a little more meat on her bones. You'll do just fine."

She took his cup and mixed his wine, and when the servers went round, she filled his plate; she found herself feeling a kindly warmth for the old man.

Priam said, "Now tell us your news, Odysseus. And I need your advice, too, friend: I have had an offer for Polyxena from

Akhilles, son of Peleus. If you were in my place, would you accept? He is noble, and I hear that he is also brave—"

"Brave he certainly is," Odysseus said, "but he has no pleasure except in killing. If I had a daughter, I'd cut her throat before I married her off to that madman."

"He has the strength of Herakles—" Hector began.

"And many of his faults," Odysseus interrupted. "Like Herakles, he's no man for women; takes a fancy to one now and then and is likely to kill her in a moment of madness. I sailed with Herakles—just once. That was enough; I got tired of his moping over his boyfriends and his sudden rages. Akhilles is too like him for my taste. There are enough fine young men in Troy —or even fine honorable Akhaians, if that's what you want for her. She looks like a nice young girl; find her someone else. That's my best advice." Then he shouted to a servant and requested that his chests be brought into the hall, and from each of them he lifted out strange and beautiful things, presenting them lavishly to Priam and to his sons and daughters. For Hecuba there was a little cup, no larger than a closed fist, of beaten gold.

"From the House of the Bulls in Crete," he said. "I found it myself in the remains of what was once the Labyrinth; the Gods know how it escaped the earlier looters."

"Maybe some God preserved it for you."

"Maybe," said Odysseus. "See the bulls?"

Hecuba looked admiringly at the cup, then passed it round the admiring circle of women. Kassandra examined it in her turn, exclaiming over the finely chiseled carvings: a bull in nets as finely incised as thread, with young men in a chariot, and a cow to lure the bull.

"But this is a priceless treasure," she said; "you should keep this for your own wife."

"I have just as many fine things again," Odysseus said with great good nature, "for my wife and my son. Never think I would give away *all* my best."

For Andromache he had a golden comb, and for Creusa a bronze mirror with gold-washed beads about the edge.

"A mirror fit for Aphrodite herself," he said. "I got this when I spent the night in the cave of a sea-nymph. All night we loved, and when we parted in the morning she gave me this because she said she'd never look in it again if she wasn't beautiful enough for me to stay with her." He winked and said, "So now you're a bride and can make yourself beautiful for your husband."

Kassandra's gift was a necklace of blue beads which looked like glass, oblong in shape, and simply made, held by a plain gold clasp at the ends.

"It is a small thing," he said, "but I seem to remember that priestesses are not allowed to wear elaborate ornaments, and this is simple enough, perhaps, that you may wear it in memory of your father's old friend."

Touched by the words, Kassandra kissed him on the cheek as she would hardly have dared with her own father.

"I need no gifts to remember you, Odysseus; but I will wear this whenever I am permitted. Where was it made?"

"In Egypt, the land where Pharaoh rules, and the Kings build great tombs which make the whole city of Troy look like a little village," he said, and she was so accustomed already to his fantastic tales that she did not know for many years that for once he was speaking only the simple truth.

The gifts bestowed, he asked Priam, "When are you going to make me free of the straits, so that I can come and go without paying taxes like those other Akhaians?"

"You are certainly different from the others," Priam temporized, "and I would be ungrateful indeed if after so many gifts I should extort more from you, my friend. But I cannot allow anyone and everyone to travel through my waters. The tax I ask of you is only to tell me what is happening in the world faraway. Is there peace in the islands where those Akhaians reign?"

"There will be peace there, perhaps, when the sun rises in the west," Odysseus said. "As with Akhilles, the Kings think of warfare as their greatest pleasure. I will go to war only when my own lands and people are threatened; but they think of battle as a pastime more virtuous than any games . . . the great game at which they would gladly spend all their lives. They think me unmanly and cowardly that I have no love for fighting, though I am better at fighting than most of them."

"For years they have been trying to provoke us to war,"

Priam said, "but I have made a policy of ignoring insults and provocations, even when they stole my own sister. You live among the Akhaians, old friend; if they make war, will you too come against us?"

"I will try not to be drawn into any such war," Odysseus said. "I am bound by only one oath. When the woman who is now Queen of Sparta was wed, there were so many suitors that none of them would yield to another, and it looked as if only a war would settle the matter. Then it was I who created a compromise, and I am proud of it."

"What did you do?" Priam asked.

Odysseus grinned hugely. He said, "Picture this: perhaps the most beautiful woman who ever borrowed the girdle of Aphrodite, and so many men standing about calling out what gifts they would give to her father, and offering to fight for her, with the winner to take bride and dowry of Sparta . . . and I suggested that she herself choose, with all her suitors swearing an oath they would protect her choice."

"Whom did she choose?" asked Hecuba.

"Agamemnon's brother Menelaus—a poor thing; but perhaps she thought he was as wise and strong as his brother," Odysseus said. "Or perhaps it was just out of love for her sister, who had been married to Agamemnon the year before. Sisters marrying brothers . . . it creates confusion in the family, or so I should imagine."

"Yet if Aeneas had a brother, I should be willing to marry him," Polyxena whispered into Kassandra's ear, "if the brother had but half of his good looks and kindliness."

"So should I," Kassandra whispered back.

Hecuba murmured in a fussy voice, "It is rude to whisper, girls; speak to the company or be silent. Anything not fit to be said aloud is not fit to be said at all."

Kassandra was tired of her mother's strictures of courtesy. She said aloud, "I for one am not ashamed of what we were saying; we said only that either of us would willingly marry a brother to Aeneas, were the brother anything like him."

She was rewarded with a swift blazing look from Aeneas. He said, smiling, "Alas, daughter of Priam, I am my father's only son; but you make me wish I were twins or even triplets, for I would willingly share a marriage cup with all three of you. What about it, my lord?" he asked Priam. "Is it fitting for me to have as many wives as you do? If you are eager to marry off your daughters, I will gladly take all three of them, if Creusa gives me leave."

Polyxena dropped her eyes and blushed; Kassandra heard herself giggle. Creusa reddened and said, "I would rather be first and only wife; yet the law permits you to have as many wives as you will, my husband."

"Enough; this is no jest," Priam said. "A King's daughters, Son-in-Law, are not to be lesser wives or concubines."

Aeneas smiled in friendly fashion and said, "I meant your daughters no insult, sir," and Priam answered, gripping his hand in a friendly, somewhat drunken clasp, "I know that well; late in a banquet when the wine has been round a few times more than is wisest, jests far more unseemly than that may be forgiven. And now perhaps it is time for the women to take your bride away, before the party grows too rough for maiden ears."

Hecuba gathered the women together and they surrounded Creusa, with their torches, and Kassandra, whose voice was the clearest, led the wedding hymn. Creusa kissed her father and he laid her hand in Aeneas'; then the women led her up the stairs. Creusa, close to Kassandra, whispered, "Can you prophesy good fortune for my marriage, Sister?"

Kassandra pressed her hand and whispered, "I like your husband well; you heard me say I would gladly marry him myself. And such good fortune as may come to any marriage in this year will surely be yours; I see long life and good fame for your husband and for the son you will bear him."

Andromache touched Kassandra's shoulder and whispered, "Why had you no such prophecy for me, Kassandra? We have been friends, and I love you."

Kassandra turned to her friend and said gently, "I do not prophesy what I wish, Andromache, but what the Gods send me to say. If I could choose prophecy, I would wish you long life and honor, and many sons and daughters to surround you and Hector in your honorable old age on the throne of Troy."

And only the Gods know how much I wish that that had been the prophecy sent me. . . .

Andromache smiled and took Kassandra's hand.

"Perhaps, my dear, your goodwill may count for more than your prophecy," she said. "And can you see enough into the future to know how long before Hector's child is born—and if it is a son? My mother would have had me bring a daughter first into the light; but here Hector talks of nothing but his son, so I too wish for a boy—and will I live through childbirth to see his face?"

With enormous relief, Kassandra clasped her friend's slender fingers in hers.

"Oh, it is a boy," she said. "You will have a fine strong boy, and you will live to guide him toward manhood. . . ."

"Your words give me more courage," Andromache said, and Kassandra felt a catch in her throat, remembering the fires which had been all she could see at Andromache's wedding. *Perhaps,* she thought, *it was madness after all and not true prophecy; this is what my mother believed. I would rather be mad than believe, in this quiet place under these peaceful stars, that fire and disaster will fall on all of these I love.*

"Kassandra, you are daydreaming again; come and help us undress the bride," demanded Andromache. "We cannot undo these knots you have tied into Creusa's hair."

"I am coming," Kassandra said quickly, and went to help the other girls at making her half-sister ready for her husband's coming. With all her heart she was glad she had foreseen for them no disaster.

20

AFTER ALL the noise and excitement of the wedding the house of the God seemed even more silent and peaceful, more separated from the disturbances of ordinary life. Ten days after

Creusa's wedding, Kassandra was summoned again to a celebration at the palace: for the birth of a son to Hector and Andromache, Priam's first grandson.

"But it is not Priam's first grandson," Kassandra said. "There is Oenone's son by Paris."

"That's as may be," the messenger said, "but Priam chooses to call Hector's son his first grandson, and as far as I know, the King has the right to choose whom he'll name his next heir after Prince Hector."

This was true; but, Kassandra thought, it was hard on Oenone to see her son passed over as was his father.

She had come to treasure the peace and calm of the Temple and resented anything which broke into it, but she got leave to pay a visit to Andromache. She found her in the elaborate suite with the murals of sea-creatures, sitting propped up on pillows, the small red-faced baby in a wicker basket at her side. She looked healthy and blooming, with a good color in her cheeks, and Kassandra was relieved; so many women died in childbirth or soon after, but Andromache looked quite well.

"What is all this nonsense about *Hector's* son?" she asked, only half joking. "It was you who went to the trouble of carrying him for the best part of a year, and you who went through all the pain and fuss of birthing him. I would call him Andromache's son!"

Andromache grimaced, then giggled. "Maybe you have the best of it, being sworn to the God and forbidden to men! After all that, I am in no hurry to welcome Hector back to my bed. Childbirth is a much-overrated pastime; I would as soon wait a few years before I try it again. And they say women are too fragile to handle weapons for fear of wounds? I wonder how brave my dear Hector would have been in *this* battle!"

Then she chuckled. "Can't you hear it now?—we change all the customs, and bards will make ballads about the bravery of Hecuba, mother of Hector! Well, and why not?—she has triumphed in that battle at least a dozen times, which means she has more bravery than I ever hope to have! They tell us about the delights of marriage . . . every girl is brought up to think of nothing else; but the delights of childbearing we are left to discover for ourselves. Ah, well . . . " She leaned over, grimaced with the pain of movement and beckoned to one of the servants to put the baby into her arms; the look of delight on her face as she held him close belied her words. "I think," she said, "my prize of battle is worth more than the sack of a city!"

"Well, I should think so," said Kassandra, touching the tiny curled fist. "What will you call him?"

"Astyanax," said Andromache. "So Hector desires. Did you know that when he is carried down to the naming-feast, he will be laid in Hector's shield and carried that way? Imagine it— what a cradle!"

Kassandra tried to visualize the infant laid at the center of Hector's great war-shield. Suddenly she shuddered and went rigid, seeing the great shield, and the child—how old was he? Surely too young for a warrior!—the child's broken body laid out as for burial. It was like a wave of icy water; but Andromache, happily holding her baby at her breast, did not see.

Kassandra closed her eyes in hopes that that would drive the bloody sight away. "How is it," she asked, "with Creusa?"

"She seems happy; she says she cannot wait to be pregnant. Shall I tell her all of what lies in store for her?"

"Don't be unkind," said Kassandra. "Let her enjoy her first happiness; there will be time enough for everything else later."

"You are right; there are enough old witches who try to spoil everything for young brides by warning them of everything in store for them in the fullness of years," Andromache agreed. "And no matter what, I would not have wanted to miss my little darling." She buried her lips in the baby's soft neck, and snuffled at him ecstatically. As when she had seen Phyllida holding her child, Kassandra was touched and almost envious.

"Is there any other news?"

"Yes; the ship of Paris has been sighted; a runner from the mountain lookout came to tell the King so," said Andromache. "Paris is your twin, but I do not think him so much like you."

"I am told we are much alike in looks," Kassandra said, hesitating. "I do not think we are much alike otherwise. There are some who think him the handsomest man in Troy."

Andromache said lightly, stroking Kassandra's hand, "I am

not among them, of course; for me no man is the equal of Hector, whether in looks or otherwise."

This pleased Kassandra; she felt herself responsible for this marriage and rejoiced that Andromache was content with her husband. And Hector had no reason to be dissatisfied either.

"And everyone thinks you beautiful," Andromache went on, "but I do not think your face would well suit a man: it is too delicate. I do not remember that you were as like as that; is he so girlish, then?"

"I don't think so, and surely he is manly enough, for he won so many events at the Games," Kassandra said. "He is a fine archer and athlete and wrestler, and a very devil in a chariot. But I think," she added with a touch of mischief, "if we were matched on the field, he would be no better warrior than I."

"My mother said," Andromache remarked, "that you had the soul of a great warrior in the body of a field mouse."

Kassandra giggled, and put her face down to the baby Astyanax; she felt she had somehow wronged him in giving way to her visions.

"May all the Gods bless him, and you too, my dear," she said.

"Will you not stay to drink to his good fortune at the naming-feast?"

"No, I think not," Kassandra said. "I will come home, perhaps, for a day or two when Paris returns. For now I will go and embrace my mother, and then return to the Temple."

She took an affectionate farewell of Andromache, knowing that she was closer to her than to Polyxena or any of her half-sisters, and went briefly to Hecuba for her blessing. Then she went to the simple rooms at the back of the house where Oenone dwelt with a couple of servants, quiet girls who had been, she knew, votaries of the River God.

Oenone was curled up in a hammock nursing her son; Kassandra came and embraced her, aware of the woman's fragility; it was Oenone, she thought, and not herself, who had the spirit of a warrior in the body of a field mouse. Oenone seemed so delicate that she would break at a touch.

"Are you well, my sister?" Kassandra asked, using the word

deliberately. She was certainly fonder of Oenone than of Creusa or even Polyxena. But when she was close to her she felt again that disturbing impulse to caress the girl, and because she did not know whether this was her own emotion or Paris', it made her diffident and shy with Oenone.

"I would have come to visit you when I was here for Creusa's wedding, my dear; but they told me you were not well enough for guests," she said.

Oenone smiled and said, "Well, now that Andromache's son is born and Hector's place is secure, I need not fear for *my* son."

Kassandra was shocked. "Surely there is no need to fear for him—"

"To be certain, I hope there is not," Oenone said, "but Hector managed to be rid of Paris, and I do not think he welcomes Paris' son or has any reason to love him."

"I think surely you misjudge Hector," Kassandra said. "He has never shown any jealousy of Paris—not to me."

Oenone laughed and said, "Oh, Kassandra, I do not think you know how much everyone values your good opinion and wishes to show you only a very best side. If Hector felt so, you would be the last to know."

Kassandra blushed. To turn the conversation aside, she picked up the baby and dandled him in her arms. "He is pretty," she said. "Is he like his father, do you think, or like you?"

"It is too soon to tell," Oenone said. "I should hope he would be like my own father, true and honorable."

Kassandra sensed the disappointment in the words, more strongly perhaps than even Oenone herself knew. She said, "He may well be like *you*; and then none can question his goodness."

"Only time will tell whether he or Hector's son would have been better fitted to rule over this city; but I truly rejoice that he will bear no such burden or such fate."

Kassandra said quickly, "Oenone, never envy the fate of Hector's son."

"What have you seen?" Oenone asked apprehensively. "No, do not tell me; I heard what you prophesied at Andromache's wedding. I wish for no such blessing on my son . . . Paris' son."

"Yes, I was talking about that with Andromache," said Kassandra. "At least, among the Amazons a son may bear his mother's name; Hector would be son of Hecuba—"

"And my child son of Oenone, not son of Paris of the house of Priam," said Oenone. "Fair enough; yet in your city, only the son of a harlot bears the name of his mother and not of his father."

Kassandra said gently, "None could call you so, Oenone, and so I would bear witness." Yet the words were meaningless, for she had no power to change matters; Andromache had been pledged to Hector before all of the city, whereas Oenone, it appeared, was Paris' wife only in that she had accepted him with her father's blessing.

"Oenone, who was your mother?"

"I never knew her name," Oenone said. "Father told me she died young. She too was one of the priestesses of the River God's shrine."

Yes; women who bear the children of Gods are more nameless even than the children of men. She kissed Oenone and promised to send her son a gift.

On the way back to the Sun Lord's house, Kassandra had much to think about. If there were men like Aeneas in the world, there might be others she would be willing to marry.

One morning she was in Phyllida's room, holding the fair-haired baby while the young mother folded an armful of freshly washed diapers and blankets. She had taken off the baby's swaddling bands so that he could kick freely and was holding the small chubby feet in her hands, admiring the soft perfection of the tiny toes and nails, putting her face down to the little feet to kiss them and caress them with her lips. She blew into the middle of his soft belly to make him laugh, and laughed herself. At this moment she was almost wishing she had her own baby to play with, though she was by no means interested in any of the preliminaries necessary for getting one.

Phyllida came and bent to reclaim her son, but Kassandra clung to him.

"He likes me," she said proudly. "I think he knows who I am—don't you, Beautiful?"

"Why should he not?" Phyllida said. "You are always ready to cuddle and spoil him when I am too busy to give him all the attention he wants."

Hearing his mother's voice, the baby began to squall and reach toward her.

"He is hungry," said Phyllida with resignation, beginning to unfasten her tunic at the neck. "And that you cannot do for me, I fear."

"I would if I could," said Kassandra, barely above a whisper.

"I know," Phyllida said, settling down with the baby at her breast.

Watching her with the child, Kassandra felt the dark waters of a vision rise and subside.

"Kassandra, why will you not tell me what you see?" Phyllida asked, staring at her fearfully.

Kassandra was silent.

This morning I have held in my arms three babes and have seen no future for any of them; what does this mean? Perhaps that I am to die and can see no future because I shall not be here to see any of them grow to manhood? If only I thought it was as simple as that . . . If I thought it was only that, I would fling myself from the heights of the city before this day's sun had set.

But that was not her destiny; a fate was approaching her, and she must live to behold it and to endure it.

She bent to kiss Phyllida and the baby too and said, not answering directly, "We must all bear our fate; you and I and the baby too. Believe me, knowing a fate makes it no easier to endure."

"I don't understand you," Phyllida said.

"I don't understand myself," Kassandra said, and went out into the courtyard of the Temple, overlooking the sea. She saw a ship there. . . . Yes, Andromache had said Paris' ship had been sighted.

It was no part of her duty to welcome Paris to the city; but something stronger than duty drew her downward.

As Kassandra walked down the long street, she saw processions forming at the ships, readying to approach the palace, and another procession coming slowly from the palace down to the shore.

Paris was driving his chariot—no doubt he had had it unloaded first so that he could make an impressive entrance to the city, in contrast to his unheralded entry to the games. Beside him in the chariot was a female figure, her identity concealed by a long veil.

Had Paris succeeded, then, in having Hesione returned to Troy? Kassandra quickened her pace slightly so that she emerged from the city gates just as Paris pulled up before them. At the same time, Priam and Hecuba, riding in Priam's best ceremonial chariot, drew up facing him. Hector stood a pace behind his father, looking something less than pleased, and Kassandra looked about for Andromache. Surely her friend would not want to miss all this excitement? She looked up at Andromache's window and saw her sitting there, with Oenone standing beside her, each with her son in her arms. Even at this distance she could see that Oenone was clutching the side of the window, white-knuckled.

Paris descended from the chariot and turned to lift down the veiled woman; then he bowed low before Priam, who raised him and embraced him.

"Welcome home, my son." He extended a hand in welcome to the veiled woman, who stood motionless beside the chariot. "You have succeeded in your mission, my son?"

"Beyond our wildest hopes."

Hector tried to look pleased. "Then you have brought Hesione back to us, my brother?"

"Not so," said Paris. "My King and my father, I bring back a prize far greater than that for which you sent me."

He brought the lady forward and pulled back her veil. Kassandra gasped: the woman was beautiful beyond imagining.

She was tall and exquisitely formed, with hair as fine and yellow as the best beaten gold; her features were like chiseled marble, and her eyes the blue of the depths of a stormy sky.

"I present to you Helen of Sparta, who has consented to become my wife."

Kassandra raised her eyes to the window where Oenone

pressed a trembling hand to her mouth, then whirled and was gone, leaving Andromache staring after her in dismay. Paris glanced upward; Kassandra could not guess whether he had seen Oenone's swift retreat.

He turned quickly back to Helen, who prompted him in a whisper; then he turned again to Priam.

"Will you welcome my lady to Troy, Father?"

Priam opened his mouth, but it was Hecuba's voice that was heard first.

"If she is here of her free will, she is welcome," the old Queen said. "Troy will give no countenance to the stealing and ravishing of women; else we should be no better than that vicious man who stole Hesione from us. And speaking of Hesione, where is she? Your mission, my son, was to return Hesione to our family; in that, at least, it seems you have failed. Lady Helen, have you come here willingly?"

Helen of Sparta smiled and touched her shining hair. It was long and loose, as only young virgins wore it in Troy, like a shining veil hardly paler than the fillet of gold which held it back from her forehead. She wore a tunic of the finest linen from the country of the Pharaohs, and her waist, which was narrow, was encircled with a girdle of disks of beaten gold inlaid with circles of lapis lazuli which echoed the color of her eyes.

Her body was full, deep-breasted, with long legs whose shape was just perceptible beneath the loose folds of the linen. When she spoke, her voice was deep and soft.

"I beg you, Lady of Troy, give me welcome and harbor here; the Goddess Herself gave me to your son, and She Herself could know no more of love than I have for him."

"But you have a husband already," said Priam hesitantly, "or did we hear falsely that you were wed to Menelaus of Sparta?"

It was Paris who replied, "She was given to him unlawfully. Menelaus was a usurper who took the lady for her lands. Sparta is Helen's own city by mother-right; her mother Leda held it, from her mother before her and her grandmother. Her father—"

"Is no father of mine," Helen interrupted. "My father was

Zeus Thunderer, not that usurper who seized my mother's city by force of arms and wed an unwilling Queen."

Priam was still suspicious. "I know little of the Thunderer," he said. "He is not worshiped here in Troy. And we are not stealers of women—"

"My lord," Helen interrupted him, advancing to Priam and taking his hand with a gesture that seemed bold to Kassandra, "I beg you in the name of the Lady to extend me protection and the hospitality of Troy. For your son's sake, I have made myself an exile among the Akhaians who have conquered my home. Would you send me back to be outcast among them?"

Priam looked into the lovely eyes, and for the first time Kassandra saw the effect Helen always had upon strangers; there was a sort of melting in his face. He swallowed and looked at her again.

"That seems reasonable," he said, but even in so short a sentence he had to breathe twice. "The hospitality of Troy has never been appealed to in vain. Surely we cannot return her to a husband who has taken her by force—"

Kassandra could keep silent no longer. She cried out, "Now, there, at least, she lies; do you not remember how Odysseus told us that she herself chose Menelaus from more than two dozen suitors, and made the others swear to defend her chosen husband against anyone who refused to accept her choice?

"Father, have nothing to do with this woman! It is she who will bring ruin and disaster on our city and our world! What does she really want here?"

Helen's lovely mouth opened in surprise; she made a cry—like a stricken animal, thought Kassandra, hardening herself not to feel sorry for the Spartan Queen.

Paris looked at Kassandra with angry distaste.

"I have always known you were mad," he said. "My lady, I beg you to take no notice of her; she is my twin sister, whom the Gods have stricken with madness, and the deluded think her a prophetess. She speaks of nothing but ruin and death for Troy, and now she has chosen to think you the cause."

Helen's wide eyes rested on Kassandra.

"What a pity that one so beautiful should suffer madness."

"I pity her," said Paris, "but we need not listen to her ravings. Can you sing no other song, Kassandra? We have all heard this one before, and we are all weary of it."

Kassandra clenched her fists. "Father," she appealed, "see reason, at least. Whether I am mad or not, what has that to do with what Paris has done? Paris cannot marry this woman; for she has a husband, whom dozens of witnesses saw her marry of her free will, and Paris has a wife. Or have you forgotten Oenone?"

"Who is Oenone?" asked Helen.

"She is no one who need ever trouble you, my beloved," Paris said, gazing into Helen's eyes. "She is a priestess of the local River God, Scamander, and I loved her for a time; but she went forever from my mind on the day I first looked on your face."

"She is the mother of your firstborn son, Paris," Kassandra said. "Do you dare deny that?"

"I do deny it," said Paris. "The priestesses of Scamander take lovers where they choose; how do I know who fathered the child she bore? Why do you think I did not take her in marriage?"

"Wait," Hecuba said. "We accepted Oenone because she bore your child . . ."

Oenone was good enough for the wife of a shepherd, son of Agelaus, but not highborn enough for Priam's son, Kassandra thought. She said aloud, "If you abandon Oenone, you are a fool and a villain. But whatever he may do, Father, I beg you to have nothing to do with this Spartan woman. For I can tell you now that it will bring down war, at least, on this city—"

"Father," Paris said, "will you listen to this madwoman rather than to your son? For I tell you now, if you refuse shelter to the wife the Gods have given to me, I shall go from Troy and never return."

"No!" cried Hecuba in despair. "Don't say that, my son! I lost you once . . ."

Priam said, looking troubled, "I want no quarrel with Menelaus' brother. Hector," he appealed, "what say you?"

Hector stepped forward and looked into Helen's eyes; and Kassandra saw in dismay that he too succumbed to her beauty. Could no man look at Helen and retain his reason? "Well, Father," Hector said, "it seems to me that you already have a quarrel with Agamemnon; have you forgotten he still holds Hesione? And we can always say that we hold her as hostage for Hesione's return. Are we nothing but a field from which these Akhaians steal women and cattle? I welcome you to Troy, Lady Helen—Sister," he said, holding out his hand and enclosing her small fingers in his big ones, "and I pledge to you that an enemy to Helen of Sparta is an enemy to Hector of Troy and all his kin. Will that content you, my brother?"

"If you take her into this city, it is you who are mad, my father!" Kassandra cried out. "Can you not even see the fire and death she brings in her train? Will you set all Troy ablaze because one man has no loyalty and desires another man's wife?" She had resolved to remain calm and sensible, but as she felt the dark waters rise to take her by the throat, she shrieked in dismay.

"No! No, I beg you, Father . . ."

Priam stepped back up into his chariot.

"I have tried to be patient with you, girl; but I have no more patience now. Get you back to the Sun Lord's house—He is the patron God of the demented; and pray to Him for kindlier visions. As for me, let it never be said that Priam of Troy refused hospitality to a woman who came to him as suppliant."

"Oh, Gods," she cried, "can you not even see? Are you all besotted with this woman? Mother, can't you see what she has done to my father, my brothers?"

Hector stepped forward and dragged Kassandra, protesting, out of the path of the chariots. "Don't stand here wailing," he said good-naturedly. "Calm yourself, Bright Eyes. Suppose it really does come to war with the Akhaian crew? Do you think we couldn't send them yelping back to those goat pastures they call their native land? War would mean disaster not to Troy, but to our enemies." His voice was compassionate. She flung her head back and gave a long wail of dismay and despair.

"Poor girl," Helen said, stepping toward her, "why have you

chosen to hate me? You are the sister of my beloved; I am ready to love you as a sister."

Kassandra jerked away from Helen's outstretched hands; she felt that she would fall down and vomit if the woman actually touched her. She stared up at Priam in anguish.

"Oh, why will you not listen to me? Can you not see what this will mean? It is not man alone but the Gods who struggle here—and no man can live when there is war among the Immortals," she wailed. "And yet you say it is I who am mad! Your madness is worse than mine, I tell you!" She whirled and ran toward the palace.

Her heart was pounding as if she had run all the way from the Sun Lord's house; she felt sick and shaking, and it seemed that she was running through flames that rose around her, engulfing all the palace in the smell of burning, the smoke . . . When hands touched her, she shrieked in terror and tried to pull away; but the hands held her tightly, and in a moment she was wrapped in loving arms. The darkness rolled away; there was no fire. She gazed in confusion into Andromache's dark eyes.

"Kassandra, my dearest! What ails you?"

Kassandra, jolted out of the nightmare but not yet fully aware of what was happening or where she was, could only stare, unable to speak.

"Sister, you are exhausted; you have been too long in the sun," Andromache said. She put her arms around Kassandra and led her into the cool, shadowed room.

"Oh, if it were only no worse than that," Kassandra gasped as Andromache pushed her down onto a bench with soft cushions, and held a cool cup of water to her lips. "Don't you think I would rather believe myself mad, or sun-smitten, if it meant I need not see what I have seen?"

"I believe you," Andromache said. "I do not think you mad; but I do not believe your visions either."

"Do you think I would invent such a thing? How wicked you must think me!" Kassandra cried out indignantly. Andromache held her close in an affectionate embrace.

"No, Sister; I believe that the Gods have tormented you

with false visions," she said. "No one could believe you malicious enough to pretend such things. But my dear, listen to
reason. Our city is strong and well defended; we have no lack of
warriors or weapons, or if it came to that, of allies; if the Akhaians should be fools enough to come chasing after this bitch in
heat instead of saying 'Good riddance to a very nasty piece of
rubbish,' why should you think they would not get more from
Troy than they ever bargained for?"

Kassandra could see the good sense in that; but she
moaned, clutching at her heart.

"Yes, Hector said something like that," she murmured,
"but . . ." She heard herself crying again, "It is the Immortals
who are angry with us!" She fought desperately to bring herself
up out of the dark waters.

"At least you know she is no more than a bitch in heat,"
she said at last.

"Oh, yes; I saw the looks she cast on Hector and even on
your father," Andromache said. "And it may well be that she is
a curse sent to our city by one of the Immortals; but if it is Their
will, we cannot avoid it."

Kassandra rocked to and fro in misery; Andromache's quiet
words and acceptance filled her with despair.

"Do you truly believe that the Gods would stoop to fight
against a mortal city? What reason could They have? We are not
wicked or impious; we have not angered any God."

"Perhaps," said Andromache, "the Gods do not need reasons for what They do."

"If the Gods are not just," Kassandra said, weeping, "what
hope is there for us?"

As if in a blaze she saw the face of the Beautiful One, the
Goddess who had tempted Paris successfully.

I will give you the most beautiful woman in the world. . . .

As she had thought then, she thought again: *But he already
has a woman!*

She raised her face to Andromache.

"Where did Oenone go?"

"I did not see; I thought perhaps she went to care for her
child. . . ."

"No; she saw Paris with Helen and ran away," Kassandra said. "I will go to her."

"I cannot see why Paris would desert her even for Helen, beautiful as she is," said Andromache—"unless some Goddess has ordained it."

"Such an unjust Goddess I would never serve," Kassandra said bitterly.

Andromache covered her ears with her hands. "Oh, don't say that," she implored. "That is blasphemy; we are all subject to the Immortals . . ."

Kassandra raised the unfinished cup and drained it; but her hands were shaking and she almost dropped it.

"I will go and speak with Oenone," she said, rising.

"Yes," Andromache urged, "go and tell her we love her and we will never accept that Spartan in her place, were she Aphrodite Herself."

Though Kassandra searched the palace everywhere, Oenone was nowhere to be found; nor was she ever again seen in Priam's house. At last, hearing the royal party on the stairs—making ready, she thought, to solemnize Paris' wedding, which, since Oenone was not there to protest it, could not be prevented —she left the palace and returned quietly to the Sun Lord's house. She had no wish to hear wedding hymns sung for Helen when they had been denied Oenone. She would have been willing to rebuke them in the name of any God, if a God had spoken to her; but nothing happened, and she had no wish to make a further spectacle of herself crying out the death and disaster that she could not but see.

VOLUME TWO——————————————

APHRODITE'S
GIFT

1

KASSANDRA SPOKE to no one, either in the Sun Lord's house or elsewhere, of Helen or Paris; but she should have known that such news would never be kept silent. Before three days had elapsed, Helen's story, and Kassandra's prophecy, were on every tongue in Troy.

There were even those who, seeing Helen's beauty, believed, or said they believed, that the Akhaian Goddess of Love and Beauty, Aphrodite, had come Herself to the city. Kassandra, if asked about this, said only that Helen was indeed very beautiful—beautiful enough to turn the head of any mortal man—and that in her own country she was believed to have been fathered by an Immortal.

She did not know or care whether anyone believed this; her own worry now was for Oenone. She hoped that the girl had simply taken her child and returned to the Temple of Scamander; but she did not believe it. At the back of her mind was the haunting fear that Oenone had somehow chosen to sacrifice herself and her son to the River God. If Aphrodite was indeed a Goddess of Love, why had She not chosen to guard the love between Oenone and Paris?

She wondered about this Goddess Aphrodite, who put such temptation into the hearts of men—and women too; it was not only that Paris had chosen and could not resist Helen, but Helen too, though Queen of Sparta by mother-right, had chosen to give herself to Paris—after having chosen her husband, as few women in the Akhaian world could do. If I were Queen, she thought, I should choose to be like Imandra and reign alone, taking no consort.

The Goddesses of Troy and of Colchis were sensible Goddesses, who ackowledged the primacy of the earth and of motherhood; but this Goddess who disrupted all things for a whim they called love—no, this was no Goddess she could ever consent to serve. And then one night she dreamed she stood in a strange Temple before this Akhaian Goddess who looked very much like the Spartan Queen.

So you have sworn you will not serve Me, Kassandra of Troy? Yet you have given your life to the service of the Immortals. . . .

Kassandra half knew that she was dreaming; she looked up toward the Goddess and saw that She was even more beautiful than the Spartan Helen, and for a moment it seemed that in Aphrodite's face was the half-forgotten beauty of the vision of Apollo Sun Lord. Could she resist the call of that love?

"I am sworn to serve the Mother of All," she said. "You are not She, and You have no part in Her worship; for You are denying Her, I think."

Faraway laughter sounded like a chiming of bells.

You too will serve Me in the end, Priam's daughter. I have more power than you, and more than the ordinary Goddesses of your cities. All women here shall worship Me, and you too.

Kassandra cried out, "No!" and woke with a start, to find her room empty and only the bright face of the sun at her window, like a mockery of the beauty she had seen.

How strange these Akhaians were; first they chose to worship a Goddess of marriage who would punish any woman for straying outside it; and then they chose a Goddess of passionate love who would tempt a woman to forsake the vows she had sworn. It was as if the Akhaians both feared and desired faithlessness in their wives—or perhaps they only wished an excuse for abandoning them.

Perhaps it was better that a child belong only to his mother. Maybe marriage and fatherhood were not good for men. A woman must care about the welfare of the child she had carried in her body, but siring children came too easily to men; they were pawns to be used for their fathers' advantage. Perhaps Phyllida had the best bargain after all; a God could have as many wives as He wished and need not cast off the old when He chose the new.

This thought reminded Kassandra that she had duties in the Temple; and while she had sworn never to serve Aphrodite, she had taken an oath to serve the Sun Lord. She should go down and join the other priestesses and priests for the sunrise greeting.

They were already gathered there, from the venerable elder healer-priests to the youngest novices; she was almost the last to take her place, and Charis gave her a patient, reproving glance. The chief priest regarded them all, and said, "In the name of the Sun Lord, I ask you to welcome a newcomer among us. He served the shrine on Delos, the Sun Lord's own isle. Give welcome to our brother, who is called Khryse."

He was well named Khryse: *golden*. He was unusually tall; almost as tall as Hector, although not so muscular or well-built. His fine features were covered all over with a fine dusting of freckles; his hair shone all the fairer because he was sun-bronzed. His smile was radiant, showing even white teeth, and his eyes a bright sea-blue.

When he spoke, his voice was strong and vibrant, with resonant echoes which strongly reminded Kassandra of the times she had heard the voice of the God. *Well has he chosen a God to serve*, she thought. *Of such a mortal might the Sun Lord well be jealous.*

"Whose duty is it today," Charis asked, "to receive and tally the offerings?"

Kassandra, recalled to her obligations, started and said, "It is mine."

"Then you will take our brother to the court and show him how they are bestowed."

Kassandra lowered her eyes shyly, almost as if she felt Khryse might read her thoughts, which, it seemed to her, were too bold.

"I thank you for this welcome," Khryse said; "but if I might first ask a favor of you, Lady . . ."

"Certainly you may ask," said Kassandra sharply when it became obvious that Charis was not going to answer. "But I can promise nothing till I know what it is you wish."

He raised his eyes so that he spoke to all of them.

"I would ask you to give shelter here to my daughter, who

is motherless," he said, and beckoned forth a young girl who was hiding among the shrubbery at the edge of the court.

At first Kassandra thought she was about eleven years old. She wore a ragged and outgrown tunic which came hardly below her knees, and her hair, the same astonishing golden color as her father's, hung in a tangled matted mass halfway to her waist.

"I have been traveling for a long time, and it is hard for a man alone to care properly for a woman-child," Khryse said, following Kassandra's eyes. "May she live here in the Sun Lord's house?"

"Certainly," Charis said, "but she is too young to be chosen as one of Apollo's maidens; time enough when she is grown to choose that path for herself if she wishes. But for now—Kassandra, will you take the child away and be certain she is properly cared for?"

"Then I shall be twice grateful to the Lady Kassandra," said Khryse, bowing and smiling at her. Trying not to look at Khryse again, she stretched out her hand to the girl.

"Come with me, dear. Are you hungry?"

"Yes; but Father said I was not to ask for anything."

"Well, you shall be fed; no one goes hungry in the God's house," Kassandra said, and leading the girl to her own room, she called a servant and asked her to bring bread and wine and a basket of fruit.

"First you must have a bath and some fresh clothes," she said, for the girl's garment was filthy as well as ragged. With the help of one of the governesses, she bathed the girl. As she was soaping the small body, she realized the child was not nearly as young as she looked; her breasts were already well formed, and there was a tangle of golden hair at her crotch. Washed clean of the dirt of the roads, she had her father's beauty, and Kassandra, asking her name, was not surprised to hear the answer:

"My mother named me Helike at birth; but Father has always called me Chryseis."

Golden. "The name suits you well," Kassandra said, "especially if your hair were not so tangled."

"I suppose it will have to be cut off," Chryseis said.

"Oh, no, that would be a shame," Kassandra exclaimed. "It is far too lovely for that." She took a comb and carefully teased out the worst of the tangles; two or three of them indeed were beyond unraveling and she had to cut them. Brushed till it was smooth and glowing, the shining hair curled over the girl's shoulders. When she was dressed in the white novice's robe, with a woven girdle of silk, one of Kassandra's own, tied about her waist, Chryseis touched it with awed fingers.

"I have never worn anything so pretty!"

"Now you look worthy to be one of the maidens of the Sun Lord," Kassandra said. "Lord Apollo will be pleased with you, as He would not be with a dirty child."

The girl still looked half starved; her hands trembled as she attacked the bread and grapes, as if she had eaten nothing for days, though Kassandra could see that she was trying to restrain herself and show good manners. She thanked Kassandra with tears in her eyes.

"While we were traveling, Father was sometimes fed at the shrines," she said, "but he did not want strange men to see me." Then, lest she seem to criticize her father, she added, "He saved something for me whenever he could."

Against her will, Kassandra was touched.

"If the governesses give leave, you may sleep in my room and I will look after you."

Chryseis smiled shyly. "And will I have duties in the Temple too?"

"Of course; no one is idle in the God's house," Kassandra said, "but until we find what you are skilled to do, we will give you such tasks as are suitable for your age." She turned to the governess. "Take her to Phyllida," she suggested, "and let her help look after the baby."

It was still early in the day when she returned to the court where Charis and Khryse were waiting for her. The old priestess was helping him to tally the offerings left in the Temple court during the night, offerings left from simple piety by citizens who had no special petitions to ask. They were making marks on tally-sticks: one mark for a jar of oil or wine, another for a tray of flat cakes, yet another for the pair of pigeons in a woven reed cage. She told them what arrangements she had made for the child.

"That was sensible," said Charis; "she'll come to no harm rocking the baby, and it will free Phyllida to return to her own duties."

"I cannot tell you my gratitude," Khryse said. "It is all but impossible for a man to care for a girl-child; if she had been a boy I might have managed it. When she was very small, it was simpler; now she is all but grown, I must watch her night and day. Among the Sun Lord's virgins I need not fear for her."

"We will certainly guard her maidenhood for you," said Charis; "but is that so important just now? I thought she was only about eleven years old."

"So did I," Kassandra said, "but when I bathed her, I saw she was older than that."

Khryse considered.

"Her mother died ten years ago," he said, "and I am sure she was not three years old. Four months ago womanhood came on her, and I did not even know what to say to a girl. It was then I decided I must leave my wandering life and settle somewhere so that she could be properly cared for. On the road I could not even keep her fed, and she was too pretty for me to let her go out as a beggar."

"Poor motherless child," Kassandra said. "I will care for her as if she were my own."

"You have no children of your own, Lady?"

"No," Kassandra said; "I am a virgin of Apollo."

She felt herself blushing at the look he gave her and said quickly, "They are beginning to bring in offerings and to consult the shrine; I must go and be ready to speak with them."

The first man had brought an offering of a jar of good wine; he asked, "Priestess, I wish to ask the God how I can get my sister well married; my father is dead, and I have been away from my village for many years serving in my King's army."

Kassandra had been asked similar questions many times; she went into the shrine and dutifully repeated the question. She did not believe it was important enough for the God to answer; nevertheless, she waited several minutes in case He had something to say. Then she returned to the waiting man and said, "Go to your father's oldest friend and ask for his advice out of friendship for your father; and forget not to give him a generous gift."

The man's face brightened.

"I am grateful to the God for His advice," he said, and Kassandra nodded to him courteously, holding herself back by force from saying, *If you had used what wit the God saw fit to give you, you would have saved yourself the trouble of coming here; but since any sensible person could have given you such an answer, we might as well have a gift for it.*

Later when Khryse asked her, "How do you know what to answer? I find it hard to believe a God would trouble Himself with such matters," she told him that the priests had worked out proper answers to the commonest questions.

"But never forget to be silent for a few moments, in case the God has another answer to be given. Even the most foolish questions—from our point of view—the God sometimes sees fit to answer," she warned him.

After a little, another man came, carrying a great basket of excellent melons, and asked, "What shall I plant in my south field this year?"

"Has there been fire or flood or any great change on your land?"

"No, Lady."

She went into the shrine, sitting for a moment before the great statue of the Sun Lord, remembering how the first time she saw it as a child she had thought it a living man. When the God did not speak to her she returned and said, "Plant the crop you planted there three years ago."

This answer could do no possible harm; if he had been rotating his crops as the headmen of most villages now advised, it would not conflict with their advice, and if he had not, it would make things no worse. As he thanked her, she felt the common exasperation; this was the safe answer for any farmer in any year, and she felt he should have known it without asking. But they would all enjoy the melons, anyway.

The morning went slowly, with only one question that gave

her a moment's thought; a man brought a fine kid as an offering, and said that his wife had just borne a fine son.

"And you wish to give thanks to the Sun Lord?"

The man shifted his feet uneasily, like a guilty child.

"Well, not exactly," he muttered. "I wish to know if this child is mine, or has my wife been unfaithful to me?"

This was the question Kassandra always most dreaded; her year among the Amazons had taught her that a man's suspicion of a woman usually meant that he did not feel himself worthy of a woman's regard.

Yet she accepted the offering calmly and went into the shrine. Sometimes this question was actually answered, apparently at random, *If you are not certain, expose the child at once.* But there was no answer, so she gave the suitable answer for such occasions. "If you can trust your wife in other ways, there is no reason to doubt her in this."

The man looked enormously relieved, and Kassandra sighed and told him, "Go home now, and thank the Goddess for your son, and forget not to make apology to your wife for doubting her without reason."

"I will, Lady," he promised, and Kassandra, seeing that there were no other petitioners awaiting consultation, turned to say to Khryse, "At this hour we should now close the shrine, and rest until the sun begins to decline; it is the custom to take a little bread and fruit before we return to see anyone who comes."

He thanked her and added, "The Lady Charis told me you are the second daughter of King Priam and of his Queen. You are nobly born, and as beautiful as Aphrodite; how is it that you serve here in the shrine when every prince and nobleman on this coast and southward to Crete must have been seeking you in marriage?"

"Oh, not so many as that," she said, laughing nervously. "In my case, the Sun Lord called me to His service when I was younger than your daughter."

He looked skeptical. "He called you? How?"

"You are a priest," she said. "Surely He has spoken to you."

"I have had no such fortune, Lady," he said. "I think the

Immortals speak only to the great. My father—he was a poor man—pledged me to the God's service when my elder brother was spared from the fever which raged in Mykenae a score of years ago. He thought it a fair bargain; my brother was a warrior, and I, he said, fit for nothing."

"That was not right," Kassandra said vehemently. "A son is not a slave."

"Oh, I was willing enough," Khryse said. "I had no talent for becoming a warrior."

Kassandra laughed a little. "Strange; surely you are stronger than I, and I was a warrior for a year among the Amazons."

"I have heard of the women warriors," he said, "and I have heard also that they kill their lovers and their boy children."

"Not so," she said, "but men dwell apart from women there; male children are sent to their fathers as soon as they are weaned from the breast."

"And had you a lover when you dwelt among them, beautiful Amazon?"

"No," she said softly. "As I told you, I am sworn as a virgin to the Sun Lord."

"It seems a pity," Khryse said, "that so beautiful a lady should grow old unloved."

"You need not pity me," Kassandra said indignantly. "I am well content with no lover."

"That seems to me the pity of it," Khryse said. "You are a princess, and beautiful, and you are kind, too—so you showed yourself to my daughter; yet you live alone here and give yourself to these wretched petitioners and serve here as any lowborn maiden might do . . ."

Abruptly he pulled her close to him and kissed her; startled, she tried to push him away, but he held her so tightly she could not escape. Her mouth was surprised at the warmth of his lips.

"I mean you no dishonor," he whispered. "I would be your lover—or your husband, if you would have me."

She pulled away frantically and ran from the room, flying up the stairs as if pursued by demons, her heart pounding and the sound of her own blood beating in her ears. In Phyllida's room she found Chryseis rocking the baby and singing to him in a small, thin voice. Phyllida was sleeping, but she sat up as Kassandra burst into the room.

Kassandra had been ready to pour out the whole story; but looking at Chryseis, she thought: *If I complain of him they will send him away; and then this child will be again at the mercy of the chances of the road.*

So she said only, "My head aches from the sun; Phyllida, will you exchange duties with me this afternoon, and take the offerings in the shrine, if I care for the baby? I can send someone to fetch you when he needs to be fed."

Phyllida agreed gladly, saying she was weary of staying indoors with the child, and it was really time he should be weaned anyhow. When she had gone, Kassandra put the baby to play in the sunshine, and sat down to think about what had happened to her.

She had panicked foolishly, she was sure; no priest of Apollo would have raped her in the God's shrine.

Surely he had meant no real harm; she had felt no such revulsion as against the tribesman who had tried to ravish her when she rode with the Amazon band. If she had not run away, what *would* he have said or done? She would not have wanted to kill him; but would he have pushed matters that far?

She did not really want to know; she liked Khryse, and felt no real anger, only a sense of helplessness. *This was not for her.* She felt within herself the surge of dark waters, and knew this was not what the Goddess willed for her, either.

2

FOR SEVERAL DAYS Kassandra managed to avoid the duty of taking the offerings; but she heard from others that Khryse was making himself popular among the other priests and priestesses. Not only was he familiar with the secret craft of bees and the art of taking their honey (though she had been told that in Crete this work was forbidden to men and allowed only to special priestesses), but he was familiar with many of the arts known in Crete and Egypt as well.

"He has traveled in Egypt," Charis told her, "and has learned the art there of marking tallies; and he has said that he will teach anyone who wishes to learn. It will greatly simplify our keeping of records, so that we can know at once what is in our storehouses without counting—even counting tally-sticks."

Others told of his friendliness, of his many tales of his travels and of his devotion to his daughter; so that she began to feel she had behaved like a little fool. A day came when she returned to her ordinary duties, and when she entered the shrine and found Khryse there to work with her, she was ashamed to lift her eyes to his.

"I rejoice to see you again, Lady Kassandra. Are you still angry with me?"

Something in his voice strengthened her resolve, told her that at least she had not imagined what had happened between them. *Why should I be ashamed to meet his eyes? I have done nothing wrong; if there was any trespass, it was his, not mine.*

She said, "I hold no grudge; but I beg you, never touch me again." She was annoyed with herself, for she had spoken as if she were asking a favor, not demanding her right to refuse an unwanted touch.

"I cannot tell you how much I regret offending you," he said.

"There is no need for an apology; let us not speak of it again." She drew nervously away.

"No," he said, "I cannot leave it at that. I know I am not worthy of you; I am only a poor priest, and you are a King's daughter."

"Khryse, it is not that," she said. "I am sworn to belong to no man save the God."

He laughed: a short, bitter sound.

"He will never claim you, nor be jealous," he said.

"As for that, I should not be the first—"

"Oh, Kassandra," he said, laughing, "I believe you innocent, but you are surely not innocent enough—or child enough—to believe *those* old tales!"

She interrupted him. "Let us not speak of such things; but

whether it be true or false that the God may claim His own, I am not for *you*."

"Do not say that," he pleaded. "Never in all my life have I desired any woman as I desire you, nor did I think I could ever want any woman so much, until I beheld you here."

"I will believe you if you say so," she said, "but even if it is true, never speak of this again to me."

He bowed his head. "As you will," he said. "Not for worlds would I offend you, Princess; I am indebted to you for your kindness to my daughter. Yet I feel that Aphrodite, She who is mistress of desire, has bidden me to love you."

"Such a Goddess sends only madness," Kassandra said, "to men and women; I would never love any man at Her bidding. I am the Sun Lord's own. And now say no more of this, or we shall quarrel in truth."

"As you will," Khryse said. "I say only that if you deny the power of the One whom all women must serve, it may be that She will punish you."

This new Goddess is created by men, Kassandra thought, *to excuse their own lechery; I do not believe in Her power.* Then she remembered her dream, but she shrugged. *I have had it so much on my mind, it is like dreaming of thunder when one hears the rain on the roof.*

"There are worshipers in the Temple, and we must take the offerings; will you teach me your new method of tallying them in writing? I have seen the picture writing of Egypt, but it is very complicated, and once, years ago, an old man who had lived there told me that Egyptian scribes must study all their lives to learn it."

"That is so," Khryse said, "but the priests of Egypt have a simpler writing which is not so difficult to learn, and the Cretan style is simpler still, for each mark is not a picture or an idea, as on the tombs of the Kings, but a *sound*, so it can be written down in any language."

"Why, how clever! What God or great man created this system?"

"I do not know," Khryse said, "but they say the Olympian Hermes, the messenger God who travels on the wings of thought, is patron God of writing." Khryse took out his tablets and tallying sticks. "I will show you the simplest signs and how to write them down; and then they can be copied on clay tablets, so when they dry we will have a record that will never perish and does not depend on any man's memory."

She learned quickly; it was as if something in her were crying out for this new knowledge, and she soaked it up as the parched ground absorbed rain after a long drought. So well did Kassandra learn the Cretan writing that she threatened to be quicker at it than Khryse; and then he insisted she must learn no more.

"It is for your own good," he insisted. "In Crete no woman may learn this writing, not even the Queen. The Gods have ordained that women are not to be taught these things, for it will damage their minds, dry up their wombs, and the world will become barren everywhere. When the sacred springs are dry, the world thirsts."

"This is foolishness," she protested. "It has not harmed me."

"Would you be able to judge? Already you have refused me, or any lover; is this not an insult to the Goddess, and a sign that already you have refused womanhood?"

"So you refuse me this out of pique at what I refused you?" He looked bitterly wounded.

"It is not me alone that you have refused; it is the great power of nature which has ordained that woman is made for man. Women alone have that sacred and precious power to bear . . ."

It seemed so ridiculous that Kassandra laughed in his face.

"Are you trying to tell me that before the Gods and the Goddess gave men wisdom and learning, men could bear children, and that because man created other things he was denied that power? Even the Amazons know better than that. They do all manner of things forbidden to women here, yet they bear children as well."

"Daughters," he said scornfully.

"Many Amazons have borne fine sons."

"I had been told that among the Amazons they kill male children."

"No; they send them to their fathers. And they know all the

arts which in tribes of different customs are reserved to men. So if women in Crete are not allowed to read, what has that to do with me? We are not in Crete."

"A woman should not be able to reason like that," Khryse protested. "The life of the mind destroys the life of the body."

"You are even more of a fool than I thought," Kassandra retorted. "If this were true, it would be even more important to teach no man, lest it destroy him as a warrior. Are all the priests of Crete eunuchs, then?"

"You think too much," Khryse said sadly. "It will yet destroy you as a woman."

Her eyes glinted with mischief.

"And if I should give myself to you, it would save me from that dreadful fate? You are kind indeed, my friend, and I am ungrateful that I do not appreciate the great sacrifice you are willing to make for me."

"You should not scorn these mysteries," said Khryse soberly. "Do you not believe that because the God has put desire for you into my heart, it is a message from the God that I should have you?"

Raising her eyebrows with scorn, Kassandra said, "Every seducer has spoken so since time began, and every mother teaches her daughter not to listen to such false nonsense. Would you have me teach your own daughter this kind of thing, that because some man desires her it is her duty to give herself?"

"My daughter has nothing to do with this."

"Your daughter has everything to do with this; my conduct is to be a model to her of virtue. Would you wish her to give herself to the first man who pleads that he desires her?"

"Certainly not, but—"

"Then you are a hypocrite as well as a fool and a liar," said Kassandra. "I liked you once, Khryse; do not complete the work of destroying all my goodwill toward you."

She walked away from him and out of the shrine. All the while they had worked together, he had not for a single day ceased his importuning. She would endure it no longer; she would go to Charis, or to the chief priest, and tell him she would no longer work with Khryse, for he had but one use for her, and that she would not allow.

*It would be simpler to leave the Temple myself. But should
I let such a man drive me away?*

It was twilight; trying to soothe her own exasperation, Kassandra moved down the hill toward the enclosure where the
priestesses were housed. As she passed by the building, a small
sound in the shrubbery disturbed her; she turned and saw two
figures, melted together in the shadows. On impulse she moved
toward them, and the man broke away and bolted. Kassandra
had not recognized him and did not really care. The second
figure was another matter; Kassandra moved swiftly and caught
young Chryseis' arm.

The girl's dress was mussed, tucked up almost to her waist,
leaving her crotch bare; her mouth was swollen and bruised; her
face reddened and sleepy. Shocked, Kassandra thought, *But
she's a child, a baby!* Yet it was clear that in what they had been
doing—and there was certainly no doubt about that—the girl
had been an all-too-willing participant.

Sullenly the girl pulled her dress down and rubbed her arm
over her face. Kassandra finally burst out, "Shameless! How
dare you stand there like that? You are a virgin of Apollo!"

Defiant, Chryseis muttered, "Don't look at me like that,
you sour, dried-up spinster; just because no man has ever desired you, how dare you reprove me?"

"How dare I?" Kassandra repeated, thinking, *And it was
because I was concerned for this girl that I concealed her father's
offense! There is no need to speculate how she came by her behavior.*

She said quietly, "Whatever you may think of me, Chryseis,
it is not my conduct at issue, but yours; this is forbidden to the
maidens here. You sought refuge in the Sun Lord's Temple;
you must then obey the rules under which the other maidens
live."

Perhaps, she thought, *it would be wisest to send forth the
worthless daughter and father together from the house of the
God.*

"Go into the house, Chryseis," she said, as gently as she
could, "and change your dress and wash yourself, or it will not
be only I who chides you." The girl had been placed in her care;
somehow she must manage it that Chryseis was not a disgrace

to the Sun Lord's house, or to Kassandra's teaching. As Chryseis went indoors, she thought, *It seems now that I am to be at the mercy of Aphrodite; will Chryseis too complain that she is under the influence of that Goddess whose business is to lure women into unruly and lawless love?*

She raised her eyes to the face of the sun high in the heavens.

"We are in *Your* power, Lord Apollo," she prayed. "Surely You are in charge of Your house and the hearts and minds of those who have sworn their lives to You. I mean no disrespect to any Immortal; but cannot You keep order in Your own place and Your own shrine?"

3

THERE WAS no immediate answer to her question; but she had not expected any. For several days she avoided the shrine, pleading illness; it seemed as if the Sun Lord's house, once so happy, had turned hostile, for Khryse was everywhere. At last she climbed the hill to the very height of the city, and there she offered a sacrifice to the Maiden, patron Goddess of Troy; her thoughts were in turmoil, and she asked herself if this was disloyalty to the Sun Lord, whose priestess she was. Yet she had been called to Earth Mother and made a priestess there too.

When she had offered her sacrifice, she felt calmer, though the Goddess did not speak directly to her. She returned to the Sun Lord's house and presented herself at the evening ceremonies, and when she saw Khryse among the priests and he smiled at her, she did not seek to avoid his gaze. It was not she who had done wrong; why should she feel ashamed?

That night her dreams were confused and dreadful; it seemed to her that a storm raged over Troy, and that she stood in the highest part of the city, at the citadel of the Maiden, somehow seeking to call the lightning bolts to strike her first, that they might not fall on those she loved. The Thunder Lord of the Akhaians strode across the great giant-builded walls, shaking His fists. The Earth Shaker, Lord of Troy, who had been called to be consort to Earth Mother, was striving and struggling to protect His city. There were the other Immortals too, and somehow she, Kassandra, had angered Them. *But I have done nothing wrong*, she protested, in confusion. If anyone had trespassed, it had been Paris. She called out to the Sun Lord to save His city; but He frowned and hid the brightness of His face, saying, *They worship Me also among the Akhaians*, and she woke with a cry of dread. When she was fully awake, she realized the absurdity of the dream—surely the Gods, who were all-wise, would not punish a great city for the foolish transgressions of a single man and a woman.

After a time she slept again; and again she began to dream. She thought she held Phyllida's baby at her breast; and she felt again the mixture of melting tenderness with horrible revulsion and despair. Something was wrong, terribly wrong. She struggled to consciousness. The touch on her breast was still there, and a dark shape bent over her, save where the light of the full moon glinted on the golden mask of Apollo. But she recognized the touch of the hand on her breast, and she opened her mouth to cry out.

The hand quickly moved from her breast to cover her mouth. "You are mine, Kassandra!" an all-too-familiar voice intoned. "Would you deny your God?"

Kassandra bit the hand, which was removed with a most ungodlike cry, and sat up, pulling her tunic back into place. "I know the voice of the God, Khryse," she snarled furiously at him, "and it is not *your* voice! Blasphemer, do you think that Apollo cannot protect His own?"

Her voice had risen considerably on the last sentence, and she heard in the hallway the voices of the other priestesses coming to investigate the disturbance. She threw herself from the bed, trying to reach the door, but Khryse blocked her way and pushed her against the wall. His attempts to hold her there, while largely successful, were not silent, and the room quickly filled with a crowd of women, including Charis, Phyllida, and

Chryseis. Khryse turned his head so that the mask stared at the group of women.

"Leave us." His voice was deep and impressive. Phyllida first gasped, seeing the mask of the God, then, recognizing the man's voice, regarded him and Kassandra with horrified comprehension. Chryseis giggled; the rest of the women looked uncertain.

Kassandra hit him, hard, in the stomach and broke away from his grasping hands.

"Vile priest!" she said in a gasp. "You dare use the semblance of the God to satisfy your lusts! You profane that which you do not understand!" She was shaking with a mixture of rage and horror. "By the Mother of All, I wouldn't lie with *you* if you *were* truly possessed by Apollo!"

"Would you not, Kassandra?" A shudder passed through Khryse's body; and then, unexpectedly—and unmistakably—the voice was that of Apollo. *You who are My chosen one—surely you cannot think I would fail to protect you from a vicious and foolish mortal?*

Kassandra heard Phyllida's cry of recognition; but the dark tide flowed over her and filled her, and she felt the surge of the Goddess rising within her. The last thing she heard was the voice of the Goddess:

Yours, Sun Lord? She was given to Me before ever she came to birth in this mortal world, or felt Your touch!

Then she knew no more.

HER BODY was propped against the wall, and every inch of her skin felt as though it had been burned. Nails clawed at her cheek and continued to rip her tunic at the shoulder.

"Murderess!" Chryseis screamed in her ear. "You have killed my father! You think yourself too good for him—you think that because you're a princess you're better than the rest of us! You act as if you were not even human! Well, you're not —you're a beast and a filthy coward . . ."

Kassandra opened her eyes. Khryse lay on the floor, dead white and very still. Phyllida was bending over him. "He's going to be all right, Chryseis," she said soothingly. "The God has taken him, no more."

But Chryseis was not listening. "She's a witch! She cast an evil spell on him!"

Charis pulled the hysterical girl away from Kassandra and thrust her into the arms of two of the other priestesses. "Get this senseless brat out of here!" Chryseis' screams echoed as she was dragged down the hallway, then mercifully faded into the distance.

Kassandra felt her body slide to the floor, but she could do nothing to stop it. Her eyes were open, but everything seemed far away and not quite real. Only a part of her self was in her body; the rest hovered over the scene, watching as Charis and the governess picked her up and laid her back in her bed. A novice brought a beaker of wine; Charis poured some of it down Kassandra's throat. Briefly it warmed her, and pulled her a bit further back into her body, but she felt terribly, unendurably cold, as if most of her life force had fled. She could see that Charis was holding her hand, but she couldn't feel the clasp of the woman's fingers. Suddenly she felt overwhelmed by homesickness for the Amazon encampment, and for Penthesilea, who had been more of a mother to her than Hecuba ever had been or would be. Tears blurred her vision and dripped down the sides of her face.

"Hush," Charis soothed, drawing up the blanket and tucking it securely about her. "Rest now, and don't trouble yourself. Time enough to sort things out in the morning."

Behind Charis, Kassandra could see Phyllida reverently pick up the mask of Apollo. Two of the priests came in quietly, conferred briefly with the governess, then carried Khryse out. His eyes were open, but he looked dazed and uncomprehending.

The priests were talking to each other as they passed her bed; Kassandra caught the words "genuine possession." But whose? Khryse's, or her own?

She woke just before sunrise, feeling as if every muscle and bone in her body had been beaten with cudgels; she lay motionless, thinking of what had happened.

One thing was certain: Khryse had—unlawfully—worn the mask of the God and had attempted to seduce her. She was not quite sure what had happened after that; she remembered Chryseis tearing at her and screaming, and then she remembered the voice of Apollo, breaking through the noise and confusion in the room, and the ill-fated words she had flung at Khryse.

"I wouldn't lie with you if you were the God Himself . . ."

Had she truly said those words to her God? Khryse had deserved them; yet her whole body tightened in grief at the thought that Apollo Sun Lord might have taken them to Himself.

Still, beyond fear or regret, she knew now the source of the dark waters: it was the Goddess who had claimed her. She had given herself to the God in all the sincerity of her first love; yet she had not been free.

The door opened and Charis came in, bending over her with tenderness.

"Will you get up, Kassandra? We are all summoned to the shrine, to discuss what truly happened here last night."

Charis brought her some wine, and bread and honey, but Kassandra could not swallow; her throat clamped shut, and she knew that if she tried to eat she would be sick.

Charis helped her to draw on her dress and brush her hair. Kassandra pinned it loosely into a braid, and followed the older priestess to the shrine, where the priests and priestesses were assembled.

One of the older priests, who had known Kassandra since her childhood, called them to order, saying, "We must find out the truth of this unfortunate incident. Daughter of Priam, will you tell us what happened?"

"I was asleep and dreaming and woke to find a man in my room. He wore the mask of the God, but I recognized Khryse's voice. He had asked me to yield to him before," she said, "and I refused him." She raised her head, looking into Khryse's eyes. "Ask the lecherous blasphemer if he dares to deny it!"

The priest asked, "Khryse, what have you to say?"

Khryse looked straight at Kassandra. He said, "I remember nothing; only that I awakened in her room with this wildcat clawing at me!"

"You did not deliberately put on the mask of the God in order to deceive the girl?"

"Certainly not!" said Khryse indignantly. "I call Apollo's self to witness—but I doubt He will come to accuse or defend me."

"He lies," Phyllida cried out. "I know the voice of the God —and I will swear that it was the voice only of Khryse! Kassandra has complained to me before that he had asked of her what was not lawful to give any mortal man! Later I heard him speak in the voice of the Sun Lord—"

"We all heard that," said Charis. "The question now is which of them, or both, or neither, blasphemed."

"I say she was guilty of refusing the word of Apollo," said Khryse. "She blasphemed; and in the name of the God we both serve—"

"Certainly she invoked the Goddess in Apollo's own Temple," said Charis, "and that is forbidden."

"I think both of them should be sent away from here," said the old priest, "for creating a scandal."

"I do not see why I should be punished," Kassandra said, "for fighting a lecherous priest who would have ravished a woman who had given herself to the God he pretended to serve. As for the Goddess, I did not seek Her protection; She comes and goes as She will. I am not party to Her quarrel with Apollo."

"I call Apollo to witness—" Khryse began hotly.

Kassandra said sharply, "And what will you do, blasphemer, if He should come to answer you?"

Arrogantly, Khryse said, "It is certain that He will not come. I sought Kassandra, yes; I serve the God, as she says she does—"

"Take care," said Charis sharply, but Khryse laughed.

"I will take that chance!"

Charis said, "We owe Kassandra protection; the maidens of the Temple are sworn to the God, and are not to be abused by a mere man, be he priest or otherwise; and certainly not by a trick of this kind."

There was murmuring in the room; Kassandra was grateful to Charis for speaking in her defense.

"One thing I ask," the old priest said. "Come here, daughter of Priam. You were heard to say to him that you would not give yourself to him even if he were possessed by Apollo in truth. Did you mean that, or did you speak in anger?"

"Since the God did not come to me, I spoke only to reject one who would have raped me in Apollo's name."

There was a blaze of light and Kassandra raised her eyes to see the brightness where Khryse had been standing.

The deep familiar voice resonated to the corners of the room:

Kassandra . . .

Beyond all question it was the voice of the God. Kassandra felt her knees loosen, and she slid to the floor, not daring to raise her eyes or speak.

This My servant did not believe I could use him this way; but now he knows better. He shall learn My power before he is much older. Leave him to Me; I shall deal with My own.

The shining Form turned to Kassandra; she trembled and bowed her head.

As for you, Kassandra, you whom I have loved: You have given yourself to My ancient enemy; yet I have claimed you and you are Mine. I will not release you; yet you have offended Me, and from you I withdraw My divine gift of prophecy. Hear My word!

The voice was filled with throbbing sadness; Kassandra, kneeling with her head bowed, felt within herself a surge of protest and resentment.

"Sun Lord, I only wish You could," she said aloud. "*I want nothing more than to be freed of that gift I did not seek!*"

She bowed as if buffeted with mighty winds; her body was a battleground, her eyes burning, the dark surging waters of the Goddess raging against the blasting heat of Apollo's wrath.

You too shall know My power!

Abruptly the presence was gone; Kassandra, released from the grip of the warring Immortals, slumped to the floor. Dimly, she knew Charis bent to lift her. As if she were floating somewhere near the ceiling of the room, she saw Khryse fall, his body jerking wildly, heels drumming on the floor and teeth chattering. Blood-flecked foam burst from his lips, and an eerie cry emptied his lungs.

And serves him right, she thought, *who thought to speak with Apollo's power to deceive one of His own . . .*

Like an echo of Apollo's voice, she heard:

I shall have use even for him in the days that will come. . . .

Shuddering with cold, she felt the dark waters withdraw, and came back as if surfacing from a very deep dive. She still could not speak; the priests were ministering to Khryse, while her own head still lay in Charis's lap.

Charis rocked her gently and whispered, "Don't cry; even if Apollo's anger is terrible, it will be good for you to be free of this dreadful curse of foresight."

How could I tell her that I wept not for the loss of the gift of prophecy? Or that it was not Apollo's anger I feared but for His love? I did not seek to be a battleground between the Immortals.

4

IF KASSANDRA had felt that the reprimand of Khryse would solve anything, she was mistaken; it seemed that her peace had been destroyed for nothing.

Nor was she the only one to seem troubled; Khryse looked pale and exhausted. He was still needed in the shrine, for he had not yet managed to teach anyone except herself enough of his new method of tallying to take his place. He had already managed to make himself all but indispensable. Most of the priests were aging; no more than thirty, he was the only priest of the Sun Lord still in the prime of his strength.

It was made no easier for Kassandra that every time she saw the sun glinting on that brilliantly gold hair, she remembered the moment when he had spoken to her in the voice of the Sun Lord. What a fool she had been, after all, she thought despondently. Surely he was capable of summoning Apollo . . . or was it she, by her appeal against the imposture, who had summoned the Sun Lord to protect her against this man she so despised? He would still have been Apollo, in whatever outer form, and had she not refused him, she might now have been carrying the child of the God. But was that what she wanted? Was that her destiny, and had she refused it?

All the same, done was done, and she could only rejoice, although with a certain bitterness, over the punishment of Khryse's presumption. *The Immortals are not mocked*, and now at least Khryse knew it.

And so do I. The Sun Lord mocks me; I, who spoke in rever- ence against what I saw as blasphemy, infringing on Apollo's chosen ones. It is I who have been punished, as much as the sinner.

It was no comfort that Apollo had intervened; now it was said (and of course the story had spread, first through the Tem- ple and then throughout the city) that she had refused the God Himself, and that in return Apollo had cursed her. The truth was known only to those who had been there that night, and, she thought almost in despair, not all the truth was known even to them.

They believed Apollo had withdrawn His gift of prophecy from her. But foresight had been hers since her earliest child- hood, and the Sun Lord could not withdraw it, for it was not His. He had only made it certain that her words would never be believed.

It was no satisfaction, either, to see Khryse viewed with the same half-frightened reverence as herself. At least once every day, sometimes two or three times, he would be seized and fall to the ground in the terrifying clutch of the falling sickness, to lie there shaking with convulsions. She had (though rarely) seen men and women and even children taken this way; they were usually regarded as a victim or favorite of the God. Kassandra began to wonder if this were not a sickness like any other. But why, then, had Khryse shown no sign of it before?

She took no satisfaction from these internal doubts and questions; if anything, she longed for her old childish belief. She was still constantly forced into Khryse's company. After a time, she realized that the episode had connected them in the

minds of most of the priests and priestesses—as if she had actually committed the misbehavior into which Khryse had sought
to seduce her, instead of their being common victims of Apollo's
wrath. *Or malice*, she thought.

*What more can the Sun Lord do to me? I am assured of His
love . . . but what of that? Is His love in any way better than His
evil will? Am I to thank Him that He did not make me too a
victim of the falling sickness?*

One day she was summoned to the court by Chryseis, who
had been set to carrying messages within the shrine. "Kassandra, you have a visitor; I think it is the princess of Colchis."

She came to the court and looked around to see Andromache, her child on her shoulder, dressed in the clothing of a
commoner. She hurried to embrace her.

"What is happening?"

"Oh, my dear, it is worse than you can imagine," Andromache said. "Everyone is under the Spartan woman's spell, even
my own dear husband; I tried to repeat to him what you said
about Helen, and he said that all women are jealous of a beautiful woman, that was all. I think you are prettier than this
Helen," Andromache added, "but no one agrees!"

Kassandra said soberly, "It is as if she wore the girdle of
Aphrodite—"

"Which, as we all know, makes men capable of thinking
only with their loins," Andromache said with a sarcastic smile.
"But women too? Do you think her so beautiful, Kassandra?"

"Yes," Kassandra blurted out, "she is as lovely as the Beautiful One Herself," and then was shocked at herself. She murmured to Andromache, almost in apology, "Since childhood I
have seen through Paris' eyes," and stopped. She could say
nothing about the curious intensity with which she had reacted
to Oenone, or Helen, not even to Andromache, who had been
brought up among Amazons and would probably understand.
"Someday," she said, "I will tell you all—but for now, tell me
what is happening."

"You did not know Menelaus had come?"

"No; what is he like?"

"No more like his brother Agamemnon than I am like

Aphrodite," Andromache said. "He came, weak and stammering, and demanded that we render up Helen to him, and Priam said, laughing, that perhaps—*perhaps*, mind you—we would return Helen when he brought Hesione back to Troy with a dowry to pay for the years she remained unwed; and Menelaus said that Hesione had a husband, who had taken her with no dowry, perhaps impressed by the fact that she was the sister of the King of Troy, and *he* at least was no stealer of women from their husbands."

"That must have pleased Father," Kassandra said, grimacing.

"Then," Andromache went on, "Menelaus told him Hesione would not return to Troy and suggested that Priam send an envoy and ask Hesione herself if she wished to return— without her child, or course, since the child was a good Spartan and belonged to Hesione's husband."

"And what said my father to that?" Kassandra asked.

"He said to Hecuba that Menelaus had played into his hands; and he sent for Helen and asked her in Menelaus' presence, 'Do you wish to return to your husband, my lady?'."

"And what did she answer?"

"She said, 'No, *my lord*,' and of course Menelaus just stood and looked at her as if she were cutting him to pieces."

"Then Priam said, 'So, Menelaus, you have had your answer.'"

"And what said Menelaus to that?" Kassandra asked.

"He made matters worse by saying, 'Will you listen to what an unfaithful whore wants? I tell you, she is mine, and I will take her,' and he tried to grab her wrist and drag her away."

"And did he?" Kassandra asked, thinking that if Menelaus had indeed acted with so much resolution, it might have impressed even Priam.

"Oh, no," Andramache replied; "Hector and Paris both jumped forward and grabbed *him*, and Priam said, 'Thank your own Gods, Lord Menelaus, that you are my guest, or I would let my sons have their way with you; but no offense shall be offered to any guest under my roof.' And Menelaus began to stammer—with rage this time—and said, 'Guard your tongue, old man, or you will have no roof from which I need to drag her.' Then he said something filthy to Helen—I would not repeat it in these sacred precincts," added Andromache with a superstitious gesture—"and flung down the cup he was drinking from and said he wouldn't accept hospitality from a—a pirate who sent his sons out to steal women."

Kassandra's eyes were wide; she had never seen anyone except his own sons defy Priam.

Andromache went on, "Then Priam asked, 'No? Then how do you Akhaians ever get wives?' Menelaus swore at him and said I don't know what all, and yelled to his servants and stormed out, saying perhaps if Priam would not listen to him he would listen to Agamemnon. And Paris had the last word . . ." Here Andromache began to giggle.

"Priam said, 'Yes, when I was a boy I sometimes told someone who teased me that my big brother would come and beat him up.' And Paris said, 'If it comes to that, Menelaus, I have a big brother too; would you or your brother care to have a word with Hector?' Then Menelaus stormed out, cursing all the way back to his ship."

Kassandra, overwhelmed, had hardly heard the last few sentences; all she could think was *It has come.* Already she could see the harbor blackened with foreign ships, the world she knew torn asunder by war. She could not stop herself from interrupting Andromache to cry out, "Pray to the Gods! Pray and sacrifice! I told my father he should have nothing to do with that Spartan woman!"

Andromache's voice was very gentle, ignoring the interruption. "Don't trouble yourself so, Kassandra, my dear."

So even she thinks that I am mad.

"What makes you think that we will not drive the Akhaians back to the islands they hold? It was one thing for those folk to defeat the simple shepherds and landless men who held their islands . . . but quite another for them to come up against the whole might of Troy! What I say is let those Akhaians look to themselves! Are we to let them think that they can go on stealing our women unpunished, but if we touch theirs, they can punish us?"

"Andromache, are you blind too? Can't you see that Helen is only the excuse? Agamemnon has been trying to find some such reason to come against us in war for many years, and now we have walked straight into his snares. Now we will have these iron-wearers trying to take all the lands that lie to the south of here. He will muster the full might of all these warlike people to . . . oh, what does it matter?" Kassandra sank down on a bench. "You can't see it because you are like Hector . . . you think war leads only to fame and glory!"

Andromache knelt beside Kassandra and put her arms around her, saying, "Never mind. I should not have frightened you; I should have known better."

Kassandra could almost hear her thinking, *Poor thing, she is mad; Apollo has cursed her after all.*

There was no way to argue with that, so she abandoned her warning and asked Andromache, "What of Oenone?"

"She has returned to the mountain, and taken her child with her," Andromache said. "Paris wished to keep the babe— his firstborn son, after all—but Oenone said he could not have it both ways; if it was *his* son, and he chose to acknowledge it, then she was his lawful first wife and this foreign woman only a second wife or concubine."

"And serves him right," Kassandra said. "It seems that Paris has neither honor nor decency; Father should have left him on Mount Ida with his sheep, if they'd have him." She was deeply disappointed in her brother; she wanted Paris to be regarded as the people of the city regarded Hector: their champion, their hero, as much for his goodness and honorable behavior as for his handsome face.

"I must return to the palace. But tell me, what will we do if there is a war, Kassandra?" Andromache asked her.

"Fight it, of course; even you and I may be glad for our weapons, if as many Akhaians rise against us as Agamemnon intends," Kassandra said, despairing.

Andromache embraced her and took her leave. After she was out of sight, Kassandra went out the highest gate of Apollo's house, climbing higher and higher, toward the Temple of Pallas Athene. As she went, sweat soaking through her tunic in the heat, she tried helplessly to form a prayer. But nothing would come, and she went on climbing.

She looked down toward the harbor, black with ships as she had seen it so many times before this. She did not know whether the ships were really there or not, but this time it did not matter. If they were not there now, they would come soon enough.

Lord Apollo! Sun Lord, beloved! If You cannot withdraw the gift and take from me this unwanted Sight, at least do not curse me that I shall never be believed!

She went up into the high Temple of Pallas Athene, at the very summit of the city, and into the shrine. Recognizing her either as Priam's daughter or as a priestess of the Sun Lord (or perhaps both), the guardians drew aside, letting her into the shrine, before the great image of the Goddess, shown as a young woman wearing the unbound locks and garland of a virgin.

Maiden, You who loved Troy, You who brought us Your priceless gifts of grape and olive, You who were here before those arrogant Thunder-worshipers and their Sky Gods and their weapons, protect Your city now.

She looked at the drawn curtains of the innermost shrine, which contained the image of Pallas, drawn from heaven, ancient and crude, and remembered the Goddess of the Amazon women.

You who are virgin like the Maiden Huntress, I come to You a maiden who has known injustice from the Sun Lord; am I to go on serving Him in this manner when He has cast me off and derided me?

She had not truly expected an answer, but deep in her mind she felt the surging motion of the dark waters of the Goddess.

Obscurely comforted, she went away down the hill to the Temple, to take up her duty of tallying the offerings.

Khryse was there as usual, marking his symbols on wax tablets, noting numbers of jars of oil, of grains—barley and millet; offerings of wine or honeycombs, of hares and pigeons and kids. She was still unwilling to look at him, although she told herself it was not she who should be ashamed.

A jar carried by one of the younger priestesses had been let fall and had broken another, so that a heap of barley and the sticky contents of a honeycomb lay intermingled, and the efforts of the young girl to clear it away had only made a worse mess; Kassandra sent her for a twig broom and a water jar, and herself took over the task of cleaning it up. She was directing the girl to get a cage of pigeons out of the way, when she heard the familiar and hated voice.

"You should not be doing this yourself, Lady Kassandra; this is work for a slave."

"We are all slaves in the eyes of the Immortals, you as well as I, Khryse," said Kassandra, her eyes on her broom.

"A correct statement; but when was the Lady Kassandra anything but correct—whatever it may cost her or anyone else?" said Khryse. "Kassandra, we cannot go on like this, with you forever afraid to look at me."

Stung, she looked up angrily into his face.

"Who dares to say I am afraid?"

"If you are not, why do you always avoid my eyes?"

Her voice was caustic. "Are you so fair an object that you think I should find pleasure in looking at you?"

"Come, Kassandra," he said, "can there not be peace between us?"

"I bear you no particular ill will," she said, still not looking at him. "Stay away from me, and I shall return the courtesy, if that is what you want from me."

"No," Khryse said, "you know what it is I want from you, Kassandra."

Kassandra sighed. "Khryse, I want nothing from you except that you leave me in peace; is that plain enough for you?"

"No," the man said, clasping her hands in his. "I want you, Kassandra; the image of you is in my mind day and night. You have bewitched me; if you cannot love me, then at least free me from your spell."

"I do not know what to say to you," she said, dismayed. "I have cast no spell on you; why should I do such a thing? I do not desire you; I do not like you at all, and if I had my way you would be in Crete, or in one of the hells, or even further away than that. I do not know how I can make it any plainer to you, but if I could think of a clearer way to say it, I would. Is that understandable?"

"Kassandra, can you not forgive me? I do not seek to dishonor you. If it is your will, I will go, humble poor priest that I am, and ask your father for your hand in marriage. You must feel some kindness for me, for you have been kind to my motherless child—"

"I would be just as kind to any stray kitten," Kassandra interrupted. "For the last time, I would not marry you if you were the last man the Gods ever made. If the alternative was to live virgin all my life or to marry a blind beggar lying in the marketplace, or even a—an Akhaian, I would choose him before you."

He stepped away, his face as white as the marble walls of the shrine. He said through clenched teeth, "Someday you will regret this, Kassandra. I may not always be a powerless priest."

His face was drawn; she wondered suddenly if he had been drinking unmixed wine so early in the day. But the wine at the priests' table was always well watered; nor did he have the flushed look he would have had in that case. His breath did not seem to smell of wine—but there was a strange scent that seemed to cling to his clothing. She could not identify it, but supposed it was some medicine the healer-priests had given him for his seizures.

She turned away, but he caught at her hand and pulled her close, backing her against the wall. His body pressed hard against hers, and one of his hands gripped both of hers painfully hard. With his free hand he tried to wrench apart her gown, his mouth jamming hard against hers.

"You have driven me mad," he gasped, "and no man can be blamed for punishing a woman who has driven him to frenzy!"

She struggled and would have screamed; finally she bit down into his lip. He jerked back and she thrust at him with both her hands, so that he tripped and fell. She stumbled as he clung to her, wrenched her hands furiously free of his, and ran. He tried to raise himself and she kicked him in the ribs. She ran from the shrine and did not stop running till she was safe in her own room.

5

KASSANDRA AWAKENED from a dream of fire sweeping up the hill of Troy toward the palace to a smell of smoke and voices clamoring in the halls of the Sun Lord's house. It was the darkest part of the night, when the moon is down and the stars are going out; but there was the smell of torches. Snatching up a cloak to cover the short tunic in which she slept, she ran out into the courtyard.

Far below in the harbor she could see dim lights from ships, and torches, presumably carried in human hands, making their way up the hill.

All she could think was *It has come*. She cried out, and then she heard the clamor of the alarm, a great wooden rattle sounded from Priam's keep. It called for women and children and the old to take refuge in the main citadel and the soldiers to turn out. She stood watching the lights moving through the city below her, and hearing the clash of weapons seized, and at last the loud voices of officers ordering soldiers to their posts.

She felt a gentle tug on her sleeve and found Chryseis standing beside her.

"What is it, Kassandra?"

"It is the Akhaians; they have come, as we foresaw," she said, and was astonished at how calm she felt. "We must make ready to take shelter in the citadel."

"My father—"

"Hush, dear; he will have to go with the soldiers. Go quickly and dress."

"But he has the falling sickness—"

"If the Akhaians take him, he will have something worse. Quickly, child." She took Chryseis' hand, and led her within, dressing her quickly in a heavy tunic against the night chill,

fastening her cloak and binding sandals on her feet. As soon as
Chryseis was dressed, they went into the courtyard. Charis was
gathering the women around her, and telling them to go down
toward the main keep of the palace.

Kassandra, the girl's hand in hers, walked quickly down the
steep road. It seemed wrong to be going *toward* the torches and
the clash of arms; surely the Akhaians would never come so
high as this: what they sought was in the palace, not up here in
the Temple. Now she could hear the chilling war cries, and the
bellowing of Hector as he rallied his men.

The other women crowded around them as Kassandra led
the way through the palace gates. The guards and soldiers were
hurrying the women inside, each one then taking up a spear
from a huge pile stacked at the entrance to the armory.

Kassandra thought of taking a spear and going down with
the soldiers; but Hector would be angry. *All the same, a time
may come when he does not despise my skill at arms.* For the
moment, she decided to go with the women. They were a disheveled crew, most of them half-dressed, having been roused
from sleep. Many of them had not troubled to dress, or do more
than clutch a blanket over their nakedness, like their children;
and babies howled or fretted in the arms of mothers or wet-
nurses. Kassandra and the other priestesses of Apollo were almost the only ones who were properly dressed for public appearance, or who kept their composure. Most of the women
were tear-stained or crying, keening and shouting for explana-
tions or for help.

Helen too stood composed among the hysterical women.
Every lock of hair was in place, and she looked as if she had this
moment come from the hands of her bath-attendant. She was
holding a small boy of five or six by the hand; he was neatly
dressed, his hair combed into place, and though his knuckles
were white as he clung to her fingers, his face was scrubbed
clean, and he was not crying.

She looked across the room with great composure, and her
eyes met Kassandra's. Then she crossed the room, threading
her way quietly through the crowding, wailing women, and
came toward Kassandra.

"I remember you," she said; "you are my husband's twin

sister. It is good to see someone who is not turned foolish with terror. Why are you not weeping and screaming like everyone else?"

"I don't know," Kassandra said. "Perhaps I am not as easily frightened; and perhaps I prefer not to cry until I am hurt."

Helen smiled. "Ah, good. Most women are such fools. Is there danger, do you think?"

"Why do you ask me?" Kassandra countered. "Surely they have not neglected to tell you that I am mad."

"You do not have the look of a madwoman," Helen said. "In any case, I prefer to make up my own mind."

Kassandra frowned a little and turned away. She did not want to like this woman or to find anything admirable in her. It was bad enough that when she looked at her she saw something of what Paris saw.

"Then you can make up your own mind as to whether there is danger," she said curtly. "I know only that I was awakened by the watchman's rattle, and I came down here to obey. I suppose, since I saw Akhaian ships in the harbor, that it has something to do with you; and so, though there may be something for us to fear, there is certainly nothing for you to be afraid of."

"You think not?" Helen said. "Agamemnon is certainly no friend of mine; his only thought would be to turn me over to Menelaus, and he would certainly stand by to see that I did not escape unscathed."

The unnaturally neat little boy clinging to Helen's hand flinched; Helen felt it, and looked gently down at him. Kassandra did not know why this surprised her; why had she thought that the Spartan woman could not also be a tender and concerned mother?

She asked, "How old is your son?"

"Five years old at Midsummer," Helen said, and beckoned across the crowded room to a thin, aristocratic-looking woman dressed in a the full skirt and low-cut bodice of a Cretan woman. "Aithra, will you take Nikos and put him down somewhere to sleep, my dear?" She kissed the child, who clung to her; but she said gently, "Go now and sleep, like a good boy," and he went without protest, trotting along obediently at the tall woman's side.

"Is that Menelaus' son?" asked Kassandra.

"Perhaps you would say so," Helen said indifferently. "I say he is *my* son. In any case, I do not choose to leave him with his father; I do not like the way he treats his children. It will not harm my daughter Hermione to be nothing but his precious gilded toy; but the only thought in Menelaus' mind is to make Nikos over in his own image—or worse yet, in the image of his wonderful brother. I sent Nikos away because someone unwisely said in his hearing that if his father came after us, he would kill us both; and Aithra also has cause to fear."

"Aithra looks more like a Queen than a waiting-woman," said Kassandra.

"She *is* a Queen," said Helen, "she is the mother of Theseus, and he sent her to me. I think somehow they quarreled. Aithra prefers to remain with me, and she treats my son as her own grandchild—which she would not do for the son of the Horse Queen," Helen said. "Now that the child is safe, I would like to know what is going on."

Kassandra said, "There is no danger here, not now; I think it would have been more sensible to leave the women of the God's house up there. Surely the invaders will not get higher than the palace keep." At Helen's side, she went into the courtyard, which looked down over all of Troy and the harbor.

The sun was just rising; Kassandra could see men fighting upward through the city.

"Look," Helen said. "Your Trojan soldiers under Hector have cut off the upward path to the palace; and now the Akhaians are looting and burning in the lower city. That is one of Agamemnon's ships, and I doubt not that Menelaus is with him." The indifferent tone in which Helen spoke fascinated Kassandra; had she no feeling whatever for her previous husband?

Flames were rising now from the seaside houses and buildings down below; houses of the poorer sort built of stacked logs and timbers were going up in flames. The houses built higher up on the hill were all of stone, and there was no way they could be set afire, but the Akhaian soldiers were running into the houses and carrying out everything they could find.

"They won't find much treasure or plunder down there," Kassandra said, and Helen nodded.

They leaned on the railing, watching the men below. Kassandra recognized one of the Akhaians, a big man who stood out as almost a head taller than his men, his crested helmet glittering as if washed with gold in the rising sunlight. He had once invaded the palace and borne off the struggling Hesione. That had been—how long? Seven years ago, perhaps? Still she shuddered and felt her stomach clench tight.

Helen said, "That is Agamemnon."

Kassandra replied, her voice only a whisper, "Yes, I know."

"Look; Hector and his men are trying to block his way back to his ship; will they burn it, do you think?"

"They'll try," Kassandra said, watching the Trojan soldiers attempting to cut off the Akhaians' leader and making him fight every step of the way back to the ship. The sun was higher now, and they could not see into the burning glare reflected off the sea; Kassandra turned away, shading her eyes.

"Let's go inside; it's cold. It is not at Agamemnon's hands that Hector will meet his fate," she said. They went into the room, where the other women were quieter now. The children had fallen asleep on blankets, and half a dozen midwives were gathered around Creusa, who was trying to tell them that she was perfectly well and was not going to go into labor just to provide them with amusement for this night.

Hecuba, wrapped in one of her oldest shawls over a ragged old house gown, had found some scraps of wool and was twirling a distaff idly; Kassandra gauged by the unevenness of the thread that it was only to pass the time.

"Oh, there you are, girls—I wondered where you had gone. What is happening down there, Daughter? Your eyes are better than mine. What was it you said about Hector, Kassandra?"

"I said it is not at the hands of Agamemnon that he will meet his fate, Mother."

"I should hope not," said Hecuba irritably. "That great Akhaian brute would be well advised to avoid our Hector!"

Some of the women had gone out onto the balcony, and now Kassandra heard them raise a cheer.

"They are going away; they have reached their ship and are making sail! The Akhaians are gone!"

"And they cannot have gotten much plunder from the houses along the shore: a few sacks of olives, a few goats perhaps. You are safe, Helen," said Hecuba.

"Oh, they will surely be back again," Helen said, and Kassandra, who had been on the very point of saying the same thing, wondered how she knew. She was no fool, this Akhaian woman, and this troubled Kassandra. The last thing she wanted was to like or to respect Helen; yet she could not help liking her.

Chryseis came up to Kassandra and whispered, "Charis has said that we may go back to the shrine; are you ready?"

"No, dear; I will stay for a while with my mother and sisters and my brothers' wives, if Charis will permit me," Kassandra said. "I will return when I can."

"Oh, they always let you do whatever you want," said Chryseis spitefully. "I am sure they would not chide you if you wanted to stay away altogether."

Hecuba had overheard this, but she was altogether too gentle a person to hear the malice in the girl's voice. She said, "Yes, they have been very good about lending you back to us, Kassandra. Be certain to tell Charis how grateful I am. I suppose with all these people sent to the palace, I should somehow find breakfast for them; will you help me, Kassandra, if your Temple duties do not summon you immediately?"

"Of course, Mother," said Kassandra, and Helen volunteered at once, "And so will I."

Kassandra was startled to see Hecuba give Helen an affectionate little pat on the cheek. She said, "I will go and speak to Charis," and went quickly away.

"Of course you must stay if your mother has need of you," Charis said, "with Creusa pregnant, and Andromache with a child still at the breast. Don't trouble yourself, Kassandra; stay as long as your mother needs you."

"What is *that*?" Andromache quavered, and hid her child's

head under her shawl, as a blow struck on the door. Others among the women trembled and cried out in fear.

"Don't be so foolish," Helen said, frowning at them in contempt. "We saw the Akhaians leave." She went and flung open the door; her face lighted, making her even more radiantly beautiful, and Kassandra knew who stood there even before she saw her twin brother.

"Paris!"

"I wanted to be sure that you and the boy were well," Paris said, looking around the room for the child. "Surely you did not leave him below while you took refuge here?"

"Of course not; he is sleeping yonder, in Aithra's arms," Helen said, and Paris smiled—a smile, Kassandra thought, that should not have been seen outside their own chamber.

"Were you frightened, my darling?"

"Not while we knew we were so well protected, my dearest," she murmured, and he clasped her hand.

"I said to Hector that he should come with me to make certain that our wives and children were safe," Paris added, "but he was too busy worrying about wine and rations for the household guard."

"Hector," said Andromache stiffly, "would never neglect his duty to his men; and I would not wish him to."

And what is Paris doing here among the women at a time like this? Kassandra knew that Hector had behaved properly; yet at that moment, she knew, every woman in Troy envied Helen her husband.

"Was Menelaus there?" she asked in an undertone.

"I did not see him, if he was," said Paris. "I told you he was too cowardly to come himself. And now we are well rid of Agamemnon."

"Don't think it," Kassandra burst out; "he will be back almost before he has time to gather his men, and next time you will not be rid of him so easily."

Paris looked at her with good-natured indulgence.

"Are you still prophesying doom, poor girl? You are like a minstrel who knows only one song to sing and wears out his welcome at every hearthside," he said; "but I am sorry you were frightened by these buzzards of Akhaians. Let us hope we have seen the worst of them."

I hope it too; he does not know how much I hope it.

"I must go and help Mother provide breakfast for all these women," she said, and turned away. It seemed incongruous that out of this terror and confusion something like a feast should come; but the men were feasting too, celebrating that Agamemnon had—for now—been driven away.

"I would rather stay with you," Paris said, "but if I do not go and join Hector and the men, I shall never hear the last of it. Forgive me, love." He kissed Helen's hand and hurried away, and Kassandra stood without moving until Andromache called to her and she went to help prepare the breakfast for the palace's unexpected guests.

6

THAT WAS ONLY the first of the raids; during the rest of that winter, it seemed to Kassandra that every time she looked down into the harbor, there were Akhaian ships lying there, and usually their raiders were in the streets, fighting. Eventually most articles of value had been carried up into the citadel of the palace, or even farther, into the Sun Lord's house, and the city was under perpetual siege.

Once the Akhaians had crept round the city, raiding Mount Ida, and before the army could be called out, they captured all Priam's cattle and most of his sheep. At the time, Kassandra was at her duty in the Temple, tallying jars of oil and noticing that the quantity, if not the quality, of the offerings had fallen off. Out of nowhere she was overcome with a surge of rage, grief and despair so immediate that she burst out in a great wail of mourning. She could not understand what was wrong until she recognized that special quality of strong emotion which always brought her into intimate communication with her brother's mind; she—or rather, he—was standing on the hillside, and before her, already covered with swarms of buzzing flies, lay the corpse of the old shepherd Agelaus.

"It was as if he tried to put his single old body, fragile as it was, between Priam's herds and Agamemnon's raiders," Paris muttered, and although Kassandra had seen the old man only briefly at the Games when Paris was welcomed to the city, she felt all of her brother's sorrow and fury.

"He had no other son; I should have stayed with him to guard his old age," Paris said at last, laying his own richly woven cloak gently over the body. At this, Kassandra was able to detach herself enough from her brother to think, *Would that you had stayed with him indeed! Better for you, for Agelaus, for Oenone —and better for Troy too!*

Paris had the body brought within the walls of Troy, and Priam gave the honorable old man a hero's funeral (indeed he had died a hero's death protecting the King's herds), with feasting and games. A few foreigners had been caught in the marketplace on the day of the first raid. They had been buried decently in the Temple of Hermes, who was the God of travelers and strangers; but there had been none to claim their bodies, no mourners and no rites beyond what was needful to placate their angry ghosts. The old herdsman was the first Trojan citizen to die in this war, and Paris, at least, would never forget; he cut his hair in mourning, and when Kassandra next saw him, at the naming feast for Creusa's firstborn, she hardly recognized her twin.

"Was this necessary? He was no more than a servant," she said, "though an old and honored one. But even so . . . "

"He was my foster-father," Paris said. "All through my childhood I knew no other." His eyes were red with weeping; she had not known he was capable of so much grief. "May the Gods forget me too if ever I forget to honor his memory."

"I did not mean to suggest he was unworthy of your mourning," Kassandra said, and at that moment she felt that in a sense he was more truly her brother than he had ever been. She had always been the undesired sharer of his feelings, an intruder; now she was beginning to know him for the person he was, faults and virtues too, and to understand him a little.

They were still standing side by side when the alarm sounded again, and from outside there was the rush of women and children to take shelter in the citadel; Kassandra went to deal with the women who were carrying heavy babies and toddlers, while Paris went, grumbling, to arm himself and join Hector's men at the wall. Next to the city gates there was an inner stair which led up inside the great wall, and here the men gathered; Kassandra, watching them, felt that perhaps she and her brother would both have been happier if they could have changed places.

She was busy all day helping to amuse the women and children and keep them quiet; confinement made them fractious, and she wondered sometimes if the men did not have a simpler time of it out there with a target at which to shoot. It would certainly, she thought, be a pleasure to take aim at some of these wretched brats—and then she stopped herself: the children had done nothing except behave as children always did. *See how wicked I am, to be provoked by these little innocents.* Yet she admitted to herself that she would like to take some of them in either hand and shake them until their little teeth rattled in their heads.

Chryseis was behaving very well; she had gathered the children round her and started them playing a romping game. And of course that was exactly what a nice young girl ought to be doing; she was playing that game so well that all the palace women petted and praised her. Yet even she left the children after a while and came up to the top of the wall of the palace where Kassandra was standing. This time the raiders had not been content to raid the lower town, but were fighting in the steep streets below the palace, making for Priam's granaries and treasuries. Soon, she thought, they must fortify the walls and keep the Akhaians out of the lower city.

If only I had my bow; I am out of practice, but I could still manage to drive back some of them before they come near the palace.

Patience; that day will come. For a moment Kassandra thought someone had spoken. Chryseis touched her arm.

"Who are the chieftains among the Akhaians? Do you know any of them?"

"I know some of them; Agamemnon, that great black-bearded man there, is their leader." As always, the sight of him made her stomach clench with revulsion. But Chryseis surveyed him with open admiration.

"How strong he is, and how handsome. What a pity he is not our ally instead of our enemy."

Trying not to show her disgust and annoyance, Kassandra murmured, "Don't you ever think about anything but men?"

"Not very often," Chryseis said blithely. "What else should a woman think about?"

"But you too are one of Apollo's sworn virgins . . ."

"Not forever," Chryseis said, "nor have I ever ridden with the Amazons, or pledged myself to hate men. I am a woman; I did not bid the Gods make me so, but since that is my lot whether I wish it or no, why should I not rejoice in it?"

"Being a woman need not mean behaving like a harlot," said Kassandra, annoyed.

"I do not think you know the difference," Chryseis said. "You would prefer to be a man, would you not? If the laws permitted, I think you would take a wife."

Kassandra was about to give a sharp answer, then caught herself . . . Maybe Chryseis was right. She said stiffly, "We have all forgotten poor old Agelaus and his pyre. He must be consumed now; his bones should be put decently into an urn for burial. I will go; Paris is my brother, and I will do this last office of respect for his foster-father."

ALL THE rest of the winter and into early spring the raids continued, day after day, and eventually, on each of the higher hills south of the city, Priam set up camps where his watchmen could see the approach of the ships and light warning beacons. So the Akhaians, landing, found nothing but bare walls and well-defended heights, and they got nothing but the journey for their pains.

Then Priam's men took advantage of a long rainy spell to repair the outer walls and reinforce the great gates; when the Akhaians began to try and fight their way up the high streets into Troy itself, they could not enter. The lower city was a labyrinth of narrow streets built in steep steps, where a defender could easily kick an assailant's feet out from under him.

"They are not finding this city quite the ripe apple for the plucking which they thought it would be," Aeneas gloated, looking out over the palace wall at the streets black with Akhaians running up and down. Even Hector, for once, had been content to let the walls defend them, and most of the women in the city, it seemed, had come out to see the sight of the Akhaians' frustration. Andromache was there with her now-toddling son, and Creusa had her infant daughter tied into her shawl. These alarms had now become so frequent an event that Hecuba no longer troubled to provide breakfast for the unwilling guests in the citadel after a night's fighting; but when Hector issued handfuls of grain and flasks of oil to his fighting men, the rule was that any woman accompanying her husband could claim a similar share.

Kassandra stood by watching the distribution of rations and said, "Tell them to bring back the flasks."

Hector protested.

"The flasks are not worth much; why be niggardly?"

"It has nothing to do with niggardliness. The potters go out to fight with the rest of the men. If this is to go on for long, there will not be enough of them to make more for every fighting day."

"I see what you mean." Hector gave the order, and no one complained. The storehouses of Troy were still high-piled with grain, and for the moment there was no shortage of food. Kassandra joined the women of Priam's house in daily refilling the little oil flasks and pouring the rations of wine. Even at the end of winter there was plenty in the palace granaries; but Hector had begun to frown over them in concern.

"How shall we do the spring sowing if they raid us every day?" he asked one night at dinner in the palace.

"Surely they will not come during spring planting," Andromache said. "At home in my country, all wars are suspended at planting and harvest to do honor to the Gods."

"But these Akhaians do not fear the Mother," Aeneas said, "and perhaps they will not honor our Gods."

"But are not all the Immortals one?" Kassandra asked.

"You know that. I know it," Aeneas said. "Whether those Akhaians know it—that is another story. From what I heard, it would not surprise me greatly if they felt war more important to them than any Gods." He smiled at her and said, "Don't worry about it, Kassandra. It is men's business."

"Yet if they come," she said, "it is the women who will suffer more than the men."

He looked surprised for a moment. Then he said, "Why, that's so; I never thought of that before. A man faces nothing worse than an honorable death; but women must face rape, capture, slavery . . . It's true: war is not for women, but for men. I wonder how a woman would conduct this war."

Kassandra said with great bitterness, "A woman would have managed never to provoke it. Then, if the Akhaians wanted the gold and goods of Troy, they would have come against us knowing they were not fighting for 'honor,' but out of greed, which the Gods hate."

"Remember, Kassandra, there are men who think of this war as a great playing field, a games-ground where the prizes are no more than laurel wreaths and honor."

Kassandra nodded. "Hector runs into every battle as if he were to win a bronze caldron and a white bull with gilded horns."

"No, you are wrong," Aeneas said; "there is nothing foolish or reckless about Hector. It is only that we all must live under the rule of our chosen God; and Hector belongs to the God of battles. But his God is not my God; war may be a part of my life, but it will never be my only chosen life." He touched her cheek lightly and said, "You look weary, Sister; there cannot be so much here for which you must fatigue yourself. The Queen has many women, and any one of them could do these small services. I think the Gods have ordained something more important for you; and we men may need your special strengths before this war comes to its end—whatever end the Gods have decreed for us."

He turned away, stopping beside his wife. She saw him bend to look inside the shawl, touching the baby's face with his finger; he said something, laughing, and turned away to go back to the men.

How different from Khryse, Kassandra thought, watching him move down the hill. *I said it at his wedding: if my father had found me such a husband, I would have been glad.*

In all my life—and I am almost the only woman of my years at the court of Priam who has not been given a husband—I have not seen any man whom I would willingly wed. Save this one, and he is my half-sister's husband and the father of her child.

She straightened her back wearily and bent again to the task of filling the little flasks of oil.

"Kassandra, you are spilling oil all down the edges; don't fill the ladle so full," reproved Creusa, coming to sit beside her. "What was my husband saying to you for so long?"

"He was asking how I should conduct this war if I were a soldier," Kassandra said, surprised into truthfulness. But Creusa only laughed.

"Well, don't tell me if you don't want to," she said scornfully. "I am not the sort of woman who is jealous if her husband says two words to another woman."

"I told you the truth, Creusa; that was one of the things he said. Also, we were wondering what we should do if the Akhaians fail to observe the sowing-truce for spring planting."

"Oh, I suppose because you are a priestess, and would know about such things," Creusa said. "But even Agamemnon could not be as impious as that. Could he?" And when Kassandra did not answer immediately she demanded, "You who are a prophetess—you should know that. Could he?"

Kassandra could not answer; but she said, "I hope not. I do not know what they do, or how they serve their Gods."

7

BUT BEING a prophetess was not enough; later the whole first year of the war became a blur in her mind of fires, raids, men screaming, burned alive from fire-arrows. A woman had wandered down unwitting into the Akhaian camp, and been abused by a dozen men. She was found screaming in delirium; the healer-priestesses of the Sun Lord's Temple fought to save her, but on the first day she seemed well enough to be left unguarded for a moment, she flung herself from the high wall of the citadel, and someone too lowborn to avoid the task had to go down and retrieve her shattered and broken body from the stones far below.

A few days before spring sowing, the priests and priestesses rose to a joyous trumpet call from the palace below, and found the harbor empty of ships; the Akhaians had gone away, leaving only a long black strip of beach, dirty and fouled from where their tents had been.

There was rejoicing in the city, even as all Hector's men went down to clean away their filth and debris. His son, little Astyanax, came too. Running about now, and prattling, he was a great pet among the soldiers; every minute he brought up some abandoned bit of rubbish he thought a treasure: a shining bronze harness-buckle, a wooden comb broken to a stub, a bit of used vellum on which someone had scrawled a crude map of the city. Kassandra took this from the protesting child and stood looking at it for a long time, wondering what enemy of Troy had made this.

"Give it back!" shouted Astyanax, reaching up for it, and Kassandra said, "No, little one. Your grandsire must see this."

"See what?" asked Hector, taking the parchment from her hand and giving it back to the child. Kassandra bent and reclaimed it, disregarding the angry child's howls.

"What is the matter with you, Kassandra? Give it to him. They are gone; there is no reason to care what rubbish they may leave behind," Hector said. "No. Stop yelling, little son, and you shall have a ride in Father's chariot."

"They are not gone for long," Kassandra said, "or, with *this*, would they have given up such an advantage?"

"You are making too much of this," said Hector. "What do you want with it?"

She traced on it the familiar markings which she could not entirely read.

"Someone from Crete has done this; and I thought they

were our allies. I must show it to him . . ." Then she thought
better of it and said, "Helen has a Cretan woman among her
entourage; I will show this to Aithra." As both a Queen and a
priestess, if any woman knew this odd kind of writing, it would
be she.

"Well, if you wish," Hector said with a shrug. "I never knew
such a woman for making much of trifles."

But Aithra looked at it without comprehension and said
that she had indeed seen such markings in Crete, but she had
not been schooled to read them.

"I cannot even guess whose hand it may be," she said.
"Perhaps Khryse will know," and Kassandra was ashamed to
explain to the dignified woman why she did not wish to confront
the priest.

But at last she took it to Charis and explained; Charis knew
why she feared and disliked Khryse, and agreed to come with
her while she consulted the priest.

Khryse examined it carefully, frowning, his lips moving,
tracing the symbols with his forefinger; then he looked up and
said, "This is no more than a map of the city; but the names are
written on it. See? This shows the Queen's chambers, the granaries, the great dining-hall, every part of the palace marked;
see, and Apollo's Temple, and here the Temple of Pallas
Athene."

"I thought as much," said Kassandra: "Can you tell me who
wrote this?"

"I cannot say who wrote this; but it was no friend of Troy.
I can say only that it was probably not a Cretan," said Khryse,
"for we are taught to make the letters differently, just a little, in
Crete."

That much, Kassandra thought, she could have guessed.
Later she took it to Priam, who paid little attention, though he
at once recognized it for what it was.

"I cannot think of a dozen men outside Troy who could
have drawn this; armed with this, it would be no task at all to
find any place in Troy," he said. "Only one who knew the palace
and the city very well could have done it, and I cannot think
that one of ourselves would have done so. Only . . ." Priam

hesitated, then shook his head. "No; he is my sworn friend and has been our guest. I cannot believe that he would betray us."

"Father, who?" she asked, and Priam, shaking his head, said "No. Only . . . No."

"Odysseus?" she asked.

"Kassandra, do you really think my old friend could be so false?"

She did not wish to think this of Odysseus; but the possibility was there. She said only, "In war men forget other oaths, Father."

"It may be. But he pledged to me that he would not be drawn into this war," Priam said. "I will not accuse him unheard. Your thoughts are filled with poison, Kassandra."

"Father, it was not I who thought of such a thing," she said, "I only asked if that was your thought."

"I am still certain that I wrong my old friend with such an idea," Priam said, "and I shall wait to ask him to his face if this was his work."

In her heart, Kassandra was certain; Odysseus, so she had heard, was full of such crafts and wiles. Yet she did not wish, either, to think he would betray his old friendship with Priam and with Troy.

There was not long to wait; the Akhaians had not been gone ten days when the ship of Odysseus was sighted in the harbor. Kassandra had come to the palace to visit Creusa and make a healing brew for her child, who was ailing with a summer fever, and afterward was summoned to the great hall. Aeneas came at once to greet her; as usual, he embraced her and kissed her cheek.

"Is it well with the child, Sister?"

"Oh, yes; there is nothing much wrong with her; I would do better to make a potion for Creusa which would cure her anxieties. Every time the wind changes, she thinks the little one is sick to death. At least Andromache has learned that babies have little upsets and it is better not to dose them too much: they will get better by themselves, and if they do not, there is time enough to call for a healer."

"I am relieved to hear it; but be patient with Creusa, Sister;

she is young and it is her first child. Come and have some dinner," Aeneas said, leading her forward. Odysseus got up from the guest-seat beside Priam and came to Kassandra; he embraced her so hard that she flinched and gave her a great smacking kiss.

"So it is my beautiful best girl," he said, "and what have you been doing these months of war? I have a gift for you: a string of amber beads which matches your bright eyes exactly; I have never known anyone else whose eyes are that yellow with just a glint of red in their depths," he added, drawing out the necklace from the folds of his tunic and putting it round her neck. Kassandra sighed, taking it off and holding it between her hands, examining the shining beads almost covetously.

"I thank you; it is very beautiful, but I would not be allowed to wear it. Should you not bestow it directly as a gift to the Sun Lord?"

Odysseus took back the necklace, frowning.

"It suits you so well; and the Sun Lord, though I have no quarrel with Him"—he made a pious gesture—"has no need of such gifts as I can give." He looked round the room, and his eyes fell on Helen, sitting modestly in Paris' shadow.

Helen said in her gentle voice, "Dear old friend, I will keep the necklace for Kassandra, and she shall have it back whenever she wants to ask for it." She was quite obviously pregnant by now, but Kassandra saw with a sigh that it seemed to make her even more beautiful. Andromache had been strong and healthy throughout, but she had looked pale and bloated, while Creusa had been sick all during her pregnancy, unable to hold down any food, and so wasted that she looked like a rat dragging about a stolen melon. Helen looked, Kassandra thought, just like one of the carven pregnant Goddesses she had seen in Colchis; or like Aphrodite if the Goddess of Love would allow Herself to be seen pregnant.

Helen took the necklace from Odysseus' hands. She said gently, almost affectionately, to Kassandra, "Who knows, my sister? You may not always be in the Sun Lord's service. I give you my word, this necklace is yours anytime you ask for it."

Against her will, Kassandra was warmed by the glow of

Helen's presence. She said, more affectionately than she intended, "Thank you, my sister," and Helen pressed her hand and smiled at her.

Priam interrupted testily, "It is all very well to stand here as my guest and bestow trinkets on the girls, Odysseus, but tell me, did I not see your ship among the raiders', and were you not among the enemy at the walls? I thought you had promised to me that you would not be drawn into war against me with those Akhaians."

"That is true, my old friend," said Odysseus, grinning and draining the wine from his cup at one draft. Polyxena came to refill the cup, and he smiled up at her—almost a leer—and patted her rounded buttocks. "Would that I were still unwedded, pretty thing; if your father could have given you to me—even if I am old enough to be your grandsire, and I am not given to seeking brides in their cradles—then Agamemnon could not have tricked me into coming against old acquaintances this way."

Priam looked politely skeptical. "I confess, my friend, I do not understand."

"Well," said Odysseus, and Kassandra reflected that Odysseus would certainly make a good story of it, truth or falsehood. "You do remember that I stood with the suitors for Helen when she wedded Menelaus. Helen, I think, has forgiven me that I was not one of her suitors—I wanted only to marry Penelope, daughter of Ikarios."

Helen smiled. "May the Gods of Truth forgive you as firmly as I have done, my friend. I only hoped I might gain a husband as faithful to me as you to your Penelope."

Odysseus continued, "And when all the suitors were fighting, it was I who created the compromise that broke the deadlock: that Helen choose for herself and that all of us take an oath to defend her chosen husband against all contenders. So when this war broke out, there was I, caught in my own trap; Agamemnon sent for me to come fulfill the oath I had taken to Menelaus."

Priam scowled, though Kassandra could tell that her father was not really angry; he wanted the rest of the story. "And what of your oath to be my guest and friend?"

"I did my best to honor it, Priam, I vow to you," said the old seaman. "I have seen enough of the world; I wanted to stay home and look after my own acres. So I had Penelope send a message that I was sick and could not come; that my wits were astray, that I was a poor madman. And when Agamemnon came, I put on my plowman's old hat, and yoked my horse and my ox together, and started to plow a field of thistle. And do you know what that"—he hesitated; "well, there are ladies present—that *Agamemnon* did?" He gave the name the force of an obscenity, and looked round to survey the effect of his story on his rapt audience. "He picked up my little son, Telemakhos— he was just toddling; about the size of your Astyanax, Hector— and he set him down in the field right in front of where I was plowing. So what was I supposed to do—plow right over the child? I swerved the team, and Agamemnon laughed to split his sides and said, 'Come on, old fox; you're no madder than I am!' and demanded I honor my oath to defend Menelaus. So I came; but believe me, it was I who sent them home to do their spring planting. They'll be back after that; I came to warn you all."

Priam had laughed as hard as anyone; then he sobered and said, "I can see how you could do no other than you have done, Odysseus. For all that, you are still my friend."

"I am," Odysseus said, and helped himself to fish and bread.

"And may you always be so," Priam replied, "as I am yours."

Kassandra narrowed her eyes, looking at Odysseus as if seeking the Sight. Try as she might, she saw only a harmless old man, genuinely torn between old friends and unwelcome neighbors with whom he must, for the safety of his own family, keep the peace. Yes, he would be their friend—as long as it was to his advantage to do so. Unless there was a good joke or a good story to be made out of his own cleverness or even treachery. No friendship would stand against that; not for Odysseus.

She quickly finished her own meal and, rising, asked her father for permission to withdraw. He gave it absentmindedly; she kissed her mother and Andromache, lifted little Astyanax in her arms and kissed him too, though he squirmed and insisted he was too big to be kissed, and left the hall.

After a minute she realized that someone had followed her. Thinking it was one of her sisters with a question to be asked of a priestess which was too private to ask before men, she stopped to wait. Then strong male arms went round her; and for a moment she rested in Aeneas' arms, before, regretfully, she drew away from him.

"Aeneas, no; you are my sister's husband."

"Creusa would not mind," Aeneas said in a whisper. "Since our child was born, she cringes whenever I come to her bed. She has no desire for me, I swear it. She would rejoice if I found love elsewhere."

"You will not find it with me," Kassandra said, sadly. "I too am sworn, my brother; sworn to the Sun Lord, and it would be a braver man than you who would contend with Him for a woman."

Aeneas said, "I will strive with Him if you want me to, Kassandra. For you I would dare even His wrath."

"Oh, hush," she said, holding her fingers over his mouth. "You did not say that. I did not hear it. But this much I will say, my dear," she went on, the endearment slipping from her lips almost without volition: "if we were both free, I would willingly have you, as husband or as lover—whatever you would. But I have seen the wrath of Apollo Sun Lord, and I would not knowingly dare it for any man; certainly not for you, whom I could well have loved."

"The Gods forbid," said Aeneas piously, "that I should contend against a God, unless you should demand it of me. If you are content to be the Sun Lord's bride and no other's . . ." He stepped back. "Be it as you will. Yet I swear by Apollo Himself"—and he raised her slender hand respectfully to his lips—"I shall be forever your faithful friend and your brother, and should you ever desire my help, I swear you shall have it, against any man—or any God."

She said, shaken, "I thank you for that; and I shall ever be your friend and your sister, whatever happens."

He held her gently by the shoulders. "Kassandra, my dear, you do not look happy. Are you truly content in Apollo's Temple?"

"If I were," she said in a whisper, "I would have run away from you before it ever came to this."

She drew away from him and went quietly out of the palace, her heart still beating so loudly she felt that Aeneas must have heard it. As she climbed the long hill toward the Sun Lord's house, she felt tears unshed pressing at her eyes.

I do not want to be false to my vows. I am sworn to Apollo, and it is He who has forsaken me; I would never betray Him with any mortal man, yet that blasphemous priest has had me disgraced in the Temple. For his sake I am defiled in their eyes when I am innocent of all wrongdoing.

Would the Goddess she had served during her time with the Amazons have taken the part of a man against Her sworn priestess? Was it only that a God, when a man and a woman contended, could not take a woman's part, whatever the rights of the matter? She was the property of the God, just as if she had married a mortal man.

Yet Khryse and I both belong to Apollo, and so we should have been equal in His sight.

She came through the great bronze doors, and the night watchman bent to her in reverence.

"You are abroad late, Princess."

"I have been at the palace with my father and mother," she said. "A good night to you."

"Good night, Lady," he said, and she went toward the rooms at the back where the women slept. She slipped out of her sandals and gown, and laid herself down to sleep.

Her eyes were still aching, and as she relaxed her muscles, she felt tears stealing unbidden down her face. The memory of Aeneas' embrace returned, and for a moment she played in her mind with the memory. If she would, she could take him from her half-sister, and Creusa would not even be angry with her; she would be pleased to be free of her wifely obligations to him. . . .

Who would be harmed if she should yield to Aeneas? Should she truly forget her vows, since she had had no good from them? Or was it that foreign Goddess of lawless love sending to tempt her? Then before her eyes the face of Aeneas was lost in the blazing memory of the Sun Lord's face, the soft, unforgettable music of His voice as He said *Kassandra* . . .

As she drifted into sleep she wondered: how could any woman choose a mere man above a God? Perhaps it was better to be forgotten or ignored by the Sun Lord than to be loved or cherished by any living man.

8

IT BEGAN to be rumored in the city that the Akhaians had given up and would not return. Kassandra knew better than that, for there were still times when she would look down from the high house of the Sun Lord, and see, for a moment, the city swallowed in flames. From this she knew that the gift of prophecy had not deserted her.

It was of no use to her or to anyone; when she spoke of it, no one would listen. *Nevertheless, O Lord Apollo, whatever may have been taken from me, a day will come when they will remember what I said and know I did not lie.*

She wondered at times, *This is only a curse, since no one believes what I say; why must I suffer in knowing and being unable to speak?* Yet when she would have prayed that the sight might be withdrawn, she thought, *Oh, no! How much worse to walk blind and unknowing into whatever the Fates have decreed.*

Yet if this was the fate of all men, how, then, did they manage to endure it?

Day after day the seas were free of warships or of raiders. Other ships came, bound northward to Colchis and the country of the North Wind, paying their tribute to Troy, and from Colchis Queen Imandra sent gifts and greetings to her daughter, and to Kassandra too.

One morning Kassandra found her snake lying dead in its pot; and this she took for the worst of omens. She had had but little time to spare for the creature lately, and blamed herself for not having seen that it was ailing. She asked leave to bury it on the Temple grounds. When this was done, Charis sent for her and set her in charge of all the serpents in Apollo's Temple.

"But why?" Kassandra asked. "I am not worthy; I tended mine so ill that it sickened and died."

"Why do we give you this task? Because you are not happy, Kassandra; do you think us blind? You are dear to me—dear to us all"; and as Kassandra made a gesture of protest, she said, "No, this is true; do you think us unaware of what Khryse has done to you? If we were free to turn him from the door, believe me, there are many who would do so. And now we have an excuse to give you a duty where you need not encounter him on every day and at every hour."

She still did not understand: why were they not free to turn him away from the Temple? He had attempted to rape a virgin of the God. It was a riddle she could not read; nor did Charis give any explanation, saying no more; evidently they were not even free to explain why Khryse had this hold over them.

There was a very old priestess in the Temple who had all kinds of serpent-lore; older than Hecuba—at least as much older than Queen Hecuba as Hecuba was older than her daughter. Kassandra, eager to avoid for the other serpents in the Temple the fate that had befallen her own snake, took to spending many hours with the old woman. Her hair was white and mostly fallen out, and her eyes sunken into her head. She suffered from a palsy of age, her hands shaking so that she could not grasp her own feeding-spoon; it was this ailment which had decreed that she had to be relieved of the care of the serpents.

Kassandra spent all her hours with the old woman, lifting her and feeding her, and when the priestess was strong enough to talk to her, learning all about every kind of snake and serpent, including many kinds no longer kept in the Temple. Sometimes Kassandra thought she would like to make a long journey simply to secure some of these stranger creatures for the house of Apollo: the ones who dwelt in the deserts far to the south, or one of the kind called Python, larger around than a child, and able to swallow a kid at a meal, or even a whole sheep. Kassandra was not entirely sure she believed in such a creature, but she liked hearing such tales, and would sit and listen all day to the old woman.

After the serpents had been fed there was little to do, except for seeing to old Meliantha's needs, and Kassandra would listen and daydream, thinking of her meeting with the Goddess as Serpent Mother in the Underworld and wondering how the story had arisen of Apollo Sun Lord slaying the Python.

The year was advancing; belated winter rains swept softly in from the sea, and on some bare branches could be seen little lumps where leaves would eventually unfold. One day she stood high atop the Sun Lord's house and heard a faraway shrill crying.

"Look, the cranes are flying north again." *I wonder*, she thought, *to what faraway land they travel, beyond the country of the North Wind.* But her companions had more practical thoughts in their minds.

"Soon it will be time for the spring planting festival," said Chryseis, and there was a greedy gleam in her eyes. "I am tired of being shut in with the women." Kassandra was struck with fear; surely with spring, the Akhaians would come. The last winter moon swelled and shrank, and there came days gray with soft rains; and a few days after the northward flight of the cranes, the clouds cleared, and the narrow new moon in the sky announced the coming of spring and the planting festival.

On the first day after the new moon, Kassandra was summoned to the palace to her mother's presence; she found her with her women, making implements for the planting rites, and a priestess of Earth Mother was there supervising the work.

Kassandra did not know what she was going to say until she heard herself saying it:

"Are you planning the festival so that the Akhaians can enjoy it? Surely to hold a festival now is only inviting them to come and despoil it!"

The priestess, an aging woman Kassandra did not know well, scowled at her.

"What would you suggest as an alternative, Lady Kassandra? We cannot refrain from planting the grain."

"Oh, I know that the grain must be sown," Kassandra said, almost frantic; "but must we draw attention to it with a festival?"

The priestess asked, frowning, "Do you expect to enjoy the gifts of the Goddess without doing Her honor?"

Kassandra, hardly knowing what to say, wanted to cry. *If the Goddess is so great and benevolent*, she thought, *surely She would give us the grain without demanding so much. Is the Earth Goddess an old market women to haggle with us—so much grain for so many songs and dances?* Since she could not say that, she said nothing at all, and knew the priestess was frowning at her with disapproval.

"What has the festival to do with you, who have chosen to remain a virgin in the house of the Sun Lord and do not pay the Goddess Her due?"

"It was not altogether by choice," she said meekly. "The Sun Lord called me, and Earth Goddess made no protest. If She had demanded of me that I serve Her, I would have obeyed."

And why did She not stretch forth Her bow to save me from the Sun Lord, then? Am I no more than a fleeing animal before the strife of these Gods?

But the priestess was still scowling at her, seeming to demand an answer, and Kassandra said, "Since I too am fed by Her bounty, I see no reason for a festival which will make the planting useless. For if the Akhaians come to destroy our festival, we will reap little from this planting."

"Are you saying to me that even the Akhaians do not pay honor to the Goddess?"

"I say only that I fear their impiety," said Kassandra. "If you believe that they pay honor to the Goddess, why not ask one of their devotees, or send a messenger to negotiate a truce and a pledge that they will not interfere with Earth Mother's rites?"

And for that fear I am badgered as if the impiety were mine own; I should learn to keep silence.

She bowed silently to the priestess, her warning given. It was no part of her duty to say more. Her mother had been looking on without speaking, and Kassandra crossed the room to join her.

"Can you not understand my fear, Mother?"

"I trust to the goodness of the Goddess; surely She can raise Her hand if She will to strike against these Akhaians," said Hecuba reprovingly. "You are too full of fears, Kassandra."

"You have served Earth Mother all these years; has She ever lifted Her hand to protect you?" asked Kassandra.

Her mother looked deeply displeased and said, "Such questions are not for women to ask; you who are a priestess should know better than to say such things. The Gods are not slow to punish those who speak against or question Them."

I should have been the one to say that, thought Kassandra. *I have lived in the Sun Lord's house and seen how He strikes— and how He protects—His own.* She sighed and said no more.

Her mother said gently, "I am not reproving you, Kassandra; but if you have found no happiness in the Sun Lord's house you should return to us here. I cannot think it entirely a good thing for a girl of your years to remain this long a maiden; if you return to Priam's house, your father will find you a husband. It would please me well to see you married and with a child in your arms. And then there would be no more of these evil dreams and prophecies to torment you."

In spite of her mother's loving tone, Kassandra felt a wave of anger so great that it choked her. *Ah, that is the remedy for all things that are wrong with women. If a woman is unhappy, or if she makes a mistake, or does not do what everyone else wants her to do, then she would be better to take a husband; and if she had a child, it would be the remedy for all her ills.* She said to her mother, "Ah, you too, Mother? When you rode with Penthesilea and her women, would you have been so quick to say that was what ailed me? Would you give me to a husband or see me pregnant just so I would not speak the truth and frighten people?"

Hecuba was dismayed at her angry tone. She patted Kassandra's knotted fingers and smoothed them gently, trying to unlock them. "Don't be angry, my dear; I don't know why you are always so angry. I only want to see you happy, my child."

"I am angry because I am surrounded by fools," said Kassandra, "and your only answer would be to make me one of them."

She stood up and flung herself out of the room. Her mother was hopeless. And yet there had been a time when she was strong and self-sufficient; Kassandra had her weapons to prove it. And why had she let her mother divert her from the real issue, which was the danger to the spring planting? Her mother had chosen to substitute for it the old issue of marriage—as if a married woman automatically gained wisdom. Andromache was certainly no wiser for her marriage to Hector, nor Creusa for being married to Aeneas.

If I thought that it could work some such great change in me, then would I be not only willing, but eager to marry!

9

A LITTLE BEFORE daybreak Kassandra heard the jingling of bells and the sounds of movement in the city below. As she raised her head, a wave of sickness rolled over her; it seemed to her that the quiet room was alive with shrieks and the clash of arms. *Oh, no,* she thought, falling back on her pillow and pulling the blanket over her head. For a few minutes she lay unmoving. She had vowed that if there was to be a catastrophe, she would be far from it when it happened; she had delivered the warning, and that was quite enough.

But outside her room, the sounds of the festival went on; soon they would come and call her, and at last she rose and dressed herself, and went to care for the Temple serpents. She half expected that on a day of such evil omen she would find them all hiding inside their pots and holes; but they seemed to be behaving exactly as always. She fetched food from the kitchens and fed old Meliantha bread soaked in watered wine. When all had been done that she could find to do, she looked over the wall and saw hundreds of women streaming down from the gates of Troy to the fertile area between the rivers. She did not put on her holiday garment, nor stop to fashion a garland for herself; but she braided her dark hair loosely to keep it out of her eyes, then left the Temple. On the path below, she recognized before her a familiar figure and a head of reddish golden hair. She hurried to catch up with the woman.

"Oenone, what are you doing here? Are there no crops to be sown on Mount Ida, my sister?"

Encouraged by her words, Oenone smiled affectionately at Kassandra; but she did not speak, and after a moment Kassandra knew, as if the other woman had told her, that she hoped for a glimpse of Paris. Kassandra could give her no encouragement or hope in this, so she lifted her hands to the chubby toddler riding on his mother's shoulder.

"How big he grows! Is he not heavy to carry on your shoulder this way?"

"His eyes are dark and he looks more and more like his father," Oenone said, not answering Kassandra's question. Indeed, the boy's eyes, smoky blue at birth like so many babies', had darkened to a glowing hazel not unlike Paris' or Kassandra's own.

Much good may that do him, Kassandra thought, so angry that she could hardly speak. Because she could not chide Oenone for this hopeless and absurd quest, she said crossly, "Go home, Oenone; tend to the crops on Mount Ida. Little good will come of this planting here. The Gods are angry with Troy. Paris will not be here; this festival is for women—I should think you knew our customs well enough by now to know that."

"Still, if there is need, I will come and pray with the others to turn away the anger of Earth Mother," said Oenone, and Kassandra knew that nothing she said would make the slightest difference.

So she said, "Let me carry the baby for you," and held out her arms for the child. He was heavy indeed, but she had offered and would not withdraw her help. A pity Paris would not come and carry his own son, she thought. Now, among the women coming down from the palace she saw her mother, and Andromache with Hector's son Astyanax, now tall enough to walk at his mother's side, clutching her skirt.

Creusa's baby, still small enough to be tied in her shawl, was slung over her shoulders. Polyxena led the group of Priam's daughters, all wearing the traditional beribboned festival tunic of maidens, their long curls floating in the breeze. They saw Kassandra and waved to her, and she did not feel churlish enough to refuse to return the greeting. If they would not postpone the festival or hold it quietly, in a way that would not attract the catastrophe she had foreseen, they might as well enjoy themselves while they could. Up the hill someone had started the first of the planting songs:

> *Bring the grain, by the winter hidden,*
> *Bring it with songs and feasting and joy . . .*

Other women took up the song. Kassandra heard Creusa's strong, sweet voice, and then the others'; but when she tried to sing she felt choked, and her own voice would not carry.

"Look," said Oenone, pointing. "The men are on the wall watching us. There is your father, my precious," she said, trying to attract the attention of the child to where Paris stood in his bright armor, the pale early sunlight reflecting off it in arrowlike rays.

The child twisted in Kassandra's arms, trying to see what his mother was pointing at; he was heavy enough to throw Kassandra off balance, so that she nearly fell.

"I had better take him," said Oenone, and Kassandra did not protest. She could see the crimson plumes that surrounded Hector's helmet, Priam's brilliant armor and Aeneas, taller than any of the other men.

They had now reached the fields; the ground had been prepared days before. The women stooped and took off their sandals, for no shod foot might tread the breasts of Earth Mother in this rite. Hecuba, wearing a scarlet robe, raised her hands for the invocation, then paused and beckoned to Andromache; the younger woman, in her own brilliant scarlet gown from Colchis, came forward to take her place.

Kassandra understood: Hecuba was an old woman, and although she had borne seventeen children, of whom more than half had survived their fifth year—a splendid sign of Earth Mother's favor—she was now passing beyond the years of childbearing, and this rite must be performed by a fertile woman, a mother. For the last years it had not mattered so much, but now, when this year's grain was crucial to the survival of the city, no chance could be taken that a woman barren with age might affront Earth Mother by her presence in the greatest of rites.

Andromache gestured, and all virgins and all others who had never borne a living child left the plowed acres. Kassandra nodded farewell to Oenone and moved toward the small stone fences and grown-over hedges of thorn and rank bushes at the edge of the field. They were far from barren; she could hear concealed within them the sound of small insects, crickets and beetles, and many herbs and plants whose uses she was beginning to know grew at the margin of the fields. She observed a narrow leaf good for curing rashes on the skin of children and small animals; she stooped to cut it, murmuring a whispered prayer to the Goddess for this bounty even outside the lands given to Her grace.

Now that the women were in the fields, the men were coming down. King Priam, the father of his people, in his richly dyed crimson loincloth, naked otherwise except for a string of purple stones around his neck, took the wooden plow between his hands and raised it high in the air; the cheer that went up was deafening. With his own hands he yoked a white donkey to the shafts of the plow; Kassandra knew that this animal had been chosen from all the beasts in Troy for the King's plowing because it was without blemish, and the owner had been highly paid.

Priam dug the plowshare into the field, and again a cheer arose as it opened a dark brown strip of fertile loam within the pale sun-dried surface of the earth. The women's voices now lifted in a new song. When Kassandra was quite a little girl, she had been told that the songs were to drown the cries of Earth Mother at being thus ravished. During her sojourn with the Amazons, she had been taught a more sophisticated theory: that Earth Mother gave food to Her children of Her free will, and the songs were only praise and thanksgiving; but even now she had to repress a shudder as the plow broke through the soil.

Now all the fertile women of the city burst onto the field;

all together they stripped off their upper garments, exposing their breasts, and made symbolic gestures of giving their milk to the waiting land, to nourish the fields. Over half of them were pregnant, from young girls just swelling with their first babies, their breasts no larger than green peaches, to women Hecuba's age who had borne a child every year or so for a generation, their long flabby breasts bared to the sky and sun.

Kassandra joined in the cry which rose to heaven:

"Earth Mother, nourish Your children, we cry to You."

Baskets of seed were relayed to all the fertile women, and they began passing them down the field, scattering the grain. Priam, shoved in rude haste to the edge of the field, stumbled, and measured his length on the soil, staining his garb. There were gasps at this evil omen, and he was picked up and borne off tenderly to where the rest of the men were surrounding the field now, watching the sowing. The sun was high, beating down with dazzling force.

"Maybe the earth would bear no matter what we do or don't do," a big rough man Kassandra had never seen before suggested. "I have been in heathen places where they know nothing of our Gods, and crops grow there too, just the same as here."

"You be quiet, Ajax; we don't need any of your foolish ideas," said a strong deep voice Kassandra identified as that of Aeneas. "Whether it has to do with the Gods or not, this is the way things are done for decency and custom; and why not?"

Thunder rumbled in the distance and clouds moved across the face of the sun. Kassandra felt the insects in the hedges grow silent. Then a few drops of rain rattled against the dry branches of the hedges, and within moments the flimsy garments of the women were flattened against their bodies. They sent up a cry: "Thanks be to Earth Mother, who sends rain to nourish us!"

The songs had quieted as the rain grew hard. Now the women finished sowing the last of the seed, and everyone, including the little girls and the women who were old and barren, ran out onto the field to assist in covering the last of the grain. Kassandra had started to run and join Oenone when a dark surge came before her eyes, and she paused, dizzy, not sure that the ground had not rocked beneath her feet.

Then there was a war cry, and she saw men in dark tunics rushing out onto the field, shouting and yelling. A man in armor seized Oenone and, flinging her over his shoulder, rushed for the dark line of ships that had appeared while all eyes were on the plowing and sowing.

By old custom, the Trojans had brought no weapons to the field; most of them now were running for the city wall where they had left them. Paris was one of the first to reappear on the wall, shooting arrow after arrow into the throng of strange soldiers. The man who held Oenone fell struggling, struck through the heart, and Oenone freed herself. There were many arrow and javelin shots, and many of the Akhaians fell; most of the others who had also seized women dropped them, and managed to reach the ships before the hailstorm of arrows cut them down. Oenone reached Hecuba's side and looked round for her child; finding him safe, she joined the small knot of women around the Queen. Kassandra was still in the protection of the hedge. She saw Helen beside Oenone, and wondered what, if anything, Paris' two wives found to say to each other. She noted, too, Helen's shapely body, obviously swollen in pregnancy.

She wondered if Menelaus had seen. If so, Menelaus would now surely rather go home and leave Helen to Paris; he would not keep fighting for the mother of some other man's child.

Kassandra, choosing her moment carefully, left the hedge and raced across the field, breathlessly crowding into the circle near the Queen, taking her place beside Oenone. All the women were looking down fearfully at the Akhaians nearing their ships. She picked out the tall beaked figure of Agamemnon; he was no monster now, only a man, rougher, stronger and crueler than most, but the sight of him still made her blood run cold.

Hecuba was looking around and counting her women. "Are you all here? Has anyone been taken?"

A group of women from the Sun Lord's house were clustered together at the fringe of Hecuba's women. Phyllida was unobtrusively counting them; she cried out, "Oh, where is

Chryseis? Was she not with you, Kassandra? I thought I saw her at your side."

"Yes, she was with me; perhaps she is still in the hedge. Shall I go back and see? All of—of *them* have gotten back to their ships, I think."

"No," Phyllida said firmly, "you must not expose yourself; remember, you are Priam's daughter, and you would be a great prize to any one of the invaders. Stay here close to your mother," she admonished, as Hecuba came and grasped Kassandra's hand.

"So you are safe? I was worried about you," Hecuba said. "How did you know they would attack us?"

"I thought it likely," Kassandra said, "and so it was."

"But they have not taken any captives," Hecuba said, "and so they have had all their trouble for nothing."

"No, we did not come off untouched," Kassandra said. "They managed to take one of the maidens from Apollo's Temple."

"Oh, how dreadful!" Hecuba said with a gasp.

Kassandra privately thought the loss a small one; the girl had been a troublemaker from the first, and it was not even certain that she was a maiden.

She was grateful that the attack had done so little harm. She decided to seek out Helen and ask when her child would be born. Once again it seemed that Helen was under the spell of the Goddess; even at the most unattractive stage of pregnancy, she seemed beautiful and glowing. It was not only Paris whose eyes followed her as bits of lint follow amber.

Helen smiled at Kassandra with such intense welcome that Kassandra felt almost weak in the knees. The favor of the Goddess was to be treasured. Without it the women here might have torn the Spartan Queen to pieces; after all, she had brought the men of Troy into the dangers of this war. *But I have no husband or lover*, thought Kassandra, *for whom I must fear.* Helen embraced her, and Kassandra returned the greeting warmly.

Strange; when she first came here it was I who pleaded to my father and mother that they should have nothing to do with her. Now I love her well, and if they sought to cast her out, I would be the first to speak in her favor. Is it the will of the Goddess she incarnates? Do I serve Her in befriending Helen? No; now, bearing a child, she must seek the favor of Earth Mother.

"When is the baby due?"

"At autumn harvest," said Helen.

"And it is Paris' child? Then perhaps," Kassandra suggested, "Menelaus will go away and be content to leave you here."

Helen smiled cynically. "If he should say it, no one would listen," she said. "Come, Kassandra, you know as well as I that my body and my adultery are only a pretext for this war; Agamemnon has been seeking a good excuse for years to attack Troy. If I sought to return to Menelaus tonight under cover of darkness, I would wager anything you like that my dead body would be found hanging on the wall and the Akhaians would keep fighting on the pretext of avenging me."

This was so likely true that Kassandra did not bother to comment. Helen said in annoyance, "There have been many times when I felt it would be best if I had been sworn a virgin to the Moon Maiden. Even now I am tempted to forswear men forever in Her shrine; would She have me, do you think?"

"How should I know?" Kassandra replied hesitantly.

"Well, you are a priestess . . ."

"All I know is that She denies no woman who comes before Her," Kassandra said, "but it seems to me that your destiny is to become a symbol of strife among men; and no one can argue with destiny."

"It would be too good to be true, I suppose, that I should be able to seek the Goddess and in Her shadow avert the known pattern of my fate," Helen said. "But how do I know it is a God who has determined this fate and not that I have simply become entangled between two willful men who care nothing for the Gods?"

"I think this is the kind of thing no one can ever know," Kassandra said. "Yet I do feel the hand of some God in this; I know how Paris was driven to seek you."

"Then you mean that this war between Troy and my people was determined by the Immortals?" Helen asked. "Why? I mean, why me and not some other?"

"If I knew that," said Kassandra, "I should then be the most favored seer of the Gods. I can only guess that the Goddess who favored you with such beauty had this purpose in mind."

"And I still ask: why me and not some other?"

"Ask as much as you will," Kassandra said, "and if you receive an answer, come and share it with me."

10

KASSANDRA DREAMED that the Gods were angry with the city and were fighting above Troy; They towered to the sky, Their spears clashing with thunderbolts, and the glare of Their great swords was like lightning. She woke to a day of heavy dripping rain, and a dull ache in her eyes.

Surprisingly, she missed Chryseis; she had grown used to the girl's company and could not help dwelling with fear and disgust on what must have befallen her in the camp of the Akhaians—they had, after all, been there for several months without their own women. Although she knew that some of the women of the town slipped out through the walls into the shoreline camp to sell their bodies, she did not suppose it was the same. However, when she thought to pity Chryseis, she found herself thinking that this had been exactly what the girl wanted; she had been eyeing the foreigners over the wall for some months now.

Dismissing the girl from her thoughts, Kassandra threw on a robe and went to care for the serpents and the old priestess.

When she entered the room set apart for the old woman and the serpents, she found confusion; two or three statues had been overturned and were lying broken about the room, and there was not a single snake anywhere. She called out—she had heard that snakes were deaf and could hear nothing, but she was not certain about that, and calling would do no harm—and old Meliantha's voice came feebly from an adjacent room: "Is that you, Kassandra, daughter of Priam?"

Kassandra went quickly to the dark inner room, where the old woman lay on a pallet.

"What ails you, Meliantha? Are you ill?"

"No," said the aged priestess, "I am dying." Kassandra saw by the dim light that her face had shrunk even further; her eyes were dimmed and covered with a white film. "You need not call out to the serpents, for they have gone; all of them. They have left us and retreated deep into the earth. Those that are still here are lying dead in their pots—look and see." Kassandra went to investigate, and saw a few unbroken pots lying in place; inside them, the serpents lay cold and still. She returned to the old priestess to ask what had happened.

"Did you not feel the anger of the Earth Shaker in the night? Not only the pots, but all my statues are broken."

"No, I heard nothing; but I had evil dreams of the anger of the Gods," Kassandra said. "Is it Serpent Mother who is angry with us?"

"No," said the old priestess scornfully. "She would not punish Her serpents to show Her anger with us; rather She would slay us for the well-being of Her little folk. Whichever God has done this, Serpent Mother had nothing to do with it."

The old woman looked so agitated that Kassandra wished to comfort her. "Will you have bread and wine, Lady?"

"No; I cannot think of such things at a time like this," the old woman said. "Dress me in my priestess' robes, and paint my face, and then carry me out into the sunlight in the courtyard, so that I may look one more time upon the face of the Sun Lord for whom I have spent my life."

Kassandra did as she was bidden, assisting the old woman into the elaborate robe of pleated linen dyed brilliant yellow with saffron. She found a pot of cosmetics and as the old woman wished, hesitantly painted her cheeks and lips brilliant red with dye, though she thought it looked grotesque. At last she stooped and picked up the old priestess in her arms and carried her into the brilliant light of the courtyard, where she laid her down on some cushions. The old woman, exhausted, lay back, and Kassandra could see the pulse in her blue vein beating away hard in her temple. Her breath was a hoarse, exhausted rasp.

"Shall I not summon a healer to you, Lady?"

"No; it is too late for that," Meliantha said. "I am glad I will not live to see the days that are coming to Troy. But you have been good to my little people, and I shall pray with my dying breath that somehow you may escape what the Fates have determined for this wretched city." She shut her eyes for a moment, and Kassandra bent forward to hear if she still breathed. Meliantha put out a wavering hand.

"Closer, my child, I cannot see your face," she said, "yet it shines before me like a star; the Sun Lord has not forsaken you." Then she kissed Kassandra with her wrinkled lips and, opening her filmed old eyes, she cried out, "Apollo, Sun Lord! Let me see Thy face bright before me!"

She trembled violently and fell back upon the cushions, and Kassandra knew she was gone.

Now it could not hurt her to be left alone, so Kassandra ran to tell Charis what had happened.

"She was the oldest of us all," Charis said. "I came here as a child of nine and she was already old then. I felt the Earth Shaker in the night, and I should have gone to her; but it was just as well. I could have done her no good. Well, we must bury her as befits a priestess of Apollo," she said, and sent the women for flowers to make garlands and for honey cakes and wine.

"We do not mourn when one of our own goes to the eternal realms," she chided the sobbing women. "We rejoice because after a long life of service the Serpent Mother has taken her. And see"—she indicated the dead snakes lying in their pots— "her little friends have gone before her to welcome her into those realms; there she can see them again and play with them, as she always loved to do."

TWO DAYS later, Kassandra heard the alarm in the city announcing an Akhaian attack, and saw the men of Troy rushing down to meet the invaders, her brother Paris among them. She was surprised at how commonplace this was beginning to seem, not only to her, but apparently to all the people of Troy. Except for the fighting men, no one seemed to pay much attention to the attacks. The smooth routine of the Temple didn't alter at all, and from the wall she could see townswomen going calmly to the cisterns with their water jars.

One nonfighting man, however, was still interested in the actions of the Akhaians. At the end of the wall nearest the fighting, Khryse stood scowling as he watched the fight. Kassandra, not wishing to deal with him, slipped away back to the maidens' rooms. *The people of Troy*, she thought, *are starting to regard the Akhaians with all the concern they would give to a sudden hailstorm. Can't they see that this will be our destruction? But I suppose that no one can live in a state of terror for years on end. No doubt I'd feel the same complacency if I did not have the visions to unsettle me.*

Shortly afterward, a messenger from the city reached her, saying that the Lady Helen was in labor and wished to see her. With Meliantha's death, Kassandra had few or no obligations in the Sun Lord's house, and so she did not bother to ask leave, but went down at once to the palace. She found her mother and sisters, except for Andromache, all gathered in Helen's rooms.

Kassandra inquired about Andromache and was told that she had taken all the littlest children to her room to tell them stories and feed them sweets.

"For if there is anything we do not need in the birthing-chamber," said Creusa, "it is the babies under our feet."

Kassandra thought she was most probably right; she wondered if it was good nature on Andromache's part, or whether she shrank from remembering her own ordeal. It did not matter; in any case, it needed doing, and Andromache's motives were not important.

The birthing-chamber was quite crowded enough as it was, and most·of the women were more obstacles to be stepped around than any kind of help to a woman in early labor; but custom demanded witnesses for a royal birth. Kassandra wondered if the Akhaians had the same custom, and resolved to ask Helen when they had leisure. At the moment, however, Helen was surrounded with so many midwives, waiting-women insistent on curling her hair or showing her some garment or piece of jewelry she might want, priestesses bearing amulets or chanting healing spells, cooks with morsels and drinks to tempt her appetite, that Kassandra could not get near the bed and resolved to wait till Helen asked for her.

Creusa had brought a lap-harp with her, and sat in the corner producing a quiet and calming background strumming. After a time Helen noticed Kassandra in the crowd and beckoned to her.

"Come and sit here beside me, Sister; this is like a festival —and so it is for most of them, I suppose."

"Like a wedding," Kassandra said. "Great fun for everyone except the ones most concerned. All we need in here is a few acrobats and dancing-girls, and someone showing off a two-headed rabbit for coppers, and a fire-eater or a sword-swallower . . ."

"I'm sure if I wanted them, Hecuba would provide them," Helen said with a droll lift of her eyebrows. Kassandra noticed that even under these trying circumstances she was ravishingly lovely.

"Acrobats and dancing-girls, at least," Kassandra said. "Priam has several of them in the palace. I'm not sure about two-headed rabbits."

"Oh, fie, Kassandra; our royal mother would not—it would be beneath her dignity to take notice of Priam's dancing-girls or flute-girls," Creusa said, between chords. Kassandra laughed.

"Don't you believe that; Hecuba's business is to oversee the food for every person under this roof. She probably knows how many olives each of them eats at dinner, which ones are greedy for honey and cakes, and which ones are careful never to get with child."

"Of course; an acrobat can put herself out of work for a year, if she gets pregnant," Helen said. "I had two girls, sisters, in Mykenae, who used to come and dance for me." It was the first time she had spoken of her old home that Kassandra could remember. "No working girl wants to be burdened with carrying and birthing. That's for ladies of leisure—like us."

"Perhaps we work hardest of all," Kassandra said. "My mother has borne and suckled seventeen children."

Helen shivered. "I am already three-and-twenty, and I have

only Hermione and Nikos; I am fortunate," she said—and then a surprised look passed over her face and she grimaced and was silent for a moment.

"That was a fierce one," she said. "I think it will not be very long now." She looked around the chamber.

Kassandra asked, "Can I fetch you something?"

Helen shook her head, but she looked sad. *She is alone here*, thought Kassandra. *Among so many women, she has no real friend from her own country.*

"Where is your lady Aithra?"

"She has returned to Crete; I would not be the cause of her exile too," Helen said, and reached out her hand to Kassandra; Kassandra held it tightly.

Helen said, almost in a whisper, "Stay with me, Sister? I do not know these women—and there is none of them I trust."

Creusa, with her free hand, pulled a stool toward them. Kassandra dropped onto it, disposing her cumbersome robes around her. She noticed that the other woman looked pale now, and drawn. Not now possessed by her Goddess, she was, Kassandra noted with detachment, quite a small woman, whose pale hair was her chief beauty; even now, it fell into smooth dazzling bands on either side of her sweat-stained face. Her eyes looked tired and a little red. Kassandra sat on the stool beside the bed letting Helen grip her hand. Creusa played softly, and music seemed to be helping—or perhaps Helen would have had an easy time of it in any case. Kassandra was curious, but did not feel comfortable asking questions; this experience was still something which seemed to have nothing to do with her.

As the afternoon sun strengthened in the room, Hecuba sent everyone away except the two senior midwives, a servant for running errands and a priestess bearing many amulets, which she came and distributed around the bed. She would have sent away Kassandra too.

"You are a maiden, Kassandra; a birth-chamber is no place for you."

But Helen clung to her hand.

"She is my friend, Mother. And she is not only a maiden,

she is a priestess. No chamber of women is forbidden to a priestess of the Mother."

"Have you brought holy serpents?" Hecuba asked.

"No; the Temple serpents all died in the earthquake," Kassandra said.

The priestess, tucking an amulet under Helen's breasts with a muttered spell, raised her head to say, "Speak not of evil omens here."

"I cannot see why the deaths of serpents in the Temple of Apollo should be an omen, good or evil, for my baby," Helen said. "Apollo is not my God, and I have no dealings with Him for good or ill. As for Serpent Mother, She is no Goddess of mine."

The priestess caught Kassandra's eye and made a sign against evil fortune. Kassandra agreed with Helen; she was accustomed to the practice which made almost any random occurrence an omen for good or bad, but she still felt it nonsensical.

The priestess went to boil a pot of water over the brazier, and the room was filled with the steamy smell of the healing herbs she cast into it. Shortly before sunset Helen gave birth to a small and wrinkled son, to whom she gave the name Bynomos.

Hecuba looked at the little wriggling form with a slight frown.

"How long have you been among us, Helen? He is small . . . never have I seen a full term babe so small. He weighs no more than a chicken trussed for the spit."

"Nor did I," said Kassandra, "as you have told me often enough. It's likely that with all the trouble and excitement—the disruption at the festival, the earthquake—no doubt this little one comes hither some days or weeks before his time. Does it matter, if he is strong and healthy?"

Helen made a face and whispered, "She simply wishes to be certain it is her own son's son. Wanton I may be, but not so much as that; I knew I bore Paris' son before we fled from Agamemnon's house. But I do not know how to tell her what she really wants to know without shocking her further."

Kassandra giggled, but she did not know what to say either.

Creusa came to take her turn at holding the baby. She said tactfully, "I think he will have his father's eyes; babies who will be dark-haired have eyes of a smokier blue than those who will be fair."

Kassandra was startled; she had not expected such support from her half-sister. As a child Creusa had always had a talent for making a bad situation worse, as well as a tendency to throw fits of hysteria if she felt herself ignored. Perhaps marriage to Aeneas was giving her more maturity than anyone had expected.

There was a step at the door, and Kassandra, recognizing it, went to let Paris in, saying, "Brother, you have another son."

"I have a son," Paris corrected; "and if you prophesy anything of evil about him, Kassandra, I shall rearrange the bones of your face so that people flee from you as from the Medusa."

"Don't you dare to make threats to her," cried Helen. "Your sister is my friend."

Kassandra took the child in her arms and kissed him. She said, "I have no prophecy given me for this child. He is strong and well, and what fate will be his in manhood is not mine to say."

She laid the child in Paris' arms; he bent over Helen, and Kassandra drew her veil over her face.

"Are you going away, Sister?" Helen asked. "I had hoped you would stay and eat the evening meal with us, since Paris will not remain in the women's quarters."

"No, I must go down to the market," Kassandra said. "Did you not hear? We lost all our serpents in the earthquake. Those who did not die forsook us, and have gone deep into the ground and will not return. Apollo's Temple cannot be without serpents; I must replace them."

"What a curious omen!" Creusa said. "What do you think it could mean?"

Reluctantly—she did not want to frighten them, nor anger Paris or her mother by repeating what they were so unwilling to hear—Kassandra said, "I think the Gods are angry with the city. This is not the first evil omen we have had."

Paris laughed. "It takes no evil omen to make snakes take to the deeps in an earthquake—it is simply the way of the serpent-kind. I have seen enough of them in the mountains. But I am sorry for the loss of your pets." He patted Kassandra lightly on the arm. "Go you to the market, Sister, and choose carefully —perhaps your new snakes will prove more faithful."

"May the Gods grant it," Kassandra said fervently, quickly leaving the room.

She decided to stop briefly and see Andromache before leaving the palace.

"Kassandra!" Andromache greeted her with delight. "I knew not that you were here. Were you summoned for the birth?"

"Yes," Kassandra replied, embracing her friend. "Helen has a son, and both are well."

"I heard the child was a boy," Andromache said. "Nurse told me when she came to get the children. But"—she grinned wickedly—" 'Helen' has a son—not Paris? For shame, Kassandra, to even imply such a thing!"

"For shame, Andromache, to put such a meaning into my words!" Kassandra retorted. "Who was your father? You know full well that I lived among the Amazons long enough to think of a child as its mother's—particularly when I have just seen him born. Now, if Paris had been lying there in labor . . ."

The two women clung together laughing. "That I would like to see," said Andromache; "and would he not deserve it well!"

Kassandra sobered abruptly, shivering. Before her she saw an image of Paris, lying convulsed with pain, on the pallet in the hut he had shared with Oenone. Oenone bent over him, wiping his sweating forehead with a cloth, and a golden breastplate lay on the floor beside them.

"Kassandra!" Hands grabbed her shoulders, guided her to a stool, and forced her head between her knees. "I am a fool to keep you standing here when you've doubtless not eaten since daybreak! Keep your head down until the faintness passes, and I'll get you some food." Andromache went to the door and called to a serving-woman, then poured out a goblet of the wine that stood on a table at the far side of the room.

"Drink this," she ordered, "and eat at least a piece of the dried fruit." She extended a plate, and Kassandra took a bunch of raisins, put one in her mouth, and forced her jaws to start chewing on it. "For once, the children didn't eat everything in sight."

"Sight." Kassandra sighed. "I wish I didn't have it."

"They're bringing up bread and meat from the kitchens," Andromache said. "That will help dispel it. My mother always used to eat hot red meat and all the bread she could hold after a major scrying. And surely priestesses wouldn't fast before ritual work if it didn't help the Sight."

"No doubt," Kassandra agreed. "And in its own way, childbirth is a ritual."

"Very true," Andromache said feelingly. "Did Helen have a hard time of it?"

Kassandra shook her head.

"It would be that way for her." Andromache made a face. "Oh, well, I suppose that if Aphrodite is going to lead her to take lovers, the least She can do is give her the art of bearing children easily. And speaking of children . . . did I see Oenone and her son at the spring planting?"

"You did, and so did I," Kassandra replied. "She came to catch a glimpse of Paris. I fear she still loves him."

"Much good may it do her," Andromache said.

A servant entered with food from the kitchen. When she withdrew, Kassandra continued, "Oenone was my friend. I feel guilty that I cannot help loving Helen. And now Paris forgets even that he has a son by Oenone."

"I think everyone loves Helen," Andromache said. "Priam himself is never gruff with her, and he is well versed in the wiles of women and not easily charmed. As for Paris—well, what could you expect? If you had the Goddess of Love for your bed, would you turn away to a river priestess—and how would the Goddess deal with you if you did?"

Kassandra shivered. "I do not like this Akhaian Goddess," she said. "May She never lay Her hands on me."

THE FIREBRAND 〔ⵔ〕 277

Andromache looked very serious. "I would not wish for that," she said. "I would be sorry to think you should never know what it is to love."

"What makes you think that I do not?" Kassandra asked curiously. "I love my brothers and my mother, my serpents, my God . . ."

Andromache smiled a little sadly.

"I am fortunate," she said; "my love is for the man I was given for my husband, and I cannot imagine loving another. From what little talk I have had with Helen, I understand it was so with her until the Goddess laid Her hand on her; and then she could think only of Paris."

"Surely, then, such love is a curse and not a gift," Kassandra said, "and I pray it may never befall me."

Andromache embraced her gently and said, "Have a care what prayers you make, Kassandra. I wished to travel forth from Colchis, and to have a husband of great honor and renown. And that prayer brought me here away from my mother and my Gods, to a city at the far corner of the earth, in these dark times." She caught up a little of the salt that lay at hand on the tray with the meat and cast it into the air with a whispered word Kassandra could not hear. Kassandra, cutting herself a small slice of the roasted meat and laying it on a piece of bread, raised her eyebrows in question.

"I prayed for you," Andromache said, "that your prayers might be answered only in the way you would have it."

Kassandra embraced her friend and said impulsively, "I do not know if the Gods ever honor such requests—but I am grateful to you."

When she had finished her evening meal with Andromache, and helped her put Astyanax to bed, she left the palace. She was strolling through the darkened stalls of the evening market when she remembered that she had intended to ask Andromache what it might mean when serpents deserted a Temple. Then she recalled that Andromache would have nothing to do with serpants.

She resolved to ask all the priestesses she could find if they knew of a lore-mistress or master, a priest or priestess of Serpent

Mother or of the Python, before she bought a single snake for the house of the Sun Lord. Somewhere in this great city of Troy there must be someone versed in such wisdom.

11

SINCE THE RAID at spring planting, Khryse had fallen into a deep depression; he neglected his assigned duties in the Temple, spending much of his time standing near the high rampart which looked down on the Akhaian camp below.

"Please go and tell him to come down," Charis said to Kassandra. "He likes you; perhaps you can persuade him that life is not over."

"It is not liking he has for me," Kassandra remonstrated; but she did feel compassion for the troubled man, and later that day she joined Khryse on the high place.

"The evening meal is prepared," she said, "and they await you."

"Thank you, Kassandra, but I am not hungry," he said. He had not bathed or shaved since the raid; he looked unkempt and dirty, and smelled of strange herbs. "How can I eat and sleep in comfort when my child has been taken? I cannot bear to think of my poor little girl down among those savage soldiers."

"You cannot improve her lot by fasting and neglecting your person," Kassandra pointed out fastidiously. "Or is it that you think that seeing you in this condition will soften the hearts of the Akhaians?"

"No, but it might soften the heart of some God," he said, surprising her with the sincerity in his voice.

"Do you really believe that?"

"Perhaps not," he said, sighing so heavily that the sound seemed ripped from the very depths of his body. "But I have no heart for food or rest when she is there. . . ."

"She has certainly not been given to the soldiers," Kassandra said; "she will be a cherished prize for one of the leaders, perhaps even for Agamemnon himself."

"Do you think that is any comfort to me?" He sounded despairing; Kassandra would have tried to speak comfort, but a surge of darkness rippled before her eyes and for a moment she did not know where she was or what she had been saying.

"Why did I guard her maidenhood so carefully all those years only to bring her here? I might as well have sold her to a brothel-keeper!"

Now Kassandra was angry.

"No; you sold her to Apollo Sun Lord, in return for a life of comfort for yourself. As for the girl, if maidenhood dwells not in the soul, it is useless to guard the body. If you wish for Apollo's protection, or for revenge, I cannot advise you. I can say only that He is unlikely to intervene when you have made yourself worthless to us all. If you want His help—or His mercy —you must first serve Him well; you cannot bargain with a God."

She stared over the rampart at the thick sea-fog obscuring the Akhaian ships below. It had come to where she hated to look on the sea because of that dark fringe of ships against the ocean's edge. Khryse turned on her with such fury that for a moment she thought he would strike her; then he restrained himself, visibly sinking back into his apathy.

"You are right," he said slowly. "I will go to the evening meal—but first I will go and bathe and restore myself to the proper appearance for a priest of the Sun Lord."

She said softly, "This is wise, my brother," and saw something kindled in his eyes that she would rather not have seen; cursing herself for her momentary impulse of sympathy, she went on her way.

EARLY THE NEXT morning there was a sound at her door, and when she went to answer it, she found one of the youngest priests, who were used as messengers within the Sun Lord's house.

"You are the daughter of Priam?" he asked respectfully. "You are wanted at once in the room at the gatehouse; a man there says he is your uncle and must have speech with you at once."

Kassandra wrapped herself in her cloak, wondering what— or who—it could possibly be. She did not know any of her father's brothers, and certainly Hecuba had none. Too late, she began to wonder if it was a trick of some sort, and when, within the room, she had a glimpse of three men in Argive cloaks, she started back, ready to call out for help.

"It is I, Kassandra," said a familiar voice, and the man pulled back the hood concealing his face.

"Odysseus!" she exclaimed.

"Not so loud, my girl; you will get us all killed!" he implored. "I must see your father—and as things are now, I could not land among these Akhaians and walk through them up toward the gates of Troy for a parley; they'd have lynched me. My ship lies hidden in a cove I discovered when I was among pirates; I stole in last night under cover of the fog, and I must speak with Priam and see if there is still any honorable way to avert this war. I thought perhaps here, in this Temple, some way could be contrived."

"But you cannot just go out at the front gate and down to the palace either," she said. "I am sure there are Akhaian eyes and ears in the market, and even here in the Sun Lord's House: pilgrims; spies in the guise of petitioners. You would be recognized at once. Let me see first if I can contrive something. For you, I am sure, my father will waive the vow he has sworn to make no civil parley with any Argive. But who are your companions?"

"Take off your cloak, Akhilles," Odysseus said, and the young man at his side put back his hood. He was not particularly tall, but had the heavily muscled shoulders of a wrestler. His hair was still worn long about his shoulders—he was not yet old enough to be shorn in manhood's rites; the hair was cloudy fair, almost silvery. The face had strongly marked features: fierce— but it was the eyes to which Kassandra returned, the steely eyes of a bird of prey.

He said to Odysseus, "You promised to take me to this war, with my soldiers; you promised, and now you talk of avoiding it

—as if there were anything honorable about the avoiding of war. That is girl's talk, not man's talk, and I have already heard too much of that!"

"Be quiet, Akhilles," said the other young man, who was taller, and slightly built, with the long, smooth muscles of a runner or a gymnast. He was a few years older than Akhilles, about twenty. "There is more to war than honor or glory; and certainly whatever Odysseus can do is guided by the Gods. If you want war, there has never been any shortage of it in any man's life. We don't need to speed to destruction—but isn't it just like you, to rush into war for the fun of it!" He smiled at Kassandra and said, "That's how this wily old pirate"—he turned his eyes affectionately toward Odysseus—"got him to come here in the first place."

"How dare you say *wily*, Patroklos!" said Odysseus in an offended tone. "Hera, Mother of Wisdom, was my guide at every step. Let me tell you about it, Kassandra."

"With pleasure," she said. "But you must all be hungry and weary. Let me call for breakfast, and you can tell me while we eat."

She summoned servants and had bread brought, and olive oil and wine, and Odysseus told his tale.

"When Menelaus summoned us all to keep our vow to fight for Helen," he said, "I foresaw this war, and so did others; Thetis, priestess of Zeus Thunderer—"

"My mother," Akhilles interrupted under his breath.

"Thetis sought to know from prophecy what would befall her son, and the prophecy stated—"

"I am weary of prophecies and old wives' tales," Akhilles muttered. "They are moonshine. I love my mother, but she is no more than an idiot, like all women, when it comes to war."

"Akhilles, if you will stop interrupting me, we will have this tale done," said Odysseus, dipping his bread calmly into the oil. "Thetis, who is almost as wise as Earth Mother, read the omens and was told that if her precious son fought in this war, he could be killed—which takes no more of Sight than forecasting snow on Mount Ida in winter. Therefore, she thought to help him escape his fate; dressed him in women's garments and concealed

him among the many daughters of King Lycomedes of Sky-
ros—"

"And a pretty maiden he must have been!" exclaimed Patroklos, "with those shoulders of his! I'd have liked to see that
darling with his hair curled and done in ribbons—"

Akhilles gave his friend a great thump between the shoulder
blades that sent him to his knees, and he growled, "Well, you've
had your laugh, my friend; mention it again and you can go
laugh at it in Hades! Not even you can say that of me!"

"Don't quarrel, boys," Odysseus said with unusual mild-
ness. "It's but a sorry joke that parts sworn friends. Be that as it
may, I too sought omens, and my Goddess told me that it was
Akhilles' fate to join in this war; but I thought perhaps he had
been made cowardly by his woman's rearing, so I gathered up
many gifts for the daughters of the King, and I spilled them all
out—dresses and silks and ribbons; but among them I concealed
a sword and a shield, and while the other girls were squabbling
over all the pretty things, Akhilles grabbed at the sword; and so
of course I brought him away."

Kassandra laughed.

"Bravo, Odysseus," she said, "but your test was not entirely
sure; I too have borne weapons—I rode with the Amazons, and
if I had been among that King's daughters, I would have done
exactly the same. One need not be a hero to be desperately
weary of the gossip of women's quarters."

Akhilles laughed with contempt.

"Penthesilea said once," she observed, "that only those who
hate and fear war are wise enough to wage it."

"A woman," said Akhilles scornfully. "What would a
woman know of war?"

"As much as you," Kassandra began, but Odysseus, looking
very tired, interrupted: "Will you help us, Kassandra?"

"Gladly," she said. "Let me go and warn my father to be
ready to meet with you tonight."

"You are a good girl," said Odysseus, embracing her, and
she flung her arms around the old man and kissed his leathery
cheek. Then, a little surprised at her own boldness, she said,
"Well, you said you were my uncle—they will be expecting it."

Patroklos said, chuckling, "I will be your uncle too, if you will kiss me like that, Kassandra."

Akhilles scowled, and Kassandra blushed. She said, "Odysseus is an old friend; I have known him since I was a little girl. I do not kiss any man younger than my father."

Odysseus said, "Forget it, Patroklos; she is sworn a virgin of Apollo. I know you. When you see her brother Paris you will forget her; they are as alike as two birds on a bush."

"A man with her beauty? I would wish to see that," said Patroklos.

Akhilles, said angrily, "Oh, is *that* one Paris? The pretty coward?"

"Coward? Paris?" demanded Kassandra.

"I saw him on the wall yesterday when Odysseus landed me with my soldiers," he said, "before I slipped away at night to join Odysseus where the ship lay hidden. I said then, these Trojans are cowards; they stand on the wall like women, and shoot with arrows so that they need not come within range of our swords."

All Kassandra could think of to say to this was "The bow is the chosen weapon of Apollo."

"It is still the weapon of a coward," said Akhilles, and she thought, *That is simply how he sees the world, all in terms of fighting and honor. Maybe, if he lived long enough, he might grow out of that. But men who see the world that way do not live long enough to learn better. It is almost a pity; but perhaps the world is better without such men.*

Kassandra's visitors were waiting for her to speak. She suggested that they remain hidden during the heat of the day; then, under cover of night, she said, she would lead them to the palace and to Priam.

"This goes against me," Akhilles said, "slinking about in disguise. I am not afraid of all the Trojans ever whelped, or any of Priam's horde of sons and soldiers; I will fight them all the way down to the palace and back."

"You young fool," said Patroklos with affection, touching his shoulder, "no one doubts your courage; but why waste yourself on that when you can await the great battle and challenge any or all of the leaders of Priam's armies? There is enough fighting ahead of you, Akhilles. Do not be so impatient." He smiled and put his arm through his friend's.

Can this be the greatest of warriors, Kassandra thought—a child proud of his new toy sword and shiny armor?

And does the survival of Troy and of our world depend on this mad child?

SHE CLOSED the door and left them inside the room, admonishing them to stay hidden. The sun was high now and Kassandra threw a shawl over her head before she went down the hill to the palace. Seldom had she deliberately sought the presence of her father, and she could count on the fingers of one hand the times she had been alone with him and not part of a family gathering.

Odysseus would not believe this, she thought, *but I who am Priam's daughter find it harder to gain access to his presence than Odysseus himself would.*

She finally went to an old steward who told her that her father was reviewing the weapons issued to the soldiers, since the Akhaians had not chosen to raid today.

"After that, Princess, he will go to the bath with his older sons, and after that he will probably drink wine in his rooms; I am certain if you went to him then he would be willing to speak with you."

She spent the intervening hours in Creusa's room, playing with the baby. Creusa warned her of the hour the men usually returned, and she went along to her father's suite, half hoping —and half dreading—to find her mother there. It would be difficult to explain her errand to Hecuba, who would not believe it suitable for a woman to have any active voice in this war— *although if this city does fall to the Akhaians*, Kassandra thought in despair, *she will suffer as much as any, and more than most.*

In Priam's suite, she found her father alone with his armorer, who was showing him some new javelins, and he broke off to look at her with displeasure.

"What are you doing here, Kassandra? If you wanted to speak with me you should have told your mother, and I would have seen you in the women's quarters."

She did not bother to protest.

"Be that as it may, Father, now that I am here, will you hear me? Would you speak with Odysseus if it would help to end this war?"

"To do that, I would speak with Agamemnon himself," said Priam. "But among the ships of the Akhaians, I have not seen that of Odysseus."

"No, it is hidden in a secret cove," Kassandra said. "Odysseus is in the Temple of the Sun Lord, and he wishes to speak with you tonight. May I bring him and Akhilles here to the palace at the dinner hour?"

"What, Akhilles too? Do you have Agamemnon and Menelaus hiding behind your skirts, ready to swarm upon us in treachery?"

"No, Father; only Odysseus and Akhilles and his friend; because Odysseus is to present Akhilles to the Akhaian leaders tomorrow, but he wished to parley with you first because of your old friendship."

"True; he has been a good friend over many years," Priam said thoughtfully. "Let him come, and Akhilles and his friend too—I have heard he never takes any step without his friend."

"I will tell them, Father," Kassandra promised, and quickly made her escape before Priam could ask more questions or change his mind. She did not bother to inform her mother or any of the palace women—there was always food enough for a dozen extra mouths at the main meal, and the very thought of entertaining Akhilles would frighten the palace women.

She returned to the Sun Lord's house quite weary, and had only time to change into her finest robes and to put on the necklace of blue faience Odysseus had given her before she went to the room where she had left her guests. Patroklos smiled at her in a friendly way; but Akhilles was restlessly pacing the floor, and Odysseus looked distressed and impatient.

"I told you, Akhilles, we cannot simply charge into Priam's house; we would not get past his guards. Even if we managed to force our way in, we would not then be received courteously as ambassadors; and this is crucial to our mission. Trust Kassandra; she will make a way for us."

"I trust no woman," Akhilles said sullenly. "For all I know, this may be a trap while she summons the Trojan guards to take us."

"I tell you she is well disposed toward us, for here she is," Odysseus said. "How went your day, Kassandra?"

"Well enough." She did not elaborate. "My father will receive the three of you as guests at the dinner hour." And now, she thought, the problem was to get them from here to Priam's great hall without encountering the spies who might be in the city.

You must all wear the cloaks of priests of Apollo Sun Lord," she said. "None would think anything of it, or question why— or whether—Priam had summoned you."

A great cloak was brought for Odysseus; in it he looked wholly unlike himself. Akhilles grumbled a bit about wrapping himself in the disguise—"as if I were afraid of any Trojan, from a simple priest to Hector's self!"

"Gods on high! Does the man think of nothing else?" Kassandra demanded.

Odysseus said, "Enough, Akhilles; when I brought you on this mission, you swore on your sacred lineage to be guided by me in all things, and now I bid you disguise yourself. Keep that promise."

Grumbling, Akhilles wrapped his cloak around his body, and Patroklos pulled it up over his head.

"They would know you in a moment by your hair. Cover it, now," he urged, draping the third cloak around his own shoulders and drawing it up to conceal his face. "But do the Sun Lord's priests really go about covered like this in this weather, Lady Kassandra? They will think we have all fallen ill with toothache!"

She could not help laughing. "Who cares what they think? The priests do what seems right in their own eyes; they may think you are about some intrigue, but they will ask no questions, and certainly they will not demand that we show our faces. And that is all that matters. Come this way; we will go out by a little-used door, the better to support the notion that three priests are on some errand they don't wish known."

AKHILLES WAS still grumbling under his breath, but Kassandra paid no attention. Swiftly she led them downward, under cover of the deepening twilight; it was still early enough in the year that the light did not linger long.

Torches flamed on the lower steps of the palace, and the great hall was ablaze with light. Priam was seated on his high seat; but he came down a few steps and welcomed the three men ceremoniously. Kassandra he ignored; she slipped into her usual seat next to Hecuba, where she could see and hear well.

Her mother patted her hand.

"I did not know we were to have you here this night," she whispered. "Is that Akhilles? He is handsome for an Akhaian; but then, my mother used to say that handsome is as handsome does. Is he as young as he looks, or is it only that he's clean-shaven and looks boyish?"

"I don't know, Mother, but I'd say he's just too young for the manhood rites of the Akhaians; sixteen perhaps, or seventeen at most."

"And this pretty boy is the greatest of their warriors?"

"So they say; I haven't seen him fight, but I'm told he is possessed by their War-God when he fights," Kassandra murmured.

Odysseus came to kiss Hecuba's hand in homage.

"And all your daughters more beautiful than ever," he remarked. "Is the lovely Helen not at table this night?"

"She is still in bed after childbirth," Hecuba told him. "And she does not really like to dine with men."

"Ah, that is a loss to us all," Odysseus said. "But if she wishes to keep to her own people's customs, I suppose it must be allowed to her. Had she a son, then?"

"Oh, yes, the finest of boys—not big, but strong and healthy; a credit to any grandmother," Hecuba said, almost purring.

Odysseus smiled and said, "If I had known, I'd have had a present for the little one. But perhaps the business we do tonight, if it comes out as we wish, will be a better present to all our sons than any string of beads." He bowed and resumed his seat as the serving-women began to pass the wine and trays of food.

Custom demanded that a guest's hunger must first be satisfied; only when the roasted kid and poultry from the spit and broiled fish, the great wheels of bread and the fruits with honey had been cleared away and the household and guests were toying with nuts and wine did Priam turn purposefully to Odysseus and say, "It is always my pleasure to have you a guest at my table, Odysseus; but tonight I understand you did not come here only to share my food. What other purpose brings you here, with your friends from the Argive country and the islands?"

Akhilles had eaten hungrily, but was restless; when he finished he had risen and was walking aimlessly about the hall, examining some ancient weapons hanging on the walls. He seemed especially intrigued by a great double-bladed ax with a handle twice as long as the height of a tall man. He looked as if he were eager to take it down and try it.

"Is this a real ax which would be wielded in battle, or is it a remnant of the Titans, Lord Priam?"

Kassandra, as a child, had been told fanciful tales of Titan warfare in which such weapons had played a part; she had always wondered if they were true, but had never dared ask. She supposed it would take an Akhilles to ask such a question of her father and get an answer.

"I do not know," he said. "For its size, it might well be a relic of the warfare against the Titans, but I cannot say it is or is not."

"It is not a weapon—at least, not for battle between mortals or even Titans," said Hecuba firmly. "It is a ritual object from the House of the Double Ax in the country of the Minoans, brought here after the great Temple fell into the sea. There are such axes no longer than my little finger; but there are many of this size, and even, I was told, larger. No one now knows their true purpose, not even in Knossos; but once I was told that the priests used them for sacrifice, when a bull's head must be struck off at a single blow."

Akhilles looked calculatingly at the length of the great ax, as if trying to decide whether it could be hefted in that way, for the shaft was more than twice his own height.

"That Temple must have had some rare big priests," he said, "if not Titans, then Cyclopeans. I do not think even your Hector could strike off the head of a sacrifice, man or bull, with such an ax."

Hector came down from his seat and joined Akhilles looking up at the weapon.

"I have always wanted to try and see if I could do just that," he said, "but when I was a youngster I was told it would be sacrilege to handle it. Now I am grown, and if there is a God to be offended, I know not who He is; I am tempted to try my strength at it." He glanced up at Priam for permission. "May we, Father?"

"I see no harm in it," the King said. "No God has forbidden it; if it is sacred to any God, He lies in His sunken Temple a hundred fathoms below the ocean, and even if He should take offense, I doubt He could or would punish you now. Do what you wish."

Hecuba opened her mouth indignantly. "This is sacrilege; the blade is sacred to Earth Mother," she said, but not loudly enough for Priam to hear, or Hector.

Hector dragged a bench over below the great ax; it took him three tries, even with his mightily muscled arms, to lift it off its hooks. He grasped it at the center of the long handle and sprange down from the bench, holding it with both hands and whirling it above his head in the open space.

Akhilles leaped forward, but Hector cried, "Get back! Clear the floor!" The blade revolved around his head faster and faster; he cried out, "Bring on your bull for sacrifice!" then slowly let it sink to the floor.

"My turn," Akhilles cried.

"Don't be foolish," Hector said sharply. "I am sure you are strong, boy, but you will rupture yourself or crack your sinews even trying to lift it; you are our guest and I wouldn't have you hurt."

"How dare you say 'boy' to me in that tone, Trojan? I will make any wager you like that I am stronger than you, and whatever you can lift I can lift," Akhilles cried, grasping the ax handle; but where Hector had had to lower it from above his head, Akhilles had to lift it up from the floor. Patroklos came and admonished him in a low voice, but Akhilles thrust him angrily away. His hands were large for his size; he clenched them round the handle and gripped hard, thrusting upward. He heaved, the veins standing out in his forehead; stopped, spat on his hands to get a better grip and heaved mightily upward again. Slowly the ax came up, till he held it balanced at arms' length over his head; then he began to spin it in the air, till it was making great sweeping circles, with a rushing sound. A cheer went up at the high table; all of Priam's sons joined in, and Hector generously led the applause.

"What God gifted you with such strength as that?" Hector asked, and without waiting for an answer, he said, "I doubt it not you are stronger than I! I wish I might face you sometime in a peaceful wrestling bout; I would rather be your friend than your enemy, Akhaian."

Akhilles' lip curled in a sneer, but Odysseus interrupted and said, "It was for this I brought these young men hither tonight, Priam. If Akhilles does not enter this combat, then you can still make peace with the Akhaians. So the oracles have said."

"I too would rather have you as friend than as enemy," said Priam. "Must we fight, then, young man? I will make you an offer: you shall marry any one of my daughters you choose, and you shall be heir to this city on an equal footing with Hector; when I die, the people shall choose freely between you and Hector as King. Come, will you avoid this terrible war as my son and heir? For if you do not join them, the Akhaians will go home."

"Even Agamemnon? Even Menelaus?" asked Hecuba.

"Menelaus knows Helen does not want him," Paris said quietly. "He will yield to Fate and to Aphrodite, knowing it is the will of the Goddess of Love."

"And Agamemnon has had evil omens," said Odysseus. "He will fight if the Gods will it, but at Aulis, where his fleet lay becalmed, he was persuaded to offer his eldest daughter as a sacrifice for the winds. She was his favorite; he feels the price was too high, and his wife has never forgiven him. I think he would be glad to withdraw from this war, if he could do so without loss of face. This prophecy about Akhilles would give him a perfect excuse, and we can have peace. And Akhilles will rule Troy with Hector, rather than both of them being killed in battle."

"I do not fear being killed in battle!" Akhilles said angrily. "But perhaps there would be renown to be won as King of Troy. As for your daughters, King Priam . . ." He broke off and sought with his eyes for Kassandra. "What about that one?"

Kassandra opened her mouth to protest; but Priam said, "That one is not mine to give in marriage; she is sworn a virgin of Apollo, and the Sun Lord has claimed her; would you contend with Apollo?"

"By no means," said Akhilles with a pious shudder. He looked again at the bench where the women sat ranged, and walked toward them; he bowed to Andromache.

"This one surely is the most beautiful."

Hector broke in with a shout. "No! She is my wife and the mother of my son!"

Akhilles' mouth drew back in his peculiar lipless grin. "I will fight you for her," he offered.

Hector said, "By no means. She is the daughter of the Queen of Colchis."

"Come, come," said Odysseus uneasily. "This war began over one stolen wife; we can't carry it on with another one. Akhilles, choose one of Priam's virgin daughters, one who is free to marry. Polyxena, who is as beautiful as the Spartan Queen—"

"The offer was not a fair one," Akhilles said spitefully. "I chose not once but twice, and was told I could not have either of the ones I wanted. Hector, why will you not fight me fairly for your wife?"

Hector chuckled and said, "I will fight you for anything reasonable, whenever you say, but I will not put up my wife in any bargain whatever; she has not deserved that of me."

"So much for Priam's fine offers," said Akhilles with a snarl of rage. "Forget it, then; I shall fight you on the battlefield, and when I have taken the city, I will take your wife."

Hector stepped forward with a menacing gesture.

"Over my dead body!"

"Well, yes; that was the idea," Akhilles said. "And I am sure she would rather have me than you."

Andromache leaned forward and whispered to Hector, who smiled and gently patted her shoulder, saying, "Should that day come, Akhilles, I cannot prevent you. But that battle will be a long time in coming."

"It is ordained by the Gods," said Akhilles, "that if I join in this war, Troy will fall."

Priam said, "Then you refuse me, Akhilles?"

Akhilles snarled, "I do; I would rather be your enemy than your ally, old man, and I will take this city myself and rule it without your help, or Hector's—and with one, two or three of your daughters if I choose."

"My sister Kassandra is a prophetess," Hector said, "and I dare say she can make a better prophecy than any of yours." He turned to Kassandra and said, "Will this bantam rooster take the city, Sister, in Apollo's name?"

Kassandra felt a spiking anger at Hector for drawing all eyes to her this way. She said, "Thus say the Gods: Akhilles will win renown before Troy, but let him beware. Akhilles, when you leave Troy this night you will never enter it again, nor will you rule it."

Now all pretense of courtesy was gone from Akhilles' snarling face.

"Oh, we have prophetesses too," he growled. "For the smallest coin they will give you a dozen prophecies—doom or triumph, whichever you choose; my own mother is as good a prophetess as any, and I'll listen to her prophecy before that of any Trojan woman of Apollo." He dragged his sword from his sheath and cried, "Here and now, if you wish, Hector, I'll have you off the throne of Troy; why waste time with the war?"

Patroklos grabbed his arms and struggled to pin them behind his back. "Your host is sacred!" he reproached.

And Hector strode forward, saying, "I would fight him here and now if he wished it; but he is my father's guest."

Priam growled, "Take him out of here, Odysseus; I received him at your request."

Odysseus came to embrace Priam and said, "Forgive me,

old friend, that I brought this wild man into your hall. I regret this with all my heart."

Hecuba said graciously, "You did your best for all of us, Odysseus. War or no war, you are always welcome here as our guest. I trust the day will come when you may come here again —and not in secret."

He bent again and lifted her hand to his lips.

"Lady Hecuba," he said. "May the Lady Hera bear witness I wish you nothing but good; and if ever a day should come when I may do you a good turn, I pray Her She will show me how to do it."

"The Gods grant it may be so," said Hecuba, smiling kindly at him. Kassandra felt a tremor; she wanted to cry out to her mother, but the moment passed. Odysseus drew on his cloak; Akhilles and Patroklos were already striding from the hall, Hector glaring at them both. Kassandra stood shuddering, for it seemed that the torchlight had become the color of blood, and blood surrounded Akhilles' fair hair like a halo.

Priam beckoned Kassandra as the Akhaians passed from the hall.

"I received these guests," he said in a tone of angry reproof, "because you asked me. You are not now an Amazon; never again presume to speak to me on such matters."

Kassandra bowed her head. It seemed to her that the smell of blood and carrion flowed out from her father and that he and she stood ankle deep in blood. How was it that he neither saw nor smelled the blood? Besides, he had bidden her never speak again to him about the war.

Never. Not while I live. Or after.

12

FOR THE NEXT several days, Kassandra watched, from the heights of the Temple, the arrival of Akhilles' soldiers; they were nicknamed "Myrmidons"—ants—and from this height they seemed indeed as numerous and ugly as insects swarming over the beach. So far, however, they made no attempt to move on the city, but marched back and forth over the plain, running, drilling and performing military exercises. Akhilles was clearly visible among them, outstanding not only for his brightly dyed cloak, but for his shining silver-gilt hair and the straight posture of his body.

A few days later, she went down to visit her mother; she was troubled by the deepening lines of age in Hecuba's face. As she approached the Queen's quarters, she was shocked by the sounds of strife; she could not make out the words, only the sound of women's voices raised in anger. As she came into the main room near the great loom, she heard the sound of a ringing slap, and a muffled cry, then Hecuba's voice, crying out, "Never!"

"Then," said a young voice, "I shall go without your leave, Lady, or your blessing either."

The voices of the women fell silent as they recognized Kassandra and drew back to give her room. It seemed that all the women in the palace were crowded there, surrounding Hecuba, who was wearing an old gown, her hair falling down from its usual coil in gray straggly locks, and one of her sewing-women, a girl Kassandra did not know by name though she had often admired her expert work.

"Here is the princess! She is a priestess; she will know what to say to her."

Kassandra came into the circle of women, who were suddenly quiet except for a murmur or two.

"What's wrong, Mother?" she asked. "What's happening?"

The young woman, her cheek reddened from the blow, spoke up proudly. She was slender and pretty, with soft brown hair which she had been interrupted in the middle of dressing, so it hung half curled almost to her waist. Her big dark eyes were shaded by long lashes.

"The God has spoken to me," she said, "and I have chosen my Lord."

"This foolish girl," Hecuba said, "this stupid child, has

taken it into her head—oh, I am almost ashamed to tell you! That any woman could so degrade, so demean herself—she is no servant or slave but well born; she is one of my best embroiderers, and I have treated her as my own daughter here in the palace. She has wanted for nothing—"

"Well, tell me, what has she done?" asked Kassandra. "Has she opened the gates for the Akhaians to invade the city?"

"No, it has not come to that yet," Hecuba admitted.

"She's mad," Creusa said. "At the feast a few days ago she set eyes on Akhilles, and since then she's talked of nothing else; how strong he is, how skilled at arms, how beautiful—if a man can be beautiful—and now something has put it into her head to go down and offer herself—"

"To the Akhaians?" Kassandra asked in consternation.

"No," said the girl softly, her eyes glowing, "to my lord Akhilles."

"Not even King Priam would send you to him as a slave," Kassandra said.

"It could never be slavery, because I love him," the girl said. "Since first I laid eyes on him I have known there could never be any other man for me in this world."

"My mother is right; you have lost your wits," Kassandra said. "Don't you realize what an animal he is, what a brute? He thinks of nothing but war, takes pleasure in nothing but killing; certainly there is no room in his life for any woman, nor the love of a woman; if he loves any, it is his comrade-in-arms, Patroklos."

"You are wrong," said the woman; "he will love *me*."

"And if he did, it would be the worse for you," Kassandra said. "I tell you, the man is deranged, mind-sick with the lust for death."

"No, I saw how he looked at me," said the young woman. "How can you say such a thing? The handsomest man the Gods ever made; such beauty must be good, too. Those eyes . . ."

With a shudder, Kassandra remembered the woman in the Kentaurs' village, her ankles pierced with a rope, defending her mutilation as an act of love. It was quite hopeless to talk to any woman in this state.

Yet she must try, if only because they were both women and therefore sisters.

"You—what is your name?" she began.

"Briseis," said Hecuba. "She is a Thracian."

"Briseis, listen to me," said Kassandra. "Can't you even see how you are deceiving yourself? This is some mad fancy put into your head by a demon, not by a God. You have invented a man from your own dreams, and called him by the name of Akhilles. Do you really believe that if you leave us and go down among the Akhaians you will mean any more to him than any harlot or slave?"

"I could not possibly love him so much without kindling some love in return," said Briseis.

Creusa came and shook her.

"*Listen* to us, you mad thing! This kind of love is a silly girl's fantasy! If you are simply hungry for a man, I will speak to my father and he will arrange a marriage for you; there are soldiers and chiefs here from all over the world, and your father is a reputable man in his own country; my father will find you a worthwhile husband."

"But I don't want a worthwhile husband," said Briseis. "I want only Akhilles; I love him. You are jealous because love has not come to you this way. If it had, you would know I can do nothing else. There is nothing in the world for me but Akhilles; I cannot eat or sleep for thinking of him—of his eyes, his hands . . ." The very sound of her voice as she spoke the name convinced Kassandra that they might as well be speaking to the wind blowing.

"Let her alone," she said hopelessly. "This is a fever like that of Paris for Helen, a curse of their Goddess of Love. She'll come to her senses soon enough once she's had him, but then it will be too late," she said.

"If only I can have him, I don't care what happens to me afterward," Briseis said, and Hecuba brushed the tears from her eyes.

"Poor child," she said, "I cannot prevent you. Go, if you will, and take the consequences of your folly. I will send to Priam, and you shall be carried down in a litter, with a message that you are a gift for Akhilles; and if he deigns to accept you, and does not throw you to the common soldiers to show his contempt for our gifts . . ."

For an instant the girl blanched, but then she said, "When he sees how much I love him, he must love me in return."

And if he should, you will be worse off than before, Kassandra thought, but she did not say the words aloud.

She watched the women dress and adorn Briseis; Hecuba even placed a golden necklace about her neck. When she was ready, Kassandra almost envied her—she looked so joyous.

Women dream of this kind of love. And then comes the rope piercing the ankles, the slavery, the degradation.

I should be in her place, Kassandra thought. *Akhilles asked for me, and he would certainly receive me as befits my rank. And then while he slept, a dagger for the throat, and perhaps an end to this war . . . the great Akhilles, conquered by no hero but by a woman, by his own passion where all the warriors of Troy could not bring about his doom.*

Is that woman meeting my *fate, my* destiny?

No; the Gods may sometimes give us what belongs to another, as Paris has the wife of Menelaus; but another's destiny none may live.

I trust this is so, I believe it; for if it is not true, I will never know how to bear my guilt.

A FEW DAYS later Kassandra descended again to Priam's palace and found Helen in the courtyard, looking down at the Akhaian camp. Her son Bynomos was running about now, and Kassandra, counting in her mind, realized that Helen had now been with them for the better part of two years. It was hard to remember the women's quarters without her, or that there had been a time when there was not war.

Three years ago I was riding with the Amazons, she thought, and wished she were back on the plains, free of city or palace walls.

Would I leave the house of the Sun Lord? He has forgotten me; He no longer speaks to me, Kassandra thought; *I am no other than any woman. But it is a God I love, not a man. . . . I sup-*

pose it is better to love a God than a man like Paris, or Akhilles. . . .

She thought of Briseis, and sought out the tent of Akhilles below; standing near it she could see the brightly colored hangings of the litter in which Hecuba had sent the girl down. And now, standing near the doorway of the tent she could make out the straight slender body of the warrior; and nearby the smaller, rounder, brightly clad form of a woman. *Briseis?* So at least he had not scorned the gift, nor thrown her to the common soldiers. Kassandra wondered if she was happy and content.

"At least she has what she most wished for," said Helen, walking to the wall and gesturing down at the girl, wrapped in her saffron-dyed veils. "So there is at least one woman in Troy who has what she most desired."

"Other than you, Helen?"

"I don't know," said Helen, "I love Paris. . . . At least, under the blessing of the Lady of Love, I loved him; but when She is not with me . . . I don't know."

So she too loves only at the will of a God. . . . Why is it that the Gods intrude into our lives? Haven't They enough to do in Their own divine realms, that They must come meddling with the lives of mortal men and women? But she only asked, "Do you think there will be a raid today?"

"I hope so; the men are getting bored, cooped up inside the walls," Helen said. "If the Akhaians do not raid us in a day or two, our men will go out and raid the Akhaians, just for something to occupy their time. . . . Why, Kassandra, what's the matter with you? You've turned pale."

"It occurred to me," Kassandra said, speaking with difficulty, "that if this war goes on for long, no son of Troy will survive to be a warrior."

"Well, I would as soon that any of my sons, were something other than a warrior," said Helen. "Like Odysseus, perhaps, to live peacefully in his home country and be a wise judge of his people. . . . If you had a son, Kassandra, what would you want for him?"

That she had never considered. "Anything," she said. "Whatever made him a happy man. A warrior, a King, a priest, a farmer or shepherd . . . anything, except a slave to the Akhaians."

Helen turned to her child and held out her arms; he came running up to her. She said reflectively, "Before this one was born, I still had it in my power—and often I thought of it—to stop this war. To steal quietly down to the camp and to Menelaus; I think then he would have agreed to go home, and when there was nothing more to fight for—or at least, no further excuse to fight—the Akhaians would have had to turn round and go back to our own islands. But now"—she shivered a little —"he would not take me back; not with another man's son at my breast."

Kassandra said quietly, "Leave him here, then, in Troy; his father will care for him, and so will I, Helen, if that is what you truly want." After she said it, she realized that Helen was almost the only person in Troy to whom she could talk these days; her mother no longer understood her, nor her sisters. She would miss Helen, if she should return to the country of Sparta.

Helen frowned. She said, "Why should I give up my own child, because Menelaus is a fool?" After a moment she added, "To tell the truth, Kassandra—unless you are under the spell of Aphrodite, there is not much difference between one man and another; but children are not so easily set aside. I am not responsible for this war; and I think Agamemnon would have made war, sooner or later, whatever I did or did not do." She sighed and let her head rest against Kassandra's shoulder. "My sister, I am not as brave as I think I am; I could summon the courage to return to Menelaus, even to leave Paris; but I cannot bring myself to leave my child." She picked up the toddler leaning against her knee, and pressed him to her heart.

"To leave your child? And why should you, after all?" asked Andromache, coming to the wall with Creusa just in time to hear her last words. "No woman could bring herself to leave a child she has borne . . . or if she could, she would be no better than a whore."

"I am glad to hear you say so," said Helen. "I was trying to tell myself that it was my duty to return to Menelaus—"

"Don't even think of such a thing," said Andromache, hugging Helen. "You belong to us now, and we would not let you go for every Akhaian down there; even if Paris and Priam and all the men wanted you to go—and they do not. The Gods have sent you to us, and we will keep you—won't we, Creusa?" she added to the other woman, who nodded and laughed.

"The Goddess has blessed you, and we will not let you go."

Helen smiled faintly. "That is good to hear. All my life men have been kind to me, but women never; it is good to have friends among you."

"You are too beautiful for women to love you much," said Andromache; "but you have been here for two years now; and unlike many beautiful women, you make no attempt to seduce our husbands."

"Why should I do that? I already have one more husband than I need; what should I want with yours?" Helen asked, laughing. "I have no great love for Troy; indeed, I would willingly see more of the world, but women cannot travel. . ."

Whenever Kassandra heard anyone say such a thing as *Women cannot* . . . she was always eager to do just that very thing. She said, "But I am about to travel at the will of my God; and if you wanted to come with me, Helen, I would willingly have your company."

"And I yours; but again, I cannot leave so young a child," Helen said. "Where do you go, and why?"

"To Colchis; to seek Queen Imandra and inquire for serpent-lore," Kassandra said. "A moon past, our serpents died or fled from us; I do not want to replace them until I am sure that nothing I did or failed to do was responsible."

She told the story, and Andromache looked wistful.

"Bear my greetings to my mother; and tell her I am happily wed and that I have Hector's son."

"Why not come and bring her your own greetings? Your son is old enough to leave with Hecuba and his father."

"I wish I could," Andromache said. "If you had told me this a month ago . . . but I am pregnant again. Perhaps this time it will be a daughter who can be a warrior for Troy."

"A warrior?"

"Why not? You are, Kassandra, and your mother before you."

"Did you not hear what Paris said, when last I would have borne my bow to the walls?" Kassandra asked in disgust. "I could shoot now—and kill Akhilles—and end this war without sending Helen forth from us. But that would not please the men; they do not want to end this war."

"No," said Andromache, "they want to win it; Hector has reserved Akhilles for himself and will never agree to any other way to end the fighting. Can you tell me when this will happen and how much longer we must fight?"

Kassandra smiled wryly. "Hector has forbidden me to prophesy doom," she said, "and believe me, I have nothing else to tell."

"Perhaps it is as well you are traveling to Colchis," Helen said. "Kassandra, my friend, the Gods have spoken to me as well as to you, and They have spoken to me nothing of disaster."

"Then may your Gods speak truth and mine be false," Kassandra said. "Nothing would please me more than to return and find Akhilles dead at Hector's hand; and all of them gone away again."

But it will not, it cannot be so. . . .

13

KASSANDRA HAD believed that once she made the decision to travel to Colchis, it would be a simple matter of getting leave of the chief priest and priestess, gathering together the clothing she wished to take with her, choosing a traveling companion (or perhaps two) and setting forth.

But it was not nearly so easy as that. She was reminded that there was officially a state of war between the Akhaians and Troy, so that it must be arranged (by lengthy messages sent back and forth from one Temple of Apollo to the next) that she travel under the Peace of Apollo, being a woman and a sworn priestess and having nothing to do with the war on either side; and she was given to understand that this was more difficult because she

was Priam's daughter and closely related to the main combat-
ants of the war. Long before the official safe-conducts and per-
missions could be arranged, Kassandra was heartily sick of the
whole idea and wished she had never thought of it. In the end,
she swore a sacred oath by every God she had ever heard of
(and some she hadn't) that she would deliver no messages relat-
ing to the war from either party, and she was declared an official
messenger of Apollo and permitted to travel wherever she
wished.

Khryse wished to travel with her, and she had some sympathy for him; he was still mourning the fate of his daughter in
the Akhaian camp, and knowing that Agamemnon had chosen
the girl for his own mistress did not help. However, though
Khryse swore to Kassandra that he would respect her virginity
as if she were his own child, she did not trust even his oath, and
refused to have him in her party. Since he was a highly respected priest of Apollo, it seemed for a time that she would not
be allowed to travel without his escort; but she finally appealed
to Charis, saying she would remain within walls till her hair
turned gray rather than travel a single step in his company; and
at last the matter was dropped.

Then Priam wished to send messages to many friends along
her path, and she had to swear that they were family matters,
or religious matters with nothing to do with the war; she could
see reason in this because travelers under religious immunity
had often taken advantage of it to spy on one side or the other.
And finally her mother refused to allow her to travel without
adequate chaperonage, so that in the end Kassandra, who
would have preferred to travel alone or with a single companion,
preferably an Amazon rider like Penthesilea, had to accept two
of her mother's oldest and most timid waiting-women, Kara and
Adrea, and to promise that on the road she would always share
her bed with them.

What can she be thinking of? she asked herself. *If I wished
to indulge myself in lechery, I would certainly not wish to travel
to the ends of the world and do so on the hard ground after
a day's riding when I could just as easily do so in my own
bed.*

But she knew it was her mother's way, and there was really nothing she could do about it; and so she accepted Hecuba's choice of women.

"For if I refuse," she said to Phyllida when at last it seemed that all the obstacles had been cleared and she would set forth the next day, "she will believe that I wish somehow to escape her supervision; and she cannot think of any reason I might wish to do so, unless it was to misbehave in some way. What is it in women that makes them suspect such things of one another, Phyllida?"

Phyllida sighed. "Experience, I suspect," she said. "Did you not tell me that you had Chryseis watched night and day and still could not vouch for her innocence?"

Kassandra knew that was true; but it made her angry. She remembered Star saying that city women were so lecherous that they must be locked up behind walls.

Women, Kassandra thought—*except the Amazons—spend their time sitting about and thinking about whom they love only because they have nothing else to occupy their minds. If they had a flock of sheep or a herd of horses to tend, they would be better off.* But that had not saved Oenone from pining, she realized, when Paris deserted her.

She lay awake much of that last night thinking about this mysterious emotion which transformed otherwise sensible women into half-wits capable of thinking only of the men who had inspired them to love.

It had been determined that she should depart at daybreak; she rose as soon as light began to appear in the sky, and breakfasted on a little bread and a cup of watered wine. She had hoped to ride on a swift horse; but her companions were too old and staid for that, so she had chosen a sedate elderly donkey and to have the older women carried in chairs. Her chair-bearers and attendants—almost guards—were strong young servants of Apollo's Temple.

She had expected to slip quietly away; but as she approached the gates she saw a little group of people gathered there: Khryse, Phyllida and a few others who wished to bid her goodbye.

Phyllida embraced and kissed her and wished her a pleasant journey and a safe return; Khryse came and embraced her too, rather against Kassandra's will.

"Come back to us soon and safely, my dear," he murmured with his lips close to her ear. "I shall miss you more than I can say. Say that you will miss me too."

She thought, *I shall miss you as I would miss a toothache*, but was too courteous to say so. "May the Gods keep you safe and bring Chryseis back to you," she said, thinking that she did not wish him ill, but she would like it if he would find himself a wife and stop troubling her. Then she clucked to her donkey and they rode forth.

Before leaving the coast they had to pass the Akhaian ships; here would Apollo's truce first be tested.

A watchman outside the Akhaian camp roused and called out; and one of the captains, lavishly armored with metal trimmed with gilt, came toward them.

"Who passes? Is the Trojan King trying to escape the city and the siege?" he taunted. "I knew they were cowards."

"No such thing," said the guards. "The lady is a priestess of Apollo and travels under His pledge of peace."

"Indeed?" the captain said, and looked into Kassandra's face so directly and rudely that for the first time in her life Kassandra could see the sense of the custom bidding the Akhaian women wear veils. "A priestess, hey? Of the Lady Aphrodite? She is beautiful enough for that."

"No; she is one of the Sun Lord's sworn virgins," said the leader of her guard, "and she is forbidden to any man save the God."

"A virgin, eh? What a waste," the man said regretfully; "but it would take a braver man than I to argue with Lord Apollo for one of his maidens. And what beauties hide inside the chairs?" he demanded, pulling back the draperies.

Kassandra was tired of hiding behind her guard. "Two of my mother's waiting-women," she said. "To care for me and see that no man offers me any offense."

"Quite safe from me, and I dare say from any man," said the soldier, drawing back respectfully.

"I'm sorry my ladies don't meet your approval," Kassandra said, "but they are for my convenience, not yours, sir; and I am on Apollo's business, not yours, so I beg you let me pass."

"Where are you going? And what business has the Sun Lord outside His Temple?"

"I am going to Colchis," she said. "And indeed, I travel on the God's business; I seek a mistress of serpent-lore so that His serpents may be properly cared for in His Temple."

"A little lady like you going so far alone? If you were my daughter, I wouldn't have it; but I suppose the God knows that what belongs to Him is safe anywhere," said the soldier. "Pass, then, Lady, and may Apollo guard you. Give me His blessing, I beg you," he added with a reverential gesture.

That was the last thing she had expected, but she extended her hands in a gesture of blessing and said, "Apollo Sun Lord bless and guard you, sir," and rode past.

She could see so far from the top of the walls of Troy that she had forgotten how long it took to travel; they camped that night and several nights thereafter within sight of the city and woke seeing the flash of sunlight on the house of the Sun Lord. She remembered her trip with the Amazons; she could hardly believe that from that hour to this, she had dwelt behind the prisoning walls of her city. Troy, her home, and her prison. Would she ever see it again?

IN THE LONG interval between proposing the trip and finally managing to leave she had had ample time for preparation, and she had had two tents made: a lightweight one of oiled linen cloth, and one of leather such as the Amazons had used in rainy weather. For the first days the weather was fine and the tent under the stars was pleasantly cool at night, although her two chaperons, interpreting her mother's instructions literally, made her sleep with her blankets spread between the two of them. Kassandra, always a restless sleeper, lay awake sometimes for hours, feeling every rock and lump of ground under the tent's floorcloth dig into her hips, hating to change position for fear of disturbing one or the other of her companions. Nevertheless, she could hear the wind and feel the cool breeze outside the tent, and at least it was different from the unchanging wind at the heights of Troy.

Day after day, their little caravan slowly toiled without incident across the great plain. They met few travelers on the road, except for one great train of wagons bringing iron bound for Troy, and when they heard that the city was under siege, they wondered if they should turn about and go northward into Thrace or even back toward Colchis.

"For the Akhaians will not trade with us for metal," said the leader. "They prefer their own kind of weapons, and most likely they will not let us pass into the city at all; then we will have to go back with only the journey for our pains; or else the Akhaians will seize our whole caravan."

Kassandra thought this very likely indeed.

"Do you know any of the Akhaians who are there?"

"Akhilles, son of Peleus; Agamemnon, King of Mykenae, and Menelaus of Sparta; Odysseus—"

"Now, that's different," said the caravan leader. "We can trade with Odysseus, same as we would with Priam; he's an honest man and an honest trader." He raised his voice to his drivers: "Looks like we'll be going to Troy after all, fellows." And then, of course, he wanted to know what she was doing, traveling without her kin, and when she answered he gave the now expected reply that if she were his daughter he wouldn't permit it.

"But I suppose your father knows what he's about," he concluded, doubtfully. And Kassandra saw no point in explaining that Priam had not been asked for his permission and had been given no chance to consent or refuse.

"Can I carry any messages for you to Troy, little lady?"

"Only to let it be known in the Sun Lord's house that I am alive and well. The message will be passed on from there to my mother and father." And with mutual expressions of goodwill and blessings they parted, moving slowly apart across the great plain like two streams in opposite directions. After a few more nights, she knew, her party would arrive within the borders of the country of the Kentaurs.

"The Kentaurs?" said Adrea, one of her chaperones.

"Oh, not the Kentaurs!" cried Kara, the other.

"Why, yes, Nurse—they live in this country and we must pass through their territory. It is almost inevitable that we shall meet one or more of their wandering bands."

But the women had been brought up on the old nursery tales.

"And are you not afraid of the Kentaurs, Mistress Kassandra?" asked Kara, and she replied "No, not at all."

She supposed that was an unwomanly answer; Kara looked as if the very fact that any woman might escape the fear of what frightened her so much actually gave offense. Kassandra sighed and finished the wine in her cup. "We must drink this up," she said, "it is beginning to turn sour and will not keep in the heat. We can get some more at the next village, in a day or perhaps two," and the rest of the talk was of simpler things.

14

TRUE TO HER prediction, they saw the Kentaurs early in the next day. At first, riding the sea of endless grass, Kassandra could see nothing; then very far away, at the edge of her vision she could see movement and shadows, and at last made out a small form . . . no, two . . . no, three, riding, dark against the golden waving of the grasses. They seemed to see her little caravan advancing, then drew together, conferring; at one point she thought they would all flee. Then they wheeled and came riding toward the Trojans.

Kassandra stopped her donkey but made no other move of withdrawal; she knew from old that one should never let a Kentaur believe you feared him or he would take ruthless advantage of it.

She said softly through the curtains of the litter where the ladies rode, "Nurses, you wanted to see a Kentaur. There is one."

"I?" said Adrea. "Not likely"; but nevertheless she thrust her head out and peered between the curtains. Kara followed suit.

"What funny ugly little men," she whispered, "and shameless; naked as an animal."

"Why should they wear clothing when there is no one to see or care? When they come into cities, they have garments they can wear if they choose," Kassandra said, and looked at the approaching band. The foremost among them was gray-haired and gnarled, his legs even smaller and more bowed than the others'. He wore a necklace of lions' teeth about his throat; Kassandra recognized him, shrunken and old as he was.

"Cheiron," she said, and he bowed from his horse's neck.

"Kinswoman of Penthesilea, greeting. When last we met, we had honey found in the wild. Our tribe is poor, these days. Many, many travelers on the plain; scare away the game, trample down wild plants. Our she-goats give no milk even for the littlest boys. We hunger much."

"We are traveling to Colchis," Kassandra said. "Can you show us the way?"

"With pleasure, if it is your wish," the old Kentaur said in his barbarous accent. "But how come ye to be riding *away* from Troy? The whole world's going there for this war, it seems. If not to fight, then to sell something to the fighters, one side or the other."

This was so true there seemed no purpose in commenting on it.

She had before leaving Troy asked the kitchens for a good half dozen loaves of bread, knowing that the Kentaurs neither grew nor ground grain and that it was a most unusual luxury for them. When it was unwrapped and given, the little man's eyes gleamed—Kassandra thought it was with real hunger—and he said, "Priam's daughter is generous. Does her husband fight in the great battles before Troy? If he does, I will gift him with magical arrows which will never fail to bring down her enemies even if they do not strike in a vital part."

"I have no husband," she said. "I am sworn to the Sun Lord and will have none but Him. And I need none of your arrows, envenomed with poison brewed from toads."

For a moment the little man looked at her and glowered; then he leaned back and broke into a great guffaw of laughter, and did something, Kassandra could not see what, that made his horse rear up and prance, and then bow down.

"Huh-huh-huh," he chortled. "Priam's daughter is clever and good; no man of all my people will harm her as she passes through my country, or anything belonging to her. Not even the old women who peer at my men lustfully from behind their curtains! But if you have no use for the old toads, give them to my men; they are no good for bang-bang"—he accompanied the meaningless syllables with a gesture which made his meaning obscenely clear—"but we could boil them for arrow poison, huh-huh-huh?"

Kassandra struggled to keep her face straight.

"By no means; I do not want to travel without my women; they are good to me," she said, "and I would not travel through your country with young and pretty ones."

"Huh; clever," he said, wheeled his horse and rode quickly away.

She held up her hand to signal that she had not finished her parley, and he wheeled back and returned a little way. She asked, "Does the wise leader of the Horse People know where Penthesilea's women pasture her mares this summer?"

He gestured and gabbled out a quick explanation. Since it would not mean going too far out of their way, Kassandra decided she would ride in that direction. Again she took leave courteously of Cheiron, who had begun sharing out the loaves with his men and already had crumbs around his mouth.

AFTER ANOTHER long day of riding in the direction the Kentaur had indicated, Kassandra saw in the distance a mounted figure. The stranger carried a bow such as Penthesilea's women bore slung across her back. Kassandra beckoned to her, and the woman approached.

"Who rides in our country with an escort of men?"

"I am Kassandra, daughter of Priam of Troy, and I seek my kinswoman Penthesilea the Amazon," she said.

The woman, clad in the leather tunic and breeches of the

tribeswomen, her long, coarse black hair knotted atop her head, looked at her suspiciously; and finally said, "I remember you as a child, Princess. I cannot leave my mares"—she gestured toward the scattered scrawny herd grazing across the spare grasses of the plain—"and it is not my place to summon the Queen. But I will send a signal that she is wanted, and if it seems good to her, she will come."

She dismounted and kindled a small fire, throwing something into the flames which emitted great clouds of smoke; she covered it, then let the smoke billow up in successive triple puffs. After some time, Kassandra saw a tall figure on horseback making its way across the plain. When the figure neared, she recognized her kinswoman.

Penthesilea's horse approached and she could see the puzzled look on the Amazon's face; after a moment Kassandra realized that her kinswoman had not recognized her. When Penthesilea had last seen her she had been a young girl; now older, robed and attired as a princess, a priestess, she was only a strange woman.

She called out her name. "Don't you know me, Aunt?"

"Kassandra!" Penthesilea's taut sun-browned face relaxed, but she still looked tense and old. She came and dismounted, and embraced Kassandra with affection. "Why do you come here, child?"

"Looking for you, Aunt." When she had last seen her kinswoman, Penthesilea had seemed youthful and strong; now Kassandra wondered how old she really was. Her face was lined, with hundreds of small wrinkles around mouth and eyes; she had always been thin but was now positively scrawny. Kassandra wondered if the Amazons, like the Kentaurs, were actually starving.

"How goes this war in Troy?" the older woman asked. "Will you shelter with us this night and tell us about it?"

"With pleasure," Kassandra said, "and we can talk at leisure about this war; though I am weary of it." She gave directions to the bearers to follow the Amazon, and herself rode at Penthesilea's side, toward a cave in a hillside; inside there were a scant half-dozen women, mostly elderly, and a few little girls. When last she had traveled with them, there had been a good half a hundred. Now there were no babies, and no young women of childbearing age.

Penthesilea saw the direction of her glance and said, "Elaria and five others are in the men's village. I was afraid, but I knew I must let them go now or I would never dare to let them go again. That's right—you didn't know what happened, did you? Then our shame has not yet been told in Troy . . ."

"I have heard nothing, Aunt."

"Come and sit down. We'll talk as we eat, then." She smiled and sniffed appreciatively. "We have not eaten this well for many moons. Thank you."

Their meal had been supplemented with dried meat and bread from Kassandra's provisions. "All the same," Penthesilea said, "we are not as badly off as the Kentaurs; they are starving, and soon there will be no more. Have you even met with any of them?"

Kassandra told about her encounter with Cheiron, and the older woman nodded.

"Yes, we can always trust him and his men. In the name of the Goddess, I wish . . ." she broke off. "Last year we arranged to go to one of the men's villages—we made an arrangement for trading metal pots, and horses and some of our milk goats, too. Well, we went as usual, and it seemed that all was well. Two moons went by; some of us were pregnant, and we were ready to depart. They besought us to stay another month, and we agreed. Then when we were ready to set out, they made us a farewell feast and brought us a new wine. We slept deeply, and when we woke—it had been drugged, of course—we were bound and gagged, and they told us that we could not leave them; that they had decided they wished to live like men in cities, with women to tend them year round, and share their beds and their lives . . ." She broke off, shaking with indignation and grief.

"Every animal has a proper mating season," she said. "We tried to remind them of that, but they would not hear. So we told them that we would consider it if they would let us go; and they said we should cook them a meal, because men in cities had women to cook for them, look after their needs. They even forced some of the women who were already pregnant to bed with them!

"So we cooked them a meal; and you can imagine what kind of meal it was." She grinned fiercely. "But some women wished to spare the fathers of their children—Earth Mother alone knows where they got such ideas. And so some of them had been warned, and when they were all spewing and purging, we made ready to ride; but a few of them forced us to fight. Well, we could not kill them all; and so we lost many of our number: the traitorous ones stayed and did not return to us."

"They stayed with the men who—who had done this to you?"

"Aye; they said they were weary of fighting and herding," Penthesilea said scornfully. "They will bed with men in return for their bread—no better than harlots in your cities. It is a perversion of those Akhaians; they say, even, that our Earth Mother is no more than the wife of the Thunder Lord Zeus. . . ."

"Blasphemy!" Kassandra agreed. "This was not Cheiron's tribe?"

"No; them we can trust; they cling, like us, to the old ways," Penthesilea said. "But when this year Elaria led the women to the men's village, we made them swear an oath even they dared not break, and we made them leave with us all the weaned children. We hide here in caves because with our strong young women away, we have no warriors to guard our herds. . . ."

Kassandra found nothing to say. It was the end of a way of life which had lasted thousands of years on these plains; but what could they do? She said, "Has there been much of a drought? Cheiron told me that food is harder to find."

"That too; and some tribes have been greedy to own too many horses, and grazed more than the plains could feed, so they would have them to sell in return for cloth and metal pots and I know not what—and so it is that those of us who treat the earth well are dying. Earth Mother has not stretched out Her hand to punish them. I know not . . . perhaps there are no

Gods who care anymore what men do. . . ." Her face looked strained and old.

"I do not understand," Adrea said. "Why does it trouble you so, that some of your women have chosen to live as all women now live within the cities? You women could live well, with husbands to care for you and look after your horses; and you could keep your sons as well as your daughters, and you need not spend all your time fighting to defend yourselves. Many, many women live so and find nothing wrong with it; are you saying they are all wrong? Why do you want to live separately from men? Are you not women like any others?"

Penthesilea sighed, but instead of the instant scornful comment Kassandra had expected, she thought for a moment; Kassandra had the feeling that she really wanted this elderly city woman who so strongly disapproved of her to understand.

At last she said, "It has been our custom that we live among our own kind and are free. I do not like to live inside walls; and why should we women spin and weave and cook? Do not men wear clothes, that they should not make their own? And surely men eat; why should women cook all food that is eaten? The men in their own villages cook well enough when there are no women at hand to cook for them. So why should women live as slaves to men?"

"It does not seem slavery to me," the woman protested, "only fair exchange; do you say men are enslaved to women when they herd the horses and goats, then?"

Penthesilea said passionately, "But the women do these things as if it were an exchange for sharing their beds and bearing their children. Like the harlots in your cities who sell themselves. Cannot you see the difference? Why should women have to live with men when they can care for their own herds and feed themselves from their own gardens, and live free?"

"But if a woman wishes for children, she needs a man. Even you, Queen Penthesilea . . ."

Penthesilea said, "May I ask without giving offense, ladies; why is it that you have not married?"

Kara spoke first, saying, "I would gladly have married; but I pledged I would remain with Queen Hecuba while she wished for my company. I have not missed marriage; her children were born into my lap, and I have shared in their upbringing. And like Lady Kassandra, I have met no man I loved enough to separate me from my beloved Lady."

"I honor you for that," Penthesilea said. "And you, Adrea?"

"Alas, I was neither beautiful nor rich; so no man ever offered for me," the old woman said. "And now that time is past. So I serve my Queen and her daughters, even to following Lady Kassandra into this Goddess-forgotten wilderness filled with Kentaurs and other such wild folk. . . ."

"So there are other reasons than simple wickedness why a woman might choose not to marry," Penthesilea said. "If it is well for you not to marry out of loyalty to your Queen, why should Kassandra not remain loyal to her God?"

"It is not that she does not marry," said Adrea; "it is that she does not *wish* to marry. How can one sympathize with a woman like that?"

This was too much for Kassandra; she exploded with words she had been repressing for days. "I have not asked for your sympathy, any more than for your company; I did not invite you to join me, and you are welcome to return to Troy, where you will be surrounded by proper women, and I shall travel to Colchis with my kinswomen and their escort," she said hotly. "I have no need of your protection."

"Well, really," said Adrea huffily. "I have known you since you were a baby, my Lady, and what I say is no more than your own mother would say, and all spoken for your own good—"

Penthesilea said peacefully, "I beg you not to quarrel; you have a long road before you. Kassandra, my dear child, even if I were free to travel with you myself to Colchis, I could not keep you safe on your road. I pray that Priam's name and Apollo's peace will do so. Perhaps it is this war; perhaps it is the spread of the Akhaian ways now that the Minoan world has fallen. You have not even told me why you are traveling to Colchis; is it simply that the Lady is your old friend, or has Priam decided to send even so far afield for allies?"

She told Penthesilea about the earthquake and the defection of the Temple serpents, and the Amazon blanched at the omen.

"Still I will trust the Sun Lord," Kassandra said. "I have none other in whom to trust; and if I can come safely to Colchis with no other safeguard than His blessing, I shall take that as a sign of His continued goodwill."

"May He bless you, then, and guide you," said Penthesilea, "and may Serpent Mother Herself await you and give you blessing in Colchis—and everywhere else, my dear."

Soon after this they went to rest; but Kassandra lay long awake.

When she slept, her dreams were restless; she was seeking something—a lost weapon, a bow perhaps—but whenever she thought she had found it, it was not the one she wanted, but was broken, or had a broken string, or something of that sort.

What was it that the Gods were saying to her? She was a priestess; she had been taught that all dreams were messages from the Gods, if she could only find the meaning. That she could not interpret this dream meant only that she was, as she had long suspected, unfit to receive the Sun Lord's favor, that He had withdrawn from her. Try as she might, she could gain from it only a faint ill omen that whatever she sought on this quest, she would not find it.

In the morning, Penthesilea bestowed gifts on her and her women—new saddles, and a warm robe of horsehide.

"You will need it, believe me, in crossing the great plain," she said. "The winters have been more severe latterly, and there still may be snow."

As she embraced her in farewell, Kassandra felt like crying.

"When shall we meet again, Kinswoman?"

"When the Gods will it. If it should ever be the will of Earth Mother that I end my days in a city, I will come and end them in Troy; that I vow to you, my child. I do not think your mother would fail to welcome the last of her sisters, nor would Priam turn me from his door. Perhaps I should come with my warriors and seek to drive forth some of those Akhaians."

"When that day comes, I will fight at your side," promised Kassandra; but Penthesilea only embraced her with great tenderness and said, "That is not your fate in this life, my love; make no pledges you cannot keep," and rode away from them without looking back.

15

THE WINTER indeed lingered long on the great plain, and within four days after they had spent the night with Penthesilea and the remnant of her Amazons, the sky darkened, and snow began to fall so heavily that Kassandra wondered how her attendants could follow the narrow and ill-marked trail at all. All that day it snowed, and all the next, and although they continued to travel, they encountered almost no sign of human life. Once, far away through the snow, they saw a watching Kentaur outlined against the horizon; but when they would have signaled to him, he wheeled his horse and galloped away.

Kassandra was not surprised; from what Penthesilea had said, she knew that the inhabitants of the great plain, never particularly willing to trust outsiders, were even less inclined to do so now. It was fortunate that she had no need to trade with them for food or any other commodities. Day after day they plodded across the plain, their animals' hooves cutting through the soggy mud where there had been frozen grass, the snow never thick enough to be a danger and the dull rains never enough to thaw more than a few inches of the frozen ground. The great steppes were empty and barren; they found little enough food to supplement their dreary travel rations, and Kassandra grew weary of riding over the empty lands, crawling under an endless sky which seemed as gray and hostile as the faces of her companions.

Day followed sullen day while the moon thinned and faded and then swelled again; how long could this winter endure? Then, soon after a vagrant sight of a full moon through ragged clouds, she woke to hear rushing winds and a heavy, thick dripping rain which seemed to be carrying away the very land itself.

The new morning brought a countryside transformed, with little rivers flowing everywhere over the surface of the ground, shining in a new strong sun, and grass springing up everywhere under warm, soft winds. It soon grew so warm that Kassandra folded away her horsehide tunic and rode in her soft cloth chemise.

On one of these spring days they came to a village. It was no more than a cluster of round stone huts on the plain; but surrounding it were fields of greening winter grain uncovered from the fast-vanishing snow. Kassandra remembered the blighted village of her journey with the Amazons years before, with so many of its children deformed. But if this was the same village, it must somehow have survived the blight, for such children as she saw looked strong and healthy. Later, though, she saw some of the older girls and boys who had only two fingers on a hand. Before this they had seen no human dwelling for eight or ten days, and when the headwoman of the village came out to meet them, she seemed glad to see them as well.

"The winter has lain long on the land," she said, "and we have seen no humans all this winter but a little band of Kentaurs, so weakened with starvation that they made no attempts on our women, but only begged us for food of any sort."

"That seems sad," Kassandra said, but the headwoman wrinkled her face in disdain.

"You are a priestess; it is your work to have compassion even for such as they, I suppose. But they have terrorized us too often for me to have any feeling save satisfaction when I see them brought so low. With luck they will all starve, and then we need never fear them again. Have you metals or weapons for trade? No one passes through here for trade these days; such metals as they have are all bound for the war in Troy, and we can get none."

I am sorry; I have no weapons but my own," said Kassandra. "But we will buy some of your pots if you still make them."

The pots were brought out, and lengthily examined; dark fell while Kassandra's party was still looking them over, and the headwoman invited them to dine at her table and continue the trading in the morning. She placed one of the stone huts at their disposal, and bade them to dinner in the central hut. The food was meager indeed—meat that seemed to be some kind of ground squirrel, boiled in a stew with bitter acorns and tasteless white roots; but at least it was freshly cooked. Kassandra, recalling the blight, was somewhat reluctant to eat here at all, but told herself not to trouble about it—*for though I am still, I suppose, of childbearing age, I am not wed, nor likely to be. And*

*in any case, while these ladies sleep one at either side of my bed,
I am scarcely likely to get myself with child.*

If this village had not somehow recovered from the blight,
she thought, *it would have vanished when every soul in it died.*

A FEW DAYS later they sighted the iron gates of Colchis, as high
and as impressive as ever, and Kassandra attired herself not in
her leather riding clothes and chemise, but in her finest Trojan
robes, dyed in brilliant colors, and had one of her waiting-
women dress her hair in the elaborate plaited headdress she
wore in the Sun Lord's Temple. At least Queen Imandra would
greet her as a princess of Troy, not as a wandering supplicant.

They were welcomed at the city's iron gates as envoys from
Troy and bidden to lodge at the palace. Kassandra, saying she
must first pay her respects at the Sun Lord's Temple, went to
His large shrine at the city's very center, and sacrificed a pair of
doves to Apollo of the Long Bow. After that, she was taken to
the palace and conducted to a luxurious guest suite, where
bath-women and dressing-maids were put at her disposal. During the long process of bathing—or rather, of being bathed—
she reflected that during the long journey she had all but forgotten the taste of luxury. She enjoyed the steaming water, the
fragrant oils, the gentle massaging of her flesh with brushes and
the soft hands of the women. Then they dressed her in fine
guest-garments and conducted her into the presence-chamber
of Queen Imandra.

She had expected that the Queen would look older; she
herself was no longer the childlike girl who had come here, shy
and tongue-tied, at Penthesilea's side. But the change was more
than she could ever have imagined; if she had met this woman
anywhere except in this very throne-room, she would never
have recognized her as the proud descendant of Medea.

Imandra had grown enormously fatter; she was imposing
rather than gross, hung everywhere with gold; but she had
ceased to adorn her fleshy body with the coils of living serpents.
Her cheeks and lips were stained with red dye, and she wore the
richly dyed robes of finespun thin cloth which came from the
land of the Pharaohs by way of the eastern roads. Her hair was

studded with jewels as always. Amid all this splendor, only the merry dark eyes were the same, almost lost in the folds of flesh.

As Kassandra entered the hall and paused to give her the ritual greeting, Imandra rose from her throne, and walked—or rather, waddled—forward.

"No, my dear, no prostrations from my kinswoman,"·she said, seizing Kassandra in a warm and scented embrace; the perfume was as familiar as the eyes. "I am more glad than I can say to see you, daughter of Priam. What a long journey you have had! No doubt you bear messages from my daughter . . ."

"From your daughter and your grandson; Andromache is a mother, and soon to be—no, by this time she has another child, if all has gone well," Kassandra said, and Imandra beamed.

"I knew it, I knew it; did I not say, my dear, that enough time had gone by that I should be twice a grandam, if my daughter had done her duty?" she asked, addressing a handsomely built young man attired in gold cloth, like an athlete or the victor of the games, who had been given a seat near her. "Tomorrow I must look in the pool of ink and try to see her child, and if all is well with her."

She took Kassandra's hands and drew her to the high table, seating herself between Kassandra and the richly dressed young man. "Now tell me everything that has happened in Troy these last years since you went from me, taking my dearest treasure with you. And what brings you so far without your kinswomen?"

"Perhaps," said the young man, "the Lady Kassandra has come to beseech our assistance in this war against the Akhaians."

"Not if she traveled under Apollo's truce," said Queen Imandra. "I know something of that, dear boy." She turned back to Kassandra. "Even so, you need not break your pledge if you have made it; without any asking, I will send to Priam all the soldiers I can find, men or women, and as much as wagons can carry of metals and weapons too."

"You are more than generous," Kassandra said, and explained her errand. Imandra smiled and kissed her.

"My own priestesses and masters of serpents shall be consulted early on the morrow," she said, "or as soon as they tell me it is an auspicious day for such things. I need hardly say that all the wisdom to be found in our city is at your command and at the command of the Trojan Apollo. You shall be free to speak with them at any time; but you must promise to pay me a long visit."

"Your Majesty is gracious," Kassandra said; she was weary of traveling and at the moment desired nothing more than a long stay in Colchis.

"Not at all, Kinswoman," Imandra replied. "Are you not my fellow priestess, and nearest of all in kin to my daughter? And my soothsayers say the child I bear now will be another daughter, and I find it a good omen that you should be here for the birth."

Kassandra had not had the faintest inkling that the Lady was pregnant; indeed, had she given the matter a moment's thought, she would have believed Imandra old beyond the age of bearing. But now she looked closely, she saw that the Queen was indeed in the early stages of pregnancy. When she had taken this in, she complimented the Queen upon her expectations, and asked, "Will this, then, be heir to Colchis in Andromache's place?"

"It will. Andromache cares nothing for queenship; you must have found that out by now," Imandra said, "and it is not hard to forget about the business of being a Queen when a woman is happy—even if that woman is a Queen. Have I not said this to you before, Agon?" she demanded.

And the handsome young man said, "Indeed, my lady."

Imandra's broad face was wreathed in a grin Kassandra could only describe as "foolish" as her eyes rested on her favorite, and Kassandra, abruptly understanding the state of affairs, was shocked; the independent Queen Imandra, Lady of Colchis, besotted with a handsome boy no older than her daughter? And besotted she certainly was; the very tone of her voice said so. He shared her plate and wine-cup, and she sought out all the finest delicacies to offer to him.

When they had dined, Kassandra sent for the chests she had carried with her and brought out the gifts Andromache had sent to her mother: embroidered hangings, bolts of richly dyed fabric, even intricately decorated bronze swords and knives; several of these the Queen, with an indifferent gesture, bestowed at once on her consort.

"But don't tell me you want to go and fight in Troy," she said firmly to him. "I need you at my side to help me bring up our daughter; and even more if the soothsayers are wrong and it is a son."

"I wouldn't think of leaving you, my lady," he said, "certainly not to fight in some faraway country. If Agamemnon or any of those fellows were to come here to try to take Colchis, that would be quite another matter."

Imandra turned to Kassandra. "Tell me about this war, and this Spartan Queen," she said. "Distant as we are, I know something about her family, of course. What sort of person can she be, to have touched off such a widespread war as this?"

Kassandra said slowly, "I had not expected to like her or respect her. But I do; I think the Gods did harshly by her when They put her in the way of my brother Paris."

"Well, she had every right to take a consort," said Imandra, with a sly smile at young Agon; "but it was her mistake not to dismiss Menelaus—or have the old sacrifice! Things should be done in order. Helen's mistake, remember, was not that she took a lover; that was her perfect right which no one could deny her. Her mother was Queen by right in Mykenae, and Sparta was Helen's to rule; her crime—and it was truly a crime for a Queen—was leaving Sparta for Menelaus to seize, and this has confused the issue. Have they given it over to her daughter to rule after her? I'll warrant they have not; Hermione is too young to be aware of her queenship. These Akhaian savages who try to bring their prattle of 'Kings' into our civilized world; and their mighty talk of *fathering* . . . as if any man could create life. The Goddess alone breathes life into children; yet some of these men are arrogant enough to say that the woman is no more than an oven in which their child—*their* child, did you ever hear such nonsense?—is cooked. That Agamemnon—may he be cursed by every Goddess and all the Furies!" Imandra exclaimed.

"He is the leader of the Akhaian armies from Mykenae itself," Kassandra said.

"Yes; you knew he was married to Helen's sister, who succeeded her mother in Mykenae? Klytemnestra was the elder twin, and very beautiful, but nothing like Helen. Klytemnestra had a daughter, Iphigenia—dedicated to Serpent Mother, and of course keeper of the shrine and high priestess from the time she was still a child. Well, when this war began, Agamemnon had sworn to aid his brother in all things, and so he had to leave Mykenae, and he was afraid that Klytemnestra would replace him as her consort; she was angry that he had dared to swear such an oath without her leave, and so she threatened that if he left her she would take her cousin Aegisthos to her bed. Agamemnon threatened to take away their son Orestes; Klytemnestra told him he might do as he would with the boy, but if he perverted any of her children with his evil Gods, she would cast his son out after him. So he made the lad a priest of Poseidon —I think it was Poseidon, the Horse God—and sent him to be fostered among the Kentaurs. When Agamemnon's armies were gathered to sail to Troy, he was delayed on shore with poor winds, and he sent to Klytemnestra that her daughter Iphigenia should come and conduct the appointed sacrifices to the winds. So she came, as priestess, and what should he do but sacrifice Iphigenia herself, on false oracles; so that Klytemnestra could not take another consort, because her younger daughter was too young to be her successor. And I have heard that this younger daughter, Elektra, has been turned against the worship of Earth Mother; and who could blame her? If she became a priestess like her sister, she might die too. But Klytemnestra has sworn vengeance; and Agamemnon will one day face the vengeance of Earth Mother. And mistake me not, he will die. The Gods are not mocked in this fashion."

"So, then, it is all a matter of whether the land shall be ordered by Kings or Queens?"

"What else? Why should men rule the hearth or the city, where woman has commanded since first Earth Mother brought forth life? The old way was best, wherein the King was led out every year to die for his people and there was no question of any man setting up his son to follow him. For thousands of years, until these Akhaian savages came to try to change our ways, that was the rule of life . . .

"And then, who knows? Perhaps there was war and a King was too skilled a leader to be made to die; or some foolish woman like myself did not wish to lose her young lover." She turned an affectionate look on young Agon. "Then these horse-folk came, and the first Kings, and set up their arrogant Gods—even the Sun Lord, who claimed to have slain Serpent Mother." Imandra yawned. "The world is changing, I tell you—but it is the fault of the women who did not keep their men in their place."

"And you think, then, this is the cause of this war?" Kassandra asked.

"My dear, I am sure of it," said the Queen. "It could never have happened in Colchis."

16

A FEW DAYS later Kassandra, lodged in the suite in the palace once allotted to the royal daughters, that same room where once she and Andromache had lain awake one night watching stars falling, was awakened by Queen Imandra herself.

"My dear, the High Priestess in Serpent Mother's Temple is willing to receive you."

Kassandra awakened her waiting-women and had herself dressed in a simple unbleached tunic, as befitted a suppliant. Adrea protested: "You are a princess of Troy and a priestess in your own right; you should go to her as an equal, my lady."

"But I go to her to seek wisdom which she possesses and I do not," Kassandra answered. "I think it is more fitting that I go to her humbly, beseeching her help."

The waiting-woman sniffed; but Queen Imandra said, "I think you are right, Kassandra. When she summons me, even I go to her with humility." Kassandra sighed with relief and bound her soft sandals on her feet. She very much disliked wearing elaborate court robes and being dressed up as a prin-cess.

Though the sun was not very high in the sky, the morning clouds had already burned off, and the heat was very strong on her head and through the shoulders of her tunic. It seemed a long walk across the city, and her feet were tired when at last they climbed the great Titan-built steps toward the shrine.

Inside, to Kassandra's relief, it was dark and cool, and there was the pleasant far-off sound of falling water. A quiet dark-robed attendant showed them into a shaded tile-floored court; at the far end there was a formal high seat where sat a large fat old woman with white hair.

"The priestess Arikia," murmured Imandra.

They advanced slowly down the room. At first Kassandra thought there was a living serpent twined about the priestess' gilt headdress; then she realized that it was only a very realistic molded and painted one of pottery, or perhaps of carved wood. The priestess was dressed in a sleeveless robe of patterned crimson cloth, richly ornamented with designs that looked like the scales of serpents; and wrapped around her waist was indeed a living snake—the largest that Kassandra had ever seen: as big around as the priestess' arms, which were very fat. The snake was coiled around Arikia's waist twice, and the old woman held the serpent's head in her hand, lazily tickling it under the chin.

She said in a soft voice which resounded nonetheless with authority: "Greetings, Queen Imandra; is this the Trojan princess of whom you told me?"

"It is, Lady," said Imandra, "Kassandra, daughter of Queen Hecuba of Troy."

Kassandra felt the old priestess' eyes resting on her, as dark and flat as the serpent's eyes. "And what do you want from me, Kassandra of Troy?"

Kassandra felt compelled to kneel down before the old woman.

"I have come from Troy to learn of you—or rather, of Serpent Mother," she said.

"Well, tell me what you seek," said the old priestess. "For you, Hecuba's daughter, I will do whatever lies within my powers."

So encouraged, Kassandra told her of the death or desertion of the serpents in the Sun Lord's house, and her unwillingness to replace them until she knew more of their care. The old woman smiled, still stroking the great snake under its chin—or the place where it would have had a chin. At last she said, "I should call all my priestesses, Kassandra, and have them come and look at you. For in all Colchis I cannot find a single young woman who wishes to learn this lore; and you have come all the way from Troy to seek it from me.

"Tell me then, Kassandra, while you are in Serpent Mother's Temple, will you give due reverence to Her?"

"I swear it, Lady."

Arikia smiled and held out her hand.

"So be it," she said, "I accept you. You may remain here, and none of our ancient wisdom shall be hidden from you while you dwell among us. You may leave her with us, Imandra; and you too may go," she said, casting her sharp eyes on Adrea. "She will need no waiting-woman in the Mother's Temple; such attendance as she may need will be given by priestesses."

Adrea said firmly, "I promised her mother, my lady, that I'd not leave her side for a single day while she was in foreign parts."

Arikia said kindly, "I cannot fault you for that, Daughter. But do you truly think she needs your chaperonage when she is in the hands of the Great Mother?"

"I suppose not, my lady. When you put it like that, where could she be safer than in the hands of the Great Goddess? But I cannot break my promise to Queen Hecuba," said Adrea reluctantly.

"Still," said Arikia, "I think you must leave her to me and the Goddess; but you may come every few days and speak with her alone and unobserved, to reassure yourself that she is safe and well, and here of her own free choice."

Imandra said, "Must she lodge in the Temple, Lady Arikia? I would be happier to have her in the palace as my guest, and she could attend at the Temple services whenever you wished for her."

"No, that will not do; she must live among us and learn to live with us and our serpents," Arikia said. "Is this disagreeable to you, Kassandra?"

"Not at all," Kassandra said. "I honor the Lady Imandra as

my mother's kinswoman and my friend; but I am more than willing to dwell in the House of the Mother as is seemly for a priestess."

Imandra embraced her, and Adrea, and they took their leave. When they had gone, the old priestess, who had observed Kassandra's close watching of the snake that was still coiled motionless about her body, asked, "Are you afraid of the serpent-folk, Kassandra?"

"Not at all, Lady." She added impulsively, "This is a very beautiful one."

"She is a true matriarch among serpents," Arikia agreed. "Would you care to hold her?"

"Certainly, if she will come to me," Kassandra said, though she had never handled such a large serpent. "She is not poisonous, I suppose?"

"Can't you tell by looking at her? Well, that is one of the first things we must teach you. But of course she is not. I would not venture to handle one of the venomous snakes like this; they are seldom so good-tempered. And they are almost never as large as this one."

Arikia held the huge snake's tail away from her body. "Look, this will make her uncoil, since she cannot brace herself against my body when I hold her like this. Hold out your hand and let her smell you." Kassandra obeyed, not flinching as the great head moved close, the forked tongue flicking in and out, just touching her hand. Then the snake moved, flowed smoothly as folds of silk along the older priestess' arm and along Kassandra's shoulders and around her waist. The big wedge-shaped head came up toward Kassandra's; Kassandra took it in her hand and began to rub gently under the chin. She was surprised to feel all the tension go out of the snake's body as the surprising weight settled round her.

"Good—she likes you," Arikia said. "It would be of little value for me to accept you here if she did not. All the same, sooner or later if she is frightened or startled while you are holding her, she may bite. Do you know what to do if she does?"

Old Meliantha in the Sun Lord's house had taught Kassandra that.

"Yes; don't frighten her more, or try to pull away, but get someone else to unwind her, beginning with the tail," Kassandra said, and held out her hand and displayed the small scars where one of the Temple serpents had chewed on it during her time as Meliantha's attendant. Arikia smiled.

"Good; but what have you to learn from us, then?"

"Oh, all manner of things," Kassandra said eagerly. "I wish to know how to find and take snakes from the wild where they breed; how to hatch them out from eggs and train them to come and go, as I have seen done; how to feed them and care for them for long life, and how to win their confidence and keep them content so they will not run away."

The old woman chuckled, holding out her hand to circle the head of the big snake.

"Good; I think here we can teach you all these things. You had better let me take her now; I am accustomed to her weight, and I do not think a slender creature like you can carry her very far. You must eat well and get fat, like me, or like Imandra, before you can more truly be a priestess of the Serpent Mother. A day may come when you will sit and display her to the people; she likes to be on display, or so it seems. One more thing: some of the girls are too softhearted or sentimental about little animals—doves, mice, rabbits—to feed the serpents. Will that trouble you?"

"Not at all; it is not I, but the Gods who have determined that some animals shall be fed on other living things; I did not create them, and it is not for me to say on what they should be fed," Kassandra replied. She had heard Meliantha say this once when a young girl in the Temple had been squeamish about feeding living mice to snakes.

"Well," said Arikia, "we must find you a room of your own, and an attendant priestess, and make you known to the rest of us who live here. You are a princess of Troy, and I hope it will not be too small and mean for you."

"Oh, no," Kassandra said, "I am eager to be one of you."

Arikia embraced her lovingly, and led her into the house of Serpent Mother.

17

THEN BEGAN for Kassandra a time like no other in her life. Since she was already a priestess, there were no wearying ordeals or trials, although as the youngest (many of the Temple's priestesses were elderly and frail, for few young women chose to serve the Serpent Mother), she was given such duties as caring for the animals being raised for feeding the serpents, cleaning pots and accepting and tallying Temple offerings. She was welcomed by everyone and treated in accordance with her station; Queen Imandra herself received no more deference, and soon Arikia came to love her as a daughter.

In many ways, her stay in the Serpent Mother's Temple was like her early years in the Sun Lord's house, with one great difference: all the devotees of Serpent Mother were women, and she had nothing like her early troubles with Khryse; the only men in the House of the Serpent were slaves, and none of them would have dared make any advances to a priestess.

She learned all that the priestesses could teach her about the ways of serpents and snakes. She soon knew how to tell the venomous from the harmless, and how to tame and handle certain harmless serpents which looked identical to certain poisonous snakes, so that any onlooker would believe that she was defying death. She herself had no fear of even the largest snakes, and soon was one of the preferred handlers; often when the enormous matriarch of serpents was carried in processions, Kassandra was one of those chosen to carry her.

Nothing of serpent-lore escaped her: how to find and capture snakes in the wild, how to feed and keep them, how to bathe them and care for them when they shed their skins. She even hatched one herself, carrying the egg between her breasts for more than a month, and sheltering the baby snake against her body when it crawled out of the egg. For this she was given the coveted title of honor among the priestesses, Snake Mother.

She seldom thought of Troy. Word came to Colchis now and again, perhaps distorted by the long journey, of how the war went. Idomeneo of Crete, and the Minoan Kings, became Troy's allies; most of the mainlanders stood with the Akhaians. The islanders, because of alliances forged when Atlantis still ruled the seas, held with Priam and the Goddesses of Troy and Colchis.

Sometimes at the full moon, Kassandra kindled witchfire and looked into her scrying-bowl by its light; and so she knew when Andromache bore Hector a second son, who died before his naval-string was healed; she wished that night that she could have been in Troy to comfort her friend's grief.

She knew, too, when Helen bore Paris twin sons, which did not entirely surprise her. Paris, after all, was a twin—and Helen too had a twin sister. It occurred to her that if she herself ever bore children, she might have twins, perhaps twin daughters. Helen's twins were strong and healthy children, though they hadn't the beauty of either their mother or father, and grew so fast that they were walking within half a year.

Before Paris' younger sons were weaned, Priam suffered a fall in a skirmish on the shore, and the thunderbolt stroke, during the illness that followed, left the right side of his face twisted and sagging, and he limped thereafter on his right foot. He made Hector the official commander of his armies—to no one's surprise. The soldiers, though they were loyal, and cheered Priam when on rare occasions he appeared before the armies, worshiped Hector as if he were Ares Himself.

Time in Colchis slipped past without incident. Kassandra was always welcomed at the palace, and Imandra often sent for her—sometimes simply for her company, occasionally to look into a scrying-bowl and tell her how it went with the war, or sometimes to search out the Amazons to be certain it did not go too badly with Penthesilea and her band. With her days filled with study and duties, Kassandra was surprised to discover that she had been gone from Troy for more than a year. Among women, birth was always a festival, and someone in the palace was always having a baby; the women sworn to Serpent Mother, however, did not marry, and most of them had taken formal vows of chastity, so there were no births in their Temple. She wondered when the Queen would have her child.

Soon she heard in the city that the Queen would walk abroad to bless her subjects in the name of Earth Mother. Kassandra vaguely remembered—it was almost her first memory—that Hecuba had done this before Troilus was born. In Troy it was simply an old custom, half-remembered and informally observed: whenever the Queen showed herself in the streets, women would rush up to her and ask her blessing. In Colchis, where the customs were kept in the old way, Kassandra was not surprised to find there was a formal procession. But surely they had left it to very late; the time of birth must be imminent. Imandra would not walk the streets but would be carried in a sedan chair, and Arikia, the earthly representative of Serpent Mother, would be carried with her, the serpents of wisdom adorning her from head to foot, so that all women in the city could seek blessing not only from the pregnant Queen but from the Serpent Mother.

"But why now? Do they want the Queen to fall into labor in the streets?" she asked.

"Well, it has happened before," Arikia said. "This would not be the first child of a Queen of Colchis to be born in the streets of the city; there will be many court midwives in the procession. But the Queen's diviners have chosen this as an auspicious day; and of course, the nearer to her time Imandra is, the more blessing she can confer."

"Yes, of course." Kassandra could understand that. It was the morning of the procession, and Kassandra, along with her fellow priestesses, was helping to dress and adorn Arikia, winding the serpent matriarch about her waist and two smaller serpents about her arms. It would be tiring for the woman, for the serpents must be held up so that the people could see them. Kassandra wished that she, who was younger and stronger, could take the older woman's place. She said so, but Arikia only said, "It is harder still on the Queen, my dear; she is as big as a python who has swallowed a cow. Perhaps next time, my dear; Imandra is an old friend, and I am happy to ride in her procession. She has been more than kind to you, too. A little more of the crimson paint on my left cheek, if you please, and some of the herbal powder to be burned in the brazier; the serpents love it, and they give far less trouble when they can smell it. Will you ride with me, Kassandra? You can feed the brazier, and stand ready to take the smaller snakes from me if they should be restless. It is not likely, but of course anything can happen."

Kassandra knew this was a privilege of which other priestesses in the Temple would be envious; but they deferred to her as princess of Troy. She went and put on her best ceremonial robe at once, and wrapped her arms with two or three of the smaller serpents, binding two others around her brow so that they formed a crown. Thus arrayed (and thinking that perhaps the statues of the legendary Medusa might have been inspired by such a serpent crown), she went out to the street and as Arikia was lifted into the high raised chair, let herself be lifted in after her.

It was cold; a high wind was blowing through the streets between the tall buildings, and all the leaves were gone from the trees and bushes. She sat holding her serpents high so that the women in the streets could see them clearly. Imandra's chair was ahead; Kassandra could see the Queen's form, heavily pregnant now, her loosened hair flowing down her back. The streets were crowded with women, many of them pregnant, rushing up to the carriages, pushing through the guards, reaching up their arms to beg for the blessing.

The wind chilled her; she was glad for the cozy weight of the serpent about her waist. The snakes were sluggish. *They do not like the cold any better than I do*, she thought, longing for the warm sun of her home.

She fell almost into a trance, looking at the tall figure of Imandra on her carriage, shadowed with the powerful magic and glamour of the Goddess. Women rushed out to hold up their hands, crying out for fertility and just the good fortune of touching the pregnant Queen who embodied the Goddess. Automatically holding up her serpents, she heard the women crying out to Imandra and Earth Mother, to Arikia, and the Serpent Mother, and then from somewhere in the crowd she actually heard someone call, "Look, it is the Trojan priestess, the beloved of Apollo!"

That brought her to sudden awareness. Was it still true? Or

had Apollo forgotten her? Perhaps it was time, she thought, that she should return to Troy and her own people and her own Gods; serving the Goddess, women were more free here, but what good was the freedom if she must dwell forever among strangers? Then her heart smote her; she was well loved here and had many friends; could she bear to abandon them and to return to a city where women were expected to defer to their husbands and brothers?

The sun grew hotter; she pulled her veil over her head and dipped her kerchief into a bowl of water to moisten the snakes' heads. "Soon, little ones," she murmured, "this will be over and you will be where it is cool and dark." One of the serpents was trying to crawl into the darkness of her dress; the crowds were thinning, so she did not try to prevent it.

The chair-bearers slowed, then came to a halt. Servants were carefully lifting Imandra down from her seat—not easily. She walked heavily toward the chair where the priestesses sat, surrounded by their serpents.

"Kassandra, my friend, will you come this evening to the palace and look for me into your scrying-bowl?"

"With pleasure," Kassandra replied. "As soon as I have cared for my serpents—if Arikia will give me leave," she added, glancing at the senior priestess, who smiled and nodded permission.

At the Temple of Serpent Mother, she helped the bearers settle Arikia down on her bed in a darkened room, then helped unwind the snakes and bathe them in the fountain in the inner court. After swallowing a little fruit and bread, she dressed herself in her simplest robe and went out again into the chill of early afternoon. It was a little warmer—what heat there was in the sun was full strength now—and the noonday streets were full of people; but none of them recognized the slight dark-haired woman in her plain tunic as the priestess who had been carried, robed and crowned in her serpents, through the streets.

The Queen's women conducted Kassandra to the royal apartments. It was pleasantly warm there, with a fire in a fireplace. Imandra was lying in a hammock, her hair unbound and her huge body mounded high against the cushions. She had shed the glamour of the Goddess and now looked weary; her drawn face would have been pale, except that she had not even troubled to remove the paint from her cheeks.

She should have kept Andromache here in Colchis instead of sending her to Troy; then she would not need to expose herself to the dangers of a belated childbearing, Kassandra thought, surprised at herself; *now she needs a daughter to rule after her in Colchis.*

As if some hint of Kassandra's thought had reached her, the Queen opened her eyes.

"Ah, Daughter, you have come to keep me company," she said. "I am glad; I think the little one"—she laid her hand across her belly—"may be born today; but at least the procession was completed and I need not give birth to their Queen in the streets. Soon I will summon the palace women—they will be cross if they are not told at once; they are entitled to their festival. Kassandra, how old are you, my dear?"

Kassandra tried to reckon up the years; in Troy they did not keep track of a woman's age once she had arrived at puberty.

"I think I shall be nineteen or twenty this summer," she said. "Mother told me I was born near to midsummer."

"A year older than my Andromache," Imandra said. "And you told me that Andromache's oldest son is old enough for his first bronze helmet and lessons in swordplay. I do not think I know any other woman of your years who is not married. Sometimes I think you should have been my daughter, since you cleave to the old ways in Colchis, and Andromache seems happy in Troy, even as an obedient wife to Hector." Her lip curled a little, almost in scorn. "But you are Priam's daughter, and a Trojan. Is it your will to remain unmarried all your days, my dear?"

"I had thought of nothing else," Kassandra said. "I am sworn to Apollo Sun Lord."

"But you are missing all that makes life worth the living," Imandra said, and sighed.

She frowned and lay motionless for a time, then said, "Will you look into the scrying-bowl and let this old woman once set eyes upon my daughter's child?"

Kassandra demurred. "Perhaps just now," she said, "you should think first of *this* child. You must save all your strength and energy until she is safely here among us, Kinswoman."

"Spoken like a priestess—and priestesses are all full of nonsense," said Imandra crustily. "I am not a maiden of fifteen in my first childbed; I am a grown woman and a Queen, and no less a priestess than you yourself, Kassandra of Troy."

"I had no thought of suggesting—" Kassandra began defensively.

"Oh, yes you did; don't deny it," Imandra said. "Do as I ask you, Kassandra; if you will not, there are others who will, though not many who see so far or so well."

Everything Imandra said was true, and Kassandra knew it.

"Oh, very well," she agreed, mentally adding *you stubborn old creature.* "Call your women," she said, "and let them prepare you for the birth. Hold me harmless of it if what I say gives you pain or sorrow; I am but the messenger, the wings of the bird on which such greetings fly." She knelt down, making the preparations for kindling the witchfire for the spell of Sight.

Imandra's women came and went in the room, making all ready for the birthing. Among them were Kassandra's two waiting-women, who came to greet her and ask quietly out of earshot of the Queen, "Are we to stay in this foreign city forever, Princess? When shall we return to Troy?"

"That shall be as Queen Imandra wills," Kassandra said. "I shall not leave her while she has need of me here."

"How can she have more need of you than your own mother, Lady? Do you truly think Queen Hecuba does not long and grieve for you?"

"You have my leave to return to Troy whenever you will," Kassandra said indifferently; "this very night if it should please you. But I have made a promise to Imandra and I will not break it." She rose and strode to the high bed where the women had placed the Queen to rest till it should be time for the birth-chair. The room was slowly filling with the women in the palace, come to witness the royal event.

"I wonder," Imandra mused fretfully, "if it ever happens that the Earth Mother sends the babe to the wrong womb? From what I know of her, Hecuba would have thought Andromache her perfect daughter, and you were always misplaced in Troy. . . . " She clung hard to Kassandra's hand. "No, don't leave me," she said; "the Gods will wait on the Sight till our eyes are ready to see."

"I do not know what the purposes of the Goddess may be, that sent me to the womb of Hecuba of Troy instead of Imandra of Colchis," Kassandra said, laying her cheek against the older woman's, "but whatever it may have been, Kinswoman, I love and revere you as if you were my mother in truth."

"I believe you do, child," said Imandra, turning her face to kiss Kassandra. "Should the Goddess take me today, as we all come under Her Wing at such times as this, promise me to stay in Colchis and rear my daughter in the old ways."

"Oh, come, you mustn't talk about dying; you will live many, many years and see this daughter with her own sons and daughters at her knees," Kassandra said. One of the serving-women handed her a cup of wine and a plate of honey cakes; she sipped at the wine absently, and put the cakes aside.

"Let me look for you into the bowl," she said, and knelt again on the stones by the kindled witchlight, casting her mind to the day when Andromache's first son had been born; Hector's face pale and excited, looking at the little creature . . .

Shadows moved in the water, flowing and congealing into Hector's face . . . the crimson plumes draggled, slimed with a wet darker crimson . . . Kassandra gasped as a sudden pain pierced her heart. *Hector!* Was he dead, or did she but see what was to come? When a city was at war, it was more likely than not that the leader of the army, who always was first among his troops in battle, should fall at the hands . . . the bloody hands of Akhilles! . . . That sneering face, pale and beautiful, beautiful and evil . . . Snow drifted across the face of the water, and Kassandra knew she saw what was to come in a future year; but which year? Kassandra had no way of knowing.

Imandra, her eyes fixed on Kassandra's face as if desperately trying to share the vision, asked, "What did you see?"

"Hector's death," Kassandra whispered. "But for a warrior there is no other end, and we have long known that this was to come; but 'tis not yet, perhaps not for many years. . . ."

"But the child," Imandra whispered—"tell me of the child!"

"When last I saw, he was healthy and well grown, and already had a wooden sword and a toy helmet," Kassandra said, reluctant to look again and see disaster, and for some reason she never doubted that this was what would come. "The omens this night are evil for the sight, Imandra; I beg you excuse me from looking again."

"As you will," said Imandra, but her face twisted with disappointment.

"I could die content if only I could see my daughter's son, even by your sight rather than my own. . . ."

Flickers of color flowed across the surface of the water; *firelight, flame across the gates of Troy . . .* and she remembered Hector's teasing voice.

You have but one song, Kassandra; fire and doom for Troy; and you sing it in season and out, like a minstrel who knows but one tune. . . .

Yes, I know Troy is to perish, but not yet. . . . I beseech You, let me see something else. . . .

The flames died; there was a flare of light, the bright sunlight reflecting on the white walls of Troy . . . melting into the angry, somber face of Khryse, distorted into the familiar lines of mourning.

Apollo Sun Lord: if I see all this in Your light, why must You show me nothing but what I already know?

Then glare, as if she were staring directly into the face of the sun; it seemed Khryse grew taller, and now Kassandra saw the blazing light of the God, and knew who now strode the walls and ramparts of Troy, terrible in His wrath; His shining bow drawn, the golden arrows shooting . . . shooting at random among Akhaians and Trojans alike, the terrible arrows of Apollo, striking. . . .

Kassandra screamed, covering her face with her hands. The vision blurred and ran like water, was gone.

"Not upon us," she moaned. "Not upon Thine own people, Sun Lord, not the wrath, not the arrows of Apollo. . . ."

Then they were all around her, shaking her, trying to lift her, holding wine to her lips.

"What did you see? Try and tell us, Kassandra."

"No, no," she cried, trying very hard to keep her voice from becoming a shriek. "We must go at once! We must return to Troy!" But dread iced her heart as she thought of the endless leagues of the journey which lay between Colchis and home.

"We must go at once! We must set out at daybreak, or even this night," she cried, reaching for her waiting-woman's hands holding her up. "We must go . . . we must not lose a moment. . . ."

She pulled herself unsteadily to her feet, and made her way to Imandra's side, kneeling there, pleading, "The Gods call me at once to Troy; I beg you, Kinswoman, give me leave to depart. . . ."

"To go now?" Imandra, her whole mind and body concentrated on the birth-throes sweeping her body, stared at her without comprehension. "No; I forbid it. You promised to remain with me. . . ."

Despairing, Kassandra realized that she could not impose her own needs upon this woman gripped in the most imperative of all callings. She would simply have to wait. She wiped away the tears she had not realized were flooding down her cheeks, and turned her attention to Imandra herself.

"Did you see my Andromache's child?" Imandra pleaded.

"No," Kassandra said soothingly, blocking from her mind the sight of the child's broken body before the walls of Troy. . . . *She had seen that before.* . . . "No, this night the Gods gave me no such sight. I saw only how ill it went with my city."

The sea black with the Akhaian ships, the walls of Troy swarmed over by the storming ants of Akhilles' armies . . . walls breaking, flames rising . . . No, not yet . . . not that final destruction, not yet . . . but worse, the terrible arrows of Apollo's wrath flying against Akhaians and Trojans alike . . .

One of the women started one of the traditional birth-songs, and after a stunned moment of silence . . . *How could they sing and behave as if this were an ordinary women's festival? But no, they had not seen blood or flames or the arrows of the angry God.* Kassandra joined in the chant, encouraging the waiting soul of the child to come into the body prepared for it, for the Goddess to release the child's body from the Queen's

imprisoning womb. Song followed song, and later some of the
priestesses danced the curious dance of the soul making its way
past the guardians of the World Before. The night wore slowly
away, and when the sky was paling for sunrise, the Queen at
last, with a shout of triumph, gave birth. The senior palace
midwife, into whose hands the child had been born, held it up,
crying out, "It is a daughter! A strong and healthy daughter! A
little Queen for Colchis!"

The women broke into a triumphant chant of welcome for
the infant, taking her to the window and holding her up to the
rising sun, passing the little naked body around the circle
of women from hand to hand that each woman might embrace and kiss the new one. Queen Imandra finally demanded, "Let me take her; let me see that she is truly strong and
healthy."

"Just a moment; we must first swaddle her against the cold,"
said the court midwife, and wrapped the baby in one of the
Queen's own shawls.

They put her, swaddled and washed at last, into Imandra's
hands, and the Queen laid her face tenderly against the little
one's cheek.

"Ah, I have waited long enough to hold you, little one. It is
like bearing my own grandchild. I know no other woman who
has borne a child at my age and lived," she said; "yet I feel as
strong and well as when Andromache was put into my arms."
She was unwrapping the baby in the compulsive way of all new
mothers, counting each finger and toe, then counting them all
over again in case she had missed one, then giving each one a
separate kiss, like a special tribute.

"She's beautiful," she said, smiling blissfully when she had
finished nudging and nuzzling the baby, and drawing a costly
ring from her finger, presented it to the court midwife: "This in
addition to your regular fee, which my chamberlain will give
you." The midwife gasped thanks and backed away, overwhelmed at such largess.

Imandra continued: "We will name her on the first auspicious day. Until then she will be my little pearl . . . since she is
as smooth and pink as one of the pearls the divers in the islands

bring from the depths of the sea. And I shall call her Pearl, my little pearl princess."

All the women agreed that this was a lovely name. It would be used until the princess was given a formal name by the priestesses, and informally all her life.

Then Queen Imandra beckoned Kassandra forward.

"Your eyes are red, Kassandra, and you do not seem to rejoice with us. Have you seen some evil omen for my child, that you do not share my joy?"

Kassandra cringed; she had been afraid that she would not be able to conceal her grief from Imandra's sharp eyes. "No, Kinswoman; I truly rejoice for your happiness," she said, bending down and kissing the little princess, "and I cannot tell you how greatly I rejoice that you are safe and well. But my eyes are always red when I sleep so little as this night; and"—she hesitated, her voice breaking—"the Gods have sent me an evil omen from Troy. I am needed there. I beg you, Kinswoman, grant me leave to depart at once for my home."

Imandra looked distressed, but the pain in Kassandra's face softened her anger. She said, "In this weather? Winter is approaching, and the journey would be terrible. I had hoped you would remain to help me raise my daughter. I had little luck in raising Andromache to be Queen after me. I put small faith in oracles or omens, yet I can deny you nothing on a day when the Goddess has sent me this beautiful daughter. Yet it is not my leave you must obtain, but that of Serpent Mother. It is to Her, not to me, that you are sworn here. And you must wait at least until I can gather gifts to be sent to Troy; for Andromache and her child, and for my kinswoman Hecuba, and not least, for you, my dear daughter."

Kassandra had known this would be required, and she told herself that the catastrophe she had foreseen could not be so imminent that a day or even a week could make so much difference. The dues of kinship and courtesy should not be ignored for one who had been so good to her as Queen Imandra. Yet her heart rebelled; everything which held her back from Troy now seemed hateful to her. She was sure that Arikia would chide her for disloyalty; but there was no other honorable thing to do. They had given generously of their knowledge and friendship; she could not, after all, steal away from Colchis like a thief.

So she braced herself and went to take leave of the Serpent Priestess.

DURING THE night and the long next day, while wagons and beasts and gifts and all that she would need on the long road to Troy were being made ready, Kassandra had time to regain some degree of calm, if only because she could not remain at that fever pitch of dread and terror and live. While she knew that the Gods had summoned her to Troy to meet whatever might be her destiny, it never occurred to her that remaining in Colchis might serve to avoid it; history was full of tales of those who selfishly thought to avoid their destiny by neglecting some duty, and inevitably brought upon themselves the very fate they feared.

The vision might not mean catastrophe; it might even mean that Apollo would not tolerate the war as it was being waged. Perhaps He would force them to some kind of truce, and all would be well.

So in the end, although truly sorry to part from Colchis and the freedom and honor she knew there, she set forth three mornings later with a high heart, glad—or at least, not sorry— to be on the road again.

18

THEIR JOURNEY began at the earliest daylight, the three women riding in a strong cart drawn by mules which Queen Imandra had provided. As the cart trundled down through the city, all was dark except for sparks from a forge, where a burly woman blacksmith worked. Adrea and Kara were openly jubilant that they were going home, although they spoke with dread of the long miles of the journey, and the dangers of bandits and Kentaurs as well as of mountain passes deep in snow, and roving wild men or women who might think they bore riches—or who would find their simple supplies of food and clothing riches enough.

Kassandra rode silently, already missing her friends in the Temple of Serpent Mother, both human and reptilian, and sorry to leave Imandra. It was hardly likely that they would meet again in this world.

As they passed through the iron gates of Colchis, a few flakes of snow were sifting down, and the skies were gray and sullen. Light grew, though the sun did not appear, and Kassandra took a last look at the high gates of the city, gleaming red in the grayish dawn light.

There could not be many women her age who had made such a journey twice in a lifetime; and if she could journey this road twice, why not three times or more? There might still be many adventures before her; and even if she rode back to Troy, there was no need to feel the walls of the city close about her again until she must.

The first night, when she and her women prepared as usual to settle down for sleep, Adrea demanded, "Are you going to sleep with that *thing* in your bed, Princess?"

Kassandra let her hand stray to the coils of the snake, warm and soft in her chemise.

"Of course. I am her mother. I hatched this snake with my own body's warmth, and she has slept in my bosom every night of her life. Besides, it is cold at night; she would die if I did not keep her warm."

"I would do much, and I have done much, for your mother's daughter," said Adrea. "But I will *not* share my bed with a snake! Can't it sleep by the fire in a box or a pot?"

"No, it cannot," said Kassandra, secretly filled with glee. "I assure you it will not bite, and it is a better bedfellow than a human child, for it will not wet or soil the bedclothes as a baby is likely to do. You will never sleep with a cleaner creature." She stroked the snake and said, "You needn't worry; she will stay close to me. I am sure she is more afraid of you than you are of her."

"No," Adrea said pleadingly. "No, please, Lady Kassandra, I can't do it, I can't sleep in one bed with that serpent."

"Why, how dare you! She is one of the Goddess' creatures, the same as you, Adrea. *You* will not be so foolish, will you, Kara?"

Kara said stubbornly, "I'm not going to sleep with any slimy snake, either. She'd be sure to crawl on me in my sleep."

"She doesn't even bite—and she wouldn't hurt you if she did," Kassandra said crossly. "Her teeth aren't grown yet. What a fool you are." She lay down, idly caressing the snake's head, which stuck just a finger's breadth out of her chemise.

"If you had the sense the Gods gave a *hen*," Kassandra said, "and would just *touch* her, you'd know she's not slimy at all, no more than a bird; she's very soft and smooth and warm." She thrust the snake, draped over her hand, at Adrea, but the woman recoiled with a squeal. Kassandra lay down, stretching out on her pillows. She said, "Well, I am weary, and I shall sleep, even if you two make fools of yourself by sleeping on the cold floor of the wagon. Make what beds for yourselves you will, but turn out the lamp and let us all sleep, in the Goddess' name. *Any* Goddess."

THEY WERE soon out of sight of Colchis, riding through the winding hills and past a succession of little villages. The days grew progressively colder, and fine snow was beginning to sift down, melting as it fell.

One morning, riding almost before the sun was up, Kassandra heard a strange, insistent wailing cry.

"Why, it's a child, and by the sound, a young one; what's a baby doing alone in this wilderness, where there could be wolves or even bears?" she said, and got down from the cart, looking around through the falling snow for the source of the sound. After a time she saw a bundle of coarse-woven fabric on the hillside: a small, well-made girl, its navel-string not healed, a dark fuzz covering its head.

"Don't touch it, Princess!" said Adrea. "It's just a baby been exposed from one of the villages; some harlot who can't raise a child, or some mother with too many daughters."

Kassandra stooped and lifted the baby. It felt icy cold in spite of its wrappings, but still kicked strongly. As Kassandra held the infant against her breast, the warmth soothed it somewhat, and the wailing ceased; it began to squirm around seeking to suck.

"There, there," Kassandra said soothingly, rocking the bundle. "I've nothing for you, poor child. But I'm sure we can find something for you to eat."

Adrea said, horrified, "Why would we do a thing like that? Surely, Princess, you aren't thinking of keeping it?"

"You would be eager to get me married," Kassandra said, "to have a baby, and now I can have one without breaking my oath of chastity, or suffering in childbirth. Why should I not take this daughter whom the Goddess has sent directly to me?" The baby felt warmer now, and dropped off to sleep against Kassandra's breast. "Surely it is a virtuous deed to save a child's life."

She had said it at first to tease Adrea; but now she began to think of the inconvenience and trouble, when the woman said, "How are you going to feed it, Princess? It's not old enough to chew hard food, and you'd have to get a wet-nurse somewhere, and drag her along all the way to Troy."

"Not at all," Kassandra said, thinking it over. "Go to that village there, and get a good healthy nanny goat, fresh in milk. Babies thrive on goat's milk." Adrea's face contorted in dismay, and Kassandra said, "Go at once; such food will be good for all of us. Or keep my snake while I go. . . ."

Thus admonished, Adrea ran for the village and came back with a young black-and-white nanny goat, strong and healthy, which at once set up a racket with its bleating. Neither of the waiting-women knew much about milking goats, but Kassandra showed them how to do it, and when they had milked a good bowlful, she fed the baby with milk dripped off the edge of her finger. The child sucked enthusiastically and collapsed again into sleep, still pulling on Kassandra's finger, a warm lump in her arms. Kassandra took a piece of cloth and rigged a sling so that when she rode the donkey the baby could travel with her on her saddle, clinging to her neck like the babies of the Amazon mothers. She decided at least for the moment to call the child "Honey" because, clean and warm and full fed, she had a sweet smell like honeycomb.

At least it would give her something to think about on the long road to Troy. And when she got there, if it did not suit her to have a child to bring up, she would make a present of her to the Queen, or to one of the Temples; young girls were always useful for the endless spinning and weaving that must be done in all households.

At first Adrea and Kara made scornful comments about "your roadside brat," but soon they were quarreling over which one should carry Honey on her lap on the long stretches in the cart, singing to her and telling her stories which she was too young to understand. She grew plump and pretty; they combed her curly hair into ringlets and made her dresses from their own clothes. Kassandra soon could not remember what life had been like without the little girl clinging around her neck when she rode donkeyback or snuggling in her lap when she rode in the cart. She seemed quickly to know who was her mother; the women were kind to her, but she would always leave them (even if they were feeding her sweetmeats) to go to Kassandra's arms. She slept curled in the back of the cart on the longer stretches of the journey, with Kassandra's snake curled up beside her, and often wanted to carry it in her own dress. When the women protested, Kassandra only laughed.

"See, she has more sense than you; she is not afraid of one of the Goddess' creatures. She is born to be a priestess, and she knows it."

Days stretched into weeks on the road as they retraced the long journey. When they came to the great plain, they kept a sharp eye out for Kentaur bands. Kassandra hoped to meet with them; she had a weakness for the riding folk, although both the waiting-women and all the escort and drivers hoped they would be spared any sight of them. But they encountered no living Kentaur, although one evening they saw a dead horse in a ditch, and clinging to him, the thin, twisted body of his rider, cold and dead; the bones, almost protruding through the skin, told them that the poor fellow had died of starvation and cold.

Kassandra's heart twisted in pity, though her driver and the women said it was good riddance and wished all his fellows a similar fate.

One evening, as they were setting up camp, Kassandra caught sight, far off, of a little group of riders: a single old man, withered and deformed from years in the saddle, and half a dozen of what seemed to be children but were probably under-nourished half-grown boys. Kassandra could not tell for certain, but she thought it might be Cheiron. She motioned to them, and called to them in their own language, but they would not approach; they kept circling slowly around the camp, too far away to see clearly, or to hear what they were saying.

"We had better set a watch," one of the drivers remarked, "or while we sleep they may approach the camp and murder us all. You can never trust a Kentaur."

"That's not true," said Kassandra. "They won't hurt us; they are much more afraid of us than we are of them."

"They should all be done away with," said Kara. "They are not civilized men."

"They are hungry, that is all," Kassandra said. "They know we have food and beasts; our nanny goat alone would give them the best meal they have had this year."

In spite of the disapproval of her women and the escort, she would still willingly have given them gifts and food, and tried to attract them near for some time, but they kept a wary distance, circling on their horses, and did not approach the camp. So as they settled down for the night, one or two of the men kept watch; and Kassandra lay awake thinking of the Kentaurs out there in the dark on their horses. In the morning, she left some loaves of barley bread and a measure or two of meal in an old cracked pot her party was ready to discard.

As they rode away from the camp, Kassandra saw that the Kentaurs were approaching; at least they would get the food—which might postpone death by starvation for only a little while. *To Honey,* she thought, *it will be only a legend, and everyone will tell how evil they were. But there was wisdom there, too, and a way of life we will not see again. Will the Amazons also go this way?*

AFTER THE almost-encounter with the Kentaurs, the road seemed long and empty; day after day they toiled across the great plain, seeing few or no travelers, the days differentiated one from another only by the waxing and waning of the moon, the changes from fine to snowy weather. In passing through the country where she would have expected to encounter tribes of the Amazons, they met with no riders at all, neither men nor women. Had all the Amazons perished, or been kidnapped to serve in the men's villages? She would have liked to send a message to Penthesilea, but had not the slightest idea how to get word to her, or even if she still lived. She sought to see her in the scrying-bowl, but could not find her.

Snow lay deep on the steppes, and it was bitterly cold. Kassandra feared for the life of her snakes in this weather; she and Honey stayed in their blankets, a brazier keeping them warm, sharing their heat with the serpents. Sometimes the snow was so deep that the cart could not travel and they were cooped up all day, with no light, little heat and unable to cook food. They had to keep the nanny goat in the wagon, too, because she could have been lost in the deep drifts.

As the months passed, there was change, too, in Honey: there were times when it seemed to Kassandra that the little girl could be seen growing between dawn and sunrise. It seemed that every day she had some new clever trick or, in growing, had developed something new to fascinate her foster-mother. A few days after the appearance of the Kentaurs, she developed her first tooth; soon after, she was able to sip her milk from a cup; and soon after that, she was eating bread soaked in milk, or soft-mashed foods fed to her with a spoon. Rather sooner than Kassandra had expected, she had a full set of teeth and was grabbing and chewing anything she could reach from everyone's plate; Kassandra could no longer set her down on the ground at their night halts, for she would crawl away and quickly make a game of disappearing for the fun of being called and chased. Finally a time came (fortunately, after the worst of the snow was past) when they had to watch her constantly lest she crawl out of the cart, even when it was moving; and soon she was running around at every halt. She was not, Kassandra thought, a particularly pretty child, but she was a strong and sturdy one, never sick, and rarely fretful even when she was cutting her teeth.

As time wore on and travel ate up the long road, they came into country with better roads, and encountered more travelers. It seemed the whole world was bound for Troy with weapons and all manner of goods to be sold to the Trojans (or to the Akhaians; it seemed that the Akhaians were now blocking all goods coming into Troy, by land or by sea). And at last, one day, they sighted the familiar outline of Mount Ida and began to travel along the Scamander toward Troy.

When they came within sight of the city, it seemed to Kassandra that another city, a spread-out city of shacks and tents and shelters, had sprung up at the foot of the great walls, and the sea was black with ships crowded into the harbor. There was a strong stench near the harbor as if the very tides had been fouled; the streets of this new-made city were clogged with carts and chariots, and as soon as Kassandra's escort brought the cart near, Akhaian soldiers, dressed in the armor she remembered Akhilles' men had worn, came at once and demanded to know her business there.

Her escort had no success in explaining, so Kassandra, who spoke the language somewhat better, got down from the cart, with Honey astride her shoulder, and explained that she was Priam's daughter, returning from a long journey to Colchis. This news, which Kassandra did not imagine would be particularly surprising, went from mouth to mouth, and finally there was a general outcry that the commander should hear it himself.

She had supposed this might be Akhilles, but instead it was the somewhat taller, stronger dark-haired young man she had seen in Akhilles' company. They spoke of him as Patroklos, and he came and addressed her with a certain degree of politeness —more, at any rate, than she remembered in Akhilles himself.

"The old King's daughter you say you are, then? Wait a minute; there's a girl in Lord Agamemnon's tent who was brought up in the palace up there, or so she says. She can tell us whether or not you're who you say you are. Wait here," he ordered, and went away.

Honey felt heavy on her shoulder, and Kassandra asked leave of one of the soldier-guards to set her down. "Stay close to me," she admonished; she did not suppose any of the soldiers would knowingly harm a child except perhaps in the heat of battle, but she was not certain, and she did not trust these Akhaians enough to wish to test the theory.

After a time Patroklos returned with a veiled woman; she put back her veil and looked at Kassandra. "Yes," she said, "this is Priam's daughter." To Kassandra's shock and dismay she recognized the girl as Chryseis.

Kassandra, however startled, was relieved to know that Chryseis was alive and well. She said, "Chryseis, my dear, I have worried about you, and I know how troubled your father must have been." Chryseis had grown tall and heavy-bodied, but she still had the astonishing blond hair that had given her her name.

Patroklos spoke to one of the soldiers; they seemed to be discussing whether they might hold her for ransom, or for exchange for one of the Akhaian prisoners.

"You cannot do that," said her main escort. "She is a priestess of Apollo and is traveling under Apollo's truce."

"Oh, is she?" Patroklos demanded. "Maybe we can do something, then, to silence that priest of Apollo who never stops complaining to the Lord Agamemnon or anyone else who will listen to him. Our own priests keep demanding we make offerings to Apollo; perhaps we should consult with her about the proper sacrifice."

He turned to Kassandra and said, "Would you sacrifice to the Sun Lord for us, then?"

She said, "I remember all too well the fate of the last priestess Agamemnon sent for to make sacrifices for you; I know who and what would be sacrificed." And she could see by their faces that this answer was not at all to their liking.

Chryseis addressed her for the first time and said, "You should not speak like that of Agamemnon, Kassandra."

"He is no friend to me, nor to my family," Kassandra said. "Nor do I owe him any duty as guest to host; I shall speak of him as I will. Why are you so deferential to his name?"

"Because he is my lord and the most powerful man of all the Akhaians," said Chryseis, "and you would do well not to anger him; we are all in his power here."

"Shall I try when I return to the city to arrange for your freedom?" Kassandra asked in a whisper.

Chryseis tossed her head. She said scornfully, "I have not asked for that. My father has been invoking Apollo for my return, but Apollo has no power here compared with Agamemnon, and I would rather belong to a man than a God."

Then Kassandra recalled her terrible vision. She found that she was trembling; then she looked at Patrokolos and said, "You have done me no discourtesy, so I will give you an honest warning; I have seen the terrible arrows of Apollo falling on this city, on Trojan and Akhaian alike." She heard her voice rising to a cry and felt the familiar heat and blaze of the Sun Lord: "Oh, beware His anger, beware the wrath of Apollo! Provoke not His dreadful arrows!"

Patroklos seemed to shrink slightly, but he frowned at her and said, "Yes, I heard you were a prophetess. Listen to me, woman; I'm not afraid of your Trojan Apollo, but it is always unwise to provoke another's Gods. I'd be inclined to let you go; our priests will probably say the same thing, and I have no love for warring on women. But it's for Akhilles himself to make the final decision." He spoke to a young boy who was watching, and told him to run for the commander.

A considerable crowd had gathered around the cart and were staring at the waiting-women. Patroklos looked up at the two elderly women and asked Kassandra, "Who are these women?"

"They are my mother's servants; my waiting-women."

"Are they, too, sworn priestesses of Apollo?"

"No, they are not; but they are under my protection and His."

Kassandra began to be uncomfortable at the way they were looking at her. She picked up Honey, who had been crawling around her feet, and held her in her arms. Patroklos said, "We have not nearly enough women in our camp to do the women's work. I will not strive with the Trojan Apollo for you, but these women are legitimately my prisoners." He went to the cart and seized Kara by the arm.

"Get down, old lady. You're staying here."

She shook him off with a furious shrug.

"Take your hands off me, you dirty Akhaian beast."

Quite deliberately Patroklos raised his arm and slapped her, not very hard, across the mouth. "I'm not quite sure what you said, but here's your first lesson, old woman; among us you don't talk that way to men. Get inside there; you'll find some clothes to mend. If you do it well, we may feed you."

Kassandra exclaimed, "I told you these women are under my protection and that of the Sun Lord! Let her go—or beware His anger!"

"And I told *you*," said Patroklos, "that I care nothing at all for your Trojan Apollo. I will honor His truce to the extent that I will not offer insult to His prophetess, but these women are my prisoners and there is nothing you can do about it."

Kassandra noticed that in the crowd there were a number of women, none of whom seemed to be at all surprised at Patroklos' words or actions. Kara cried out and began to run, heading for the gates of Troy; Patroklos motioned to one of the soldiers to bring her back, and said to Chryseis, "Here, you, you speak her language; tell her what I said. No one will abuse her if she does her work well. And you might repeat what I said to Priam's daughter; she doesn't seem to understand very well either."

Chryseis began to repeat Patroklos' words to Kara, but Kassandra interrupted.

"Tell the Akhaian captain that I understand what he said perfectly well; but these women are my handmaidens, and under the protection of Lord Apollo just as I am myself; he cannot take them from me."

"Do you think you are going to stop me, Princess?" the man inquired, and dragged Adrea out of the wagon. "Now, this one, she's too old for bedding, but I'll wager she can cook; Akhilles has been saying he wants someone to wait on that woman he keeps in his tent. Send her over to Briseis, somebody."

One of the men standing about said, "What about the baby? She looks strong and healthy—shall I get her?"

"Gods of Hades, no," said Patroklos, as Kassandra's hand tightened on her dagger. "She's still wetting her clothes; do you think we will hang about in Troy till the brat is beddable? Forget it." He said to Kassandra, "Be grateful that you are under Apollo's protection; I suggest you climb into your cart and be on your way. But not quite yet." He motioned to his men and said, "Strip the cart; the food we can use, and other things."

The men at once began swarming all over the cart, hauling out provisions and throwing them down. Kassandra had nothing to say; she knew they would not listen. After a time, as she knew they would, they got into the blanket rolls, and began to unfold them on the ground; then a soldier jumped back with a shriek as the largest of the serpents uncoiled before him. He grabbed at his spear, but Kassandra cried out a warning in his own language.

"No! She is sacred to the Sun Lord; do not dare to touch her!"

The man staggered back, as pale as death; Kassandra had been in Colchis so long she had forgotten the terror with which the creatures were regarded in the islands. Now she reached inside her dress and encouraged the serpent there to crawl slowly out. It circled her waist and flowed along her arm, as the soldiers drew back one by one, gripped by superstitious terror.

"A—aaahhhh! Look there! what has come by her sorcery!"

"Don't be fools," said Patroklos. "In our country priestesses are taught to handle them too; but don't lay a hand on her. We don't want them here. Go," he said to Kassandra, "and take your damned pets with you."

Kassandra knew she would get no better. Kara and Adrea were kneeling and weeping; Kassandra went to them and said softly, "Don't be too frightened; do as they say and don't make them angry. I swear by Apollo, I'll get you back." She had no great love for either of the waiting-women, but they were under her protection, and were dear to her mother.

Now she could see reason for Apollo's anger. She would speak at once to His priests.

19

AS THE CART clattered across the space before the walls of Troy, Kassandra realized that all the sentries on the walls must have seen what had happened. The plundering of a cart must not be an unusual occurrence, or they would have interfered, at least by shooting arrows down into the Akhaian camp. No doubt better-informed travelers with goods bound for Troy knew enough to do as she should have done, and approach from the landward side.

Kassandra still had the serpents destined for the Sun Lord's Temple. She herself was unharmed, and the Akhaians had not seriously threatened Honey. Matters could have been worse. But she realized that the level of hostilities had escalated; she should have had the forethought to inform herself of how the war was progressing.

In front of the gates an armed Trojan soldier stopped her, and after a moment she recognized Deiphobos, Priam's son by one of his palace women.

He bowed.

"The main street is too steep for the cart, Princess," he told her. "You will have to have it driven around to the landward side. But for you we will open the small gateway beside the great gate. The great gate itself is never opened now for fear the Akhaians will rush it; so long as it stays shut, it can't be breached —unless some God or other, Poseidon perhaps, decides to break it," he added quickly, making a gesture against evil luck.

"May that day be far," Kassandra said. "Can you find some-one to take the cart to the Temple of Apollo? There are serpents for the Sun Lord's house in the cart, and they must not be frightened, or allowed to get too cold."

"I'll send a messenger at once to the Sun Lord's house," Deiphobos promised her courteously. "Will you go at once to the palace, Sister?"

"Yes; I am longing to see my mother," Kassandra said. "I hope she is well?"

"Queen Hecuba? Oh, yes; though like us all, she grows no younger," said Deiphobos.

"And our father? He lives still in health? I heard he had suffered some illness . . ."

"Word came of this as far as Colchis? He suffered the stroke of the God; he is lame, and his face stricken on one side," the young officer told her. "And now Prince Hector leads the armies of Troy."

"Yes, that I had heard," Kassandra said, "but on the long road from Colchis I had no news at all, nor was the journey favorable for the Sight; for all I knew, he might have died since then."

"No, I rejoice to say that though he grows old, he is well enough to come out every day on the wall to see what happens," Deiphobos said. "As long as Priam still leads us, Hector will not be too foolhardy. Akhilles"—he made contemptuous gesture toward the Akhaian camp—"is always trying to lure Hector out to single combat; but my brother has more sense than that. Besides, we all know how Agamemnon played a filthy trick on his own daughter, so it's not likely they'd observe the rules of single combat; more likely they'd rush him ten or more at a time. You can't trust an Akhaian as far as you can throw him; they say, if one of 'em kisses you, count your teeth, thieving bastards. But I see they let you through safe. . . ."

"Safe, but I encountered their thieving ways," Kassandra told him. "What they did not steal they left only because they feared Apollo's serpents—and I do not think that was from any reverence for the God, but only fear of the serpents themselves. And they have taken both of my mother's waiting-women—who were not Apollo's servants but mine, or rather Hecuba's."

Deiphobos came and gently patted her shoulder.

"Never fear, Sister, we'll get your waiting-women back. But let me send to the Sun Lord's Temple for men to unload your cart, and for you, an escort up to the palace; it isn't fitting for a princess to walk alone through the city. Better yet, let me send to the palace for a sedan chair; it's what the Lady Andromache uses when she comes down to greet Hector every day before the battles start."

Kassandra wanted to protest that she was certainly capable of walking; but Honey was heavy in her arms, and she agreed to use the chair.

Before long, servants in the distinctive robes of the Sun Lord's house appeared, and Kassandra gave careful instructions about the serpents, promising that she would herself come to supervise their care after she had greeted her parents. Then Deiphobos conducted her through the side gate into a small guardhouse. There he fetched her refreshment while she awaited the chair that was to carry her to the palace.

She was unaccustomed to the sun's glare, its heat even in this season. It soon seemed frighteningly hot to her. Also, she was worried about Kara and Adrea.

Honey was crawling on the floor of the little guardhouse; Kassandra noticed that she was getting her tunic very dirty, and her knees not much less so, but she was far too tired to care.

Deiphobos guided her attention to a small stairway carved out from the stone which actually led up inside the wall.

"Would you care to have a look from the top of the wall? You can see everything that goes on in the Akhaian camp from here. The King is coming down now to have a look—he comes every day about this time," Deiphobos said. "I hear his guards." He glanced at Honey. "The baby will be safe here," he said. "She's big enough that no one will step on her." He picked up a spear that was leaning against the wall, and slung it in his belt. "There—nothing else she can hurt herself with. Come along."

Kassandra followed him up the narrow steep stairs; he turned back at the top to give her a hand up. It was true: from here she could see all through the Akhaian camp. He pointed out to her the large ornamented tent that was Agamemnon's, the somewhat smaller but more ornamental one that belonged to Akhilles and Patroklos, the quarters of Odysseus, which looked as if he had moved a ship's cabin ashore. "And many others. There's a long roster of the ships out there which belong to the Akhaians—some bard was making a song about it," he said. "To hear them tell it, every hero from the mainland has turned up to help Agamemnon and his crew. There's a sizable list of our allies too, but I don't suppose you're interested in that."

"Not particularly," Kassandra confessed. "I heard enough about both sides in Colchis."

"Colchis," he said thoughtfully. "Come to think of it, Colchis hasn't come out for either side; why hasn't their King sent soldiers for Troy?"

"Because Colchis has no King," Kassandra informed him. "Colchis is ruled by a Queen; and this last year she has been pregnant; her heir—a daughter—was born just before I left."

"No King, and a woman's rule? It seems a strange way to manage a city."

Before he had time to say anything more, the sound of soldiers approaching interrupted them, and Priam, accompanied by several of his soldiers—many of whom Kassandra recognized as the sons of his palace women—came up on the top of the wall.

It was well she had been warned by the Sight; otherwise she might have recognized her father only by the rich cloak he wore. He had been a hale and hearty man with fresh color, verging on middle age; now she saw an old man, his skin grayish and wrinkled, his face fallen away at one side with a drooping eyelid, the corner of his mouth sagging. His speech too was heavy and thick.

He demanded of Deiphobos, "What was going on in the Akhaian camp this morning? Was it those Akhaians intercepting weapons again? If this keeps up, we'll be melting down our old swords to make new ones. We need a couple of wagonloads of iron from Colchis, but we'd have to arrange special escort or bribe someone to let it through . . ."

He broke off and said, "How many times have I told you: no women here unless the Queen herself is present to make certain they behave themselves? You know as well as I do, the kind of women who come here to gawk at the soldiers—"

Kassandra said, "No, Father; it is not Deiphobos' fault; he offered me shelter from the sun and a view from the wall after the Akhaians captured my wagon . . ."

She did not finish, but she did not need to; Priam recognized her and said, "So you have come back like an ill omen, Kassandra! I thought you had determined to pass the rest of the war in Colchis—one less woman for me to worry about should the city fall. But your mother has missed you." He came and dutifully kissed her on the forehead. "Do you mean that the Akhaians dared to break Apollo's truce?"

As a small child, Kassandra had found Priam's anger terrifying; now he simply sounded peevish, like an overgrown spoiled child. She said gently, "It doesn't matter, Father; no one has been hurt, and Apollo's property—including me, I suppose—is quite safe. And as soon as my chair is here, I shall go and reassure my mother."

"You are strong and healthy; why should you need a chair to carry you?" he demanded crossly.

The war is not going as he wishes it, she translated to herself, and said demurely, "Yes, Father, I am sure you are right."

"Your chair is waiting for you," Deiphobos said, and Kassandra saw it drawing up inside the wall. She went down the stairs and picked up Honey, wishing she could find a way to have the baby washed and fed before taking her to her mother; but there was no help for it now. She herself was disheveled from long traveling, and from the interlude in the dusty Akhaian camp, as well as from holding the dirty child; but there was no help for that either. *And why should I put on my finest robe and tidy my hands and face for my mother?* she asked herself. But when she was brought into Queen Hecuba's presence, and saw her mother's disapproving stare, she knew.

"Well, Kassandra! My dear, dear daughter!" Hecuba exclaimed and came to embrace her, then drew back with a little grimace of dismay.

"But what have you been doing with yourself, my dear? Your dress is a disgrace, and your hair—"

"Mother, after my encounter this morning with the Akhaians, it is fortunate they even left me a dress to wear before you," she said with a smile. "I fear that the gifts I brought from your kinswoman Imandra were left in the Akhaian camp."

Hecuba looked deeply distressed. "They did not—offer you insult?"

"Nobody raped me, if that's what you mean," Kassandra said, laughing.

"How can you make a joke of such a thing?" her mother demanded.

Kassandra said, kissing her, "Why, how can I do anything else? They are fools, all of them; but there is foolery enough in Troy, if it comes to that."

Hecuba's eyes fell on the child in Kassandra's arms.

"Why, what's this? A child, and such a young one . . . her hair . . . it curls the way yours did when you were that age. . . . Why, what . . . Who . . . How—?"

"No, Mother," Kassandra said quickly, "she is not mine—or rather, I did not bear her; she is a foundling." Hecuba still looked skeptical, and Kassandra, sighing—Why was her mother always ready to think evil of her?—said, "Would it be easy to find a man who would share my bed when it was occupied by a serpent—even one so small as this?" She reached inside her dress for the one that always coiled there during her waking hours.

Hecuba gave a little scream. "A snake—and in your very bosom!"

"She is my child far more than the baby," Kassandra said, laughing, "for I hatched her myself from an egg; but anyone in my train can tell you how I found Honey on a hillside in a snowstorm, cast out to die by some mother who chose not to rear a girl this year."

Hecuba came and looked closely at the child. She said, "Now I look well, she is not at all like you."

"I told you that."

"So you did. I am sorry; I would not willingly believe . . ."

Not willingly, perhaps, but you would have believed it, Kassandra thought.

But then her mother asked the question she had been evading: "And where are Kara and Adrea?"

"In the tents of Agamemnon and Akhilles," she said, "but not by choice." She explained what had befallen them.

"So we must somehow arrange to ransom them—or exchange Akhaian prisoners for them, perhaps," she said.

"Arrange to exchange for them? Why should we do business with the Akhaians?" asked a familiar voice, and Andromache came into the room. "Oh, Kassandra! My dear sister!" and she flew to embrace her, ignoring the dirt on her robe. "So you have returned! I knew you were not traitorous enough to remain all through the war in Colchis! What a darling baby!" she exclaimed, staring at Honey. "Is she yours? No? Oh, what a shame!" Then she saw the snake and recoiled a little.

"So you are still at your old game of playing with serpents! I should have remembered."

Honey, seeing the snake, began to cry and reach out her hands for it. Kassandra, laughing, allowed the little girl to wind it about her waist. Andromache shrank away with a glance of revulsion, but the child's delight in the snake was unmistakable.

"Why not get her a kitten, Kassandra?" Hecuba suggested. "It would be an altogether more seemly pet."

Kassandra laughed. "She is content with such pets as I give her; you should see her with our very matriarch of serpents— the one who is almost as big around as she is."

"Are you not afraid—snakes have not very good eyesight— the snake will make a mistake and swallow her by misadventure?" Andromache protested.

But Kassandra said, "They know their own; Honey has fed her with doves and rabbits. But, Mother, this is not a proper subject for your rooms."

Hecuba asked, laughing, "The snake—or the baby?"

"Both," Kassandra replied, hugging her mother again. "Let me call someone to take her away for a bath and clean clothing. She will be prettier then; and besides, she has had nothing to eat since early morning." Then, with a glance at Hecuba for permission, Kassandra summoned a servant to take child and snake to the house of the Sun Lord.

"I too should present myself there soon, I fear," she said, "although I am sure they would gladly give me leave to pay my respects to my mother and my family. And I would like to see Helen's sons," she added.

"Ah, Helen's sons," Hecuba said drily. "There are jokes in the Akhaian army that Helen is raising up an army for Troy."

"As I cannot for Hector," said Andromache, and her eyes were full of tears. "But that Akhaian woman, no sooner has she whelped than she is in pup again."

"What a thing to say," Hecuba protested. "You had bad luck, that is all. You have borne Hector a fine son, and every man in the army knows his name and admires him. What more do you want?"

"Nothing," Andromache said, "and just between us women, I am glad enough to be spared the business of bearing every year or two; I told Hector that if he wishes for fifty sons like his father, he must get them as his father does. But so far he wishes only to share my bed and even refused one of the captured Akhaian women. Perhaps I am not as fond of children as Helen, but I would like to have a daughter before I am too old. And speaking of daughters, Kassandra, did you know that Creusa had named her second daughter Kassandra?"

"No, that I had not heard," Kassandra said, and wondered whether it had been Creusa's doing or that of Aeneas.

"And now before you go," said Andromache, "tell me of my mother."

Kassandra told Andromache of the birth of the heir to Colchis; and Andromache sighed.

"I wish that I might go to Colchis, so that Hector might be King there; perhaps when this wretched war is over that can be arranged."

"Imandra feels that her little pearl princess will be reared to be Queen," Kassandra said. "And Hector would not be content to sit at the foot of the throne, as your mother's consort does, and amuse himself in hunting and fishing with his companions."

Andromache sighed.

"Perhaps not; but he would get used to it, I suppose, as I have gotten used to keeping indoors and spinning until my fingers are sore," she said restlessly. "Now that you have returned, Kassandra, perhaps we can manage some excursions outside the walls . . ."

"If the Akhaians allow it . . ."

"Or if they get tired of sitting outside the walls and throwing rocks at the guards," Andromache said. "That is about all they have accomplished in the last few months; though once or twice they have tried to storm the walls, and even brought extra-long ladders. But Hector had the idea of emptying the big soup kettle boiling for the guards' dinner over their heads, and they went

down a great deal faster than they had come up, I assure you."
She laughed heartily. "Now they always keep a great kettle of
something boiling up there, and if it is something no worse than
soup, the assailants are lucky. Last time it was oil, and they have
not tried again since then; ai, the screams we heard that night
from the Akhaian camp! All their healer-priests were out chanting, and sacrificing to Apollo, until past dawn. That will teach
them to come sneaking up the wall when they thought all the
guards were sleeping!"

"You do not bear weapons now—but you have not lost
your taste for warfare," Kassandra commented.

"I have a child to protect," Andromache replied; and Kassandra remembered that she herself had indeed been ready to
kill when the soldiers threatened Honey.

"And I many children, but they are all of an age to fight for
themselves," Hecuba said. "And now, Kassandra, tell me: when
you passed through the country of the Amazons, did you encounter our kinswoman? And had Penthesilea any message for
me?"

"I saw her only on the outward journey," Kassandra said,
and told her mother about the meeting with the Amazons, and
how many of the women had chosen to settle into villages with
men. Then, more troubled, she told about the starving Kentaurs on the return journey, and that she had seen no sign of
any women of the tribes.

"May the Goddess be with her," said Hecuba fervently. "I
have no sense that she is dead; and I think I might know. We
have been as close as if we were twins; but she is four years
younger than I. It is not beyond all possibility that one day we
may see her in Troy."

"May that day be far off," Kassandra said, "for she told me
that if the war went desperately against us, she would come and
end her days in Troy." And with a curious flicker of the light, as
if the sun had gone behind a cloud, she saw Penthesilea riding
through the gates of Troy . . . in triumph, or in defeat? She
could not tell; the vision was gone, and they spoke of other
things.

At last she rose and stretched herself. "I sit like any old

gossip among women," she said, "and I have duties awaiting me in the Sun Lord's house. But it has been good to gossip and be idle"—and, she thought, to talk of women's matters like the raising of children. She had once thought it must be very boring, but now, having a child of her own, she was beginning to understand that such woman's talk could be absorbing. *But to speak of nothing else for a lifetime* . . .

"It is not every day that you return from a journey of such length," Andromache said. "Helen will want to see you, and show you her babies—and Creusa to show you your namesake. She is more like Polyxena than like you, with red hair and blue eyes—and as pretty as if Aphrodite had laid the gift of beauty in her cradle. She will marry a prince, if this war leaves any of us alive to think about marriages."

"I think no one will ever call my little one beautiful," Kassandra said, "but to a mother I suppose even the plainest children are lovely. In any case, I intend, if the Gods are kind, to send her to Penthesilea to be brought up a warrior. I still wish I might have been."

"Oh, you cannot mean that, Kassandra," said Hecuba, coming to embrace her in farewell.

"Can I not? Mother, if any of Imandra's gifts have survived the Akhaians, I will send them to you as quickly as the cart can be unloaded," she said, and took her leave. Andromache said she would walk with her a little way.

"For I get out so seldom, and Hector is always very troubled if I go out alone; but he cannot refuse me the chaperonage of his own sister," she said discontentedly. "I often walk with Helen, but she did not come today: Paris took a small wound in the last fight—nothing to worry him, but enough to give him a good excuse to stay indoors and be cosseted. Otherwise I am sure she would have come to greet you."

After a short distance they parted, Andromache returning down to the palace and Kassandra turning up toward the Sun Lord's high house.

She had started across the courtyard to check on the snakes when she encountered Khryse. He looked weary and worn; there were new lines in his once-handsome face, and lines of dull silver in his fair hair. It was hard to realize that there had been a time when in this Temple there had been those who considered him nearly as handsome as the Sun Lord Himself.

He recognized her at once, and cried out in welcome.

"Kassandra! We have all missed you," he exclaimed, and came quickly to embrace her. She would have recoiled, but it was not unpleasant to see a familiar face and to know herself so welcomed; so she allowed the embrace, but at once regretted it, and managed to twist her face so that his kiss fell only on her chin.

Quickly disentangling herself, she retreated out of reach.

"It seems that all has gone well with you while I was absent," she remarked. "You look well and thriving." Not for worlds would she have told him that it was his face in an oracle which had prompted her to return to Troy.

"But that is not true," he said. "Never again shall I have health or joy until the Gods choose to restore to me my poor dishonored child."

"Khryse," said Kassandra gently, "is it not near upon three years that Chryseis has been in the camp of the Akhaians?"

"I care not if it is a lifetime," Khryse said passionately. "I will mourn and protest and cry out to the Gods—"

"Cry, then," Kassandra said, "but expect not that They will hear. It is your own pride you mourn and not your daughter," she went on sharply. "I saw her this morning in the Akhaian camp; she seems well and happy and content, and when I asked if I should try to arrange for her exchange, she told me to mind my own affairs. I truly think she is content to be Agamemnon's woman, even if she cannot be his Queen."

Khryse's handsome face grew dark with wrath.

"Have a care, Kassandra; you say this to hurt me, and I believe not a word of it."

"Why should I wish to hurt you?" she asked. "You are my friend, and your daughter was like my own child. Think only of her happiness, Khryse, and leave her where she is. I warn you, if you press further in this matter, you will bring down the wrath of the Gods upon our city."

His face twisted in anger.

"And I am supposed to believe you have my good at heart? You care nothing for me—I who have so long loved you . . ."

"Oh, Khryse," she said, holding out her hands to him in absolute sincerity, "please, please, don't begin to talk of this again. Why must you think I wish you ill because I do not desire you?"

"Then what would you do if you did wish me ill? When you have destroyed any kindness I might have in my heart . . ."

"If such kindness is destroyed, why do you say it is my fault? Cannot a man take any woman seriously unless she is willing to lie with him?" she asked. "I speak to you in all friendship, Khryse; do not press this matter."

"You are willing to see my daughter disgraced, and insult offered to Apollo—"

"In the name of all the Gods, Khryse, the question is not what you feel, but what your daughter feels," she said in exasperation, remembering Chryseis' proud look when Patroklos had turned to her for help in translation. But she did not wish Khryse's anger to make more trouble; there was already enough bitterness, and this could only make it worse. She spoke with what friendliness she could summon. "If you do not believe me, why not go down to the camp of the Akhaians—they will honor Apollo's truce for His priest—and ask her for yourself if she feels disgraced. If she wishes to leave Agamemnon, I swear to you, I shall go to Priam and leave nothing undone to have her released or exchanged. But if she is happy with Agamemnon and he with her . . . Believe me, she is no prisoner; they were calling upon her to translate when they took my waiting-women from me, and they are elderly women who truly do not wish to remain in the camp of the Akhaians. But I promise you: if Chryseis wishes to return, I shall do everything I can before the King and the Queen."

"But the disgrace—my daughter to be Agamemnon's concubine . . ."

"Cannot you see that you are unreasonable? Why is it so disgraceful for her to be Agamemnon's woman? And if this makes you shudder so with shame, why were you so eager to convince me that it would do no harm if I should be yours? Is it different for your daughter than for Priam's daughter?" she asked harshly, losing patience at last. Now he was really angry, and she was just as well pleased; it meant she need no longer fear that he would try to grab at her.

"How dare you mention my daughter as if she were like you?" he charged her angrily. "You do not care what happens to my daughter. As long as you can follow your own unnatural ways and refuse to give yourself, to humiliate a man—"

"Humiliate you? Is that what you think?" she said wearily. "Khryse, there are hundreds of women on this earth who would be happy to give themselves to you. Why should you choose one—perhaps the only one—who does not want you?"

"I did not choose to desire you," he said, glaring at her, "but I find I wish for no other. You have bewitched me, out of some evil wish to humble me; I . . ." He stopped, gulped and said, "Do you think, sorceress, that I have not tried to break this spell you have cast on me?"

For a moment Kassandra almost pitied him. She said, "Khryse, if you are under a curse, some other has done it and not I. I swear by Serpent Mother and by Earth Mother and by Apollo Himself, whom we both worship, I bear you no malice and no evil will, and I will entreat any God to free you from any such spell. I want no power over you, and I would bless your manhood, provided you find some other woman on whom to exercise it."

"So you still have no pity on me? Even knowing what you have brought me to, you still deny yourself to me?"

"Khryse," she said, "enough. I am awaited above, and I must show myself to Charis and to the priestesses. I wish you good night."

She turned away, but he muttered between his teeth, "You will be sorry for this, Kassandra; even if I die for it, I swear you will regret this."

I traveled all the way to Colchis and back to escape this man's bitterness; and I return no better off than I left, except that his wrath has had two years to grow.

Lord Apollo, was it Your will that I give myself to this man I dislike so much? And she wondered, almost frightened at her own thoughts, *Even if Apollo demanded it, would I have given myself to Khryse?*

But He had not demanded it. And Khryse—he was always a troublemaker; must she be part of his troublemaking?

20

KASSANDRA LAY awake much of the night, mentally going over her argument with Khryse, wondering what she should have said. Surely he would at last have seen reason, had she been able to find the right words.

Finally she decided that in his current state he probably was not capable of reason at all. Was any man, when a woman was concerned? Certainly, Paris had not shown much reason when it was a question of Helen . . . and he already had a virtuous and beautiful wife who had given him a son, and from what she had heard, that was what men wanted most.

But it certainly was not only men; women themselves seemed to lose all reason when men were concerned. Even Queen Imandra, who was strong and independent, and Hecuba, who had been brought up as an Amazon, had shown little reason when it was a matter of their men. *As for Briseis, or Chryseis,* Kassandra thought, almost with contempt, *they are like puppy dogs, rolling over with all four feet in the air if their master but gives them a pat.*

Perhaps the question is not why they do so, but why do I feel no desire to do so?

She shifted her weight on the bed to make room for the serpent which coiled slowly around her arm. It was good to be sleeping in a bed rather than on the hard floor of the cart; and with her last thought she reminded herself to check the cart and make certain which of Imandra's gifts, if any, had survived the Akhaian soldiers. Their fear of serpents might have kept them from exploring the depths of the cart.

She woke at sunrise. Honey was playing at the foot of the bed, letting the serpent flow around her waist and down along her arms. She bathed the child and found her some breakfast, then went to the top of the Temple where the first rays would strike the heights of Troy. She thought she should go up to the Temple of the Maiden today, and greet her friends among the priestesses there, and perhaps offer thanks for her safe return to Troy. But before she had a chance, she noticed Khryse among the assembled priests come to greet the sunrise.

He looked even worse than the night before, his features swollen and his eyes reddened as if he had not slept. *Poor man, she thought, I should not taunt him or expect him to be reasonable when he is in so much misery. It may not make sense for him to suffer like this; but when did that ever stop anyone from suffering?*

Charis was speaking with him; she saw Charis point to one and then another of the priests, saying, "You, and you, and you —no, not you, you cannot be spared." As Kassandra approached them, Charis beckoned to her.

"I understand from what Khryse says that you actually saw his daughter in the Argive camp yesterday when you passed through. Are you certain it was really Chryseis? It has been some years, and she was a growing girl when she—left us."

"When she was cruelly stolen from us, you mean," Khryse added savagely.

Kassandra said, "Why, yes, I am sure; even had I not recognized her, she recognized me; she addressed me by name and warned me against angering Agamemnon."

"And did you say this to her father?"

"I did; but the message made him angry," Kassandra said. "He as much as accused me of inventing it to torment him."

Khryse said sullenly, "You know she has always had a grudge against me."

"If I were going to invent a tale to annoy Khryse, I could make up a much better one than that," Kassandra said. "I tell you, it happened exactly as I have said."

"Well, then, you had better go with them to the Akhaian

camp," Charis said. "He is resolved to go down and in Apollo's name demand the return of his daughter from the Akhaians; they too have priests of Apollo and observe His truce."

Since this was exactly what she had suggested that he do, she was not surprised, except that he had not done it months or years ago. But she supposed that he had first exhausted all other remedies, whatever they might have been.

There were a good three dozen of them in the ceremonial robes and headdresses of the Sun Lord when at last they started down the long streets and arrived at the great gates of Troy. The guard was unwilling to open the gates, but when Khryse explained that they wished to parley with Agamemnon to arrange a prisoner's return in the name of Apollo, the guard sent a herald to arrange a meeting. Then they stood in the hot sun for the best part of an hour, until they saw a tall, strongly built man, with thick black curly hair and an elaborately curled beard, approaching them with long, purposeful strides.

Kassandra had been as close as this to Agamemnon before; as always, horror and revulsion flooded her body. She stared at the ground and never raised her eyes, hoping he would not notice her.

He did not. He stared belligerently at Khryse and said, "What do you want? I am not a priest of Apollo; if you wish to arrange a festival truce or some such matter, your business is with my priests, and not with me."

Khryse stepped forward. He was taller than Agamemnon, his head imposing even with his blond hair faded, his features strongly carved. His voice, deep and strong, rang out imposingly: "If you are Agamemnon of Mykenae, then my business is indeed with you. I am Khryse, priest of Apollo; and you are holding my daughter prisoner in your camp; she was taken three years ago at spring planting."

"Oh?" Agamemnon inquired. "And which of my men is holding this woman?"

"Lord Agamemnon, her name is Chryseis; and I believe it is you who are holding her. In Apollo's name, I declare myself ready to pay such ransom as is suitable and customary; and if you do not wish to release her, then I demand you pay me her bride-price and that we see her married with all proper formality."

"Oh, you do, do you?" Agamemnon retorted. "I wondered what you wanted, all dressed up for ceremony. Well, Khryse, Priest of Apollo, listen here: I intend to keep her myself; and as for marrying her, I can't, because I've already got a wife." He gave a great sarcastic bellow of laughter.

"So I suggest you and your friends march right back inside Troy before I decide that I could use a few more women in the camp." His eyes swept across the ranks of priests and priestesses. "Most of your women seem to be too old for bedding; I seem to have the only pretty one. But we could use a few cooks and wash-women."

"You deliberately persist, then, in this insult to Apollo Sun Lord? You continue in this insult to His High Priest?" Khryse demanded.

Agamemnon spoke slowly, as if to a young child or a simpleton.

"Listen well, Priest," he said. "I worship the Sky Thunderer, Zeus, and the Earth Shaker, Poseidon, Lord of Horses. I will not interfere in the affairs of Apollo; He is not my God. But by the same token, your Apollo would be well advised not to interfere with me. This woman in my tent is mine, and I will neither release her nor pay a bride-price; and that is all I have to say to you. Now go."

Controlling his anger, Khryse replied, "Agamemnon, I lay my curse on you; you are a man who has broken the sacred laws, and no child of yours shall honor your grave. And if you do not fear my curse, then fear the curse of Apollo, for it is His curse I lay upon your people, and you shall not escape it. His arrows shall fall upon you all, I so declare."

"Declare anything you like," Agamemnon said. "I have heard the rage of my foes before this, and it is of all sounds the most welcome to my heart. As for your Sun Lord, I defy His curse; let Him do His worst. Now get out of my camp, or I shall tell my archers to use you all for target practice."

"So be it, my lord King," said Khryse; "you shall see how long you can scorn the curse of Apollo."

One of the archers cried out, "Shall I shoot the insolent Trojan, Lord Agamemnon?"

"By no means," Agamemnon said in his rich, deep voice. "He is a priest, not a warrior. I do not kill women, little boys, eunuchs, nanny goats, or priests."

The laughter from the ranks of archers robbed Khryse's exit of much of its dignity, but he strode firmly away without looking back; one by one the priests and priestesses followed him. Kassandra kept her eyes lowered, but she could feel, for some reason, Agamemnon's eyes on her. It might only be that she was the youngest of the women from Troy, almost all the other priestesses chosen being well past fifty; but perhaps it was something more. She knew only that she did not want to meet Agamemnon's glance.

And Chryseis went to this man—willingly!

They climbed through the city to the balcony of the Sun Lord's house, which looked down upon the plains before Troy. Khryse had disappeared briefly from among them; when he reappeared, he was wearing the golden mask of the God, and bearing the ritual bow. Suddenly it appeared that he grew taller, more imposing; the eyes of all the Akhaians below were lifted to where he stood. Khryse raised his bow and cried out, *Beware, you who have offended My priest!* and Kassandra realized Who stood there beneath the mask, and the voice, strong and resonant and more than human, rang throughout Troy and to the farthest corner of the Akhaian camp below:

This is My city, Akhaians; I solemnly warn you.

My curse and My arrows shall smite every man among you,

If to My priest you return not the one so unlawfully taken.

Beware of My curse and My arrows, I warn you, you chieftains impious!

Even Kassandra, who was familiar with the voice of the God, was paralyzed with terror. She could not have moved a muscle nor spoken a word.

Quickly the form who at once was and was not Khryse shot three arrows into the air. One of them fell directly upon the roof of Agamemnon's tent; another before the tent of Akhilles; the third into the very center of the camp. Kassandra watched, feeling a dreadful stillness, as if she had watched all this before. It was as if she were very far away, and a thick wall of glass, or the weight of an ocean, rippled before her, cutting off what she saw and heard.

Apollo's curse! It has come upon us, O Sun Lord!

Was this a curse on the Akhaians alone?

But yet, she thought, *if the Akhaians are cursed, somehow we will suffer for it; we are at their mercy. I wonder whether Priam realizes that. If he does not, I am sure that Hector does.*

Then slowly she began to be aware again of what was going on around her: the glare of midday, the light reflected off the city walls and the plain below, the laughter and jeers of the Akhaians. They seemed to think this a charade, a gesture; it never occurred to them that perhaps Apollo Himself had cursed their people and their army.

Or did I dream it?

Whatever the truth, there were things to be done. She went to the Temple and was set to the task of accepting and tallying the offerings. After an hour of counting and tallying up flasks of oil and wheaten loaves she felt as if she had never been away from Troy.

She worked till sunset. When she had finished with the offerings, she went to care for the serpents and to see what places had been found for them. Then she went to Charis, the most senior priestess, and told her that alone she could not easily care for so many snakes if she had other duties as well; she asked for someone to train to help her with them and learn serpent-lore. Charis asked if Phyllida would be satisfactory to her.

"Yes; she has always been my friend," Kassandra replied, and Charis sent for Phyllida and asked if it was acceptable to her.

"I will teach you everything I learned in Colchis," Kassandra promised, and Phyllida seemed pleased.

"Yes, and if we work together, our children can grow up as brother and sister," Phyllida said. "It was I who bathed your little one yesterday and gave her her supper. She is very quick and clever, and someday she will be pretty too."

Kassandra suspected that Phyllida had said this to flatter her, but it did not altogether displease her. When it had all been arranged, they went out again to look down into the Akhaian camp. The glare and heat of the daytime had subsided, and a light wind had sprung up; they could see blowing dust in the Akhaian camp, and the forms of many people, some of them clad in the white robes of the servants of Apollo.

"So they were not quite as casual about it as they seemed," Phyllida said. She had not taken part in the mission to the camp, but she had heard all about it, and Kassandra could see it had lost nothing in the telling. "Look," she said, "they are performing rituals to purify the camp and appease the Sun Lord."

"Well they might, if they scorn His curse," Kassandra said.

"I do not think it is the soldiers who scorn His curse," Phyllida said. "I think it is only Agamemnon himself; and we know already that he is a godless man."

"What are they about now?" Kassandra asked.

"They are building fires to cleanse the grounds," Phyllida said, then shrank back at the great cry of mourning that rose from the Akhaians. They had dragged out a body from one of the tents and were casting it into the flames.

It was too far to hear the words of the cries of despair, but they had heard such cries before. Phyllida gasped, "There is plague in their camp!"

And Kassandra said, in horror, "This, then, is the Sun Lord's curse!"

EVERY MORNING and evening for ten days they watched as bodies of plague victims in the camp were burned; after the third day, the bodies were dragged a long way down the shore and burned there, for fear of contagion. Kassandra, who had seen the dirt and filth and disorder within the camp, was not surprised that there was sickness, though she did not make light of the Sun Lord's curse, and she knew the Akhaians believed in it. At sunrise, at high noon and again at sunset, Khryse strode the battlements of Troy, wearing Apollo's mask and carrying His bow, and whenever he appeared there were cries and shrieks for mercy in the Akhaian camp.

Priam proclaimed that every Trojan soldier and citizen must appear each morning before the priests of Apollo, and that anyone who showed signs of illness was to be confined alone to his own house. This isolated a few people with bad colds, and one or two men who had been indiscriminate in exploring the women's district. He closed two or three brothels and also a filthy market, but there were no signs, so far, of plague inside the walls of Troy. He declared a holiday for prayers and sacrifices to Apollo, imploring that the city continue to be spared the curse. However, when Khryse begged for audience and asked Priam also to request the return of Chryseis, he answered him sharply: "You have called a God to your side, and if that is not enough, what more do you think a mortal, even the King of Troy, could do?"

"You mean you will do nothing to help me?"

"Why should it matter to me what becomes of your wretched daughter? I might have felt a fellow father's feeling, had you asked three years ago when first she was taken, but you have not appealed to me before this; I cannot believe you are much in need of my help—except perhaps to boast that the King of Troy is your ally," Priam said.

Khryse said hotly, "If I called down Apollo's curse on the Argive camp, I can as easily curse Troy—"

Priam lifted his hand to stop him.

"No!" he thundered. "Not a word! Raise a finger or speak a syllable to curse Troy, and by Apollo's self, I swear I will myself have you flung into the Akhaian camp from the highest rampart of the city!"

"As Your Majesty wishes," Khryse said, bowed deeply and went away. Priam scowled, his feathers still ruffled.

"That man is too proud! Did you hear him—threatening to curse Troy itself!" He looked around to his advisers in his throne room. "Should he ask audience again with me, make certain that I have no time to speak with him!"

Kassandra was not displeased with the interview. Still at the back of her mind had been an old fear: that if Khryse, as he once threatened, were to go to Priam and ask to marry her, her father would be pleased to thrust her, even unwilling, into marriage—any marriage—and would find no reason for refusing an apparently respectable priest of Apollo. Now that she knew that Priam found Khryse almost as distasteful as she did herself, she breathed a sigh of relief.

21

TEN DAYS they watched the plague raging in the Akhaian camp. On the tenth day the soldiers dragged out a noble white horse and sacrificed it to Apollo, and some time later, a messenger with Apollo's serpent staff came up to the city and asked for a truce for the purpose of speaking with Apollo's priests.

"A delegation will come down to the camp," he was told. Khryse, of course, was first among them. Kassandra did not ask if she might join the group; she simply slipped away to put on her ceremonial robes and went with them.

Agamemnon, Akhilles and several of the other leaders, among whom Kassandra recognized Odysseus and Patroklos, were drawn up in ranks behind the priests of Apollo. The chief priest among the Akhaians, a lean, sinewy man who looked like an athlete, approached Khryse.

"It seems," he said, "that the Immortal is angry with us after all. But I ask you, colleague, will you accept some gift from us?"

Khryse said, "I want my daughter back, or properly married to the man who took her, to whom she went as an innocent maiden . . ."

Agamemnon snorted, but said nothing; he had apparently agreed to let the priests speak for him.

"It cannot be expected," the priest began, "that the King of Mykenae would agree to marry a prisoner of war, when he already has a Queen."

"Very well," said Khryse, "if he will not marry my daughter, I want her back, and a proper dowry with her, since she is no longer a virgin and I cannot find a husband for her without a dowry."

The priests conferred for a moment. Finally they said, "Suppose we were to offer you the pick of all the women from all the cities we have sacked in the countryside, maiden for maiden?"

"Do you think I am a lecher?" Khryse asked, his voice simmering with indignation. "I am a grieving father, and I call upon Apollo to right the wrong done me."

"Well, Agamemnon," said the Argive priest, "it seems that there is no alternative; we must act with simple justice, and restore the man's daughter."

Agamemnon stood up to his full height and folded his arms. "Never! The girl is mine."

"But she isn't," said the priest. "You took her when there should have been a truce, at the spring planting, and for that impiety the Earth Mother is displeased."

"No woman, even a Goddess, tells me what I may not do," contradicted Agamemnon. Kassandra noticed a visible shiver through the ranks of the men, and Odysseus in particular looked displeased.

"The Immortals," Odysseus said, "hate such pride as belongs only to them, Agamemnon. Come, give the girl back, and pay the girl's father her lawful bride-price."

"If I give up the girl . . ." For the first time Agamemnon hesitated, noticing that his fellow chieftains were regarding him with anger. "If I give up the girl," he repeated, "why should all you others keep the prizes you have won, and laugh at me? You, Akhilles; if I am forced to give up mine, will you give up the woman in your tent?"

Akhilles snarled, "I was not fool enough to steal mine from a priest of Apollo, and bring us all under a curse, Agamemnon. My woman came to me because she liked me better than any of Priam's sons inside Troy. And since I came to Troy to please you, Agamemnon, when by right I should have been fighting at the side of my Trojan kinfolk, I don't see why my woman should come into this at all. She is a good girl; she came to me of her free will, and she is skilled in all kinds of women's work. I had thought to take her home with me—should I ever return from this war—and make her my wife, since, unlike you, I did not have to marry some old hag of a Queen to get the rule of her city."

Agamemnon set his teeth; Kassandra could see that he was trying very hard to keep hold of his temper.

"As for my Queen," he said, "I remind you, my Queen is the twin sister of that Helen who was thought beautiful enough that her loss should start this war. And if she was also Queen in her own right of a great city, did that make her worth any less? She has borne me noble children; and let that be enough about her."

"Yes, enough," said the chief priest. "Agamemnon, you swore an oath you would do whatever was needful to save us from this plague; so we have determined that the girl Chryseis must be returned to her father. We will all make up the dowry he asks."

Agamemnon's fists were clenched, and his jaw set so hard Kassandra wondered if his teeth would shatter.

"Do you all say this," he demanded, "in spite of all I have done for you? It would serve you all right if I said 'Get another to lead your armies.' You, Menelaus—do you too stand with these people to rob me?"

The slight, brown-haired man with a small curly beard shifted uneasily from foot to foot. He said, "I would rather not suffer Apollo's wrath for your impiety—or your bad luck or bad manners—in taking a girl who should have been let alone."

"How was I supposed to know the damned girl's father was a priest, or to care if I did know? Do you think we spent our time discussing her father?" Agamemnon raged.

The priestess behind Kassandra compressed her lips against a giggle and muttered softly, "It's for certain you did not spend it in learning manners," and it was Kassandra's turn to tighten her mouth against a snicker. Agamemnon's head swiveled toward the women, and he seemed angrier than ever.

"Very well," he said. "Since you all connive against me that I shall be robbed, take the girl and be damned. But I shall then be repaid by having the woman in Akhilles' tent."

Akhilles sprang out from the midst of the Akhaian ranks and yelled, "No! You'll take her only over my dead body!"

"I suppose I could arrange that if you insist," Agamemnon said lazily. "Patroklos, can't you control this wild boy? He's hardly old enough to mix in men's affairs. Come, Akhilles, what do you need with a woman at your age? I'll send you the box of toys I gathered for my own son."

Kassandra's eyes narrowed. *Agamemnon should not have said that; Akhilles is young, but not young enough to be taunted that way without getting his own back.*

The chief priest of the Trojans said, "Khryse, have you a cloak for Chryseis? With plague here, she may not bring any garment into our camp; what she is wearing must be burned before she enters Troy, and her hair cut off."

Khryse produced a long robe and a cloak. "Burn what clothes these folk have given her," he said. "But her hair too?"

"I am sorry; it is the only way to be certain she does not carry the plague," said the priest. Agamemnon came back from his tent with Chryseis, and Khryse stepped forward to embrace her. But the chief priest stopped him.

"Let the women undress her and take her clothing to be burned, first," he said, and Charis and Kassandra moved to Chryseis, the other women making a circle about her to hide her as her Akhaian dress and overdress were stripped away and cast to the ground. With dignity, Chryseis ignored them. But when Charis unbraided her hair and took out a knife to cut it, she moved away.

"No. I have borne all else, but you shall not make a mock of me by shorn locks; I feel no need of purification or penance!"

Charis said gently, "It is only for fear of plague; you come from an infected city into one so far clean."

"I haven't the plague nor have I been near anyone who has it," said Chryseis, weeping. "Don't cut off my hair!"

"I'm sorry; we must," said Charis, seizing the long hair and cutting it off to the nape of her neck. Chryseis was sobbing inconsolably.

"Oh, look what you've done! What a figure of fun I shall be, with everyone laughing and jeering! You have always hated me, Kassandra! And now you have done this to me. . . ."

"What a foolish child you are," Charis said brusquely. "We have done as the priests bade us, no more. Don't blame Kassandra." She laid the robe Khryse had brought over Chryseis' shoulders. "I have no pin; you will have to hold it together over your breasts."

"No," Chryseis said sullenly. "If you don't have a pin, it can fall open for all I care."

Charis shrugged. "If you want every Akhaian soldier gazing on your naked breasts, that is your affair," she said, "but it might distress your father. For his sake, hold your robe so your modesty is preserved."

She signaled to the women to open a gap in their circle so that Chryseis could approach her father. Agamemnon took a step toward her, but Odysseus held him back, speaking to him urgently in an undertone.

22

THE DAY AFTER Chryseis had been returned to Troy, Kassandra was summoned to dine with her parents at the palace; she supposed that Priam wished to hear how the parley had gone. Besides the King and Queen there were Creusa and Aeneas, Hector and Andromache, with their little son, and Helen and Paris with her children. Nikos, a handsome boy, was a year older than Hector's son; the twins were running around, but were no particular trouble, as each had his own nurse who kept him under reasonable control.

It seemed to Kassandra strange that the years of war had made little change in the palace dining hall. The paintings on the walls were a little faded and cracked; she supposed that the palace servants who might have been repainting them had other duties, if they were not among the army. There were many kinds of food, including fresh fish—although indeed, there was not much of this. Andromache told her that the Akhaians had dirtied the harbor so that the finest fish stayed farther out at sea;

and no one could be spared to go out with the fishing boats through the blockade of the Akhaian soldiers.

"And when a boat does go out," she added, "the Akhaians draw it onto shore and take most of the best fish."

But there was an abundance of fruits and barley bread and honey; and wine from the grapes plucked from the vines that grew as plentifully as weeds all through the city.

Priam insisted that Kassandra repeat every word exchanged in the negotiations. He shook his head angrily when he heard of Agamemnon's arrogance and said, "I have seen no more plague victims in the Argive camp; and may the Gods grant there come none to our city. So the girl is safely back among us; what will her father do with her now?"

"I do not know; I have not asked him," Kassandra said, thinking, *nor do I have any intention of doing so, and do not care.* "I suppose," she said, "he will find her a husband with the dowry the Akhaians gave. They seemed eager to placate the Sun Lord. And after the plague who can blame them?"

"I suppose that none of the Akhaian leaders died in the plague?"

"None that I know about," said Aeneas. "Certainly neither Agamemnon nor Akhilles suffered; but they came almost to blows as soon as Chryseis left the camp; and at the end, Agamemnon stalked off to his tent and Akhilles to his; it seems there was a quarrel . . . ."

"There was," Kassandra said, and told them how Agamemnon had insisted that if his woman was taken from him, he would be repaid with Briseis; and what Akhilles had said to this.

"That explains what I saw later, though of course I did not know what it meant," Aeneas said. "A few of Agamemnon's soldiers went to Akhilles' tent, and there was some sort of fight between them and Akhilles' men; then Odysseus came and talked with them all for a long time. After that, Akhilles' soldiers were tearing down banners and decorations; it looked as if they were packing to go home."

"May that be what the Gods will," said Hector. "Agamemnon is an honorable enemy; Akhilles is mad. I prefer to fight sane men."

Kassandra had her namesake, Creusa's daughter, in her lap. She said, "I do not think any man who would fight in this war is sane."

"We all know what you think, Kassandra," said Hector, "and we are tired of hearing it."

"Hector, do you truly think we can win this war? If the Gods are angry with Troy—"

"I have seen no sign of Their anger," said Hector. "Now, it seems that the Sun Lord, at least, is angry with the Akhaians; with Akhilles gone, I have no fear of the rest of them. We will fight them and win honorably, and then we will make a truce and live at peace with them—if we are fortunate, for the rest of our lives."

"And what will happen to us?" asked Paris. He was sitting beside Helen, who was feeding one of the twins mashed fruit with a bone spoon; she looked quiet and peaceful; lovely, Kassandra thought, but without any trace of the uncanny beauty she had shown when she was inhabited by Aphrodite.

"If peace comes to us," Andromache said, "there will be peace for you as well, and you may make such lives for yourselves and your children as you desire."

"It will be a dull world without war," Hector said, yawning.

Paris disagreed. "I have already had as much war as I care to see. There must be better things to do with a life."

"You sound like our sister," Hector said. "But peace will come, like it or not; if all else fails, there's peace in the grave, and an end to all fighting and talk of honor."

Kassandra said wryly, "It sounds like a heaven specially designed by Akhilles' God."

"No heaven for me, then," Paris said. "Enough to fight here; I don't intend to spend the afterlife doing it."

"You mean you wouldn't *choose* to spend the afterlife doing it," Hector remarked. "I'm not so sure we will be given our choice."

At this moment there was a loud outcry; the children had been playing at the far end of the hall, and there were whacking sounds from wooden swords and loud childish shrieks; Hector and Paris saw that little Astyanax and Helen's son Nikos were sprawled on the floor, struggling and punching at each other, both shouting incoherently, their faces red and tear-stained.

Helen and Andromache each ran to reclaim her son, and when they returned, each with a wailing small boy under her arm, Hector motioned to the women to set the boys down.

"Here, here, lads, what's all this? Isn't there enough war outside the gates; must we have it at dinnertime too? Astyanax, Nikos is our guest in Troy; a guest deserves our hospitality. Besides, he is smaller than you. Why do you beat him?"

"Because he is a coward like his father," Astyanax scowled, digging his fists in his eyes.

Nikos kicked out at his shins, and Astyanax muttered, "Well, *you* said it, Father."

Hector struggled to keep his face straight. "No, Astyanax; I said that his father, Menelaus, was an honorable enemy; Paris is not his father, you know. And besides"—he raised his voice, as both boys began yelling at once—"whoever said what, there is always a truce at dinnertime. If Agamemnon himself came to this table, it would be my duty as an honorable man to feed him if he was hungry; the first duty we owe the Gods is hospitality. Do you hear me?"

"Yes, sir," muttered Astyanax, and Hector turned to Helen.

"Lady, I beg you to keep your son in order at dinnertime, out of respect to my father and mother, or send him away with his nurse," he commanded.

"I will try," she murmured. Paris looked like a thundercloud, but he did not venture to contradict Hector; no one did, these days.

Kassandra applied herself to the honeyed fruits which had appeared in her dish at the end of the meal, and asked Priam, "Has there been any sign that Mother's waiting-women can be exchanged or returned?"

"Not yet," Priam growled. "That damned priest's daughter —a plague on her, for all Apollo took her part," he added with a pious gesture—"has brought all other negotiations to a stop so sudden that if it were a chariot we'd all be head over heels in the road! When we can, we'll try again, but just now I'm afraid there's no hope."

Creusa rose, cradling her child in her arms. "I must take the little one to bed," she announced to the company at large. "Helen, will you come with me?"

Kassandra rose too.

"I too will say good night," she said. "Mother, Father, good night, and thank you; I have certainly dined better at your table than in the refectory of the priestesses."

"Don't see why it should be that way," Priam said thickly; "they get the best of everything up there."

Aeneas said, "By your leave, sir, I will walk through the city with the Lady Kassandra; it's late, and there may be riffraff about, now that all the decent able-bodied men are with the soldiers down below."

"I thank you, but really, Brother-in-Law, it's not necessary."

"Let him go with you, Kassandra," Hecuba commanded firmly. "It will ease my mind; Polyxena was not with us tonight because the Temple of the Maiden could spare no man to escort her."

"Why, where is Polyxena?" Kassandra asked. She had noticed her sister's absence, but for all she knew, Polyxena might have been married to some King or warrior at the far end of the world.

"She serves the Maiden Goddess; it's a long story," Hecuba said in a tone indicating that long story or short, she had no intention of telling it now. Kassandra kissed her mother and the children, and let Aeneas, rather than a servant, fold her into her cloak. Hector rose too, embracing his wife and son, and at the palace doors took leave of Aeneas and Kassandra.

"You are prettier than when you went to Colchis," he said kindly. "There is some ballad which calls you beautiful enough for Apollo to desire; if you wished, I am sure Father could find you a husband, without all the nonsense that drove Polyxena into the Temple of the Maiden."

"No, dear brother; I am happy in the house of the Sun Lord," she replied; but she returned his embrace with real warmth, knowing he meant her well.

It was not particularly dark as they moved up the steep

streets, for the moon was rising, round and bright. Aeneas paused at one point to look out over the plain where the Argive army lay.

"If Agamemnon and Akhilles had not quarreled, this is the sort of night when it would hardly be wise for Hector to dine at home with his family," Aeneas said. "Usually, these last three years, on nights with a full moon we have had an attack from seaward. But look, everything is dark down there—except in Akhilles' tent, where, I dare say, they are still arguing over their wine."

"Aeneas, what's all this about Polyxena?"

"Oh, Lord," he said, "I don't know the whole story; nobody does. Akhilles—well, Priam offered her to Akhilles, hoping to make trouble in the Akhaian ranks. Your father—after that, he went about saying she was as beautiful as the Spartan Helen, and he would award her to the most powerful—"

"What? Polyxena, as beautiful as Helen? Is his eyesight failing with age?"

"I think he was trying to make trouble with the Akhaians; he offered her to the King of Crete—"

"Idomeneus? But I heard he was joined with Agamemnon on the Akhaian side. It's treachery, of course; the Minoan folk have been our kinsmen and allies since before Atlantis sank."

"Well, however it may be, Priam tried to offer her as wife to many of the island people; but all those who wanted to accept were among the supporters of the Akhaians. And in the end, Polyxena rebelled—"

"Rebelled? But Polyxena has always done whatever she was told," Kassandra protested.

"And so she did; but she said at last that she felt like a pot being hawked at the market; and a cracked pot which no one would buy, at that—and vowed to serve the Maiden Goddess. Where she is to this day. Priam was angrier with her than when you went to serve the Sun Lord."

"I should think so," Kassandra said. "Since I was a very little girl, Father always thought of me as a rebel; but when Polyxena disobeyed, it must have been as if a child's pet rabbit had turned and bitten him."

"Yes, exactly like that, I think. Your mother was very distressed."

"Yes," Kassandra said, "Mother brings us up to think for ourselves and then is shocked and upset when we do it. I'm glad my sister made her own decision."

They strolled quietly up the steep street. Kassandra stumbled in the darkness and Aeneas quickly caught her.

"Mind your step!" he admonished. "It's a long fall!"

His arm was around her; he was not wearing armor, only tunic and cloak, and against her body he felt warm and strong. She let him support her for the next few steps; but when she would have drawn herself upright, he tightened the clasp of his arm around her waist, and bent his face to hers. In the dark their lips just met before she pulled away.

"No," she said, entreating, drawing herself away. "No, Aeneas. Not you too."

He did not free her at once; but he raised his head, and said softly, "Since first I set eyes on you, Kassandra, I have wanted you. And somehow I thought that this—this was not altogether distasteful to you."

She said, and discovered that her voice was shaking, "If it had been otherwise . . . but I am sworn to chastity, and you are the husband of my sister."

"Not by my own choice, not by Creusa's," Aeneas said softly. "We were wedded by the will of my father and yours."

"Still, it is done," Kassandra said. "I am not Helen, to abandon a pledge of honor . . . " but she let her head rest against his strong arm. She felt weak, as if her legs were no longer holding her firmly upright.

Aeneas said quietly, "I think too much is said of honor and duty. Why should Helen remain faithful to Menelaus? She was given to him with no thought for her happiness. Are we put on this earth only to carry out our duty to our families? Are we not given life by the Gods so that we my create lives for ourselves for some good to our own hearts and minds and souls?"

"If you felt like that," Kassandra asked precisely, drawing herself upright a little (she felt cold away from Aeneas' arm), "why did you agree to marry her in the first place?"

"Oh, I was younger then," Aeneas said, "and all my life I had been told it was my duty to marry whatever princess was found for me; and at that time I believed still that one woman was very much like another."

"And are they not?"

"No," Aeneas said violently. "No, they are not. Creusa is a good woman, but you are as unlike her as wine to spring water. I say nothing against the mother of my children; but at that time I had never seen a woman who was more to me than any other, one I truly wanted, one who could speak as an equal, a comrade. Kassandra, I swear, if before I married Creusa I had had the opportunity to speak a dozen times with you, I would have told Priam and my father that I would marry no other woman under the skies—that I would have you or go unmarried to my grave."

She felt stunned. "You cannot mean this; you are making fun of me," she murmured.

"Why would I want to do that?" he demanded. "I did not—I do not—want to disrupt my life, or trouble your peace, or hurt Creusa; but I think that Goddess of Love who played such a cruel trick on Paris has chosen to throw discord my way as well, and I felt I must say to you, once, what I felt."

She put out her hand, hardly knowing she was doing so, and touched his; he clasped his fingers strongly over hers. He said softly, "When first I saw you, Kassandra, seated among the girls with your eyes cast down modestly, I knew all at once that it was you I wanted, and that I should have stood up at once and proclaimed it to Priam and to my father. . . ."

The thought made Kassandra smile.

"And what would Creusa have said to that?"

"I should not have let that matter to me," Aeneas said. "I was the one whose life was being cast into the balance. Tell me, Kassandra, would you have had me for a husband? If I had refused Creusa and demanded you instead—as the price of my fighting for Troy—"

Her heart was beating as wildly as his agitated words. "I don't know," she said at last. "Whatever I might have said or done then, it's too late for thinking about it now."

"It need not be too late," he said, and drew her into his arms. She did not know that she was crying until Aeneas' finger wiped away a tear.

"Don't cry, Kassandra; I don't wish to make you unhappy. But I cannot bear to think that now I have found that you are the one I love, there can never be anything more for us than this."

He enfolded her in an embrace so rough, so completely compelling, that nothing outside seemed to exist at all; she was drowning, suffocating, wiped away into nonexistence; incapable of thought. Nevertheless, after a time that seemed too long— but very short—she pulled herself upright and onto her own feet, wiping her eyes with her gown. *So that is what it is like.*

She knew her voice was shaking as she said, "You are my sister's husband; you are my *brother*."

"By my own immortal ancestress! Don't you think I have chewed on that until it sickens me?" he muttered. "I can only beg you not to be angry with me."

"No," she said, and it sounded so foolishly inadequate for the moment between them that she began helplessly to giggle; "no, I'm not angry with you, Aeneas."

He pulled her again into an embrace she could not and did not want to fight off; but this time there was caution too, as if he were taking great pains not to hurt or frighten her. He said against her ear, "Tell me you care for me too, Kassandra."

"Oh, Gods," she said helplessly, "do you have to ask?" Her mouth was crushed so tightly against his that she wondered how he could understand her words.

"No," he said, "I don't have to ask, but I need to hear you say it. I don't think I can stand to go on living unless I hear you say it."

Suddenly Kassandra was filled with the most unbelievable sense of generosity. It was in her power to give him something he wanted so much. She leaned forward again against him and whispered, "I do care for you. I think—I think I have loved you since first I saw you." And she felt him move softly against her as if it were where he had always wanted to be. He was touching only her fingers; but that touch was somehow closer than an embrace. She wanted him to hold her again; yet she knew that if he did, she and she alone would be responsible for whatever happened.

She said softly, "Aeneas . . ." and stopped.

"What, Kassandra?"

"I think," she whispered with a sense of overpowering wonder—"I think I only wanted to hear myself say your name."

He tightened his arms around her, but gently, as if he were afraid the slightest touch would break her. He said, "My little love. I don't know—I'm not sure what it is that I want, but it is not to seduce you into my bed; *that* I can have from anyone, anytime. I love you, Kassandra. I wanted to tell you, to try to make you understand. . . ."

"I do understand," she said, tightening her hand on his. Above them the moon swung so brilliant that she could see his face as if by daylight.

"Look," he said: "all the fires are out in the Akhaian camp. It is very late. You must be weary; I should let you go."

It *was* late. She drew a little away from him, feeling cold out of his arms, and offered him her hand. He bent over her very close, but he did not kiss her again. He whispered, "Good night, my little love, and the Goddess keep you. I will stand here till I see you safe inside the gates of the Sun Lord's house."

She climbed the last steps alone and knocked at the gate, which was opened from inside.

"Ah, Princess Kassandra," said one of the Temple servants, as he opened the gate; "you are returning from dining with your parents at the palace? Did you walk up alone?"

"No; the Lord Aeneas escorted me," she said, and the young man thrust out his head.

"Would the Lord Aeneas like a lighted torch for the way downward?"

"No, thank you," Aeneas said courteously. "The moon is very bright." He bowed to Kassandra. "Good night, my sister and my lady."

"Good night," she said, and when she was out of hearing, she heard herself whisper, "Good night, my love."

She was stricken with dismay. She had sworn—knowing nothing of it—that she would never serve the Goddess Aphrodite nor succumb to this kind of passion.

And now she was like any other of that Akhaian Goddess' servants.

23

AKHILLES' SOLDIERS were loading their ships; the quarrel in the Akhaian camp had evidently not subsided. One of Priam's favorite agents, an old woman who sold cakes in the Akhaian camp and came back inside the walls every day about noon for a new supply (and a long talk with the Captain of the Watch), reported that Akhilles had not stirred from his tent. Patroklos had tried to dissuade the soldiers from leaving, but without much effect.

Patroklos, she said, was liked by all the soldiers, but they all felt their loyalty was to Akhilles, and if he had decided to give up the fight, they would give up too.

Halfway through the morning, Kassandra went down to the wall to see for herself, along with most of the women of Priam's house: Hecuba, Andromache, Helen and Creusa.

They listened to the old cake-woman's report and wondered what this would mean to the Akhaian cause.

"Not much," said Paris, who this morning was Captain of the Watch. "Akhilles is a maniac for fighting, but Agamemnon and Odysseus are the brains of the campaign. Akhilles is great in single combat, of course, and drives his chariot like a hellion; those Myrmidons of his would follow him in a charge over the edge of the world."

"What a pity someone can't persuade them to do it," Creusa murmured. "That would solve most of our trouble—with Akhilles at least. Does anyone know a friendly Immortal who would appear in Akhilles' form and lead his men off on an urgent mission somewhere on the other side of the world, or convince them they're desperately needed at home?"

"But the point is," Paris said, ignoring her, "that that is all Akhilles has in his favor: he's crazy for the kill. He doesn't know a damned thing about strategy or war tactics. Losing Akhilles from the war, having him go home like a little boy saying "I'm not playing anymore," is no great blow to the Akhaians. It would be far worse for them, and better for us, if they lost Agamemnon, or Odysseus, or even Menelaus."

"What a pity we can't think of some clever way to get rid of one of them," said Hecuba.

"It almost happened," said Paris. "This quarrel between Akhilles and Agamemnon meant they would have to lose one or the other. Losing Akhilles distressed the soldiers—he's their idol—but the leaders knew they couldn't lose Agamemnon or the whole campaign would fall apart. Why else do you think they let him take Akhilles' girl? They know how important Agamemnon is to the whole campaign. Why do you think Akhilles is sulking? He's been shown very clearly that he's not nearly as important—not to anyone—as Agamemnon."

"Well, something is going on down there," Helen said. "Look, there is Agamemnon—with Menelaus tagging behind him, as usual—and his herald."

Kassandra had seen the herald before: a tall young man who was perhaps too slightly built to be of much use with sword or shield, but who had a splendid bass voice which he could make ring through the entire camp. *Waste of a fine musician*, Khryse had once said; and indeed he would have made a splendid minstrel or singer.

Now Agamemnon was giving him orders, and the herald was striding clear across the camp and—yes—toward the foot of the wall. Paris took his tall loop-shaped shield, settled his helmet down on his head and went out onto the wall. The herald shouted: *"Paris, son of Priam!"*

"That is I," Paris said, his voice sounding small and young after the herald's trained and resonant tones. "What do you want with me? And if Agamemnon has a message for me, why does he not come within range of the walls himself, instead of —like a coward—sending you, whom I may not lawfully shoot?"

He went on, laughing, "When will they declare an open hunting season on heralds? I think they should all be exterminated, like Kentaurs."

"Paris, son of Priam, I bear a message for you from Menelaus of Sparta, brother of Agamemnon, Overlord of Mykenae—"

"I know perfectly well who Menelaus is," Paris interrupted him. "You don't need to explain, nor rehash all our grudges against each other."

"Oh, let the poor man give his message, Paris," Helen said, in a voice that carried clearly. "You're making the poor child nervous. He wants at least to sound like a warrior, if he can't fight like one. He might wet his tunic if you go on, and think how embarrassed he'd be before all these women."

"Well, if you have a message from Menelaus, go on and give it," Paris said. The herald, blushing, visibly pulled himself together and straightened.

"Hear the words of Menelaus, Lord of Sparta: 'Paris, son of Priam, my quarrel is with you, not with Priam or with the great city of Troy. I now propose that we settle this war in a single-combat challenge before all the assembled soldiers of Troy and the Akhaians. And that, if you kill me or I surrender, then you shall keep Helen and such goods of mine as you may have, and my men, including my brother Agamemnon, will be pledged not to fight further, not even to avenge me, but to take their ships and sail away from Troy forever, and this war be at an end. But if I kill you or you surrender, then Helen shall be turned over to me, with her goods and gear, and we will take her home without asking any of the spoils of Troy other than this. How do you say? What is your answer?' "

Paris stood at his full height and said, "Say to Menelaus that I have heard his offer; and I will consult with King Priam and with Hector, the leader of the Trojan armies. For it seems to me that there are many causes in this war other than Helen; but if my father and my brother wish to settle it in this way, then I am agreeable."

There was a rousing cheer from both sides as Paris dropped down out of sight and came back into the little corner of the wall where the women had been watching. Helen stood up without words and kissed him.

Paris said, "Whew! What was the point of that? Menelaus knows as well as I do that there's more to this war than Helen. How did Agamemnon manage to entice him into this arrangement? Or is it a trick to get me out from behind the wall?"

"I would credit Menelaus with the spite to do it," Helen said, "but not with the wit to think of it."

"Well, how do you think Priam would have me answer?" Paris asked. "Or Hector? Hector would probably welcome this chance to have me out of the way so he can conduct the war as he pleases."

"You wrong your brother, my boy," Hecuba said.

"May you always think so, Mother," Paris replied, "and may I always be at hand to argue the point."

"The heart of the matter is that you can't fight Menelaus," said Kassandra.

"Why not? Do you think I am afraid of him?" Paris argued.

"If you are not, you are a greater fool than I ever thought you were," Andromache said.

"But Hector will so welcome the settling of this war by single combat," Kassandra said, "that he will probably have Paris accept—but only on the condition that he challenge Agamemnon instead."

"Well, he might offer to fight Menelaus in my place," Paris said. "I'll lend him my cloak, and all the armies are welcome to think it is I."

"Whatever Hector will think, you may ask him yourself, for here he comes," Andromache said. Hector and his warriors were coming through the streets of Troy toward the gate. There were about a hundred and fifty armored soldiers, and others dragging Hector's chariot down the steep streets, to harness it at the gates so that Hector might mount it and ride out. He saw them from a distance on the wall and came up to speak with them.

"What's happened?" asked Hector. "I heard some yelling in the streets. . . ."

Hecuba told him quickly about Menelaus' challenge, and Hector frowned.

"It's probably the best we can do with Akhilles out of the picture," he said. "Are you going to fight him, Paris?"

"I'd rather not," Paris said. "I don't trust him to meet me in single combat; I think it's more likely that he's trying to lure me out to have me shot down by a dozen archers, or ambushed."

Hector scowled.

"Damn you, Paris, I never know whether you're talking cowardice or plain common sense."

"I don't think there's that much difference," said Paris. "I take it that means you want me to get out there and fight him."

"Is there any question about that?" Kassandra could tell from Hector's expression that he could not imagine why Paris was not so eager that he wasn't already strapping on his weapons.

"Well, yes," Paris said. "If I kill him, they'll all go away and you'll never have a chance at Agamemnon or Akhilles. That would spoil your fun, wouldn't it?"

"And if he kills you?"

"I was trying not to think about that," Paris said. "I doubt that *that* would particularly spoil your fun; but they'd certainly gloat over you while they carried off Helen and anything else they happened to fancy in Troy. And as I say, it might not be the kind of fair fight you'd feel honor bound to give Akhilles if he challenged you."

"Helen," Hector said, "you know Menelaus better than any of us; is he likely to abide by his word?"

She shrugged. "I would think so; I doubt he could think up a trap. Of course, I have no idea what Agamemnon may have thought up; *that*'s another matter entirely."

"Well, Paris, it's for you to choose," Hector said. "I can't force you to fight him; on the other hand, I don't want to be responsible for refusing the challenge."

Paris looked down to where Menelaus in his crimson cloak was still pacing up and down before the wall. He said, "Helen, what do you want me to do? Shall I fight him for you?"

"Hector will give you no peace unless you do," she said shrewdly, "so I think you had better. But we must manage a way of escape for you; perhaps we can persuade some Immortal to intervene."

"How will you do that?" he asked.

"You had better not know," she said; "but I do not think that the Goddess of Love and Beauty brought me here to be dragged home in disgrace at the tail of Agamemnon's cart. But as you fight, keep watch, and one way or another we will get a rope ladder over the wall. And if the Goddess gives you a moment to get to it—well, do not let the opportunity pass unless Menelaus is already dead at your feet."

Paris shrugged, went to the wall and shouted down to Menelaus that he would meet him in an hour, if he wished.

Then he put on his armor and went down to the field with Hector. When they saw him in the chariot, the Akhaians broke out into a cry.

"What are you going to do?" Kassandra asked, approaching Helen. Helen grasped Kassandra's hands.

"You are his twin sister and a priestess," she said. "Now join me in chanting and praying that the Sea-Born may send us one of Her sea-fogs. Hecuba, I beg you, if you love your son, send for a strong rope ladder; we cannot ask the Goddess to do for us what any ropemaker could do for a copper coin."

Hecuba dispatched a messenger for a rope ladder, and when it came, Helen went and stood with Kassandra at the very edge of the wall, watching Paris and Menelaus arming themselves while their heralds exchanged insults.

Menelaus and Paris paced carefully around, marking off the circle into which no other fighter on either side might enter while either of them lived. That done, they bowed to each other ceremoniously. A trumpet sounded, and they began to fight.

"Chant!" Helen urged. "Pray! Beseech the Goddess to send us Her sea-fog!"

The women began to chant. Kassandra was so busy watching the men swing their swords that she could hardly form the words of the prayer, though this was simple magic enough. At first the men seemed fairly evenly matched. Paris was taller and had a longer reach; but though Menelaus seemed to have grown soft from inactivity, he was as quick as a mongoose. They circled

THE FIREBRAND 393

each other, exchanging blows, carefully taking each other's measure but not yet seriously joined in battle.

Kassandra's eyes ached. Was it dust in the battle circle before them? Or was it actually a swirl of sea-fog drifting up from the shore? She could not be sure. Helen stepped to the edge of the wall and let the rope ladder down; she had hooked it for security around the edge of the wall's stones. Then she rose to her full height and called aloud: "Menelaus!"

He turned his eyes upward briefly and stopped in midstroke. Helen slowly unfastened the neck of her garment and let it drop till her breasts were bare.

As she stood without moving, it seemed to Kassandra that the air was filled with faint glowing golden sparkles, as if the veil between the worlds grew thinner. Helen, touched with that golden shimmer, seemed to gain height and majesty and to glow from within with a beauty beyond anything human. It was no woman but the Goddess Herself standing on the wall.

As for Menelaus, he stood as if his feet had taken root in the earth beneath them.

Not so Paris. As his eyes fell upon Helen standing there in the form of the Goddess, he broke away, sprinting for the foot of the wall. From the ranks of the Akhaians came a great cry of awe and longing; then Paris was atop the wall and pulling up the ladder. With everyone's eyes on Helen—or rather, on the Goddess—Kassandra realized, probably no one had seen him climb the ladder at all. He bundled it up and tossed it down inside.

Helen still stood unmoving, her body glowing with light. Then in the flicker of an eyelash, the illusion—if it had been illusion—was gone, and it was only Helen who stood there, her face a little sunburnt, fastening up her dress. She came to Paris and said, "You are wounded."

"Nothing serious, Lady," he said, his eyes still wide; but the stripe of red just outside the edge of his leather armor was dripping now.

She said, "Come along; I'll care for it," and led him away.

There were shouts from the Akhaians now.

"Paris! Where did he go? Coward!"

But through and beyond it all there were cries of, "The

Goddess! She appeared before us on the wall! The Beautiful One, the Sea-Born!"

Hector's chariot rumbled back through the gate, and the next minute he was striding up the stairs built into the wall. He looked around and demanded, "Where is he, then?"

Hecuba said, her voice quavering, "Did you not see the Goddess take him?"

"That's what they said in the Akhaian ranks," said Hector, "and when I asked my own charioteer, he swore he had seen Aphrodite stoop down from the walls and fling Her cloak over Paris and snatch him away. As for me, I don't know what it was I saw; maybe just the blaze of the sun in my eyes. Where is Helen?"

"When the Goddess returned Paris here, She saw that he was bleeding," Andromache said, "and took him to Her rooms to bandage his wound; by now they're probably in the bath."

"I don't doubt it a bit," Hector growled; "but I wish if Goddesses are going to interfere, They'd wait till things were properly settled. If the Goddess came Herself to snatch Paris to safety, I wish She'd snatched Menelaus—and Helen too—all the way back to Sparta. If She's capable of the one—and notice, Immortals, I'm not impious to say She couldn't do it—She's capable of the other. Kassandra, what did you see? Are *you* going to tell me fairy tales about the Goddess on the wall snatching him away?"

For a moment, Kassandra was overjoyed: Hector had appealed to her as if she were a trustworthy witness.

"Not a bit of it," she said. "But it looked to me as if Menelaus had some kind of vision; he stopped fighting and stared at the wall, and Paris ran for his life."

Hector sighed and said, "Well, it's too late for any more fighting today; but wait till this gets around. But of course, if the Goddess intervened—even by giving Menelaus a vision—no one can blame Paris."

But he did not sound altogether convinced.

VOLUME THREE

POSEIDON'S
DOOM

1

By TWILIGHT everyone in both armies, and most of the civilians in the city, had heard the story, which of course did not grow less in the telling.

According to most of the eyewitnesses, the Goddess had appeared on the city wall and snatched Paris from under Menelaus' very sword, delivering him from a certain death-stroke; in one version, Menelaus had sliced Paris in one stroke from chin to pelvis, and the Goddess had healed him at a touch; She had bound up his wounds with nectar and ambrosia and transported him into Helen's very chamber.

Kassandra, when asked, replied only that she was not sure what she had seen; the sun had been in her eyes.

Privately she was certain that somehow the Goddess had intervened. But she was no longer certain quite how it had happened, although she was perfectly sure that for a moment at least, Helen had worn the semblance of the Goddess. It would not be, after all, for the first time.

For two days the city talked of nothing but the duel, and the supposed intervention of the Goddess. Hector and Aeneas came back from councils saying that the Akhaians were insisting that Menelaus had won the duel because Paris had fled, wounded.

"What did you answer them?" Priam asked eagerly.

"What do you think? We said that it was obvious that Paris had won, since the Goddess had intervened to save his life," Hector replied.

Kassandra, who had watched from the walls during part of

the day, remembering her own arms-training and thinking that she could probably do as well as most of the Akhaian soldiers or any of the Trojans, asked, "What was that all about this afternoon? I saw two soldiers I did not know stand out for combat, and before they ever got to fighting, one of them started unarming and ended by stripping off his clothes down to his loincloth. Did they decide to wrestle instead of fighting with swords?"

Aeneas chuckled.

"Oh, no," he said. "Do you know Glaucus the Thracian?"

"I have spoken with him," Helen said. "He was the sailing-master of one of the ships that brought us here."

"Well, he stood out and challenged any Akhaian to give him a fight, and Diomedes accepted. So they began calling out their lineage, in order to find out if they could meet honorably in single combat, and before they reached their great-grand-fathers, they discovered they were cousins."

"So did they decide not to fight?" Kassandra asked.

"Didn't you see?" Aeneas asked.

"No; I was called away to the Temple. One of the great serpents is about to shed her skin, and needed special care; a serpent is blind at this time and cannot be handled by strangers," Kassandra said.

"They agreed they must fight for the honor of it; but they decided to exchange armor. Diomedes said that his ordinary armor was not handsome enough for an honorable gift, so he sent back to his ship for a precious set of silver armor with gold inlay, and then of course Glaucus had to trade around with his comrades for a fancy set to give him a gift of equal worth. They sounded like a couple of old men in the flea market haggling over the value of some trinket, and it went on and on—and of course they did the fighting in their old battered fighting armor, with the two fancy sets hanging up to be admired. . . ."

"Who won?" asked Helen.

"I have no idea; I think they knocked each other down a time or two, and then it got too dark to see, so they embraced each other, thanked each other for the handsome gifts and went off to dinner."

Hector chuckled. "No advantage either way, I suppose; but

it passed the afternoon. Of course, we had nothing better to do anyway today; until the councillors on both sides have decided whether Paris or Menelaus won *their* duel, everything else is simply for amusement anyhow. Glaucus and Diomedes would have done better to make it a wrestling match; at least we could have had some bets on that one. I've been tempted to challenge Big Ajax to wrestle—he's the biggest man on the Akhaian line. I don't know if he can wrestle—"

"He can," said young Troilus. "He won the garland for wrestling at their Sacrificial Games."

"Then I shall certainly challenge him," said Hector.

"Watch out you don't get an elbow in the face; his specialty is breaking teeth," Troilus said.

At dinner, Hector asked Priam, "Sire, what will happen if the Council decides that Menelaus won the duel?"

Priam shrugged.

"Nothing," he said. "The Akhaians will refuse to accept the decision and the war will go on. They don't want to settle; they're not going to give in till they break down the walls of Troy and sack the city."

"Why, you sound like Kassandra, Father."

"No," said Priam, "I know what Kassandra thinks." But for once, as Kassandra raised her eyes, struck again by that terrible fear, and the vision of Troy in flames which came between her and the living world, Priam smiled at her kindly, as if to try to dispel her fears. "I have heard her say often enough that she believes that they will destroy us. But that is not true."

"*Can* they break the walls of Troy, Father?" Paris asked.

"Not unless they can persuade Poseidon to help them with an earthquake," Priam stated.

Now Kassandra felt it through all her body: the walls would fall to the wrath of Poseidon, His earthquake. She should have known all along that no ordinary efforts of men could break the walls of Troy; only a God could tear down the great high citadel.

"Then we should sacrifice to Poseidon as soon as possible," Hector said, "for He is the only God who can help us."

"Yes," Kassandra said quickly, "let us make sacrifices at once to Poseidon and beseech Him to aid us in our cause! Is He not one of the guardian Gods of Troy?" Not knowing what she was going to say until she heard it flooding through her mind like a scream of anguish, she cried, "Paris! You—oh, beware of the earthquake! Sacrifice to Poseidon! Make Him pledges, for it is you He will destroy—destroy—destroy!"

She stopped herself by main force, actually clamping her hands across her lips. Priam scowled at her in anger and disgust.

"Haven't we had enough of this, Kassandra?" he demanded. "Even at your mother's dinner table? Can't you even make up your mind which God is to destroy the city? I really think you must be mad."

She could not speak; the lump in her throat was so great that it took all her strength merely to breathe. She swallowed and felt tears flooding down her face. Helen came and wiped her face with her veil, and the tenderness in the gesture disarmed Kassandra so that she could only stare at her brother's wife and whisper, "It is you He will destroy."

"My poor girl," Hecuba said, "the Gods still torment you with these visions. Leave her alone, Helen; there is nothing you can do for her. Kassandra, get back to the Temple; among your companions there, I am sure that the priests have remedies against such seizures as this."

Priam said firmly, "Never again prophesy here, Kassandra. I have spoken; so let it be done."

Unable to control her sobbing, Kassandra rose and ran out of the hall, fleeing up through the streets. After a time she became aware of footsteps following her upward, and she redoubled her pace, but the steps quickened to follow her, and then gentle hands seized her and brought her to a stop.

"What's the matter, Kassandra?" asked a man's voice. She gasped in panic, and at first struggled wildly against his grasp; then, realizing it was Aeneas who held her, she relaxed and stood silent. "Can't you tell me?" he asked. "What's really wrong?"

"You know what they say: that I am mad," she said dully.

"I don't believe that for a moment," Aeneas said. "Tormented by a God, perhaps; but not mad, nor anything like it."

"I don't know the difference," she said. "And I cannot keep

silent; when the Sight comes to me, I must speak. . . ." She heard her own voice shaking so that the words were almost indistinguishable.

"Perhaps," Aeneas said gently, his arm around her, "all those who see farther than the rest of us are considered mad by those who can see no farther than tomorrow's breakfast. When you ran away, I was afraid for you—afraid you would fall and hurt yourself. I do not for a moment believe that your wits are astray—you seem perfectly sensible to me; nor do I see why it should be considered madness to warn our people that the Gods are eager to destroy us. Ever since I came to Troy it has seemed to me that we are under the shadow of one angry Immortal or more, and I too seem to smell the danger of destruction on every wind."

He kissed her gently on the cheek. "Now, can you tell me what it is that you see?"

She looked him straight in the eye, filled suddenly with certainty. "I have seen that you will survive the danger; I have seen you leave Troy alive and unwounded."

He patted her shoulder gently. "That is good to know, of course. But that is not why I asked you. Come, let me take you up to the Sun Lord's house." They climbed silently for a few moments. Then he said, "You truly feel there is no hope for Troy in this war?"

"I knew that the moment Paris brought Helen here," she said, "and believe me, this is not malice; I have come to love Helen dearly, as if she were my own sister born. I knew it when Paris entered Troy's walls at the games; Hector was right to wish to send him away, but for the wrong reasons. Hector feared that Paris would try to make himself King; but that was not the danger. . . ."

Aeneas stroked her cheek. He said, "I do not share your Sight, Kassandra, but I trust you; you are speaking the truth. You may be mistaken, but you are not doing this from malice or from madness. And if this is what you see, of course you must say what the Gods have given you to say." They had reached the Temple gate; he embraced her and said, "When you speak, I will listen always, I promise you."

"I think," Kassandra said, "that some Immortal began this war—but I think Aphrodite has had Her chance to aid or to destroy us; and now it seems to us that it is not She, but the strife of other Gods that threatens us. When Father said that no mortal could pull down the walls of Troy, I knew he spoke the truth. It will not be to the hands of the Akhaians that we will fall, but to the hands of the Gods; and I do not know why They should destroy our city."

"Maybe," said Aeneas, "the Gods do not need reasons for what They do."

She whispered, "That is what I am beginning to fear."

2

THE CLIMATE of Troy was considerably warmer than that of Colchis; the serpents Kassandra had brought from Imandra's city were more active here, and she spent much of her time caring for them.

For this reason, she did not hear immediately when the Council determined that neither Paris nor Menelaus had won the duel, but that a truce would be proclaimed while it considered the matter further. Kassandra knew it would make no particular difference—both sides were resolved to continue fighting—so she paid little heed. She was still concerned with the serpents when the word came that the fighting had been resumed. Later, someone told her that the truce had been broken when one of the Argive captains—later claiming that the Maiden Goddess had prompted him—had shot an arrow at Priam, which pierced his best robe and came near to killing him.

A few days later, from the safety of the wall, she and the other palace women watched the gathering of Hector's forces, both chariots and armed foot soldiers. She heard among the women that Aeneas had accepted a challenge from Diomedes, the Akhaian who had fought with Glaucus.

Creusa did not take it very seriously.

"I have not heard that Diomedes is a fighter to worry about," she said. "This nonsense about exchanging gifts—what was that except an excuse for talking instead of fighting?"

"I would not count on that too much," said Helen. "Granted, that day they were both playing a game; but I have seen Diomedes when he is really set for fighting, and I think perhaps he is stronger than Aeneas."

"Are you trying to frighten me, Helen?" Creusa asked. "Are you jealous?"

"My dear," Helen said, "believe me, I have no interest in anyone's husband but my own."

"Which one?" asked Creusa unkindly. "Two lay claim to you, and no one in Troy talks of any other woman."

"I am not to blame if they have nothing to do but mind the affairs of their betters," Helen said. "Tell me, is there any woman in Troy who claims I have spoken one word to her husband that could not be repeated before my mother and his?"

"I do not say that," Creusa muttered, "but you seem to take pleasure in showing yourself to all men as the Goddess—"

"Then your quarrel is with *Her* and not with me, Creusa; I am not to blame for what She does."

"I suppose not—" Creusa began, but Kassandra interrupted.

"Of course not; don't be silly, Creusa. Is it not bad enough that the men down there are at war? If we women begin to fight with one another too, there will be no good sense left anywhere in Troy."

"If the Gods and the Goddesses are quarreling, how are we to remain free of entanglement?" asked Andromache. "I think perhaps the Gods take pleasure in seeing us fight, as They take pleasure in fighting Themselves. I know Hector's greatest pleasure is battle; if this war stopped tomorrow, he would weep."

"What troubles me is that he seems to welcome it," Helen said. "One would think he sought to be possessed by Ares. Kassandra, you are a priestess; it is true that men can be possessed by their Gods?"

She thought of Khryse and said, "It's true enough, but I do not know how or why it happens. Not, I think, merely by their wishing for it. Helen, I have seen you overshadowed by the Goddess. How can it be brought on?"

"Why, don't tell me that you wish to show yourself as Aphrodite?" Helen said, laughing. "I thought you were one of Her foes."

Kassandra made a pious gesture.

"May it be far from me to be the foe of *any* Immortal," she said. "I do not serve Her, for it seems to me that the Beautiful One is not a Goddess as Earth Mother and Serpent Mother and even the Maiden are Goddesses."

"When is a Goddess not a Goddess?" asked Helen with a droll smile. "I don't think I understand you, Kassandra."

"I mean that the Goddesses of your Akhaian folk are different from the Goddesses of our people," Kassandra said. "Your Maiden Goddess—the warrior, Athena—She is just such a Goddess as a man would invent, because they say She was not born of any woman but sprang in full armor from the head and the mind of Zeus; yet, for all Her weapons, She is a girl with all the domestic virtues, who would make some God a good wife. She tends to Her spinning and weaving and is patron of the vines, both the olive and the grape. Would not a man create a warrior maiden just like this—brave and virtuous, but still obedient to the greatest of Gods? And your Hera—She is like our Earth Goddess, but your people call Her only the wife of Zeus Almighty and say She is subject to Him in all things, while to us Earth Mother is all-powerful in Herself. She brings forth all things, but Her sons and Her lovers come and go, and She takes whom She will; when the God of Death took Her daughter, She brought the very Earth to a standstill, so that it neither bore nor brought forth fruit. . . ."

"But we too have an Earth Lady," said Helen: "Demeter. When Hades took Her daughter, She brought, they say, a winter of fearful cold and dark; and in the end Zeus said that the girl must return to her mother—"

"Exactly," Andromache interrupted. "They say that even Earth Mother is under obedience of this great Zeus. But there's no sense to it. Why should the Earth Goddess, who was before all else and all-powerful, be subject to any man or any God?"

"Well, if you are going to argue as to which of the Gods is most powerful," Helen said, "is it not the forces of love which can disrupt all else in men's lives—and women's too—and make them blind to all else—"

"Create disorder and disruption, you mean," Kassandra said.

"You speak that way only because you have never come under Aphrodite's sway, Kassandra," said Andromache, "and if you defy Her, She will make you suffer for it."

Surely this was true; Kassandra remembered the shocking conflict she had felt in Aeneas' arms. *You do not know She is already making me suffer.* But she could not speak of that, not to any of the women here.

"May that be far from me," Kassandra said. "I defy no one —certainly no Immortal." Yet even as she spoke she remembered that Khryse had called her defiance a defiance of Apollo's self. Was it so, or was he only—like all men—vengeful against a woman who would not serve him and his lust? And she had— if only in a dream—defied Aphrodite's power.

"Even Apollo Sun Lord," she said, with a little thrill of dread, as if she flung a challenge even in the Sun Lord's face, "is said to have slain Serpent Mother, and taken from Her Her power. Yet surely of all men, he who slays the woman from whom he sprang is most wicked—and would the Immortals allow in a God what is most wicked in man? Were this true, Apollo would be no God but the most evil of fiends—which He surely is not."

"And as for Earth Mother creating a year in which no fruit or flowers came forth, and no crops would bear," Helen said, "in the year in which Atlantis sank beneath the ocean, so my mother's father's father said, there were great earthquakes, and great clouds of ash covered the sun; in that year, it might be said, there was no summer, for the very foundations of the earth had been shaken. But whether it was the doing of any God, who can say? It would not be surprising if men thought that Earth Mother had betrayed them, and sought to put an end to Her misbehavior by giving Her an overlord who would make Her serve men as She ought."

"I do not think," Creusa interrupted nervously, "it is well for us to stand here questioning the ways of the Immortals. They do not look to men to make an accounting of what They do, and if we seek to question Them, They may seek to punish us for it."

"Oh, nonsense!" Kassandra said. "If They were as stupid and jealous of Their power as all that, why would anyone serve Them at all?"

"Do you, who are sworn to serve the Gods, not fear Them at all?" Andromache asked.

"I fear the Gods," Kassandra said, "not what men say They are."

IN THE Sun Lord's house, the serpents—so Phyllida told her when Kassandra went to see her charges—seemed unusually disturbed. Some of them withdrew and would not come to be handled or even bathed; others were drowsy and sluggish. As she went from one to another, trying to decide what was troubling them, she remembered the earthquake when Meliantha had died. Was this a warning of just such another blow from the hand of Poseidon?

I should send a message to the palace, she thought; but when she had last spoken prophecy there, she had been mocked and taunted, and Priam had forbidden her to speak it again. *I would not be believed if I did send a warning,* she thought. And then she knew, without the shadow of a doubt, that she must not refuse to hear the voice which sent her the warning. Not that she could do anything to stay the hand of whatever God might send the earthquake, but that some of the worst of its fury might be averted. Distraught, she caught up a cloak and cried to Phyllida to try to soothe the serpents in whatever way she could. Phyllida had put her own son and Honey to bed, each of them hugging a restless snake. As Kassandra bent to caress each of the children, her mind filled with pictures of the roof collapsing; she swiftly gave orders that beds be made up for them in the courtyard, where if any building should fall, they would not be crushed beneath it.

Then she ran into the courtyard and cried out, "O Lord Apollo! Hold off the hand of Thy brother who shakes the earth!

Thy serpents have given me Thy warning; let all Thy servants hear!"

People came running out at her cries. Khryse demanded, "What is happening? Are you ill? Are you smitten by the hand of the God?"

Kassandra fought to control the intolerable shaking of her body. She struggled to speak rationally, make her words even.

"The serpents in the Sun Lord's house have given me warning," she shouted, knowing that she sounded distraught, or worse. "As they did when Meliantha died, they are restless and trying to escape; the earth will shake before morning. Whatever is precious must be rescued; and none should sleep beneath a roof this night, lest it fall upon them."

"She is mad," Khryse said. "We have known for many years that she raves in prophecy."

"All the same," said one of the elder priests, "whatever she may or may not know of the Gods, in Colchis she learned the ways of serpent-lore from a mistress of that art. If the serpents have given her warning—"

Charis commanded, "The warning is given; we may not disregard it. Do what you will, or suffer the consequences; as for me and mine, I will make my bed under the open sky, which will not fall upon us yet, at least."

The sky was already dark; torches were brought, and the priestesses went quickly about the task of removing out-of-doors anything that might be endangered by the falling of stone or walls. Khryse still grumbled; it was to his advantage, she knew, to have it thought that nothing she said was true.

She ran toward the gates. "Open the doors," she cried. "I go to warn the folk of the city, and Priam's palace!"

"No!" Khryse cried out. "Stop her!" He stepped toward her, and reached out to grab her arms, to prevent her forcibly from leaving the Temple. "If warning must be given, sound the alarm; that will bring the folk out of their houses without making it seem that we are all God-smitten and bestirred without reason except a foolish girl's dreams."

"Touch me at your peril! I go as the Gods determined, to warn them!"

Her cry shocked him enough that he let her go, and she darted through the door before he could stop her. Once in the street, she screamed at the top of her voice: "Take heed! The serpents of the Sun Lord have given warning: the earth will shake! Take such shelter as ye can find! Let none sleep beneath roofs, lest they fall!"

People, roused by her cries, came flooding out their doors. Driven by a terrible urgency, she ran on, calling out her warning over and over. She heard behind her cries and shouts, some saying, "Hark to the warning of Apollo's priestess," and others grumbling, "She is cursed by the God; why should we believe her?"

It was as if she were filled with fire: she was driven, burning with the heat of the warning that cried and raged within her. She fled down the streets, shrieking her warning over and over again. When she came to awareness of where she was, she was standing in the forecourt of the palace, her throat raw, and a dozen or more of the palace folk were standing and staring at her. Hoarsely she gasped out her tale.

"Let none sleep under a roof; the God will shake the land and buildings will fall—will fall. . . . Helen, your children . . . Paris . . ." She grabbed his shoulders; he thrust her away roughly.

"Enough of this! I swear, Kassandra, I have heard too much of your evil prophecies! I will silence you with my own hands!"

His hands clasped around her neck; her consciousness wavered, and almost with relief she felt the hovering darkness take her in a great burst of light exploding somewhere inside her head.

HER THROAT ached; she put her hand weakly to it. A gentle voice said, "Lie still. Take a little of this."

She sipped at the wine, coughed and choked, but the insistent hand stayed until she swallowed again. It cleared her head; she was lying on the flagstones, and her head felt as if it had been cloven with an ax. Aeneas bent over her and said, "It's all right. Paris tried to choke you, but Hector and I stopped him. If anyone can be called mad—"

"But I must speak with him," she insisted. "It is his children —Helen's . . ."

"I'm sorry," Aeneas said, "Priam has ordered all the palace folk to bed; he says you have disturbed them all too many times and has forbidden anyone to listen to you. But if it is of any comfort to you, I have ordered Creusa to sleep out in the courtyard with the baby; and I think Hector has heeded you, too, for he says that whatever you may or may not know of the ways of the Gods, you know the ways of serpents. Now drink a little more of this and let me take you back to the Sun Lord's house. Or if you will, you may stay here and share a bed with Creusa and the baby."

She wanted to weep at the love in his voice; she knew it was this, and not any great belief in her warning, which had prompted him to this kindness. She got to her feet, feeling as if every bone in her body had been beaten with wooden cudgels. "I must go back," she said, "and see the folk in the Temple, and the serpents, and my daughter. . . ."

"Ah, yes, Creusa told me you had a little girl. A foundling, I suppose?"

"Yes, as it happens; but how did you know?"

"I know you too well to imagine you would ever disgrace your family by having a child outside of honorable marriage," he said; and she thought, *Even my own mother did not trust me as much as that.*

"Well, then, will you walk up with me?"

"Gladly," he said, "but you ran out without your cloak. Let me fetch you one, or you will be cold." He brought her a long, thick garment which she had seen Creusa wear, and she wrapped herself in it. The night had grown chilly, and even in the heavy cloak she shivered, less from cold than from some subtle danger which remained in the air. It was as if far beneath the ground she could hear the very earth groaning; a heaviness weighed intolerably on her mind and heart. She could hardly summon the strength and will to put one foot before the other, and she leaned on his arm. Then, when he bent to kiss her, she moved away.

"No, don't," she said. "You should go back—you have a wife and a child at risk to care for when it comes. . . ."

"Don't remind me of that," he said, and drew her within the curve of his arm again. After a moment he said, "I love you, Kassandra."

He was touching her gently in that way she found so disturbing, and she drew away from him.

He said softly, "My poor little love. I swear, if only I had the right, I would beat Paris for hurting you so. If he ever touches you again, I swear he'll find it the most dangerous thing he ever did. It is not his place to rule you."

"He does not realize that," she said. They had reached the great bronze gates of the Sun Lord's house, but she did not go inside. Sitting on a low wall, she said, "I have no husband, so my brother thinks it is his right to direct me. I suppose, to those who do not see and hear what I do, my prophecy must sound like madness. They try to protect themselves against it by refusing to believe. I am just as ready as anyone else to ignore what I do not want to know."

"Yes, I have seen that," said Aeneas, gently and meaningfully, and drew Kassandra against him under his cloak. She let him kiss her, but sighed with weariness, so that he let her go. He said, "We will talk of this again tomorrow, perhaps—"

"If there is a tomorrow," she said with such exhaustion that he blinked in astonishment.

"If tomorrow should not come, I will regret even beyond death that I have not known your love," he said, so passionately that Kassandra felt her heart clutch as if a fist had squeezed it.

She said in a whisper, "I think I would regret it too. but I am so tired . . ." and she began to cry.

He kissed her gently and said, "Then let us pray there will be a tomorrow, my love," and let her go. The weight of the trembling world felt as if it were about to crack and descend on her uneasy head as she watched him walk away.

Inside the Sun Lord's house, people wrapped in blankets were sleeping in the courtyards. All seemed peaceful—except for the violent throbbing in Kassandra's head, which made it seem as if her every step were taken on rolling waves. She went up to the court of the serpents; there the children slept, and Kassandra lay down beside Honey, taking the child in her arms.

She imagined the earth as a great serpent coiled about the waist of Serpent Mother, whom she saw as a woman large and stately like Queen Imandra. The ground seemed gently to rock beneath her, and as she drifted into sleep she half expected the coils to wind around her too.

Instead, she seemed to drift through clouds, acres and fields of cloud, and a great expanse of sky; and at last she drifted unseen to the surface of a great mountain, and knew that she stood alone on the summit of the forbidden mountain where the Gods of the Akhaians gathered, and heard the distant sound of thunder as They spoke. She saw Zeus Thunderer as a tall and imposing man in the prime of life, with a full graying beard; it seemed that little flares of lightning moved around His hair like a wreath as He spoke.

"Now that this absurdity of a duel between Paris and Menelaus is over, it is obvious that Menelaus has won; I suggest that We bring this foolish war to a close and get back to Our proper business."

"How can You say Menelaus has won when he did not kill Paris?" inquired Hera. She was a tall, imposing woman, rather stout, with hair dressed in a crown about Her head. "I insist that Troy be brought to destruction; its rulers and its people do not properly serve Me. Also, I am patron Goddess of Marriage; and Paris has personally insulted Me, and fled to Troy, where Helen has been received as Paris' wife without any rites or sacrifice to Me."

"All the same, they pay homage to Me, and I have blessed their love," said another Goddess in gleaming garments, Her hair crowned with roses. Kassandra knew from Her resemblance to Helen that this was the golden Aphrodite.

Hera sniffed and said, "Your rites are not those of lawful marriage."

"No, and I am proud of it," Aphrodite said, "for Yours are only the tiresome bonds of Law and Duty. Paris and Helen do honor to real love, and I am on their side."

"You would be," said Hera. "Nevertheless, I am Queen of the Immortals, and it is My privilege to demand the destruction of Troy."

*Zeus looked distressed at Her tone, as harried as Kassandra
had seen Priam look when his women were arguing. He said, "My
dear Hera, no one questions Your right to demand that. But it
must be done properly; We cannot simply destroy the city. If the
Trojans can defend their city, they cannot simply have it taken
from them. Athene—"*

*Kassandra saw the helmeted Battle Maiden, with Her flash-
ing spear like an Amazon's, as Zeus beckoned to Her. But it was
the regal Hera who spoke:*

*"Go, My child, and counsel the Akhaians; they are dis-
heartened and about to sail away. Bid them resume the fighting,
and tell them that I, Hera, will not allow them to be defeated."*

*"This seems to be against all wisdom," the tall and solemn
Athene said gently, "for the Trojans have done no wrong. And
the Akhaians are proud. If You give them the city of Troy, I tell
You, they will commit such evil acts in their pride and wickedness that they will offend every God known to mankind. But I
have no choice but to obey Your voice, Royal Lady." She bowed
to Hera and flew away, and Kassandra, watching the flaming
light of Her helmet, like a comet, found herself standing on the
plain before the city of Troy where Athene came to rest. Before
Her, a great white stallion blocked Athene's way to the Akhaian
camp.*

*Athene said, "Poseidon Earth Shaker, what do You do here?"
and the figure of the horse rippled like an image underwater and
became first a Kentaur—half man, half horse—then a tall and
strong man with seaweed for hair.*

*Poseidon, brother of Zeus, seemed to speak with His godly
Brother's thundering voice.*

*"You have been sent to betray My city; I will not let You
enter it." As He spoke, He stamped his foot; a great roll of thunder followed, and the ground shook. . . .*

Kassandra awoke in the serpent court, with the two children still sleeping at her side. But the ground was rippling like
water, and she could hear the sound of thunder—or was it
Poseidon's stamping feet? She screamed aloud, and Honey woke
and began to whimper. Kassandra sheltered the child in her
arms and watched the great arch above the gates rocking back

and forth in the gray light of dawn; then it crashed to the ground.

In the corner of the courtyard a lamp had been placed; it rocked and fell over, and a tongue of flame licked at the cloth on which it stood. Kassandra leaped up and extinguished the fire. All over the Temple there were cries and shrieks of terror. The ground was heaving upward and buckling; a great crack opened in the earth, raced across the courtyard and closed again. Kassandra watched silently, feeling the great weight in her mind dissolve. It had come; she was delivered of it.

If they had sacrificed to Poseidon, might He have held back His hand? She did not know and could not guess. She put down the jug of water with which she had doused the fire, and ran down through the courts. Several of the buildings had indeed collapsed, including the dormitory where the maiden priestesses would have been sleeping; so had the post that supported one of the bronze gates of the Sun Lord's house, which now hung twisted on its hinges. The Temple was a ruin. Kassandra looked down into the city from the gap at the gates; houses had fallen into rubble and fires were springing up everywhere.

Should she go down into the palace? No; she had given her warning there, and Priam had forbidden any to heed her; neither he nor Paris was likely to be well pleased if she came saying "I told you so." *But she had. Why were people so unwilling to hear truth spoken?*

Slowly she went back into the Temple of Apollo. At least her own people had listened to her warning; it seemed that all had survived, and the few fires had quickly been put out. She could do no good in Priam's palace. She went back to the children. They would have been frightened by the quake and would need her.

3

THE REBUILDING of the Sun Lord's house began almost at once. So many buildings had been destroyed, and some on such a scale that, Kassandra thought, it would demand the fabulous reputed strength of the Titans to set the walls up again. Some of the great stones could not be restored with the labor now obtainable; too many of the able-bodied men in the city were out there fighting Akhaians under Hector's command.

Thanks to Kassandra's timely warning, no lives had been lost in Apollo's Temple. A few of the priests had been injured—broken legs, twisted shoulders, a shattered ankle—by falling over stones that were no longer where they were supposed to be, and there were a good many burns incurred in the extinguishing of fires. One or two of the serpents had escaped in the confusion, or taken refuge under fallen stones, and had not yet been found. One of the oldest priestesses had gone mad with fright and had not spoken a rational word since; the others treated her with herbal potions and played soothing music, but the most experienced healers felt it unlikely that she would ever fully recover her wits.

Still, comparatively, Apollo's household had escaped lightly. In the Temple of the Maiden, it was said, some priestesses had died when the roof of their dormitory fell in. No one knew how many, and Kassandra was frantic about her sister Polyxena, but had no leisure to seek news of her. She comforted herself with the thought that if Polyxena was dead, word would be sent to her.

As always, the city's poorest districts, with their flimsy wooden houses and inadequately guarded open fires, had suffered the most. Had the quake come a few hours earlier the havoc would have been worse, but since the hour was late, fires lighted for cooking the evening meal had mostly been extinguished.

Still, a dreadful number of dead lay in the streets, except where the burning houses had given them funeral pyres. Some corpses still were lodged under fallen buildings which would have to be torn down to recover them, as the ghosts of the unburied dead all too frequently sent pestilence in revenge. The priests of Apollo worked night and day, but it would take time, and everyone feared the vengeance of so many unburied corpses.

Nor had Priam's palace escaped unscathed. The buildings were of Titan stone that had resisted even the strength of Poseidon's fury, but one room had collapsed—the room where the three sons of Paris and Helen were sleeping. Most of Priam's family, including Paris himself and Helen, were uninjured.

Helen's son by Menelaus, young Nikos, had been hiding with his playmate Astyanax from their nurses. The two children had been sleeping in a courtyard out-of-doors (which they had actually been forbidden to do), and both boys had escaped unhurt—and unpunished. Still, the palace was plunged into grief for Paris' sons, and the truce had been briefly extended for the rites and burial of the children.

Kassandra went down to join in the mourning in the women's quarters of the palace—since none of the boys had been as old as seven, the warriors would take no official notice of their death, little children still being under the women's care. Paris was there, attempting to comfort Helen. She looked pale and weary, and Nikos, who had been officially committed to his father's care only a few days before, was there too, as if to remind his mother that she still had a son.

Helen came at once to Kassandra and embraced her.

"You tried to warn me, Sister, and I am grateful to you."

"I am so sorry," Kassandra said. "I only wish—"

"I know," Helen said. "This grief is not new to me. My second daughter did not live; she was a year younger than Hermione, and two years older than Nikos. She never breathed, and when Nikos was born strong and healthy, so that I had both a Queen for Sparta and a son for Menelaus to bring up as a warrior, I swore I would bear no more children; but nothing went as I had decided."

"It seldom does, in this world of mortals," Kassandra said.

Paris approached them in time to hear this and said with an angry glare at Kassandra, "So have you come to gloat to us?"

"No," she said wearily, "only to tell you how very sorry I am."

"We need not your sympathy, you crow of ill omen!" Paris said wrathfully. "Your very presence brings us more evil fortune!"

"Be quiet, Paris! For shame!" Helen said. "Have you forgotten that she came to try to warn us of Poseidon's wrath? Or what welcome she had for her pains?"

Paris only scowled; but Kassandra thought he did look somewhat ashamed. Well, she could live without his good opinion; she would rather have Helen's.

The children were duly cremated and their ashes properly entombed. The truce lasted two more days and then was broken by a Trojan captain (he, like the Akhaian who ended the truce before, said that one of the Gods had prompted him, though he refused to say which one), who let off an arrow and wounded Menelaus, painfully, but (unfortunately, Priam said) not fatally. If Menelaus had been killed, the King said, the Akhaians would have had a good excuse to end the war and go home. Kassandra was not so sure; perhaps the Gods were really eager to destroy the city as she had seen in her—had it been only a dream?

Only the women were troubled by the end of the truce; Hector, Kassandra thought, was glad to get back to the fighting. In his chariot he led forth the Trojan armies the next day, riding up and down the long line of foot soldiers, encouraging them while the Akhaians were gathering for battle. The women, as usual, watched from the wall.

"Hector is certainly the finest charioteer," said Andromache, and Creusa laughed.

"You mean he *has* the finest charioteer," she said, "and I think Aeneas comes at least close to that. Who is Hector's charioteer? He drives like the wind—or a fiend."

"Troilus, Priam's youngest son," Andromache said. "He wanted to take part in the fighting, but Hector wanted the boy under his own eyes. He's worried because he is no more than twelve, and still unseasoned in battle."

"Does Hector really think Troilus will be safer in his chariot? It seems to me that that is where the fighting will be thickest, and certainly Hector will have no leisure to protect him," Kassandra said, but Andromache only shrugged. "Don't ask me what Hector thinks," she said.

Of course, Kassandra thought, Troilus was nothing to her, only her husband's youngest brother. She would mourn his death, but only in the same way that she grieved for Helen's children; from family duty, no more.

Helen still looked wasted and worn with sorrow, her eyes red and burning, her hair lusterless; she had hardly troubled to pull it back out of her eyes, much less to scent it and brush it with oil. She wore an old bedraggled gown; it was all but impossible to recall the incredible glowing beauty that had inhabited her as the Goddess of Love. Yet Kassandra remembered, with the tenderness she always felt for her sister-in-law. Was this a sign of Paris' neglect? Was it that he cared so little for his children? She could guess Helen was grateful that her firstborn had not been lost in the earthquake, yet she sensed that Paris' sons were dearer to Helen than the son she had borne Menelaus.

She turned her eyes down to the battlefield, where Aeneas was riding up and down the line in his spendid chariot, calling out what she imagined was a challenge. Battle among opposing armies, she had seen, often took the form of a series of duels between champions. It was not at all like the pitched battles she had fought when she rode with the Amazons, battles that were a muddle of fighting in which you killed as many as you could, any way you could.

"There," said Creusa, "he has found someone to take his challenge. Who is that?"

"Diomedes," said Helen.

"The one who exchanged armor."

"The same, yes," Andromache said; "but I think Aeneas is a stronger fighter, certainly with that chariot and those horses."

"His mother was a priestess of Aphrodite—some say Aphrodite's self," Creusa said, "and she gifted him with these horses when he came to Troy. . . . Look, what's going on?"

Below them, Diomedes had ridden like a madman at

Aeneas, and managed with his spear to overturn the chariot, tumbling Aeneas out on the ground. Creusa screamed, but her husband sprang to his feet, evidently unharmed, his sword out and ready. But Diomedes had cut the harness of the horses and seized their reins; it was obvious from his gestures that he claimed horses and chariot as his prize. Aeneas shouted in protest and rage, so loudly that the women could clearly hear his voice, but not the words. He turned on Diomedes, and as they watched, he seemed before their eyes to grow taller, and his head to glow with a shining aura; it flashed through Kassandra's mind, *Why, I did not know his hair is the same color as Helen's!* Then she knew that she saw before her the beautiful Goddess Herself, turning on Diomedes in the fury of an Immortal. Diomedes visibly flinched—he had not been prepared for this. But his courage did not fail; he dashed at the towering form of Aphrodite and thrust with his sword, wounding the form of the Goddess in the hand.

Abruptly it was again Aeneas who stood on the field, screaming like a woman and shaking his hand, from which blood was pouring. Diomedes did not lose the advantage, but put up shield and sword in defense. Aeneas, however, attacked strongly, and after a moment Diomedes went down full length on the ground; a few seconds later, Agamemnon and four of his men were backing up Diomedes, driving Aeneas off in a fury of blows. Hector's chariot dashed by, and Hector jumped to the ground, briefly engaged Agamemnon in a wild exchange of swordplay and lifted Aeneas into his chariot. They dashed back toward the gates of Troy, while a handful of Hector's soldiers drove off Agamemnon and his men from Aeneas' chariot and managed to recapture the horses.

"He's hurt," Creusa cried, and ran down the stairs. The other women followed in haste, just in time to greet Hector's chariot. Hector swung down and motioned them away.

"Get back so we can get these gates closed, unless you want Agamemnon and half the Akhaian army in here," he said; the women surged back and the men joined hands pushing the gates closed, cutting down one luckless Akhaian soldier who was trapped inside.

"Throw him over the wall to his friends," Hector said. "They want him, and we don't."

Creusa was holding Aeneas tightly, summoning healers to bandage up his hand. He seemed dazed; but when Kassandra came and took over the bandaging, he smiled up at her and asked, "What happened?"

"If you don't know," said Hector, "how are we to tell? You were fighting Diomedes and suddenly you stopped . . ."

"It was not you but Aphrodite," Helen said. "She fought through you."

Aeneas chuckled. "Well, I don't remember anything except being in a rage at Diomedes for trying to claim my chariot and horses; the next thing I remember, my hand was bleeding and I heard someone scream—"

"That was you," Hector said; "or the Goddess."

Aeneas laughed. "The Beautiful One," he said, "screaming all the way back to Olympos, I daresay, to sit in Zeus Thunderer's lap and tell Him all about the nasty men fighting. I hope the Thunderer commands Her in no uncertain terms to stay off the battlefield from now on; it's no place for ladies—not even when they're Goddesses," he added.

Kassandra continued tying up his hand.

His eyes smiled at her. To her he still bore the glamour of the Goddess, and her heart beat faster. If he sought her again, she knew she would not be able to resist him. *Is this the revenge of the Goddess because I would not serve Her? Has Aphrodite conquered me,* she wondered, *when Apollo could not?*

She had finished the bandaging; it was with reluctance that she let go of his hand. There was a little stall nearby where the soldiers bought bread and wine at midday; Hector went to it and brought back two goblets of wine and gave one to Aeneas, who shrugged it away. Creusa said, "Drink it; you have lost blood," and he shook his head.

"I've cut myself worse and lost more blood shaving," he said; but he sipped at the wine after all, and laughed. "I wonder if they will tell the same mad tales as they did when the Goddess appeared when Paris fought Menelaus."

"No doubt," Kassandra said. He was looking straight at her. "The Akhaians seem to like that kind of story."

"Well, the Gods will do as They will, and not as we ask Them to," Aeneas said. "Yet by my divine ancestress, I wish They would go away and let us get on with the war. It's not Their business, it's ours."

"I think perhaps it is Their business more than ours," Helen said, "and we have very little to say about it."

"But why? Why should the Gods care who wins a mortals' war?" Andromache asked.

Hector shrugged. "Why not?"

And to that not even Kassandra ventured an answer.

"There was a time," Hector said, "when I believed that we were altogether at the mercy of the Akhaian troops. But now that Akhilles has abandoned them—"

"That can hardly go on for long," Helen said. "I cannot imagine the great Akhilles remaining for long sulking in his tent like a little boy . . . "

"But that is exactly what Akhilles is like," Aeneas said. "A cruel, arrogant schoolboy. There might be something great and heroic about falling to a madman, but a brainsick child is something else."

Hector said without changing expression, "We must not question the decrees of the Gods."

"If the Gods make decisions that would be set aside as the decisions of the mad," Aeneas replied, "perhaps They are not to be obeyed blindly. Perhaps"—but he lowered his voice and looked around fearfully as he spoke—"perhaps They are testing us to see if we have the wit to stand against Them."

"Maybe They are headstrong like Akhilles," Helen said, "and if They cannot have Their own way in a game They will smash all the playthings."

"I think it is like that," Hector said; "and we are the playthings."

4

FOR THE NEXT few days Kassandra heard the war news from the old cake-woman. It seemed that Akhilles remained in his tent, never showing his face even to encourage his companions; and the war dragged on without much change. Hector fought a prolonged duel with Ajax; they battled till it became too dark to continue, and neither had the advantage. Agamemnon tried a bluff, threatening to pull out of the war too, if Akhilles would not fight; but the Akhaians greeted this threat with so much glee, rushing for their ships and starting to pack up their gear, that he had to spend much of the next day coaxing his men to come back, offering them gifts and bribes to continue fighting.

Kassandra drifted that night in confused dreams of Olympos. Hera, tall and proud, stood and demanded help in destroying the city of Troy.

"Zeus has forbidden Us to intervene," said the tall Athene, somber and sad, "although He has allowed Me to counsel the Trojans, if they will but listen to My wisdom. Why do You hate them so fanatically, Hera? Are You still jealous because Paris did not award the crown of beauty to You? What did You expect? Aphrodite is, after all, the Goddess of Beauty; I learned long ago that I could not compete with Her. And why should You care what a mortal thinks?

"Then You, Poseidon!" The proud Lady turned to the hairy Sea-God, thickset, bearded, muscled like a swimmer. "Let Me have Your help in destroying the walls of Troy. Zeus has ordained it, and when it is done He will not be angry."

"Not I," said Poseidon. "Not till the time ordained has come. I know better than to conspire with a woman against the will of Her husband."

Thunder flashed as Hera stamped Her foot and cried out, "You will regret this!" But Poseidon had taken the form of a great white stallion and galloped away along the shore; the pounding of His hooves sounded like the crash of waves along the seawall the Akhaians had built.

Kassandra woke in dread, hearing the sound of Poseidon's rage, wondering if it presaged another earthquake; but all was quiet in the Temple, and at last she slept again. In the morning she found that a few vases and dishes had fallen from tables and shelves, and a lamp had overturned, but had burned itself out on the stone floor without setting anything afire; if there had been an earthquake, it had been a very small one, hardly more than a shrug of the God's shoulders. The Immortals seemed to have the same unresolved squabbles as those inconclusive duels between the soldiers, which settled nothing. Well, they—the soldiers—were only human and could hardly be blamed for behaving foolishly; but Kassandra would have thought the Gods would have something better to do.

She resolved that this day she would stay away from the city wall; she had seen enough of these duels, and she supposed that with Akhilles still hiding in his tent, there would be nothing happening yet again. It was surprising, she thought, how much time she had wasted of late gossiping with the other women watching from the walls.

Honey was outgrowing her frocks. Kassandra spent the morning looking through her own possessions and inquiring of the priestesses; perhaps there would be something suitable among the offerings that she could use to make her daughter some clothes. She was given a piece of saffron-dyed material (which she thought would look pretty with the little girl's dark curls and lively dark eyes) from which she could fashion a gown and kerchief. The child would still need sandals; she was running everywhere now, and after the big earthquake the courts were full of rubbish on which she could hurt her feet. Kassandra started to call a servant to go to the market to fetch leather for sandals, then decided to go herself and take the child.

Honey was big enough now to scamper along beside her, and to understand that she was to have sandals like a big girl; Kassandra enjoyed the feeling of the small chubby hand in hers. Sagely she examined the sandals displayed for sale; the prices were not, it seemed, exorbitant. She arranged to try a sturdy pair on the child, and finding them well built and satisfactorily fitting the little feet, allowed Honey to choose which pattern she liked best.

"And for you, Lady?" the sandalmaker asked. By habit Kassandra started to say no, then followed the man's gaze to her feet. Her sandals were much worn, thinning at the sole, and one strap mended and remended. Well, after all, she had worn them to Colchis and back.

"Well, these sandals have been halfway around the world; I suppose they deserve to be honorably put out to pasture like an old mare," she said, and allowed him to show her several pairs, all of which were too large. At last he measured her foot and said, "The Lady has such a little foot; I must make a pair to your measure."

"I did not design my own foot," Kassandra said, "but if you will make me a pair by this pattern"—she indicated the most nearly fitting of the sandals he had shown her—"that will do nicely. Meanwhile, I suppose you can simply mend the strap of these yet again."

"I don't think it will hold together; it has been sewn so often," he protested. "If the Lady will be content to wait in my humble shop but half an hour, the new ones will be ready. May I send for a glass of wine for you? A slice of melon? Some other refreshment? No? Something for the child?"

"No, thank you," Kassandra said; Honey too must learn to wait patiently when necessary. She stood watching the man trimming the soles of the sandals that had been just a little too large, repositioning the straps and stitching them with his thimble and heavy leather needle. He had an iron needle, which, she thought, must be why he did such fast work; bronze needles could not pierce the leather so readily. She wondered whether he had had it smuggled in past the blockade, or whether he traded with the Akhaians. It was probably better not to know. Such commerce was forbidden; but if Priam's city wardens were to thrust into prison everyone who traded illegally, there would be no trading at all, and commerce in the city would come completely to a halt.

Already many foodstuffs were hard to come by after the long siege; what had saved the city was the gardens inside the walls, where grapevines and olive trees were the sources of wine and oil, and vegetables could be grown. Many houses had caged doves or rabbits, previously kept for sacrifice; now these were eaten, and kept away the most acute hunger. Bread was in short supply except for the soldiers' mess and the palace, though some wagons of grain had been brought in overland, avoiding the Argive ships, during the truce.

Now that the truce was officially over, would it mean a tightening of the siege? Or would the Akhaians get tired of fighting without Akhilles, and go away again? That might be the best that could happen.

But if they felt they had the Gods on their side—and there Kassandra's thoughts broke off in the old confusion: why should the Gods meddle in men's affairs? Well, Hector's answer had been simply Why not? Anyway, she had been asking that same question since the beginning of the war, and she had had no answer—except in her dreams. *Dreams! what good were they?*

Yet her dreams had sent her warning of the great earthquake; she should, then, trust them. Anyway, she had no choice. The dreams were *there*; she ignored them at her own peril—and for all she knew, the peril of Troy and her world.

She had drifted into reverie when she heard a great commotion in the streets; Hector's chariot raced down through the city toward the lower gates. To Kassandra, watching from her bench inside the sandalmaker's shop, it seemed that half the population of Troy emptied itself into the streets to watch. After so long, one would think they would take it for granted and go on about their business. But there was as much enthusiasm evident as on the first day he had paraded before his troops. Well, that was nice for Hector, she thought, not entirely without sarcasm, and would have turned away; but the sandalmaker brought her new sandals and stood watching Hector's chariot instead of helping her put them on.

"He drives his chariot like the very Battle-God himself," he remarked. "Princess, he is your brother?"

"Yes; the son of both my mother and my father," she replied.

"Tell me, what is he like? Is he truly as much a hero as he seems?"

"He is certainly brave and a valorous fighter," she said. *But was it bravery or simply a lack of imagination? Paris could sim-*

ulate bravery, *but only because he feared being thought a coward more than whatever else it was he feared.* "But more than that," she said, "Hector is a good man, apart from being a good fighter. He has other virtues than bravery." The man looked a little startled, as if he could not imagine any other virtues. "I mean he would be worthy to admire even if there were no war."

And that, she thought, could hardly be said of any of her other brothers; they seemed little more than animate weapons, without much thought for what they were doing or why. Paris had some good qualities—although he seldom showed them to a sister: he was kind to Helen, showed kindness as well as respect to his aging parents and had been a loving father to his children while they lived. He was kind even to Helen's son by Menelaus. Aeneas too had this kind of character—*or do I think so only because I love him?* she asked herself. The sandalmaker still lauding Hector's attributes, Kassandra said, "He will be pleased to know that he is so well thought of in the city" (which certainly was true), paid for her purchases and stepped out into the street. She immediately had to snatch Honey out from under the feet of the crowds blocking the way and surging back from the street where four chariots, driven by Aeneas, Paris, Deiphobos and the Thracian captain Glaucus, were thundering down in the wake of Hector's toward the great gate.

Had Priam decided to send his best champions against the Akhaians regardless of the fact that Akhilles was not with them —or in hopes of luring Akhilles forth? The thought revived her curiosity; Honey was already trying to run after the crowd, so Kassandra went down toward the wall and once there, up the stairs inside to the women's favorite observation point.

As she had expected, she found Helen, Andromache and Creusa there with Hecuba. They all greeted her with affection. Helen, she observed, looked less worn. Soon she confided to Kassandra that she believed she was pregnant again.

Andromache said, "I do not see how any woman could in good conscience bring a child into the world when there is this great war. I said so to Hector, but he only answered that this is when children are most needed."

"And children die when there is no war," Helen said; "I lost my second son to a midwife's carelessness, and three of my sons died in an earthquake. They could have fallen to their death bird's-nesting on the rocks, or been trampled by an escaped bull at the games. There is no safety for children anywhere in this mortal world; but if we all decided not to bear children because of that, where would the world be?"

"Ah, you have more courage than I," said Andromache. "Just as Paris is more daring with his chariot than Hector—look how he races out of the great gate!"

It was hard to tell which man was driving most wildly; all five chariots exploded out of the gate almost at once, Hector's foot soldiers streaming after them. The Akhaians had not yet formed any battle lines; Kassandra saw the chaos and disorder of the Argive camp as the troops sprang out between their tents, yelling, searching for weapons. The line of chariots thundered down on the camp, and on through. Now she saw that each chariot bore a brazier of coals and something else—tar? pitch? —and an archer swiftly preparing arrows by dipping them into the blazing stuff, and shooting at the lines of ships that lay in the harbor beyond the camp. For a few minutes, while trying to bring down the chariots, the Akhaians did not see the objective of the attack; then a great cry of rage rang out—but by this time the chariots were actually on the beach and several of the ships already ablaze.

Hector's foot soldiers were well organized, attacking the still-surprised troops of Agamemnon.

Ship after ship, each with a blazing arrow in the folds of its furled sails, took fire, with sailors unready to fight the flames jumping overboard and adding to the confusion. Now Hector's men turned their attention from the ships to the armies' tents. There were screams and immense confusion all through the camp as men tried halfheartedly to organize ways of fighting the inferno and tended to the wounded. One of the ships (she heard later it had a cargo of oil) had already burned to the waterline and sunk. A great cheer went up from Hector's men.

The Trojan chariots were surrounded now by Akhaian foot soldiers trying to pull the riders down; but the archers continued to shoot their fire-arrows into the tents until the women on the wall could not see into the Akhaian camp at all through the smoke. Another ship sagged and settled down into the harbor, the flames subsiding in the water.

The women cheered; then there was a commotion among the guards along the wall, and Trojan soldiers ran past them to a vantage point where some archers were stationed. There were loud yells, a combination of cheers and jeering cries, and a great crash. When the captain of archers came back, Andromache asked what had happened. Saluting her respectfully, he said, "At first we thought it was Akhilles himself and that he'd picked this time for a diversion. 'Twasn't him, though; it was that friend of his—what's his name—Patroklos; climbed right up the west wall where there're stones loose from the earthquake."

"Did you get him?" Andromache asked.

"No chance, Lady; we sent a good few arrows whizzing round his head, though, and he lost his balance and slid down. Then his archers returned our fire and covered him while he showed us a good pair of legs back to their camp," the soldier replied. "Shame we missed him; if he'd wound up with an arrow through his gullet, maybe Akhilles *would* get discouraged and take off home."

"Never mind," Andromache said; "you did the best you could. And at least he didn't get into the city."

"Begging your pardon, Lady, *best we could* won't be good enough for Prince Hector," said the soldier pessimistically. "But I reckon you're right: nothing to do about it now, and no use worrying about what we can't mend. Maybe he'll give us another chance one day and we'll pick him off."

"May the War-God grant it," said Andromache. The women looked out over the wall again; the chariots had withdrawn now from the camp and were racing back toward the gates of Troy; Kassandra, though she could not at this distance distinguish one chariot from another, counted them and noted that they were all there. The raid on the ships, then, had been a total success.

Below them the watchman shouted, "Ready there to open the gates!" and they heard the creaking of the ropes that opened the great gate. Helen and Andromache went down the stairs to greet their husbands; the other women remained behind.

Hecuba approached Kassandra, and she asked, "The King was not with the chariots?"

"Oh, no, Kassandra," said her mother; "his hands no longer serve him to drive. The healer-priests have treated him with their healing oils and spells, but every day it grows worse. He can hardly tie the laces of his sandals."

"I am sorry to hear it," Kassandra said; "but for old age, Mother, there are no healing spells, even for a King."

"Nor, I suppose, for a Queen," Hecuba said, and Kassandra, looking sharply at her, realized how frail her mother was, her back stooped and so thin that her bones seemed to protrude from the skin. Her complexion had always seemed fresh and bright; now it was grayish and sallow, and her hair a dirty streaked yellowish-white. Even her eyes seemed to have faded.

"You are not well, Mother."

"Well enough; I am much more troubled about your father," Hecuba said. "And Creusa; she is pregnant again, and there is likely to be a scarcity of nourishing food in the city this winter. The crops were not good, and the Akhaians burned so much of what there was."

"There is food enough in the Sun Lord's house," Kassandra said. "What is shared out for me and for Honey is always more than we can eat; I will try to see that Creusa has enough."

"You are good," Hecuba said gently, reaching out to stroke her hair; her mother had rarely caressed her since she was a very small child, and Kassandra felt warmed.

"We have not only food but healing herbs in plenty; you must always come to me if anyone at the palace is ill or in want," she said. "It is taken for granted that we'll share what we have with our families. I will send some herbs for Father, and you must steep them in hot water, and soak a cloth, and apply the hot cloth to his hands. It may not cure him, but it will ease his pain."

Hecuba looked past her to Honey, who was sitting on the wall, playing with some pebbles. Kassandra remembered a similar game when she was very small; she and her sisters, the other daughters of the royal house, would choose nice round little stones and set them in niches on the wall to bake, as if they were buns or loaves, examining them every few minutes to see if they were cooked enough. She smiled at the memory.

The chariots were inside the walls now, and the gates closing. Hecuba asked, "Will you come and dine at the palace? Though you will surely be better fed in the Sun Lord's house . . ."

"I think not tonight," Kassandra said, "though I thank you; I will send the herbs down by a messenger. I hope they do Father good—we cannot spare his strength in these days. Not even Hector is fit to rule Troy, even if he should survive his father." She stopped herself, but Hecuba had heard and stared at her in shock.

She did not speak. Kassandra knew what she was thinking:

So she believes that Hector may die before his father, old and ill as Priam is. What more has she seen?

The charioteers had left their chariots; Hector and Paris, accompanied by their wives, came up the stairs, and Aeneas joined Creusa. Kassandra picked up Honey; if she did not intend to join them this night at the palace, it was time to take her leave.

Creusa came to her and said, "I will walk with you to the Sun Lord's house, sister."

"I would be glad of your company; but the sun is still high in the sky. I need no escort," Kassandra protested. "You should not tire yourself with that long climb."

"I will come," Creusa insisted. "I would like to speak with you."

"Very well, then; as I said, I am glad of your company," Kassandra said. Creusa gave her small daughter to a servant, instructing the woman to take her home, and to feed her if Creusa had not returned by her suppertime; then she joined Kassandra, who was tying on Honey's broad-brimmed hat against the sun.

"She is well grown for her age," she said. "How old is she now? When was she born?"

"I am sure Mother has told you that I am not certain,"

Kassandra said, "but she cannot have been more than a few days old when I found her, and I left Colchis near the middle of last winter."

"Nearly a year then; she must be close to my own daughter in age," Creusa said; "yet she is taller and stronger, and already walking beside you like a big girl. Little Kassandra still crawls on all fours like a puppy."

"Well, those who know children best say that each one walks and talks when the time is right for her—some early, some late," Kassandra replied. "Mother says I was early to walk and talk, and I remember things that must have happened no later than my second summer."

"That's true," Creusa said. "Astyanax did not walk or even talk till he was past two years old; I know Andromache was beginning to wonder if he had all his wits."

"That must have been very worrying," Kassandra agreed. She felt confused; surely Creusa had not undertaken this long climb to speak with her about the growth and feeding of little children, when the palace was filled with so many nurses to consult.

Whatever it was, Creusa was finding it hard to come to the point; but just as Kassandra was beginning to wonder if Creusa had somehow found out what she had said to Aeneas (but how? some spying servant? She would swear they had not been overheard) and to feel vaguely guilty, Creusa said, "You are a priestess and they say you are a prophetess; it was you who gave warning of the great earthquake, was it not?"

"I thought you were there when I gave the warning," Kassandra said.

"No; Aeneas came and told me not to sleep under a roof that night, and to take the children outdoors," her sister said. "What have you foreseen?"

Creusa knows as well as I do that I have seen death, and the destruction of Troy, she thought, but she was sure her sister had some reason beyond the ordinary for asking. She said, hesitating, "Are you sure you want to know? Priam has forbidden anyone to listen to my prophecies. It might be better not to anger him."

"Let me tell you, then, why I ask," said Creusa. "Aeneas told me that you prophesied that he would survive the fall of Troy."

"Yes," said Kassandra, embarrassed. "It seems the Gods have work for him elsewhere; for I have seen him departing unharmed, and behind him Troy in flames."

Creusa's hands flew to her bosom in a strange gesture. "Is this true?"

"Do you believe I would lie about it?"

"No, no, of course not; but why should he be chosen to be spared when so many will die?"

"I do not know; why were you and your children spared when Helen lost three sons in the great quake?"

"Because Aeneas heeded your warning and Paris would not."

"That is not what I meant," Kassandra said. "No one can say why the Gods choose one to die and another to live; and perhaps those who live may not be the most fortunate."

I wish I were sure that only death awaited me, she thought, but she did not say so to Creusa.

"Aeneas has ordered me to leave the city as soon as I can, and take the children," Creusa said. "I am to go, perhaps, to Crete, to Knossos or even farther. I was thinking I should refuse to go, to say that my place was at his side, come war or death; but if it is true that he is certain to survive, then I can understand why he wants me to go . . . . so that we may meet in safer country when the war is over."

"I am sure he is thinking only of your safety."

"He has been strange lately; I wondered if he had found himself another woman and wanted me out of the way."

Kassandra said through a dry mouth, "Even if it should be so, would it matter? Since almost everyone in the city is to die in its fall . . ."

"No, I suppose not; if one of them can make him happy for a little time," Creusa said, "and they are all going to die anyway —why should I care? So you think I should go?"

"I cannot tell you that; I can say only that there are few who will survive the city's fall," Kassandra said.

"But is it safe to travel with a child so small?"

"Honey could not have been more than a few days old when I found her, and she survived and thrived. Children are stronger than we think."

"I thought only that perhaps he wished to be rid of me," Creusa said. "But you have made me understand why it is best that I should go. Thank you, Sister." Unexpectedly, she put her arms around Kassandra and hugged her hard. "You too should forsake the city before it is too late. You did not make this war with the damned Akhaians, and there is no reason you should perish with the city. I will ask Aeneas to arrange that you too be sent away."

"No," Kassandra said; "it seems that this is my destiny, and I must abide it."

"Aeneas speaks well of you, Kassandra," Creusa said. "He told me once you were more clever than all of Priam's officers together, and that if you were in command we might even win this war."

Kassandra laughed uneasily and said, "He thinks too well of me, then. But you must go, Creusa; gather together your possessions and be ready to depart whenever he can find you a ship, or whatever means he may find to take you and the children to safety."

Creusa embraced her again. She said, "If I am to depart soon, we may not meet again. But wherever destiny may take you, Sister, I wish you well; and if Troy truly does fall, I pray that the Gods may preserve you."

"And you," Kassandra said, kissing her cheek; and so they parted. Kassandra watched her sister out of sight, knowing in her heart that she would never see Creusa again.

5

SINCE THE BATTLE when five of the Akhaian ships had been burned to the waterline and others greatly damaged, the Akhaians had drawn their blockade so tight that—as Hector said—a crab could not have crawled into the city. For that reason, Aeneas made no attempt to get Creusa away by sea; she was sent in a cart around to the landward side, and along the coast for many miles past the blockade, where a ship would take her first to Egypt and then to Crete. Kassandra watched her depart, and thought that if Priam had any sense he would order all the women and children out of the city. However, she said nothing; she had done her best to give warning.

Even the landward side of the city was no longer completely safe. A wagonload of iron weapons from Colchis was intercepted and brought into the Argive camp with great celebration. Soon after, a small army of Thracians, coming overland to join Priam's forces, was waylaid by Akhaian captains—rumor said by Agamemnon and Odysseus themselves: all the horses were stolen, and the Thracian guards murdered.

"This isn't war," Hector said; "this is an atrocity. The Thracians were not yet part of Troy's armies and Agamemnon had no quarrel with them."

"And now he never will have," said Paris cynically.

This touched off another attack by the Akhaians, led by Patroklos, who again climbed the walls at the head of his own men; the Trojans managed to repel them, and Patroklos was reported wounded, although not seriously.

At Kassandra's earnest petition, the people of the Sun Lord's house built an altar and sacrificed two of Priam's finest horses to Poseidon. Another earthquake could pull down every wall and gate of Troy and leave the city open to the besieging forces of the Akhaians. This was now Kassandra's only fear; she knew it must come, but if the Trojans put all their efforts into the placating of Poseidon, He might still hold His hand.

The Akhaian forces fought without their greatest warrior; Akhilles still remained in his tent. Now and again he would come forth—not dressed for battle—and walk about the camp, morosely alone or in company with Patroklos, but what they talked of, no one could say. Rumors brought by spies said that Agamemnon had gone to Akhilles and offered him first choice of all the city's spoils for himself and his men, but Akhilles had answered only that he no longer trusted any offer Agamemnon might make.

"Can't blame him," Hector said. "I wouldn't trust Agamemnon as far as I could heave him with one thumb. Damned convenient for us, though, this quarrel in the enemy camp; while they're fighting each other, we have time to repair our walls and get our defenses together. If they ever make it up, and decide to work together, then God help Troy."

"Which God?" Priam asked.

"Any God they haven't already bribed to be on their side," Hector said. "Suppose Aeneas and I got into some sort of fight, and refused to work together?"

"I hope that we never find out," Aeneas said, "for I suspect that on that day we would have doomed ourselves more quickly than the Gods could doom us."

Priam pushed restlessly at his plate, on which were only a sparse assortment of vegetables and some coarse bread.

"Perhaps we might arrange a hunt on the landward side," he said. "I would be glad of some venison or even rabbit."

"I had not thought I would hear you say that, Father. We were glutted with meat for so long when the goats had to be slaughtered for lack of fodder; we kept only a few for milk for the smallest children," Hector said. "The pigs can eat what is left from the tables, and there are still some acorns in the groves; but now there is little left. Perhaps we can hunt. . . ."

"I think the pigs should be killed too," said Deiphobos. "This winter we will need the acorns for bread; we should set all the young people not old enough to fight to gathering them and laying them away. It will be a hungry winter, whatever we do or do not do."

"What is being done in the Sun Lord's house?" asked Aeneas. "You sit there so still and wise, Kassandra. What says Apollo's wisdom?"

"It does not matter what you do." Kassandra spoke without thinking. "By winter Troy will have no more need of food."

Paris took one great stride toward her. He roared, "I warned you, Sister, what I would do if you came here again peddling your evil news!"

Aeneas caught his arm in mid-swing.

"Strike someone your own size," he snarled; "or strike at me, for I asked the question which prompted the answer you do not want to hear!" He added gently, "Is it so bad, Kassandra?"

"I do not know," she said, staring helplessly at them. "It might even be that the Akhaians will be gone, and there will be no more need to hoard food. . . ."

"But you do not think so," he said.

She shook her head; they were all staring at her now. "But things will not go on as they are now for long, that I know. A change will come very soon."

It was growing late; Aeneas rose. "I will go and sleep in the camp with the soldiers," he said, "since my wife and children have gone."

Hector said, "I suppose I should send away Andromache and the boy, if there is so much danger here."

Paris said, "Now you see why I feel that Kassandra should be silenced at any cost; she is spreading so much hopelessness inside Troy that before we know it all the women will have gone; and then what are we to fight for?"

"No," Helen said, "I will not go; for better or worse I have come to Troy, and there is no longer any other refuge for me. I will remain at Paris' side as long as we both live."

"And I," said Andromache. "Where Hector has courage to remain, there will I remain at his side. And where I remain, my son will remain."

Kassandra, remembering that Andromache had been reared as a warrior, thought that perhaps Imandra would be proud of her daughter after all. *I wish I had her courage*, she thought, then remembered that Andromache did not know what lay before them. Perhaps it was easier to have courage when you could still believe that what you feared would not come to pass. In her ears were the thunders of Poseidon, and she could hardly see across the room for the fires that seemed to rise.

Yet the room was quiet and cool, and all the faces surrounding her were kind and loving. How much longer would she have them around her? Already she had lost Creusa; who would be next?

She knew she should stay inside the Sun Lord's house; but

she could not keep away from the palace, and every day she watched with the other women from the wall, so that she was one of the first to see the people exploding into the spaces between the houses so swiftly that for a moment she wondered if it was another earthquake. Then the cry went up.

"Akhilles! It is the chariot of Akhilles!"

Hector swore violently and ran up the stairs to the lookout point on the walls.

"Akhilles has come back? The worst news we could have—or is it the best?" he said roughly, hastening to where the women stood watching. "Yes, right enough, that is his chariot"—and he shaded his eyes with his hand. Then he turned away, scowling.

"By the Battle-God! That is not Akhilles, but somebody else wearing his armor! Akhilles' shoulders are twice that wide! Maybe that boyfriend of his. The armor doesn't even fit him. In the name of Ares, what is he playing at? Does he really think he can deceive anyone who has ever seen Akhilles fight?"

"I suppose it is a ruse to hearten Akhilles' men," said his charioteer, young Troilus.

"Whatever it is," Hector said, "we'll make short work of him. I might hesitate to face Akhilles, even on a propitious day; but the day has never dawned when I would be afraid to face Patroklos. Perhaps, youngster, I should put my armor on you and set you in my chariot and send you out to take him on."

"I will do it gladly if you will allow it," said the boy eagerly, and Hector laughed and clapped him on the shoulder. "I daresay you would, lad; but don't underestimate Patroklos as much as that. He is not at all a bad fighter; not in my class or Akhilles', it's true, but you're not ready for him yet; not this year and probably not next year either."

He called his armorer, who came and strapped on his best armor; then the others heard the creaking of the gate as Hector rode out.

"This frightens me," Andromache said, hurrying to the best vantage point for watching. "Great Mother, how that wretched boy drives his chariot! Has Hector taught him neither caution nor good sense? They will both be flung out in a moment!"

The two chariots rushed together like rutting stags coming together in the height of the season. Troilus was kept busy with the Myrmidons who rushed against the chariot. He fought back one after another while Hector awaited the champion. Then he sprang out along the axle of the chariot, leaving Troilus to defend it, and faced the man decked out in the brilliant gold-decorated armor of Akhilles.

Hector's sword swung up to meet the Akhaian, who rushed at him, swinging. One swift step and Patroklos was down; but as Hector rushed in to finish him off, the youth scrambled up as if the heavy armor were a feathered cloak, and backed away. The men exchanged a flurry of blows so rapid that Kassandra could not see that either of them had the least advantage. A small shriek from Andromache told her that her husband had taken a wound; but when she looked, she saw that Hector had recovered himself at once and was thrusting violently enough that Patroklos was retreating toward his chariot. His sword drove hard into the place where the armor met the armpiece, then came free in a shower of blood. Patroklos staggered back; one of the Myrmidons caught him around his waist and lifted him bodily into the chariot; he was still standing, but swaying and white-faced. His charioteer—or was it Akhilles' charioteer?—slapped at the horses, and they galloped back toward the beach and the Akhaian tents with Hector in hot pursuit.

Troilus loosed an arrow which struck Patroklos in the leg, and he lost his balance and fell; only the quick grab of the charioteer kept him from being flung out of the chariot. Hector motioned to Troilus to abandon the pursuit; Patroklos was either dead or wounded so gravely that it was only a matter of time before he died. Hector's chariot turned back toward Troy; Andromache started to dash down the stairs as she heard the creaking of the ropes that opened the great gate, but Kassandra held her back and they waited until Hector came up the stairs. His arms-bearer came and began to help him out of his armor, but Andromache took his place.

"You're wounded!"

"Nothing serious, I assure you, my dear," Hector said. "I've had worse wounds in play on the field." There was a long gash in his forearm, which had not injured the tendon; it could be dealt with by cleansing with wine and oil and a tight bandage. Andromache, not waiting for a healer, began at once to care for it, and asked, "Did you kill him?"

"I'm not sure whether he's dead yet, but I assure you, nobody really ever recovers from a thrust to the lungs like that one," Hector said, and almost at the same minute they heard a noise from the Akhaian camp: a great howl of rage and grief.

"He's dead," Hector said. "That's one in the eye for Akhilles, at least."

"Look," said Troilus—"there he is himself."

It was indeed Akhilles himself, wearing only a loincloth, his great shoulders bare and his long pale hair flying. He strode from his tent and toward the walls of Troy. Just out of bowshot he paused and, raising his clenched fist, shook it at the walls. He shouted something, lost in the distance.

"What did he say I wonder?" Hector asked.

Paris, who was unarming close by, said, "I suppose some version of 'Hector, son of Priam'—with a few choice remarks about your ancestry and progeny—'come down here and let me kill you ten times over!' "

"Or, more likely, ten thousand times," agreed Hector. "I couldn't quite make out the words, but the tune is clear enough."

"So now," said Paris, "shall we celebrate?"

"No," Hector said soberly, "I do not rejoice; he was a brave man and, I think, an honorable one. He may have been the only one to keep Akhilles' insanity within bounds. I am sure that the war will go the worse because he is no longer among them."

"I can't understand you," Paris said. "We've done away with a great warrior, and you're not delighted. If I'd killed him, I'd be ready to declare a holiday and a feast."

"Oh, if all you want is a feast, I'm sure we can arrange that somehow," Hector said. "I'm sure many will rejoice; but if we kill off the decent and honorable foes among the Akhaians, we will be left to fight the madmen and rogues. I fear no sane man, but Akhilles—that is another matter. I probably mourn Patroklos as much as any man save Akhilles himself."

Aeneas went and looked over the wall. "Where is Akhilles? He's gone."

"Probably back in his tent trying to get Agamemnon to call off the fighting for a few days of mourning."

"This would be the time to hit them hard," said Paris, "before Akhilles recovers: while they're still disorganized."

Hector shook his head.

"If they ask a truce, we are honor bound to give it," he said; "they gave us a truce to mourn *your* sons, Paris."

"I didn't ask for it," Paris snarled. "This isn't war, this careful exchange of honors; it's some kind of dance!"

"War is a game with rules like any other," Priam said. "Wasn't it you, Paris, who complained that Agamemnon and Odysseus had broken the rules when they seized the Thracian horses?"

"If we're going to fight," Paris said, "let us try to win; I see no point in exchanging courtesies with a man when I'm trying to kill him and he's doing his best to return the favor."

Both Hector and Paris started speaking at once. Priam demanded, "One at a time," and Hector shouted the louder.

"These 'courtesies,' as you call them, are all that make war an honorable business for civilized men; if we ever stop extending these courtesies to our enemies, war will become no more than a filthy business, run by butchers and the lowest kind of scoundrels."

"And if we are not going to fight," Paris said, "why do we not settle our differences with an archery contest, or games such as boxing and wrestling? In this case it seems to me that competition would make more sense than a war; we are competing for a prize."

"With Helen as the prize? Do you think she would be willing to be the prize in an archery contest?" scoffed Deiphobos.

"Probably not," said Paris, "but women are usually disposed of as prize to someone's greed, and I don't see why it should make so much difference."

IT WAS EARLY the next day when Agamemnon, in the white robes of a herald, came under a peace flag to Priam's palace, and as a peace offering brought Hecuba's two waiting-women, Kara and Adrea, who had been taken from Kassandra when she entered the city. Then Agamemnon asked Priam, in honor of the dead, to grant a seven days' truce because Akhilles wished to hold funeral games to honor his friend.

"Prizes will be given," he said, "and the men of Troy are welcome to compete and will be considered for prizes on even terms with our own people." He added after a moment that Priam would be welcome to judge any contests for which he felt qualified—chariot racing perhaps, or archery. Priam thanked him gravely, and offered a bull as a sacrifice to Zeus Thunderer, and a metal caldron as a prize for the wrestling.

After Agamemnon had soberly accepted the gifts and gone away with courteous expressions of esteem, Paris asked disgustedly, "I suppose you're going to compete in this farce, Hector?"

"Why not? Patroklos' ghost won't begrudge me a caldron or a cup, or a good bellyful at his funeral feast. He and I have no more quarrel now; and if I'm killed at the final sack of Troy, if there is one, we'll have something to talk about in the Afterworld."

6

DEATHLY SILENCE hung over Troy all the next day, and over the Akhaian camp. At midafternoon, Kassandra went down to the city wall; she could see into the camp and as far as the beach full of ships from the high edge of the wall of the Sun Lord's house, but from there she could not hear anything or tell what was taking place.

Andromache was at the wall with Hector and others of Priam's household. They welcomed Kassandra and made room for her where she could see what was happening. "This would be the best time to attack them and burn the rest of their ships," Andromache suggested, but at Hector's fierce look she drew back.

"I was joking, my love; I know you are incapable of breaking a truce," she said.

"*They* did," Paris reminded them. "If I had been killed and we had sought a truce for my burial, do you really think they would not storm us at the very height of the feast? Odysseus and Agamemnon are probably urging them right now to make an attack when we least expect it."

"The camp looks almost deserted," Kassandra said. "What are they doing?"

"Who knows?" Paris said. "Who cares?"

"I know," Hector said. "The priests are laying out Patroklos' body for burial or burning; Akhilles is mourning and weeping; Agamemnon and Menelaus are plotting some way to break the truce; Odysseus is trying to keep them from fighting loudly enough for us to hear; the Myrmidons are setting up for the games tomorrow—and the rest of the army is getting drunk."

"How do you know that, Father?" asked Astyanax.

Hector said, laughing, "It's what we would be doing if the shoe were on the other foot."

At this moment a young messenger, in the dress of a novice priest of Apollo, came up inside the wall.

"Your pardon, nobles; a message for the Princess Kassandra," he said, and Kassandra frowned. Had one of the serpents bitten someone, or one of the children fallen into a fever? She could think of no other reason she should be summoned; her Temple duties for the day, never very pressing, had been performed, and she had been given leave to absent herself.

"I am here," she said. "What is wanted?"

"Lady, guests have arrived at the Sun Lord's house; they came by the mountains to avoid the Akhaian blockade, and they seek you. They say the matter is of very great urgency and cannot be delayed."

Puzzled, Kassandra bowed to her father and withdrew. As she climbed to the Temple, she wondered who it might be, and why they should seek her out. She went into the room where visitors were entertained; in the darkness of the room after the sunlight, the strangers were only a half dozen indistinct forms.

One among them rose and came toward her, opening her arms.

"It rejoices my heart to see you, child," she said, and Kassandra, her eyes adapting to the dimness of the room, looked into the face of the Amazon Penthesilea.

Kassandra fell into her enthusiastic embrace.

"Oh, how glad I am to see you all! When I came from Colchis there was no sign of you, and I believed you were all dead!" she cried.

"Yes, I heard you had been seeking us; but we had gone to the islands, seeking help and perhaps a new home country," Penthesilea said. "We found it not, so we returned, and I had no way to send word to you."

"But what are you doing here? How many of you are here?"

"I brought with me all of us who remain who have not chosen to go and live in cities under the rule of men. We have come to defend Troy against her enemies," Penthesilea said. "Priam told me once, many years ago, that before he would send to women to help in the defense of his city, Troy would indeed be fallen on evil times. Perhaps by now I know better than he how evil is the case in which Troy finds itself."

"I do not know if my father would agree with you," Kassandra said. "The army is rejoicing because Hector has just killed the second-most-dangerous fighter in the Akhaian army."

"Aye; they told me in the Sun Lord's house," Penthesilea said. "But I do not think Troy any the nearer safety because Patroklos lies dead."

"Kinswoman," Kassandra said gravely, "Troy will fall, but not to the hand of any man. Do you think, then, that we can contend with the hand of a God?"

Penthesilea smiled in her old way and said, "It is not the destruction of the walls that we need fear, but the destruction of our defenses. Troy could be defeated and sacked, and if it is the will of the powers above that this should happen . . ." She broke off and held out her arms to Kassandra, who went into them like the child she had been.

"My poor child, how long have you been alone with this? Is there no one in Troy, soldier or King or priest, to trust your Sight?" she asked, holding her like a child against her meager old breast. "None of your kinsmen or brothers? Not even your father?"

"They least of all," Kassandra murmured. "It angers them when I speak doom for Troy. They do not want to hear. And perhaps, if I can offer no way to avert this fate, but can only say it must come . . . perhaps they are right not to dwell on it."

"But to make you suffer all this alone . . ." Penthesilea began, then broke off and sighed. "But now I must present myself with my warriors to Priam, and greet your mother, my sister."

"I will take you to the palace that he may welcome you," said Kassandra.

The old Amazon chuckled. "He will not welcome me, my darling, and the more desperately he needs the fighting skills of my women, the less welcome I will be," she said. "The best I can hope for is that he will not refuse us; perhaps I have waited late enough that he will know how badly he is in need of even a few good warriors. Mine number twenty-four."

"You know as well as I that Troy cannot afford to spurn any help from any source whatever, even had you brought an army of Kentaurs," Kassandra said.

Penthesilea sighed and shook her head. "There will never be such an army again," she said sadly. "The last of their warriors are gone; we took in half a dozen of their youngest boy children, after their horses died. Now villagers scratching the ground for a harvest of barley and turnips pasture their goats and swine where once the Kentaurs roamed with their horses; our mares too are perished, save these last pitiful few. There are few horses now on the plains near Troy, I see. The wild herds have been captured by the Akhaians or by the Trojans themselves."

"Apollo's sacred herd still roams free on the slopes of Mount Ida; none has ventured to touch them," Kassandra reminded her. "Even the priestesses of Father Scamander have not ventured to lay a bridle on their heads." But this made her think of Oenone, and she wondered how she fared. It had been years since she had caught sight of the girl; now the women of Mount Ida never came down to the city even for festivals. Paris never spoke of her and as far as Kassandra could tell, never thought of her, even though, now that Helen's children had been killed, Oenone's child was his only living son.

She said, "You and your women must be weary from travel; I offer you the hospitality of the Sun Lord's house. Let me bring you servants who will conduct you to a bath, and if you wish for guest robes—"

"No, my dear," Penthesilea said. "A bath would be more than welcome, but my women and I will present ourselves in our armor and riding leathers; we are what we are and will not pretend to be otherwise."

Kassandra went to make the arrangements, then to prepare herself to dine at the palace. She sent word that she would be bringing guests, but only to Queen Hecuba did she disclose their identity. As kinswomen she knew they would be welcomed, but she knew Priam had no love for the Amazons. Even so, the laws of hospitality were sacred and she knew Priam would never violate them.

In defiance, she thought of robing herself in her old riding leathers and bearing weapons; Priam would be angry, but she wished to identify herself with the Amazons. But when she took the old clothes from her chest, the soft undertunic would not even go over her head; it had been made for the girl she had been when she rode with the Amazons. The leathers were old and cracked, and would not fit her either; why had she kept them all these years? The girl she had been was gone forever.

Lying at the bottom of the chest was her bow of wood and horn; she could still draw that, she supposed; and she had kept her sword and dagger bright and free of rust. *I could still ride, and I am sure I can still fight if I must*, she thought, *even though I now have no Amazon garments; perhaps before my city falls I may still draw weapons in her defense. It is not clothing but weapons and skill that make an Amazon.* She saw and felt herself—though she had not moved a muscle—fitting an arrow to the great bow, drawing the cord back and back, letting the arrow fly . . . *but at whom? She could not see the target where the arrow sped. . . .*

Nevertheless, it heartened her to think she would not stand helpless in the final defense of Troy. Kassandra put away her weapons in the chest—the leathers she would throw away, or better yet, keep them for Honey one day. She dressed herself in a fine gown of woven linen from Colchis, and put her best golden earrings—they were made in the form of serpent heads —in her ears. She added a golden bracelet and the necklace of blue beads from Egypt, and went down to meet her guests.

They had been joined by a tall armored man; with surprise she recognized Aeneas.

"I came to escort you, Kassandra," he said, "but I have been talking with your guests. We will be grateful to have the Amazon archers to defend the main tower; we will station them on the walls . . ."

"I am at your disposal," Penthesilea said, "and I have an old grudge against the father of Akhilles; once at least I will ride out against the son."

Kassandra felt again the clamping darkness squeezing its fist around her throat, so that she could neither speak nor cry out.

"No!" she whispered, but she knew that none of them could hear her.

Aeneas said in a friendly manner, "Well, Hector is our commander; it will be for him to say where he wishes you to fight. We can settle that in a day or two. Shall we go?" He offered his arm courteously to the Amazon Queen, and they left the room, walking down toward the palace. It was not yet quite dark, and Penthesilea looked with dismay at the rubble still blocking the streets. A few wooden shelters had been hastily flung up, but the town still looked as if a giant's child in a fit of temper had kicked over a box of his toys.

Aeneas said, "My father has told me many tales of the wars between the Kentaurs and the Amazons. There was a minstrel at our court who used to sing a ballad about them . . ." He hummed a few phrases. "Do you know the song?"

"I do indeed; if your minstrels cannot sing it, I will sing it for you myself," Penthesilea said, "though my voice is not what it was when I was a girl."

Moving through the courtyards, Kassandra studied the small band of Amazons. Penthesilea had aged more than a year or two since their last encounter on the road to Colchis. She had always been tall and thin; now she was gaunt, her arms and legs all taut, ropy sinew with no remaining ounce of softness anywhere. She still had all her own teeth, strong and white; one could hardly have described her as "an old woman."

None of the others were as old as Penthesilea; the youngest, Kassandra reckoned, was hardly into her teens, a slight girl who looked as strong and dangerous as her own bow.

This is what I could have been; what I should have been. Kassandra regarded the young warrior with ill-concealed envy. *At least she need not sit idly while the defenses of her city fell apart.*

"But you have not been idle," said Aeneas softly, and she wondered—though she never knew for sure—whether he had read her thoughts or whether she had whispered them aloud. "You are a priestess, a healer. It is not only the fighters who serve a city at war." He slid his arm around her waist, and they walked entwined the rest of the distance. When they entered into Priam's great hall, the herald called out their names:

"The Princess Kassandra, daughter of Priam; the Lord Aeneas, son of Anchises; Penthesilea, warrior Queen of the Amazon tribes, and two dozen of her ladies—er"—the herald coughed to cover his confusion—"of her warriors—how shall I say it, my lady—"

"Peace, donkey," said Penthesilea. "None of us have more wit than the Gods have given us. Your King and Queen know who I am." But she was smiling and good-natured even while the herald fumbled to dry his sweaty palms on his tunic.

Hecuba came down from her high seat, bustling toward her sister, and took her into her arms.

"Dearest sister," she said, and Penthesilea returned her embrace.

Priam rose too and took several steps from the high seat, embracing Penthesilea exactly as his wife had done.

"You are most welcome, Sister-in-Law; every hand that can raise a weapon is welcome to us this day. You shall have your choice of all the booty of the Akhaian camp with the other warriors, that I promise to you. Anyone who gainsays this is no friend to me," he said, with a sharp and meaningful look at Hector.

"Father, have we come to this?"

"I would welcome the Kentaurs themselves to fight against Akhilles' army," said Priam. "Tell me, Sister, what weapons have you brought?"

"Two dozen warriors, and we are all armed with swords of iron from Colchis," Penthesilea said. "Every one of us skilled with the bow as well; not one of my women but will shoot out the eye of a running stallion at a hundred paces."

"Will one of yoú enter the archery contest in the funeral games tomorrow?" Paris asked. "Akhilles has offered the best of the captured chariots, and to the best archer, the great bow of Patroklos himself."

"He would not award that to a woman," Hector said. "Not though she outshot Patroklos himself."

"He is sworn to award the prizes to the victor."

"Nothing is sacred to Akhilles," Penthesilea said. "I would be willing to compete if only to show that to all his men; but he might surprise me. But I have neither wish nor need for a chariot; and my own bow is sufficient to my needs." She laughed. "I am not in this war for gold or booty; what would I do with a woman captive?"

"If you win enough booty in this war, you could reestablish your cities," Andromache said, "or go and found a city of your own somewhere, as my mother's people did with Colchis."

"There are worse thoughts," said Penthesilea. "I will consider that. If I win this great chariot, then, Priam, will you ransom it for gold?"

"If he does not," Hecuba said, "I will. You will be well paid —you and all your warriors."

The wine cups went round again, all the men laughing and joking, each saying in which contest he would compete, and what he would do with the prize if he won it.

"You should seek to win one of the women, Aeneas," said Deiphobos. "Someone to warm your bed while Creusa is in Crete."

"No," said Aeneas, raising his cup. "Should I win a captive woman, I will send her to Crete as a maid to wait on Creusa and help her care for the children; she will be paid an honest wage, that someday she may be able to purchase her freedom. I like not this passing round of women as prizes. No more than Penthesilea would I desire any woman who does not come to me of her free will."

Over the rim of the golden cup his eyes met Kassandra's; she knew what he was asking of her and what her answer would be.

KASSANDRA AND Aeneas moved slowly up the hill toward the house of the Sun Lord; there was no moon and the streets were dark except for the occasional spilled light from the inside of one of the houses. Kassandra stumbled over a loose stone, and Aeneas put his arm around her, steadying her steps—or perhaps, she thought, seeking an excuse to hold her; she was not certain she had not stumbled for an excuse to cling to him. Although the night was warm, he wrapped his cloak round them both; and she was overwhelmingly aware of the warmth from his body.

She was not precisely frightened; but she was nervous and a little troubled. For so many years her life had been the life of a priestess, and virginity had been at the very center of that life. She found herself remembering all the arguments she had mustered against Khryse, and wondered if she was behaving like a hypocrite: now that she had resolved to surrender, she was surrendering to her sister's husband. But she had Creusa's own word that it did not matter; she need have no scruples on Creusa's account.

And as for the God? She had long ago lost the belief that it would matter to Apollo Sun Lord what she did. He had long abandoned her; but if He had spoken to forbid this step, even now, she knew she would not defy Him. There was within her a small glowing center of angry desolation: *He did not care*; it did not even matter to Him that one of His chosen was to abandon her pledge to Him.

But that thought was buried very deep indeed; on the surface of her mind there was room for nothing except Aeneas.

They were approaching the great gates; a priest stood there to guard the entrance and exit, and she stopped and turned away so that he would not see her.

"We cannot go in there," she said. "If I take you inside and do not bring you out again immediately . . ."

He understood at once.

"No, indeed," he said. "You must look to your reputation; I would not endanger it, Kassandra. Perhaps we should have remained in the palace this night. . . ."

"No," she said softly, "I would not want that. I am not ashamed—it is not that—"

"But you must not cause a scandal," he said, and walked toward the low wall where it fell away to the streets below. Kassandra felt awkward; she had not thought of this till this moment. Penthesilea and her women had left the palace earlier, and Kassandra had seen no one in the streets. She had brought out Akhilles and Odysseus in the cloaks of novice priests; but she could not do that with Aeneas, even if she could somehow lay hands on a cloak. She frowned, trying to think of a way to take him in unseen; letting him depart again in the morning was no particular problem. She said in an undertone, "There is a place where the wall crumbled away in the great earthquake; even the little children can climb it. It has not been repaired because all the workmen have been put to repairing the city gates, down below. This way," she said, and led him along the outer wall. It was nowhere very high, and there had once been a door at the side; it had been blocked up only a generation or two before, and when the old arch crumbled, it had left a pile of easily scaled rubble which no one had thought it necessary to guard or observe. Even in her long skirt Kassandra found it easy to climb, though the stones turning under her feet and those of Aeneas behind her rattled loudly.

She thought she was probably not the first of the Temple women to bring a lover in this way; it was the sort of thing she would have expected of Chryseis. She did not want to think of herself in the same terms as that alley-cat girl; but she must accept it; she was no better. She gave Aeneas her hand to steady him as he stepped down and felt her breath catch in her throat; she had so often chided Chryseis in her mind for this kind of thing.

If Creusa does not object—and if the Lord Apollo does not speak to prevent it—then there is no one, man or woman or God, to be offended, she told herself firmly. She led him along the deep shadows at the edge of the wall; and rather than conducting him to the door of the priestesses' dormitory and through the corridor to her room, took him to the window that opened from the street, and stepped through.

Inside, it was dark and still, a single rushlight burning on a platter—just enough for them to see her bed and the pallet where Honey usually slept. As she approached the bed, Kassandra saw the little girl's dark head on the pillow; and as she bent to lift her, a long blunt form uncoiled upward, eyes gleaming like two flat pebbles. She saw Aeneas recoil and said softly, "She will not harm you; she is not poisonous."

"I know," Aeneas said. "My mother was a priestess of Aphrodite, and shared her bed with stranger things than snakes. Your pet will not trouble me."

"I can put her in the child's bed if you like," Kassandra said, lifting Honey and laying her on the pallet; the child whimpered, and Kassandra sat with her, crooning softly to soothe her back to sleep.

"It does not matter to me," Aeneas said, "but I am a stranger to her; perhaps she will spend a quieter night in the child's bed." Kassandra felt heat rising in her cheeks as she rose and picked up the snake, laying her down close to Honey; the serpent glided down, wrapping her coils close around Honey's waist. Reassured by the familiar touch, Honey slept, and Kassandra came back, taking Aeneas' cloak and laying it aside.

"I did not know your mother was a priestess of Aphrodite," she said, and Aeneas replied, "When I was a child, they told me my mother was Aphrodite's self. Later, I knew who she really was and came to know her as a mother. I am not surprised if she seemed like the Goddess Herself to my father; she was very beautiful. I think the priestesses of Aphrodite are chosen for their beauty."

"And if they serve the Goddess," Kassandra said, "She would certainly lend them Her beauty."

"It cannot be only that," Aeneas said, "or you would long ago have been chosen to Her service."

The remark made her shiver. Was she, then, being deceived into the service of that Goddess who thrust the disorderly worship of carnal love into the lives of men and of women? Was it, then, that despised Goddess who sought now to lay a hand on her and win her away from the pledge she had made to Apollo?

Already she had seen how Aphroditè disrupted the lives of those who worshiped Her. Aeneas was Her child; did he worship Her too?

She could not ask him these things. He sat on the edge of her narrow bed, drawing off his sandals. She came to him and he reached for her, with a single gesture pulling the pin from her hair and letting it fall free to hide her face and all her questions. It no longer mattered. All the Goddesses, whatever Their names, were one, and she should serve Them as every woman served Them.

She heard the rustling of the snake as it shifted its coils. Aeneas reached for her, his arm around her waist.

"It is no wonder you have remained so long a virgin, with such a guardian of your chastity," he murmured, laughing. "Have all the Sun Lord's maidens such chaperones to safeguard them?"

"Oh, no," she said, laughing, and lay back in his arms. Then she raised herself to extinguish the rushlight. Darkness filled the room and she heard him laugh again, softly. Beyond the laughter she heard, very far away, a ripple of thunder, then the sudden rush and rattle of rain outside.

"Shining Aphroditè, if I must serve You like all women, after so many years of refusing Your service, lay then some of Your gifts on me," she whispered, and felt a shimmer of light around her—or was it only a random flicker of the lightning outside as Aeneas touched her in the dark?

AT DAWN she slipped quietly from her bed, to sit at the window, remembering and savoring every detail of the night. Soon the winds at the summit would blow away the pearly mists in the city below.

At the highest point of the Sun Lord's house the wind already roared noisily around the walls; and Aeneas stood, not yet armed.

"There is no reason for arming, if I am to compete in wres-

tling and boxing," he said. "I will take on any contestant save
Akhilles himself. I dreamed last night . . ."

Kassandra asked, "Did the God send you a lucky dream?"

"Whether lucky or unlucky I do not know," said Aeneas.
"My good fortune, it seems to me, I have already won." He bent
and kissed her. "Promise me: you have no regrets, my beloved?"

"None," she said. It no longer mattered to her. So many
years she had waited to give herself, refusing even, as she
thought, the Sun Lord's self; and here in the midst of war, in
the shadow of death, she had found love and knew it could not
last. When Honey at the far end of the room stirred and cried
with some nightmare, she ran quickly to quiet the child. She
soothed her gently, rocking, crooning to her, and saw Honey's
eyes turn to the unfamiliar figure in the room; she was suddenly,
confusedly glad that the little girl was too young to voice her
surprise or curiosity.

Now as they stood close together, she thought of all the
other women of Troy who for all these years had been fastening
on their men's armor and sending them out to fight—*or to die*
—and that for once she shared the concerns and fears of these
women.

She helped him to buckle the final strap on his breastplate;
the rest of his armor would be donned in the field. The trumpet
which blew at dawn to summon the men had not yet sounded;
and this morning it was uncertain whether it would be heard at
all. Only those who were competing in Patroklos' funeral games
need rise or go out this day, although a careful watch would be
kept in case the Akhaians attempted to break the truce.

"Come, kiss me, love; I must go," he said, holding her tight
in a last embrace; but she protested, "Not yet; shall I find you
some bread and a little wine?"

"I must breakfast with the soldiers of my mess, sweetheart;
don't trouble yourself." He hesitated and held his face against
her cheek. "May I come to you again tonight?"

She did not know what to say, and he mistook her silence.
"Ah, I should not have . . . your brothers are my friends, your
father my host . . ."

"As for my father or brothers, there is no man in all of Troy to whom I must account for my doings," Kassandra said sharply. "And your wife, my sister, said to me when we parted that she begrudged you nothing that would make you happy."

"Creusa said that? I wonder . . . well, I am grateful to her, then. I could have told you that, but better you should hear it from her." Impulsively he caught her to him again. "Let me come," he begged. "We may not have much time . . . and who knows what may happen to either of us? But these days of the truce . . ."

All over Troy, she thought, women fresh from their men's beds were fastening on armor, using these last little delaying moments and kisses, trying not to think of the vulnerability of the flesh they had caressed.

Aeneas stroked her hair. "Even with Aphrodite I now have no quarrel—for it was She, I think, who brought you to me. I shall sacrifice a dove to Her as soon as I can."

There were doves enough in Apollo's shrine; but Kassandra felt a certain reluctance to suggest he buy one of them. Aeneas in one way had stolen something belonging to Apollo—though she did not know now and had never known why it should have belonged to anyone but herself. Then she told herself sharply not to be foolish; she was certainly not the first of the Sun Lord's maidens to take a man to her bed, and would hardly be the last. She stood on tiptoe to kiss him and said, "Until tonight then, my dearest love."

She went to the high railing to watch him as he went down through the city. It was hardly full light yet; the clouds were blowing across the plain before Troy, and there were only a few figures astir in the streets: soldiers, gathering for the morning meal.

She was weary; she should go back to bed. But she wondered how many of the women in the city who had just sent their lovers or husbands to battle—or, today, the mock-battle of the games—could calmly go and sleep. She went into her room, finding Honey still buried in her blankets, and dressed herself swiftly. She did not want to walk about the courts; for some reason she was certain that she would encounter Khryse, and she felt that he would be instantly aware of what had happened and that she could not endure his gaze. She had lately allowed Phyllida to take over the care of the serpents, so there was no reason to go to the serpent court.

With surprise she realized that what she felt was loneliness; she had always been so solitary, and in general so accustomed to that state that it was rare for her to crave company. Then she remembered that there was now one person in the Sun Lord's house to whom she could actually say all that was in her heart.

A few of Penthesilea's women had been assigned a room not far from Kassandra's; the mass of them were in a courtyard nearby, where they were sleeping on rolled blankets. One or two were awake, and breakfasting on bread and the harsh new wine that was made within the Temple. Penthesilea, as befitted their Queen, was in a little room alone at the far end of the hall. Kassandra traversed the ancient mosiac of seashells and spirals, tiptoeing quietly so as not to wake the sleepers. She tapped lightly at the door; the old Amazon opened it and pulled her inside.

"Good morning, dear child. Why, how worn and sleepless you look!" She held out her arms, and Kassandra went into them, weeping without knowing why.

"You needn't cry," Penthesilea said. "But if you *will* cry, I would say you have reason enough; I know you left the banquet with Aeneas last night. Has that rogue seduced you, child?"

"No, it is not like that at all," Kassandra said angrily, and wondered why Penthesilea smiled.

"Oh, well, if it is a love affair, why do you weep?"

"I—don't know. I suppose because I am a fool, as I always knew women were fools who play these games with men, and talk of love, and weep . . ." *And now*, she thought, *I am no better than any of them.*

"Love can make fools of any of us," Penthesilea said. "You have come later to it than most, that is all; the time for weeping over love affairs is when you're thirteen, not three-and-twenty. And because when you were thirteen you were *not* weeping and bawling over some handsome young slab of manhood, I thought you would be such a one as would seek lovers among women, perhaps . . ."

"No, I had no thought of that," Kassandra said. "I have, known what it is to desire women," she added thoughtfully, "but I thought perhaps it was only that I had seen them through Paris' mind and his eyes." She remembered Helen and Oenone and how deeply she had been aware of them; something in her, whatever happened, would always feel a strong affection for Helen. This was something altogether different and not at all welcome; it enraged her that she could make such a fool of herself over a man to whom she could never even seek to join her life.

She was crying again, this time with rage. She tried to put something of this into words; but Penthesilea said, "It is better to be angry than to grieve, Kassandra; there will be time enough to grieve if this war goes on. Come, help me arm, Bright Eyes."

The old pet name made her smile through her tears.

Kassandra picked up the armor, made of overlapping boiled and hardened leather scales and reinforced with plates of bronze; it was decorated with coils and rosettes of gold. She pulled it over the old Amazon's head, turning her gently to fasten the laces.

"Should any harm come to me in this war," Penthesilea said, "promise me my women will not be enslaved or forced to marry; it would break their hearts. Pledge me they will be free to leave unharmed, if your city survives."

"I promise," Kassandra murmured.

"And should I die, I want this bow to be yours; see, I even have a few Kentaur arrows, here at the bottom of the quiver. Most of my women now use metal-tipped shafts, because they can pierce armor like mine; but the arrows of the Kentaurs— you know the secret of their magic, Kassandra?"

"Aye—I know they use poison. . . ."

"Yes: little-known poisons brewed from the skin of a toad," said Penthesilea; "and they will kill with even a slight wound. Few of your foes will wear armor head to toe, even among the Akhaians. They are—shall we say—a way of evening the disadvantage that we women have in the way of size and strength."

"I shall remember that," said Kassandra; "but I pray the

Gods I shall not inherit your women nor your bow, and that you shall bear your weapons till they are laid in your grave."

"But my bow will do no good in my grave to anyone," said Penthesilea. "When I am gone, take it, Kassandra; or lay it on the altar of the Maiden Huntress. Promise me that."

7

THE AKHAIANS made no effort to break the truce during the seven days of funeral games for Patroklos, nor during the next three days, which were devoted to a feast at which the prizes were distributed. Kassandra attended neither the games nor the feast, but heard about them from Aeneas. He won the javelin-casting, and gained a gold cup. Hector was disgruntled because he had entered the wrestling, and he had been beaten by the Akhaian captain called Big Ajax, but was a little comforted by the fact that his son Astyanax won the boys' footrace, though he was smaller than any other boy in the contest. "What did he win?" Kassandra asked.

"A silken tunic from Egypt, dyed crimson; it's too big for him, and too fine to be cut up for a child, but he can wear it when he is grown," Aeneas said. "And at the end of the feast, they thanked us for our company at the games and said they'd meet us on the battlefield in the morning. So let us sleep, love, for they will blow the horn to rouse us an hour before daylight."

He stretched out and drew her into his arms, and she put her own around him joyfully. But after a moment she asked, "Was Akhilles there?"

"Aye; Patroklos being killed has made him even more angry than any insult from Agamemnon," Aeneas said. "You should have seen him look at Hector; it was as though he were the Gorgon and could turn your brother to stone. You know I'm no coward, but it's just as well it's not my fate to go up against Akhilles."

"He's a madman," Kassandra said with a shudder, then stopped further talk by pulling Aeneas' head down to her own and kissing him. They fell asleep in each other's arms; but after a time it seemed to Kassandra that she woke and rose . . . no, for, looking back, she could see herself still in the bed, still lying entwined in Aeneas' arms.

Light as a ghost, she drifted through the Temple, hovering where the Amazons still sat wakeful in their rooms, sharpening their weapons; drifted down to the palace, into the rooms where Paris and Helen lived, Paris sleeping heavily, Helen with tear-stained cheeks wandering through the room where her children had been killed. *She still has Paris; but is this enough? If we are defeated, what will become of her? Will Menelaus drag her back to Sparta, only to kill her?* For a moment it seemed to Kassandra that she saw the Akhaian captains casting lots for the conquered women, dragging them on board the black ships which filled the harbor so full of filth and dread . . .

No; that was no more than a dream; it might never happen after all. The death of Patroklos and the return of Akhilles had changed some tide in the currents of what might befall, she knew that; now even the Gods must make new plans. The night appeared to sparkle with glimmers of moonlight, and it seemed, as she drifted ghostlike down toward the Akhaian camp, that great Forms drifted through the dark. No mortal thing, she knew, could see her in her present guise, but the Gods might catch sight of her as she spied in this world of ghosts. . . .

She had no idea where she was going, but for some unknown reason a firm sense of purpose drove her on. She lingered a moment in Agamemnon's tent, where he lay sleeping. He was not really larger than life-size—only a narrowly built, mean-looking man with a troubled look on his face. This man was married to Helen's sister, and had offered his own daughter as sacrifice for a fair wind. . . . Did the Gods of the Akhaians truly demand such hideous things, or did they have priests who said so to suit their own corrupt purposes? She supposed that an evil man was evil everywhere, and among the Akhaians it must be easier. As she lingered, he rolled over on his back and opened his eyes; it seemed to Kassandra that he could see her—and perhaps if he was dreaming, he could.

He said in a whisper—though she did not think he actually spoke—"Have you been sent to tempt me, maiden?"

She replied, "You are only dreaming I am here. I am the spirit of the daughter whom you sent to death, and may the Gods send you evil dreams." She drifted through the wall of the tent, but behind her she heard him wail in sudden terrified waking. She would not wish to be he this night.

She moved on and found herself in the tent of Akhilles. The Akhaian prince was awake, stretched on his back, his eyes wide open; and lying on a stretcher at the other side of the tent lay the body of Patroklos. Kassandra did not understand; he should surely have been burned, or buried—or even exposed to the great scavenger birds, as was the custom of some of the tribes of the great steppes. Yet the body had been embalmed, and Akhilles kept vigil beside it. His strange pale eyes were swollen as if he had been weeping for a long time, and he was crying audibly.

"Oh, Mother!" he cried out through his sobs, and Kassandra had no idea whether he was invoking his earthly mother or calling upon a Goddess, "Oh, Mother, you told me that Zeus Thunderer had promised me honor and glory, and look what has happened to me: taunted by Agamemnon—and now my only friend is gone from me!"

She thought, *You should have been the kind of person who could have more than one friend in a lifetime.* She heard him moan wordlessly again and then cry out to Patroklos: "How could you leave me? And what shall I say to your father? He told you to stay at home and mind the affairs of your own kingdom; but I pledged to him that no harm would come to you, and that I would bring you home covered with honor and glory! Aye, I will bring you home—but there is no honor or glory for you now." His sobbing became uncontrollable.

For a moment Kassandra almost pitied the Akhaian prince's grief; but she had heard too much of his mad battle-lust. He killed without mercy, inflicting as much suffering as he could; but when it came his turn to suffer he had little bravery. If he had come out and fought for himself, this would never have happened; Patroklos had been killed for being where Akhilles should have been. Suddenly she knew what she had come to do.

"Akhilles," she called softly, imitating the accent she had heard in the Akhaian camp.

He sat up, staring around him, his eyes rolling with terror.

"Who calls me?"

"Ghosts have no names," she said, deepening her voice. "I am numbered among the dead."

"Is it you, Patroklos? Why have you come to haunt me, my friend? Why do you stay here rather than passing to your rest?"

"While I remain unburied I cannot rest; my spirit remains to haunt those who compassed my death."

"Then go and haunt the Trojan Hector," Akhilles cried in terror, his eyes almost starting from his head. "It was his sword cast out your life, not mine!"

"Alas," Kassandra wailed, "I remain here for I was killed in your armor, and in that place which should have been yours in battle"—and then, with sudden inspiration, "Do you love me no more because I have passed the doors of death?"

Akhilles wailed, "The dead have no more place among the living; reproach me not, or I shall die of grief."

"I do not reproach you," Kassandra moaned in the sepulchral voice. "I leave that to your own conscience; you know I died the death that should have been yours."

"No!" Akhilles cried out. "No! I will not hear this! Help! Guards!"

What the devil! she thought. *Does he truly believe that his guards can cast out a ghost?* Four armed men rushed into his tent.

"You called us, my prince?" asked the first of them, avoiding looking at the body of Patroklos where it lay.

"Search the camp," Akhilles commanded. "Some intruder has entered unseen and spoken dreadful things to me in the voice of Patroklos. Find him and drag him here, and I will have his eyeballs on sticks to roast! I will tear out his gizzard and fry it before his eyes! I will—but find him for me first!" He shook his fist, and the men rushed out.

Her mission finished, Kassandra drifted after them, and

heard one of them say, "I knew it. He's been mad since he shut himself up in his tent, and it's driven him further out of his senses, it has."

"Do you think there's a spy?"

"I wouldn't wear meself out looking, lad," said the first speaker cynically. "Inside his poor sick brain, that's where ye'll find yer intruder."

Kassandra would have laughed if she had been capable of it. Like a wraith of fog she moved up the long hill to the windswept heights of Troy, and silently slipped downward and merged with her body, still wrapped in Aeneas' arms.

She slept without dreams.

Now THAT she had a man among the warriors, Kassandra felt more strongly than ever the impulse that sent the women down to the wall to watch the fighting. She left Phyllida to care for the serpents, and the other priestesses to the task of healing the wounded. This morning the line of chariots seemed more brilliantly painted and polished, weapons shining with a more terrible menace than ever before. Hector was leading, flanked by Aeneas and Paris, armored and imposing as if they were the Gods of War in person. Behind the line of chariots came long lines of foot soldiers in their polished leather armor, with their javelins and spears. She thought, if she were among the Akhaians and saw this formidable host approaching, she might well run away.

The Argive troops, already lined up along the earthworks they had built between the plain and the shoreline where their ships were beached, did not flinch even when Hector gave the command to charge, and the Trojan war cry rang out. The chariots thundered forward, toward the unbreaking Argive line. The Akhaians loosed a flight of arrows and, in one concerted movement, the Trojan shields went up; most of the arrows fell harmlessly on the roof thus formed by the shields of the Trojans. A second flight of arrows quickly followed the first; one or two soldiers in the ranks fell, or stumbled out of line back toward the walls; but this did not interrupt the charge of the chariots.

A great cry went up from both ranks; at the top of the

earthworks stood a great bronze chariot adorned with gilded wings and a rayed sun, and in it a glittering figure: Akhilles had joined the battle, dominating the line of Akhaians as a rooster dominates a henyard; everyone on either side of the battle seemed smaller and drabber by contrast.

Shouting, he raised his mighty shield and charged down the earthworks at Hector like a Fury. Jumping out of the chariot, he cried his challenge. Hector was ready to oblige him. He cast his javelin, which rebounded from Akhilles' shield; then, sword in one hand and shield in the other, swiftly engaged Akhilles in combat. Even from where she stood Kassandra could feel the shock of that first blow, from which both men reeled back, staggering, several feet.

She knew that Andromache was beside her, clutching at her arm so strongly that her nails dug into Kassandra's skin. This battle had been inevitable from the moment Patroklos was killed.

Kassandra shrieked with excitement. Behind the foot soldiers, who swept along to catch the Akhaian soldiers between the chariots, came the horses of the Amazons. Their arrows and swords dispatched many of the foot soldiers. Hector, engaged with Akhilles, now seemed taller and more formidable; Kassandra felt it was not her brother, but the shining War God Himself. Hector wounded Akhilles and the Akhaian went down. A cheer from the Trojan ranks seemed to revitalize him, and he was up again, beating Hector back toward his chariot. The Trojan prince jumped up and was fighting Akhilles from the step of the chariot, then pivoted the wheels and knocked Akhilles down as he rode almost over him. Akhilles recovered and flung his javelin. It rebounded from Hector's armor, but he followed it up with a mighty sword-slash that struck Hector in the neck.

Hector slumped in the chariot. Troilus grabbed the reins and knocking Akhilles down again, made a dash for the walls. Then the Amazons with their spears swept toward Akhilles; but he was surrounded by at least two dozen of his own Myrmidons, who made a solid wall of shields around him. The Amazons were forced to retreat, for although they cut down ten or twelve of Akhilles' men, there were always more.

The Myrmidons reached Hector's chariot when it was already under the walls of Troy. Then storming after them came Akhilles in his own chariot, with only one horse—he had cut the other loose. He crashed his chariot deliberately into Hector's, spilling young Troilus out onto the ground. The boy landed on this feet and went down beneath the swarming Myrmidons. Andromache was screaming; Kassandra turned to quiet her, and when she looked back again, Akhilles had the reins of Hector's chariot and was racing back toward the Akhaian lines with Hector—or his body—still inside.

Troilus was fighting for his life. One of the Amazons swept up to him, killed three of Akhilles' men and snatched Troilus into her saddle. Paris and Aeneas were in hot pursuit of Akhilles, but the men atop the earthworks repelled them with what seemed a wall of javelins, on which their horses were impaled. The Amazon charge cut down the javelin wall, and rescued Paris and Aeneas, but their overturned chariots were in Akhaian hands. Akhilles, with Hector and his chariot, had vanished from sight.

It took a hard-fought hour for the Trojans to make their way back to the gate, even covered by arrow-fire from the walls; and Andromache met them.

"You couldn't even recover his body?" she shrieked. "You left it in their hands?"

"We did our best," said Paris; he had lost most of his armor, and was leaning on his charioteer, bleeding from a great sword-cut across the thigh. "But with Akhilles leading his men—"

"Akhilles! Curse him forever! May his bones rot unburied on the shores of the Styx!" Andromache broke into a high wild scream of lamentation: "Hector is dead! Now let Troy perish indeed!"

Hecuba joined in the keening: "He is dead! Our greatest of heroes is dead! Dead or in Akhaian hands—"

"Oh, he's dead all right," Aeneas said grimly.

"Galls me to admit it, but without the Amazon charge we would *all* have been dead," said Deiphobos, who had lifted down Troilus from the Amazon saddle and was half carrying him, examining his wounds. Hecuba hurried to him and took him in her arms, beckoning for a healer-priest.

"Ah, my sons! My Hector! My firstborn and my lastborn in a single hour! Ah, most fateful of all battles! It has begun," Hecuba wailed, and crumpled senseless. Kassandra ran to kneel by her, suddenly terrified that the shock had killed her mother too.

"No, Troilus is alive," said Aeneas, lifting the old woman gently. "You must be strong, Mother; he will need your good care if you are not to lose him too." He turned Troilus over to a healer-priest, who restored him to consciousness with a sip of wine, then examined his wounds. Women were handing wine around; Aeneas took one of the cups and gulped it.

"I think tomorrow I will take careful aim at Akhilles from the walls and try to get him off the field before we even venture out."

"He can't be killed that way," Deiphobos said. "That armor of his is God-forged; arrows bounce off it like twigs!"

"Not God-forged," said Penthesilea, "forged of solid iron. Have you any idea what it must weigh? Even my women's metal-tipped Skythian arrows cannot penetrate it."

Paris said in disgust, "There's an old tale that Akhilles is protected by spells so that no wound inflicted by a mortal can bring him down."

"Let me but get a weapon into his flesh," said Aeneas; "I'll guarantee to kill him. But we must go up and break the news to Priam; the worst news of all this year."

Kassandra said between her teeth, "We should have expected this. Hector killed Patroklos; Akhilles was ready for him the moment he put foot outside the wall. This was not war but murder." And silently she wondered if there was that much difference.

"We must go to Akhilles at once," Aeneas said, "perhaps even before we tell our father, and ask a truce to bury and mourn our brother."

"Do you really think they will give it?" asked Paris sarcastically. "You think too well of them."

"They *must* grant it," said Aeneas. "We gave a truce for Patroklos' funeral games."

"If it comes to that," said Andromache, "I will go myself and kneel to Akhilles and beg back the body of my husband."

"They will return it," said Aeneas. "Akhilles is always talking of honor."

"Only his own, I notice," Kassandra said.

"Well, then, his own honor will prompt him to do the honorable thing," Aeneas said. "They know me; let me go, then, with a delegation of Hector's own guard to bring home his body."

"We must tell Father first," said Troilus, rising from the healer's ministrations, very pale, his head wrapped in bandages. "If you wish it, I will tell him; I am to blame; I let him fall into Akhilles' hands."

Hecuba embraced him fiercely. "No blame to you, my love. I rejoice that you did not follow him into death." She added, "But yes, go to Priam; nothing could comfort him for the loss of our firstborn but the knowledge of the son we still have to bless us. . . ."

"I will go and tell him," Paris said. "But first gather all my brothers; all of us who live still shall stand before him and be ready to comfort him."

"And I," said Kassandra, "I will go to the Maiden's Temple and tell Polyxena; she and Hector were close in age, and they loved each other well."

They had begun to set out on their various errands, when Andromache went to the wall and let out a high, wild shriek.

"Ah, the fiend, the monster! What is he doing now?"

"Who?" Kassandra asked, but she already knew; fiend, monster could be only one person. She rushed to the wall.

The sun was high. It was not yet noon; it had only seemed that they had watched the great battle for half of a day. There was a great cloud of dust on the plain before Troy; it cleared a little and she could see the chariot of Akhilles, with Akhilles himself standing upright, driving his matched horses. And in the dust at the tail of the chariot, a figure whose armor clearly revealed its identity.

"Hector! But what is he doing?" she demanded.

It was all too clear what he was doing; he was dragging Hector's corpse in the dust behind his chariot, as he raced fiercely in circles around the plain. The Trojans watched, frozen in horror.

"Why," said Kassandra, "he *is* mad, then. I thought . . . "
She had thought they called him mad rhetorically; but surely a
man who could thus abuse the corpse of a fallen enemy—even
an enemy who had slain his dearest friend—must be mad in
truth.

Why, he is not fit to be let out without a keeper, she thought
with a shudder.

Aeneas said, "Why, this goes beyond even revenge; the man
is inhuman."

"Demented with grief, perhaps," said Kassandra. "He loved
Patroklos beyond reason, and when his friend died, he lost the
last of all ties to sanity."

"Still, this must be stopped," Aeneas said. "We must send
to the Akhaians—Odysseus, at least, is a reasonable man—and
get back Hector's body before this comes to his father's ears."

"So," said Andromache, with clenched fists, "I am to stand
here and watch this and not go mad myself with grief; but
Priam, a man and a King, must be shielded from the very word,
let alone the sight . . . " She flung back her head and screamed,
"I will go down myself, if I must, and I will persuade that man
with a horsewhip that he cannot do this thing before all of
Hector's kin!"

"No," Paris said, embracing her gently. "No, Andromache,
he would not listen to you. I tell you, he is mad."

"Is he? Or is he feigning madness so that we will offer him
a greater ransom for Hector's body?" Andromache asked. Kassandra had not thought of that.

At last Troilus, taking with him two or three of Priam's
other sons, went up to tell the King that Hector was dead, while
Paris and Aeneas armed themselves and drove forth in a chariot
with Priam's favorite herald. They tried in vain to make Akhilles
hear them, but he simply went on whipping up his horses into a
frenzy and refused to listen to a word the herald said.

After a time they stopped and conferred and went on to the
main Akhaian camp to speak with Agamemnon and the other
captains. Eventually, looking discouraged, they returned to
Troy.

Andromache rushed at them. "What did they say?" she
demanded, though it was obvious they had had no success;

down on the plain, Akhilles' chariot was still dragging the body around in circles. It seemed he meant to go on at least till sunset, perhaps longer.

Aeneas said, "They will do nothing to stop Akhilles; they said he is their leader, and he must do as he will with his own captives and prisoners. He killed Hector and the body is his, to ransom or not as he chooses."

"But that's monstrous," Andromache said. "You hesitated not at all to grant them a truce for mourning Patroklos! How can they do this?"

"They didn't want to," said Paris. "Agamemnon could not look me in the eye. He knows they are violating all the rules of warfare—rules which they themselves made and we agreed to honor. But they know they have no chance of triumphing without Akhilles; they angered him once, and they will not risk making him angry again."

The sun had slanted down considerably, and the plain of Troy was now partly in the long shadow of the walls. Paris said, "There is nothing for it but this, then: we must go out and fight for his body." He called his arms-bearer and started putting on his armor.

"Summon the Amazons; their charge and their arrows can cover us. They are fierce fighters, fiercer than any man," Aeneas said. "I will vow my best horse to the War-God if He grants us that we win Hector's body."

"I'll vow more than that if He grants me Akhilles," said Paris. "Hector and I were not always close, but he was my elder brother, and I loved him; and even if I had not, kinship's dues would forbid me to stand by and see his corpse dishonored. Even Akhilles can have no quarrel with the dead."

Kassandra said, "I remember how Hector said he and Patroklos would have much to talk about in the Afterworld."

"Aye," said Aeneas somberly. "If Akhilles paused to think, he would know that Hector and his friend would feast side by side as comrades in the halls of the Afterlife."

"I trust it is no God's will I meet Akhilles as a comrade on the other side of death," said Paris grimly. "Or I swear, unless I learn something there that I have not been given to know in this life, I shall disrupt the peace of that world itself when I meet Akhilles there."

"Oh, hush," said Aeneas. "None of us know what we shall think or do past that gate; but in this world, we all have been properly taught that enmity ends at death, and what Akhilles now does is an outrage and an atrocity—as well as being plain bad manners. He should show respect for a fallen foe; you know that, I know it, the other Akhaians know it. And I give you my word, if Akhilles does not know it, I shall be happy to give him a lesson, here and now. Are the soldiers armed and ready?"

"Yes," called Paris. "Open the gates."

Priam came slowly through the ranks and went to the wall where the women stood. He himself was as white as death, Kassandra thought, and he had been weeping.

"If you rescue the body of my son for honorable burial," he said, as Aeneas passed him on his way down to the gate, "it needs no saying that you may ask whatever reward you will."

Aeneas knelt for a moment before him and kissed the old man's hand.

"Father, Hector was my brother-in-law and my brother-in-arms; I want no reward to do for him what I know well he would be the first to do for me."

"Then the blessings of every God I know how to call be upon you," said Priam, and as Aeneas rose, embraced him quickly and kissed his cheek. Then he let him go, and the men went down to the gate.

As Troilus would have joined them, Hecuba cried out, "No! Not you too!" and caught at his tunic; but Troilus pulled away, and Priam motioned to the Queen to let him go.

Hecuba collapsed weeping. "Cruel old man! Unnatural father! We have lost one son today; will you lose another?"

"He is no child," Priam said. "He wishes to go; I will not forbid him. I would not make him go if he wished any excuse to stay; but you should be proud of him."

"Proud!" she raged, looking down on the chariots as they raced out through the gates. "There is more than one madman here!"

8

KASSANDRA HAD SEEN the Amazons fight many times before; she wished that she were riding forth with them. Yet if she had thought the morning's fighting fierce, that was nothing to the ferocity of this battle for Hector's body.

Time after time the Trojan soldiers made what seemed like a suicidal dash at Akhilles' chariot, trying to overturn or crash it and cut free the body; but the joined forces of Hector's soldiers and the Amazons could not come near him. It seemed that the War-God Himself rode with Akhilles, and more than a dozen of the soldiers and seven of the Amazon warriors died in these charges before Agamemnon's charioteers, led by Diomedes and the strongest of the Spartan archers, came and drove them off a final time.

When it was almost too dark to see, at last the Trojans retired; and when Troilus fell to an arrow shot by Akhilles himself, Aeneas finally yielded and called off the attack, carrying Troilus inside the walls.

"He didn't want to live," Hecuba wept over his body. "He blamed himself—I heard him—that his brother died. . . ."

In the flaming sunset, the cloud of dust behind Akhilles' chariot was undiminished. "It looks as if he means to keep that up all night," said Paris. "There is nothing else we can do."

"I can probably see better in the dark than his horses," said Aeneas. "We might try again by moonlight. . . ."

"There is no reason to do that," said Penthesilea. "You have one brother now to bury and to mourn; tomorrow will be time to think again about Hector."

Hecuba, kneeling before Troilus' corpse, raised her face, swollen with tears, looking suddenly twenty years older.

"If I must, I will go to Akhilles and beg him, for the love of his own mother, to let me bury my son," she said. "Surely he has a mother and pays honor to her."

"Do you truly think anything human gave birth to that monster?" wept Andromache. "Surely he was hatched from a serpent's egg!"

"As a keeper of serpents, I resent that on their behalf," Kassandra said. "No serpent was ever wantonly cruel; they kill only for food or to defend their young, and no serpent ever made war against another, whatever God they may serve."

"Let us leave it for tonight," Andromache said; "perhaps a new day may bring him reason." She turned from the wall, deliberately looking away from the sight of Akhilles' chariot and the cloud of dust where Hector's body was hidden. She raised Hecuba gently by the arm and, Kassandra noted, taking a good deal of the older woman's weight. Together the two went up the steep street toward the palace.

Kassandra bent over the lifeless body of Troilus. She remembered when he had been born, what a sweet red round-faced baby he had been, squalling and thrusting out his little fists. How her mother had prayed for another son, and how happy she had been when he had arrived. But then she had always been happy with every son born in the palace, even those born to the concubines; the Queen was always the first to have every baby in her arms, however humble the mother.

Well, she had promised to tell Polyxena; she went slowly up the steep streets of the city toward the Maiden's Temple. The winds at that height dragging against her cloak and hair, she reached the outer court, where the statue of the Maiden stood.

She had now spent so many years as a priestess that she had almost ceased to trouble herself about the nature of Gods or Goddesses, whether They were truly from some place beyond humanity, or whether They were from some soul of humankind seeking to worship the greater virtues and the divine within. Yet now, looking at the serene face of the Maiden, she wondered again; could anything, human or divine, be brought unmothered to birth, and was not that very concept a blasphemy against all that was divine? She herself had brought no child to birth; yet within her the unfed passion for motherhood had brought Honey into her arms, and she knew she would protect her with her very life, as any other mother would do.

With her own mother she now shared a passionate grief. She had been guilty of underestimating Akhilles; she should have known that his madness made him ever more dangerous, as even a house dog may turn vicious and untrustworthy.

Yet if she had offered warning, she would not have been listened to.

One of the attendants of the shrine recognized her and came to ask deferentially how she could serve the daughter of Priam.

"I would speak with my sister Polyxena," she said, and the servant went at once to fetch her.

Before very long, she heard a step and Polyxena came into the room, at the sight of Kassandra's face crying out, "You bear evil news, Sister! Is it our mother, our father—"

"No; they live still," Kassandra said, "though I know not what this news will do to them in the end." Polyxena, now a tall woman in her late twenties, still had the soft face of a child. She came and embraced Kassandra, weeping.

"What do you mean? Tell me."

"Hector . . ." Kassandra said, and felt herself almost at the edge of tears.

"The worst," she said. "Not only Hector, but Troilus." Her throat closed and she could hardly speak. "Both dead in a single hour, at Akhilles' hands; and that madman drags Hector's corpse behind his chariot and will not hear of giving up his body for burial. . . ."

Polyxena burst into sobs, and the sisters clung to each other, united as they had not been since they were little children.

"I will come at once," Polyxena said. "Mother will need me; let me but fetch my cloak." She hurried away, and Kassandra reflected sorrowfully that this was true; she could not comfort her mother. Even Andromache was closer to Hecuba than she was. All her life it had been so: that of all their children Hector was closest to their parents' hearts, and Kassandra the least loved. Was it only that she had always been so different from the others?

It broke her heart that even in this dreadful moment she could not turn to her mother. Because she could always retain her composure and because she was not beside herself with grief, it would never have occurred to anyone that she herself was in need of consolation. Her bottomless, tearless sadness seemed to her mother, she knew, cold and inhuman, quite unlike the aspect of a woman at all.

Polyxena returned, in the pale cloak of a priestess, with something tied in a cloth at her waist. Her eyes were red, but she had stopped crying; however, Kassandra knew she would weep again at the sight of their mother's tears.

I wish that I could; Hector is worthy of all the tears we all might shed for him. And she wondered, despairing, *What is wrong with me, that for all my grief I cannot weep for my dearest brothers?*

Yet in her heart a small rational voice said, *Hector was a fool; he knew Akhilles was a madman who did not abide by any civilized rules for warfare, and nevertheless for something he called honor he rushed to his death. This honor was dearer to him than life, or Andromache or his son, or the thought of the grief his parents would feel.* And for all the horror of it, she could not feel any additional disgust or dismay at what Akhilles had done to his corpse. Hector was dead, and that was bad enough. What could make it worse?

And we are all going to die anyhow; and few of us as quickly or mercifully. Why do we not rejoice that he is spared further suffering?

Polyxena handed Kassandra the cloth, and she felt something hard within it.

"What jewels I have," she said. "Father may need them to ransom Hector's body. Akhilles is just as greedy for gold as for what he calls glory; perhaps this will help."

"He is welcome to mine too," said Kassandra, "though I have few: only my rings and my pearls from Colchis."

Together they went down the hill toward the palace. It was growing late; the low sun was hidden behind a heavy bank of cloud, and the brisk wind held a smell of rain. On the plain, there was no sign of Akhilles' chariot; he had given up his gruesome revenge, at least for the night.

"Perhaps they will make a foray in the dark to rescue him," Polyxena said. "Or if it rains, Akhilles may agree to accept a ransom; he will not want to drive a chariot all day in a storm."

"I don't think it will make any difference to him," Kassandra said. "It seems to me that the sensible course would be to accept this and do what he does not expect: let him keep Hector's corpse; then muster all our forces tomorrow and throw everything we have into an all-out attempt to kill Akhilles and Agamemnon and perhaps Menelaus as well."

Polyxena stared at her in utter dismay, the beginning rain mingling with the tears on her cheek.

"I beg of you, Sister, say nothing like that to our mother or father," she said. "I did not think even you could be so heartless as to leave Hector unburied in the rain."

"It is not Hector who lies unburied," Kassandra said fiercely; "it is a dead body like any other."

"I do not know if you are very stupid, or simply very malicious," Polyxena said, "but you speak like a barbarian and not a civilized woman, a princess and a priestess of Troy." She turned away her eyes, and Kassandra knew she had only made things worse. She looked away from Polyxena to hide the tears in her eyes, while knowing perversely that Polyxena would think better of her for them. They did not speak again.

When they reached the palace, a servant (Kassandra noticed that the old woman's eyes were as swollen and red as her mother's—everyone down to the kitchen drudges had loved Hector, and all the palace women remembered Troilus as a small petted child) took their sodden cloaks, dried their hair and feet with towels and showed them into the main dining hall.

It looked almost the same as always—a roaring fire casting light around the room and branched candlesticks spreading brilliance by which the paintings on the walls wavered as if seen underwater. The carved bench where Hector habitually sat was empty, and Andromache sat between Priam and Hecuba, like a child between her parents.

Paris and Helen were nearby, their hands clinging. They came to greet Polyxena, who went to kiss her parents. Kassandra sat down in her accustomed place near Helen; but when the servants put food on her plate she could not swallow and only nibbled at a dish of boiled vegetables and drank a little watered wine. Paris looked sad, but Kassandra knew that he was very well aware that he was now Priam's eldest son by his Queen and commander of the armies. *If there is to be any hope for Troy, someone must disabuse him of that notion*, she thought. *He is no Hector.* Then she was astonished at herself; she had known so long that there was no hope for Troy: why did these unconquerable thoughts of hope keep rising again and again?

Did this mean her visions of doom were simply hallucinations or brain-sickness, as everyone said? Or did it mean that somehow with Hector gone there was new hope for Troy? No, *that* was certainly madness; *he was the best of us all*, she thought, and knew that someone—Paris? Priam?—had actually said it aloud.

"He was the best of us all," Paris said, "but he is gone, and somehow we must manage the rest of this war without him. I have no idea how we will do it."

"It is in essence your war," Andromache said. "I told Hector he should have left it to you all along."

Someone sobbed aloud; it was Helen. Andromache turned on her in sudden rage.

"How dare you! If it were not for you he would be alive, and his son not fatherless!"

"Oh, come, my dear," Priam said in a conciliatory tone, "you really mustn't talk like that to your sister—there is enough grief in this house this night."

"Sister? Never! This woman from our enemies, from whom all out troubles have arisen—look, she sits and gloats because now her paramour will command all Priam's armies. . . ."

"The Gods know I do not gloat," Helen said, stifling her tears. "I grieve for the fallen sons of this house which has become my house, and for the grief of those who are now my father and my mother."

"How dare you . . ." Andromache began again; but Priam took her hand and held it, whispering to her.

"How would you have me prove my grief?" Helen stood up and came to Priam's high seat. Her long golden hair was unbound, hanging over her shoulders; her blue eyes, deep-set in her face and shadowed with weeping, were luminous in the candlelight.

"Father," she said to Priam, "if it is your will, I will go down to the camp and offer myself to the Akhaians in return for the body of Hector."

"Yes, go," said Hecuba swiftly, almost before Helen had finished speaking, and before Priam could answer. "They will do you no harm."

Andromache chimed in, "It might be the one good act of a lifetime and atone for all else you have done to this house."

Kassandra was riveted to her seat, though her first impulse was to rise up and cry out "No, no!" Nevertheless, she remembered what she had prophesied when Paris first stood at the gates of Troy: that he was a firebrand who would kindle a fire to burn down all the city—a prophecy repeated when he had brought Helen here. That was long ago; she no longer blamed Helen for what would come to the city: that was the fate ordained by the Gods. And her father and brothers—even Hector himself—they had not heeded her then; and whatever she said, they would certainly do exactly the opposite. Better to keep silent.

Priam said gently, "Helen, it is a generous offer, but we cannot possibly allow you to do this. You are not the only cause of this war. We will ransom Hector's body—with all the gold of Troy if we must. Akhilles is not the only captain of the Akhaians. Surely there are some there who will listen to reason."

"No." Andromache rose and stood looking at Helen with a somber gaze; Kassandra realized that some people would think her more beautiful than Helen, though her beauty was of a different kind—dark where Helen was fair, lean where Helen was rounded. "No, Father, let her go, I beg of you. You owe me something too; I have borne Hector's son. I beg you, let her depart, and if she does not, drive her forth with whips. This woman has never been anything but a curse to all of us in Troy."

Paris rose to his feet. "If you drive out Helen," he declared, "I go with her."

"Go, then," cried Andromache wildly. "That too would be a blessing to our city! You are no less a curse than she! Your father did well when he sought to send you away."

"She is raving," Deiphobos said roughly. "Helen shall not go from us while I live; the Goddess sent Helen to us, and no other roof shall shelter her while my brothers and I live."

Priam looked down the hall. "What shall I do?" he asked half aloud. "My Queen and the wife of my Hector have said to us—"

"She must go," Andromache cried. "If she remains here, I will depart this night from Troy—and I call upon all the women of Priam's house to go forth with me; shall we remain under one roof with her who has cast our city down into the dust?"

"And yet the walls of Troy stand firm," Paris said. "All is not lost." He rose and came to Andromache, taking her hand gently and raising it to his lips.

"I bear you no grudge, poor girl," he said. "You are distraught with your grief, and no wonder. I'll answer that Helen shall hold no malice toward you."

Andromache jerked away.

"Women of Troy, I call on you, come forth from the accursed roof that shelters that false Goddess who would bring us all to ruin and slavery. . . ." Her voice had risen, high and hysterical; she picked up a torch and cried, "Follow me, women of Troy. . . ."

Priam rose in his place and thundered, "Enough! We have trouble enough without this! My child," he said to Andromache, "I understand your pain; but I beg you, sit down and listen to us. Nothing would be solved by driving Helen forth. Soldiers have fallen in battle long before Hector was born—or I." He reached out to embrace Andromache, and after a moment she collapsed against his breast, sobbing. Hecuba came to enfold her in her arms.

"Peace," she said somberly. "We have Troilus to mourn and to bury before the sun rises; and you women, collect your jewels to offer for Hector's ransom."

Kassandra, joining the women as they gathered together to assemble by Troilus' body, found herself wondering whether Andromache had been justified. Andromache alone among the women did not follow Hecuba; she remained at Priam's feet, crying out desolately, "I have not even a body over which to mourn." Then she raised her voice and called out, "Let not Helen touch Troilus' body, Mother! Know you not the old tale, a corpse will bleed if his murderer touches it?—and he has little blood left to spare, poor lad!"

9

ALL NIGHT Kassandra heard the rain and wind, beating and tearing around the high palace of Priam, as the women of the royal household wailed for Troilus. They washed and dressed his corpse, covered it with precious spices and burned incense to cover the sickly smell of death. In the gray lull between darkness and sunrise they ceased their nightlong mourning to drink wine and listen to a song from one of the minstrels in the room. She praised the beauty and bravery of the dead youth, singing that he had been felled because his beauty was such that the War-God desired him, and took the form of Akhilles in order to possess him.

When the song ended, Hecuba called the musician to her and gave her a ring as a memento of her noble elegy, and one of the women persuaded her to sit down and rest, and to drink a cup of warmed wine with spices. Helen, who had also accepted a cup, came and sat beside Kassandra.

"I will go and sit somewhere else if you do not want to be seen talking to me," she said, "but it seems I am not welcome anywhere among the women now." Her face looked thin, even haggard, and pale—she had lost weight since the deaths of her children, and Kassandra noted dulled strands within the gilt of her hair.

"No, stay here," Kassandra said. "I think you know I will always be your friend."

"All the same," Helen said, "my offer was sincere; I will return to Menelaus. He will probably kill me, but I might have a chance to see my only remaining daughter once before I die. Paris thinks we will have other children; and indeed, I had hoped—but it is too late for that. I think he wanted our son to rule Troy after us."

She looked half-questioning at Kassandra, and Kassandra nodded, with a shocking sense that by agreeing with what Helen had said, it was as if she willed that the doom be so.

In the last years she had grown accustomed to this feeling,

and knew its foolishness; the guilt, if guilt there must be, belonged only to the Gods, or whatever forces there were which made the Gods act as They did. She raised her cup to Helen and drank, feeling the heaviness of the wine strike her hard at this unaccustomed hour; and she had eaten but little the day before. Helen seemed to echo her thoughts, saying, "I wonder if the Queen is wise to serve so strong a wine unmixed when we are all half fainting with grief or hunger; these women will all be raving drunk in half an hour."

"It is a matter not of wisdom but of custom," Kassandra said. "If she served less than her best, they would question her love and respect for the dead boy."

"It's odd," Helen said reflectively, "the way people think, or refuse to think, about death. Paris, for one—it seems as if he thinks that since our children have died, perhaps the Gods will accept the sacrifice of their lives and spare ours."

"If a God would accept the innocent to expiate the sins of the guilty, I could have no reverence for Him; and yet there are some peoples who do believe in Gods who accept the sacrifice of innocent blood," Kassandra said. She added, almost in a whisper: "Perhaps it is an idea the Gods—or fiends—put into all men's heads; did not Agamemnon sacrifice his own daughter on the altar of the Maiden for a fair wind to bring his fleet to Troy?"

"It is so," said Helen, softly, "though Agamemnon will not now hear it named, and says the sacrifice was of his wife's—my sister's—doing, a sacrifice to her Goddess. The Akhaians fear the old Goddesses, saying they are tainted. The bravest of men flee in terror from women's Mysteries."

Kassandra looked round the shadowed room, where the women were drinking and talking in little groups.

"I wish somehow we could inspire them with this terror now," she said, and remembered how she had visited Akhilles' tent in a trance—or only in a dream? The thought stirred in her mind that perhaps she still might have some such access to the mind of the Akhaian hero; she would attempt it at the first opportunity. She raised her cup silently and drank; Helen, meeting her eyes over the rim, did the same.

There was a sudden strong draft in the room; the door

opened and Andromache stood there, holding a torch with long flaming streamers blowing in the strong wind from the corridor. Her long hair was dripping with rain and her dress and cloak sopping. She came through the room like a walking ghost, softly chanting one of the funeral hymns. She bent over Troilus' wrapped body and kissed the pale cheek.

"Farewell, dear brother," she said in her clear reedy voice. "You go before the greatest of heroes, to speak to the Gods of his eternal shame."

Kassandra went quickly to her and said softly, yet audibly, "Shame done to the brave is shame only to the one who commits the crime, not to the one who suffers it." Yet Hector had willingly fought Akhilles, playing that game of one scoring on another. *He did only what his whole life had taught him to do.*

She poured a cup of the spiced wine—it was heavy now, even less diluted than what had been in the pitcher when it was fuller. Perhaps it was better; Andromache would go from here to sleep and some ease of her horror, if not of her grief. She set the cup in her cousin's hand, smelling on her breath the heaviness of wine—wherever she had been, she had been drinking.

"Drink, my sister," she said.

"Ah, yes," Andromache said, tears spilling down her face. "With you I came to Troy when we were girls, and you told me, as we came here, so many stories of how brave and handsome he was. My child was born into your hands. You are my dearest friend for all our lives." She embraced Kassandra and clung to her, swaying, and Kassandra realized that she was already drunk. Kassandra herself was not unaffected by the wine she had drunk; she sensed Andromache's restlessness and her seeking.

Andromache bent again to kiss the dead face of Troilus. She said to Hecuba, "You are fortunate, my mother, that you can adorn his corpse and weep; my Hector lies moldering in the rain, unmourned, unburied."

"Not unmourned," said Kassandra gently. "All of us mourn for him. His spirit will hear your tears and lamentations, whether his body rests here or yonder with Akhilles' horses." Her voice broke; she was thinking of a day soon after Andromache had come to Troy, when Hector had forbidden her to bear weapons and threatened to beat her. She had spoken to try to comfort Andromache, but suddenly she wondered if she had made things worse. Andromache's eyes were cold and tearless. Kassandra guided her toward the seat; but when Andromache saw Helen there, she drew back, her lips baring her teeth in a dreadful masklike grimace which transformed her face almost into a skull.

"You, here, pretending to mourn?"

"The Gods know I pretend nothing," said Helen quietly, "but if you prefer it, I will go—you have the better right to be here."

"Oh, Andromache," Kassandra said, "don't speak so. You both came to this city as strangers, and found a home here. You have lost your husband, and Helen her children, at the hands of the Gods; you should share sorrow, not turn and rend one another. You are both my sisters and I love you." With one hand she drew Helen close; with the other arm embraced Andromache.

"You are right," said Andromache; "we are all helpless in Their hands." She snuffled and drank the last of her wine. Her voice was unsteady as she said drunkenly, "Sister, we are both victims in this war; the Goddess forbid this madness of men should sep—separate us." Her tongue stumbled clumsily on the words, and they were both weeping as they embraced. Hecuba came to enfold all three in her arms; she was crying too.

"So many gone! So many gone! Your precious children, Helen! My sons! Where is Hector's son, my last grandchild?"

"Not the last, Mother; have you forgotten? Creusa and her children were sent to safety; they risk nothing," Kassandra reminded her. "They are all out of range of Akhilles' madness or the Akhaian armies."

Andromache said, "Astyanax is too old for the women's quarters; I cannot even comfort him, nor seek to find comfort seeing his father in his face." Her voice was sadder than tears.

"When I lost—the little ones," Helen said shakily, "they brought Nikos to me for comfort; I will go, Andromache, and bring your son to you."

"Oh, bless you," Andromache cried.

Kassandra said, "Let me take you to your room; you do not want him here among all these drunken women."

"Yes, I will bring him to you there," Helen said. "You still have your son, and that is the greatest of all gifts."

One by one, or in twos and threes, the women, exhausted with grief and the strong wine, were slipping away to their beds. Only Hecuba, and Polyxena in her priestess' robes, took their station at Troilus' head and feet, there to remain until those came who would give his body to the earth. Kassandra wondered if she too should remain; but they had not asked her, not even to do the service of a priestess in purifying the chamber of death. Andromache and even Helen needed her more; she knew she was as alien among the women of Troy as were the Colchian and the Spartan woman.

She stayed with them until Helen had slipped into Paris' rooms and found Nikos and Astyanax. They had both been crying. Astyanax' face was filthy and smudged with tears; someone had evidently told him of his father's death and had tried to offer the child some solace. Helen took both boys to the well at the center of the courtyard and washed their faces with the corner of her veil.

Astyanax fell gratefully into his mother's arms, then said, bewildered, "Don't cry, Mother. They told me I was not to cry because my father is a hero. So why are *you* crying?"

Helen said gently, "Astyanax, you must help to dry your mother's tears; it is now your business to care for her, since your father cannot."

At the child's touch Andromache dissolved drunkenly into tears again; Helen and Kassandra took her to her room, put her to bed and tucked the boy in at her side.

"Nikos will stay with me," Helen said. "Oh, why do they take them from us so young?" But when she took Nikos in her arms, he pulled indignantly away.

"I'm not a baby, Mother! I shall go back to the men."

Smothering her sobs, Helen said, "As you like, child; but embrace me first."

Grudgingly Nikos complied, and ran away; Helen, tears streaming down her face, watched him go, unprotesting.

"Paris has done no better with him than Menelaus," she observed. "I do not like what men make of boys—making them like themselves. Thanks to the Gods Astyanax has not yet become ashamed to stay with his mother," she said, staring out into the hard gray rain that howled outside the palace.

"Kassandra!" she said suddenly. Her voice was so filled with dread and she clutched so abruptly at the other woman that Kassandra almost dropped the torch. "If we fall into the hands of the Akhaians, what will happen to my son? Perhaps the Trojans will stop at nothing to make sure Menelaus cannot reclaim him!"

"Are you saying that you think my father or brothers would kill the child to prevent his being taken back to Sparta?" Kassandra could hardly believe her ears.

"Oh, I cannot really believe it, but—"

"If you believe that, then perhaps you should indeed return to Menelaus, and take the child to safety," Kassandra said. "Surely he would welcome you if you came with his son. . . ."

"And I thought Nikos would be so much better off in Troy; that Paris would make a better father to him than Menelaus," Helen said sadly. "And he was, Kassandra, he was; but now . . . he seems to hate him because he is alive when our own sons died. . . ." Her voice broke and for a moment, clinging to Kassandra, she wept.

"Then you will go—?"

"I cannot," Helen said numbly. "I cannot persuade myself to leave Paris; I tell myself that it is the will of the Gods that I stay till this is all played out between us. He no longer loves me, but I would rather be in Troy than Sparta . . ." She let her voice trail away into silence, then said, "Kassandra, you are weary; I must keep you no longer from your bed. Or will you return and watch by Troilus?"

"No, I do not think they want me there," Kassandra said. "I will return to the Sun Lord's house."

"In this rain? Listen to this storm," Helen said. "You are welcome to sleep here if you will. You can sleep in my bed—it is less than likely Paris will come in now; they will all have drunk so much in honor of Hector's spirit that they would lose their way on the stairs. Or I will have the maids make up a bed for you in the other room."

"You are very kind, Sister, but the servants will all be sleeping by now; let them rest," Kassandra said. "The rain will clear my head." She picked up her cloak and put the hood over her head, then embraced Helen and kissed her. She said, "Andromache did not mean what she said to you."

"Oh, I know that; in her place I should feel the same," Helen said. "She is afraid; what will become of her now, and Astyanax? Paris has already decided that he will succeed Priam, and leave no place for Hector's son; and if Paris should somehow bring this war to a good end—"

"There is no chance of that," said Kassandra. "Yet you must not be afraid, Helen; Menelaus has not fought all these years for revenge."

"I know that; I have spoken with him," Helen said, surprising her. "I know not why, but it seems he wants me back."

"You've spoken with him? When?" She started to ask how, but remembered that as Paris' wife Helen could go where she would, even down into the Akhaian camp. But why should she go and confer with the captains among the enemy? she thought suspiciously, then mentally absolved her friend of treason. It was no more than reasonable that Helen should wish to bargain for her own fate and that of her son.

She said, "If you speak with him again, ask him if there is something he can do to influence Akhilles and have Hector's body returned to us."

"Believe me, I have tried and will try again," Helen said. "Listen, the rain is slackening a little; if you go now, perhaps you will be home before it starts to come down hard again."

She kissed Kassandra again, and went down to the heavy front gate of the palace with her. Kassandra went out into the icy rain. Before she had climbed half a flight of the long stairs, it began to beat down with renewed fury, and the wind tore at her cloak like a wild beast's claws.

She thought for a moment, regretfully, that she should have accepted Helen's offer of a bed. Aeneas would be feasting and drinking with the men, and would be unlikely to join her tonight. But there was no point in turning back now; she struggled upward against the storm.

As she turned into the street of the Sun Lord's house, she heard a light step in the street behind her. After so many years of war she was nervous of strangers, and turned to see, in the pale light of the torches hung up over the gateway, the face and cloaked form of Chryseis. Even in the torchlight she could see that the girl's dress was rumpled and stained with wine, and the cosmetics on her face were smeared. She sighed, wondering in what strange bed the girl had spent much of the night and why she had bothered to leave it in such a storm. *She looks like a cat after a night of wandering—except that a cat would have washed her face.*

The watchman at the gates of the Sun Lord's house greeted them with amazement ("You are abroad late in this cruel weather, Ladies"), but no one had ever shown curiosity about Kassandra's comings and goings; she reflected that she might have had as many lovers as Chryseis, and no one would have known or cared. As they climbed the steep courtyard toward their rooms, located near the highest part of the Temple, she slowed her steps to match the girl's.

"It is growing so late it is almost early," she said. "Do you want to come into my room and wash your face before you are seen like this in the Temple?"

"No," Chryseis said, "why should I? I am not ashamed of whatever I do."

"I would spare your father the sight of you like this," Kassandra said. "It would break his heart."

Chryseis' laughter was brittle as breaking glass.

"Oh, come, surely he cannot still cherish any illusions that I came from Agamemnon's bed a virgin!"

"Perhaps not," Kassandra said. "He cannot blame you for the fortunes of war; but to see you like this would distress him."

"Do you think I care for that? I was well content where I was, and I wish he had minded his own affairs, and left me there."

"Chryseis," Kassandra said gently, "do you have any idea how dreadfully he grieved for you? He thought of little else."

"Then the more fool he."

"Chryseis . . ." Kassandra looked at the girl, wondering what was in her heart or if, indeed, she had one. She asked at last, curiously, "Doesn't it shame you at all, to stand before all men in Troy and know that all men know and recognize you for having been Agamemnon's concubine?"

"No," Chryseis said defiantly, "no more than it shames Andromache to have all men know she is Hector's, nor Helen to have it common knowledge that she belongs to Paris."

There was a difference, Kassandra knew, but she could not muster her thoughts to tell this confused girl what it was.

"If the city should fall," Chryseis said, "all of us will be given into the hands of some man or other; so I give myself where I choose while I still can. Will you, Kassandra, keep your own maidenhood so that it may be taken by a conqueror by force?"

For that I cannot fault her at all. Kassandra could not speak; she only turned and went into her own room.

Inside, some neglectful servant had left the shutters wide open; the rain and wind were beating in through the windows. Honey's pallet was sodden, and the child had rolled off the quilts and onto the stone floor against the wall to escape the rain. Even so she was soaked.

Kassandra closed the shutters and took the child to her own bed. Honey felt as cold as a little frog and whimpered when Kassandra lifted her, but did not wake. Kassandra wrapped her in blankets and rocked her, holding her close against her breasts until she felt the icy little feet and hands beginning to warm, and at last Honey was sleeping the heavy sleep of any healthy child.

She put the little girl down and lay down herself beside her, wrapping them both in her warm cloak. The noise of the storm outside the closed windows was muffled, but still rattled the shutters with its force. She closed her eyes, trying to move her spirit forth from where she lay.

To her surprise, once she had slipped free of her body, moving her consciousness away from the bed and through the window, she had no awareness of the storm, only a deep silence; on the level where her spirit now moved there was no weather.

As swiftly as thought she glided down the hill into clear moon-light, flying over the plain between the gates of Troy and the earthworks that guarded the Akhaian camp.

Under that impossible moonlight, shadows lay sharp and black on the plain, silent and untenanted except by a single drowsing night watchman. Paris was right, she thought: they should have flung all their forces at the camp by night. Then she remembered that in the physical world the Akhaian earth-works were better guarded by the pouring rain than by all the watchmen in the world. She could see a dark-shadowed struc-ture which she recognized as Akhilles' chariot, and a blurred shape which had to be Hector's bound body. Her first thought was gratitude that in this analogue of the Afterworld—and how had she come to walk so handily in this world of the dead when she was still among the living?—Hector's body was not battered by rain and howling wind. And as she thought of him, he was standing there before her, smiling.

"Sister," he said, "it is you. I might have expected to see you here."

"Hector . . ." She broke off. "How is it with you?"

"Why . . ." he stopped and seemed to consider. "Better than I ever expected," he said. "The pain is gone, so I suppose I am dead. I remember only being wounded, and thinking this must be the end; then I woke, and Patroklos came and helped me to rise. He was with me for a while, and then he said he had to stay with Akhilles, and went away. After that I went to the palace tonight, but Andromache could not see me. I tried to speak with her and then with Mother, to tell them I was all right, but neither of them seemed to hear me at all."

"When you were living, did you ever hear the voice of the dead?"

"Well, no, of course not; I never learned how to listen for it."

"Well, then: that is why they could not hear. What can I do for you, my brother? Do you want sacrifices or—"

"I can't imagine what good it would do," Hector said. "But do tell Andromache not to cry; it feels very strange not to be able to comfort her. Tell her not to mourn; and if you can, tell her I will come soon and take Astyanax with me. I would like to leave him to take care of her, but I have been told—"

"By whom?"

"I don't know," Hector said, "I can't seem to remember; perhaps it was Patroklos—but I know well that my son will come to me very soon, and Father, and Paris. But not Andromache; she will stay there a long time." He advanced to her, and she felt the faint touch of his lips against her forehead.

"I will bid you farewell too, Sister," he said, "but have no fears, there will be much to suffer, but I promise you, all will be well with you."

"And Troy?"

"Ah, no; it is already fallen," he said. "See?" And he turned her around, with gentle insubstantial hands, and behind her she saw a great heap of rubble, with flames rising, where once Troy had stood. But the sound of such destruction . . . how could she not have heard it?

"There is no time here," he said. "What is, and what is to be, are all one. I do not understand all these things," he said fretfully, "for tonight I walked in the halls of my father's palace where they were feasting, and now look, the city has been fallen for a long time. Maybe when I was on earth I should have inquired of those who know these things, but there never seemed to be time. But now I see Apollo and Poseidon—look, They are striving with each other for the city," he said, and pointed to where above the fallen walls it seemed that two monstrous figures, spanning the clouds, stood and battled, Their flesh glowing like lightning.

She shivered at the sight of the beloved face of the Sun Lord, crowned by brilliant golden curls; would He turn and see her walking in the forbidden realms? Resolutely she turned back to Hector's shadowy form.

"What of Troilus? Is it well with him?"

"He was with me for a little; he came running out just a little behind me," Hector said. "But he remained at the palace with Mother; he was trying to tell her not to grieve. He would not believe that he could not make her hear him. Perhaps she would listen to you if you told her; she knows you are a priestess and wise in such things."

"Ah, I do not know if she will listen to me either, dear Brother," Kassandra said. "She has her own opinions and no room for mine. But for the sake of our parents and their peace of mind . . ." She stopped to consider. "I came here to try and perhaps frighten Akhilles into releasing your body for ransom; perhaps you would do better than I at that."

"Do you think he'd be afraid of ghosts? He has killed so many, he must live with them surrounding him at all times," Hector said, "but I will go and see what I can do. Go back, Sister, back to your own side of that wall which now rises between us, and tell Mother and Father that they should not waste time grieving; they will be with me soon enough. And be certain to tell Andromache not to grieve: I will be waiting here for our son; and tell *him* not to be afraid: I will be ready to greet him. She would not want him to live in the days that are coming now."

Hector turned away from her and drifted toward the tent of Akhilles. After a moment he turned again, and already, she thought, he looked distant and strange, a man she did not know. "No, do not follow, Sister; our ways part here. Perhaps we may meet again, and understand each other better."

"Am I not to join you and Troilus, and our mother and father?"

"I don't know," he said. "You serve other Gods; I think if you pass death you may go elsewhere. But it is given to me to know that here our ways part, for a long time if not forever. May it always be well with you, Kassandra." He embraced her, and she was surprised to feel the strength of his embrace. This was no ghost, but as real as she was herself. Then he was gone, even his shadow vanishing on the plain.

10

TOWARD MORNING the rain stopped, and was replaced by strong winds. Kassandra drifted into and out of sleep, where again and

again she dreamed she tried to follow Hector's ghost toward the
tent of Akhilles, where the Akhaian roused to stare and gibber
in terror at the sight of Hector walking in and out through the
tent walls, laughing at him; or else found herself in Agamemnon's tent. The King stared wildly up at her and tried to seize
her, but she drifted out of his arms as if she were made of mist,
and he shouted with rage and lunged after her, howling with
frustration.

When at last she woke, faint sunlight was coming through
the shutters, and Honey was staring at her in amazement. She
wondered if she had been talking or crying out in her sleep. She
seldom slept this late, but of course she had been awake till
almost dawn. Dressing quickly, she tried to cling with her memory to the messages Hector had told her to give; she knew how
quickly, like half-remembered dreams, such experiences faded.
She was just tying the belt of her dress when Phyllida ran in.

"Kassandra, come at once; the serpents—"

"I cannot, I have a message to deliver," Kassandra said. "I
trust that you can do whatever needs to be done."

"But—"

"Well, quickly then—have they run away or all crawled into
their homes?" she demanded, suddenly afraid that this would be
the dreaded earthquake warning; it was sure to come soon—
only, please the Gods, not today, not today!

"Well, no, but—"

"Then don't trouble me; I have weighty matters on my
mind and cannot stay to talk. Take Honey with you; dress her
and give her some breakfast—I'll come and tend to her when I
can," she said, and ran out of the chamber and down the hill.

As she went downward, she stopped briefly to look over the
wall; once again Akhilles' chariot was circling on the plain, his
horses whipped to their greatest speed. The inert bundle of
Hector's body was being dragged behind; yet her Sight was now
so clear between worlds that she could see him, a bright shadow
standing at the edge of the field, laughing at the foolish thing
the Akhaian captain was trying to do. She knew what he found
so funny; and as she came down to her parents, standing on the
wall in the usual place above the gates, she laughed aloud.

Hecuba's eyes, almost swollen shut with crying, turned to her angrily.

"How can you laugh?"

"But can't you see, dearest Mother, how foolish it all is? Look, there in the shadow of the earthworks: Hector is laughing at Akhilles' foolishness—look at the sun shining on his hair."

Hecuba gave Kassandra her resigned *But of course, she is mad and cannot be expected to feel anything like a normal person* look, but Kassandra seized her mother's arms.

"Mother, what I tell you is true; last night I spoke with Hector in the Land Beyond Death, and I tell you all is well with him."

"You dreamed it, my darling," said Hecuba gently.

"No, Mother dear, I saw him as I see you, and touched him."

"I wish I could believe you. . . ." Tears gathered slowly and dropped from the old woman's eyes.

"Mother, truly, you must believe me! And he said to tell you that you must not grieve—"

"Last night I could almost have believed it—I thought once that I heard Troilus' voice—"

"You did, Mother, I tell you you did!" Kassandra cried out in excitement, full of her message. "I did not see or speak with Troilus, because Hector said that he stayed with you, trying to comfort you, trying to make you hear him."

Hecuba said slowly, "When Polyxena and I were too weary to watch longer—already the sun was rising—I stepped into the garden for a moment, and I thought I felt Troilus touch my hair as he did when he grew too tall to kiss me except on the top of the head. He was such a sweet little boy, the dearest of all my sweet boys . . ." Her eyes filled and spilled over again, and Kassandra hugged her mother close.

"He was certainly at your side," she said; "I swear it to you."

"And Hector—you say he too is at peace—but how can his spirit be free when we have not his body to give it decent burial and pay honor to his spirit?" Hecuba demanded. "And if it be so, then why have funeral rites been ordained by the Gods?"

"I know only what I have seen, Mother."

"It is no use," said Hecuba despairingly, after considering this for a time. "I cannot think of his spirit as free while I see his poor body . . . Look how the dust rises, even after a full night of heavy rain!" she exclaimed, and began to cry again.

Kassandra tried to dry her mother's tears with her veil, chiding her, "It would break Hector's heart to see you cry like this. Akhilles cannot hurt him now, whatever he may do. Even if he should cut up Hector's body and feed it to his dogs, it would not harm the part of Hector we knew, not at all."

Hecuba cringed and looked sick. "How can you say such things, Kassandra?"

"I am sworn by Apollo to speak the truth; to those who will not hear it I can only say that this does not excuse me from speaking it," Kassandra replied, wondering why only her mother could make her this angry even—or especially—when she was trying to say nothing that could upset her.

"But here you are saying that we could feed our Hector to the dogs—"

"Mother, I said no such thing!" Kassandra was furious now, but with an effort she kept her voice steady and calm. "You did not hear me aright! I said only that if Akhilles in his madness should do such a thing it would make no difference to Hector, but only to us."

"But you were saying—I heard you—that we did not need to give him funeral rites," Hecuba said, and Kassandra sighed as if she were dragging a very heavy weight uphill.

"Mother, I do not think funeral rites matter at all to Hector or to the Gods, but only to us," she repeated, as if she were trying to explain to Honey why she could not eat a dozen cakes.

Hecuba thrust out her chin. "And I say this is only one of your wild notions," she said, and turned away.

"Yes, very likely, Mother," Kassandra said, stifling her rage. *She is old; I cannot expect her to understand anything that is new to her.*

"But I beg you to say nothing like that to Andromache, Kassandra; she has already enough grief to bear without that."

"Without what?" asked Andromache, stepping up to the wall in time to hear the last words.

"I was saying to her," Kassandra began, and Hecuba flashed an angry *Don't you dare* glance at her; Kassandra realized that the argument with her mother had made her forget the exact words she had intended to speak.

She said wearily, "Only that in a vision last night I spoke with Hector and he bade you be comforted, because he is content and at peace, whatever they may do to his body." There was more; Hector had bidden her to say to Andromache—what? That he would come to take his son . . . *but no! I can't say to her that her son will die, when she has lost Hector too . . . she . . . what was it . . . that she wouldn't want her son to live in the days that are coming. . . .*

Andromache was watching her with arched-brow skepticism; Kassandra said, "He bade me say that—that he would remain to watch over his son."

"Much good that does either of us," Andromache said, with the wide-open eyes of suppressed tears, "when he has left us."

"But he does not want you to cry and grieve," Kassandra said. "It cannot help him now."

"Every seer and soothsayer tells us that," Andromache said, and she sounded bitter. "I had hoped for something better from you, Kassandra, if indeed you can see beyond death."

"I speak as the God bids me speak in such words as people are willing to hear," Kassandra said, and turned away. Out on the field, Akhilles went on whipping his horses in an ever more maniacal fury.

All day, as the sun rose and declined over Troy, this went on. Twice Paris led out a party to try to capture Akhilles' chariot and Hector's body, and twice the troops of Agamemnon drove them off again; three of Priam's lesser sons by his palace women were killed, and at last they realized Akhilles was simply too well protected.

"No more," Priam said after the third attack. "The sun is setting; when it is dark, I will myself go down to Akhilles and try to bargain with him to ransom my son's body."

How foolish, Kassandra thought, *and how useless; Hector is not in that lump of rotting flesh out there tied behind Akhilles and his damned chariot.* Why could she see this when her parents could not? Should they not be wiser than she was? It frightened her that they were not.

She felt ill and faint; she had stood all day by her mother and had not even partaken of the hard bread and oil portioned out to the soldiers at noon. She went and ate a little bread, washing it down with a few sips of watered wine, then went with Hecuba, who was assisting Priam's body-servants to dress him in his richest robes.

"If I go to Akhilles without robing myself in my finest," he said, "he may believe I do not think him worthy of honor. I don't, of course, but I don't want him to think so."

"I'm not so sure, Father," Paris said; he was standing beside his father, trimming his beard meticulously with the scissors Helen used for her tapestry. "Perhaps that madman's vanity would be more flattered if you went to him robed simply in mourning, as a suppliant."

"Yet showing him the gold of Troy may arouse his greed if we cannot appeal to his honor," Andromache said.

"We can hardly appeal to his honor," said Paris. "It seems obvious to me that he has none. The question is how we can best persuade him to give us Hector for burial."

"I will go to him as a suppliant," Priam said. Already he was energetically tearing off his robes. "Bring me the plainest garment I own. Also, I will go to him alone."

"No!" Hecuba cried, falling to her knees before him in an agony of despair. "We have already seen he has no respect for customary honor, or Hector would even now be in his tomb! If you go within his reach, he will certainly kill you or mistreat you, and perhaps offer the same kind of insult to your corpse that he has offered to Hector's. You cannot go to him unguarded."

"If I must, I will go first to our old friend Odysseus, who will bring me safely to Akhilles," Priam said, "and we know he wants the good opinion of Odysseus; he will offer me no insult in his presence."

"That's not enough," Hecuba declared, clinging tightly to his knees. "If you are bent on this folly you shall not take a single step; for I will not let you go at all."

Priam tried to shake her loose, but she would not be dislodged. He stood scowling crossly.

"Come, my lady," he said at last, "what would you have me do, then? If I go to Akhilles with armed men, he will only think I am challenging him to single combat; is that what you want?"

"No!" Hecuba cried, but she refused still to loose her hold.

"Well, then, what do you want me to do? Why can a woman never be reasonable?" Priam demanded.

"I don't know, my lord and my love; but you're not going down to that madman alone!"

"Let *me* go," said Andromache with quiet dignity. "Let him explain to Hector's widow and to his child why he will not ransom him."

"Oh, my dear—" Priam began, but Hecuba started up in indignation.

"If you think I'd let you take my grandson within a league of that fiend—"

"A better thought," Helen said: "take a priest—if only as a witness before the Gods; Akhilles fears the Gods—"

"Better yet," said Priam, "I will take two priestesses, Kassandra and Polyxena. One serves Apollo and one the Maiden, so whichever Immortal Akhilles fears may witness his impiety."

He turned to Kassandra and said, "You are not afraid to go with your old father into Akhilles' presence, are you, girl?"

"No, Father," she said, "and I will go unarmed if you will, or weaponed; have you forgotten I was trained as a warrior?"

"No," Polyxena said in her childish voice, "no weapons, Sister; we go barefoot with our hair unbound, praying for his mercy. It will flatter his vanity to have us kneeling at his feet. Go and robe yourself in an unadorned white tunic without embroidery or bands, and comb out your hair—or better yet," she added, seizing the scissors from Paris, "cut it in token of mourning." She hacked vigorously at her long reddish curls, disregarding her mother's cries of protest. Then she began to cut away Kassandra's, and as Kassandra looked, shocked, at the waist-length tresses lying on the floor, she exclaimed, "Do you begrudge Hector your vanity?"

I wouldn't if I thought it would make a fingernail's worth of difference to Hector, Kassandra thought, but was wise enough not to say the words aloud. She let Polyxena take off her rings and the necklace of pearls she wore; her sister then stripped off her own jewels. Priam kept only one large and beautiful emerald ring on his finger—a gift for Akhilles, he said—and removed his own sandals. Kassandra took a torch in her hand, and Polyxena another, and with their father they went down from the palace. At the gates of Troy, Priam bade his servants turn back.

"I know you do not want to desert me," he said, "but if we cannot do this alone it probably cannot be done at all. If Akhilles will not listen to a grieving father and sisters, he would not listen to the whole armed might of Troy. Go back, my children."

Most of them wept, and cried out with grief and fear for him; but at last, one by one, they turned back and the three suppliants went through the opened gates, and began moving deliberately, by the light of their two torches, across the plain.

The ground was still muddy underfoot from the last night's rain; and it was very dark, for the sky was covered with thick clouds which now and then opened to show a withering moon. Kassandra shivered in her plain robe, the cold rising up through her muddy feet, and wondered if the sky would open for a further downpour. Such a useless errand, and yet if it gave peace of mind to her father, how could she refuse?

Priam moved slowly, she noticed, with a pain at her heart, as if his legs would hardly carry him and he were borne along by his strength of will alone. *Will this, then, be his death? Oh, damn Hector for having the bad luck and the bad sense to go and get himself killed!* she thought, stumbling along behind Polyxena with her eyes so full of tears that she could hardly see where she was going.

Was Hector still here on this plain, bound somehow to that lump of decaying flesh tied behind Akhilles' chariot? Why did he not come and speak with them, forbid his father to humble himself to Akhilles? No, Hector had bidden her farewell and said they would not meet again. If she had told her father and mother that she had seen the ruin of Troy, would they have believed her? Or would it have made them even more eager to see all things done in order while there was still time enough?

A solitary watchman challenged them: "Who goes there?"

Priam's voice sounded thin and quavering; Kassandra had never realized quite how old and feeble he sounded.

"It is Priam, son of Laomedon, King of Troy; I seek a parley with the Lord Akhilles."

There was a muttering of voices, and after a time a lantern flashed on them.

"My lord of Troy, you are welcome, but if you have an armed guard you must leave them here."

"No guard at all, armed or unarmed," Priam said. "I come only as a suppliant to Akhilles; my only company is my two young daughters."

It made them sound, Kassandra thought, as if they were little girls, not grown women past twenty. As if explaining this, Priam added, "They are both sworn priestesses, one of Apollo and one of the Maiden; not the wives of warriors."

"Why are they here, then?"

"Only to support our father if his steps should stumble by the way," said Polyxena, as the torch flashed in their faces.

Kassandra added, "I am known to the Akhaian captains; I was present at the negotiations for the return of Chryseis, daughter of Apollo's priest." After she said this she wondered if she should have mentioned it; Akhilles had not come out of that encounter so well that he would wish to be reminded of it.

But the watchman evidently didn't know or didn't care about that. He said, "Let them come, then," and lowered the torch, saying, "Follow me."

He led the way across the ground, rutted by chariot wheels, toward the light that streamed from the tent of Akhilles. Inside was warmth and even a certain degree of comfort; chairs covered with furs and skins, tapestry hangings and a table spread with fruits and wine. Akhilles sat at the center of the tent, looking as if he had arranged himself to give audience. At the far end of the tent, in the shadows between the light of half a dozen lamps, lay the shrouded and mummified figure of Patroklos, just as Kassandra had seen it in her vision. Nearer the door stood Agamemnon, and beside him Odysseus with a cup of wine in his hand; they looked as if they had been set up for a tableau. Akhilles was apparently just fresh from his bath; he looked very clean, his skin as pink as a little child's; his hair, which had been cut short, silver-gilt in the light, was being combed by a slave, whom Kassandra recognized as her mother's woman Briseis. As his gaze fell on Priam, he put up his hand to stop the combing, and the woman drew back.

"Well, my lord of Troy," he said, his thin lips stretching back in what Kassandra thought of as a grin of contempt, "what brings you out on a night like this?"

As if he didn't know perfectly well! But it was obvious to all of them that Akhilles was all set to enjoy this. Priam came forth into the lantern light; Kassandra and Polyxena drew together, watching him. Priam knelt clumsily down, extending his hands in a pleading gesture toward the younger man.

"Oh, my lord Akhilles, I am sure I need not say to you why I have come; I beg you to yield up to me what is customary and proper, and give me the body of my fallen son Hector for proper burial."

Akhilles' facial muscles barely twitched into a slight smile. Priam rushed on, "You are so valiant, sir; you have fought long; but all these years of battle, we have returned your dead to you that their bodies may be given to the fire and their spirits sent off properly to the Afterworld."

"Hector angered me," Akhilles said. "He really should not have had the arrogance to go up against me, whom the Gods have sworn to protect."

Priam stopped and swallowed; he could not think what to say to that. Kassandra clenched her fists under her hanging sleeves.

And he dares speak of arrogance?

Priam said at last, "My lord Akhilles, a warrior challenges the finest opponent he can. And he has fallen; you who are so powerful, can you not be merciful to Hector's wife and child as well?"

"No," said Akhilles, "I can't."

He stopped, and Kassandra could hear them all listening for his next word; but he was so silent for so long that she thought he intended to leave it at that. But then he said, "I have sworn that I will have the revenge that has been given to me."

Priam leaned forward and laid his hands on Akhilles' knees. His words rushed out of him.

"Prince Akhilles, you must have had a father once; can you not for your own father's sake be merciful? Hector was the eldest of my sons; I was proud of him as your father must have been of you. And when the gallant Patroklos fell in battle, Hector did not seek to keep his body; he honored a brave fallen foe! He came to the funeral games for Patroklos, because, he said, Patroklos would not begrudge him a good dinner; and he said that he looked forward to having much to talk about with Patroklos in the Afterlife. They were both warriors, and when the battles of this world were over he trusted they would be friends as fellow warriors. Let us lay Hector to rest as you will bury Patroklos."

Akhilles looked toward the shadowed corner of the tent, and Kassandra saw that his eyes were suddenly filled with tears. She could see emotions chasing themselves over his features: hatred, scorn, pity, sorrow; but the sorrow predominated. Her father had evidently found the one thing that might cut through the arrogance and scorn. Akhilles said slowly, "You are right, my lord of Troy; Patroklos has a friend, then, in the Afterlife. Guard!" he snapped out. "Go out and bring us the body of royal Hector!"

The soldier bowed to the ground and fled.

Akhilles said, "You spoke of a ransom? What ransom do you offer me, then?"

Priam muttered, "That is for you, noble Akhilles, to say." He drew the ring from his finger and set it on Akhilles' finger. "First I offer this as a gift to you with my thanks."

Akhilles stroked it consideringly. He said with his cruel smile, "I suppose Hector is worth more to you than a few captured chariots."

The madman is enjoying this. It was obvious to Kassandra that he was contemplating something outrageous. Priam mumbled, "I have sworn that I will pay without haggling whatever you ask, Prince Akhilles."

Akhilles rubbed his chin, evidently intending to extort the most drama he could from the scene. "Agamemnon—what should I ask for ransom?"

"Get a good one," Agamemnon said carelessly. "The King of Troy can afford anything you ask; his city has half the riches of the world within its walls."

Odysseus interrupted and said clearly, "Your nobility will be measured by your generosity, Akhilles; will you allow a Trojan to outdo you in generosity?" His face was turned away; Kassandra thought that he was ashamed. She wished that they could have dealt with Odysseus alone.

"It's easy to see what a friend to the Trojans you have always been, Odysseus," said Agamemnon. "I have not forgotten how we hardly persuaded you to fight on our side at all."

"Half the riches of the world," murmured Akhilles, looking greedily at the ring. "But still, I do not want to be too greedy; what would I do with half the wealth of the world? I will ask, then, only the weight of Hector's body in gold."

"You shall have it," said Priam, unflinching. "I have sworn."

But this is unsufferable, Kassandra thought; *no such ransom has ever been asked or paid in the whole history of warfare.* Only Akhilles would have ventured such a thing. Odysseus made a sharp movement as if he were about to protest; but he did not speak. Kassandra knew why: a wrong word might touch off Akhilles' madness, and then there would be no ransom at all.

Priam said, "It shall be weighed out before your eyes at dawn before the walls of Troy, Prince Akhilles, to the last ounce." Priam bowed so that Akhilles could not see the angry contempt on his face.

Akhilles smiled; he had what he wanted, and he had it before his allies.

"Will you drink with me to the bargain, then, my lord of Troy?"

"Thank you," Priam said; it was all too obvious he would rather have spat in Akhilles' face, but he raised the cup the prince set in his hand and took a few swallows, after which he passed the cup to Polyxena and then to Kassandra, who put the cup to her lips without drinking; she knew it would choke her.

"May I then have Hector's body, that his mother and sisters may ready it for burial?"

"It shall be returned to you washed and decently shrouded, anointed with oil and spices, at dawn before the walls, when the ransom is paid," Akhilles said.

"Akhilles, in the name of Zeus Thunderer!" Agamemnon burst out. "The King of Troy makes no niggling bargain! Give him what he came for!"

"I did not think a father would wish to look on the body as it is now," said Akhilles, deliberately, watching Priam's face as he spoke. (A *cruel child, pulling the wings off nesting birds.*) "I would have it made seemly for his mother to look upon."

"My Lord Akhilles is as kind as we believed all along he was noble," said Kassandra quickly. *Yes, just exactly as we believed.* "Let it be so. At dawn then, Lord Akhilles," and she pulled at her father's sleeve. Priam's head was bent, and he was weeping. She steadied him, and Polyxena took his other arm as they went out of the tent—quickly, so that Priam would not hear the laughter of Akhilles behind him.

11

As SOON as they returned to Troy, Priam set all the people of the household to frenzied activity, stripping the palace of golden ornaments, demanding the golden necklaces, earrings and rings of the women and gold cups from the table, even before he opened the treasure room, and had the gold carried up to the walls.

Priam sent for a priest from the Sun Lord's Temple to rig up a pair of scales. It was Khryse, and for once he was genuinely too busy to take the slightest notice of Kassandra as he worked with pulleys and weights. She watched him work, understanding the principles of what he was doing, but knowing she had not the skill with her hands or knowledge to do it herself. When he had the strange-looking balance strung up, he asked her to lie on one of the platforms so that it could be tested.

"Just pretend you are a dead weight," he said.

"As you like." She took her place, watching as the people of the household piled gold on the other part of the scale. She was surprised at the smallness of the heap that balanced her, lifting her slowly into the air. He saw her look and said, "Gold is heavier than most people think."

She was sure Akhilles knew to the fingerweight how much gold he would be getting. She began to sit up as they took off the gold and piled it up.

"Your weight in gold, Kassandra," Khryse said: "if it were mine, I would offer it all to you for a bride-price."

She sighed and said, "Do not begin that again, my brother."

He looked crestfallen. "Must you always destroy any hopes I might have for happiness in this world?"

"Oh, if what you want is a wife," she said with an angry laugh, "there are women enough and to spare in Troy."

"You know that for me," Khryse said, "there is no woman save you alone."

"Then I fear you will live and die unwed," Kassandra said firmly, "even if yonder gold were your own and you could dower me with it." She slid to her feet, looking at the heap of gold which equaled her weight. She had never greatly cared for jewelry, and she could only marvel that this cold stuff excited so much greed in so many people. Somehow, even knowing Akhilles as she did, she had not thought he could be swayed with gold alone; she had thought he might attempt some additional humiliation on the royal house of Troy.

Above them, lighting the top of the stones, the sun was rising; she stepped to the top of the wall and extended her arms silently in the morning salutation to the Sun Lord.

"Sing the morning hymn, Kassandra," Khryse urged. "Your voice is sweet, but we so seldom hear it lent to us now, even for Apollo's sake."

Stubbornly she shook her head; if she sang, he would accuse her again of trying to entice him. "I prefer to sing only in the presence of the God alone," she murmured, and was silent.

Priam, coming with his servants and another basketful of gold—even though the precious stuff barely covered the bottom of the basket, it was so heavy that it had to be carried between two men—said, "Well, priest, are the scales ready?"

"They await your pleasure, my lord."

"My pleasure? You fool, do you think I take any pleasure in this business?" Priam demanded crustily. He was still wearing the white robe of a suppliant, streaked with mud from the earthworks; his bare feet were caked with mud.

Polyxena whispered to him, but Priam said aloud, "Are you saying that for that villain Akhilles I should bathe and comb my hair and put on fair garments, as if this were a wedding and not a funeral? And I care not if this is the chief among the Sun Lord's priests, he is no less a fool for all that!"

Kassandra covered her mouth with her fingertips; it would be unseemly to smile at this moment. Surely there was little to smile about, except the discomfiture on Khryse's face; it seemed to her that her father spoke with the peevish sound of senility.

Priam motioned to the servants to put the basket down by the rest of the gold. "Now we await Akhilles' will. It would be like him to drive such a degrading bargain as this and make us wait all day—or not to come at all."

"He made the bargain before witnesses," Polyxena reminded her father. "*They* will make him come. They are eager to get on with this war, now they don't have Hector to face."

There was silence while Priam's household slowly gathered on the wall, Hecuba and Andromache standing on either side of the King.

Kassandra was not sure exactly what it was that she expected: perhaps Akhilles' chariot galloping at his usual breakneck speed toward the walls. She looked into the rising sun till her eyes ached.

Khryse stood at her side and put his arm under hers as if to lend her support; she was exasperated, but did not want to draw attention to herself by moving away. The priest said, "They are astir in the Argive camp; what are they waiting for?"

"Perhaps to humble my father further by seeing him faint with exhaustion from the heat," she murmured. "Khryse, compared with Akhilles, Agamemnon is surely noble and kindly."

"I know little of him," Khryse said, "but enough to know I

would not willingly see the fate of Troy in his hands; and Priam's health and strength are now all the hope we have for Troy."

Little hope that is, she thought, but remained silent. She had no wish to discuss her fears for her father with anyone, and certainly not with a man she distrusted.

"Look," Polyxena said, and pointed, barely raising her arm. Far out on the plain, figures were moving; as they came nearer, Kassandra made out Akhilles, his pale hair shining in a blinding streak of sunlight. He was walking at the head of a small procession; behind him, eight of his soldiers carried a body on a pallet —it could only be that of Hector—and behind them came a half dozen Akhaian chieftains, in full armor, but bearing no weapons.

At least, for once Akhilles has kept his word. She let out her breath, only now realizing that until she saw Hector's body she had not for a moment expected him to do so.

They were nearer now; she could make out individual faces and even see the details of the embroidery on the pall that covered Hector's body. Akhilles bowed before Priam and said, "As I promised, my lord of Troy, behold the body of your son."

"The ransom awaits you, Prince Akhilles," Priam said, and went to the pall, folding back the heavy covering to expose the face. "First let me make certain that it is truly the body of my son. . . ."

Hecuba came to stand beside him as he rolled back the pall, with Penthesilea ready beside her should she need support. Kassandra was braced to hear her mother break into wailing or shrieking, but she simply nodded gravely and bent to kiss the cold white forehead. Priam said, "The scales have been set up by a priest of Apollo Sun Lord who is skilled in such things. If you would like to check the weights for yourself—"

"No, no," said Akhilles with a bizarre geniality, "I know very little of such things, my lord."

Khryse said, conducting Akhilles to the edge of the scales, "You worked against your own best interest, Prince Akhilles, when you allowed Hector's body to become so mangled; in perfect condition it would have brought you more gold." The jest seemed gross and inappropriate. Kassandra wondered, looking at Khryse's shaking hands and the overbrilliant pupils of his eyes, if he had been drinking unmixed wine, or a brew of wine and poppy seeds, so early in the day that he had forgotten in whose presence he was.

Priam turned pale and said stiffly, "Let's get on with this." He gestured, and the body of Hector was hoisted up to lie on the platform. Priam's slaves began to scoop out the gold onto the other platform, a few pieces at a time. Akhilles watched, barely smiling, as the platform bearing the body trembled and began to rise from the ground. Kassandra wondered if the other watchers found the scene as grotesque as she did.

The scale quivered and, briefly, shook hard, so that the bound corpse slid to one side, but it did not fall off. On the heights above Troy the wind was rising; but here below the walls, the air was agonizingly still—still enough to smother breath. It occurred to Kassandra that nowhere in the city did she hear the sound of a single bird's song. Was this a part of the warning such as she had been given before? Was Poseidon about to strike? Let Him strike, then, and end this obscenity, this travesty of decency and honor. She fixed her gaze firmly on one of the pulley ropes and would not look away. The rope trembled as she watched, and a few gold ornaments fell off. *Oh, come, Poseidon, is that the best You can do for Hector?*

One of Priam's slaves scooped up the ornaments and re-placed them. He added a heavy gold breastplate, and the plat-form bearing the gold sagged down, now obviously outweighing the body.

"Too heavy," Priam said, and removed it, replacing it with a multistranded gold necklace.

"A hair too light now," said Akhilles, his eyes dwelling cov-etously on the breastplate. Polyxena stepped forward, pulled her long gold-wire earrings from her earlobes and flung them onto the platform. The scales trembled, then stopped still, evenly balanced.

"There," she said; "it is enough. Take your gold, and go."

Akhilles looked from the gold to Polyxena, his eyes brightening.

"For the gold, a golden girl would suffice," he said. "King

Priam, I will forgive you half the ransom for this woman, even if she is one of your slaves or concubines."

"I am Priam's daughter," Polyxena said, "and I serve the Maiden, who is no friend to lust even in a King or a King's son. Be content with your gold and your pledged word, Prince Akhilles, and leave us with our dead."

Akhilles clenched his lips tight, and Kassandra saw a vein throbbing in his forehead. He said between clenched teeth, "Is it so? Then will you give her to me—honorably, in lawful marriage—in return for a three days' truce to bury your son? Otherwise, the war will resume at noon."

"No!" The voice of Odysseus boomed out from among the silent ranks of Akhaian chieftains. "This is too much. Akhilles, honor your word, as you have sworn, or you will find yourself fighting *me* at noon. We pledged Priam three days' truce for Hector's funeral, and so it shall be."

Akhilles glowered, but said, "So be it," and raised his hand to his men. They shared out the gold in baskets, each carrying one, and marched away across the plain the same way they had come.

Kassandra did not stay to hear the planning of the funeral games, pleading duties in the Temple; she must go at once and see what the serpents portended. No one else had apparently noted the touch of the hand—or the fingertip—of Poseidon. She went quickly up the long steep way toward the Sun Lord's house. After a moment she was aware that Khryse was following her. Well, let him follow; he had just as much a right to enter the Sun Lord's house as she did herself. But he did not approach her or speak until they had passed through the great gates.

"I know what is in your mind, Princess," he said. "I felt it too. The God is angry with Troy." He looked pale and haggard; what *had* he been drinking so early? Something, perhaps, to sharpen his visions, if not his ordinary wits?

"I was not certain that I felt it," she began. "I was not sure I did not dream or imagine it."

"If you did, then I too dreamed," he said. "It is now only a question of time; how long can Apollo Sun Lord delay the full fury of Poseidon's blow? I too have seen Them struggling for Troy. . . ."

Recalling her own vision, she said, "It is true. No mortal can break the walls of Troy. But if a God should breach them . . ."

"There is an army outside more powerful than all the might of Troy," Khryse said. "And our greatest champion awaits his funeral rites, while they have at last three warriors greater than our best."

"Three? I grant you Akhilles, but—"

"Agamemnon, who could best Paris and Deiphobos together if he must, and Odysseus and Ajax are the equal of Hector, though neither ever bested him."

"Well," said Kassandra, wondering where this was leading, "while our walls stand it does not matter; and if it is foreordained that they must fall—well, we will meet that fate when it comes."

"I do not want to remain and see the city fall. If I were a warrior I would stay and fight; but I was never trained to use weapons, and I would be no help even to defend myself—far less the ones I love. Will you come away with me, Kassandra? I do not want you to die when the city falls."

"I wish I had only death to fear."

"I mean to go to Crete in the first ship I can find, and I have heard there is a Phoenician ship standing out to sea down beyond the cove," Khryse said. "Come with me and you need fear nothing."

"Nothing, that is, but you."

"Can you never forgive me that moment of folly?" Khryse demanded. "I mean you all honor, Kassandra; I will marry you if you will, or if you are still resolved not to marry, I will swear any oath you like that we shall travel as sister and brother, and I will lay not so much as a finger's weight on you."

But I would not trust your oath, not even if you swore by your own mother's virtue, she thought, and shook her head, not unkindly.

"No, Khryse. Believe me, I thank you for the thought. But the Gods have decreed that I have something more to do in Troy. I do not know yet what They have ordained for me, but no doubt They will tell me when it lies before me."

"You certainly will be of no use as one more spear when the city falls," said Khryse. "Are you staying to comfort your mother and sister when they are carried off as captives of the Argive captains? What good will that do them?"

Kassandra looked sharply at him. He looked as if he had not touched food for a long time, yet he had not quite the look of starvation alone. Her heart ached for him; she did not love him as he wished, but she had known him for a long time, and no longer wished him ill.

A moment's touch of the God now would kill him, she thought, and was saddened.

"If that is the only task the Gods lay on me," she said firmly, "then that is the one I will fulfill."

"It seems hardly worth going alone to Crete or Thera," said Khryse. "You could come with me as you went to Colchis, to study serpent-lore; or to Egypt, where priestesses are always welcome. In Egypt there is always much building going on, and always work—as at Knossos—for a man who is handy with weights and measures. I have heard they will rebuild the palace that was reduced to rubble with the last touch of Poseidon Earth Shaker."

"Then don't go alone," Kassandra said. "Take Chryseis with you. She has never been happy here. And you do not want her to fall captive again to Agamemnon's bed, do you?"

"It is not Chryseis that Agamemnon wants," said Khryse, "and you know it as well as I do."

Kassandra shivered, hearing the sound of truth in the priest's voice; but she said, "I abide my fate as you, my brother, abide your own; go, then, to Knossos or Egypt, or wherever your fate leads you, and all the Gods keep you safe there." She moved her hand in a gesture of blessing. "I wish you nothing but good; but we part here, Khryse, and forever."

"Kiss me but once," he pleaded, dropping to his knees before her.

She bent and lightly laid her lips against his wrinkled forehead, like a mother kissing a small child.

"May you bear the Sun Lord's blessing wherever you go; and remember me with kindness," she said.

She climbed up past him, leaving him still kneeling and dumb in the street. *His wits are no longer sound*, she thought;

perhaps it is a mercy. He will suffer less when his fate strikes him; it cannot be long now. Not for any of us.

IN THE HALL of the Serpents she found the priestesses all running about half dressed, struggling to recapture the snakes; this morning quite a number of them had deserted their proper places and taken refuge in the garden. One or two of the most docile, on being rounded up and carried back to their places, had bitten the handlers. Kassandra was dismayed. Phyllida had indeed tried to tell her of this, but she had not listened. The omen was bad indeed; but the time to be afraid had passed.

"The Sun Lord did not send His people a false warning," she said. "The hand of Poseidon Earth Shaker did in fact strike us; but only the lightest of blows. Listen, the birds are singing once more; the danger is past, at least for this day."

Nevertheless, some of them looked troubled.

"The great snake, the Mother of Serpents, has not come forth for her food for three days," said Phyllida. "We have tempted her with mice and newborn rabbits, then a young pigeon, and even with a saucer of fresh goat's milk." (This last was a rare delicacy now in Troy, where so many goats had had to be slaughtered for lack of fodder; what milk remained was kept only for young babies, or for women in early pregnancy who could tolerate no other food.) "What does this omen portend, Kassandra? Is the Mother angry with us? And what can we do to turn away Her anger?"

"I do not know," she said. "I have not been given any message from the Goddess to say She is angry with us. I think perhaps we should all put on festival robes and sing to Her." (That at least could do no harm.) "And then we shall all go down and perform a dance of devotion at Hector's funeral feast."

This brought exclamations of pleasure from the women; as she had supposed, it quickly banished their fears about the omen. But Phyllida, who had learned from Kassandra much of the serpent-lore of Colchis, delayed for a moment when the others had gone to change into their robes.

"This is all very well, my dear; but what if the great serpent refuses to feed again?"

"I suppose we must simply accept it as the most evil of omens," Kassandra said. "Even the Mother of Serpents is but a beast, after all; and no beast starves itself without reason. I have force-fed smaller serpents; but I do not feel equal to the task of force-feeding this one; do you?" Phyllida silently shook her head, and Kassandra nodded. "So all we can do is offer her such food as may tempt her most, and pray she will see fit to take it."

"In short, exactly what we would do with one of the Immortals," Phyllida said with a cynical smile. "I wonder more and more: what good are the Gods?"

"I don't know either, Phyllida; but I beg you not to say that to the other girls," Kassandra said; "and I suppose we had better go and put on our dancing robes too."

Phyllida patted her cheek; she said, "Poor Kassandra; you cannot feel much like dancing and feasting when Hector lies dead."

"Hector is better off than most of us still living in the city," Kassandra said. "Believe me, my dear, I rejoice for him."

"None of my kin are fighting," said Phyllida, "and it is so long since I feasted that I would be joyful about it even if the feast were in honor of my own father. So we will dance for Serpent Mother and in memory of Hector, and I hope one gets as much good out of it as the other." She slipped away, and Kassandra bent before the great artificial cave in the wall that had been built for the great snake.

She hesitated to be certain that Apollo would not speak to forbid her entry, then crawled inside with a lighted torch in her hand to investigate. The ancient serpent knew her smell and would not harm her; but she would not willingly approach a lighted torch either. Inside the cave, in the semidark, Kassandra smelled the ancient smell which brought fear to the very center of the bones of humankind; but she had been trained to ignore that.

She crawled on, avoiding a patch of filth in the cave. Snakes were cleaner than cats under normal conditions; this one would not have fouled her own place if all were well. She began to

make out the great heap of scaled coils, and murmuring soothingly, she crawled on. She put out a hesitant hand and stroked
gently; but in place of the warm scales she anticipated, she
touched what felt like cold pottery. She pressed more firmly.
Unstirring beneath her hand, the Great Serpent lay dead.

*So that's why she didn't come out to eat. The omen was
worse than the girls knew,* Kassandra thought, sighing and lying
for a moment quietly at the side of the dead creature. She found
herself wondering: if she went out onto the gray plain of death
where Hector lingered awaiting his son, would she find the Serpent Mother there, and would the snake speak to Her priestess
in a human voice?

Well, it would make no difference; if she had occasion to
cross that plain again, maybe she would find out; there were so
many questions to be answered about death, she could never
understand why anyone should fear it or face it with anything
except eager curiosity.

She crawled backward out of the cave and placed the
lighted torch in a stand before it, a signal not to disturb the
occupant. Phyllida came back and asked, "Did you go into
the cave? Is it well with her?"

"Very well," Kassandra said steadily. "She has cast her skin
and must not be disturbed."

Phyllida was relieved. "Oh, but you haven't changed your
robe—nor put on your dancing sandals."

"Oh, Hector will not care about my robes," she said, "and
I can dance barefoot as well as in my sandals."

As the girls gathered again in the shrine, she led them
through the steps of the dance, which was older than Troy. At
the finish, she cried out the final wailing cry, murmuring under
her breath a prayer for the old snake; then wondered: was it
proper to pray for the soul of a beast who probably had none?
Well, if she had a soul she was welcome to the prayer, and if
not, at least it would do her no harm.

"And now for the feast," she said, and led the women down
the hill to the palace.

Priam had not expected them, but they were welcomed
anyway, and Hecuba was pleased that they had come for this

tribute to Hector. Kassandra stood at the center of the dance, watching as the long spiral of the women, with their white robes fluttering, wound around her and then led the unwinding of the coils of the ancient dance of the labyrinth. When the dance and song came to their end, Kassandra signaled the priestesses to help in filling the cups of the guests before they sat down, and herself poured a cup of wine and bore it to Penthesilea. Weary and heartsore, she felt there was no one else in this hall to whom she could speak except the old Amazon. Not even to Aeneas, though he smiled and beckoned to her, could she bear to speak.

Penthesilea did not trouble her with questions; she simply pulled her down on the couch beside her and shared her cup of wine. Not till then did she ask: "What is it, little one? You look so weary. It is not only grief for Hector?"

Kassandra felt tears welling up in her eyes. To everyone else in Troy she was the priestess, the bearer of burdens, the answerer to whom all questions must be brought. It never occurred to anyone that she might have fears or questions of her own.

"There are times when I wish I too had chosen to be a warrior," she blurted. "I cannot see what use it is to anyone that I am a priestess."

Penthesilea's voice was stern. "Our lives are often chosen for us, Kassandra."

"Then why is it that some people are able to choose?"

"I think perhaps some of us have the choices made for us by the choices we have already made—if not in this life, then in another," Penthesilea said.

"Do you really believe that?" demanded Kassandra.

"Oh, my dear, I don't know what I believe; I only know that like all of us, I do the best I can with the choices offered me at any moment," said Penthesilea, "and so do you. But you should not sit here discussing all the ins and outs of life's vagaries with an old woman; look, Aeneas has been trying and trying to catch your eye. A few minutes with your lover will do more to cheer you than all of my philosophy."

It might be so, thought Kassandra, but she resented it. Nevertheless, she looked at Aeneas and returned his smile. He rose and came to her and accepted another cup of wine—although she noted that it was so diluted that it was more water than wine.

"The dance was lovely; I have never seen anything like it before," he said. "Is it one of the old dances of Troy?"

"Yes, it is very old," she told him. "But I think it may be from Crete; it is the labyrinth dance—the spiral of the coils of the Earth Snake. It has been danced in the Sun Lord's house since before He slew the Great Serpent, they say."

And once again, the Great Serpent lies dead, and the Sun Lord gave us no warning or omen, she thought, overwhelmed by her dread. . . . What could all this mean? Surely the death of Hector was only the beginning of a procession of evils. . . .

Aeneas was bending over her anxiously, troubled by her distress. She did not want to frighten him too; with him she might even find some surcease from this endless despair.

"Let me bring you something," he said. "You have hardly tasted of the feast; and there is roast kid and lamb—Priam has spared nothing, and Hector would not want you to be miserable; wherever our dear brother may be, we can be sure it is well with him, and will be none the better for our mourning."

This sounded so near to what she had been trying to say that she was overjoyed; *at least Aeneas understands when I speak; I need not try to fight my way through a mountain of fear and superstitious nonsense about death!* His face seemed to glow in the torchlight. She remembered that she had seen him coming undamaged from the ruin of Troy; he was going to live, and the light in his face was simply the light of life, where the pallor of death lay over everyone else.

"I want nothing to eat," she said, though a little while ago she had been hungry.

"Well, then, let us get out of this hall of mourning. All the Gods may witness I loved Hector, but I do not see how his fate or our understanding of it can be bettered by people sitting around and eating till they can hardly move, and drinking themselves into a stupor," he said, and slipped his arm around her. Enlaced, they went out onto the balcony and looked down into the dark expanse of the Argive camp; there were a few scattered lights, but all else was dark.

"What are they doing down there?" Aeneas asked.

"I don't know; I may be a prophetess, but I cannot see that far," she said. "Building an altar to Poseidon, I should think. But it is too late for that, and they should know it."

"Perhaps their soothsayers are not as good as you are," he said, holding her tightly. "Kassandra, let me come to your room. . . ."

She hesitated, but finally said, "Come then." Tomorrow would be enough time to deal with dead serpents and dying cities.

On their way up the steep street, a star fell, with such a dizzying sweep across the sky that for a moment it felt as if it were the earth that tipped; and she clutched Aeneas' arm, remembering how she and Andromache had watched falling stars in Colchis when she was only a young girl. Since that night, though she had watched the skies diligently, she had not seen another falling star until this moment. Was it a portent of some kind? Or did it mean anything at all?

"What is it?" Aeneas asked, bending over her and speaking with great tenderness.

"Only the star."

"Star?" he asked. "I saw nothing, my love."

Now I am imagining things. Enough, then, for tonight, she said firmly to herself, and drew Aeneas into her room, knowing with a sudden stab of pain that it would be the last time.

12

THE TRUCE, rather to Kassandra's surprise, was not broken by the Akhaians. None of them competed in Hector's funeral games—except for an anonymous Myrmidon who entered the wrestling, threw four successive opponents (ending by pinning down Deiphobos), pocketed the golden cup given as a prize and vanished without revealing his name. Gossip in the city later credited him with being one of the Immortals in disguise, but he wasn't. Paris said he had seen him in the ranks and he was just a common soldier. Trojans and Akhaians both stood watching the various events and applauding the winners in a fine sportsmanlike way.

Penthesilea insisted on competing for the prize in archery, which caused some trouble when she won handily against all comers, including Paris, who had obviously marked out that prize for himself. He protested, but no one upheld his objection; since Paris had been heard often to say that no man alive could best him at archery, several of Priam's younger sons (who were not at all sorry to see their brother beaten for once) insisted he had no right to complain at being beaten by a woman.

On the third morning Kassandra woke early, hearing with relief the sounds of many birds singing loudly in the gardens of the Sun Lord's house; at least there would be no substantial earthquake this day.

She went early to the palace—Penthesilea had moved from her quarters in the Sun Lord's house—and helped dress the Amazon in her armor of hardened leather with metal plates.

"All of us will be fighting, and this day we—we Amazons, that is—will throw all our forces against Akhilles," she said. "We have fought for many years. One warrior, be he never so fierce, cannot lay us all low."

"I wish you would set yourselves to attack someone less formidable," Kassandra said, troubled. "There are enemies enough; such men as Menelaus and Idomeneos need killing too. Why not go against Agamemnon? Why must you challenge the pride of the Akhaians?"

"Because if Agamemnon or Menelaus is killed, Akhilles is still there to inspire the troops, but if Akhilles is dead, they will be like a hive of bees when the queen is gone," Penthesilea said. "The Myrmidons, at least, will be completely demoralized; remember when Akhilles was still sulking, they hardly fought at all, and they certainly did not fight like the well-disciplined army they are now."

"Oh, I can understand why you feel this way," Kassandra said, "but this is not even your war. I wish you would all leave before this day's fight."

Penthesilea looked her straight in the face. "Have you had an omen, Bright Eyes?"

"Not really," Kassandra said, then realized she should have said yes; maybe the Amazon would have believed her. She flung her arms around Penthesilea and began to cry.

"I wish you wouldn't" was all she could say. She clung to the older woman, weeping, and Penthesilea scowled.

"Come, now, where's the warrior I myself trained?" she asked. "You are behaving like a weak house-bred woman! There —that's right—dry those bright eyes, my love, and let me go."

Reluctantly, Kassandra wrenched herself free, trying to stifle her sobs. "But Akhilles is invulnerable; they say a God protects him and no man can kill him."

"Well, Paris boasted that no man could beat him at archery," Penthesilea said with a droll smile. "Perhaps that only means it is reserved for a woman to kill him. And if I am not ordained to do it, perhaps another of my women may do so to avenge me. Darling, no mortal man is invulnerable; and if any God protects such a monster, then such a God should be ashamed. We have given too much power to Akhilles; he is a man like any other."

Nevertheless, he did kill Hector, Kassandra thought, but there was nothing to say, for Penthesilea was right. They walked together, surrounded by the other Amazons, to where the horses and chariots were forming up for the attack.

Penthesilea put her arm around Kassandra's waist.

"Why, child, you are still shaking!"

"I can't help being afraid for you," Kassandra said in a muffled voice.

Penthesilea frowned at her; then her voice altered to tenderness. "This can be no part of a warrior's life, Bright Eyes. I don't want anyone to see you weeping like this. Come, darling, let me go."

I can't bear to see her go! She will never return. . . . But Kassandra reluctantly unwound her arms from her kinswoman's waist. Penthesilea kissed her and said, "Kassandra, whatever may happen, know that to me you have been more than a daughter, and dearer than any of my lovers. You have been my friend."

Kassandra stood aside, watching through a blur of tears as her aunt swung up into her saddle. The Amazons closed ranks about her, talking in low tones of battle strategies; then the gate swung open and they rode out.

Kassandra knew she should go to her mother in the palace, or to the Temple to oversee the serpents—all was in confusion there now that the death of the Great Snake was known; but instead, she went up onto the wall to watch as Penthesilea and her group rode forth against the Akhaians. Half a dozen of the Trojan chariots rode out first, directly engaging the massed forces with spears and swords. Then like thunder the charge of the Amazon horses raced down on Akhilles and his men.

They came together with a shock of spears clearly heard by the women on the wall. When the dust subsided, two of the Amazons were lying on the ground, their horses fallen. One scrambled to her feet and cut her assailant down with her spear; the other lay motionless, her horse struggling and rolling away, trying to rise. An Akhaian soldier saw its struggles and quickly cut its throat, then knelt over the fallen woman to wrench off her fine armor. Kassandra saw that Penthesilea had survived the first charge; her horse had taken a spear wound, but was still on its feet.

The Amazon Queen swung her mount and charged right through a cluster of Akhilles' soldiers, knocking them aside, killing more than one with her spear-thrusts. Kassandra saw the very moment when Akhilles became aware of her: when she cut down a man who must have been one of his own personal body-guards. She saw the leap he made, facing the Amazon as if inviting her to get down and fight him face to face.

Penthesilea dismounted to face him head on, sword to sword. She was actually taller than he was, and had a longer reach with the sword. They clashed together, with a flurry of sword-strokes too swift to follow. Akhilles reeled and for a moment went down on his knees. He made some signal, so that his men rushed in and immediately engaged all the other warrior women. Then, swiftly as a striking snake, he was up, his sword moving almost too quickly to be seen. Penthesilea retreated a few steps until she stood against her horse's flank. Then his relentless sword pressed her until she went down. Kassandra heard the breath sob out of her as Akhilles fell to the Amazon's side. What was the madman doing? He tore at her clothes in a frenzy, leaned forward and, as they watched in horror, violently raped the corpse.

Monstrous, she thought. *If only I had my bow!* Akhilles had finished and was fighting off the four Amazons who had come to attack him. He struck down two of them at once, then took down another with a spear, wounding her so that, reeling away, she was cut down by one of his soldiers. The remaining women made a desperate rush to recover Penthesilea's body; but they were hopelessly outnumbered, and within a few more minutes not a single Amazon warrior remained alive. The soldiers rounded up and led away their surviving horses. In a single hour of battle, the last of a tribe with all their culture and their memories had been wiped out, and that fiend Akhilles had carried out the final insult to a warrior who dared challenge him. Kassandra did not believe for a single moment that he had been overcome by lust; it had been a cold-blooded act of contempt.

It would have been fitting, she thought, if Apollo had let fly His arrow at that moment to take him in the very act of overweening pride. The God who loathed excess in revenge or even in war would have been the perfect avenger. Akhilles, Kassandra realized, no longer qualified as an honorable opponent in battle; he was like a mad dog.

But the Gods stand by and will do nothing. If Akhilles were indeed a mad dog, she reflected, *someone would come and kill him, not to avenge the dead but to protect the living, and to put the poor maddened beast out of its misery.*

And if Apollo will not act, it is not for nothing that I am sworn to serve Him—if only by doing what a more innocent priest would expect the God to do. For the first time since she had knelt and prayed as a young girl to the Sun Lord to accept her, she knew clearly why she had come to the Sun Lord's house. She looked one last time at the body of Penthesilea lying shamefully stripped and bared on the field, then turned away; she had done all her weeping that morning when she begged Penthesilea not to go, and had no more tears.

She went up into the Sun Lord's house and to her room;

from the chest there she took her bow, a gift from Penthesilea, elaborately gilded and inlaid with ivory like the Sun Lord's own. She strung it with a plain arrow—she might need it to get the range—and into her quiver she put the last of the envenomed arrows which the old Kentaur Cheiron had made.

Kassandra realized she was shaking from head to foot. She went down into the kitchens and found herself some stale bread and a little honey, forcing herself to eat. The women were gathered there baking fresh bread for the funeral feast of the Great Snake, and besought Kassandra to wait for the fresh baking, but she refused everything except a mug of watered wine. They were all astonished at seeing their priestess armed, but they forbore to ask her questions; in her status as an elder priestess her doings were assumed to have a good purpose, no matter how mysterious or obscure, and could not under any circumstances be challenged.

Then, deliberately, she went down into the most secret room of the Temple, and from a chest to which only a few of the high priests and priestesses had the keys, she took a certain robe adorned with gold, and the golden Sun Lord's mask. With hands schooled to steadiness, she put them on and tied the strings.

She was not entirely sure whether what she did was the highest of sacrileges—she thought of Khryse putting on these things in an attempt to cajole an inexperienced girl into serving a lust he could not satisfy any other way—or whether she was serving the honor of Apollo by doing what the God ought to be doing and would not.

Sandals were a part of the costume; gilded sandals with small golden wings attached to the heels. She laced them on, wishing they were really winged so that she could fly down over the Akhaian camp. Silently she climbed to the balcony which overlooked the battlefield, remembering how Khryse had stood here in the aspect of Apollo to shoot down the arrows of plague into the Akhaian camp. He had cried out, too, in Apollo's voice.

The bodies of the Amazons lay at the center of clustering clouds of flies. The horses were gone; the Trojan chariot riders and foot soldiers who had marched out this morning had retreated within the walls of Troy. Akhilles strutted in the midst of his own guards, apparently waiting for someone to come and challenge him to a fight. Couldn't his own soldiers see that the man had gone outside every limit of sanity and decency? Yet they still respected him as their leader!

She did not cry out as Khryse had done; Apollo had given her nothing to say, even though He was the God of song. Perhaps someone else would make a song about this, but it would not be with her words. She simply strung the bow, took careful aim at Akhilles and let fly. The arrow fell a little short; but now she had the range. The Akhaian hero had not seen the arrow and continued his strutting between the chariots. Now where to shoot when the iron armor covered so much of his body? She looked up and down to see that though the helmet covered face and hair, on his feet he wore sandals which were no more than a couple of narrow strips of leather. So be it, then; she let fly at his feet.

The arrow struck his bare heel. He evidently thought it no more than an insect bite, for she saw him bend to brush it away; then he drew out the shaft and looked about to see where it had come from. One by one the Trojan soldiers looked up at the Temple to see what Akhilles' Myrmidons were staring and pointing at. Kassandra stood motionless; she was probably out of ordinary bowshot when it had to be directed straight upward, even if anyone had the courage to shoot an arrow at what could have been the God. She felt completely invulnerable, and even if an arrow had come out of the blinding noon, she had accomplished what she set out to do.

Akhilles was still standing, gazing upward at the source of the arrow, apparently unaware of the nature of his wound; but after a time she saw him reach down and claw at his foot, signaling one of his men to bind it up. Well, let them try; she knew that even if they should now cut his foot off—and that had been tried for small localized wounds such as this—the poison had entered his blood, and Akhilles was already a dead man.

For a few more minutes he strode arrogantly about the field; then he stumbled and fell. He was on the ground now in convulsions. There was confusion in the Akhaian camp—and then a great cry of rage and despair went up, not unlike the death-cry raised over Patroklos. Down on the city walls where the other women were watching there were cries of jubilation, and at last a great shout of thanksgiving to Apollo. But by this time Kassandra had slipped down from the wall and was in the secret room returning the mask and robe to their locked chest. When she came out again, the people of Troy were crowding to the wall, pushing and shoving to find out what had happened.

"One of the Akhaian leaders is dead," someone told her. "It may even be Akhilles. Apollo Himself appeared, they say, high on the walls above Troy, and shot him down with His arrows of fire."

"Oh, did he?" she replied, sounding skeptical, and when the story was repeated, said no more than "Well, it's about time."

13

NOW THAT AKHILLES was gone, a mood of confidence swept through Troy; everyone was looking forward to a swift end to the war. There was no formal period of mourning, and no funeral games; Kassandra suspected that among the Akhaians there was little genuine mourning, though some ritualized wailing arose around the funeral pyre. She remembered Briseis, who had gone to Akhilles of her free will, and wondered if the girl mourned the lover she had idealized. She almost hoped so. Even for Akhilles, it was not just that there should be no one to mourn.

Yet Agamemnon, who had assumed command of all the Akhaian troops, and even commanded the Myrmidons to go on fighting, seemed to have no doubt of the final outcome of this war. The Akhaians began building an enormous earth-rampart to the south, from which they might assault the wall partially tumbled in the last earthquake. It was a few hours before the

Trojans noticed what they were doing, and when they did, Paris ordered all available archers to the highest wall to shoot the soldiers down. The Akhaians worked for a considerable time under cover of extra-large shields held over their heads, but as the shield-bearers were shot down one after another, faster than they could be replaced, the Akhaians finally gave up the attempt and withdrew the builders.

Kassandra had not watched Akhilles' funeral pyre, nor the battle of the archers, though the women in the Sun Lord's house reported every move to her. The Temple was in mourning for the great serpent, and would continue to be so for a considerable time. Serpents of this variety were not found on the plains of Troy, and they must send forth to the mainland or to Colchis or even to Crete for another one. Privately, Kassandra believed that the death of the serpent was an omen not only of the death of Akhilles, which it had so briefly preceded, but of the fall of Troy, which could not now be long delayed.

She spoke of this one night in the palace when she had gone down to see her mother.

Hecuba had never really recovered from the death of Hector. She was appallingly frail and thin now, her hands like a bundle of sticks; she would not eat, saying always, "Save my portion for the little children; old people do not get as hungry as they do"—which in fact sounded sensible enough, but there were times when Kassandra thought her mother's mind had gone. She spoke often of Hector, but seemed not to realize that he was dead; she talked as if he were out somewhere about the city, overseeing the armies.

"What are the Akhaians doing now?" Kassandra asked Polyxena.

"They have felled a good many trees along the shoreline, and are hacking them into lumber; I spoke with the woman who sells honey cakes to the Akhaian soldiers, and she said they spoke of a plan to build a great altar to Poseidon and sacrifice many horses to Him."

Poseidon would indeed be a friend to those Akhaians, if they should persuade Him to break our walls; and their soothsayers know it, if they have persuaded the attackers to invoke the Earth Shaker.

She rose from Polyxena's side and went to speak with Helen. She had learned long ago that Paris would not listen to her but could sometimes be approached through his wife. Helen greeted her with her usual affectionate embrace.

"Rejoice with me, Sister; the Goddess has heard my grief and will send us another child for the ones I lost to Poseidon's blow." When Kassandra did not smile, she begged, "Oh, be glad for me!"

"It is not that I am not glad for you," Kassandra said slowly, "but at this particular time—is it wise?"

Helen's pretty smile was full of dimples. "The Goddess sends us children not as we will but as She wills," she reminded Kassandra; "but you are not a mother, so perhaps you do not yet understand that."

"Mother or not, I think I would try to choose a better time than the end of a siege," Kassandra said, "even if it meant sending my husband to sleep among the soldiers when the moon was full or the wind blowing from the south."

Helen blushed and said, "Paris must have a son; I cannot ask him to take Nikos as his heir and set the son of Menelaus upon the throne of Troy."

"I had forgotten that particular foible," Kassandra said, "but I had believed that Andromache's son was to rule after Hector. Has Paris, then, resolved to usurp that place?"

"Astyanax cannot rule Troy at eight years old," Helen said. "It goes ill with any land where the King is a child; Paris would have to rule for him for many years at least."

"Then perhaps it would be better for Paris to have no son," Kassandra said, "so that he would not be tempted to overthrow the rightful heir." Helen looked indignant, so Kassandra added, "In any case, Paris already has a son by the river priestess Oenone, who dwelt with him here as his wife till you came from Sparta. It is not right that Paris refuse to acknowledge his first-born."

Helen frowned and said, "Paris has spoken of her; he says there is no way to be certain that he fathered Oenone's child."

Kassandra saw the look in Helen's eyes and decided not to pursue this further.

"That is not what I came to say. Have they more horses in

the Akhaian camp than are needed to draw Agamemnon's chariot and the chariots of the other Kings?"

"Why, I've no idea; I know nothing of things like that,"
Helen said, and leaned across the table to touch Paris' hand.
She repeated the question to him, and Paris stared.

"Why, no; I don't think so," he said. "They've been trying
to capture the horses from our chariots, even at the cost of
leaving gold or leaving the chariots themselves."

Kassandra said urgently, "If they are building an altar to
Poseidon, you don't suppose the Kings are going to sacrifice the
horses that draw their own chariots, do you? I beg you to set a
double watch on all the horses of Troy, wherever they are sta-
bled."

"Our horses are all well within our walls," Paris said uncon-
cernedly, "and the Akhaians can no more get at them than if
they were in the stables of Pharaoh of Egypt."

"Are you certain? Odysseus, for instance, is crafty; he might
by some ruse inveigle his way inside the walls, and get the horses
out," she said, but Paris only laughed.

"I don't think he could get inside our gates even if he could
manage to disguise himself as Zeus Thunderer," Paris said.
"Those gates will not open to man or Immortal; even for King
Priam or myself it would be difficult to persuade anyone to open
them after dark. And if he did get in somehow, how do you
think he would get out again? If Agamemnon wants horse sacrifices, he will have to sacrifice his own, for he'll get no Trojan
ones."

Kassandra thought he was dismissing the possibility a little
too lightly, but there was no way to continue; Paris would not
admit the fallibility of his defenses, certainly not to his sister. If
he would be the only one to suffer from this casual attitude, she
would have said no more, but if he was wrong all Troy would
pay; so she urged, "I beg you, set extra guards around your
horses for a while at least," and repeated what Polyxena had told
her.

"Sister," Paris said, not altogether unkindly, "surely there
is enough women's work for you to do that you need not concern yourself with the conduct of the war."

Kassandra pressed her lips together, knowing that Paris was certain to ignore whatever she might say.

Kassandra could hardly stand guard on the horses herself; but she spoke to the priests in the Sun Lord's house, and they agreed to set a watch upon the royal stables.

Late that night the alarm was sounded from the walls, and Paris' soldiers, roused, caught half a dozen men, led by Odysseus himself, leaving the royal stables. The guards, who had not recognized the Argive general, said that he had come into the stable with a royal signet and an order to take half a dozen horses to the palace. They had believed him a messenger from Priam himself, and had given up the horses without protest. Only when they had gone did one of the priests of Apollo notice the Akhaian sandals that they were wearing, suspect a trick and sound the alarm.

Paris ordered the deceived guard hanged, and when Odysseus was brought before him, said to him: "Is there any reason I should not hang you from the topmost wall of Troy for the horse-thief you are?"

Odysseus said, "In my country, we hang woman-stealers, Trojan. If you had not shown us all how fast you could run, you would now be nothing but bare bones hanging outside the great walls of Sparta, and none of us would have had to leave our homes and come and fight here for all these years."

Priam had been hastily roused from sleep; he looked unhappily at his old friend and said, "Well, Odysseus, you're still a pirate, I see. But I see no reason to hang you. We've always been willing to accept ransom for captives."

"What ransom do you want?" Odysseus asked, looking only at Priam and ignoring Paris.

"A dozen horses," Paris said.

Odysseus waved a hand. "There they are," he replied, and Paris scowled at his effrontery.

"Those are our horses already. We will have a dozen of yours."

Odysseus said, "Have you no piety, friend? Those horses have already been dedicated to Poseidon. They are not mine to give back; they belong already to the Earth Shaker."

Paris sprang up, ready to aim a blow at him; Odysseus deflected it easily.

"Priam, your son is lacking in the manners of diplomacy; I would rather deal with you. You can take those horses back if you are willing to risk angering Poseidon Earth Shaker with your stinginess; but I swore to sacrifice those horses to Him. Do you really think He will favor Troy if you rob Him of His sacrifice?"

Priam said, "If you have vowed those horses to Poseidon, they are His. I will not be more stingy than you with a God. These horses are for Poseidon, then, and a dozen more from your people to ransom you."

"So be it," Odysseus agreed, and Priam called for his herald to send the message to the Akhaian army. Agamemnon, however, would not be pleased, Kassandra thought. She wished Odysseus no harm; in spite of his place with the enemy host, she could not help thinking of the old pirate as a friend—as he had been in her childhood. She still had, in one of her boxes, the beautiful string of blue beads he had given her years before.

As Odysseus took his departure to arrange for the actual exchange and delivery of the ransom, Paris said to his father, "You fool! Are you really going to give those horses for sacrifice? What are Odysseus' promises to you? You don't believe he was going to sacrifice them, do you?"

"It may well be," Priam said; "and what have we to lose? We need Poseidon's goodwill too; and we will be getting a dozen more for Odysseus' ransom, so we have lost nothing."

"I don't think they will do the God half as much good as they would do our armies," Paris still grumbled; but when Priam made up his mind there was nothing to be done.

The next morning, before the walls of Troy, the horses were sacrificed to Poseidon. Kassandra watched the slaughter, troubled; Priam hardly seemed strong enough. She remembered such sacrifices in her childhood, when Priam had been strong and vigorous enough to strike off the head of a bull with a single blow. Now his shaking hands could scarcely close on the ax, and after he blessed the weapon, a strong young priest took the ax and completed the sacrifice, chanting invocations to the Earth Shaker.

As the halfway mark was reached and the sixth horse fell to the ground, there was a small sound like a very distant thunderclap, and the ground beneath them rolled slightly. An omen? she wondered. Or was Poseidon simply acknowledging His sacrifice?

Apollo Sun Lord, she implored, *can You not save this city which has been Yours for so long, even if You first took it from Serpent Mother?*

The glare of the sun was bright in her eyes, and the well-known voice seemed to crash in her ears like the distant surf.

Even I cannot contend with what the Thunderer has decreed, child. What is to come must come.

The sacrifice went on, but she was no longer watching. What was the use of sacrificing to Poseidon if He was bound by the Thunderer—*who is no God of mine, and no God of Troy's* —to destroy the people who sacrificed to Him, while Apollo Sun Lord stood helplessly aside as the Earth Shaker ravaged the city —*His own city?*

If this was all ordained anyhow, why sacrifice and petition the Immortals? Defiance struggled in her, never again to be wholly silent, the old cry still unanswered: *What good are these Gods?*

It seemed now that high above the city, as she had seen once in her vision, two mighty figures, fashioned of cloud and storm, stood toe to toe like wrestlers, struggling and casting blows of lightning and thunder at each other. The sound seemed to slam through her consciousness. She swayed, her eyes fixed on the battling Immortals.

Then she stumbled and fell, but lost consciousness before she touched the ground.

When she woke, she was lying with her head in her mother's lap.

"You should have stayed out of the midday sun," Hecuba reproved gently. "It was not right to make a disturbance at the sacrifices."

"Oh, I don't think the Gods cared that much," said Kassandra, pulling herself upright through the stabbing pain behind her eyes. "Do you?" But seeing the faintly bewildered look on her mother's face, she was sure the Queen did not understand what she was talking about; she was not sure herself. "I am sorry; I meant no disrespect to the Gods, of course. We are all here to do Them honor; do you think They will feel in honor bound to return the courtesy?" But all she saw in Hecuba's eyes was the old look—the look that said *I don't understand you.*

"What in the name of all the Gods are they doing out there?" Helen asked.

"Polyxena heard that they're building an altar to Poseidon," Kassandra replied.

Down below, on the open space which had been so long a battlefield, what looked like the whole Akhaian army was lugging lumber, and under the protection of a veritable wall of lashed-together leather shields, hammering and sawing frantically.

"Their priests drew up the plans," said Khryse, strolling up to join the women.

Paris came toward them and bent down to kiss his mother's hand.

"It looks unlike any altar I have ever seen," he said; "more like some form of siege machine. Look, if they build it this high they could shoot down over the walls, or even climb over into the city, like boarders on a ship."

Hecuba seemed troubled by the tone of his voice. She demanded, "Have you spoken to Hector about this?"

Paris bent his head and turned away, but not before Kassandra could see that his eyes were filled with tears. "How can you bear it when she talks like that?" he murmured.

"The question is not how we can bear it, but that she must," Kassandra said sharply. "You at least can go out and try to avenge the ills that have broken our mother's mind and are breaking down our father's. Tell me, can they really build that thing high enough to climb into the city?"

"Probably; but they shall not while I live," said Paris. "I must send to rally all the remaining charioteers and archers." He kissed Helen, and went down the stairs. Soon after, they heard the battle cry as Paris and the remaining chariots dashed breakneck at the structure, shooting flights of arrows that all but darkened the sky. The wild charge actually knocked off one corner of the structure, sending it down with a crash, and half a dozen men fell screaming to the ground.

The Akhaian soldiers broke and began to run, with Trojans in hot pursuit in their chariots, cutting them down as fast as they could. When they were in full retreat and appeared to be trying to run as far as the ships, Paris called off the chase and rode back to the unprotected structure. Finding a barrel of tar on the site and sloshing it liberally about, he set the whole construction alight. As it burned, the Trojans heard the cries of Agamemnon uselessly trying to rally his men, and they rode back inside the walls before Agamemnon could assemble the Akhaians together for a renewed attack.

The Trojans on the walls were cheering wildly. It was the only battle they had clearly won since the burning of the Akhaian ships. Paris came up and knelt before Priam.

"If they want to build an altar to Poseidon, they will not build it on Trojan ground, sir."

"Well done," said Priam, embracing him heartily, and Helen came to help him out of his armor.

"You're wounded," she said, seeing him flinch as she removed the vambrace from his upper arm.

Paris shrugged; the movement made him flinch again.

"An arrow wound. It didn't touch a bone," he said.

"Kassandra," Helen said, "come and look at this; what do you think?"

Kassandra came and folded back the sleeve of Paris' tunic. It was a flesh wound, a small depression just above the elbow. Purple and puffy, like pouting lips, it had already closed, and from it a drop or two of blood oozed.

"It is not, I think, too serious," she said, "but it should be washed in wine and bathed with very hot water and herbs; if a puncture wound closes too quickly, it can be serious. At all costs it must be kept open and made to bleed freely to cleanse it."

"She is right," said Khryse, bringing a flask of wine, which he began to pour over the wound; but Paris grabbed the flask.

"A waste of good wine," he said, and poured it into his mouth instead, making a wry face. "Ugh, not even fit for that. Might be good to wash my feet with."

Khryse shrugged. "There is better wine for the drinking in

the Sun Lord's house, Prince Paris; this is a poor vintage kept for cleansing wounds. Come and have some of the better vintage while we tend you."

"Better yet, come to our rooms in the palace and let me tend you," Helen said. "You have had enough fighting for one day—and there is nobody left to fight."

"No," Paris said, walking to the wall. "I hear Agamemnon; he's got some of those archers of his to attack again. Let's go down and drive them off. Already they say I spend too much time in your boudoir being cosseted, my Helen; I am weary of a coward's reputation. Here, tie this up with your scarf and let me go." He pulled his armor together over the bound wound and was off down the stairs. They heard him shouting to his men.

"Oh, why did he have to have a damned attack of heroism right now?" Helen said angrily. "And if it was really an altar to Poseidon, do you think the God will be angry because he burned it down?"

"I don't see what else he could have done, whether the God is angry or not," Kassandra said. "Perhaps the Earth Shaker will remember all those nice fat horses that we gave Him courtesy of Odysseus a couple of days ago."

"I pray it does not hamper his riding and shooting," Helen said. "When he comes back—if he survives this charge—I will take him off to be tended by the best of the healers."

"I will go and send our best healer-priests to the palace for him, Lady Helen," Khryse said, and went off up the hill. Kassandra watched the charge; Paris fought like a madman, as if the War-God's self inhabited him, and she lost count of how many of the Akhaian soldiers he cut down and left bleeding on the ground.

"I have never seen him fight like this before," Helen said.

Pray you never do again, Kassandra thought.

"Maybe the wound is as slight as he says; he seems not to be favoring the arm at all."

"He rides like Hector himself," said Priam, watching him from the wall. "We have all been unjust to the boy, thinking him less heroic than his brother."

Helen shut her eyes as a sword came down toward Paris; he

parried the blow at the very moment when it seemed it must strike his head from his shoulders. It was the last blow; a moment later Agamemnon's men broke and ran, running as if they did not mean to stop until they reached their ships. Paris yelled as if he were going to chase them into the water, but before long he called off his men.

"If there is a bullock, have it killed for the men's dinner," he said to Hecuba, as he came up the stairs to the waiting women. "I have never seen such fighting."

Helen hurried to embrace him. "Praise to Aphrodite that you are safe still!"

"Yes, She is still watching over us; She did not bring you here to Troy only to abandon us now." Paris looked down at the ashes of the structure the Akhaians had been trying to build.

"If this is dedicated to any God, I pray He will forgive me. Now, if you will find that healer, my Helen, I will be glad of his good offices; my arm aches." He leaned on her as they went down into the palace, and Kassandra looked after them with dread.

"You had better go," said Khryse. She had not heard Khryse come back. "You are as good a healer as any in the Sun Lord's house."

Kassandra was not sure of that, but did not know how to say so. "You saw the wound closer than I; you know how bad it is," he added. "I do not like such wounds even when they look harmless." She hurried off to Paris and Helen's chambers, only to be told that her services were not required.

That night was quiet, but in the morning the scaffolding had been raised again and the Akhaians were hammering and sawing away as if they had never been interrupted.

"Well, we'll make short work of that, as we did yesterday," said Deiphobos, who had come out this morning with Priam. The old man leaned heavily on his son's shoulder. "Where's Aphrodite's gift to womankind this morning? Still hiding behind Helen's frilled skirts?"

"Be quiet," Priam said sharply. "He had a wound yesterday; perhaps it is worse or he has taken cold in it." He summoned one of the younger messengers and said, "Go to Prince Paris if you please, and ask why he is not here with his army."

"A wound," said Deiphobos scornfully. "I saw that wound; a cat-scratch or more likely, a love-bite."

The boy hurried away and came back looking pale. He bowed to Priam and said, "My lord, the lady Helen asks that the priestess Kassandra come and look at her brother's wound; it is beyond her power to cure."

"My father," Deiphobos said, "have I your leave to take out the chariots and drive off these ants as Paris did yesterday?"

"Go," Priam said, "but when Paris is healed, you will give over command to him again; nothing that is his will ever belong to you."

"We'll see," said Deiphobos. He saluted Priam and left.

Kassandra went down into the palace, through the halls which seemed, this morning, dank and cold and still, with wisps of sea-fog hanging in the air. In the rooms allotted to Paris and Helen, Paris, half-clad and very pale, was lying on a pallet, muttering. Helen, at his side, trying to bathe the wound with steaming water scented with herbs, sprang up and came to Kassandra.

"Aphrodite be praised that you have come; perhaps he will listen to you when he will not to me," she said. Kassandra came and drew back the veil with which the wound had been covered. The whole upper arm was grossly swollen, the puncture still obstinately closed and weeping clear fluid; the arm looked purplish, with red streaks fanning down toward the wrist.

Kassandra drew breath; she had never seen an arrow wound quite like this. She said, "Have the priests of Apollo seen this?"

"They were here twice in the night. They told me to bathe it with hot water, and said it should probably be burned with a hot iron; but I had not the heart to make him suffer that, when they could not promise that it would cure him," Helen said. "But just in the last hour he seems worse, and he does not know me now; until a few minutes ago he was yelling to the servants to bring his armor, and threatening them with a beating if they would not help him get up and put it on."

"That is not good," Kassandra said. "I have seen worse wounds heal, but—"

"Should I have let them burn him?"

"No; if I had been there I would have said to dress it with wine and sweet oil; and sometimes I have known a poultice of moldy bread, or of cobwebs, to cleanse a puncture wound," she said. "The healers are too quick with their hot irons; I might have cut it last night to make it bleed more freely, but nothing more. Now it is too late. The infection has taken hold, and either he will live or he will die. But don't despair," she added quickly. "He is young and strong, and as I told you, I have seen worse wounds heal."

"Is there nothing that can be done?" Helen asked wildly. "Your magic . . ."

"Alas, I have no healing magic," Kassandra said. "But I will pray; I can do no more." She hesitated and said, "The river priestess Oenone—she was skilled in healing magic."

Helen sprang up in excitement.

"Can you not send for her?" she implored. "Beg her to come and heal my lord! Whatever she asks, it shall be hers; I promise it."

But the only thing she wishes for, you have already taken from her, Kassandra thought. She said, "I will send a message to her; but I cannot promise that she will come."

"But if she loved him once, could she be cruel enough to refuse him her help, if it meant his death?"

"I don't know, Helen; she was very bitter against him when she left the palace," Kassandra said.

"If I must, I—Queen of Sparta—will kneel before her with ashes in my hair," Helen said. "Should I go to Oenone, then?"

"No. I know her; I will go," Kassandra said. "You pray and sacrifice to Aphrodite, Who favors you." Helen embraced her and clung to her.

"Kassandra, surely you do not wish me evil? So many of these women of Troy hate me—I can see it in their eyes, hear it in their voices. . . ." Helen's voice sounded almost like a pleading child's, and Kassandra touched her cheek gently.

"I wish you nothing but good, Helen; that I swear to you," she said.

"But when first I came to Troy you cursed me—"

"No," Kassandra said, "I foretold truly that you would bring sorrow on us. The fact that I saw the evil does not mean that I caused it. It was the doing of the Immortals, and no more of your doing than mine. No one can escape the working of Fate. I will go now to the headwaters of the Scamander and find Oenone, and implore her to come and heal Paris."

Khryse greeted her as she left the palace. She looked at him in surprise; this morning she had forgotten and simply taken his presence for granted.

"I thought by now you would be on a ship bound for Crete or Egypt," she said. "Why have you not gone?"

"There may still be something I can do for the city which has sheltered me, or for Priam who has been my King," Khryse said, "or—who knows?—even for you."

"You should not stay for me," Kassandra said. "I would be glad to know you are safe from what will come."

"I want nothing," he said in a queerly sober tone, "except that you should know at last, before the end comes for us all, that my love for you is true and unselfish, desiring nothing except your good."

Why, that's true, she thought, and said gently, "I believe you, my friend; and I beg you to go to safety as soon as you can. Someone must remember and tell the truth about Troy for those who come after; it troubles me that in legends, our children's children should come to think of Akhilles as a great hero or a good man."

"It is not likely to do us any harm, or Akhilles any good either, whatever they may say or sing of us in times to come," Khryse said. "Yet if I survive, I swear I will tell the truth to anyone who will listen."

Kassandra climbed quickly to the Sun Lord's house and took off her formal robe; she put on an old dark tunic, in which she could come and go unheeded, solid leather sandals and a heavy cloak which would keep out wind or rain. Then she went quietly out the small abandoned side gate and took the road up toward Mount Ida, along the drying stream of the Scamander. The track was beaten now into a road; many horses and men had come this way, and the water which had once run strong and clean was muddied and fouled. When last she had taken this path—how many years ago now?—the water had been clear, the path almost untrodden.

Even now, had her errand been less urgent and desperate, she would have enjoyed the journey. The sun was hidden by clouds, the tops of the tree-clad hills lost themselves in thick rolls of mist and the light winds promised rain and probably thunder. She went up quickly; but although she was a strong woman, the grade was so steep that she was soon out of breath and had to stop and rest. As she climbed, what had been a river ran thinner and clearer, and no man or horse had polluted the pathway or the water. She knelt and drank, for in spite of the clouds and wind, it was hot.

At last she reached the place where the water sprang forth from the rock, guarded by a carven image of Father Scamander. She struck the bell which summoned the river nymphs, and when a young girl appeared, asked if she might speak with Oenone.

"I think she is here," the girl said. "Her son was ill with a summer fever; she did not go down to the sheep-shearing festival with the others."

Kassandra had forgotten that it was so near to shearing-time.

The child went away, and Kassandra sat down on a bench near the spring and enjoyed the silence; perhaps when Honey was older she might come here to serve among the nymphs of the River God. A pleasant place for a young girl to grow up—not, perhaps, as pleasant as riding with the Amazons, but that was no longer possible. Kassandra began to understand that she had hardly begun yet to feel her grief for Penthesilea. She had been so busy with vengeance and then with other deaths that her grief had had to stand aside for more leisure to mourn.

It will be a long time before I can mourn for my brother, she thought, and wondered what she had meant by it.

She heard a step behind her and turned; at first she hardly recognized Oenone. The slender young girl had become a tall and heavy woman, deep-breasted, her dark curls coiled low on her neck. Only the deep-set eyes were the same; but even so, Kassandra hesitated when she spoke the name.

"Oenone? I hardly recognized you."

"No," Oenone said, "none of us are as young and pretty as we once were. It's the princess, is it not—Kassandra?"

"Yes," she said. "I suppose I have changed too."

"You have," Oenone said, "though you are still beautiful, Princess."

Kassandra smiled faintly. She said, "How is my brother's son? I hear he has been ill."

"Oh, nothing serious—just one of those little disorders that come to children in the summer. He will be recovered in a day or two. But how may I serve you, Lady?"

"It is not for me," Kassandra said, "but my brother Paris. He lies dying of an arrow-wound, and you have such skill in healing—will you come?"

Oenone raised her eyebrows. At last she said, "Lady Kassandra, your brother died, for me, on the day when I left the palace and he spoke not one word to acknowledge his son. All these years, for me, he has been dead. I have no wish now to bring him back to life."

Kassandra knew in her heart that she should have anticipated this answer; that she had had no right to come here and ask anything of Oenone. She bowed her head and rose.

"I can understand your bitterness," she said. "And yet—he is certainly dying; can your anger be still so great? In the face of death?"

"Death? Do you not think it was like death for me, to be sent forth without a word, as if I were a penny harlot in the streets of Troy? And all those years not a word to his son? No, Kassandra, you ask if my anger is so great? You have not begun to know anything about my anger, and I do not think you want to know. Go back to your palace, and mourn your brother as I have mourned him all these years." Her voice softened. "My anger is not toward you, Lady; you were always kind to me, and so was your mother."

"If you will not come for Paris' sake, or for mine," Kassandra pleaded, "will you not come for my mother's sake? She has lost so many of her sons . . ." Her voice broke and she bit her lip hard, not wishing to weep before Oenone.

"If it would make any difference . . ." Oenone began. "But now, with the city about to fall into the hands of an angry God —ah, it surprises you that I know that? I am a priestess too, Lady. Now, go home and care for your child—send her to safety if you can; it will not be long now. I bear no ill will even toward the Spartan Queen, but I can do nothing for Paris. When he deserted me, he outraged Father Scamander—who is one with Poseidon."

It had never occurred to Kassandra before that the River God, Scamander, should be an aspect of Poseidon Earth Shaker. But Paris had forsaken the River God's priestess for the daughter of Zeus Thunderer—and he had presumed to judge in a controversy between the Immortals, abandoning his own country's Gods to serve the Akhaian Aphrodite.

"I bear no guilt for his death," Oenone continued; "his fate is on him as are yours and mine on ourselves. May your Gods guard you, Lady Kassandra." She raised her hand in a gesture of blessing, and Kassandra found herself walking away down the hill, feeling like a peasant woman dismissed from the royal presence.

Downhill, her return took less time, and when she returned to the palace, she heard the sound of wailing. Paris was dead. Well, she had expected it. Despite her encouraging words to Helen, she had been sure that with such a wound he could not long survive.

Moving to the balcony to look out over the plain where the Akhaian armies were building, she could now see the rough outline of what the scaffolding surrounded. It rose, huge, clumsy, unmistakable: the great wooden form of a horse.

So this is their altar, she thought: the very form of Poseidon Earth Shaker Himself. Do they think this horse will kick down the walls of Troy, or that it will summon the God to do so for them? How childish.

Then, without knowing why, she was seized with a sharp fit of shivering, so that she had to wrap her cloak around her in spite of the brightness of the sun. The figure of the horse—or of the God—struck her through with terror, although she was not sure why.

14

EVEN BEFORE the funeral rites were held for Paris, Deiphobos went to Priam and demanded command of the Trojan armies; when Priam protested, he said, "What choice have you, Sire? Is there anyone else in Troy, save perhaps Aeneas? And he does not belong to the royal house of Troy, and is not Trojan born."

Priam only stared, embarrassed, at the ground.

"Perhaps you would like to give the armies to your daughter Kassandra, who was once an Amazon?" Deiphobos asked, sneering.

Hecuba spoke up clearly and almost loudly, for the first time since Hector's death.

"My daughter Kassandra would command the armies of Troy no worse than you," she said. "You were a cruel and greedy child, and you are a proud and greedy man. My lord and King, Priam, I beg you to find some other to command the forces of Troy, or it will be the worse for all of us."

But they all knew there was no other. None of Priam's other surviving sons was old enough, or experienced enough, to lead the armies. When Deiphobos was called out before the troops and Priam formally handed over the command to him Deipho-bos said, "I will take this command only if I am given Paris' widow Helen, as my wife."

"You are mad," Priam said. "Helen is by right Queen of Sparta, not a prize to be handed from man to man like a con-cubine."

"Is she not?" asked Deiphobos. "Have you not had enough of the trouble a woman can make when she is left to choose with which man she will share her bed? Helen will marry me and be cheerful enough about it, won't you, Lady? Or would you rather go back to Menelaus? I could arrange that if you prefer it."

Kassandra saw Helen shudder; but she only said to Priam in a low voice, "I will marry Deiphobos if you wish me to, Sire."

Priam looked embarrassed. He said, "If there were any other way, I would not ask this of you, Daughter."

She threw herself into the old man's arms and embraced him. "It is enough that this is what you wish for me, Father," she said.

He held her gently, and there were tears in his eyes. He said, "You have become one of us, child. There is no more to say."

"Well, if that is settled," Deiphobos said loudly, "set forth the marriage feast."

Hecuba protested. "Is this any time for feasting, with Paris lying dead and not yet laid to rest?"

"There may be no time for feasting hereafter," Deiphobos insisted. "Should I alone of all Priam's sons go to my wedding unfeasted and unhonored?"

"There is little enough to honor here," said Priam, under his breath; only Hecuba and a few of the woman heard him. Nevertheless, he called the servants and ordered that the stores of wine be brought out and a kid be killed and roasted, and such foods as could be quickly prepared be set forth.

Kassandra went with the palace women, including Deiphobos' mother, to choose any fruits ready for harvest and set them out on platters. She agreed with Hecuba that this was no time for feasting, but if this wedding had to be, it should be made to look like a matter of choice rather than coercion. If Helen could put a good face on it, who was she to complain?

But for all the food and the hastily summoned minstrels, the wedding was joyless enough. The knowledge that Paris lay dead above cast gloom over the palace. Long before the bride and groom were put to bed together, Kassandra excused herself and withdrew. Looking down at the lights, she thought that perhaps the common folk of Troy, enjoying the gifts of food and wine sent down to them from Priam's palace, actually believed that this was a genuine festival. If they criticized Helen, it was only for her willingness to be given again in marriage when her husband had yet to be buried. Well, she thought, let them enjoy themselves. There may not be much more for them to enjoy.

And indeed, the funeral rites for Paris were held on the morrow—veiled Helen grave and pale, and nine-year-old Nikos standing small and serious at her side. He had insisted on cutting his hair for mourning. "I know he was not my father," he said, "but he was the only father I have ever known, and he was kind to me." His attempt not to cry tore at Kassandra's heart.

Once the ceremonies were completed, Deiphobos, with a look of relief, said briskly, "Now that's done, we'll go down and deal with that horse as Paris did. Start with a barrel of good hot tar or some pine-pitch and a few fire-arrows. We'll make short work of it. What do you think of that, my wife?"

Helen's voice was barely audible: "You must do as seems best to you, my husband."

She looked submissive and quiet, like any of the Trojan soldiers' wives, with little trace of the Goddess-given beauty they all had come to take for granted. The words were submissive too, the very ones she might have spoken to Paris; but it occurred to Kassandra that with this obedience she was mocking him. Deiphobos did not seem to think so; he looked at her with satisfaction and pleasure: now he had what he had always envied, Paris' wife and Paris' command. Well, if this marriage had brought happiness to at least one person, then it was not all bad.

This had not been demanded of Andromache; she had been allowed a decent time to mourn Hector. Why could Helen not have been allowed that same privilege?

Yet Helen had acted to show all women that they could do as she did; they should be grateful to her and admire her.

Deiphobos was gathering his charioteers, briefly discussing strategy with them. Kassandra watched Helen say farewell and bid him take care in battle, exactly as she had done with Paris.

Was it that Helen was so accustomed to catering to a man's will that it made no difference to her who the man was? Or was she only so stricken dumb with grief that nothing mattered anymore? *If I had loved as she loved Paris, and he was taken from me—look at Andromache! I love Aeneas well; but when he is gone from me, I remain myself. If he were to die, rather than leaving me to return to Creusa's side, I would mourn his death beyond measure; but it would not destroy me as Hector's death destroyed Andromache.* Was Andromache mourning Hector, then, or only the loss of her place as Hector's wife?

The charioteers rushed forward, making a charge through the workers who were pulling down the scaffolding around the monstrous wooden horse; they scattered and ran, about a dozen of them falling under the wheels of the chariots. There was a queer bitter smell in the air which Kassandra could not identify, and as the charioteers came close to the Horse, their flights of fire-arrows went toward it, but they did not ignite.

Agamemnon's soldiers attacked from the shadow of the scaffolding. The Trojans in their chariots fought strongly, but they were driven back to the walls. As the gates were opened for them to retreat inside Troy, there was a battle to prevent Agamemnon's men and what looked like a host of Akhilles' now-leaderless Myrmidons from crowding in and flooding the streets. A few forced their way in, but they were cut down in the narrow streets, and Deiphobos' men got the gates shut.

"It looks as though we will have a siege again," Deiphobos declared. "At all costs now we must keep them out of the city, which means these gates must not be opened. The one thing that monstrosity out there does is keep us from a good view of what's happening in their camp and field. We can't even burn it; they've soaked it with something so it won't burn, maybe a mix of vinegar and alum. Burning the scaffolding before may have been a mistake; it warned them that that was the first thing we'd try to do."

"If it is intended to be our God Poseidon," Hecuba said, "would it not be a sacrilegious act to burn it?"

"I think I'd burn it first and make my peace with the Earth Shaker afterward," Deiphobos said; "but it won't burn now."

"But we can burn it eventually?" asked Priam.

"Well, Sire, I'm certainly going to try my best," Deiphobos answered. "We can try shooting arrows covered with pitch and hope enough of the stuff will stick. I keep wondering if they've put this thing up here to give us something to think about so that we'll not notice what else they might be doing, like trying to tunnel under our walls from the landward side, or climb to the Maiden Temple and attack from up there."

"Do you think they could do that?" Hecuba asked fearfully.

"I'm sure they'll try, Lady. It's up to us to keep ahead of whatever tricks that Master of Sneaks, Odysseus, might be thinking up while we've got our eyes and our minds on that wretched *thing* out there." He looked at the Horse with loathing and shook his fist at it.

The image of the wooden Horse wandered that night through Kassandra's dreams. In one nightmare it came alive, rearing like a stallion and pawing at the ground; then it kicked out, and the stroke of its mighty hoof battered down the main gate of Troy, while from the Horse an army poured, raging and pillaging in the streets. Its head rose black and dragonlike above the flames that consumed the city. When she woke, so intensely real had the dream seemed that Kassandra went out in her night-shift to the balcony where she looked down over the plain below and saw the Horse solid and wooden and lifeless as ever in the pallid moonlight. It was not even nearly so large as it had seemed in her dream. *It's just a thing of wood and tar,* she thought, *harmless as that statue by the Scamander.* A few pale torches burned before it—homage to Poseidon? She recalled the vision in which she had seen Apollo and Poseidon battling hand to hand for the city, and went inside to the shrine to kneel and pray.

"My lord Apollo," she implored, "can You not save Your people? If You cannot, why are You called a God? And if You can and will not, what kind of God are You?"

And then, terrified at the form of the prayer, she fled the shrine. She was suddenly aware that she had asked the last question anyone ever asked of a God, and the one that would never be answered. For a moment she was afraid she had committed blasphemy; then she thought, *If He is not a God, or if He is not good, then what is there to blaspheme? He is said to love Truth; and if He does not, then all of what I have been taught is false.*

But if He is not a God, what was it I saw battling for the city? What was it that overshadowed Khryse, or Helen?

If the Immortals are worse than the worst of men, small and petty and cruel, then whatever They are, They are not for mankind to venerate. She felt bereft; so much of her life had been spent in the intense passion for the Sun Lord. *I am no better than Helen, but I chose to love a God Who is no better than the worst of men.*

She went back to the walls and stood there, numb with horror, as the sun rose for the last time over the doomed city.

15

BEFORE HER lay the plain of Troy in the early sunlight. Within the city no one was stirring; outside, a few torches guttered weakly against the sunrise.

The silence was absolute. Even the distant line of the sea beyond the Akhaian earthworks lay dead calm and molten as if the very tide itself had ceased to pull upon the land. The reddish overcast of the sky was like faraway flames swallowing the last dim flicker of the setting moon. It was again as in her dream: the wooden Horse before the walls seemed to rear upward, pawing with monstrous hooves at the city.

She screamed, hearing her own voice die unheard in her throat, and then screamed again, pressing against the silence until at last, she could hear her voice as if it were tearing her throat open: "Oh, beware! The God is angry and will strike the city!"

It was as if behind the dead silence she could hear great roiling waves of sound as if Apollo and Poseidon, in their struggle for the city, had broken the deadlock and Poseidon had thrown the Sun Lord down.

Her screams had not been unheard; already women were flocking out of the buildings in all stages of undress.

"What is it? What's the matter?"

Kassandra was dimly aware of what they were saying.

It is Kassandra, Priam's daughter. Don't listen to her: she is mad.

No, heed what she says. She is a prophetess; she sees . . .

"What is it, Kassandra?" asked Phyllida calmly, speaking to her soothingly. "Can you not tell us quietly what it is that you have seen?"

She was still screaming out words. She tried to listen to herself—for she was as confused as her hearers, and it seemed as if her head had been cloven with an ax—and she thought, *If I were listening, I would believe I was mad too.* Yet in spite of the confusion, one part of her mind was clear, with the icy clarity of despair, and she struggled to bring that part into focus and to ignore the part that was a chaos of panic and terror.

She heard herself crying out, "The God is angry! Apollo cannot conquer the Earth Shaker; the city walls will be destroyed! Our own God will do what the Akhaians could not do in all these years! We are lost, we are destroyed! Hear and flee!"

But of what use was a warning? It was upon her that no one would escape, that she could see only death and disaster. . . . She became aware that she was fighting Phyllida's restraining hands and her friend was saying gently to one of the other priestesses, "Give me your sash to tie her, lest she do herself some hurt. Look, her face is bleeding where she has scratched herself." She passed the cloth carefully around Kassandra's hands.

Kassandra said desperately, "You need not tie me; I will not hurt anyone."

"But I fear you will harm yourself, my dear," Phyllida said. "Go, Lykoura, bring me wine mixed with syrup of poppy seeds; it will calm her."

"No," Khryse said, striding toward them. He roughly shoved Phyllida away and pulled the sash from Kassandra's hands. "She needs no drug; no soothing draft can calm her now. She has had a vision. What is it, Kassandra?" He laid his hands on her brow and said in a strong, stern voice, looking compellingly into her eyes, "Say what the God has given you to say; I pledge by Apollo, none will lay hands on you while I live."

But you are as powerless now as your Sun Lord, she thought frantically.

"Listen, then," she said, trying to silence her beating heart with the pressure of her clasped hands at her bosom. "The Earth Shaker has overthrown the Sun Lord as He will overthrow our city. We will feel Earth Shaker's rage more strongly than we ever have before. Not a wall, not a house, not a gate, not the palace itself will escape.

"Warn the people to flee, even into the arms of the Akhaians! Cover the cooking fires; make sure no lamp is near to the stores of pitch or oil. Let no one remain within doors, lest his body be broken by falling stone."

Khryse said sternly, turning toward the women, "We may still have a little time. Go quickly and release the serpents, any that have not taken flight already. Then two of you go to the palace and inform the King and Queen that we have had evil omens and bid them flee to open ground. They may not heed, but we must do what we can."

"It will avail nothing," Kassandra cried out, trying to stop herself even as she spoke. "None can escape the wrath of Poseidon! Let the women take refuge in the Temple of the Maiden; She may have some pity on us."

"Yes, go," Khryse said to the women. "Take the children there, and remain beneath the open sky till the quake subsides; there perhaps you can hide from our foes if they break into the city. There are great spoils to loot in Troy, and they may not climb that far." He held Kassandra as she began to recover her senses; in her head there were sharp pain and a drowning sensation, as if she looked out at the world from deep underwater. "I must go, Kassandra, and do what I can to spread the warning. Do you want that soothing draft? Will you take shelter in the Sun Lord's courts or will you go down to the town? What can I do to aid you?"

She found that Khryse's voice came to her as if across the plains and legions of the dead; but when she spoke, her own voice was calm.

"Thank you, Elder Brother, I need nothing. Go and do what you must, and I will go and make certain my child is safe."

Khryse walked away, and Kassandra went to her room. Honey slept there, still curled in blankets, but Kassandra noted that the snake was gone. Wiser than humans, it had sought refuge in some secret place known only to the serpentkind. Kassandra bent and gently shook the child, waking her. Honey put her arms up to be lifted, and Kassandra dressed her quickly.

Somehow she had to get the child safely out of Troy before the invaders broke through the walls.

She said, "Come, darling," and took Honey's hand. "We must go quickly."

Honey looked confused, but obediently trotted along beside Kassandra as they crossed the compound. Hurrying up toward the Maiden's Temple with Honey's hand in hers, she stumbled, and strong hands picked her up.

"Kassandra," said Aeneas, "it has come. This was your warning?"

"I thought you had left the city," she said, trying to steady her voice.

"Surely you cannot stay now," he said. "Come with me; I shall find a ship bound for Crete—"

"No," she said. "Come—quickly. The Gods have forsaken Troy."

She led him swiftly into the innermost shrine of the Maiden's Temple; there were a few priestesses there, and she cried out to them: "Quickly, extinguish all the torches—yes, even the sacred flame! The Gods have deserted us!"

She herself, releasing Honey's hand, took the last torch and crushed out the fire that burned before the Maiden, and as the priestesses were rushing out of doors, she tore down the curtain.

"Aeneas, this is the most sacred object in all of Troy; take it." She drew forth the ancient statue, the Palladium, and wrapped it in her veil. "Carry it across the seas, wherever you may go. Build an altar to the Goddess and establish the sacred fire. Tell the truth of Troy." He moved as if to draw away the veil and behold the sacred object, but she stayed his hand.

"No, no man must look upon it," she said. "Swear you will carry it to a new Temple and there consign it to a priestess of the Mother. Swear!" she repeated, and Aeneas looked into her eyes.

"I swear," he said. "Kassandra, you can have no further reason to remain. Come with me—a priestess should be the one to take this beyond the seas."

He bent to embrace her; she kissed him wildly, then drew back.

"It cannot be," she said; "my fate lies here. It is yours to leave Troy unwounded and alive. But go at once, and all our hopes and all our Gods go with you."

"You must not stay here—" he began.

"I pledge to you, I shall leave Troy before the sun rises again," she said. "It is not death that awaits me; but I am not free to go with you. The Gods have decreed otherwise."

He kissed her again and took the wrapped bundle.

"I swear it by my own divine lineage," he said. "I will do your will—and Hers."

Kassandra's eyes blurred with tears as he hurried out of the Temple.

She had hardly crossed the court when inside her head she heard a great roar. The ground swayed beneath her feet; she stumbled and fell with Honey in her arms, and lay still, her body pressed against the suddenly unstable earth which rippled and bounced beneath them. Her only emotion was not fear but rage: *Earth Mother, why do You let Your sons play this way with what You have made?*

The movement seemed to go on forever, under the frightened sobs of the child in her arms. Then it subsided, and she realized that the sun was still only a fraction above the horizon; the quake could hardly have lasted more than a few moments. Honey's crying had subsided to a soft hiccuping.

Kassandra looked behind her, and saw that the sound she had heard had been the walls of the Sun Lord's house collapsing inward. Hardly a building in the enclosure was still standing. Of the main building where they dwelt, no more than a heap of rubble was left. Certainly nothing could be salvaged from there. There was a muffled screaming; someone had been trapped inside under the fallen stones. Kassandra looked helplessly at the pile—she could not with all her strength have budged a single stone—and very soon the sound ceased.

Somewhere in the gardens, a bird began to sing.

Did this mean it was over?

As if in answer, the ground seemed to shudder and rock again, and then was still. Stunned, Kassandra walked toward the vantage point where last night she had looked down on the plain.

The great gate and front wall of Troy had fallen, and in the midst of the battered rubble of wall and gate, Kassandra saw the wooden Horse lying, one leg raised grotesquely as if it had indeed kicked the wall down with its great hooves. The torches had set the scaffolding on fire and it was burning fiercely; but against the Horse itself, the flames licked in vain. Flames were rising from the poorer quarter with its wooden houses. It was the vision she had seen first as a child, the vision no one had believed: Troy was burning.

Through the gap in the fallen wall, Akhaian soldiers were already pouring in in floods, rushing into still unfallen houses and leaving laden with everything they could carry. Where could she hide? More important, where could she take Honey? One building within the compound of the Sun Lord's house was still standing: the shrine. There might be food there, remnants of the offerings of the day before. She was conscious, to her own shock, of a sudden fierce hunger. She went inside, and paused: if there should be another quake, the building might collapse. Then she saw that the statue of the Sun Lord had fallen, and beneath it, crushed, lay a human figure. Approaching with a numb curiosity—there was nothing to be done—she saw that it was Khryse who lay there.

At last, she thought; *now the God has truly struck him down.* She knelt beside the fallen man, closing the wide-open eyes, then rose and passed on.

In the room behind the statue, where the offerings were kept, she found loaves of bread—quite stale, but she ate one, dividing it with the little girl, who seemed stunned and did not cry. She thrust another into the fold of her robe—she might need it—and stopped to consider. The Akhaians were already plundering the lower town. Had the palace fallen? Had they all been killed—her parents, Andromache, Helen? Were there any Trojan soldiers left alive to halt the sack? Or were she and her child the only ones left alive to watch the devastation?

She listened for any sound that would prompt her to think that someone else remained alive in the Sun Lord's house, but there was only silence. Perhaps people still lived in the palace below. Had they heard the warning in time to get out into the courts or gardens?

Although the sun was now quite warm, she shivered. Her warm shawl—every stitch of her clothing except the shift she stood in—was buried in the ruins of the Sun Lord's Temple.

She should go down to the palace; although she was aware of the Akhaian soldiers in the city, she was desperately anxious to know if her mother still lived. She picked up Honey and began to run down the street.

The way was blocked with rubble and the debris of partly fallen houses: the people she met were mostly stunned-looking women, like herself half-clad and barefoot, and a few half-armed soldiers who had risen early to join Deiphobos. When they saw she was heading for the palace, they followed her.

The palace had not collapsed. The front doors had, and some of the carvings had fallen away, but the walls were still standing, and there was no sign of fire. As she approached she heard a loud wailing, and, recognizing her mother's voice, began to run. On the flagstones of the forecourt, heaved up and uneven now, she saw Priam lying—dead or senseless: she could not tell. Hecuba bent beside him, wailing; Helen, wrapped in a cloak, Nikos at her side, and Andromache, clutching Astyanax in her arms, were with her.

Andromache raised her eyes to Kassandra and said fiercely, "Are you content, Kassandra, that the doom you prophesied has come on us?"

"Oh, hush!" said Helen. "Don't talk like a fool, Andromache. Kassandra tried to warn us, that is all. I am sure she would rather have left all this unspoken. I am glad to see you unharmed, Sister." She embraced Kassandra, and after a moment, Andromache followed suit.

"How is it with Father?" asked Kassandra. She went and bent over her mother, gently lifting her up. "Come, Mother, we must take refuge in the Maiden's Temple."

"No! No, I will stay with my lord and King," Hecuba protested, her wails turning to sobbing.

Andromache embraced her, and then Astyanax came and put his arms around Hecuba, saying, "Don't weep, Grandmother; if any harm has come to Grandfather the King, then I will look after you."

"Hush, love," Helen said, as Kassandra knelt beside her father, taking the cold hand in hers, and raised a closed eyelid. There was not the faintest stir of motion or life; the eyes were already filmed over. She knew she should join Hecuba in ritual keening, but she only sighed and let his hand fall from hers.

"I am sorry, Mother," she said. "He is dead."

Hecuba's cries began again. Kassandra said urgently, "Mother, there is no time for that; Akhaian soldiers are in the city."

"But how can that be?" Hecuba asked.

"The walls were broken in the earthquake," Kassandra explained, desperately wondering if they were all lacking in wits, or senseless with shock—had they heard nothing? "Already they are plundering in the streets, and they will surely lose little time in coming here. Where is Deiphobos?"

"I think he must be dead," Helen said. "We heard Mother cry out that Father had fallen down in a fit, or a faint. We came at once, and Deiphobos carried him out of his room into the court here, then ran back seeking his own mother. Then the first shock came and the floors fell in and I think some of the roof as well. I had snatched up Nikos and ran out with him after Deiphobos."

"And so we six are alive," said Kassandra, "but we must hide somewhere, unless we wish to fall into the hands of the soldiers. I do not know what is the Akhaian custom with captive women, and I do not think I wish to."

"Oh, Helen has nothing to fear from them," said Andromache, staring fixedly at the Argive woman. "Her husband will soon be here to claim her, I am sure, and deck her in all the jewels of Troy and lead her home in triumph. How fortunate for you that Deiphobos died just in time—not that you care."

Kassandra was appalled at her spite.

"This is no time to quarrel, Sister; we should be glad if one of us need not fear capture. Shall we take refuge in the house of the Maiden? That is where we sent the women from the Sun Lord's house and I am sure it is still whole." She put her arm around Hecuba and said, "Come, let us go."

"No, I stay with my King and my lord," said the old woman stubbornly, dropping again to her knees beside Priam's body.

"Mother, do you truly believe that Father would want you to stay here to be captured by some Akhaian lord?" Kassandra asked in exasperation.

"He was a soldier to his death; I will not abandon him the moment he has fallen," Hecuba insisted. "You are a young woman; go and take shelter somewhere they will not find you, if there is such a place in Troy. I stay with my lord; Helen will be with me. Even the Akhaians would offer no insult to the Queen of Troy. We have fallen to a God and not to them."

Kassandra wished she felt half that sure. But they could already hear the soldiers approaching, and she seized Honey's hand. Astyanax was in Andromache's arms, protesting, struggling to get down, but his mother paid no attention.

"Let us hide in one of these mean houses along here; they would never think of looking in here, where there would be nothing to plunder," Andromache suggested, but Kassandra shook her head.

"I will entrust myself and my daughter to the Maiden of Troy. If our Gods have deserted us, perhaps the Goddesses will not."

"As you wish," Andromache murmured. "I no longer believe in any Gods. Farewell, then. Good fortune to you." She wedged herself into the smallest and dirtiest of the houses, and Kassandra, with Honey, ran on up the hill, to the highest point of Troy, where the Maiden's Temple stood untouched, the statue in the forecourt still unfallen. Kassandra quickly set Honey down and flung herself at the feet of the statue; surely no man, not even an Akhaian barbarian, would venture to make bold with any woman who took refuge here.

She heard the voices of the other women in one of the inner rooms. In a moment she would join them.

"Ah, there she is!" It was a cry of triumph in the barbarian tongue of the soldiers. Two armored men burst in the door. "I wondered where all the women had gone."

"This one will do for me; it's the princess, Priam's daughter. She's a prophetess and a virgin of Apollo—but if Apollo had wanted to protect His virgins, He'd have done it. You want to check in the inside room for some more of them?"

"No," replied the other, "I'll take the little one. When people think they're big enough, they're too old for my taste. Come here, little girl, I've got something nice for you."

Kassandra turned in horror, to see a giant soldier beckoning to Honey. "No!" she shrieked. "She's only a baby! No, no—"

"I like them that way," said the big soldier, grinning, and made a lunge at the child, ripping away her dress. Kassandra flew at him, using nails and teeth to tear Honey from his arms; a savage kick sent her flying half senseless into a corner of the room. She heard Honey screaming, but could not move; her limbs were so heavy she could not stir a finger. She felt the other man seize her and struggled violently; a blow across the face from the man's arm sent her back as all the strength poured out of her like sand from a torn sack.

She kept on hearing Honey's helpless cries until, even more terribly, they stopped. She was aware—though she could neither move nor speak—when the man tore away her shift and shoved her down onto the marble paving.

Goddess! Will you let this happen in Your very shrine before Your eyes? she implored—and then in shock remembered: she no longer honored the Immortals; why should the Maiden protect her?

But Honey has done no wrong, and she is a baby! If the Maiden sees this and cannot prevent it She is no Goddess. And if She can and will not—

Then fierce pain ripped her apart as the man thrust violently into her, and she felt darkness closing in on her.

She felt herself step out of her pain-racked body, conscious of the man still jerking away at her limp form, of Honey naked and torn, bleeding on the stone, still moving a little, whimpering through bruised lips. She rose and moved away, stepping over the flat and featureless plain. The sun had dimmed into the grayness that was all that was here. She walked down through the plain that was, and was *not*, the city of Troy where the wooden Horse had kicked down the walls and, though no longer on its feet, rose still whole and nightmarish over the dead city.

She saw others on this plain: Akhaian soldiers, a few of the Trojans. They seemed confused, looking about for a leader. Then she saw Deiphobos, half clad, still carrying his mother in his arms, his face and hands singed with fire. So they had died together, as Helen had suspected.

He tried to call to her, but she had no wish to speak to him. She turned and hurried the other way, wondering what had happened to Andromache.

There was Astyanax, his head bleeding, his clothing torn. He looked stunned, but as she watched, his face brightened, and he began to run across the plain, crying out in joy. She saw him swept up into Hector's arms and smothered in kisses. So Hector had claimed his son; she was not surprised that the Akhaian soldiers had not let him live. Andromache would grieve; she did not know that her son was with his father, as Hector had promised. Kassandra hoped the child had not known too much terror before he met his end on an Akhaian spear—or had they hurled him from the walls?

Then she saw Priam, standing tall and imposing as she remembered him from when she was a little girl. He smiled at her and said, "The city's gone, isn't it? I suppose we're all dead, then?"

"Yes, I think so," she said.

"Where's your mother, my dear? Not along yet? Well, I'll wait for her here," he said, gathering himself together to look around. "Oh! There's Hector and the boy . . ."

"Yes, Father," she said, feeling a lump in her throat; he sounded so happy.

"I think I will go and join them; if you mother comes, tell her, will you, love?"

But this can't be all there is to being dead, she thought. *There must be more to it. . . .*

She looked up and saw, standing directly before her, Penthesilea, unwounded, smiling, her face shining, surrounded by half a dozen of the warrior women who had fought with her on that last day. Laughing for joy, Kassandra ran into the Amazon's arms. She was surprised to find that her kinswoman felt as solid and strong and warm as on the day she had embraced her when she went out to fight before Troy and to die at Akhilles' hands. Kassandra spoke her surprise aloud.

"Then I suppose Akhilles must be here somewhere too."

"I would have thought so," said Penthesilea, "but he seems to have gone to his own place, wherever that may be."

Beyond Penthesilea the plain of the dead faded away, and Kassandra could see what looked like blinding light—twice the brilliance of the Sun Lord as she had seen Him in her first overpowering vision; and through the light, she made out the form of a great Temple, larger than the one where she had served in Colchis, and even more beautiful.

She whispered in awe, "Is that where I am to go?"

Beyond the light she began to hear music: harps and other instruments, swelling and filling the air with harmony like a dozen—no, a hundred voices, all joined together in song, clear and high and coming closer. This was what she had thought the Sun Lord's house would be. Khryse was standing in the doorway, beckoning to her; his face was free of the dissatisfaction and greed she had seen in it, so that he was at last what she had always believed him. He held out his arms, and she was ready to run into them, as Astyanax had run to Hector.

But Penthesilea was standing in her way—or was it the Warrior Maiden Herself, wearing the armor of the Amazon? She held Honey, laughing and unwounded, by the hand. *So she is dead too.*

"No," Penthesilea said; "no, Kassandra. Not yet."

Kassandra struggled to form words. It was the place she had seen in her dreams, the place where she had always known she belonged. And not only Khryse, but everyone she had loved was there, awaiting her, waiting for her voice to fill the place open in that great blended choir.

"No." Penthesilea's voice was sorrowful, but inflexible, and she held Kassandra back as one restrains a small child. "You cannot go yet; there is still something you must do among the living. You could not leave with Aeneas; you cannot come with me. You must go back, Kassandra; it is not time for you."

The beautifully molded face under the shining helmet was beginning to break up into a sunburst of brilliant sparkles. Kassandra fought to keep it in focus. "But I want to go . . . the light . . . the music . . . " she said.

The light was fading, and around her was darkness; she was

aware of a ghastly smell, like death, like vomit; she was lying on the dirt floor of some kind of rough shelter. *Then I'm not dead after all.* Her only emotion was bitter disappointment. She fought to hold on to the memory of the light, but already it was disappearing. She was conscious of pain in her body. She was bleeding, and part of what she smelled was her own blood on her face and covering her shift. The man who had raped her was lying half across her body. It was his vomit she smelled, and slowly, as if surfacing from a very deep trance, she heard a familiar voice and saw a face—hook-nosed, black-bearded— that had haunted her nightmares for years.

"I told you she was the one I wanted," said Agamemnon. "Look, she's breathing again. If you'd killed her I'd have had you flayed alive; you knew she fell to me in the casting of lots, but you had to try and get ahead of me. You always were spiteful, Ajax."

Kassandra felt agony through her whole body; agony mingled with despair.

So I am not dead after all; the Maiden saved me. For this!

16

SHE LAY still, too miserable to try to move.

"Honey?" she whispered painfully, through the rawness in her throat. But there was no answer. She remembered seeing the pitiable little body, bleeding and broken, flung aside by the man who had used her.

She must be dead now. I hope she is dead now. Yes, she is with Penthesilea.

She will be looking for me there.

I don't want to live. I want to be back there with Penthesilea, and Father . . . and the music. . . .

But she could feel her own breathing, the loud intrusive beating of her own heart. She would live. What was it Penthesilea had said? "There is still something you must do among the living." . . . *Had it been to care for Honey, I would have gone back—not willingly, but without complaint. But she is gone, I cannot help her now. Why am I here and everyone I love gone before me?*

She dimly made out that she was lying on the floor of a small building, and around her were boxes and bundles and bales of piled-up goods: silks, rich cloaks, tapestries, vases and pottery, sacks of grain and jars of oil—all the riches of the plundered city. Andromache lay close to her, face down, covered with a coarse blanket. Kassandra made out her face in the dim light. Her eyes were red and swollen with crying. She opened them and looked at Kassandra.

"Oh," she said, "you are awake; they said when they brought you here that you were dead, and Agamemnon would not admit it."

"I was sure I was dead," Kassandra said. "I wanted to be dead."

"And I," Andromache said. "They took Astyanax."

"Yes, I know; I saw him—running to his father's arms."

Andromache considered this for a moment. She said, "Yes, if anyone could see beyond death, I suppose it would be you."

"Believe me, he is free, and happy, and with his father," Kassandra repeated. Her voice caught at the memory. "They are better off than we are; I wish I were where they are now."

After a moment she said, "Why are we being held here? What is to become of us? Where is this place?"

"I am not sure; I think it is where the Akhaian captains are making ready to load the ships," Andromache said.

"Listen," Kassandra said, cringing; "someone is coming." She could hear the fall of heavy footsteps on the ground. But she had lost the preternatural Sight of the trance state, and she felt dull and sick, locked into her ordinary mortal senses. There was a foul taste in her mouth. "Is there any water here?"

Andromache sighed and stirred, then sat erect. She reached for a jar and carried it carefully to Kassandra, who drank till she was no longer thirsty. She had to sit up to drink, and felt as if her head would split off and roll away. She helped

Andromache to replace the jar and lay down again, exhausted by only that small movement.

Kassandra said, in a whisper, "Honey is dead too. They tore her from me in the very shrine of the Maiden; and raped her, baby that she was . . . " Her voice broke.

Andromache's hand closed over hers. "I know how you must feel, even though she was not your own child."

Kassandra said dully, "She was my own as much as any child could have been."

"You say that, because you have never borne a child," Andromache said. She pulled her cloak over her face again.

"Are you all right? Have you been harmed?" Kassandra persisted, trying to break through Andromache's lifeless despair.

Andromache turned over to face her. "No, they did not lay a hand on me. I suppose they have taken me because it helps their pride to think of Hector's wife a slave," she said. "As for my child—if he had been the son of a lesser man they might have let him live. . . ." After a moment she asked, "But what of you? You have been hurt. . . ." She reached out, stopping short of touching the bleeding cut on Kassandra's forehead. "Were you—beaten as well as . . ."

"Raped? Yes," she said. "I thought—I hoped that I was dead. But for one reason or another, I—was sent back."

She remembered painfully Penthesilea's words: *There is still something you must do among the living.* But what? They would not have sent her back simply to comfort Andromache and tell her that her son was safe with his father. But what else? Could she somehow avenge herself on Agamemnon? Ridiculous; not all the armies of Troy could cast him down, and she was no more than a single woman, wounded and ravished.

A dark form blotted out the light through the door, and a rough voice said, "All right, you, in there with the others," and someone was pushed inside, stumbled and fell at Kassandra's side: a woman, small and frail. She moaned and raised her head painfully.

"Kassandra? Is it you?"

"Mother!" Kassandra sat up and embraced her. "I thought you were dead. . . ."

"And I heard Agamemnon had taken you. . . ."

"He has claimed me," Kassandra said, trying to speak steadily, "but they have not loaded the ships yet; so at least we have a few moments to say farewell."

"They are still quarreling over the spoils," Andromache said bitterly, sitting up to embrace Hecuba. "Including us."

"I do not know where I am to go," Hecuba said, "nor what good I should be, old as I am, as a slave."

"At least, Mother, you need not fear being made a concubine," Andromache said.

Hecuba laughed a little, then said, "I never thought I should find anything to laugh about again. But you two are young; even as slaves, you may still find something good left in life."

"Never," Andromache said. "Oh, let us not begin to quarrel about which of us has suffered most!"

Kassandra froze, whispering, "Someone is coming."

It was Odysseus; his broad body seemed to fill the whole doorway. The guard at the door asked him, "What do you want, my lord?"

"One of the women in here belongs to me. I lost at the draw, but maybe it isn't all loss; my wife, Penelope, would be angry with me if I brought home a young and pretty slave."

"Oh, misery," Hecuba whispered, clutching at Kassandra's hand. "And he was so often a guest at our fireside. I cannot bear this humiliation!"

Odysseus came in and bent over the women. His voice was not unkind.

"Well, Hecuba, it seems you're to come with me. Don't be afraid; I have no quarrel with you, and my wife has less." He gave her a hand to help her rise, which she did stiffly. Then he bent over Kassandra and whispered, "Don't be afraid for your mother. I'll take good care of her; she'll never be homeless while I live. I'd have been willing to take you home too, Kassandra, but Agamemnon was bound and determined he'd have you, so it looks as if you'll be a King's mistress."

"Who is to take Andromache?" Kassandra asked.

"She goes to the country of Akhilles to his father, as part of his estate."

"It could be worse," said Andromache grimly.

Hecuba asked, "And Polyxena?"

Odysseus looked down. He said, "She is a companion to Akhilles himself."

"What can that mean?" Hecuba demanded, but Odysseus cast down his eyes and would not meet her gaze.

Kassandra, however, had seen it in his eyes, and blurted it out: "She is dead, sacrificed, her throat cut and her body cast on Akhilles' pyre as if she were some animal. . . ."

Odysseus flinched; Hecuba demanded, "Is this true?"

Odysseus said, "I would have spared you that knowledge. Akhilles had offered to marry her; so they sent her to join him in the Afterworld."

Kassandra said gently through Hecuba's cry, "Don't grieve, Mother; she is better off than most of us, and you will be with her soon."

Hecuba dried her eyes with her dress.

"Aye, better off than any of us," she said. "The Afterworld cannot but be better than this, and soon I shall be with my lord and King and the father of my sons. Well, lead on, Odysseus." She stooped quickly to embrace Kassandra. "Goodbye, my daughter. May we meet again soon."

"It cannot be too soon for me," said Kassandra, as they parted. She lay down, trying to rest her aching head on a bundle of canvas. She knew she would not see her mother again this side of death, and Hecuba would not be alone there.

The light moved slowly across the floor; it must be past noon. Had it been only this morning the city had fallen? It seemed like weeks—no, years.

The light was growing duller when she heard an Akhaian voice say apologetically, "You don't have to wait in there with them, Lady," and a soft, courteous protest in a familiar voice.

Then a slender form stepped inside the shelter, saying softly, "Who is there?"

"Helen?" Kassandra sat up. "What are you doing here?"

"I would rather be here than thrust aboard Menelaus' ship for all the sailors to gape at," said Helen. "He will come and fetch me when the ship is ready to sail."

Kassandra lay down again. She knew she should feel some

resentment toward this woman, but Helen had only followed her own destiny as she, Kassandra, followed hers. Helen stared, appalled, at Kassandra's still-bleeding head.

"Oh, how awful!"

"It's all right, I'm not much hurt," Kassandra said.

"And you, who deserve the worst of all, have not been touched," Andromache said bitterly. "Why, you're even properly dressed." She looked with resentment at the fresh rust-colored gown, the neatly fastened cloak with gold clasps and belt.

Helen's smile was faint. "Menelaus insisted. And he sent Nikos away with the soldiers, saying I wasn't fit to have the care of a child."

"At least your son still lives," Andromache muttered.

"But he is lost to me," Helen said. "And Menelaus has sworn that if this one lives"—and Kassandra remembered that Helen had confided to her that she believed herself to be pregnant again—"he will expose it. Believe me, Andromache, I would rather be going into the hands of a stranger, even if the men threw dice for me. Menelaus will doubtless make me feel his fury for the rest of my life; I would rather be buried peacefully here at the side of Paris, whom I loved."

"I do not believe that," said Andromache grimly. "I am sure you would rather have some new man to captivate with your beauty." She turned away from Helen and did not speak again.

Kassandra held out her hand to Helen and the other woman clasped it. She said, "I wonder, do all the women in Troy hold me responsible . . . ?"

"I don't," Kassandra said.

"No. And I found friends in Troy," Helen said, bending down to kiss Kassandra. "I wish I had never come here to destroy you all. . . ."

"It was Poseidon who did that," said Kassandra, and they were silent, holding hands like young girls. It was not very long before steps sounded outside and Menelaus stooped to come in the low door.

"Helen?" he said.

"I am here," she said meekly, and Kassandra looked up into

the blaze of light that seemed to fill the little hut. Helen's hair was brilliantly golden, and about her was the radiance she had borne when she stood upon the walls of Troy: the very aura of the Goddess.

Menelaus blinked as if his eyes were dazzled. Then, unwillingly, he bent and murmured, "My lady and my Queen." As if he were afraid to approach her, he offered his arm, and she stepped slowly toward him.

They left the hut, Menelaus following Helen a half pace behind.

It was growing dark outside when at last Kassandra saw the familiar form of Agamemnon thrust his head inside the hut.

"Priam's daughter," he said, "you are to come with me; the ship is ready to sail."

Now what am I do to? Submit? Fight? There is no help for it. It is Fate.

She rose and he took her arm, not roughly, but with a certain proprietary pride. He said, smiling tentatively, "I asked for you alone, from all the spoils of Troy; believe me, I will not ill-treat you, Kassandra. It is no small thing to be the beloved of a King of Mykenae."

Oh, I believe it, she thought. It occurred to her that Priam might, if Agamemnon had not already been wedded to Helen's sister, very well have given her in marriage to this man. What lay before her now, except for a few formal rites and the blessing of her kin, would not be much different from that. A wife to any Akhaian was no less a slave than any slave in Troy. She shivered; and he turned to her solicitously.

"Are you cold?" he asked. He bent and picked up a cloak from a pile of plundered garments that were stacked in the hut, a blue one she had never seen before.

"Wear this," he said magnanimously, draping it around her shoulders. He guided her over the rough ground, down to the water's edge, and held her hand as she stepped onto the ship. The deck swayed as he led her across it; it was bigger than it had looked from the walls of Troy. The rowers at their oars looked up at her curiously as she tried to walk without tripping over the cloak. On deck there was a small tent, something like the tents in which the Akhaians had camped during the war. He lifted the flap for her to step inside. There were soft rugs, and a lamp burning.

"You will have privacy here," he said ceremoniously. "We will sail with the tide, two hours before dawn." He left her, and she let herself fall on the rugs, feeling the gentle up-and-down sway of the deck. She wondered if she could slip to the other side of the ship, slide off into the water and drown. But no, surely she was watched, and they would seize her before she got to the water. Besides, she had been told that she was not to die, so she would only be sent back again.

She lay back, trying to resign herself to the moment when Agamemnon would come to her.

He could not be worse than Ajax. And she had lived through that. She would live through this too.

17

AT LEAST she was no longer retching. Kassandra dragged herself out of the tent on deck and into the fresh evening air. She still could not bear the thought of food; the very idea gave her a warning spasm; but she managed to stay upright this time, on her knees—the motion of the ship made it unthinkable to stand without an undignified fall—and looked curiously at the shoreline and the small rocky islands they were passing.

It seemed they had been at sea forever; last night she had seen the new moon, slim and pale and welcome because she knew it appeared in the southwest and gave some direction—now that she could note directions at all—to the trackless, directionless sea. She thought that her confusion had added to the sickness; there was nothing but a sick and whirling body in the center of a vortex of heaving ocean and lurching deck. At first she had been so ill nothing had mattered—not the smells of the sea or the sounds of the rowers, not Agamemnon's use of her uncaring body, not the food she regularly refused. At first, she had believed it was mostly the aftermath of the blow she had had from Ajax—head injuries often caused both nausea and confusion, and when it did not subside in a reasonable time she thought that it was the motion of the ship.

Now—counting time from the moon—she had begun to wonder, with dismay and revulsion, if she might be pregnant. When she had first taken Aeneas to her bed, she had not thought much about it. The priestesses were taught ways to avoid such things if they chose; but these arts often failed, and aboard the ship she had been too ill to heed them. She had been resigned to the fact that sooner or later she would find herself with child by Aeneas. But the possibility that this might be Aeneas' child was very small indeed; since the blow on the head she had a certain amount of trouble remembering exactly when he had last been with her, or when she had last seen evidence that she was not pregnant. So it was probable that this was the child of Agamemnon—or worse, of Ajax, who had taken her first. Kassandra rarely listened to girls' gossip, but she had heard them saying often enough that one was not likely to get pregnant the first time with any man. But she had seen evidence, whatever they believed or hoped, that once was quite enough. If she had to choose, she would hope it was Agamemnon's child: him she detested, but it was not he who had taken her by force over the body of her dead child. The fact that she was recognized as his chattel and prize of war was not pleasing to her. *All my life I feared him*, she thought, remembering her first vision when she was a child, but at least he had behaved no worse than custom allowed in such cases.

It was an evil custom certainly, but he had not invented it, and it would hardly be reasonable to blame him for following his tradition. If she had been given by her parents in marriage to this man, he would have used her no worse, and probably no better.

He was, she supposed, no more reprehensible than any other Akhaian; as they were reckoned, she supposed he was considered a good man. She even realized that he had actually been frightened by her continuing sickness; at first he had tried to gentle her out of it, reassuring her that it was always this way. at the beginning of a voyage and that she'd soon grow used to it, encouraging her to get into the fresh air; when it did not subside, he left her alone a good deal, for which she was dimly grateful.

She thought sometimes that he might be trying to show her kindness. Once when she had vomited all over him (without apology; she had not asked him, nor given him leave, to bring her on this voyage at all) he had not beaten her—as she half expected (she had seen him beat one of his servants for spilling his clean shaving water)—but had called for fresh water to rinse her mouth, and had held her in his arms, covering her with a fresh cloak and trying to soothe her to sleep again.

That had been early in the voyage, while she was still in a mad confusion and rage of hatred; she would not look at him or speak, and he had soon stopped trying to engage her in conversation about the lands they passed. Now she wished she had encouraged him in this talk—it might be useful if she should ever escape. She could not return to Troy—there was nothing to return to—but she might go to Colchis, where Queen Imandra, or any priestess in the house of Serpent Mother, would welcome her, or to Crete; and in the islands there were many Temples where a priestess skilled in the healing arts or the lore of serpents might find shelter.

She was not closely guarded, perhaps because at first it had been so obvious that between the head wound and seasickness she was incapable of walking, let alone attempting any kind of rebellion or escape.

Now, lying on the sun-flooded deck outside the tent she shared with Agamemnon, listening to the slow drumbeat which kept time for the rowers, she thought, *It is more than that. It would never occur to them that a woman might think of escape.* A week ago when they had gone ashore on a little island to find fresh drinking water, they had left her unguarded. She had not tried to escape then—she could see that the island was so small that she could not possibly have hidden anywhere or found shelter. If anyone had lived there, to ask for shelter would have been to bring down the wrath of Agamemnon on the hapless peasant who might take pity on her. Only if there had been a shrine of the Maiden—or of the Sun Lord—would she have dared claim sanctuary.

She might do that still, if she could find such a shrine, although she supposed Agamemnon might legitimately claim her as a fair prize of war. Scant sympathy was shown to runaway slaves, and she could no longer claim to be a princess, since Troy had fallen. Everyone who spoke of her (she had overheard Agamemnon's soldiers and servants) seemed to think there was no reason she should not be content with him for the rest of her life.

She realized that she was allowing her mind to wander to keep from thinking seriously about the fact that she was probably carrying Agamemnon's child. Should she tell him? Not at once; it would please him too much, and he might think she was making some kind of claim to his sympathy or kindness.

Agamemnon was at the stern of the ship, standing beside the man who held the steering-oar. He was dressed, as were all his men, in a simple loincloth of bleached coarse linen; but the gold torque round his neck and the ornaments he wore, no less than his military bearing and air of command, made it obvious who was King and who were the servants.

He saw her seated in the shadow of the sail and strode across the deck.

"Well, Kassandra, I am glad to see you awake," he said. "The sea is calm, and the sun will do you good. When we went ashore for drinking water this morning"—she had been asleep and only dimly aware of the cessation of motion—"my men gathered some fresh grapes; perhaps you would like some of them?" Without waiting for her answer, he shouted to the four serving-women who spent most of their time huddled together at the stern gossiping. "You, there"—Kassandra had no idea of the women's names because Agamemnon never spoke to them by any name except "Girl" or "You"—"bring us some of those grapes. You greedy little beasts haven't eaten them all, have you?"

"Oh, no, my lord," murmured the tallest of them, and rose. From an enormous basket she seized four or five bunches of small wild grapes, laid them on a silver tray (Kassandra had seen it in the palace; Hecuba had used it for grapes too because it was etched with vines) and brought them across the deck.

The girl knelt before Agamemnon; he gestured for her to offer them to Kassandra first. She looked familiar; had she seen her in the streets of Troy somewhere in that other life?

"Princess . . ." she whispered, her eyes humbly cast down. It made Kassandra wonder what had happened to Chryseis when the city fell. She reached out and broke off a few grapes from a bunch, and bit into one. The juicy tartness was pleasant, and she swallowed, hesitantly, half expecting the queasiness to break over her again. Agamemnon had taken a bunch and was eating them with relish. His teeth were large and white and strong—*just like a horse's*, Kassandra thought with fascinated revulsion. She had to turn away to avoid a convulsive spasm, but she managed to swallow a few grapes, and did not feel immediately compelled to vomit.

"I am glad to see you eating again," Agamemnon observed. "Seasickness seldom lasts this long, and when you are in health you will be as beautiful as when I first saw and desired you."

She realized that he thought it would please her; he was trying to be friendly. Well, she seemed to be bound to him for a time at least; certainly if she was pregnant she must put aside all thought of escape until after the child was born. And it would be foolish to force him to consider her an enemy and perhaps keep closer watch on her, as he would certainly do if he thought she was considering escape.

But does he really believe that I will love him and obey him as a husband when he has murdered my brethren and my parents and my city?

It appeared to be exactly what he thought.

"Will you have more grapes?" he asked, and selected a bunch from the tray. She nodded and ate a few more. After a moment she started to speak; but she had not spoken a word since she came aboard, and now her voice failed her. She had to clear her throat twice before speaking.

"How much longer will we be aboard this ship?"

He looked startled, as if he had grown so used to her refusal to speak that he half believed she *could* not. But he said amiably enough, "I can well believe you are weary of travel. It is never possible to tell how long the journey will take; it we have fair winds and fair weather, we might arrive before the moon has fulled twice more. If we have bad weather and the winds are against us, we might not arrive before the worst of the winter."

She wished she had not asked; the thought of two more months on shipboard appalled her. And what would happen to her when they came to Mykenae?

That thought must have passed visibly across her face, because he said reassuringly, "You must not be frightened. My wife, Klytemnestra, is a gracious lady, and she would never treat badly one who had been a princess in Troy. She does not think she must prove her own royalty by treating others as her inferiors. Everyone in our house, servant or slave, is treated as custom demands, neither better nor worse."

It would not have occurred to Kassandra to be afraid of Klytemnestra. She was the twin of Helen, and Kassandra had loved Helen and found her a friend. Now it occurred to her that Agamemnon himself was afraid of his wife and that was why he thought she might be.

Was he afraid because she was the Queen of the land and he had become King only as her consort? She still might cherish her anger with him over the evil trick he had played in sacrificing her daughter Iphigenia to the God of the winds; after all, Iphigenia had been her eldest daughter, and Klytemnestra would have thought of her as her heir.

Kassandra remembered old crude jokes about shrewish countrywomen greeting faulty or drunken husbands with blows over the head from a winnowing fan or a dough roller; did Agamemnon fear some such greeting?

She looked at him and saw that the fear was deeper and blacker than that. For an instant it seemed as if there were blood smeared on his face that would never wash away; she told herself it was only the light of the setting sun. And if she truly saw blood, what wonder? He was a bloody man, a warrior who had slain hundreds in his long career.

She put the grapes aside, and shifted her weight; the roiling nausea, which had subsided for a little while, came back. She sighed and dragged herself back into the deck tent, glad to be again at rest. No, there was no way now to hide from the knowledge. She was with child, whether by Agamemnon or by another, and sooner or later he would have to know it.

That night the weather broke; the north wind rose and battered the ship so hard that even after the sail was lowered, high waves swamped the tent on deck and Agamemnon gave orders for everything to be lashed down. Kassandra was too sick with the rolling and pitching of the ship even to be terrified; she lay clutching a safety rope which Agamemnon had made fast about her, vomiting and at intervals wishing that the ship would be cast on the rocks or the tent washed overboard so that she could drown and be at peace.

The storm continued many days, and even when it subsided she wanted nothing more than to lie on deck and pretend she was dead. Her one hope was that the violence about her would bring on a miscarriage. This did not come to pass. Rage alternated with despair; what would she do with a child in captivity—bring it up as another of Agamemnon's slaves?

The day finally came when, as she had known he eventually must, Agamemnon looked at her and said, "You're carrying."

She nodded sullenly, not looking at him, but he smiled, and stroked her hair. He said, "My beautiful, have you forgotten my promise, that you are not my slave but my lawful consort?" He had indeed said something like that, but she had paid no more attention than she did to anything else he had said while she was still vomiting every hour or so. "You must not be afraid for our child; I pledge you my word that it will not be a slave but will be acknowledged and brought up as my son. I do not trust the children of Klytemnestra. Our son will be shown how much I value his mother, who was a princess of Troy."

She was dimly conscious that he was trying to please her; that he considered himself very generous and indulgent. Did he actually believe she could be led to thank him for treating her as a human being?

She supposed some women might be grateful not to have been treated worse, since such was his unlimited power. She raised her eyes and said, unsmiling, "That is kind of you, my lord." For the first time afraid of what he might do, she spoke the words she had promised herself never to say.

They pleased him, as she had known they would; men were so easily deluded and flattered. He smiled and kissed her. Going to one of the many great chests in which he kept the spoils of Troy, he took from it a gold necklace with four strands, each formed of many small links and engraved plates.

He stooped and put it about her neck.

"This befits your beauty," he said. "And if your child is a son, you shall have another to match it."

She had wanted to fling it back in his face. What arrogance, to give her as a gift some small part of what he had stolen from her family! Then she thought: *If I escape him, this necklace, with the links pried off and sold one at a time, would carry me to Colchis or even to Crete. Creusa is there, and perhaps Aeneas; she has only daughters and might be glad of a son, even if Agamemnon had fathered it.*

How will he feel if instead of the son he wants he has only a daughter? That would almost please her, she thought, *to give him what he does not want;* but then she asked herself, *Who would choose to have any child born as a girl into this world, to suffer at the hands of men what all women suffer?*

And then at the thought of a little girl like Honey, even one fathered by Agamemnon, her heart softened. If this child was a girl she would take her to Colchis, so that she might be reared where she need never be a slave.

Days passed, and as she had seen in other women who were in the hands of the Life Forces, she grew sluggish and heavy on her feet, unwilling to rise, though Agamemnon, now that he knew of her pregnancy, was gentler with her. Every day when weather permitted he escorted her about the deck, insisting that she must have some air and exercise. Once he expressed a hope that they would reach Mykenae before she was delivered.

"We have excellent midwives there, and you would be safe in their hands," he told her. "I do not know if any of these women on the ship know anything about such things."

One of them had been her mother's waiting-woman and

the chief of the palace's midwives; but she did not tell Agamemnon that. She did, however, contrive secretly to speak to the woman and tell her what had happened.

"Oh, well, Princess," the woman said, "if you give him a son he'll cherish you all the more; you'll be safe in Mykenae as mother of the King's son."

Secretly Kassandra had been hoping the woman would share her outrage, and she had intended to ask if the old woman could produce for her an herb potion which would cause her to miscarry. It confirmed her belief that women everywhere conspired with their oppressors.

Once when Agamemnon was sitting beside her, speaking of their son, she asked, "But do you not have a son by Klytemnestra? And being the eldest, would he not take precedence?"

"Oh, yes," Agamemnon said with an evil smile, "but my Queen values only her daughters; she pretended to believe that one of them would follow her as Queen. She even sent our son to be fostered away from the palace, so that I could not school him in the ways of king-craft."

That, Kassandra thought, was the best thing she had ever heard of Klytemnestra. She had wondered how Helen's sister could ever have brought herself, even for reasons of political expediency, to marry a man like Agamemnon. But perhaps her people had given her no choice, or had wanted a King, who commanded iron, to rule over their war parties.

"Our son, Kassandra, might rule after me over the city of Mykenae," he said to her. "Does that not please you?"

Please me?

But she only smiled at him; she had learned that if she smiled, he took it for agreement and was better satisfied than if she spoke.

There was at this season no good weather on the sea, but endless rain and wind, and every time they sailed a little way toward where they wanted to go, the winds would rise and beat them back so that they were always in danger of being driven onto the rocks.

Frequently Agamemnon had to head out into open water to avoid being driven onto a shore that would destroy the ship; it seemed that with days and months of sailing, they were no nearer to where they wished to go. One day, after a fearful hard-driving wind had blown them about for many days out of sight of land, a morning calm left them drifting. A sailor came to Agamemnon saying that they had sighted a stream of green water like a separate current in the sea. Agamemnon went on deck cursing, and she heard him shouting at his men; when he came back he was furious, his face drawn and dark with rage.

"What is the matter?" she asked him. She was lying on the deck, trying desperately to keep down the little bread and fruit she had eaten for breakfast.

He scowled and said, "We have sighted the outpourings of the Nile—the great river of the country of the Pharaohs. Poseidon, who rules the sea as well as the earthquake, has driven us far from home, and onto the shores of Egypt."

"That does not seem a catastrophe," she said. "You were saying that we were gravely in need of fresh food and fresh drinking water. Can they not be had here?"

"Oh, yes; but the word of Troy's fall has been spread all about the world now, and much gold will be expected for supplies," he muttered. "And everyone has told a different tale about what happened . . ."

"People do not know that Troy fell not to might of arms and soldier-craft, but to the earthquake," Kassandra said. "You can tell them what tale you will and they will not be rude enough to doubt it."

He scowled at her; but at that moment a cry came from the lookout in the bow that land had been sighted. Agamemnon went forward and soon returned to say that they had indeed reached Egypt.

Some of the men were sent ashore and eventually returned, bearing an invitation from Pharaoh to dine at the palace. Kassandra had hoped to lie alone in the tent, simply enjoying the cessation of the sea's motion, but it was not to be. Agamemnon drew from his chests an assortment of silken robes.

"Wear any one of these that pleases you, my dear; and I will send one of the women to dress you and braid your hair with jewels; you must be beautiful—yes, as beautiful as Helen herself —to honor me at the court of Pharaoh."

For the first time, she pleaded with him. "Oh, no, I beg of

you: I am ill—do not ask it of me. I have sought nothing from
you, but for the sake of the child I am to bear you, spare me
this. It will be easy to tell them that I am ill; do not parade me
as a slave before this foreign monarch."

"I have told you again and again," he said, sounding less
angry than sorrowful, "that you are not slave but my consort.
Klytemnestra has never pleased me, and when you bear my son
you shall be my Queen."

She wept in despair; he argued, cajoled and finally stormed
out of the room, saying in a tone of command, "I'll not argue
with you further; dress yourself at once, and I'll send a woman
to you."

She lay helplessly weeping, and roused only when the
woman who had been Hecuba's midwife came into the tent.

"Now, now, Princess, you mustn't go on crying like this,
you'll hurt the baby. I've brought you this." She held out a clay
cup with a potion that steamed with fragrance. "Drink it; it'll
settle your stomach, and you'll be beautiful to dine at the palace."

"You are a wicked woman," Kassandra flung at her. "Why
should Agamemnon have his way always? Why have you come
to be his most loyal servant? Can't you give me something that
would make me so sick that even he knows I cannot go?"

The woman looked shocked.

"Oh, no, I couldn't do that; the King would be very angry,"
she said, "Mustn't make the King angry, mistress."

Enraged, but knowing there was no help for it, Kassandra
let the woman dress her; she refused to choose a gown and let
the woman put her into a striped dress of crimson and gold silk
which she had seen her mother wear at palace banquets. She
drank the potion, which did make her feel better—or maybe it
was only her anger. Let Agamemnon parade his captive princess; what did it matter? If Pharaoh—who, she had heard, had
well over a hundred wives—knew anything about the fall of
Troy, he would know she was not here of her own free will; and
if not, it would not matter.

18

"THERE IS no relying on the winds at this season," said the bald man who called himself Pharaoh, and was regarded as a God incarnate by his court. "It would please us if you remained as our guest until the seasons change and the winds can be depended on to bear you to Mykenae, or wherever you wish to go."

"The Lord of the Two Lands is gracious," Agamemnon demurred, "but I had hoped to make my way home before that."

"Pharaoh gave this advice to the noble Odysseus, when he guested with us, and Odysseus ignored it," said one of the courtiers. "Now word has come that bits and pieces of Odysseus' ship have been cast up on the rocks of Aeaea; he will never be heard from again."

"Well, well, I suppose it is better to come late home than to arrive early on the shores of nowhere," said Agamemnon, "and I accept your gracious invitation, for myself and my men." Kassandra knew he was annoyed; this meant that he would have to ransack his chests of worthy guest-gifts for Pharaoh, and if they stayed too long he would not get any of his plunder home at all. They were not the first from Troy to be cast on these shores; Pharaoh's hall already displayed recognizable spoils from the city, including the statue of the Sun Lord from the shrine.

In the next few days Kassandra discovered that a few of the priests and priestesses of the Temple of Apollo had taken refuge here, though none of her closest friends to whom she might have appealed. She would have been overjoyed to know that Phyllida, or even Chryseis, was alive.

Egypt was hot and dry, and filled with bitter winds from the desert, which could wipe out all signs of life if people did not take shelter at once; even in Pharaoh's great stone palace the damage could be seen.

Nevertheless, at least it was on land, and better than being daily battered by wind and sea.

Kassandra was glad of the respite. The Egyptians gossiped

about Agamemnon, and one of the waiting-women told her secretly that everyone in Egypt knew that after the death of Iphigenia, Klytemnestra had sworn vengeance and had openly taken a lover, a cousin of hers named Aegisthos, and was living with him in the palace at Mykenae.

Kassandra's attitude was simply "Well, why shouldn't she? Agamemnon, away in Troy, was no good to her as a husband."

But these Egyptians also worshiped male Gods and felt a man's wife must do what he bade her, and that the worst thing that could happen was for a wife to lie with anyone but her husband. If it was a King's wife, then the Queen's behavior brought disgrace upon the whole country. Kassandra could only hope that Agamemnon would not hear the story and have another grievance. He spoke often of putting Klytemnestra away and making Kassandra his lawful Queen, and that was the last thing Kassandra wanted.

She even heard that Klytemnestra, feeling young again when she had taken Aegisthos to her bed, had to all purposes disinherited her remaining daughter, Elektra, by marrying her off to a lowborn man who had been the palace's swineherd or something of that sort. People who venerated Queens generally felt that a Queen past the age of childbearing should abdicate in favor of her daughter—and the people of Mykenae accordingly believed that Klytemnestra should have married Elektra to Aegisthos and allowed Elektra to take her place as Queen. It was agreed by everyone that Elektra's marriage was to a man no one could possibly have accepted as King.

Agamemnon finally heard the story—not about Klytemnestra's lover; everyone was careful that no breath of that should reach his ears—but about Elektra's marriage. And about that he was angry.

"Klytemnestra had no right to do that; it was as if she had presumed my death. Elektra's marriage was mine to make, a dynastic marriage which would have brought me allies. Odysseus had spoken of marrying her to his son Telemachus, and now that Odysseus' ship is lost, Telemachus will need powerful allies if he is to hold Ithaca against those who would like to take it," he said.

"Or I might have married her to the son of Akhilles—he

was never formally married to his cousin Deidameia, but I heard he seduced the girl and she bore him a son after he went to fight in Troy. Well, when I come home, Klytemnestra will learn that I mean to set my house in order and that her rule is at an end," he said. "Elektra as a widow will be just as valuable a marriage pawn; the girl cannot be more than fifteen or so. And it is your son and not Klytemnestra's son Orestes who will sit on the Lion Throne when I am gone."

Kassandra had noted that the Akhaians thought much of their sons' coming after them; it seemed to be how they coped with the thought of death, for they seemed to have no concept of an afterlife. No wonder they had no code of decency; they seemed not to believe their Gods would hold them responsible in the next life for anything they did in this one.

THE DAYS in the calm Egyptian land were all so much alike that Kassandra was hardly aware of the passing of time; only by the growth of the child within her did she have any awareness of the days that were hastening by. At last the season was sufficiently advanced that Pharaoh said they might set sail; but that very night Kassandra fell into labor, and at sunrise the next morning she gave birth to a small male child.

"My son," Agamemnon said, picking up the baby and looking carefully at him. "He is very small."

"But he is healthy and strong," said the midwife eagerly. "Truly, Lord Agamemnon, such small children often grow up as big as those who are larger at birth. And the princess is a narrow woman; it would have gone hard with her to bear a son of a proper size to be yours."

Agamemnon smiled at that and kissed the baby. "My son," he said to Kassandra; but she looked away from him and said, "Or Ajax'."

He scowled, not liking to be reminded of that possibility, and said, "No; I think he has a look of me."

Well, I hope you enjoy thinking so, she thought; *it will not make the poor child prettier.*

"Shall we name him Priam for your father, then? A Priam on the Lion Throne?"

She said, "It is for you to say."

"Well, I will give it thought," Agamemnon said. "You are a prophetess; perhaps we can think of a name full of good omen." He stooped and laid the baby back to her breast.

But there are no good omens for a son of Agamemnon, she thought, remembering that Klytemnestra and her new King awaited Agamemnon at home. This son, no more than Klytemnestra's son Orestes, would never sit on the Lion Throne of Mykenae.

She felt a familiar far-off humming in her head, and the sun blinded her eyes. The child seemed to weigh less in her arms—or was it that her arms had released him? She had believed the Sight was gone from her forever; she had not managed to save her people or her loved ones with her prophecy, and had thought herself free of it at last.

Now she saw the great double-bladed ax that cleft the head of the great bulls in Crete, and Agamemnon staggering, with his eyes full of blood.

She clasped her hands to her eyes to shut out the sight.

"Blood," she whispered, "like one of the bulls of Crete. Go not to the sacrifice. . . ."

He leaned down to stroke her hair.

"What did you say? A bull? Well, for this fine gift no doubt I should give a bull to Zeus Thunderer. But not here in Egypt; we will wait for that till we reach my country, where I have bulls in plenty and need not pay the outrageous amounts of gold the priests here demand for sacrificial animals. I think Zeus can wait till then for the proper sacrifices; but when you can get up you may take a couple of doves to their Earth Mother in thanksgiving for this fine son."

Maybe that was all I saw, she thought, *a sacrifice somehow gone wrong*—but all at once her malice was gone; she had hated and despised him, but now she saw him among the dead and wondered if after death he must face all the men he had slain in battle. Hector had said that when he crossed the gate of death he was first greeted by Patroklos. But it would be different for Agamemnon, as it had been somehow different, she knew, for Akhilles.

She lingered abed, knowing that as soon as she could walk, Agamemnon would set sail for the port of Mykenae. And she had been so sick every day of the voyage which had brought them here that now she was in terror of the sea.

She finally decided to call her son Agathon. Before his birth, she could not imagine loving a child conceived like this one, and she had begun to suspect that a good part of her sickness during pregnancy was just revulsion against the very thought that this parasite of rape had fastened on her from within and would not be cast forth. If he had turned out to have been poisoned by her loathing, with two heads or a marred face, she would have thought it only fitting.

And yet he lay on her breast so small and innocent, and she could not see anything about him that was like Agamemnon. He was just like any other newborn child, very small indeed, but everything about him was perfectly formed, down to hands with exquisite little fingernails, and a tiny toenail on each toe.

How strange to think that this soft little being, who could lie at the center of his father's great shield and leave room for a good-sized dog, might grow up to bring down a mighty city. But for now he was all softness and milky fragrance, and when he nuzzled at her breast she could not help thinking of Honey helpless in her arms. Why should this perfect little creature be blamed for what his father had done?

But she knew that just as Klytemnestra had done, she would be sure to send this son away so that Agamemnon could not school him in king-craft. She found no pleasure in the thought that her son might one day sit on the Lion Throne. She did not wish her son to be brought up as the Akhaians brought up their sons.

She supposed that Helen by now had borne Paris' last son, and she wondered if Menelaus had carried out his threat to expose the child. It was the sort of thing he would do; these Akhaians seemed to care only for their *own* sons, as if a child could be anyone's except the mother's who bore it.

Even Agamemnon had no knowledge whether this child was his or Ajax'—or, for that matter, Aeneas'. She would take care not to remind him again of that. This was *her* son, and no man's. But she would hold her peace and let Agamemnon think it his if he wished, for its safety.

She gathered the babe up in the swaddling clothes that had

been provided in Pharaoh's palace, and went through the streets of the city with one of the women of the royal household who had borne a child the day before. In the Temple of the Goddess —a repulsive statue of a woman with huge breasts like a cow, and the head of a crocodile—she sacrificed a pair of young doves, and kneeling before the statue, tried to pray.

She was a stranger in this land and a stranger to this Goddess. She supposed there was not so much difference between the Goddess of crocodiles and the Goddess of snakes; but no prayer would come, nor could she look even a little way into the future and see whether it would be well with her child.

She should seek the Sun Lord's house; here in Egypt, the Sun Lord was the greatest God, and He was called by the name of Re. But she still mistrusted the God who had been unable— or unwilling—to save her city, and would not approach Him.

If He could not save us, He is not a God; if He could and would not, what sort of God is He?

The next day Agamemnon's goods were prepared and loaded, he gave final guest-gifts to Pharaoh, and they departed.

Kassandra had been in terror of renewed seasickness; but this time she felt only a little queasy the first night the crew lifted anchor. The next morning she felt perfectly well. She ate fruit and the hard ship's bread with good appetite, and sat on deck with the baby at her breast. The illness, then, had been a side effect of her head injury and then of her pregnancy.

She knew nothing of ships and sailing, but Agamemnon seemed pleased with the strong winds that day after day drove them across the clear blue waters. The baby proved as good a sailor as his father. He suckled strongly, and it seemed that she could see him growing every day, his small hands becoming more formed, his nose and chin, from mere blobs, taking a real shape. She felt that perhaps, considering the shape of his chin, he might be Agamemnon's child after all. His father liked to hold him and joggle him in his arms, trying to make him laugh. This was the last thing she had expected. Well, Hector and even Paris had enjoyed playing with their children. Painful as it was to admit it, Akhaians were not greatly different from other men.

One morning, just as it was getting light, she had gone on deck to rinse the child's swaddlings in a bucket of seawater and spread them to dry. The ship was silent except for a single steers-man at the stern, for the winds were strong enough that the rowers were not needed except for maneuvering at close quarters to land.

She looked from horizon to horizon; the sea was peaceful, and they were passing between two shores. One was a high mountain rising steeply above them, its shadow reaching almost to the ship itself. On the other side was a long, low, treeless headland. Suddenly on the side of the mountain a streak of fire flared upward to the sky, like a flower of flame blooming there. The steersman let out a shout of exultation and yelled for one of his fellows to come and steer.

Agamemnon appeared on deck and shouted to the crew, "There it is, my brave lads! The beacon on our own headland! After all these years, we've come home at last! A bull to Zeus Thunderer!"

The sunlight glinted in his eyes—*as red as blood*, Kassandra thought. Her own eyes felt strained and dry, and it struck her that he should hardly be so overjoyed at coming home: who knew what he would find there?

She came to the rail, the child in her arms, and stood beside him.

"What is it?"

"When I left home," he said, "I gave orders that a great pile of wood should be made on the headland, and a watchman kept there at all times. When I set sail, I sent a message by a swift courier that a watch should be kept for my ship. Now we have been sighted, and word will be sent to the palace; a feast and a welcome will be prepared for us.

"It will be good to be home again. I am eager to show you my country and the palace where you will be Queen, Kassandra." He took the child from her, bending over the little face and saying, "Your country, my son; your father's throne. You are silent, Kassandra."

"It is not my country," she said, "and it is certain Klytemnestra will have no joyful welcome for me, eager as she may be to see you again. And I am afraid for my child: Klytemnestra—"

"You need not fear anything like that," he said arrogantly.

"Among the Akhaians, our women are dutiful wives. She will not dare say a word of protest. She has had a free rein while I was away; she will soon learn what I expect of her, and she will do as she is told or be the worse for it, believe me."

"It is cold," she said. "I must go and fetch my cloak."

"It seems warm and fine to me," he said, "but perhaps it is because this is the port of my native city. Look, now you can see the palace on the hill, and the walls, built by Titans centuries ago. The port here is called Nauplia."

She went to fetch a cloak and stood beside Agamemnon at the prow, letting the woman who had been her mother's midwife take the baby.

The great sail had been lowered, and the rowers had taken their places to maneuver the ship in the harbor; it glided smoothly along inside the sheltered waters in the lee of the headland.

Now she could see a number of people collecting along the pier. As the ship drew in close, one man raised a cheer, and Agamemnon's soldiers, clustered along the side of the ship, began waving and yelling to people they recognized on shore.

But for the most part the watchers were silent as the ship drew slowly closer to the pier. To Kassandra the silence seemed ominous. She shivered, although the rich cloak she wore was warm, and took the baby back from the serving-woman, to clutch him close against her body.

The prow of the ship bumped gently against the land. Agamemnon was the first to step ashore; at once he fell to the ground and solemnly kissed the stones of the pier, crying in a loud voice, "I give thanks to the Thunder Lord who has returned me safe to my own country!"

A tall red-haired man with a gold torque about his throat stepped up to him and said with a bow, "My lord Agamemnon, I am Aegisthos, a kinsman of your Queen; she has sent me with these men to escort you with great honor to the palace."

The men closed in around Agamemnon and marched away. It looked to Kassandra as if he were a guarded prisoner rather than a King receiving an escort of honor. Agamemnon was scowling—she could see he had little liking for this. Nevertheless, he went with them unprotesting.

One of the men on the pier climbed aboard and came to Kassandra. "You are the daughter of Priam of Troy? The Queen sent word you would be coming and you were to be shown all regard," he said. "We have a cart for you and your child, and your woman."

He gave her his hand and helped her ashore, settling her in the cart with the baby on her knees and the serving-woman crouched at her feet.

In spite of this luxury—and the road up to the palace was so steep that she had dreaded climbing it on foot—Kassandra felt uneasy. The stone walls of the great palace, almost as massive as the fallen walls of Troy, seemed to frown above her, deep in shadow. They passed under a great gate above which two lionesses, painted in brilliant colors, kept watch face to face. As the cart trundled through the Lion Gate, she wondered if they represented the ancient Gods of the place or were Agamemnon's private emblem. But they were lionesses, not lions, and anyhow, Agamemnon had come here as a consort of the Queen in the old way. Klytemnestra's symbol, then?

Ahead of the cart marched Agamemnon and his honor guard with Aegisthos. Just inside the Lion Gate was a city built on the hillside on the same pattern as Troy: palace, temples, gardens, one above another, the walls rising in many terraces and balconies. It was beautiful; yet it seemed shadowed darkly, the depths of the shadow falling on Agamemnon where he walked at the center of the soldiers.

On the steps of the palace, a woman appeared, tall and commanding, her hair, elaborately dressed in ringlets fresh from a curling iron, flaming gold in the morning sun. She was dressed richly in the Cretan style, a laced bodice low across her breasts, a flounced skirt dyed in many colors, one for each flounce.

Kassandra saw at once the close resemblance to Helen. This would be her sister Klytemnestra. The Queen came through the escort and bowed low to Agamemnon; her voice was sweet and clear.

"My lord, a great joy to welcome you to these shores and to the palace where once you ruled at my side," she said. "We have long awaited this day."

She held out her two hands to him; he took them ceremoniously and kissed them.

"It is a joy to return home, Lady."

"We have prepared a celebration and a great sacrifice suitable to the occasion," she said. "*I can hardly wait to kill you.*"

No, Kassandra thought in shock, *that cannot have been what she said; but it is what I heard.*

What Klytemnestra had actually said was "I can hardly wait to see you take the place we have prepared for you."

"All is prepared for your bath and the feast," Klytemnestra said. "We are entirely ready to *see you lying dead among the sacrifices.*"

Once again Kassandra had heard what Klytemnestra was thinking, not what her lips had actually spoken. So again foresight, undesired, had come upon her.

Klytemnestra gestured Agamemnon toward the palace steps.

"All is prepared, my lord; go in and officiate at the sacrifice."

He bowed and began to walk up the steps. Klytemnestra watched him go with a smile which made Kassandra shudder. Couldn't he *see*?

But the King moved without hesitation. Just as he reached the great bronze doors at the top of the stairs, Aegisthos, armed with the great sacrificial ax, flung them open and thrust him inside. The doors closed after him.

Klytemnestra came down the stairs to the cart. She said, "You are the Trojan princess, Priam's daughter? My sister sent word to me that you were the one friend she had found in Troy."

Kassandra bowed; she was not sure that Klytemnestra's next move would not be to thrust a knife through her heart.

"I am Kassandra of Troy, and in Colchis I was made a priestess of Serpent Mother," she said.

Klytemnestra looked at the baby on her breast. She said, "Is that Agamemnon's child?"

"No," said Kassandra, not knowing whence came the courage which bade her speak so boldly, "he is *my* son."

"Good," said Klytemnestra, "we want no King's sons in this land. He may live, then."

At that moment, a great shout arose from within the bronze doors; someone thrust them open from inside, and Agamemnon appeared in flight at the top of the steps, with Aegisthos behind him, bearing the great double-bladed sacrificial ax. He whirled it high and brought it down into the fleeing King's skull. Agamemnon staggered and tripped over the edge of the stairs, falling and rolling down the steps almost to Klytemnestra's feet.

She screamed, "Witness, you people of the city: thus the Lady avenges Iphigenia!"

There was a tremendous cheer and cry of triumph; Aegisthos came down with the bloody ax and handed it to her. A few of Agamemnon's soldiers started a cry of outrage, but Aegisthos' guard quickly struck them down.

Klytemnestra said fiercely to Kassandra, "Have you anything to say, princess of Troy who thought perhaps to be Queen here?"

"Only that I wish I could have held the ax," replied Kassandra, gasping in a wild joy. She bowed to Klytemnestra, and said, "In the name of the Goddess, you have avenged wrongs done to Her. When a woman is wronged, She is wronged too."

Klytemnestra bowed to her and took her hands. She said, "You are a priestess, and I knew you would understand these things." She looked into the face of the sleeping child. "I bear you no grudge," she said. "We will have the old ways returned here. Helen has not the spirit to do so in Sparta, but I do. Will you remain here and be the Lady's priestess then? You may enter Her Temple if you will."

Kassandra was still breathing hard, her heart pounding at the suddenness of her release. Through Klytemnestra's features she still saw the hunger for destruction; this woman had avenged the dishonor offered the Goddess, but Kassandra still feared her. The Goddess took many forms, but in this form Kassandra did not love Her. Never before had she faced so strong a woman: princess and priestess. For once she had encountered a force stronger than her own.

Or did she but see in Klytemnestra the ancient power of the Goddess as She had been before male Gods and Kings invaded this land? She could not serve this Goddess.

"I cannot," she said, as calmly as she could. "I—this is not my country, O Queen."

"Will you return to your own country, then?"

"I cannot return to Troy," Kassandra said. "If you will give me leave to depart, Lady, I will seek my kinswomen in Colchis."

"A journey like that, with a baby still at the breast?" Klytemnestra asked in astonishment.

Then a curious change came across Klytemnestra's face. An unearthly peace relaxed the sharp features, and she seemed to glow from within. A voice Kassandra knew well said, *Yes, I call you home. Depart at once from this place, My daughter.*

Kassandra bowed to the ground; the word had come. Still she had no idea how she would travel or what would become of her; but she was once again under the protection of the Voice which had called her first when she was no more than a child.

Truly had the priestess in Colchis said, *The Immortals understand one another.*

"I beg leave to depart at once," she said.

And Klytemnestra replied, "Whom a God has called we must not detain. But will you not have rest, fresh clothing, food for yourself and the babe?"

Kassandra shook her head. "I need nothing," she said, knowing that with the gold Agamemnon had given her she was well provided. She wished to accept nothing from Klytemnestra —or from the Goddess of this place.

She departed within the hour.

Her child tied in her shawl, she went to the harbor, where she would find a ship to take her and the baby on the first step of the arduous journey halfway to the world's end, which would bring her at last to her kinswoman Imandra and the iron gates of Colchis. And above all, she was no longer blind and deprived of Sight; she was herself again, and after all the sufferings she knew the Goddess had not yet forsaken her.

On the docks a woman approached her, clad in a ragged earth-colored tunic, her face covered by a tattered shawl.

"Are you the Trojan princess?" she asked. "I am bound for Colchis, and I have heard you are going there."

"Yes, I am, but why—"

"I too seek Colchis," the woman said. "A God has called me there; may I bear you company?"

"Who are you?"

"I am called Zakynthia," the woman said.

Kassandra stared at her and could see nothing. Perhaps the woman was bound to her by Fate; in any case, no God forbade it. And even Klytemnestra had doubted her ability to make this long journey alone with an unweaned child. With a sigh of relief she unslung the shawl in which she had tied her son, and passed him over.

"Here," she said. "You can carry the baby till I need to feed him again."

EPILOGUE

THE WOMAN was soft-spoken and obedient, even submissive; she cared for the baby, rocking him and keeping him quiet. Kassandra, prey to renewed seasickness, had little opportunity to pay much attention to her child or the woman, though she did watch unobserved for several days to make certain that the servant—about whom, after all, she knew nothing—could be trusted not to ill-treat or neglect the baby when no one was watching. But she seemed conscientious, attentive to the infant, singing to him and playing with him as if she were really fond of children. After a few days Kassandra decided that she had been fortunate in finding a good servant to care for her child, and relaxed her vigilance somewhat.

And yet Kassandra began to suspect her companion was not what she professed to be. Underneath the ragged garments the woman seemed strong and healthy; Kassandra could only guess her age—perhaps thirty or even more. When Kassandra was near she was modest in her manner, but her voice was rough and hoarse, and her demeanor with the sailors and crew was free as an Amazon's. Then one day on the deck, Kassandra saw a stray wind blow Zakynthia's garments hard against her chest, and it seemed that her bosom was too flat to be womanly. Her legs, Kassandra noticed, were hairy and muscular; and her face looked as if it had never known cosmetics or smoothing oils. The thought came to Kassandra that perhaps it was possible Zakynthia was not a woman, but a man.

Why would any man, she wondered, have sought her out in woman's guise? Yet if he was a man, she thought, he might try to have his way with her—although, catching a glimpse of her own reflection in a basin of water, she could not imagine that any man would desire her as she was now: pale from seasickness, dressed in ragged garments, her body still shapeless after childbirth. Even so, she took to sleeping with Agathon in her arms; if the suckling at her breast did not deter a ravisher, probably nothing would, except her knife.

One night of storm, when the ship was tossed about like a cork on the heavy waves, Zakynthia spread her blanket close to Kassandra's and offered to take the baby into her own bed. The waves slammed their blanket rolls together, sliding them first uphill and then downhill in the cramped little cabin, until at last Zakynthia, who was larger and heavier, took Kassandra in her arms.

Kassandra, sick and weary, felt nothing but relief at the shelter her companion's body offered against the constant battering.

After this incident some of her fear subsided; surely no ordinary man would have ignored such an opportunity. She began to consider other possibilities. Perhaps he was a eunuch, or a healer-priest under vows of chastity. But why, then, did he wear women's garments and profess himself a woman? Finally she decided that it did not matter and after a time it occurred to her that she no longer cared whether her companion was a woman or a man; he or she was simply a friend she trusted and was beginning to love. The baby loved her companion too, and was willing to leave his mother's arms to be held and rocked by Zakynthia.

When at last the ship came to shore and they disembarked, she sought through the market for horses.

"But surely, Lady," said the merchant, "you will not travel overland, with a baby and a single servant, into the country of the Kentaurs."

"I did not know any of them remained alive," Kassandra said. "And I am not afraid of them." She hoped that on their journey they would meet some of that vanished race. She bartered a single link of gold for horses and food for the journey; she also bartered for a cloak for herself which could double as a blanket for sleeping, or as a tent.

"We should also have another tunic for you, Zakynthia," she said, turning over in her hand a remnant of woven cloth which might make a cloak for the child. "You are so ragged that you might be a street-sweeper. And as for me, I have been thinking that before we go on, perhaps I should cut my hair and wear a man's garment. The babe can soon be weaned, and surely they raise goats hereabout. It might be somewhat safer for traveling in this wild country. What would you think of that? You are taller and stronger than I; you would perhaps be more convincing as a man."

Her companion stood very still, but she had heard the caught breath of consternation before the other said quietly, "You must do as you think best, Lady; but I cannot put on a man's garment nor travel as one."

"Why not?"

Zakynthia did not meet her eyes.

"It is a vow. I may say no more."

Kassandra shrugged. "Then we shall travel as women."

KASSANDRA LOOKED UP at the gates of Colchis and remembered the first time, as a young girl in the Amazon band of Penthesilea, she had seen them. She had changed and the world had changed; but the great gates were just the same.

"Colchis," she said quietly to her companion. "The Gods have brought us here at last."

She set Agathon on his feet; he was beginning to toddle at last. If the journey had not been so long, she thought, he might have been really walking already; but she had been forced to carry him much of the time instead of letting him crawl or walk around. He was almost two years old now, and she could see in the strong development of his little chin, in his dark eyes, and dark curly hair, that he was Agamemnon's son.

Well, at least he would not be trained into Agamemnon's version of manhood.

It had been a long road; but not, she knew now, endless, as it had seemed. They had traveled overland mostly at night, hiding by day in woods and ditches. She had worn out several pairs of shoes and the clothing she wore was threadbare; she had had little opportunity to replace it.

There had been encounters on the road with soldiers—veterans of the sack of Troy—but she had seen and heard nothing of the Kentaurs; most of the people to whom she spoke of them believed they were only a legend, and either frankly accused her of telling tales or secretly smiled with contempt when she said she had seen them in her youth.

They had hidden from wandering bands of men, bribed themselves free, used their wits and sometimes their knives to get out of danger. They had gone cold and hungry—sometimes food was not to be had even for gold—and had stopped once or twice for a whole season to find work as spinners, or as handlers of animals.

Once they had traveled for a time with a man who was exhibiting "dancing" serpents. They had joined once or twice with other lone travelers, and had lost their way for long distances.

And after so many adventures that Kassandra knew she would never dare to try to recount them, they had arrived safely in Colchis.

She picked up the child again as they walked through the gates. She knew she looked like a beggar-woman. Her cloak was the same one with which Agamemnon had covered her on board his ship—once crimson, but now faded to a grayish colorlessness. Her gown was a shapeless tunic of undyed wool, her hair loosely bound with a scrap of leather thong which had once been used to tie a sandal. Zakynthia looked even worse, if possible; less like a beggar-woman than some kind of ruffian. Her sandals were worn almost through, and she would have had to find another pair in Colchis even if it had not been her destination.

But they had managed to keep the child well and warmly dressed. His tunic—though he was outgrowing it—was from a good piece of wool which she had bought two towns ago and was fastened with a pin made from one of her last bits of gold, and his sandals were stout and strong. Sometimes she thought he looked less like Agamemnon than like her brother Paris.

"Now we are at journey's end," she said to her companion.

She asked a passerby the way to the palace, and asked if Queen Imandra still reigned here.

The woman said, "Yes, though she is growing old; there was a rumor from the palace that she was mortally ill, but I do not believe it." She stared at Kassandra's threadbare cloak and asked, "And what can the likes of you want with our Queen?"

Kassandra merely thanked the woman for her help and did not answer. She set off for the palace. Zakynthia picked up the child and carried him.

Climbing the palace stairs, Kassandra nervously smoothed her hair with her fingers. Perhaps she should have stopped in the market and provided herself with proper clothing to visit the Queen.

She spoke to the guard on duty—an old woman guard whom Kassandra actually recognized from her stay so long ago in Colchis.

"I would like audience with Queen Imandra."

"I'm sure you would," said the woman, sneering, "but she doesn't see every ragtag and bobtail who comes looking for her."

Kassandra called the woman by name. "Don't you know me? Your sister was one of my novices in the house of Serpent Mother."

"Lady Kassandra!" the woman exclaimed. "But we heard you were dead—that you had perished at Mykenae; that when Agamemnon died, Klytemnestra murdered you too."

Kassandra chuckled. "As you see, I am here alive and well. But I beg you to take me to the Queen."

"Certainly; she will rejoice to know you survived the fall of

Troy," the woman said. "She mourned for you as for her own daughter."

The woman wished to take her to a guest chamber to make her ready for her audience; but Kassandra refused. She bade Zakynthia await her, but her companion shook her head.

"I too was bidden here by the hand of the Goddess," her companion said. "And I can reveal only to Imandra why I have come."

Eager to know her fellow traveler's story, Kassandra agreed. A few moments later, she was in her kinswoman's arms.

"I thought you dead in Troy," Imandra said. "Like Hecuba and the others."

"I thought Hecuba went with Odysseus," Kassandra said.

"No; one of her women made her way here and said Hecuba died—of a broken heart, she said—as the ships were loading. It is just as well; Odysseus was shipwrecked, and no one has heard of him since, and 'tis now close on three years. Andromache was taken back to one of the Akhaian Kings; I cannot remember his barbarian name, but I heard that she lives. And this is your child?" Imandra picked up the little boy and kissed him. "So some good came from all your sorrows?"

"Well, I have survived and made my way here," Kassandra said, and they fell to talking of other survivors of Troy. Helen and Menelaus were still reigning in Sparta, it seemed, and Helen's daughter Hermione was betrothed to the son of Odysseus. Klytemnestra had died in childbirth a year before, and her son Orestes had killed Aegisthos and taken back Agamemnon's Lion Throne.

"And have you heard anything of Aeneas?" Kassandra asked, remembering, with a sweet sadness, starlit nights in the last doomed summer of Troy.

"Yes, his adventures are widely told; he visited in Carthage and had a love affair with the Queen. They say, when the Gods called him away, she killed herself in despair, but I believe it not. If any Queen was fool enough to kill herself over a man, so much the worse for her; she cannot be much of a woman, and still less of a Queen. Then the Gods called him to the north, where, they say, he took the Palladium from the Trojan Temple of the Maiden, and founded a city."

"I am glad to hear he is safe," Kassandra said. Perhaps she should have gone with Aeneas to his new world; but no God had called her. Aeneas had his own fate, and it was not hers. "And Creusa?"

"I fear I do not know her fate," Imandra said. "Did she even escape Troy?"

Kassandra began to wonder. She remembered parting from Creusa, but it had been so long ago she wondered if she had dreamed it. All things surrounding the fall of the city were like dreams to her now.

"And you remember my daughter Pearl," Imandra said. "Come here, child, and greet your kinswoman."

The child came forward and greeted Kassandra with such poise that Kassandra did not kiss her as she would have done with any other child her age. "How old is she now?" she asked.

"Nearly seven," Imandra said, "and she will rule Colchis after me; we still keep to the old ways here. With good fortune, that will never change."

"There is not that much good fortune left in the world," Kassandra said, "but it will not change tomorrow nor the day after."

"So you are still gifted with the Sight?"

"Not all the time, nor for many things," Kassandra said.

"So what do you want of me, Kassandra? I can give you gold, clothing, shelter—you are my kinswoman, and you are welcome to remain in my house as a daughter—that would be most pleasing to me. I know the Temple of Serpent Mother would hail you as the chief of their priestesses."

Klytemnestra too had made her such an offer; but she knew it was too late to spend her life within walls.

"Or if you wish," said Imandra, "I will do as your father should have done long since, and find you a husband."

Kassandra said fiercely, "I am as little inclined as ever to be some man's property. In less than a year with Agamemnon I had a lifetime's worth of that."

Zakynthia suddenly interrupted; she came forward and fell prostrate before Imandra.

"O Queen," the rough voice entreated, "it was laid on me by the Goddess to come to this city for your help. The Gods have called me to found a city, and I cannot do it alone. At first I thought the Goddess had sent me here to know if any of the Amazons yet survived, for She sent me a vision that only such a woman could assist me in this task."

"And who are you?" asked Imandra.

"My name is Zakynthos," said the one Kassandra had known as Zakynthia. "Is there none left of the Amazon women who could help me to found a city where the Goddess is served without Gods or Kings? I would not have an ordinary wife after the fashion of the Akhaians, but one who can serve as a priestess in the city. Yet I have heard there are no more such women."

"No," Kassandra said, "no Amazon survived that last battle, in which Penthesilea died."

"I cannot accept that," Zakynthos said, putting back the veil he had worn as a woman. "Now I am free of my vow, I will search the world over if I must."

"What was your vow?" Imandra asked.

"To live as a woman until I came here to Colchis, so that I might know the life women must lead," he said. "Before I had worn women's garb three days, I knew why women must go in fear, and so I sought protection from the Trojan princess—and in her company as we traveled I discovered why women seek to be free of men. She needed no man's protection or help."

"Yet," Kassandra said warmly, "the protection you gave me —sharing my journey and my burdens . . ."

"But it was not because I was a man," Zakynthos said, "and again and again, I swore I would search the world over, if I must, for a woman in whom the Amazon's spirit still lived."

"And so," Imandra said, "have you not found one?"

"I have," said he, and turned to Kassandra, "and I have come to know her well."

Kassandra laughed and said, "I have long outlived any desire for weapons, Zakynthos. Yet—how will you found your city?"

"I will sail far to the west into the great sea and there find a place where a city can be built," he began. "Outside these accursed isles where men worship Gods of iron and oppression . . ."

Listening, Kassandra could not but remember Aeneas; this had been his desire too. She would willingly have helped him fulfill it, and Zakynthos seemed to have been fired by that same spirit.

"I seek a world where Earth Mother will be worshiped in the old ways," he said with enthusiasm. "It is She who has given me this vision, a dream of a city where women are not slaves, and where men need not spend their lifetimes in war and fighting. There must be a better way for both men and women to live than this great war which consumed all my childhood and took the lives of my father and all my brothers—"

"And of mine," Kassandra said.

"And of yours."

Zakynthos turned and knelt again before Imandra. "I beseech you as this woman's kinswoman, give me leave to take her in marriage."

Imandra said, "But marriage is one of the evils which came with the new ways; who am I to give her to you, as if she were a slave?"

Zakynthos said with a sigh, "You are right. Kassandra, we have traveled far together; you know me well. Will you continue to travel with me—to build a world better than Troy?"

Kassandra, thinking of their long journey together, said slowly, "But, like other men, you will want a son . . ."

"I have carried your son at least half this long way in my arms," he said. "If I can be a mother to your son, do you doubt I can be a father to him too? For I think if I sought the world over I could not find a woman more suited to my purposes. And I think perhaps it would suit your purposes too," he added, smiling. "Do you wish to sit here at Imandra's court and spin thread?"

"It does not trouble you that I was forced to be Agamemnon's concubine and that I bore him a child? All men will know," she said. He smiled very gently, and again she thought of Aeneas.

"Only as much as it troubles you," he said. "And as for the boy, he is *your* son, and you have seen how well I love him. Someday we may have others for whom I can be both father and mother as well . . ." His voice was very tender as he added, "I would like to have a daughter like you."

She had spent too much of her life with the idea that she could never marry; yet this war had taken all her kindred and she had no place of her own. And the Amazons too were gone, as Troy was gone.

Their new city might be one where men and women need not be enemies, where the Gods were not the implacable enemies of the Goddess. . . .

If Troy could not last forever, there was no assurance that the new city would. But if for her lifetime's work she could have a share in building a city where men did not deform their sons into fighters so that they need not follow cruel Gods into battle, or their daughters into men's playthings, then her life would be well spent.

She remembered the young girl she had been, seated in the Sun Lord's house and dealing out wisdom to the petitioners. What had she said then?

I give such answers as they could give if they could trouble themselves to use such wits as the Gods gave them, she remembered. But she had added, *Before I speak, always, I pause and wait in case the God has another answer to be given.*

She listened within her heart, but there was only silence, and the memory of a God's burning smile. Might a day come when like any dutiful wife she would see the face of the God in her husband? She looked at Zakynthos. He was no Sun Lord, but his face was honest and kind. She could hardly imagine a God speaking through him, but at least what he said would not be cruel or capricious. Agamemnon had been no worse than Poseidon; Paris had set Troy aflame at the bidding of a Goddess more cruel and capricious than any man. The worst of men, in her lifetime, had been no worse than the best of Gods. And what evil they had done, they had done at the bidding of Gods made in their own image.

She listened, but no God's voice spoke to forbid her; she knew at that moment what her answer would be, and already her heart was racing forward across the great sea to a new world which, if it was no better than the old, would at least be as much better as men and women could make it.

"Let us go, Zakynthos, to search for our city. Perhaps one day those who come after us will know the truth of Troy and its fall," she said, and took his hand in her own.

Somewhere, a Goddess smiled. She did not think it was Aphrodite.

POSTSCRIPT ───────────────

THE *Iliad* has nothing to say of the fate of Kassandra of Troy. Aeschylus in his *Agamemnon* presents her as a sharer in his death at the hands of Klytemnestra; it was regarded as perfectly permissible to introduce characters from the *Iliad* if their fate had not become a part of that poem. Euripides shows Kassandra as one of the Trojan captives; interestingly, she is the one woman who suggests revenge on their captors, but it is also made clear that she is insane. Yet another dramatic appearance shows Kassandra as leading the women of Troy in a heroic mass suicide.

However, tablet #803 in the Archaeological Museum in Athens reads as follows:

ZEUS OF DODONA, GIVE HEED TO THIS GIFT
I SEND YOU FROM ME AND MY FAMILY—
AGATHON SON OF EKHEPHYLOS,
THE ZAKYNTHIAN FAMILY,
CONSULS OF THE MOLOSSIANS AND THEIR ALLIES,
DESCENDED FOR 30 GENERATIONS
FROM KASSANDRA OF TROY.

ACKNOWLEDGMENTS ─────────

I WISH to acknowledge especially the help of my husband, Walter Breen, who assisted materially in the research for this book, and whose knowledge of classical Greek—both language and history—was of invaluable help in creating this story, particularly including the quotation from the Athens museum which ends this book, providing historical basis for the fate—and the very historical existence—of Kassandra of Troy, from whose viewpoint this story is told.

Readers will be likely to raise challenges: "That's not the way it happened in the *Iliad*." Of course not; had I been content with the account in the *Iliad*, there would have been no reason to write a novel. Besides, the *Iliad* stops short just at the most interesting point, leaving the writer to conjecture about the end from assorted legends and traditions. If the writers of Greek drama felt free to improvise, I need not apologize for following their excellent example.

One further apology: Walter's knowledge of the language persuaded me, in the name of linguistic "correctness" and rather against my better judgment, to use classical transliterations rather than the more familiar Latinized forms; hence Akhaians for Achaeans (the term "Greek" was not known then), Akhilles for Achilles, and worst of all, Kassandra for Cassandra. To me the difference is appalling and changes the whole meaning of the name and character. A cow or a crow would not, after all, be the same creature if called a kow or a krow. To those whose aesthetic sensibilities are as acute as mine, and to whom the look of a name on the page alters its very essence, I can only express my apologies. Linguistics and aesthetics are, after all, very different philosophies, and the discordances between them will never be resolved—at least, not by me.

I also acknowledge my debt to Elisabeth Waters, who on the

many occasions when I was "stuck" with the "what happens next" blues never failed to help me find the most constructive answer, and to the other members of my household who suffered all through the fall and the sack of Troy with me.

Marion Zimmer Bradley